*SLAVES AND MASTERS . . .*

**TAMBOURA:** born a prince in the jungles of Africa and sold into slavery; his beauty and nobility draw him into a forbidden alliance with blonde Alix, his owner's mistress.

**ALIX:** a French countess, driven to become the most celebrated madam in New Orleans.

**DON CESAR:** an egocentric patrician whose wealth is the weapon he uses to turn whims into law.

**DRUM:** son of Tamboura and Alix, who becomes the star performer in the melees given in his mother's brothel, and the most invincible prize-fighter in the South.

**HAMMOND MAXWELL:** hates white women and black men, and owns the great slave-breeding plantation, Falconhurst, presided over by an elegant, enigmatic woman he acquires in a strange transaction.

**DRUMSON:** sold by his grandmother to sire slaves at Falconhurst, where the evils from the past and the present explode in a thunderous slave uprising.

*With savage power and unflinching detail, DRUM sweeps away the old myths of the benevolent master, the fragile Southern Belle and the humble, happy slave.*

**Other Fawcett Books by Kyle Onstott:**

**Mandingo**

**Master of Falconhurst**

***and with Lance Horner***

**The Tattooed Rood**

**Falconhurst Fancy**

**The Black Sun**

***and by Lance Horner***

**The Mustee**

**The Street of the Sun**

# DRUM

by Kyle Onstott

*A Fawcett Crest Book*
FAWCETT PUBLICATIONS, INC., GREENWICH, CONN.
MEMBER OF AMERICAN BOOK PUBLISHERS COUNCIL, INC.

THIS BOOK CONTAINS THE COMPLETE TEXT OF THE ORIGINAL HARDCOVER EDITION.



A Fawcett Crest Book reprinted by arrangement with The Dial Press, Inc. and Denlinger's Publishing Company, Middleburg, Virginia.



Ninth Fawcett Crest printing, November, 1967

Published by Fawcett World Library,
67 West 44th Street, New York, New York 10036
Printed in the United States of America

This volume is dedicated, with his permission, to my good friend and valued collaborator

LANCE HORNER

to whom I am profoundly obligated for the assistance he has given me and without whose insistence, aid, and persistent encouragement the book would never have been finished.

# book one

## chapter i

THE AFRICAN SUN exploded in a blast of white-hot heat that seared the earth. It tore at the face, the head, the vitals, and parched the throat. Tamboura paused to wipe away the stream of sweat that ran down into his eyes and dripped into his mouth with the salty taste of his own body. He shifted the weight of the slain antelope buck on his shoulders, while with the tip of his tongue that was like a darting arrow of red flame he licked the moisture from his thick, dark lips. The green flies that had departed momentarily from the carcass alighted again to gorge themselves with blood.

Tamboura was proud of his kill. His light wooden lance had penetrated the animal's jugular vein on his first throw, and he had now completed his last task—that of killing the meat for his own feast. Although the spear had served him well, he looked at it with contempt and his lips twisted in disdain at the light shaft and the fire-sharpened end encrusted with dried blood.

Balancing the slain buck with one hand behind him, he raised the other and hurled the stick away from him. It was an awkward cast because of his burden, but it landed many paces away and stood quivering in the ground. He spat after it and cursed it, calling down upon it the avenging spirits of his ancestors and his own particular spirit. It was a stupid boy's weapon—a worthless plaything! Tomorrow! Ay, tomorrow, after the circumcision ceremonies of tonight, he would have an iron-tipped spear, the spear of a man, a real hunter.

Tamboura squinted to see through the shimmering heat waves and, shielding his eyes with his hand, peered across the stubble of sunburned grass and dusty tamarisk shrubs to where a huge baobab tree lifted a stubby umbrella of leaves above a squat barrel-like trunk. Beneath it there would be shade from the fierce sun and rest from his heavy burden.

Strong as he was, with the elastic vitality of youth, he stumbled under his burden as he quickened his steps to a trot, the sooner to reach the beckoning shade. Then he slid the carcass with its buzzing flies from his shoulders and dropped to the ground, welcoming the cool dryness of the leaves against his back. Even under the tree the dappled light was dazzling, and when he closed his eyes his lids served only to change the stark whiteness of the light to a fiery red. He reached down to unknot the sweaty strip of soiled cloth from his loins. Once it had been gay and gaudily patterned with red and white arabesques—the Midlands cotton mills of England knew what "the stinkin' niggers" liked—but now it was grimy and sweat-stained, a faded gray. He folded its musky wetness and laid it across his eyes, glad of the welcome darkness it afforded.

He stretched, grinding his narrow buttocks down into the comforting leaves. Ay! It was pleasant to lie under the shade of the big tree with a sense of accomplishment behind him and the even greater anticipation of what the evening would bring. This was the day he had yearned for, lived all his life for and for which he had patiently taken the taunts and patronizing jibes of the young hunters. This was his day. Yesterday he had left the camp of the pubescent boys, with no provisions to eat or drink, only the obligation to slay an animal for his feast. He had sustained himself with the locusts he had caught with his hands, and fat white grubs he had found under a stone. He had bathed in the warm water of the river, carefully examining his body for any disfiguring pimple or defect, anointing his skin from a little leather flask of palm oil. He had had the good fortune to slay his meat offering on the first throw. Now he would not be cheated out of his initiation as he had been last year and the year before. He knew he had seventeen years instead of the fifteen his brother Mandouma claimed for him.

The notches on the pole of his spirit in his brother's hut—the pole with the carved lion on top—had counted up to fifteen two years ago but Mandouma, head man of the village, had erased one mark and done the same thing again last year. Both Mandouma and his son, Bansu, had insisted there were only fourteen marks. That was because his brother hated him and so did Bansu, Tamboura's nephew, who was three years older than he. Well, they and that dirty bitch, Zarassa, Mandouma's wife, were all the family he had and if they hated him, he could hate equally well in return. Once there had been eight brothers between Mandouma and Tamboura and now they were all dead. Only the eldest and the youngest were alive, and that meant that when Mandouma joined the hunters in the sky, Tamboura would be head man of the village with all the honors and authority of king. It was the law of the Hausa nation that a brother succeeded rather than a son but the greedy Zarassa and the foppish Bansu did not want that. Zarassa was half Arab and she cared little for Hausa laws. She cared only for her son, and she had soft-talked Mandouma into hating his brother. Yes, they had almost succeeded again this year, but they could not soft-talk old Kanili, the witch doctor. Two years ago he had believed them, even last year, but this year Kanili took one look at Tamboura and scoffed at their assurance that he had only fourteen rainy seasons to his life.

They had tried to deny him the rite of circumcision which was rightfully his for they did not want him to sit in the councils of the village and gain the confidence of the hunters and the elders. But old Kanili was his friend! Neither Mandouma nor the half-caste Bansu had dared dispute the old witch doctor a third time. So, Tamboura had left the hut of his brother to sleep in the communal hut of the initiates, all younger than himself, for the last six months. During that time, he had studied with old Kanili, learning of his own spirit—the spirit of Earth whose sign was the lion. Tamboura was glad he was of the earth spirit for that meant he would be a hunter. Those whose marks were the crane were of the spirit of the air to hunt birds; those with the mark of the crocodile were of the spirit of water to spear fish and hunt the crocodiles, but those of the earth proudly bore the sign of the lion and were hunters of beasts.

To Tamboura, Kanili had taught the secrets of the earth —how to hunt the animals, how to make things grow from the soil, and perhaps most important of all how to renew his strength from his great mother earth by lying on his back and letting her power seep through his skin. Someday soon, when Tamboura had learned to use the iron-tipped spear, he would stalk and kill a lion alone and then the lion's spirit would enter into him. He would have all the power and bravery of a lion and perhaps, if the spirit were really within him, the lion's mane would grow on his cheeks and chin and cover his belly with a mat of black hair.

Atunoo, one of the young hunters of the village, had killed a lion and it was a marvel the way the hair grew on his body. Tamboura envied him for he was a real lion-man. To kill a lion was much more difficult than killing a foolish crane with flapping wings or a sleepy crocodile. Mandouma was a crocodile—that's why he was so lazy and why he let Zarassa influence him instead of knocking out her teeth and teaching her obedience. And Bansu was a crane—that's why he walked stiff-legged like a bird and twittered like one, hanging beads around his neck and braiding copper wire to make even more bracelets for his skinny arms. Ay! Tamboura was glad he was a lion spirit for the lion spirits were the real men who were able to scatter their seed ten times a night and breed a thousand sons.

It was cool under the baobab—cool and quiet and restful, with a hint of a breeze which rustled the leaves above him and fanned the sweat from his skin. He knew that he was not far from the *kraal* for he could see the tops of the silk cotton trees that grew there. There was time to linger a little longer; he was not due back at the village until sundown, which would give the women plenty of time to skin the buck and roast it for the big feast that would follow the secret rites which they were forbidden to witness. Tamboura's mouth watered at the anticipation of the roast meat, the yams, the locusts in honey and the cassava bread.

But in spite of all his bravery, he shivered with an involuntary twitching of all his muscles. He would not admit it even to himself but he dreaded the pain the evening would bring. Some boys feared it so much that they ran away from the *kraal* and became outcasts in the bush. That there was pain he was well aware, for all the men boasted of how they had endured it and how it had seared them like a white-hot fire. Sometimes the knife didn't cut clean the first time and old Kanili had to saw and saw until the skin came away. Then it was more painful and left a ragged and disfiguring scar. But Kanili now had a new knife—a sharp one of steel—which he had bought from the slave traders. He had promised that with the new knife there would be a clean cut the first time and he had demonstrated how easy it would be with Tamboura for there was more than enough skin to get a firm grasp. And then . . . Kanili had whispered a secret! The millet beer that Tamboura would drink before the ceremony contained a white powder dissolved in it which would dull the pain.

Ay! What was a little pain compared to the glorious fact that it would make him a man? The last two years had been difficult ones, for his body had ached with desire which could not be fulfilled. As he was now, no girl of the village would let him touch her. He was unclean and he would contaminate any girl or woman whom he entered. Tamboura removed the sweaty loincloth from over his eyes and looked down over his body, hating the thick rosette of black skin which marked him as still a boy. After tonight, it would be gone and he could strut before the other men in the council house, removing his loincloth as they did and displaying the unshrouded organ of his manhood with pride. But even more than the pride he would take in his virility was the freedom he would have to court the girls of the village when they slipped away into the darkness of the trees after the pulsating rhythm of the full moon dances. Then all the men of the village, aflame with the desire the drums had instilled, forgot wives and marriage vows and grabbed the first warm flesh they found in the darkness and bore it to the ground. Once Tamboura had almost succeeded but the woman had discovered his boyhood and clawed his face, spitting on him and cursing him for trying to defile her. But not after tonight!

When the cut had healed, he knew the first girl he would take for himself—Iba, the sleek daughter of Layoumba. As children they had played together like young animals. Although he had not seen her for six months, he remembered how the points of her breasts would press hard against him when he drew her close to him while they were hiding in the tamarisk bushes. But that was only playing! She would not let him do what his throbbing urgency demanded. Never! She would only stroke him, slowly at first and then violently until he tingled in every muscle of his body and the blood exploded in his head. Then suddenly it would be all over and he would run from her in disgust. Now it would be different! Ay, by the very spirit of the lion, he swore it would be. She would be the one who would run from him but he would catch her, not once, not twice but ten times, maybe twenty times as he had heard Atunoo, the hairy lion-man, boast.

His hands wandered down over his body, reveling in its hardness, and it was with difficulty that he removed them.

Bah! He was no longer a child. Such things were for boys, not the man that he almost was. After tonight! Ay, after tonight! He stood up, the better to resist the temptation that had lured his hands.

Tamboura was tall for his seventeen years—tall and big-boned, with hands and feet that seemed too large even for his big frame and promised even more growth. The adolescent curves of his body had almost disappeared and the sharp cleavages of definition between his muscles were showing. Twin, rounded curves broadened his chest. Somewhere back in his ancestry he too had a sprinkling of Arab blood, for his face lacked the rotundity of the pure Negro and there was a suggestion of high cheekbones. His nose, short in length and starting wide between his eyes, came down in a straight line, flattening to broad but sensitive nostrils. The lips were thickened but not ill formed, dully tinged with red and damply smooth. They parted to disclose a row of large, white, even teeth. His body glistened with palm oil and sweat like a piece of blue-black steel, smoothly glabrous except for the close-fitting skullcap of black velours which covered his head, reaching at the sides almost to his eyebrows. His eyes were velvety soft like those of the antelope he had slain—circular discs of copper brown, set in a creamy white which seemed overlarge in contrast to the dark skin. There was a hint of the Arab ancestor, too, in the long eyelashes and the strongly cleft chin.

Having put Iba out of his mind, he was now able to tie the loincloth, and he reached down and eased the slain beast up onto his shoulders again. It was later than he thought. The sun was nearing the horizon in a mass of rose and violet clouds and he must hurry. Rested now, and refreshed by his contact with his spirit Earth, he started off at an easy lope, the polished hooves of the antelope clicking a tattoo that timed his footsteps. Soon he reached the yam and manioc patches which marked the outer boundary of his village and with them the grass disappeared in a path of beaten dirt. He passed the stockade where he heard the plaintive singing of the slaves his village had captured and he smiled to think how he too would raid the villages beyond the river and bring back captives whom he could trade for yards of cloth, sharp knives, bugle beads and all the luxuries which his primitive civilization had not been able to produce.

People he had not seen in his six months' absence from

the village passed him on the path. The women, knowing that this was the night of his celebration, greeted him with good-humored bantering; the men, with frightening threats of the painful ordeal he must undergo; the young boys with envious looks. And the girls . . . ay, the girls only dropped their eyes with a false modesty which allowed them to estimate the bulge of his loincloth in anticipation of dancing nights to come. He returned their greetings in kind for now; being only a few hours away from man stature, he could speak to all as an equal, giving no offense.

Further down the path, he entered the gate to the stockade which surrounded his village. High on the poles were the bleached skulls of his ancestors' conquests in battle. No new skulls had been added for many years, for today it was more profitable to capture a man alive than to kill him and the taste for human flesh had long been forgotten.

Inside the stockade, in front of her father's hut, Iba was grinding millet. She knelt before the stone mortar, letting the pestle rise and fall rhythmically, her upstanding young breasts tapering to pointed nipples, rising and falling with the motion of her arms. Tamboura saw the glance she stole in his direction and knew she was conscious of his coming, and so he added a bit of hip-swinging swagger to his walk. He spread his arms wide and back to grasp the hooves of the antelope, the better to broaden his shoulders. As he neared her, she glanced shyly up at him, then coquettishly lowered her eyes with the same shameless modesty the other girls had employed. He felt her eyes tracing the soiled arabesques of his loincloth and he rejoiced in the involuntary response which riveted her attention even more avidly.

Balancing the burden on his back, he squatted on his heels until his eyes were level with hers.

"After tonight?" His question was more of a command.

She giggled and turned her eyes away but only momentarily. "After tonight there will be blood," she taunted him.

"But the blood will stop."

"And after the blood there will be a soreness."

"But the soreness will not endure. And then . . . ?"

Now she avoided his eyes. "And when the soreness has stopped, it will be the night of the dance," she sighed. "But," she tossed her head, "it is the night that I have promised to another."

He relinquished his burden and grabbed her hand. The force of his grip made her drop the pestle.

"You are hurting." Iba made much of trying to pull her hand free from his grasp.

"I shall hurt more unless you take back your words. You are promised to nobody but me. When you quit the dancing, you will wait for me beyond the *kraal,* by the garden of your father."

"Why should I wait for you?" She was still struggling.

"Because I choose you as my first and I shall not disappoint you. And you? You know that you desire me and that there will be no other."

She snatched her hand away and in so doing she deliberately brushed it across the now tautly stretched loincloth. "There is a possibility." Her eyes met his and she smiled.

Tamboura straightened up with the energy of hidden springs in his knees. Unable to contain himself, he bounced on his toes. The heavy burden was no longer heavy and he ran from her to the largest hut in the *kraal.* It faced the clean-swept circular dance compound of hard-beaten earth with the black fire circle in the center. In front of the hut were the carved tree trunks of his ancestors' spirits. He slipped the buck to the ground.

"Mandouma, my brother!" he called out. "Come, the buck that I have killed for my feast tonight is here at your door." He waited until his brother appeared, a man possibly in his forties, for the black wool was graying at his temples, although his powerful body foretold that which Tamboura's promised.

Mandouma stood in the doorway, looking down at the antelope. He noted the single wound in the neck.

"A good kill," he admitted grudgingly. "With one throw of the spear. Go now to the house of Kanili to prepare yourself for the blood sacrifice that will make you a man." He waited in the doorway until he saw Tamboura run across the dancing ground and enter the hut of Kanili. With his bare foot he kicked the buck's head, studying the wound, then re-entered the hut.

A woman's voice, that of his wife, Zarassa, whined from the semidarkness.

"The cub has returned."

"That he has." Bansu languidly raised himself up on one elbow from the pile of skins on which he was lying. "Of course the little lion has survived all the ordeals of preparation and of course he has slain his meat offering for the feast. Now what shall we do?"

The dim light that entered the doorway glinted on the knife that Zarassa tossed to Bansu.

"No, woman, not that!" Mandouma reached down and picked up the knife. "His blood is my blood and it cannot be spilled by me, and not by you or my son. His spirit would haunt us and torture us."

"Then let him live!" Zarassa stamped her foot. "Yes, let the brat live and let him grow up to plot against you and wish for your death that he may be king. Let him take the place your own son should rightfully have; you know that Bansu can be nothing as long as Tamboura lives. Not until he dies can Bansu sit at your feet in the council and echo your words. I say that Tamboura must die."

Zarassa could not see the quick raising of Mandouma's hand in the half-light, but the sharp crack of it against her teeth caused her to reel and fall to her knees.

"Shut your mouth, woman! It is as big as a crocodile's and clatters like the dried pods on a tree. There are other ways."

"What other ways, my father?" Bansu rose languidly to his knees, swaying slightly in his slender elegance. The tone of his words mocked his father.

Mandouma pointed out through the doorway.

"Go, climb the highest tree in the *kraal* and tell me what you see. No," he shook his head, "you are not man enough to climb it, so I shall tell you what you would see. You would see a circle of little fires where Ama-jallah, the Arab slave trader, camps with his caravan for the night."

"The slave trader." Zarassa was rubbing the sting from her mouth. "What has that to do with us?"

"We have eighteen captives in the stockade whom we will trade with him tomorrow; also the young hunter Sabumbo, whose father sells him to pay the debts for his new young wife."

Zarassa clapped her hands. "Then get me a length of red cloth with bugle beads to trim it—the brightest red he has and beads that are many colors."

"And a mirror to see myself in." Bansu stood up. "But not one with a paper edge. I want one with a metal rim that stands by itself."

Mandouma's hand menaced his son. "You are stupid, both of you. All you can think of is worthless finery. Don't you understand? Tonight we will deliver Tamboura to him."

Bansu's wide grin showed his teeth gleaming white in

the darkness of the hut, but his grin vanished in an instant.

"Consider, my father," he said. "The brat's a pet of Kanili's. If you sell him, Kanili will put a curse on us all."

"And need Kanili know about it unless you blab it to him?" Mandouma's tone emphasized his son's dull-wittedness. "Listen! Tonight after Tamboura has been anointed white with the clay, will he not be brought here to his own hut for the blessing of his family and for the drugged beer? Will I not then, as his brother and sponsor, escort him to the circle around the fire and hold him in my arms while the knife cuts him?"

"Yes," Bansu agreed. "So you did with me."

"And how you screamed." Mandouma spat on the floor. "You disgraced me and your ancestors. But that is past. Tonight when Tamboura drinks his beer here, it will have a triple portion of the powder that kills the pain. It will make him sleep. We will carry him off to the Arab but we shall not sell him, we shall give him. Then we shall tell Kanili that Tamboura suddenly turned coward and became one of the craven ones who fear the knife and flee to the bush. Many boys have done so in the past."

"Kanili will know better. He knows the brat is brave."

"Kanili will not be able to prove it."

"But why give him away?" Zarassa was indignant. "He is worth at least a bolt of cloth, a copper kettle, a mirror for Bansu and a gourdful of beads."

The motion of Mandouma's hand silenced her.

"Him I shall not sell. He is the son of my father. I give him to Ama-jallah on one condition—that he hide him until the caravan is many hours on its journey from here tomorrow. We shall never see him again and the elders will burn the pole with his marks and his spirit, for those who flee the knife are adjudged dead. He will be gone and his blood will not be on my hands or yours, nor will we receive any profit from his body."

Zarassa crept across the floor of the hut and flung her arms around Mandouma's knees, slavering his thighs with her kisses. Bansu came over and laid his arm around his father's shoulders, but Mandouma kicked the woman so that she fell backwards on the floor, and angrily thrust his son's arm away.

"And when he is gone, you will both shut up. 'Get rid

of Tamboura'—'Kill Tamboura'—'The brat did this, the cub did that, punish him, flog him, poison him.' I'm sick of it and weary of your badgering. Perhaps with him gone we shall live in peace." Mandouma stalked angrily out of the hut.

## chapter ii

SLOWLY, PAINFULLY, Tamboura struggled through vast, frightening quagmires that grew, wavered and diminished into wet, slimy malformations that curtained him from reality. But his consciousness plodded on and up through the miasmic silt until at length he was able to open his eyes and behold something quite as unreal as the narcotic-inspired horrors from which he had just emerged. There was a continuous motion which kept his head a-bobbing, and a darting pain which seemed centered in his ankles and wrists. The parched dryness of his lips and mouth extended far down into his stomach and the throbbing in his head made him feel as if the top of his skull had been sliced off and birds were picking out the insides like ravens around a burst calabash. An eerie light of alternate white and red stripes, which seemed like hot bars of metal, enveloped him.

As he gradually became more aware of his surroundings, he discovered that the bobbing of his head was caused by the motion of the horse he was riding. The pain in his ankles came from the straw rope which was fastened to one ankle, pulled tautly under the horse's belly and tied to the other ankle. Both his wrists were secured to the high wooden pommel of the saddle with leather thongs and spread over him was a smothering tent-like affair of red and white striped material, supported on thin bamboo poles. He had seen such a contraption in the slave caravans when some True Believer of Allah carried one of his favorite wives along with him, and took care that she be shielded from the view of profaning eyes.

He struggled vainly, pulling at his wrists to free himself, but the thongs only dug deeper into his already raw flesh. His feet, too, were securely anchored. Now he could view his body, which had been so gaudily painted with clay the night before. The white clay was streaked with his own black skin where the sweat had soaked through and run down his body in serpentine meanderings. The sticky clay reminded him of the ceremony of the night before. He remembered no pain and strangely enough he felt none now —at least not where pain should be. By spreading his arms as wide as his bound hands would allow and leaning as far back in the saddle as he could, he was able to look down at himself. Now he understood why there was no pain. There had been no cut. He was exactly the same as he had been before.

It was all so difficult to understand. That it was day now was certain—the light and heat of the sun proved it. But the ceremony was to have taken place last night and by rights he should now be waking in the hut of Mandouma, sore but happy. Instead he was . . . where was he?

Suddenly he had an impulse to scream out, to raise his voice in a shrill cry of fear that would summon someone or some thing to him—a hand to raise the striped canopy, a knife to cut the binding thongs, an arm to stop the plodding of the horse, a voice to explain where he was and why. But a man did not scream. A man did not cry out in his grief and bewilderment. Tamboura stifled the outburst and tried to remember what had happened the night before.

He had left Mandouma's hut and gone across the dance compound to the hut of Kanili, rich in the knowledge that he had killed his antelope with one fling of the wooden spear. Yes, he had bragged about it before the other boys. Kanili had only grunted, but that was sufficient praise from the old witch doctor. Kanili was kneeling before one of the boys and beside him on the floor was an iron trade kettle, filled with a viscous white mixture. This he had smeared over the boy until the lad's whole body gleamed with a white phosphorescence in the firelight of the hut, except for the one vital spot which must of course remain black. Then he had dipped his finger in a bowl of red clay and drawn jagged lines down from the boy's shoulders over his thighs to his ankles. Once finished, he dismissed the boy, cautioning him to stand still and not sit down. Kanili had brushed aside the next boy in line and beckoned to Tamboura to take his place. It seemed to Tamboura that the witch doctor took special pains with his ornamentation. In addition to the jagged lines on his hips and thighs, Kanili drew a crude representation of a lion between his nipples, then, muttering to himself, he had opened a small box, dipped his finger in an azure powder and further decorated his body.

When the last boy had been painted, they had all lined up and one by one, starting with Tamboura, they had been taken to the huts of their fathers. The village was deserted. All of the women, who were forbidden to witness any of the rites, were outside the stockade preparing the feast, and the men sat rigid and formal in their huts, waiting to welcome the initiates.

Mandouma and Bansu greeted Kanili with the rich-speaking words used on such occasions and welcomed Tamboura into the hut. With unwonted graciousness, Bansu took the carved wooden dipper down from a shelf and Mandouma filled it with the yeasty millet beer from a large gourd. He too seemed kinder than usual, and when Tamboura knelt before him and Mandouma laid his hands on his head to bless him, his voice was almost tender.

"May you be a brave hunter, my brother. May you slay many beasts, despoil many virgins and father many sons." Mandouma handed him the cup.

Tamboura drank. He remembered the bitter taste of the beer. He remembered sitting on the floor with his back against his spirit pole and then . . . after that he could not remember anything.

And now he was here, although he did not know where *here* was. Time passed. Just how much time, Tamboura did not know but the heat inside the flimsy tent was stifling. Heat and pain—wrist pain and ankle pain. Flies settled on the blood that seeped from his wrists where the leather thongs had bit into the flesh. His head ached, his back ached, and the muscles in his arms and legs were cramped with immobility. Time passed and still, in his agony and bewilderment, he refrained from opening his mouth.

His own brother had done this to him! Of this he was sure; or, if not his brother, then certainly his brother's wife or son. He was now an outcast from his own village, branded with the mark of a coward, for he had not faced the knife. But crowding out the resentment and hatred which he felt for his brother and the bitch Zarassa and the mewling Bansu was the crowning disappointment that he had not reached his long-hoped-for man status. Now, he was certain, he never would. Not only was Iba left behind, untried and untouched, but never, during his whole life, would he ever taste the delights of any woman, for no woman would ever have him.

His homesickness was as nothing compared to the terror that a lifetime of unsatisfied desires engendered. A whole vicious circle of thoughts whirled in his head—his grief at not being a man, his homesickness, his fear, his hatred and his pain—combining, twisting and growing into new thoughts that almost erased the pain, the heat and the flies.

The horse plodded on, until the striped shadow of Tamboura's head was directly beneath his body. Suddenly the slow motion of the horse ceased and he heard a word in a tongue with which he was unfamiliar but which he could somehow understand. Then a hand, with long, black bony fingers and spatulate nails reached inside the tent and rested for a moment on the flesh of his thigh. It was removed and soon his legs were free. The hand reached inside again, this time followed by a deformed cranium, covered with thick black moss, growing low over a forehead which shadowed small, squinting yellow-white eyes and a pair of large nostrils like two black holes gaping above thick, rubbery lips. A quick slice of a steel knife severed the leather thongs and the hand developed into an arm, long and powerfully muscled, which grasped Tamboura around the waist and slid him off the saddle onto the ground. The long confinement of his legs had made them useless and he was unable to stand. He crumpled to the ground.

The ground! He remembered old Kanili's teachings. If he could but lie there, flat on his back for a few moments, he would regain his strength. He was allowed to remain while the big Negro prodded him with the thick, horny nail of a dirt-encrusted big toe.

"You stay here, boy. Don' you run 'way. I go fetch Amajallah."

"No need!" a voice called. Tamboura could see the finely made slippers of yellow leather coming across the dusty beaten trail. "I saw you take him down, Akeem. Has he come to himself?"

"He wake, great lord." The rubbery lips parted in a grin. "He wake but he no stan'."

"He'll stand quick enough." A hand disengaged itself from the folds of the white robe and a thin whip curled through the air to wrap itself around Tamboura's belly. "He'll stand and in an hour, when the cattle have been fed, he'll walk along with the rest. Get him up! Feed him! If he refuses to eat, pry his jaws open, put a stick between his teeth and cram the food down his throat. He looks to be in prime condition and I want to keep him that way. Then tie him into the caffle."

"Yes, great lord." The Negro prodded Tamboura again with the same offensive toenail. "Great Emir say get up, stand on feet and eat. You come along by me. I get you food. You eat. Then we go. Get up."

"Yes, up!" The thin whip snaked out again. "We have a schedule to meet. Can't be delayed because of one half-grown whelp. We must reach the river before sundown. The canoes will be waiting."

Tamboura looked up to see the hand that held the whip. It was a delicate hand, blue-veined on a dark skin that was not black but a deep olive, with almond-shaped nails that were carefuly pared. He looked up from the hand, across the folds of the white robe to the face above it. He saw a youthful face with a beauty that was marred by cruelty. Its main feature was a prominently aquiline nose that seemed to stretch the skin so tightly across the bridge that the effect was almost painful. Dark eyes, under even darker lashes, looked down at Tamboura. The thin, moist lips parted and the Hausa words came slowly, for although Hausa was the language spoken for intercommunication between most of the tribes of interior Africa, its pronunciation was always difficult for one not born to it.

"You are Tamboura. I am Ama-jallah, the son of the Sultan of Zinder. This is my slave caffle and you are now a slave. You are no longer the brother and heir to King Mandouma. Here you are nothing but an animal, less in value even than the horse you were riding. Obey me and come peacefully and you will not be hurt. Try to escape, try to kill yourself, try to stop eating or any of the other tricks your people know that bring self-destruction and you will be punished. I will have you flogged until your flesh falls from your bones in chunks of raw meat and I will leave you on the ground for the ants to devour."

Tamboura managed to get to his knees and the big black hands of Akeem reached down and lifted him up. The delicate brown hands of Ama-jallah felt Tamboura's body, sliding over the streaked clay and the sweat. They gauged the muscles, the framework, the chest, the belly and the thighs. They lifted and weighed the genitals and noted the hood of skin, forcing it back, then releasing it.

"It is well your tribe are not true believers. When will they learn that conversion to Islam will protect them from being slaves?" The hands left Tamboura's body. "Prime condition. Better than we usually get." He seemed to be speaking to himself.

"Akeem!" Ama-jallah beckoned the black close to him and wiped the sticky clay and sweat from his fingers onto the broad back of the Negro. "To work!" He turned and started back to where the hands of the slaves were being untied so that they could feed themselves. At a distance of about three paces, he turned. Once again the whip sang through the air and Tamboura felt its sting as it wrapped around his shoulders. But he did not heed it, for suddenly pain, discomfort, heat, everything he might feel was consumed in the flame of his anger. He watched the elegant ripples of the white robe leave without a change of expression.

"You come, boy," Akeem motioned to him. "You come, eat."

Tamboura followed him mechanically, sat where Akeem pointed for him to sit, dumbly accepted the mess of boiled yams and cassava that was placed before him on a broad leaf. He had no desire for food but he recognized strength in the meal, so he ate, slopping the food into his mouth with dirty fingers, chewing and swallowing without tasting. After the food there was water, a small cup of it, hot, greenish and stinking of the goat skin in which it had been carried, but he drank it greedily. His haunches were on the ground and he knew his earth spirit was helping him because he could feel his strength returning. Suddenly there was a crash in the underbrush and he saw the tawny flesh of a lioness, awakened from her midday sleep by the halt of the caravan and now prowling as near as she dared to scent these strange invaders. The brief glimpse he had of her hindquarters as she leaped through the underbrush gave him further reassurance. His spirit was following him and protecting him. For the first time, he squared his shoulders and looked around.

Seated not far away from him was a face he recognized. It was that of Sabumbo, the young hunter from his own village. He had been orphaned and lived with his uncle, and now his uncle, in his senile desire for a young wench from a neighboring village, had sold Sabumbo into slavery to pay the price of his young bride.

His own hands and feet both untied, Tamboura crept down the line, glad of a face that he knew and a mind that encompassed his own village and knew the familiar names and the gossip about them all. He squatted on his heels beside Sabumbo, whose feet were bound with a grass rope. Sabumbo looked up at him, recognized him and spat on the ground before turning his face away.

"Coward!" Sabumbo spat again. "Afraid of the knife!"

"What mean you that I am a coward?" Tamboura's anger so very near the surface met the other's words. "Say that again and I will. . . ." His rage exploded into wordlessness.

Sabumbo, like all the young men of the village, was a tall, muscular young buck, perhaps a year or so older than Tamboura. He turned his vapid and rather stupid face toward Tamboura and laughed with derision.

"My feet may be bound but my hands are not. I suppose you would hit me and then run as you did from the knife last night."

"Now you say it a second time. I did not run from the knife last night. Think you that if I had run I would be here?"

Sabumbo considered Tamboura's question and saw some logic in it. His thick lips pressed closely together and, as understanding came, he nodded slowly.

"A slave caffle would be a strange place to run to, but perhaps it would be better than being a renegade. For myself, I do not mind too much being here. But for you! Had you been afraid, you would have run to the bush and joined up with the renegades. No, I do not think you would have sold yourself into slavery."

"And I did not. I remember nothing after I drank the millet beer in my brother's hut. Bansu, my brother's son, gave it to me."

"And then your brother came to the group at the fire with downcast eyes and beating his chest. He said that you had fled, afraid of the knife. He said that your blood had turned to water and that you had disgraced him. Ah, Tamboura, it begins to make sense. It was they who drugged your beer and sold you into slavery to get rid of you."

"So that Bansu may be the next king." Tamboura crept closer to Sabumbo. "I think you are right. I know it, Sabumbo! And now?" He gazed around him. "What now?"

"Now we are slaves. We're heading down the river and we'll be sold like so many head of cattle."

"It's bad, Sabumbo?"

The hunter nodded. "Squat here, boy." He edged over to make room for Tamboura. "When they tie us again, they'll not notice and they'll tie you behind me. That means we can be together on the march. We're from the same village and it makes us like brothers. We can help each other."

Tamboura squatted beside him and they continued to talk. Soon Akeem came along, knotting the rope that led from neck to neck. He recognized Tamboura, but merely proceeded to secure him behind Sabumbo. He slipped a wide hoop of woven bamboo over Tamboura's shoulders and tied his hands to it, letting it fall free around the hips. The big black was not unkind. When he saw the raw cuts the thongs had made, he tied Tamboura's hands loosely, and when he looped and fastened a length of grass rope around each ankle he allowed enough slack for a normal step.

The brief rest had renewed Tamboura's strength and the assurance of seeing the lion in the brush, and being with Sabumbo, had renewed his courage. He had never known Sabumbo well as he was in a different age group but now, in truth, he felt as close to him as to a brother. Although the anger in his heart had not died, he began to feel better. Up in front of the long line of slaves, he saw them striking the awning which had been set up for Ama-jallah's meal and he watched the Arab mount the horse which had been brought for him. Tamboura turned and regarded the young slave who was tied behind him. The fellow grinned back at him with a row of white teeth. At the rear of the line of slaves, perhaps some two hundred in all, there were horses and riders.

Ama-jallah rode down the line of the kaffle, flicking his whip idly at the standing men. Tamboura stood out from the rest because of the remnants of white clay which still adhered to his body. The Arab checked his horse briefly and glanced down appraisingly at the boy. The dark Arab eyes approved. His lips curled in a half-smile. All of his male slaves were fine muscular specimens but this one was different. He was the brother of King Mandouma; generations of selected blood lines had produced this rich young body with its promise of prodigious strength, its long clean limbs, its powerful arms and the face of classic barbaric beauty. Ama-jallah's love for a bargain was satisfied. This, the best slave of the whole lot, had cost him nothing, not even a single bead. The boy was a Hausa, what's more a Royal Hausa, and the Hausas along with the Mandingos and the Fantis were the best breed for slaves. Strong, powerful, but gentle if they were gentled, almost doglike in their devotion to a master who treated them well! And this boy would be a breeder—one could be sure of that; breeders were what they wanted in the big market across the sea. It was whispered along the slave coast that soon there might be a law prohibiting the transport of slaves across the water, so the foreign owners were breeding them themselves against that day. This boy would bring a good price. One had only to look at him to know that there were a thousand sons in his loins.

The thin whip curled out gently and fell across Tamboura's shoulders but there was no sting in the lash. It was more of a caress.

Ama-jallah turned his horse and rode to the head of the line. Somewhere up front a drum began to beat with a slow, monotonous rhythm that started the men in the caffle moving their feet in time to its beating. There was a shout and the drum spoke with a series of hard blows. Tamboura saw the man in front of Sabumbo step ahead, then Sabumbo, and he timed his steps to those of his brother from the village. One step, then another and another and another. He did not know where he was going, but somehow it did not matter. He walked along, carrying the burden of his grief and anger which rested far more heavily on his shoulders than the antelope of yesterday. He walked. The drum beat and he walked and all he saw was the rope that led from Sabumbo's neck to his own and the drops of sweat that oozed from the skin of Sabumbo's back, gathered, joined and trickled down the deep channel to spread out over his buttocks and fall to the ground of Africa.

## chapter iii

THE SUN was spreading a palette of purple, gold and flame, just before sinking out of sight, when they reached the river. It was not like the shallow, sandy-shoaled little stream which circled about Tamboura's village. That was hardly a river; during the dry season, the crocodiles had scarcely enough water to cover their backs. This was the big river, the one Tamboura had heard about but never expected to see. This was Africa's river of mystery, the mighty Niger, which flowed slowly down to the sea like a stream of viscous oil in a tunnel of verdigris.

During the latter part of their day's journey, the whole aspect of the land had changed. It was no longer hot and sunburned, with dusty trails, parched grass, stunted tamarisk and thorn, but violently green, dark and miasmic. The trail changed from dust which rose like a cloud and settled on their bodies to oozy mud which spurted between their toes. The fierce blaze of the sun was lost, strained through a thick canopy of leaves overhead, and the hanging lianas were arm-thick, like immense snakes hanging straight down from the lofty trees. Only rarely did they see a splotch of sky and then it disappeared as something glimpsed briefly from the bottom of a well whose sides were damply green and unwholesome. The hot steamy stillness was oppressive; the eerie quietness was enhanced rather than disturbed by the chattering of parrots in the branches above and the humming of thousands of insects below. A sooty cloud of gnats and midges like the smoke of a campfire of green wood followed them, settling on their faces and bodies until their skin crawled with a fluttering, devouring life that bit into it, inflamed their eyelids, crawled deep inside their ears and nostrils and even into their mouths, so that when they swallowed, their spit was grained with insects. With their hands bound to the bamboo rings, they were helpless to do anything but walk on, on, on, forever in time to the metronomic beat of the drum which had now become a part of themselves.

There were a few women in the rear of the caffle—all young, some pregnant and others carrying children in their arms. Whatever their condition, they were forced to keep up with the men, and when one woman, heavy with child, met her time along the road, the column halted only long enough for her to be cut out of the line. For a few moments she groveled in the slime, arching her swollen body with high-pitched moans until the knife of the flat-faced Akeem slashed at her throat and her spasms stopped. Again his knife slashed, this time at her belly and the child was laid bare. He nipped the cord with his teeth and handed the baby to a woman who was toting her own infant, relieving her of it and handing it to an unencumbered female. The mother reached for the newborn baby, examined its sex and when she found it was a boy, put it to her breast. The whole episode had taken only a short time. The caffle was retied, the corpse already thick with insects was abandoned, and they were on their way again.

Ama-jallah had kept to his schedule. Now there were calls in the near distance, and the sound of water. The Arab rode on ahead, soon to return and whip the long line of the caffle into a quicker step. They were almost trotting when they arrived at a clearing by the side of the river where a sand spit ran out into the water. Black against the yellow sand were lined the canoes—the big wooden canoes that required twelve men to paddle each one. Tamboura could not count beyond the fingers of both hands but he could see that there were more canoes than he had fingers.

Akeem and his helpers quickly untied the hands of the slaves from the bamboo hoops, which were then piled high over a stake to await the return of Ama-jallah. After that the grass ropes were removed and they were free except for the rope which led from neck to neck. More food was awaiting them and this time it was not even put on a leaf. Instead they held out their cupped hands to receive it, and slobbered it into their mouths like animals. But more welcome even than the food was the water, which was plentiful and clean. They were led out on the sand spit and allowed to lie flat on their bellies and drink as much as they wanted. It was warm and tasted of mud but it was clean and refreshing. Then they were made to squat ankle-deep in water and relieve themselves if they could.

The whips stood them on their feet again and the Kru canoe boys, who had been awaiting their arrival, walked down the long straggling line of the caffle, counting on their fingers. When they had counted off both hands three times, they cut the neck-binding rope and marched their thirty men off to a waiting canoe. Although the canoes were large enough to accommodate twelve paddlers, it was a tight squeeze to force thirty men into such a limited space. The end man in the line was whipped into the canoe after it had been shoved off into deep water. He was boosted over the side and held down with his legs spread wide apart. The next man climbed in and was pushed up as closely to the first man as possible, his buttocks grinding against the other's groin, his elbows resting on the other's knees. And so it went, one after another, until the canoe was packed tightly with men, buttock to groin, each immovable from the hips down. Now, for the first time, the metal accouterments of slavery appeared. A light chain was run along the gunwales of the canoe and handcuffs of iron were spaced along the chain, snapped over the wrists of the slaves and locked, thus immobilizing hands and arms as well as legs and feet. From the loaded canoe, a strong rope ran to another canoe which accommodated the Krus and a certain amount of baggage. One by one the canoes were loaded, and they started off down the river.

The whole operation was managed with the utmost economy of motion. The Krus were experts at their trade. They constantly plied the river from its delta to various spots which were used as rendezvous for overland caravans, meeting them and taking the slave caffle down to the various factories on the shore, then returning with the trade goods and meeting another caravan.

Night came quickly with an impenetrable blackness through which neither moon nor stars could be seen. With the night came hordes of mosquitoes, and now Tamboura began to be glad for what little was left of his clay anointing of the night before and for the mud which had hardened on his back after the brief rest when he had stretched out full length on the earth during the childbirth. He was seated between Sabumbo and the young slave who had grinned at him, somewhere in the middle of the canoe. With hands and feet both immobilized there was no way to ward the insects off, but by leaning forward and brushing his head against Sabumbo's back, he could rid his brother of some of the pests, and he was grateful for the almost metallic scraping of the hair of the man behind him on his own back.

After an hour, every muscle in his body cried out for relief. As the interminable night wore on, Tamboura found some relief by leaning forward and resting his head on Sabumbo's shoulders and then, when aching muscles began to cramp in this position, he leaned back and rested his head on the chest of the fellow behind him, whose name he discovered to be M'dong. He felt closer to Sabumbo, however, because of their common background, and each found that talking helped to pass the long sleepless hours of the night. It kept up their spirits and quieted their unknown fears.

"As for myself, I do not mind, Tamboura," Sabumbo admitted. "Life in the village held nothing for me after my father and mother died. I went to live with my uncle and from that day on I planned to get away even if it meant taking a woman from another village and being a slave to her family, because I had no goods with which to pay her bride-price. The old man and the old woman didn't want me, although she was never unkind to me when I was a kid. After I became a hunter, she died and then the old man began to get jealous because the girls wanted me and not one of them would go into the bushes with him after the dances."

"You can't blame them," Tamboura said. "He was too ugly and too old."

"Too old and too limp," Sabumbo laughed. "But he got the idea that Kanili could put new strength into him. He had the witch doctor working over him for nights at a time, feeding him pepper broth and dancing around the hut until at last—I don't know if it was the spirits or the pepper broth—he managed to be a man again. Then he started to look around for a new wife but not a girl or woman in the village would have him. So he went over to Bingtu and found a young girl whose father's eyes opened wide when my uncle promised him three bolts of cloth, two trade kettles and a gourdful of bugle beads."

"And where did your uncle think he would get all that wealth?" Tamboura was familiar with his reputation as the poorest and the stingiest man in the whole village.

"The old fellow had the gift of tongues and he soft-talked them into it with promises." Sabumbo's head was on Tamboura's chest and he shook it violently to dislodge the mosquitoes. "The old fellow was not so stupid after all and it was not all soft-talking because he knew I would fetch that amount when the next slave caffle came along. Not only would he get the goods to buy his new wife but he would get rid of me at the same time."

"Did you know?" Tamboura shifted one leg and managed to stretch a muscle. He sighed with relief.

"No, but what good would it have done me? I had no way to escape except to the camp of the renegades, and believe me, their life is worse than a slave's. They have no women in their camp except some worthless wretches they capture by raiding a village and they wear them out in a week. So I stayed on but it was even worse when he brought this woman back to the hut. You never saw her because you were away from the village in the camp of the boys. She was young with a soft, smooth body. Well! You know what happened."

Tamboura thought for a moment. "No."

Sabumbo laughed. "Every night after my uncle had sweated and groaned and worked over her for a long time without accomplishing anything, he would be so tired out, he'd fall off to sleep, and then she'd crawl over to my mat. Believe me, after what I'd been listening to, I was standing as straight and strong as my own spirit pole—ready and waiting for her. And after what she'd been through she was ready for all I had to give her. So she got knocked up and the old man went all around the village, crowing like a cock and saying now he could prove that he had regained his youth. Everybody was laughing at him behind his back. They all knew I was the one who had done it. One day somebody told him as much, and then. . . . Well, that's why I'm here."

Tamboura felt the flame of hot anger searing him again at the thought of Sabumbo's betrayal and his by their own people.

"This isn't too good but it won't be too bad either," Sabumbo said, as if he had read Tamboura's thoughts. "We go down the river and then we get on a big canoe, so big that there are no paddles but it has white wings like a bird. I've heard tell about it. Then that big canoe takes us to another world where all a man has to do is to raise children from more women than there are leaves on a tree. He can eat and sleep all day and take on a stready stream of women all night. That's the life I want. It's better than staying in our little village and having nothing but my uncle's wife and a girl once a full moon after the dances. I'd never have goods to buy a wife of my own."

There was a long silence while Tamboura turned the prospects over in his mind. What had he back in the village? It was his home, yes. But what kind of a home would it be in his brother's hut with the three of them always against him? True, some day he would be king but that might be a long time away. Mandouma was still young and he was not brave like the other brothers. He never took chances in hunting or on slaving expeditions to faraway villages. *Maybe I am better off,* Tamboura thought. The picture Sabumbo painted of an endless stream of women every night was certainly appealing. But . . . his heart sank. No matter how many women there were, he would not be able to do anything with them. He was still uncut and . . . unclean.

He sighed deeply. "It will be all right for you, Sabumbo, my brother, and it would have been all right for me if they had but waited another day and I could have become a man. Now, as long as I live, no woman will ever have me."

"You speak stupid words, my brother. Stupid words! In our little village, you could not have had a woman had you stayed there as you are now, but our custom does not extend to all the villages in Africa or even to all the Hausas. 'Tis said that our custom came from the filthy Arabs, like the one that has us now. No, my brother, believe me, in some villages you would not be able to have a woman if you *were* cut."

"He speaks the truth, boy." M'dong had been listening to the conversation and joined in. "In my village, which is many days' walk from yours, we do not have the custom. Once a man who was cut like that was captured by our hunters and brought to the village. Our women saw him and tore him to pieces. They said he was not only unclean but incomplete. Do not let it bother you. I have had plenty of women, sometimes ten in a night. So too will you."

"Is that true, Sabumbo?" Tamboura felt a great joy that wiped out all his weariness and pain. "Is it true what M'dong says?"

"It is, Tamboura, it is."

"I swear it by my spirit," M'dong answered. " 'Tis said that women prefer a man who is uncut and also that a man gets more pleasure."

"Then I shall go with you willingly, Sabumbo. We shall see that other land you speak of and together we shall sire thousands of children. I have no regrets about leaving the village." He hesitated. "Well, just one."

"And what is that, my brother?"

"I was thinking of Iba, the daughter of Layoumba. Do you remember her?"

"The little bitch with the pointed tits?" Sabumbo laughed.

"The same."

"Then have no regret." Sabumbo laughed again and this time Tamboura could feel the contractions in Sabumbo's body against his chest. "Of all the girls in the village, she was the poorest and the most worthless."

"You have had her?"

"Once I tried and I never chose her again. You have missed nothing there. She lets a man do nothing at all and if he tries, she squeals and whines and fights back until he loses all desire. All she wants to do is play with her fingers."

"I know the kind," M'dong confirmed Sabumbo's words. "Once in a while you'll find one like that."

"Then if what you say is true, Sabumbo, I go with not even one regret." Tamboura sat up straight. "Perhaps tomorrow we shall reach the big water and see the canoe with the white wings. It will take us out of this world to another where we shall sleep all day and lie with women all night. Now I am happy, Sabumbo."

"Then sleep, little brother." Sabumbo shifted his legs as much as possible, rolled his head into a more comfortable position on Tamboura's chest and became quiet. Tamboura did the same, turning his cheek against the warm, damp flesh of M'dong. They slept in spite of leg-ache and arm-ache and back-ache.

But morning did not find them at the sea. The next morning they were still on the river and the next and the next, until eight mornings had passed with only a short rest each day when they were unchained and allowed to get out of the canoe so they might walk the kinks out of their cramped muscles on some sandy riverbank, and eat, drink and relieve themselves.

# chapter iv

Don Fernando Francisco Bernardo de Llariñago y Tait, better known as Mongo Don from Accra to Calabar along the Gold Coast and even as far down south in Africa as Loanda, slowly opened his eyes and shuddered. Mongo Don hated everything along the Gold Coast with the possible exception of the good solid pounds sterling it had enabled him to pile up to his credit in the offices of Tait & Llariñago, Factors, of Liverpool. But most of all, upon awakening, he hated himself with a bitter, nameless loathing that encompassed everything he had ever done or touched. He looked with disgust at the gray cotton sheet—grayed not because it was unclean, but because of the continued washings in the water of the Niger; at the unkempt bed; the hard-packed dirt floor which, no matter how often it was swept, looked exactly like what it was—dirt. Even more contemptible was the sweaty form of the Negro wench, sleeping soundly beside him, her breath still reeking of rum, her tight black cap of wiry wool peppercorned into little mounds, a drool of saliva hanging from her thick lips and her skin almost livid in the morning light. His own aging body, with the long gray hairs plastered with sweat to his bony chest, and his whole emaciated frame were equally repulsive to him. With supreme disgust, he edged away from the sweating black curves so closely plastered against him, to allow a passage of air between his own sticky body and that of the woman. She grunted like an animal disturbed in its rest and shifted her body so that her back was to him. He cursed her silently and then, unable to stomach any longer the impassive sleep of his companion, drew up his knees and placed his bunioned and misshapen feet with their long yellow nails against the middle of her back and pushed.

She slid from the bed and landed on the floor with a dull thud like a sack of grain but the scream that rent the air was high-pitched and was immediately followed by a string of curses, rich in the many-voweled syllables of Hausa. Still dazed, she hoisted herself to her knees, rubbed her eyes with the back of her hands and began a lower-keyed howling which further served to tauten Mongo Don's already strained nerves.

"You no love-a Jobeena more?" she wailed.

"Shut your blabbering mouth and get out, you black she-elephant." He pointed to the doorway. "Out! Do you hear me?" He half rose in bed and threatened her with a weakly clenched fist. "Out, or by every dirty heathen god from here to Ethiopia, I'll flatten your goddam nose even flatter than it is now." His cursing was in cultured English, betrayed only by a lisping Spanish accent.

Jobeena stopped her howling, cutting it off abruptly on the rising crescendo of one final shriek, reached down to pick up a shapeless mass of once-red cloth, now faded to a dirty pink, and slipped it over her head. The garment fitted itself snugly to the full, voluptuous curves of her body but it could not hide the coarseness of her face, the cropped hair, the spreading nostrils and the thick lips. Her skin lost its grayness as the full light of the sun hit it through the half-open shutters, making it gleam in stripes of brown and black.

Jobeena scratched under her arms as she regarded the unhealthy whiteness and blotched redness of Mongo Don's body on the bed. "I go, Masta Mongo," she said. There was an equal contempt in her voice. She had a lover among the slave guards and much preferred the violent thrusting of her Negro to the weak efforts of this old man. But her compliance to the white man meant money. Her black man could pay her only in pleasure.

"Yes, get out." Mongo Don felt he could not look at her another moment. "And don't come back tonight, at least not if that covenanting Scot arrives for his cargo. Stay away until he gets t'hell out of here. I've no mind for a lecture on 'sinnin', fornicatin' and adulterin'.' "

"Yes, Masta Mongo, I don' come back while he's here."

"And tell Blackanna to send me a cup of coffee and some bread and tell her to fetch Mister Jonathan."

"Yes, Masta Mongo."

"And now, get moving!" He waited impatiently for her to leave and close the door behind her, then started to scratch his legs, covered with the dry red scabs of some tropical fungus.

Dammit! He wished he were back in Havana. He was fed

up with Africa and rum and black wenches and slave trading, worn out with carrying the whole responsibility of the factory on his shoulders. What did he have Jonathan out here for? How could the young squirt learn the business if he never knew what to do without being told? But no, Jonathan was a good lad and learning fast. Already he had relieved him of much of the work. By the bleeding wounds of Christ, he was sick of it all! His mind stretched ahead to some future morning in Havana when he could wake up in a civilized bed in a civilized room beside a civilized white woman—or at least an octoroon—who didn't smell of vegetable butter and sweat. They could eat a civilized breakfast together and then he would leave her and devote the rest of his day to his painting. Absently he scratched at the red incrustations on his legs until the blood came.

Dammit! He'd never last another year in this hell-hole. Fever and scabs and wasting away! Rum and slaves and haggling slave captains! Arabs and more slaves and more haggling! Heat and malaria and dirt, no matter how hard one tried to keep the place clean. And now, on top of all these other things, a day's work ahead of him. The *Augustus Tait* was due to anchor in a day or two and that Bible-shouting Captain MacPherson would soon be coming ashore in his long boat, preaching out of his mouth one minute and fingering the wenches all over the next. Wanted to see if they were fit! Wanted to see if they were virgins! Ay, *la virgin sanctissima,* the only virgins they ever had were those under ten years old and one couldn't be too goddam sure about them, either. The little sluts started spreading their legs back in their native villages when they were about twelve and after that not a one of them could pass any virginity test. All the Captain wanted was an excuse to finger them. Oh, to hell with it all! And to make matters worse, runners had come the night before from Ama-jallah, that goddamned Arab princeling. He would arrive today, expecting to be kowtowed to like the King of Spain.

Ama-jallah, the half-breed son of the Sultan of Zinder! Sultan of Shit! Half Arab and half Negro, living in a mud palace and calling himself a Sultan. And his high-nosed son with all his affectations of elegance—his embroidered slippers, his robes of white muslin and his strings of pearls! Bah! The bastard—and he probably was a bastard—wouldn't know an El Greco from a Velasquez!

Velasquez, El Greco, Goya! Boucher, Fragonard, Largillière! How Mongo Don loved the names and the great paintings they stood for. He looked at the half-finished canvas propped up on an easel in the corner. Yes, he hated that too. How could a man paint a white woman when he had not seen one in seven years? Velasquez? Bah, he couldn't have painted one either. Seven years of thick lips and wide nostrils and hair like wool! What was that verse his English mother had taught him?—"Bah, bah, black sheep, have you any wool?"

No need to ask the stinking blacks that question. All they had was wool—wiry, close-cropped and rough. Nothing a man could run his hands through and let cascade through his fingers like strands of silk; nothing he could sink his face into and smell the faint and indescribably delicious aroma that exists only in the beloved's hair. Wiry wool and stinking armpits. Mongo Don shuddered. How he hated Africa. And yet, did he? Africa had eluded him, escaped him. There was something grand and wonderful, something regal and majestic about Africa but he had never been able to find it. There was strength and beauty if he could just glimpse it, if he could. . . .

He was daydreaming again and there was work to do. Get the guest house ready for Ama-jallah! Probably the bastard had the same kind of kinky wool on his head but he knew enough to keep it covered with a turban of white muslin. Oh well! What was it he had to do? Get the guest house ready; have it swept and garnished. Spread the divan with new cloths. Take down the rotting curtains and put up new ones. Go to the warehouse and pick out the blasted presents that royalty—black-blooded and black-skinned royalty—expected. But wait. . . . Jonathan would do that. Jonathan knew enough now to take over the chores and let his uncle relax. Relax! He knew what would relax him. If he could paint one picture, just one picture, and feel that he had put a soul into it, he would be happy.

Mongo Don shifted his long, lean shanks over the edge of the bed, groped under it with one hand for the porcelain chamber pot and sat on the very edge of the thin mattress, letting the slow stream trickle down. He sighed and shook his head. He'd like a bath but he didn't have time. He needed a shave but that would come later. The gray bristle of his beard scratched his hand as he rubbed his face and he wondered if it had scratched Jobeena's smooth skin last night. He hoped it had. From the wardrobe he pulled out a pair of clean pantaloons which, like the sheets, had once been white but were now a dusty gray, slipped them on, and put his feet into thonged sandals. There was a rap at the door.

"Come in," he called, lifting his arms to his shirtsleeves.

The door swung open slowly, propelled by the black foot of a naked Negro urchin. He bore a tray covered with a grayed white napkin, which was immediately whisked out of his hand by the man behind him. A playful slap on the fat little rump of the boy sent him scampering away.

"Time you were here, Jonathan," Mongo Don grumbled. "There's a lot of work to be done today."

"Already started, sir." Jonathan Danson was the exact opposite of Mongo Don. Where the Mongo was old and ravaged by his years on the Gold Coast, Jonathan was young and pinkly fresh as though he had stepped out of a Devonshire cottage on a misty October morning. One could never imagine there was any blood relationship between the two, but Jonathan was Mongo Don's great-nephew, fresh out of the Liverpool countinghouse which owned and controlled the slave factory here at Yendo Castle in the Niger Delta. Mongo Don represented the Spanish side of the family which, in the previous generation, had married with the English to found the Llariñago-Tait dynasty. Now they owned not only the vast warehouses, piers and offices in Liverpool and Havana but three factories on the Gold Coast of which Yendo Castle was the largest, as well as the fleet of sturdy slavers which plied back and forth across the Atlantic. From Liverpool they came to Africa, loaded with gaudily printed cottons, copper kettles, iron pans, bugle beads, cheap mirrors and all the other claptrap of trade goods. Then back across the Middle Passage to Cuba, loaded with their most precious cargo—slaves—and carrying also ivory, wax, oil and gold. Once they had discharged their living cargo in Havana, they filled with tobacco, rum, sugar and rare Cuban woods for the return journey to Liverpool. There was a cargo waiting in every port and a ready profit from each one but the biggest profit of all was from the black sons and daughters of Africa whose seed would soon spread across all the new world.

"Already started, sir," Jonathan repeated so cheerfully that it made Mongo Don wince just to look at him. "The compound's been swept, the guest house cleaned—"

"New curtains?" Mongo Don raised his head, hoping that this particular item might have been missed.

"New curtains that will knock Ama-jallah's eyes out. Special chair set up for His Highness on the porch alongside yours and gifts lined up for his inspection."

"What gifts?"

Jonathan ticked them off on his fingers. "One brass clock, one crystal chandelier with a hundred wax candles—"

"Change them to tallow, the stinking Sultan will never know the difference."

"Yes, sir," Jonathan nodded, "and one bolt of rose damask—"

"Silk or cotton?" Mongo Don was hoping to catch the boy in some error.

"Silk on a cotton warp, sir, but it looks like silk." He waited for Mongo Don to nod his head in approval before he continued. "Twelve bottles of assorted French scent and twelve cases of Cuban rum."

Mongo Don spat on the floor. "The bastards say their religion prohibits them from touching liquor, but I notice they always lap it up."

"The Sultan of Zinder finds it a powerful medicine," Jonathan winked, "and twelve Sheffield spoons, a brass crown with glass jewels and three second-hand French court gowns."

"For Ama-jallah's three wives. What if he has a fourth by now?"

"We've others in the storehouse."

Mongo Don sipped his coffee and broke the hot bread into chunks, which he dipped into the strong brew and then sucked into his mouth. He was unable to chew with his stubble of broken teeth.

"And food for the caravan?"

"Ten goats slaughtered and hung for the slaves. Three sheep for Ama-jallah's *cous-cous*." He stopped suddenly.

Mongo Don held up a warning finger for silence.

"Hark! Can it be the bastard's coming now?"

"Either that, sir, or all hell's broke loose on the river. Listen!" Jonathan cupped his hand to his ear and his foot instinctively started tapping to the beat of the drum which set the stroke for the first canoe. A volley of shots was fired, causing all the pigeons in the compound to take flight, followed by another that started them off as soon as they had settled. There was a loud banging of kettles, accompanied by bursts of song from the Krus and even a chorus of feeble shouts from the canoe loads of slaves, who had sensed they were nearing their final destination.

The noise of the arrival had aroused the whole of Yendo

Castle, free and slave, village and factory. Although the arrival of a slave caravan from the interior was not as exciting as a ship from overseas, it meant a break in the monotony of the lives of the factory slaves and the villagers. Their bare feet could be heard padding across the compound, and by the time Mongo Don and Jonathan had arrived at the landing stage there were perhaps a hundred people crowded around and onto the jerry-built bamboo piers that straggled out into the river.

The first canoe, partially tented with the same striped fabric which had shaded Tamboura on his first day, with its Krus glistening with palm oil, swept up to the pier with a flourish, where it was moored by half a hundred black hands eager to reach out and draw it closer. There was a flutter beneath the awning and it parted to show Ama-jallah, resplendent in pure white muslin and reeking of cheap French perfume. A board was laid from pier to canoe and he walked over it—carefully so as not to lose his balance; slowly, to retain his dignity; and majestically, to impress the cadaverous, unshaven Spaniard and the young, pink-cheeked Englishman.

They greeted each other in Hausa, using the stilted phrases of Islamic courtesy, and after the greeting all waited expectantly until a volley of shots was fired from the factory. Meticulously Ama-jallah counted the shots on the fingers of his hands. Twenty-one! He beamed his satisfaction. Only royalty received that salute. It put him in a good mood and he walked along between Mongo Don and Jonathan, making sure that they measured their gait to his, not he his to theirs. In deference to him, they walked a step behind him as they progressed slowly up the path that led by the barracoons, past the whitewashed log walls of the factory, the warehouses, the offices, and across the hard-packed earth of the clean-swept compound to the Mongo's porticoed home, bordered by a row of feather-duster palms which gave no shade but did manage to decorate with a fluff of greenery.

Mongo Don allowed Ama-jallah to ascend the steps of the wide-roofed portico first. He motioned to the ornate chair, beribboned and decorated with tufts of dyed ostrich plumes and swags of varicolored beads, in contrast to his own chair which was not decorated. Ama-jallah seated himself, carefully arranging his robes. He spoke for the first time since he had left the pier. His Hausa words were slow but fluent.

"May Allah bring peace to your household, Mongo Don."

"And may you find peace here, Your Highness."

They sat silently for several minutes as Ama-jallah studied, with seeming indifference, the gifts lined up on the edge of the porch. His dark eyes glittered with cupidity. When Mongo Don motioned to Jonathan to bring the gifts, the Arab scanned them one by one, apparently without interest, although the crystal chandelier did cause him some wonderment.

"To hang in your father's throne room," Mongo Don explained, realizing how incongruous it would look, hanging from the rafters under the thatched roof of a mud hut.

Ama-jallah graciously accepted the explanation without giving any indication that he had never seen such an implement of civilization before. But he seemed satisfied and he reached inside his *djellabah* to draw out a parchment, covered in Arabic script. He read from it slowly and apologetically as though the mere mention of business was beneath his royal dignity.

"One hundred and thirteen slaves, consisting of ninety-eight young men between the ages of fifteen and twenty-seven years. Fifteen women, four with babies, six pregnant and five virgins. Seventy-two prime tusks of ivory. Six bales of ostrich and other plumes. Gold dust and nuggets in a quantity to be weighed."

He allowed the paper to flutter from his hands as an evidence of its worthlessness. Jonathan retrieved it and handed it back to him but he waved it away with utter unconcern.

"With your permission, Your Highness"—Mongo Don was sufficiently humble although he was inwardly cursing the arrogance of this would-be princeling—"we shall have the slaves unloaded and taken to the barracoons and the other goods delivered to the factory."

A languid right hand, slightly raised, was Ama-jallah's consent. He rose slowly and called for his slave Akeem who squatted at the foot of a palm tree. With a short nod to Mongo Don and an even shorter one to Jonathan, he descended the steps and made his way across the compound to the guest house, where he had stayed several times before and where he knew he would find two slaves, male and female, carefully selected for his use.

Mongo Don and Jonathan watched his studied progress across the compound.

"Arrogant young pup!" Jonathan wrinkled his nose in the Arab's direction.

"But our best supplier—always prime merchandise! Brings

only fine strong young men and that's what they want in Cuba these days. They're breeding slaves over there now—afraid of the Abolitionists in England. Must tell him to be on the lookout for more wenches. They want them too."

"Wenches didn't used to bring much."

"No, but they will from now on. Keep Ama-jallah buttered up. Doesn't cost anything but a sacrifice of your own pride. Keep him eating out of your hand by making him think that he and his black papa are the most important personages in Africa. It costs little and you'll gain much."

"It goes against the grain." Jonathan's straightforward bluntness could not stomach the affectations of the Arab.

"What do you care as long as it piles up good solid English pounds for you in Liverpool? And now to work, Jonathan. Send the men from the warehouse to unload the canoes and lose no time in unlocking those poor wretches. Cattle they may be but even a dog can suffer pain. Take them to the empty barracoon that we cleaned and fumigated last week. Don't put them in with the slaves that we have been holding. Give them preferential treatment these first few days to condition them. Let them rest all the afternoon. At sunset have them chained and taken down to the stockade in the river and let them wash themselves. Issue a bucket of soft soap for every canoe load and make sure they wash their heads, to get rid of the lice. I only hope none of this lot have crabs. After they've rested, give them a good supper—a hearty stew of meat and vegetables, then issue them a couple of kegs of palm oil so they can rub each other down. Clean, oiled, rested and their bellies full, they'll condition quickly and think they're in heaven. By tomorrow, you'll see no unhappy wretches but a grinning, happy bunch of prime slaves, Ama-jallah always brings the best—Hausas, Fullahs and sometimes even Mandingos."

Jonathan started to leave, to follow out the Mongo's commands. He knew exactly what to do himself but he realized it gave his uncle a feeling of authority to tell him and he suffered it good-naturedly.

"And guards?" Jonathan asked, already knowing the answer.

"Two in each corner blockhouse and have others walk the rounds outside the stockade tonight. The poor bastards are too lame and tired to run away but we'll take no chances."

Mongo Don turned and walked into the house, passing through the long common room with its litter of shabby, though once ornate, furnishings and into his bedroom. He looked at the canvas propped against the easel, the simpering face, the rosebud lips, the delicate blonde hair and the staring blue eyes. Why torture his soul? There wasn't a white woman in a thousand miles except some broken down whores in Calabar. And, after all, why should he paint a white woman? He knew he'd never see one again. He'd never last the year out.

His hand smeared the wet paint over the canvas, which he lifted off the easel and regarded with mingled hatred and sorrow. His fist crashed through it and he threw the torn daub to the floor. A sudden spell of dizziness caused him to grab one of the bedposts for support. Then slowly, walking like a man in a dream, he went into the other room and returned with a larger canvas on a stretcher and stood it against the easel. Its blank whiteness mocked him. There was, he knew, some message which he wanted to paint on it but what it was he did not know. It had something to do with Africa and it certainly was not the simpering grace of a heartless coquette. Something deeper, richer, greater and grander than that must be put on the canvas while he was still able —something that would tell the world about these last seven years, some monument he could leave behind him. It would not tell about the heat and squalor and flies; it would not depict a black wench with her thick lips, nor an avaricious young Arab Prince. Instead it must be something big, something wonderful, something strong and vigorous.

But, as always, it eluded him. He fell back on the unmade bed. The sheets reeked of Jobeena's musk and it nauseated him but he was too weary to get up. If he called her back tonight, as he probably would if MacPherson didn't arrive, he must tell her to scrub her armpits and douse them with scent.

# chapter v

Exhausted as he was, Tamboura had felt the contagion of general excitement as the canoes neared their destination. With the hope of liberation from the days of cramped travel, he was shouting as lustily as the Krus themselves when their boat, the third in the line, was maneuvered up to the rickety wharf by the towing canoe, and the many black hands reached out from the wharf to secure it. No sooner were they alongside than their handcuffs were loosened and they were helped out. Their legs were so cramped they were scarcely able to stand but they managed to propel themselves stiff-legged along the slippery bamboo flooring of the pier and at last onto solid ground. For the first time since Tamboura had left his home village, he was not bound in any way—his feet and hands were free and there was no constricting rope around his neck.

Led by a Negro guard, wearing an old scarlet military jacket and nothing else, they were taken to the neighboring barracoons. These were an extensive part of the settlement of Yendo Castle, heavily stockaded by tree trunks of hard wood as thick as a man's thigh, sunk deeply into the ground with some fifteen feet standing clear, the tops axed into sharp points. Metal chains bound them together and at the corners there were sentry boxes raised above the stockade. A wide door of metal-bossed planks opened on well-oiled hinges and they filed in. Within the stockade there was nothing but a cleanly swept hard dirt compound, but the walls of the stockade were lined with a double tier of wooden shelves, covered by a thick thatch of roof.

As their contingent entered, they could see the other two canoe loads which had preceded them, already stretched out on the shelves, and they were quickly assigned their spaces, two men to a shelf. Tamboura and M'dong were on the upper tier; Sabumbo and the fellow who had been in front of him in the canoe—a young Fullah by the name of

Khandago—were on the lower tier. They lost no time in resting their aching limbs on the hard, clean planks which, although not as comfortable as their beds of hides at home, seemed nevertheless a paradise after the constrictions of the canoes. They even had the comfort of a wooden log, securely spiked to the bed, for a pillow. For a few moments before sleep came they luxuriated in the joy of stretching out at full length, easing their cramped and swollen muscles. But who could keep awake after the many weary nights on the river, sleeping only in fitful snatches between the mosquitoes, the rigid immobility and the physical nearness of a hard male body in front and behind? Tamboura scratched where the insect bites itched the worst, settled his head more comfortably against the log pillow and dropped off into a deep sleep.

He was not disturbed until late afternoon when M'dong, who was already awake, shook him and pointed to the same red-jacketed guard who had led them in. The man was now going from shelf to shelf, waking the men. He had no whip and he was rough but not vicious. The whole policy of the slave factory was to treat the men well during their first days. Unshackled, with a bed to sleep on, food in his belly and no work to do, a man would usually be sufficiently happy not to miss his home village. There were new friends to make, new sights and new experiences to interest him. He was soft-talked into the coming joys of passage on the big ship and exhilarated by the prospects of becoming a stud in another world where his only duty would be to serve an uninterrupted procession of women all night and sleep and eat all day. It was a gratifying prospect and most were willing to undergo the curtailment of their liberty within the stockade in order to gain the greater reward that was promised to them.

They were told to scramble out from their bunks and line up. Once again, Tamboura inserted himself between Sabumbo and M'dong. Instead of the grass rope which had bound their necks together, a thin chain with equally spaced neck-rings was passed from one to the other and each neck was snapped into its collar.

The big door of the stockade opened and they were led down to the river, where another stockade had been erected out into the water, more for the purpose of keeping the crocodiles out than keeping the slaves from escaping. Here they were told to walk out into the water until it reached their knees. They were furnished with bunches of grass and some slimy stuff which Tamboura had never seen before but which made a white lather all over his body when he applied it. Unlike the white clay, it did not stick to his skin but washed off when he sat down in the water. The clay which Kanili had applied to Tamboura's body had worn off days ago, and now it seemed as if his skin had been thickened by a layer of sweat, dead insects and the unwashed excretions of himself, M'dong and Sabumbo. After so many days of filth and sweat it was good to be clean again.

They scrubbed themselves with the handfuls of grass and washed each other's backs, making a game of it and sloshing the water over one another's heads. The hours of rest, the joy of physical cleanliness and the cool water had almost restored them to normal, and when, dry and clean, they were led back to the barracoon, the iron collars and chains were removed and they were given palm oil to rub themselves with. Here again, teamwork was employed, and M'dong's hand anointed Tamboura's back, rubbing the oil deep down into his pores, so that his body shone like polished ebony.

Then, and most welcome of all, they were fed with a plentiful stew of meat and vegetables, flavored with salt and little peppers. It was served in large wooden bowls—one bowl to each four men—with round thin circles of cassava bread to mop it up. Between Tamboura, Sabumbo, M'dong and Khandago, there was no quarreling for the chunks of meat. They showed their village training by each graciously insisting that his neighbor take the largest piece and their only remarks were words of disapproval of him who took the smallest. After they had finished the stew, they were given limes to suck and water to drink and told that they could sleep again.

His stomach full, his body clean and oiled, his arms and legs unrestrained, Tamboura lay down on the hard planks contented and happy. His village and all that it contained had receded far into the background and the first poignant nostalgia had been dissipated. He slept soundly and dreamlessly until, in the pre-dawn chill, he awoke to find himself shivering and crept closer to M'dong who, without waking, pulled Tamboura close to him and with some mumbled words enveloped him in his arms. Secure in his friend's warmth and protection, Tamboura slept again until the bright sun made him open his eyes.

The whole compound was stirring and the sleepy slaves sat up one by one and hung their legs over the edges of the shelves. Tamboura extricated himself from the tightly enveloping arms and legs of M'dong and slid down from the shelf. Sabumbo and Khandago were already awake and up, sitting on the edge of their bunk, contentedly scratching themselves in the sun. They saw the big door open and a huge, steaming cauldron wheeled in. As Tamboura was the youngest, it was his lot to take their bowl across to have it filled. Embarrassed by a healthy morning erection, he hesitated to go until he saw that most of the men were in a like condition. Comparing himself with the others and noting his own superiority, he joined in the procession, strutting pridefully and a little arrogantly to the laughing comments of his fellows. While he waited for his bowl to be filled, his tumescence subsided. But even in this condition, he noted that he still had the advantage, and he walked back to his companions as peacock-proud as he had left them.

This morning there was no meat, but the food was warm and tasted good and it filled their stomachs comfortably. After they had finished eating, the doors of the barracoon opened to admit a procession so strange and unusual to Tamboura and his companions that they could only regard it with eyes wide and mouths agape. There were so many things they had never seen before that it seemed they had been transported to a land of miracles. Several of the factory slaves carried in a strange wooden affair, painted white. It consisted of a wall of boards, higher than a man's head, atop a platform which was about waist-high from the ground and had two steps leading up to it. The white background of boards had horizontal black and red stripes running the width of it, which was about that of a man with his arms extended.

As though this marvel were not enough, other slaves appeared lugging a huge wooden stool, gaily trimmed with feathers, colored silks and beads, which they set down a few paces in front of the strange wooden affair. Then came another stool, this one as big as the first but devoid of decorations, which was placed beside the first. Following this, two more slaves entered, each bearing a huge umbrella, one of a plain, dark green stuff and the other as gaily ornamented as the stool. Another black entered with a low table, agleam with brightly polished brass things which he placed between the two big stools, and the slaves with umbrellas took up their positions in the rear. Tamboura was certain that the strange things were stools for he had seen such wooden things to sit on in his own village, but he had never seen such large ones with a back to lean against and places to rest one's arms.

While they were all regarding these marvels and chattering among themselves, he saw Ama-jallah enter, flanked by two white men. White men! Yes, he agreed with M'dong that they were white, although one, the younger, was whiter than the other. And, perhaps most remarkable of all, the younger one had hair the color of the sun and it grew long and fine. His white cheeks were tinged with pink, his nostrils small and his lips red and thin instead of dark and thick. They were, Tamboura thought, quite the strangest looking men he had even seen—unreal and ghostly—and he noted that the older man looked sick and unhappy, for his deep-set dark eyes looked around the compound with a lack-luster gaze.

Ama-jallah took his place on the decorated seat, the older man on the plain one, and the young man with yellow hair stood between them and behind the table. The slaves with the umbrellas adjusted them so that the three men were in the shade and then the older man spoke to the same slave who wore the funny cloth garment of red with the gold trimmings. He came trotting around the edges of the compound, waking up those who were still sleeping and making everyone get up and stand straight before his shelf. When they were all standing, he started the line marching and it advanced slowly across the hard-packed earth. As they neared the white-painted wooden platform, the first man was told to mount and stand, facing the two seated men.

He was young, and Tamboura remembered seeing him in the canoe ahead of his. He could tell that the fellow was frightened. He was shivering and shaking as he mounted the platform with reluctant steps. Tamboura could not blame him for nobody knew what might happen to the fellow. This might be some strong magic of the white man which would kill. But nothing happened, at least nothing of importance. The black boy stood there and the red-coated Negro pushed his head up against the stripes on the wall behind him, while the seated white man spoke to the young fellow behind him and he did something with a little stick on something white which he held in his hand. Then the old man spoke to Ama-jallah and the red-coated Negro led the young black over to the two men. He had to get down on his knees in front of the old man, who went all over his body, opening his mouth and putting his fingers inside, running his hands with careful explorations over arms, shoulders, chest and head. Then, at a word from Red Coat, the boy stood up and the white man called him close to where he was sitting. Again his hands explored the fellow's body, sliding down his thighs, feeling the calves of his legs, even lifting and examining those private parts of a man which no other man should ever touch. However, no harm happened to the fellow and he was dismissed with a nod of the white man's head. Then it was another's turn and another's and still many others' before Tamboura found himself standing at the foot of the steps that led up to the white platform. He mounted, and although the others had remained there for only the time it took to draw ten breaths, he was kept there longer, standing first on one foot and then on the other, while the three men drank something that was poured out of a brass pot into some strange white cups. He was so near he could hear them talking and he could even understand their strangely accented Hausa words.

"If they're all as good as these first ones, Your Highness, you've brought as fine a lot as usual." It was the old man who was speaking to Ama-jallah.

"I do not bother with old ones, weak ones, sick ones or those who have been scarred in battle or have defects. It does not pay. It's too much work to get them here and it takes as much trouble to bring an old man as a young one." Ama-jallah glanced up at the platform and noticed Tamboura standing there, whom he remembered. The boy had been a good bargain; he had paid nothing for what was undoubtedly the best slave of the lot.

"See that." Ama-jallah's languid hand motioned to Tamboura. "That's what I mean. You could scour the length and breadth of Africa and find nothing better. Young, well-built, well-hung and handsome. Yes, even royal African blood, for he is the son of old King Tooma and the brother of King Mandouma. Royal Hausa! I'll want a premium on him."

Tamboura saw the old man put down the white thing he was drinking from and raise his head. His eyes looked straight into Tamboura's. For a long time, the space of three breaths, they looked at each other, and finally the man beckoned to Tamboura to come to him. Tamboura came and knelt before him as he had seen the others do and he could feel the moist warmth of the man's hands as they passed over his head, around his ears, opened his eyelids and then his mouth. He tasted the strange acrid taste of the man's fingers as they entered his mouth and felt his teeth. He saw the man's hands and felt them as they gauged the muscles in his arms and the thickness of his chest, and he knew that he had pleased the man for the long fingers gave his nipples a little pinch—not enough to hurt them but playfully.

Again the hands started their investigations, down across his belly, into the little patch of hair, lifting the genitals, even pulling back the dewlap of skin which Tamboura hated so. He weighed it in his hands and laughed, speaking in some unknown tongue to the yellow-haired man standing behind his chair. The yellow-haired man laughed back. Then Tamboura had to turn around while the white man grasped his buttocks and pulled them apart and held them there a brief moment. That was all, but strangely enough, as the Negro in the red coat motioned for him to leave, the white man stopped Tamboura and spoke to him.

"What is your name?" he asked in Hausa.

"I am Tamboura, the brother of Mandouma."

"And your spirit, Tamboura?"

"I am of the Earth and my spirit is the lion."

"It's a brave spirit. Tomorrow, this man here"—the white man pointed to Red Coat—"will come and fetch you. He will bring you to my hut. Do not be afraid, nothing will harm you."

Ama-jallah leaned forward in his chair and smiled. It was a confidential smile but at the same time libidinous and salacious. One eye closed knowingly.

"You like the boy, Mongo Don? I didn't know that you had an affection for boys. Ah, but he is very beautiful, is he not? One cannot blame you. I was tempted myself on the way here. When one's *hareem* does not travel with one. . . ." He spread his hands wide in a gesture of helplessness.

Tamboura heard the old man sigh, and when he spoke to Ama-jallah he was not soft-talking him as he had been all along. His words were angry words but he spoke them softly and they did not sound sufficiently angry that Ama-jallah might take offense.

"Not what you're thinking, Your Highness. This boy nor any other has ever appealed to me that way, but suddenly I see something wonderful. I see something more than a slave I am buying from you to ship to Cuba. Here in this one perfect specimen, I see all Africa, all the dignity and beauty and grandeur of this stinking hell-hole. It must have taken many generations of carefully selected breeding to produce a specimen like that."

"The family of King Mandouma is a very ancient one in Africa, Mongo Don."

"It must be to produce that. No, Your Highness, I have no desire to initiate this youth into the practices you mention. Instead I would preserve him in all his vigor and manliness. I have a desire to paint him."

Ama-jallah smiled. "He was painted when he was brought to me—painted with white clay and red stripes for his initiation into manhood."

"I do not mean to paint his body like that. I would draw his likeness in colors. I am inspired, Your Highness. I shall paint a portrait of him."

Ama-jallah bowed his head and held up an admonitory finger to Mongo Don. "Ah, but that is forbidden. Our Prophet writes that no delineation shall be made of man or beast or any living thing."

"But I do not subscribe to Islam, Your Highness, and seeing that this boy is your slave, although soon to become mine, I do not believe that he does either, for I know that the sons of the Prophet may not be sold into slavery."

Tamboura understood the words that the two were speaking but he could not understand their meaning clearly. He only knew that he had pleased the white man, who was not unkind, and that the white man would reward him.

## chapter vi

TAMBOURA WAS AWAKE with the first bright streaks of the sun. Turning on his side, he looked out over the light-flooded compound. He did not know at what hour he would be sent for but he wished to be ready, so he slid down from the shelf without disturbing M'dong or the others and walked across the compound to the latrine. On his way back, he stopped at the open keg of palm oil, dipped his hands in it and carefully oiled his body, rubbing it well into his skin so that it shone. Beside the keg of oil, he discovered a palm frond which had fallen into the compound and he idly stripped the leaves from it as he walked along. Sitting in the warmth of the sun, he shredded the fronds and started weaving a small flat envelope for no reason except to pass the time. But gradually a purpose came to his work. During the days on the water he had had no contact with his spirit Earth, and as his fingers plaited the palm, he resolved never to be separated from his spirit again. His deft fingers finished the little container and he scraped up some of the hard-packed dirt and placed it inside, sealing the packet with a tightly woven closure. Then he painstakingly braided a fine strand of palm, which he fastened to the small amulet and hung around his neck. From now on, merely by touching it, he would have contact with Earth, and he knew that his spirit would not desert him.

Gradually the occupants of the shelves roused themselves, nudged their bedmates awake and swung their legs over the edges of their bunks. The morning priapic parade wended its unhurried way to the latrine, accompanied by the usual good-natured bantering. It was not long before the outside door opened and the kettle of food was wheeled inside. Red Coat, still wearing his single garment which seemed to be his only possession, stood beside the kettle, his eyes shaded with his hand, looking around at the mass of young Negroes—one scarcely identifiable from the other in their black nakedness. He spotted Tamboura and beckoned him to approach, ladling out a bowl of the slop that now served as breakfast. As Tamboura held up the bowl, Red Coat bade him eat and told him that when he left, Tamboura was to accompany him. Tamboura had scarcely time to carry the bowl to his friends and dip his fingers into it before Red Coat summoned him. He led Tamboura down to the river, gave him more of the slimy stuff that whitened his body in the water, told him to wash himself clean, then handed him grass to dry his body with. Tamboura's morning toilet had been wasted, as the oil was all washed off, but even without the oil his body gleamed. Red Coat made him squat down so that he might see if he had any lice in his hair and then examined the small patch of hair on his body to see if he had crabs. He found Tamboura free from vermin and told him to follow.

This time they did not stop at the gate of the barracoon but continued on past the high wooden walls of the warehouses and offices up to the white-pillared portico of the Mongo's house. Red Coat told him to wait and went inside. While Tamboura was waiting, leaning against one of the porch pillars, he saw a door open and a Negro girl come out. She was engaged in pulling her dress down more snugly over her hips and smoothing it with her hands. Surprised at seeing him she halted, inspected him carefully and then walked over to him, swinging her rounded hips under the thin cotton of her dress. He thought she was the most beautiful and desirable girl he had even seen and he wanted to speak to her but his very desire to speak made him hopelessly tongue-tied. She sidled up closer to him, her breasts straining the thin cloth of her dress. Her lips smiled an invitation to him and she slowly raised her skirt above her waist in a gesture of invitation. She did not speak and neither did he, but she dropped her dress and her finger lightly touched his forehead, traced a warm line down his nose, lingered for a moment on his lips, then dropped to his chest where it remained even longer before starting on its downward path. He felt it creeping across his belly, exploring his navel and then it went as far as it would go. She smiled up at him.

"Sleeping with you would be much nicer than with old Mongo." Her eyes danced and her hand caressed.

Tamboura started to speak but the words never came. A door opened out onto the portico and a voice called out.

"Jobeena, you bitch! Leave him alone. Get going!" It was the Mongo. Jobeena snatched her hand away and started off across the compound like a startled zebra. The Mongo, walking slowly and clutching the wall of the house for support, followed the same path along the porch that Jobeena had taken and came to Tamboura.

"Come, lad, follow me." His voice had lost the sharp edge of anger with which he had yelled at Jobeena.

They walked back along the portico and through a door into a room, the like of which Tamboura had never seen before. The shabby elegance, the worn rococo chairs, the dusty rugs and the paintings of white women on the walls all seemed too wonderful for him to grasp. He followed the Mongo to a corner of the room where a big piece of white cloth was stretched on a wooden frame. Tamboura was frightened—not of the man, who treated him kindly, but of the unaccustomed surroundings, the strange pieces of furniture which seemed ready to leap out at him, the painted pictures on the walls that smiled at him like so many spirits from another world, and the closed-in feeling which oppressed him. He was trembling and the Mongo noticed it. He laid a reassuring hand on Tamboura's shoulder.

"Nothing to be afraid of, boy." He was soft-talking Tamboura while he gently maneuvered him up against a wall to stand before a piece of rich, dark-green cloth which fell from ceiling to floor. Two huge ivory tusks curved upwards from carved wooden bases on the floor, gleaming ghostly pale in the subdued light. Mongo Don placed Tamboura between them, stretching his arms out so that a hand grasped each tusk. From a wicker basket, filled with moist dark earth, Mongo Don spilled a mound on the floor around Tamboura's feet.

"Your spirit, boy," the Mongo said as he distributed the earth around Tamboura's feet. He reached for a small box on a nearby table, opened it and sprinkled the earth with gold nuggets and dust. From another basket, he took an armful of plumes—the black of ostrich, the blue of heron, the downy white of marabou, the rose of flamingo, the jewel colors of parrot, and the glistening eyes of argus bird. These he arranged carefully behind Tamboura and then from a chest he took the striped pelts of zebras, the tawny hide of a lion and the delicate long white hair of monkeys and added them to the colorful plumes. He walked away, his eyes fixed on the naked boy, surrounded by the precious things which Africa offered to the world—her rich dark earth, her gold, her ivory, her plumes, and between them, rising above them, dominating them, her most precious product of all, her black manhood. Mongo Don backed to the other side of the room slowly, using the backs of chairs to support him, and pulled up one of the bamboo curtains so that the strong light of the sun flooded Tamboura.

"And now, my boy, stand there and do not move if you can help it. Stand as long as you can and when you are tired tell me and you may rest."

Tamboura understood and remained as still as possible while the Mongo faced him with the stretched white cloth between them. Tamboura saw him take a little stick with a bunch of hair at the end in one hand and a large flat object covered with little mounds of color in the other. The Mongo dipped the little stick into the color and made strange motions, which Tamboura could not see, on the white cloth.

A brass box, with a swinging round brass plate below, ticked away on the wall, like a deathwatch beetle hidden in the thatch of a hut. Tamboura's eyes were fastened on the slowly swinging pendulum as he watched its regular course. It seemed to quiet him and he let his thoughts slip away to the same moon-dappled tamarisk bushes and the warm flesh which were his favorite daydreams. There was nothing to do but stand and dream while the Mongo kept on with his mysterious work. After a while, Tamboura's muscles began to cramp and he felt as uncomfortable as he had felt in the boat, but he did not move until the Mongo spoke to him.

"Rest, boy, you've been standing for over half an hour. You're an excellent model. Now rest for a few minutes and then you can stand again for me." He went to a swinging pottery jar which oozed moisture, tipped it and filled a cup with cool water for Tamboura, who gulped it greedily while the Mongo stretched out at full length in a chair. Tamboura walked around the room, getting the kinks out of his legs, and looked at the strange objects until the Mongo called him back and he resumed the same position once more between the ivory tusks. Thus passed the morning, until the sun had shifted and Tamboura was no longer in the light, but the Mongo opened another blind and the room became lighter although the sun did not hit Tamboura directly. Still the Mongo worked—faster now, as though he were fighting against time. Tamboura posed and rested, posed again and rested again time after time. During one of his rests, the Mongo motioned to him to sit down on one of the big stools. He sat gingerly, aware that his body was covered with sweat and fearing to soil the shabby brocade.

"I am going to send you back to your village, Tamboura." Mongo Don smiled as he spoke. "Not for you the long trip to Cuba. You must return to your home and become King."

"No, Mongo, no," Tamboura pleaded, "do not send me back. My brother will kill me and if he doesn't succeed, his wife surely will. Let me go with the others in the big canoe with white wings."

"So that's it." Mongo Don nodded his head gravely. "I thought as much. Your own family sold you into slavery. Well, then, how would you like to stay here with me? You can work for me here in the house and I will treat you well."

"No, let me go on the big canoe, Mongo. Let me go with M'dong, Sabumbo and Khandago."

Mongo Don leaned forward in his chair. "And why do you want to go on the big ship, Tamboura?"

"Because they tell me that in this new land I shall have many women, Mongo, and"—he hesitated—"I have never yet tasted the joy of a woman. I am anxious to know."

"According to what I hear from Cuba, you'll have plenty of chance there. Well then, if you wish, I shall send you on the big canoe, but I shall also send a letter by the Captain that you are to be delivered as my gift to a good friend of mine in Havana. He will be kind to you and it will be better than the cane fields. Now, come, let's get back to work." He stood up impatiently and went back to stand behind the canvas as Tamboura took his accustomed place against the wall.

Later, after many ticks from the brass box on the wall, the white man with the yellow hair came in followed by a fat black woman with a big tray covered with a napkin which she put down on a table and left.

"Come, Jonathan." Mongo Don, his face wreathed in smiles, took the young man by the arm. "Come and see what I have already done. The whole figure is outlined and I have finished the face. At last I have done something of which I am proud. Look, Jonathan, here is Africa!" He led Jonathan around to look at the canvas. "Rest, Tamboura."

Tamboura slumped onto the floor. He was unable to understand the strange words the Mongo spoke.

Jonathan studied the canvas carefully. He knew little about art but he sensed that here was something real, something genuine. He saw no simpering white woman with roses in her hair and pearls at her neck. He saw something primitive, almost brutal, but what he saw was compelling and startling. From the dark, gold-spangled earth of Africa, the long strong legs of Tamboura rose, hastily but surely sketched. They supported the narrow waist, the broad shoulders and the powerful arms, the column of neck and the face. Ah, it was at the face that he looked, for the face was finished. The body was that of a magnificent animal but the face was human, so human that it almost spoke. This was no stray head of cattle, no black beast of burden; instead it was a man, a human being. From the face which was so superbly finished, Jonathan looked down over the sketched body to its startling nakedness.

"It's wonderful, Uncle, but where can you hang it? Surely you cannot take it to Havana and hang it where ladies might see it."

"I care not where it hangs, Jonathan, and perhaps it will never go to Havana as I fear I shall never return, but I feel I have accomplished something. Praxiteles would have done the boy in black marble. Titian would have painted him as the black Magus. Raphael would have used him as the symbol of Africa, as have I. Having done this, my mind finds a strange peace, Jonathan. I think I have solved the riddle of Africa." He stopped and smiled at Tamboura. "Come here, boy."

Tamboura circled the big white screen and gazed upon it with palpitating terror. He saw himself, as he had seen himself in Bansu's mirrors, and he was frightened anew. The Mongo had taken his spirit and put it on this piece of cloth. He sank to his knees, his arms wrapped around the Mongo's legs.

"You have stolen my spirit, Great Mongo." The boy was sobbing with terror. "Now I shall never see it again." He felt the Mongo's warm hand on his head and heard the words the man soft-talked to him.

"No, believe me, I have not stolen your spirit, Tamboura. Instead, see, I have given you two spirits. This one will remain here in Africa while you take your other one to the new land. This spirit will stay to avenge itself on those who have sold you. See, Tamboura, instead of having one spirit, you now have two. You are more of a man that you were before because it isn't every man who has two spirits."

Tamboura stood up and looked at the portrait. The man was right. One Tamboura would go across the sea and this other one would remain here. His sobbing ceased and his lips parted in a smile to show the white crescent of his teeth. He stood up and came closer to the portrait.

"But this Tamboura has only a head. His legs and arms are not solid."

"They will be soon," Mongo Don assured him. "And now let us eat."

Jonathan had been watching silently. "I leave you now, Uncle." He was speaking in English so Tamboura did not understand. "I know not what has happened to you but I am glad because you seem happy."

"I am, Jonathan; nobody knows the joy it brings an artist to feel that he has really painted something worthwhile. It gives him a feeling of supreme satisfaction. And now, leave us, for I am impatient to finish my work, which is far more important to me than haggling with Ama-jallah, which you can do as well as I."

After Jonathan left, Mongo Don ate and gave what was left to Tamboura who ate the strange food without savoring it. The flavors were foreign to his taste, although the sweet things were good. During the long afternoon, he posed while Mongo Don worked. The shadows crept to the other side of the room and still he stood. Mongo Don left his work to open another curtain, but as he started across the floor, he fell, suddenly and without warning, with a strange gasping sound on his lips.

Tamboura did not dare to move because the Mongo had not told him to rest. He regarded the figure of the white man on the floor. Perhaps he was resting—Tamboura did not know, but he seemed to be stretched out in a most unusual position if he was resting. One arm was curiously doubled under him and his head had fallen onto the board with the colors on it, which streaked his face with black and brown and vermilion. For a long time, Tamboura looked at the Mongo on the floor without moving from his position. Then he decided on a brave venture. He relaxed his hold on the ivory tusks and let his hands fall to his side. This action brought no response from the Mongo, so Tamboura stepped out from between the tusks on tiptoe and took a few tentative steps in the direction of the man on the floor. Still the man did not move.

Tamboura walked over and knelt beside him. The white man's eyes were open but he did not see. Then Tamboura knew the Mongo's spirit had departed. He sat back on his heels and howled—the same high-pitched keening he had heard from the people of his village when the spirit of one of their family departed. How long he sat there howling he did not know, but he heard the door open and the fat black woman came in, rushed over to the Mongo's body and took one look at it. She ran out and soon the room was full of people and the young man with the yellow hair had them lift the Mongo's body and place it in the next room. Nobody paid any attention to Tamboura and he crept back to his place between the tusks. He did not know where to go or what to do but he sensed that he belonged there, where the Mongo had placed him.

Jonathan, coming out of the room where they had carried the Mongo, noticed him. His Hausa words were slower and less easy to understand than the Mongo's.

"Come, Tamboura, I will take you back to the barracoon. The Mongo is dead, do you understand?"

Tamboura nodded. "His spirit has departed. Yes, I know."

Jonathan led the bewildered boy out onto the porch and scanned the sea of black faces lined up a few paces from the porch. He saw the identifying color of the red coat and called to the slave.

"Take this boy back to the barracoon," he said. "Let him be with his friends."

## chapter vii

TAMBOURA WALKED ACROSS the compound to seek the security and comfort of the barren shelf that was now his only home, and the welcome voices of his companions. They listened while he told them of all the strange things that had happened to him—of the ivory tusks and the black dirt sprinkled with gold nuggets, the plumes and the hides, and of the hours of standing while the Mongo worked. He told them of the second Tamboura which had been taking shape on the cloth and explained to them how it was a second spirit to be left behind in Africa while he himself went across the water. He mentioned the Mongo's offer to return him to his village if he so desired.

"You did right not to go back," Sabumbo agreed. "It is better to take your chances with us." And the others added their words of confirmation while they all marveled at the reproduction of Tamboura's spirit and looked at him in reverence, for they had never seen a man who possessed two spirits before.

But most important of all was the strange story of the Mongo's death. Perhaps Tamboura's second spirit had already started to avenge him by slaying the Mongo. If so, they argued, it must be a strong spirit, far stronger than even Tamboura himself. Tamboura became frightened and the others showed their fear, too, but the practical M'dong calmed them. It was good, he told them, that Tamboura's other spirit had such remarkable power that it could strike a man dead so quickly. Since it was to remain in Africa, it could not harm them once they were on the big canoe, headed for another land.

And Khandago, after thinking the matter over, fully agreed with M'dong. He said he was glad he was not Mandouma, for certainly, after having killed the Mongo, Tamboura's spirit would head up the river after Mandouma. They were all glad they were not in Mandouma's place and they regarded Tamboura with open envy.

During the night they did not sleep much, for the community outside the stockade was not sleeping. There was a continuous keening and wailing both from the village and from the factory. The drums of the village beat all night and the *conjo* in the village, spurred on by the rum, did not die down until sunrise. Then there was silence and the day that followed was quiet as the villagers slept off their drunken stupor. Nobody appeared with breakfast and the men did not eat until late in the afternoon when an indifferently stewed mess was brought in and slopped into their bowls. Nor were they let out of the barracoon again to wash themselves.

For three days and three nights, nothing happened to break the day-and-night monotony of their existence. Then, on the fourth day, they were rewarded with something different. This time there was no fanfare, no decorated chairs, no coffee table and no umbrellas. The yellow-haired white man was accompanied by another white man, even more unusual in appearance, for this one had a bushy beard as red as flame. He was a huge man, towering above the other, and he spoke in a language which they did not understand, but they knew from the tone of his voice that he was not soft-talking, because his words rasped and burred with a deep throaty resonance.

No sooner had he entered than things began to move in the barracoon. Red Coat hastily lined them up and once again they passed through the humiliating process of inspection, although on this occasion they were not required to mount any steps or stand with their heads back against the lines. The big red-bearded man merely passed his hands over them brusquely, quickly and impersonally, looked in their mouths and eyes, cursorily handled their genitals and then slapped them on the rump to start them along. Three or four of them, after the big red-bearded man had looked at them, were told to step out of the line, and after the examination was ended and the white men had departed, they were led out of the barracoon by Red Coat. Tamboura never saw them again nor knew why they had been dismissed, but M'dong remembered that one man coughed every night and Khandago said that one of the others had developed a limp.

Later that day, along towards sunset, Red Coat returned and separated all the men into two groups. Those on the top shelves were told to stand on one side of the compound and those on the lower shelves to remain in their bunks. M'dong and Tamboura passed across to the opposite side, leaving Khandago and Sabumbo behind. They did not know that they were not to see each other again and so there were no leave-takings, except for a wave of the hand and the usual grins. After pushing the slaves into a semblance of a line, Red Coat separated them into groups—as many in each group as the fingers of both hands. Once again the iron collars, connected by the chain, were placed around their necks.

Tamboura resented the restriction as much as he did the humiliation of being handled. For days now, since the journey in the canoe, he had been free. Even on the day he had been taken to the Mongo's hut, he had had no shackles or fetters. With the iron collar around his neck he began to fear, but M'dong quieted him by reminding him that the last time they had been so treated it had been merely to take them to the river to bathe.

Indeed, that is where Tamboura thought they were going, for they were led, one caffle of ten at a time, down to the river. But instead of being led to the shore, they were taken out on the bamboo pier again, where a canoe was waiting for them. This was not as big a canoe as the one in which they had made the trip down the river and there were only four Krus to a canoe. Once they were in and seated, instead of heading up the river from the direction in which they had come, the canoe started down river, rounding a bend and out into more water than Tamboura had ever seen before, for here there was nothing but water as far as he could see. Nothing but water—except for a canoe that seemed so enormous it was scarcely believable. Even at a distance, it towered out of the water. Tamboura nudged M'dong, who was behind him. It had white wings on it!

This then was the big canoe that was to take them away from Africa to that other land and with this knowledge they became happy and anticipatory. They speculated on what delights this marvel might hold in store for them and they tried to elicit information from the Krus. The only answer they got was a disparaging laugh from these men who, because of their ability to handle canoes, were not slaves but paid servants of the factory. Secure in their immunity, they were not above torturing the hapless occupants of their canoes with dire threats of what was in store for them.

The canoe started pitching in the eddy of currents caused by the outflowing river and the incoming tide. It was hard to keep their position in the boat and as they lunged forward the length of chain stopped their headlong plunge, making the collar bite deep into their throats, choking them and cutting off their breath. They tried to steady themselves as best they could in a misery of gasping and choking.

"That there's the *'Gustus Tait.*" The Kru, who wielded his paddle between Tamboura and the slave ahead of him, was grinning at their discomfort and determined to make them even more uncomfortable. "Hit's de bes' slaver in de Cubee-Africee trade. She load up at B'wambo Cas'le with five hunnerd slaves jes like yo' po' boys. Thaz why she no take all de barracoon. On'y room for fifty mo'."

"She good boat," the Kru behind them volunteered. "She al'ays clean but dat ol' Cap'n MacPherson, he a debbil. He a debbil with a red beard, that one. Man say he have de long tail under him's pants. Man say he like to skin black boy ev'y mornin' an' eat him's balls fur b'eakfas'. Thaz why he so stron', that debbil cap'n. He al'ays looking for black boy with big balls so's he kin eat 'em." The fellow smacked his lips together with gusto.

Tamboura released his hold on the side of the canoe to cover his groin with his hands. Again he was afraid; he was sure he would be first choice for the Captain's morning meal.

"An' that debbil cap'n,"—another grinning Kru took up the story—"he love to string a boy up by his toes and whup him—whup him til' de meat fall off'n him's back in chunks. Den he fro him ober de side of de ship for de sharks to eat. Yo' boys know what sharks is?"

They shook their heads in denial. They were too frightened to speak.

"They big fishes, long as this canoe." The Krus were enjoying the discomfiture of their passengers. "And teef! One dem dere sharks, he jus open his mouf and . . . snap!" The Kru brought his teeth together the better to demonstrate. "Man's leg gone down in shark's belly."

Once having started they were anxious to embroider their tale with more vivid details. "Yeah! Cap'n MacPherson sure do like to feed black boys to sharks. Likes to see them big fish snap black boy's head right off. Yo'uns better be careful 'cause if Cap'n MacPherson don' skin yo' and eat yo' balls, he a'goin' to whup yo' down and make yo' dinner for them sharks." He cackled with high-pitched glee.

"An' Cap'n MacPherson clean." The Kru missed a stroke as he turned to Tamboura. "He so clean he make yo' boys work all'a time. Ev'y day, you down on yo' han's and knees, stonin' that deck and makin' it shine white and if'n it not white, Cap'n MacPherson"—he paused and turned again to the paddler behind him. "What 'at debbil cap'n do to black boy what don' work hard? You tells 'em."

The Kru aft rolled his eyes back into his head so that only the whites showed. "That," he declared emphatically, "am de wors' of all! Better be skunned alive and have yo' balls et. Better be whupped and fed to de sharks. You know what dat debbil cap'n do to black boys who don' work? Firs' he put one thumb in yo' eye and, plop, out comes de eye and he eats it. Then he put thumb in odder eye and, plop, out it come and he eats dat. Then he take big trade knife and he slice off'n yo' tongue and he eat dat; den yo' ears but he don' eat them 'cause they tough and he fro dem to de fish. Den, li'l piece by li'l piece, he cut all de meat from yo' bones and he sit dere and chaw on meat til yo's all gone. Co'se you kaint see him 'cause you ain' got no eyes. Ay! Thaz turrible! But that Cap'n MacPherson, he sure have damn clean ship so don' none of yo boys go a-shittin' on de deck."

By this time, both Tamboura and M'dong were paralyzed with fear. All of their anticipatory joy had departed and they cowered on the floor of the canoe, choking from the collars, nauseated by the pitching, and quaking with terror. Suddenly Tamboura felt a resurgence of his spirit. His hand touched the woven bag of earth at his neck. He invoked not only his own spirit but the spirit which he had left behind him on the canvas in the big hut of the Mongo. He felt better, safer, more secure. His spirit was great. It had already killed the Mongo white man and it would protect him now against this other—the one with the red beard who had so impersonally examined him back in the stockade.

As they came close to the ship, it reared a high black wall above them, and from it they could hear a continuous wailing—hundreds of voices coming from the inside like the hum of bees from a tree, lifted in a dirge of sorrow and hopelessness. They not only heard the ship but they smelled it, a rank, putrid effluvium that far outstank the latrines in the barracoon. It was a stench of old sweat and male excrement, of human fear and nameless horror, an odor so overpowering in its festering pollution that it struck their already weak stomachs like an iron spear entering their vitals, causing them to retch and swallow their sour vomit.

The canoe drew alongside the ship—a sheer wooden wall

of black wood with blacker holes along its sides, each one emitting the wailing and the stench. From the high deck above, a rope net dangled to the water, and as the Krus caught it to steady the canoe they told the slaves to grab hold of it and hoist themselves up. They clambered aboard, over the rail, onto the shining white deck just as the last rays of the African sun were sinking into the sea in a whirlpool of violent colors. Taking their places alongside the rail, they lined up, joined by the chain from collar to collar.

The sight of the red-bearded man standing there, now a most awful reality, brought back the frightening stories. Again Tamboura covered himself with his hands, cursing for the first time the generosity of nature and hoping that he would not be the captain's first choice as he felt so sure he would be. But the captain scarcely looked at them, except to count them and make a mark with a little stick on a piece of paper. Another white man, dressed in a blue suit with gleaming brass buttons, barked at them in garbled Hausa and told them to follow him. They walked over the white deck to where a yawning black hole appeared. Here the stench was more sickening and the howling from below more audible. Tamboura could understand some of the words which a slave, deeper- and stronger-voiced than all the rest, was shrieking.

"Oh, take me back! Take me back to my wife and sons. Take me back to my village by the river. Let me go! Let me go."

Another voice joined his—a high wavering tenor—and took up the lament.

"Loose me and let me go, Mongo man. Loose me and give me a spear and let me show you how good my aim is. Loose me and let me plunge my spear in your evil heart, Mongo man, for I too am a man and not an animal to lie here and rot in my own filth."

They descended the steps into the steaming heat, into the horror of the dim light below, into the putrid smell, into the concentration of fear and bitterness and sorrow. The white man unhooked a lighted lantern whose flickering flame did little to dispel the gloom but sufficed to bring to light row after row of shining black legs and pink-soled feet on one side of a narrow strip of deck and matte-black skulls on the other. When the rays of the lantern struck the eyes of the men stretched out on the floor, they glowed back like the eyes of animals at night and the moaning rose to a higher key with impassioned pleas for release, pleadings for water, protests of sickness, discomfort and heartache. But the man with the lantern disregarded all the supplications and led the ten-man caffle down the narrow aisle between feet and woolly heads to where there was a small vacant space on the floor.

He unlocked the collar of the first man and told him to get down on the deck. The poor wretch, his wits completely addled, did not understand the quick command. It was repeated and this time accompanied by a quick lash from the quirt which dangled from a leather loop around the white man's wrist. The slave yelped with the sudden pain and slid to the floor writhing, but the white man's boots kicked him into submission and up against the body of the man already chained there. He moved the slave as close up to the other man as possible, then reached down and flopped him over on his side so that the slave's body fitted snugly to that of the man already there—spoon-fashion—belly to back and groin to rump. A chain with iron shackles, spaced at equal distances, ran along the floor and once the man had adjusted the slave's body sufficiently close to that of his neighbor so that he could not get his hand between them, the shackles were slipped over the wretch's ankles and snapped shut. Another chain at his head, far heavier than that which now linked them together, had similar but heavier collars and one of these was closed around the fellow's neck.

One by one they took their turns. The light collars were taken off, they knelt on the floor, slid down to fit their bodies into the curves of the man already there, then felt the snap of the shackles on their feet and the ring close around their necks. When it came Tamboura's turn, fortified by the knowledge of the strength of his dual spirits, he glared back at the white man and would not kneel. But the sting of the quirt, cutting across his chest, then lifted again and biting into his legs, proved to him that his combined spirits were no match for the impersonal brutality of this man with the whip. He knelt as he had seen the others do and accommodated his body to that of the man already there, a Mandingo whom Tamboura had spoken with once or twice in the barracoon. He felt his legs become immobilized by the shackles, and his neck restricted by the heavy collar and the hard boards under him. Within a matter of breaths, M'dong was down on the floor beside him and Tamboura felt the welcome assurance of M'dong's strong arm encircling him. With no place to put his own arm, he laid it across the shoulders of the Mandingo.

The feeble illumination of the lantern departed with the white man and they were left alone in the blackness, with the smell, the heat, the wailing and the fear. The hard boards of the deck were beneath them, a body pressed closely against their bellies and another against their backs. Ay, this was far worse than the canoe! This was the end, Tamboura felt. He had lost his faith in his own spirit as well as the one he had left behind on the Mongo's canvas. Now he could only pray for one thing—death. He started sobbing, adding his wails to the hundreds of voices which were moaning in a long-drawn-out cadence of utter despair.

He felt M'dong's arm tighten around him.

"Do not be afraid, Little Hunter. We are strong. They do not want to kill us. Remember, we are to be breeders of men."

"And do not believe all that those hyenas in the canoe told you." The Mandingo in front of Tamboura half turned his head to speak. "Those Kru bastards are craven cowards. They have sold their spirits to the white man for strong drink. Cowards they are, not hunters. All they know is to paddle canoes." He paused for a moment and his hand groped in the darkness for Tamboura's. "No, do not be afraid, Little Hunter. My name is Omo. In my village I was the apprentice to the witch doctor and already I know much magic. Now you will be quiet and you will sleep and not be afraid."

"I fear only one thing." Tamboura felt somewhat reassured by the Mandingo's words and his sobbing subsided to a whimper.

"And what is that?" M'dong asked.

"That the big man with the red beard will—" Despite himself Tamboura broke into sobs again. "—that he will eat those which I have tomorrow morning."

"Then fear no more." Omo managed to laugh despite his own fear and discomfort. "Think you that they would be taking us across the water to be breeders of men if they were to despoil us of those very things which would make us so?"

M'dong, who was himself fearful, found courage in the Mandingo's words. "Ho, ho," he laughed himself, echoing Omo's laughter, "Omo is right, Tamboura. The Krus were just trying to frighten us. See, Little Hunter, we have not been harmed. 'Tis true that this place stinks like the armpits of an old woman; 'tis true that these boards are hard and my legs already ache from the irons; 'tis true that your butt makes a hard lump against my stomach and that the fellow behind me forces himself up against me, but do not despair, Little Hunter. We are not women that we should weep and wail and demean ourselves."

"You speak words of wisdom," Omo replied. "What is your name? I would know you for you are brave."

"My name is M'dong and he between us is Tamboura."

"Then sleep, M'dong and Tamboura. And I will give you dreams of a fair land, watered by a broad river, abounding with beasts that are awaiting your spear. Or I will give you dreams of beautiful women, taken at the full of the moon."

"May I have those?" Tamboura asked. His sobbing had stopped.

"You may, Little Hunter, but if I give you those dreams, you must promise me one thing." Omo managed another laugh which sounded almost sacrilegious amid the univeral moaning.

"And what shall I promise you, O Giver of Dreams?"

"That in your dream, you do not think I am the woman you are holding in your arms."

It was M'dong's turn to laugh. "Ay, but you would be sorry, Omo. Take my advice and give him dreams of wild beasts and spears. It would be safer for you."

Whether it was Omo's magic or his own natural recuperative ability from mental as well as physical pain, Tamboura slept on the hard boards with his feet chained, an iron collar pinching his neck and the sweaty bodies of his companions pressed tightly against him. He slept in the heat and the reeking miasma that rose from hundreds of beslimed bodies. Sometime during the night the air freshened and a breeze came through the opened ports. There was a rattle of chains as the anchors were hoisted. The rocking of the ship increased. Africa receded to a dim dark line on the horizon and then vanished.

# chapter viii

TAMBOURA HAD SLEPT only fitfully in the new and strange surroundings. Despite Omo's boasted witchcraft, his dreams were not of beautiful maidens under the tamarisk bushes but rather of discomfort from sleeping without his pillow of wood, trying to adjust his legs so that the irons would not chafe him, and shifting his cramped body to accommodate it to the pressure of Omo's body in front and M'dong's at his back. All the men were lying on their right side and they discovered that slipping their right arms under the necks of the men in front of them eased their neighbor's head as well as their own arms. Their left arms lay stretched alongside their body or across the man in front of them. Their position was the result of an efficient study made in Liverpool to determine the minimum space a sleeping man could occupy. It was found that by sleeping the slaves on their sides space would be conserved, because four men on their sides took less room than three men on their backs. The right side was chosen because it was felt that that position would be less damaging to the heart. Yes, Negroes had hearts the same as other cattle.

In those days when slave trading was legal and even English royalty dipped their fingers in black profits, the conditions of the slavers were not regulated by humane methods but merely by those that were considered the most efficient. Later, when public opinion had overruled the rich merchants of Bristol and Liverpool and banished the slave trade forever, at least legally, the smuggling of slaves brought indescribable suffering to the transported blacks. But while English law upheld the traffic, slaves were not knowingly ill treated. They were a cargo and it behooved the master of the vessel to stow his cargo as compactly and as efficiently as possible. Slaves were valuable and it was most important that as many as possible should survive the hardships of the Middle Passage in good condition in order to bring a good price. To this end, the ships were kept scrupulously clean; the men were fed as well as the limited variety of foods which were then transportable allowed; and they were given as much fresh air and exercise as possible. Some small efforts were also made to entertain them. They were treated with all the consideration of valuable livestock, which is exactly what they were. Certainly in the eyes of the slavers they were not human. Only white men were human beings—Negroes were cattle, more valuable than a milch cow or a steer but not quite as valuable as a fine horse. They possessed a certain amount of intelligence, it was admitted, which enabled them to speak and possibly think in a limited way, but it was agreed that they were certainly devoid of human emotions. A good slave was like a good dog—obedient and faithful with a dumb love for his master and, like dogs, he was permitted three pleasures—eating, sleeping and fornicating—all three, of course, at the will and discretion of his white master.

A watery green light penetrated the open ports of the slave deck of the *Augustus Tait* the morning after she sailed from Yendo Castle. When Tamboura awoke, the stability of land had vanished and now there was such a rolling and pitching that at one moment he was pressed tightly against Omo, with M'dong's weight against his back. In the next moment, he was lying against M'dong and Omo was pressed against him. The movement was continuous: over, pause, back, with unerring regularity. Tamboura's head ached with dizziness and his stomach churned in resurgent nausea. It was hard to contain his swollen bladder, and when he felt the warm stream from M'dong spattering his legs he too let go and, in turn, copiously watered Omo. There were no recriminations for each realized the other was powerless. Tamboura felt relieved and now he had only to fight the rising nausea and hope that he would not cover Omo's back with the filth of his vomit.

By this time they were all three wide awake but in their misery and sickness they did not speak, afraid to open their mouths for fear of disgorging the puke that rose in their throats. The wailing had died down but there was a continuous, restless moving of legs and rattling of chains. After a long while they heard the heavy wooden grating being removed from the hatchway and saw the thick-soled leather boots of a white man on the steps. Above the boots there came blue pantaloons, then a red sash, a white shirt and finally the face of the same man who had chained them the night before. He was followed by two other white men—these in white pants and striped shirts. Without looking at the slaves, one of them went to the forward bulkhead and waited for the other to go aft. There was the sound of metal scraping against metal as the long chain was unlocked, followed by its clanking progress as it was pulled through the leg-irons of the men. Sometimes the chain caught and would not pass through, and then one of the sailors would have to free it, with a liberal amount of cursing and a few well-directed kicks at the slave involved to make him straighten out his legs. The collars were also removed, and this took even longer. But the men were deft in their work through long experience, and before many minutes had passed, Tamboura and his companions heard the Hausa words 'get up.' They tried to stand, clutching at each other to keep from falling with the roll of the ship, even more nauseated now that they were standing than they had been lying down. But it was a relief to change their positions, and when they heard the thumping of a drum they fell into step as they had on the long trek before they reached the canoes. The chained wretches on the other side bemoaned the fact that their turn had not arrived to be freed, while the long line which included Tamboura slowly snaked along the deck. He had to duck his head to avoid hitting it against the crossbeams, for the space between decks was only a finger's breadth more than his height. His footsteps, paced by the drum, shuffled along in the dim light of the 'tween-decks, then up the steep stairs and out onto the main deck where the bright sun, shining on the white deck, dazzled him and caused him to put a shielding hand to his forehead.

Tamboura's control of his stomach was more difficult now and the vomit surged up in his throat, making it almost impossible to restrain it. His eyes sought the consolation of something steady and immovable but he saw only the prow of the ship, rising and falling, and beyond that nothing but water, white-flecked and bright blue, shimmering under the incandescent sky and the blaze of sun. He brought his eyes back to the sloping deck. A huge cauldron, with the embers of a dying fire in the pit beneath it, sent up clouds of steam. Standing beside it were two other sailors, one with a long wooden ladle and the other with a supply of wooden bowls. As the line shuffled past, each slave was handed a wooden bowl which he presented to the sailor with the ladle, who filled it with a steamy mixture of boiled yams, thickened with manioc. The sight of the food was too much for Tamboura. With the wooden bowl in his hand, he reached out to have it filled but when the food was slopped into it, he could restrain himself no longer. The vomit that was in his throat gushed out, spattering the white trousers of the sailor and making a puddle of sour slime on the white deck.

"You goddam nigger bastard!" The sailor's face was purple with rage. "Puke on me, would ye, ye savage son of a bitch." The wooden ladle crashed against the side of Tamboura's head stunning him so that he fell to the deck. Omo, who had already filled his bowl and started away, turned quickly, slipped in Tamboura's vomit and lost his balance, the bowl spilling its contents to mix with Tamboura's defilement of the white deck. M'dong, his own bowl upraised, stood still, not daring to move.

The sailor, now incoherent from cursing at Tamboura, kicked at the recumbent form beneath him, and with each kick Tamboura yelped like a tortured dog. The confusion brought the blue-trousered man running.

"What's happened here, Belknap?"

"That goddam nigger puked all over me and I let 'im 'ave it across 'is bloody 'ead. Cain't let them get away with nothin' like that, Mister Moore. If they sees that one pukes on me, the whole fuggin' line will puke on me when they pass—jest fur spite."

"All right, Belknap." Moore, the second mate, reached in his red sash and drew out a silver boatswain's whistle, whose succession of shrill notes brought several sailors running.

They were a brutal-looking lot, recruited from the docks and shanghaied from the alehouses of Liverpool. Their quick response to the boatswain's whistle was prompted by their sadistic hope of wreaking vengeance on someone—or, as they thought in their own minds, *something*, for Negroes were not human—more unfortunate than themselves. That the something they were about to harm had feelings, felt pain and could scream and sob with anguish only made it all the more interesting.

"String him up to the grating and give him ten lashes." Moore pointed to Tamboura, still stretched out on the deck. "A taste of the cat will teach him to swallow his puke after this. Let me know when he's strung up." He turned to the two sailors at the cauldron. "When this lot has finished eating, cook up another mess for those below and send Mr.

Johnson to me so that he can get this lot to sluicing out the slave deck while the others are eating."

The sailor grabbed Tamboura's ankles and pulled him across the deck to where the heavy wooden grating which had covered the hatchway was upended and belayed against a bulkhead. Tamboura felt his body scraping across the deck; felt himself lifted and held against the grating; felt ropes passing around his wrists; felt the strain in his groin as his legs were spread far apart and his ankles tied. His spread-eagling took but a few moments but it was long enough to make him feel how alone he was—a single entity of hopelessness in a sea of fear. The fear had chased the sickness from his body; his nausea had departed, crowded out by fright. He strained at the ropes but they were secure, and with each futile straining he heard the white men laugh. Fear gave way to hatred; as fear had superseded sickness, so now hatred cast out fear. His eyes saw nothing but the white painted boards of the bulkhead through the little squares of the grating, and soon he heard the voice again of the man they called Moore.

"Trussed up, is he?"

"Ay, sir!"

"Then ten lashes. Count ten between each lash. If he faints, douse him with a bucket of water and wait till he comes to. Never lash a man after he passes out. The discipline is wasted. I will count. Get ready!"

Tamboura heard the single word "one."

There was a whistling sound and from out of nowhere a streak of flame coursed along Tamboura's back. It bit deep into his flesh, searing him with a stinging pain that caused him to contract his whole body in a spasm of agony and throw his head back in a howl of torment. He heard a meaningless staccato of evenly spaced words—"One, two, three. . . ." After a few more words, the pain hit again, only this time it was sharper, for it had struck on flesh that was still quivering from the previous lash. He experienced another convulsion and his howl turned into a piercing shriek.

Again the fateful words started, "One, two three . . . ," and this time Tamboura sensed how many more there would be. But the full quantity was never spoken.

"One minute, Mr. Moore!" Tamboura recognized the burring voice of the man with the red beard. Now it had come! Now what he feared even more than the lashes on his back was about to happen. He could not see, but he was sure that the man had a knife in his hand. It was as he had dreaded—he would supply the captain's morning meal.

"Why are ye a-poonishin' this mon?" The captain's voice continued.

"Beggin your pardon, sir, it was necessary to discipline him. He puked all over Belknap as he was being served his meal."

"Puked, eh? The bairn's nae but seasick. Once when I was a-sailin' in the passenger trade, I had a grand English ladyship puke on me brand-new uniform. But think ye that I trussed her up and lashed her? Furthermore, are ye nae aware, Mr. Moore, that all punishment on this ship is by me own orders?"

"Yes sir."

"Then why did ye take it upon yeself to order this 'ere floggin'?"

"Because you were 'aving breakfast, sir." Moore was humbly respectful with an oily subservience. "I didn't want to disturb you. You 'ave always said that the punishment must immediately follow the crime because the niggers don't know what they are being punished for if it is delayed, so I. . . ."

"So ye yoosurped me authority, Mr. Moore! Ken ye not that the mon ye have strung up there is valuable? We transport him all the way from Africy to Cuby for sale. Nae mon wants to buy himsel' a nigger with swellin' welts on his back. It forewarns that the slave's a stubborn, wicked one."

Tamboura could hear the tramp of shod feet on the deck coming nearer to him. He felt a warm, rough hand passing over his back but its touch was gentle. The captain's voice spoke again.

"Fortune was along wi' ye, Mr. Moore. The varmint's hide has nae been broken and the welts will disappear. From now on, Mr. Moore, confine you punishments to short rations and chains. I will attend to other discipline. As this is your first voyage wi' me, I'll only warn you this time. Now, untie him."

The ropes slackened and Tamboura's body slid to the deck on his stomach. He turned over on his back and looked up. It was exactly as he feared. The captain stood over him, a white cloth tied around his neck, a knife in his hand, whose brightly polished steel blade caught the sun and reflected it in a dancing point of light on the deck.

"No, Mongo man, no!" Tamboura's Hausa words sounded

strange even to himself, but in his fright he had wits enough to point to the knife.

"Nae what, me lad?"

"Do not cut them off and eat them."

"Cut what off and eat what?" MacPherson occasionally allowed himself to smile and he did so now.

"My balls."

MacPherson's smile broadened and he started to laugh.

"Ye've no cause to think me a cannibal, boy. I've no desire to chew on your knockers, be they fried or biled." He looked down at Tamboura. "But if I had, undootably yours would be the first I'd choose." He flourished the knife, then stuck it in his pocket. "Them demned Kru boys been a-scarin' ye? Then fear nae mair, lad, your knockers are safe as fur as me appetite is concerned. Come, get to your feet."

Tamboura managed to stand.

MacPherson looked at him, scrutinizing him carefully.

"I've seen ye a-fore."

"Yes, Mongo man." With the knife hidden in the captain's pocket, Tamboura felt braver. "You passed your hands over me in the compound."

MacPherson scratched his head. "It's nae there that I saw ye. One nigger always looks pretty much like another but somehow, lad, ye look familiar to me." His hand continued to scratch "Ah, now I ken," he laughed again, "ye're the same mother-nekkid laddy that poor Mongo Don was a-paintin' when he died. I saw the picture back at Yendo. Yes, ye are, the verra one."

"I am, Mongo man. That is my spirit which remains in Africa."

"And a demned good likeness too." He beckoned to one of the sailors.

"MacQuoid, carry on as usual. Have the niggers pull up the buckets of water and douse each other. I want them clean —as clean as sea water can make them. Issue them fresh water and limes. We'll have no scurvy on this trip. Then take the varmints below as soon as the other gang is readied to come up. Sluice the slave deck and have it stoned. There's a fair wind and it will blow some of the demned stench out. During the two days in port it got pretty filthy below, but get it clean. See to it that the varmints put some elbow grease into the stonin'. When they are through, bring them back up here on deck for an hour of sunshine after the second lot has finished a-stonin' this deck."

"Aye, aye, sir." MacQuoid stepped lively to issue the metal buckets, each one on a long rope, which were lined up alongside the rail.

"And you, Tangley," MacPherson beckoned to another sailor. "When this lad has been doused and scrubbed, take him to the infirmary and spread ointment on his back. Excuse him from work today. Let him sit here in the sun till chain-up time."

Tamboura's back pained and smarted from the two bites of the cat but he welcomed the pailful of salt water that M'dong poured over him and Omo's fingers were gentle as they scrubbed the sensitive welts. He felt clean and refreshed and afterwards, when the sailor called Tangley had applied the ointment, the fiery sting subsided. Back on deck, he found a sunny corner and seated himself on a capstan. Much to his amazement, he saw black women, dressed in shapeless, faded cotton garments, walking back and forth on a small upper deck aft, partially screened by a wooden grating. They interested him so intensely that he saw little else, although he noticed a dark look on the second mate's face whenever he walked by. Tamboura was reassured once again. His spirit was working for him. He touched the little plaited amulet at his neck with the soil of Africa in it. This time, the spirit that he had left behind in Africa had helped him, even at a distance.

Tamboura's gang were below, holystoning the slave deck. He watched the other gang come up, line up for their food and then douse themselves with water as he had been doused. Not a few of them puked over the rail but none of them besmirched the deck as he had. Then—and this was something he had never seen before but was to learn well during the voyage—some of the men were issued square bricks and knelt down with them on the deck, scrubbing the boards as others poured water over it. The water dried quickly in the hot sun and the purity of the deck's whiteness attested to Captain MacPherson's excellent housekeeping.

Tangley, the sailor who had taken Tamboura aft to the infirmary, came to fetch him. He was a young chap with a trace of the purple heather of Scotland still coloring his cheeks. His face had not as yet been coarsened by the vices of the Liverpool docks and the Havana waterfront. He studied Tamboura for a moment before Tamboura became aware of his presence. Tangley's unconscious reaction to the slave's savage beauty and the unexpressed desire it engendered in him made him almost gentle. He knew few Hausa words so he spoke haltingly, but his words were soft-talking.

"You come along with me, boy." His hand reached out, felt the warmth of Tamboura's shoulder and, attracted by the sun-warmed soft pliancy of the skin, slid down Tamboura's back, gently fingering the welts. "You feel better now, boy?"

"I and my spirit are both better." Tamboura resented the white man's fingers on his flesh. Although they did not molest him, there was something about them that was unwelcome. It caused his skin to crawl, but he endured them. He rose and followed Tangley below. The slaves on Tamboura's side had been already chained down and the second section were now lying down to have their fetters fastened. Tamboura pointed to the vacant space between M'dong and Omo.

"That is mine." He walked to the narrow space and inserted himself between M'dong and Omo. Tangley snapped the fetters around his ankles, then knelt and secured the collar. He could not resist touching Tamboura's cheek before he stood up and left. Tamboura watched him go, hating him as he now hated all white men; hating them despite Mongo Don's creation of his other spirit, despite Captain MacPherson's kindly intervention and the implied caress of Tangley's hands. White men, Tamboura had discovered, were his enemies. He was suddenly aware of the vast, unbridgable gulf between black and white. A white man could be kind if he wanted something. Mongo Don had wanted to paint him and he was kind; Captain MacPherson wanted to sell him, so he was kind. Tangley was kind because he wanted something, too, but just what it was, Tamboura did not understand.

He pillowed his head on M'dong's arm and slipped his own arm under Omo's head. M'dong's fingers pinched his nipple but it was only playful evidence of camaraderie, not like the lingering fingers of Tangley. Omo turned his head as much as possible to look at Tamboura.

"Yours is a strong magic, Little Hunter, far stronger than any I know."

"Yes, my spirit is strong," Tamboura admitted, "but it is not strong enough. Had it been really strong, I would not have received the whip twice. I must work to make it even stronger."

"And how will you do that?" Omo asked.

"The hatred that I had for my brother and his wife and son, I shall leave to my second spirit that remains in Africa. That will clean my heart so that I can fill it with hatred for all white men. Then, indeed, will my spirit become strong, because from now on I shall hate every white man I see."

"And how about white women?" M'dong asked.

Tamboura had never considered that. He did not even know if there were white women. Then he remembered the paintings he had seen on the wall of Mongo Don's house. But those were not real women.

"Are there white women?" he asked.

"Surely there must be," Omo answered, "for if there were not white women, there would be no white children. These men we have seen must have had mothers."

Tamboura considered the matter. Surely if there were white women, they must be ugly creatures, pale and spiritless as ghosts. He wanted none of them, and yet. . . . He remembered the gold hair, the pearls and the half-revealed bosoms in the paintings he had seen. Perhaps he did want them. He would wait until he had seen one before making up his mind.

He thought about the matter as he sought sleep, but something troubled him. He wanted to ask Omo, but the regular rise and fall of Omo's chest under his arm told him that he was sleeping. Perhaps M'dong would know.

"M'dong?"

"Yes, Little Hunter."

"I would ask you a question."

"Yes, Little Hunter."

"If I fathered a child from one of the women of my village, the color of the child's skin would be black. Am I right, M'dong?"

"You are right, Little Hunter."

"And if a white man fathers a child from a white woman, the child will be white."

"It would be white." M'dong was not quite sure but he did not want Tamboura to guess his ignorance.

"Then, M'dong, if I father a child from a white woman, what color would it be?"

This time M'dong had to confess his ignorance. He visualized a man white from the waist up and black from the waist down. Or perhaps he would be black of face and white of legs. Then, it might be that one side would be white and the other black. He did not know.

"I do not know, Little Hunter."

"But, M'dong, if we go to this other land to be breeders of

men, may it not be possible that we shall cover white women as well as black?"

Again M'dong could not answer.

"I do not know."

But Tamboura did. He felt a deep instinctive certainty.

"I shall, M'dong. I shall. And when the white woman gives birth to my son, it will be my son, even though it be striped like a zebra."

# chapter ix

One day followed wearily after another in a deadly monotony of sea and sun, slowly sliding from dawn to day and then from dusk to night. Sometimes the sea was glassy smooth and the sails hung limp; at other times it piled up in waves and the wind played through the cordage, plucking at the ropes and making a weird, unearthly music.

The food became tasteless and then worse than tasteless. Some of the slaves refused to eat, but it did them little good to refuse. Captain MacPherson wanted no merchandise with ribs showing through a covering of skin. Those who spurned their food were thrown to the deck and held down with one burly sailor squatting on their chests and another on their legs. Stubborn jaws were pried open and a solid inch-long piece of wood was wedged between their teeth. Then the food was crammed into their mouths so that they had no choice but to gag and swallow.

Tamboura and his friends ate the insipid stuff rather than suffer the torture and humiliation of having it pushed down their throats. The yams and the limes had long since disappeared, and now in the place of these there was only a slimy, gray, farinaceous slop which they somehow managed to get down. Once Captain MacPherson himself came along as their gang was being fed. He had his own bowl filled with the stuff and ate it with relish before them.

"Guid Scotch oatmeal," he said, smacking his lips. "N'aer hurt man nor beastie."

Encouraged by his example, they ate the gray mess, but none of them smacked their lips. They remembered the feasts in their villages, and their mouths watered as they recalled the roasted flesh of antelopes, the crispness of locusts cooked in vegetable butter, the delicate flavor of river fish, the cool juices of tropical fruits and the round loaves of cassava bread. Some of the men who came from the more remote tribes of the interior also missed the pink flesh of their fellow creatures when, after a raiding expedition on a hostile village, some plump young warrior among their enemies had been cooked for a big feast.

After the second week water was rationed—only a small cup a day for each man, and that warm and greenish, alive with wigglers. But they drank it as they ate their food, without relish, merely to keep alive.

As the journey wore on, the captives were allowed greater liberties. No longer were they chained at night. Certain of the slaves—the biggest and most powerful, if seldom the most intelligent—were issued patched pantaloons and armed with wooden clubs. Clothed with the authority of white men, they were often more assiduous in keeping discipline than the sailors had been; they needed little provocation to clout some luckless fellow slave over the head. Fortunately for Tamboura's section, their watch was a big, lazy Eboe who, despite his huge size, was as gentle as a kitten.

Even with their nostrils accustomed to the stench of the ship, the odor grew worse as the days wore on. The slave deck was painstakingly scrubbed each day, but try as a man might, he was not always able to get to the privies—mere holes which overhung the water aft—and his only way of relieving himself would be on his neighbor and on the floor. With some five hundred slaves packed into the low-ceilinged quarters, there was never a time when they were free from dung, vomit and urine, except possibly immediately following the morning scrubbing.

On two widely separated days—Sundays according to the Christian calendar about which, of course, the Negroes knew nothing—they were all assembled on the upper deck. Then the captain and the sailors appeared in fresh, clean clothes. The sailors sat stiffly on chairs in the front row while the captain stood up and harangued the gathering with his eyes on the small black book in his hand. The slaves could not understand a word he said, although from time to time he would look up from the book and point to them. When he had finished, the sailors all stood up and chanted and then they were dismissed. The whole affair was incomprehensible to Tamboura, but anything became a welcome relief in the monotony of existence.

They never saw the women who were on board except through the grating, and that was too far away for the men to catch more than a glimpse of faded cotton frocks. Even on the nights when the captain permitted them a *conjo* up on deck and the men danced to the accompaniment of drums, kettles, and pans, the women did not appear. The dancing served to work off the men's energies, but without the women afterwards, it all became pointless. After the frenzy of the drums on those nights, Tamboura knew that strange things happened between some of the men in their tightly packed quarters. He could hear the gasps for breath and the low moaning. But he felt safe between M'dong and Omo, even though at times M'dong's hands had a way of straying down over his belly and Omo's buttocks would often press tightly against him. Violent friendships with their attendant jealousies sprang up among the slaves and on several occasions bloody fights broke out. Only a fear of punishment kept the violence at a minimum. The men fighting were soon brought down by the guards' clubs, and they were made to endure a day's agony spread-eagled on the grids, without food or water.

One morning the waking captives sensed a subtle change in the air. Above the reek of sweat and excrement, a new odor drifted in on a fresh breeze. It smelled of earth and trees and rotting leaves. It was so pungent it could almost be tasted and it stirred the slaves into a new restlessness. They could hardly wait for the grating to be removed, and when they were once up on deck they could see birds circling the ship. Far off, on the port side there was a low-lying purple strip which came nearer and nearer until they could distinguish the white line of surf on the sand and the bright green of palms receding into the purple mountains. They passed vast acreages of shimmering, waving green, with blotches of white which betokened houses. At one time they were near enough to a jutting headland to see men—black men like themselves—following a high-wheeled cart pulled by plodding white oxen. A wave of restless enthusiasm ran through the ship. Even when night came, the breeze still brought the odor of earth across the dark water, and once, along toward dawn, they heard, faintly over the black waves, a cock's clarion call greeting the new morn.

The next day about noon, they saw a grim fortress of rock topped by a scarlet and gold banner. Then, with sails flopping idly, the ship rounded the promontory of the fortress and they saw the vast city of Havana spread out before them, glittering in white, rose, turquoise and green. It was an incredible sight to eyes that had been accustomed to grass huts and leafy trails, this pile upon pile of masonry and streets and people. They sailed between the grim piles of El Morro and La Punta and into the landlocked lake that was the harbor of Havana. The anchor chains rattled and the ship stilled, its voyage ended.

Much to their chagrin, the slaves were herded below decks, and locked in irons again. But something told them this time it would not be for long. They sensed that they had reached the end of their long journey and the brief glimpse they had had of the multicolored city spread out before them in the sun seemed to promise sufficient reward for all they had suffered. Now at last they were here, although they did not know where *here* was except that it had a strange name—Cuba.

M'dong drew Tamboura closer.

"We are here, Little Hunter. Tonight we shall be bedded with women. Ay! I hope there will be plenty of them."

"And I," Omo chuckled. "How about you, Little Hunter?"

Tamboura could not laugh. Both M'dong and Omo knew that he had never had a woman, so he let them laugh for him.

They remained in chains until late afternoon when they heard the welcome sound of the grating being opened. This time it was Captain MacPherson himself, his mates and several sailors, who descended the stairs. The collars were unlocked and the fetters taken from their legs. Again the light chains and collars were put on and they were separated into groups of ten. Then, up the steep stairs for their last sight of the whitely gleaming deck they had scrubbed day after day on the long journey. Two sailors stood beside a pile of folded garments and as they filed past they were handed patched and darned pantaloons, cut off at the knees. There was only one size—big—and to hold them up they were given lengths of hempen twine to tie around their waists. The pantaloons felt uncomfortable after the nudity of the voyage but the men were proud of them, for here was a concrete evidence of a new life. They went over the side of the ship on the same nets they had used to board it, only now, instead of encountering the Krus and their canoes, they stepped into wide boats with blacks at the oars who spoke a strange language that was not Hausa.

The boats, filled with two or three caffles of ten men each, left the ship and headed for the city, drawing up to a low pier of heavy wooden planks, quite different from the jerry-built construction of bamboo which had welcomed them at Yendo Castle. Here the slaves disembarked and lined up in caffles of two abreast for a march through the streets, just as the sun was painting the Morro behind them in vivid pink. The narrow streets with their abundant life, the happy laughing people, the donkeys, the white men in strange clothes, and an occasional glistening *volante* stirred their imagination. But far more interesting and eye-compelling than any other sight was the first white woman they saw. She was young, pretty and undoubtedly a whore, and she was leaning over the table of a sidewalk *cantina* talking to a white man. The very miracle of her existence stirred Tamboura. He could see the outline of her breasts under her dress and the curve of her hips and the line of her calves. Ay! so there really were white women! They existed and they were far more beautiful than any girl he had ever seen before. He became more certain than ever that some night he would meet one in the tamarisk bushes after the full moon dance and that he would father a son by her. He turned his head to eye her as long as possible and his hand stole up to the woven amulet around his throat. His spirit would help him.

With all the wonder of the streets of Havana, they had little regret for the Africa they had left behind, but their excursion was of short duration. Soon they reached a low-lying building of peeling stucco which presented a blank wall of masonry to the street. The entrance was barred by a double set of iron gates. As they halted in front of these, Moore, who was leading the procession, disappeared inside through an open wicket in one of the large gates. In a few moments he returned with a tall Negro, dressed quite as raggedly as they were. The gates slowly opened and Moore yelled at them to follow.

Inside there was an ancient stink which surpassed even the reeking odors of the slave deck. On the ship the frequent scrubbings and the cleanliness of sea air had diluted the stench, but here it was the accumulation of generations. The courtyard, paved with broken stones and strewn with litter, was surrounded by a continuous row of tall iron gratings. One by one these were opened, and a ten-man caffle entered each cell. When the slaves were inside, the collars and chains were taken from their necks and then the iron doors were closed behind them.

That was all. They had landed, they had had a brief glimpse of another world of light, color and freedom, and now once again they were imprisoned. But the cells were roomy and they had sufficient space to lie without touching each other. After the long, cramped nights at sea it was a blessing not to feel the pressure of a hot, sweaty body against the hot sweatiness of one's own. M'dong pre-empted the corner nearest the grating which gave a view of the courtyard, and through habit and the desire to be together, Omo and Tamboura followed him. They established it as their *querencia*—their own particular spot. Soon after their arrival they were fed a tasty stew of meat and vegetables, followed by oranges and limes—a welcome relief after the days of the porridge they had come to loathe. And there was fresh water—all they wanted to drink.

As the shadows lengthened, an obese man, so fat that he had to be supported by two Negroes, made his plodding way around the courtyard, stopping at each grating. One of the blacks supporting him spoke to the slaves in their own language and told them to line up at the grating. The fat man looked them over, his small eyes making a quick and expert inventory before he passed on to another cage. After that, they slept.

What a relief it was to be able to lie on one's back or on the left side. But the body enforces strange habits and the men found they were only comfortable lying on their right side, as they had slept all during their long voyage. When they awoke in the morning, they were in the same tightly packed position as on shipboard. Tamboura's arm was under Omo's head and he was lying on M'dong's arm, with their bodies pressed closely together.

Three days and three nights passed. They were given water for bathing and oil for their bodies; they were exercised in groups in the patio and fed better and more generously than they had been since the first night at Yendo Castle. Each day they had some sort of meat, stringy and tough but flavorsome, and cooked with vegetables, with fruit to follow it. Their bodies filled out and their skin became sleek and glossy again.

The welts had completely disappeared from Tamboura's back and once again it was smooth as satin. He cleaned his teeth with the rind of limes, bit his fingernails off evenly, and painstakingly rubbed his toenails against the stone floor until they were smooth and even. They were all connoisseurs of their own bodies and spent much of their day attending to them. In truth, they had nothing else to do; their bodies were their only possession.

Soon after they had eaten, on the morning of the fourth day, two white men appeared, immaculate in starched white clothes. Tamboura had never seen such elegance before and his eyes popped as he saw the gold rings on their fingers, and their glossy long black hair tied behind with a narrow ribbon. He admired the closely woven hats of white straw and the highly polished shoes. Ay! someday he too would be dressed like that. The men made a slow circuit of the courtyard, accompanied by the fat man who bowed and grinned at them. One by one the gates opened and the slaves inside stepped out. The older of the two men gave only a quick look at most of the slaves awaiting his inspection and shook his head, but occasionally he would point to one particular man and have him step apart from the rest. When they arrived at Tamboura's cell, they stopped and looked at all ten of the slaves. The older man, his lips pursed, eyed them, then pointed to Omo.

"A Mandingo?" he asked. The fat man ducked his head in a series of nods and smiles and spouted words which were meaningless to Tamboura, whose turn it was next.

"Royal Hausa?" The man seemed astonished.

Again the fat fellow went through his fawning ritual.

It was M'dong's turn, and the man looked him over and smiled. He motioned for the three of them to step forward and dismissed the others. Together with those he had chosen from the other cages, they were lined up and told to shed their breeches.

Now the younger man took over. He examined them carefully, running his hands over their bodies, making them squat and leap in the air, throwing a stick down the length of the patio for them to run after. Then came the part that Tamboura hated, when the hands of the white man touched his genitals, hefted them, examined them, and pulled back the flap of skin. The fingering angered and excited him. The three men walked away and left them standing there but soon the younger man returned. The cell that Tamboura had occupied was emptied and the men selected were put into it.

Meanwhile the slaves of the fat man had been busy, knocking together a wooden platform at the far end of the patio and later placing rows and rows of wooden benches before it. Around noon the courtyard began to fill with white men, some in stiffly starched white suits and some in dusty garments, who looked as if they had come from far off.

The door of the cage occupied by Tamboura and his companions was unlocked and they were told to shed their breeches and line up outside it. Here they stood while many of the white men came and examined them. It was the same procedure—hands run quickly over arms and flanks, eyes spread open and fingers inserted in their mouths. And always the same anger-creating abasement of having white fingers paw at that which they had been taught to consider sacred and private.

Time and again Tamboura had to kneel and rise, turn and bend, open his mouth, jump in the air, squat down and spring up, submit to the same humiliation as the white fingers felt, weighed and examined. His hatred of the whites, generated in Africa and grown on the voyage, was inflamed by the gross liberties these men took with his body, their smiles, smirks, grins and guffaws. Only for one white man did he feel some grudging respect—the older man who had come earlier in the morning and had now returned. This one only looked at Tamboura but did not touch him, except to lay a hand on his shoulder and say something to the young man who accompanied him.

Gradually the assemblage took their seats on the wooden benches and the fat man was hoisted up onto the platform where he sprawled in an oversized chair. The first caffle of ten men—the contents of the first cage—was led up the steps of the platform and placed in a row at its front.

The fat man began to speak and as he spoke the men below answered him, some in a loud voice and some by merely a nod of the head or by lifting a finger. Tamboura could not understand what was happening, nor could M'dong nor Omo. Finally there was a lull, and the fat man banged on the table three times with a wooden mallet. Then he pointed to a man seated below him and the caffle was led down from the platform, taken back to its cell and locked inside.

Soon it was the turn of those in Tamboura's cell to be led up the steps and to stand in line before the many faces looking up at them expectantly. The talk started. Arms were raised, heads were shaken, nods were given. The fat man talked back to those below him, raising his voice to a strident whine, and still they kept shouting at him. To Tamboura it seemed that there was more excitement than there had been with the other lots. He recognized the white man who had put his hand on his shoulder, and his younger companion who had examined him earlier. The older man was sitting quietly amid all the commotion, merely holding up one finger from time to time.

As he tried to figure out the strange ritual in which he was somehow involved, it dawned on Tamboura that he, along with the others beside him, was being sold. If so, he hoped it would be to the quiet man sitting down there. For some reason, he seemed to hate him less than the others. He caught the man's eye and smiled at him, and the man smiled back.

The usual lull was followed by the banging of the fat man's hammer on the table. He spoke once, twice, a third time. There was a hushed silence.

"Sold . . . to don César and his son, don Gregorio."

Tamboura and his companions descended the steps of the platform and as they came down the young man met them. He was surrounded by others who were slapping him on the back, shaking his hand and talking to him. Extricating himself from his well-wishers, don Gregorio led Tamboura's group away. But this time they were not locked in their cell. They were told in fairly intelligible Hausa to put on their breeches and follow him.

Outside the patio they saw a sumptuous high-wheeled carriage, followed by a long wagon drawn by four mules. Seated in the carriage was the older white man. Don Gregorio got in beside him, and then a Negro who spoke Hausa ordered the slaves up in the back of the wagon and they set off through the streets of Havana.

The big wagon almost completely filled the width of the narrow streets and the walkers on the sidewalks had to stand in doorways while they passed. Tamboura, along with the others with him, was happy. Once more they were out in the life and gaiety of the city and there was much of interest to see and talk about. Soon they passed under a gate of masonry and the houses became fewer and there were more trees. The air was fresh and sweet, the sun shone and the trees looked like dripping fountains of bright flame-colored flowers. Birds sang, and colored butterflies sparkled in the clear air. From time to time they passed black men like themselves on the road who stopped and waved at them, sometimes calling messages to them in Hausa. As they went farther from the city, they saw tall fields of cane on both sides of the road, and as the stalks undulated in the breeze it reminded them of the ocean they had so recently left. It was hot but the breeze cooled their skin and they chatted together excitedly. They were neither manacled nor shackled and for once they were riding and not walking. Verily this country was a fair one, clean and orderly and well cared for. There was a tropical exuberance to the landscape but it was neither the unkempt jungle nor the sun-parched plains of Africa. It was green with grass and trees and cane and colorful with flowers. Enormous white houses sat far back from the road behind long rows of palms that lifted their acid green fronds high on straight gray pillars.

The road dipped down to ford a shallow stream and the carriage and wagon halted. The driver told them to get out and they lay flat on the sandy bank, drinking the clear running water. Then they were told to scrub themselves clean, which they did with the fine white sand in the river, and they dried themselves in the sun. The driver lifted the seat of the wagon and handed them big chunks of some spongy white stuff with a brown crust, and said they should eat it. None of them had ever seen it before, but eat it they did and it tasted good. After relieving themselves in the bushes, they piled back into the cart, washed, fed, and refreshed. Tamboura had noticed that all the time they were sporting in the water the two white men kept their eyes on them, while they were talking to each other. Tamboura felt they must be discussing him, for he saw the older man point directly to him and, as he had done during the sale, he grinned at the younger man, who nodded his head slightly in return.

The road continued and the sun behind them sank in a violent swirl of golden clouds. Darkness came soon and with it a chill that made them huddle together for warmth. The deep indigo of the sky changed to a velvet blackness, sprinkled with stars which vied with a pale disc of moon to silver the road ahead of them. Over the black fields, thousands of tiny pricks of light came and went in circles of pale light from the fireflies. The only sounds were the wheels of the wagon crunching on the gravel of the road, the voice of the young man singing in the carriage ahead of them and the steady hum of the insects of the night.

Tall white masonry posts appeared like ghostly sentinels out of the darkness and the carriage turned in between them. They followed up a long road, white in the moonlight, except where it was striped by the shadows of the palms. Lights twinkled ahead and a white man, escorted by two blacks with *flambeaux*, came out to meet them. The carriage drove up to the house and the two men got out. The young man took a seat beside the driver of the wagon, which continued around the big white house and down along a street of palm-thatched huts in front of which groups of Negroes were sitting. From the door of each hut a yellow light gleamed, gilding the faces of the Negroes when they walked in front of it.

The wagon stopped and the young man jumped down. He carried a piece of paper in one hand and walked over to a lighted doorway to study it. In the unknown tongue, he spoke to the driver and he in turn told the slaves to get down out of the wagon. A Negro from one of the huts appeared with a lantern which he handed to the white man, who held it high, examining the faces of Tamboura and his companions. He signaled them again to untie the string which held up their breeches and lowered the lantern to scrutinize their bodies.

"You," he tapped Tamboura on the shoulder. "Over here." Again he passed down the line and sent M'dong and Omo over to where Tamboura stood. "Come along with me," he said in his halting Hausa and they followed him, leaving the others under the guard of the driver.

He marched them down the street a short distance to where an old woman sat in the shadows before one of the huts, surrounded by the vague forms of other women.

"Mama Baba," he called out, "I've brought you three strong sons from Africa. Do you want them?"

The old woman stood up with some difficulty, for she was so enormous she seemed to be a part of the dark earth itself arising.

*"Si, Señor!"* she laughed in a high pitch of excitement. "Three sons are what I have been wanting and my three young girls want them even more. I've had no men in my hut for many months and these girls sure been itching for a man. Bless you don Gregorio and bless don César for buying them for my little posies."

"Well, here they are!" He left them standing there as he walked away.

The old woman waddled over to them, her arms widestretched, a broad grin on her face. Her immense arms engulfed them and her breasts, like soft, overripe melons, pressed against them. Her Hausa was rapid and fluent.

"I'm your Mama now. I'm your Mama Baba. Ay! what fine sons I have and what are your names?"

"I am M'dong." He stepped up, his breeches in his hand. She embraced him separately and her excited cackle became a shriek of pleasure. Her big arm nudged him into the light from the door.

*"Ay de mi! Ay de mi!* Maria Luz, here is a man for you—a fine man. He's strong and vigorous and I hope he beats you and knocks some sense into your silly head."

A young woman arose and stepped boldly forward from the shadows. She was tall and comely and the light from the door turned her brown skin to gleaming copper. Mama Baba took her hand and placed it in that of M'dong. Together they retreated to the bench in the shadows.

"Put on your breeches, man," the old woman called after them. "Can't have you sitting out front of my *bohio* naked."

"And you, big boy?" She brought Omo into the light and ran her hand over his shoulders.

"I am Omo."

"He, he!" She shrieked louder than she had over M'dong. "A Mandingo! I can tell it to look at you. *Ay de mi!* We are blessed this night. You Mandingo boys sure are scarce."

"Yes, I am a Mandingo," Omo answered proudly.

"Whee, makes me wish I was young again." Mama Baba gave Omo a nudge with her elbow which nearly threw him off balance. "I guess I'm not too old to enjoy it, but I've got something you'd like better than fat old Mama Baba. Graciella, come here, you lucky girl, and see what don César bought for you. Mandingos are scarce—we have only eight on the whole *finca* and now you have one for your own. How the other girls will envy you. Mandingos are *muy hombre—muy, muy hombre."*

A smaller girl, well rounded, with a saucy grin which showed the white crescent of her teeth, stepped out. She did not wait for Mama Baba to put her hand in that of Omo's. She flung her arms around his neck and touched his lips to hers. He did not respond, for it was something new to him.

*"Besame!"* she cried out in Spanish. "Ay, Mama, he does not kiss me back."

"Of course not. Well-brought-up African boys do not know

how to kiss—only the riffraff have learned it at the white settlements. But you can teach him, Graciella."

Tamboura was left alone as Omo and his girl joined M'dong and Maria Luz.

Mama Baba drew him over into the light.

"You are not Mandingo, boy, but you are even finer than Mandingo. *Por Dios!* You are Royal Hausa. *Ay de mi!* What a pretty boy you are. And young! Now I am glad I saved Pia for you." She left him standing in the light and went to the bench and took the hand of the last girl. "Pia, come, see what don César bought for you. Look!"

She led the girl into the light coming through the open door, and as Tamboura looked at her he was filled with desire. She was small, light-boned and slender, brown instead of black, and her hair, instead of being a close skullcap of wool, was a finger-length long and tied all over her head with varicolored threads. Her breasts under the shapeless gown were well rounded and their nipples strained against the thin fabric. Her lips were delicate, her teeth small and white, and when she looked up at him her eyes were like two dark pools of mystery.

"What is your name?" she asked in Spanish.

Mama Baba interpreted for her. "She speaks only Spanish, this little one, but you will learn it quickly."

"I am Tamboura." His throat was dry but he found the words to answer.

"Tamboura?" she repeated. "Tamboura? *Ay, entiendo. Tambor! Me llamo Pia y ahora voy a tocar el tambor.*"

"She say your name is the Spanish name for *drum*. She say that tonight she is going to play on the drum."

*"Si, Tambor,"* she nodded, still smiling, and came closer, pressing her body tight against his, while his hands came to rest on the firm curves of her hips. He smelled a strange delicious odor, for she had rubbed her skin with the leaves of the lemon verbena—the *reina luisa*. It was an intoxicating scent and it combined with her nearness to arouse him. When she stepped back, Mama Baba took one look at Tamboura and threw her hands high over her head with a shriek of delight.

"Put on your breeches, boy, or every hot-blooded bitch on the *finca* will be fighting over you." She let her arms fall and turned to enter the hut, her monstrous body still heaving with laughter. "Inside all of you. I've kept the pot steaming since this afternoon, for don Gregorio said he would return with three boys for my girls. Come in."

The hut was larger inside that Tamboura had anticipated, but there was none of the clean-swept simplicity that had marked the huts of his village. Here all was disorder, chaos and dirt. Long festoons of cobwebs hung from the smoke-blackened ragged thatch of the roof. The uneven floor of hard-packed dirt was littered with scraps of decaying food, crumbles of dried palm from the roof and the discards of daily living which remained where they had fallen. One corner held a low shelf of hard-baked mud with a sunken hole, reddened by dying embers, on which an iron pot simmered. Along one wall the floor was strewn with matted grass and rags. The open door and two small windows did little to dispel the odor of human bodies which had accumulated from the countless couples who had met, twisted, slavered and copulated on these makeshift beds. Yet the strong musk which permeated the hut, although at first offensive to nostrils which had been accustomed to the perfumed freshness of the tropic night, was strangely stimulating. It carried a scent of women that was strongly aphrodisiac to the three men.

Mama Baba pointed to the pile of grass and rags. "This for you lovers. I sleep over here." She pointed to a low wooden framework in the other corner. "These girls are ignorant, they speak only Spanish and you will learn it quickly but tonight you will have no need for words. Come eat, for you will need your strength and I know you are anxious that I put out the candle. *Ay de mi!* I know what the weeks on shipboard are like for many years ago I traveled the Middle Passage myself. And I know what it's like in old don Solano's slave barracoons; that's where don César's papa bought me. But now you can forget all that for you are here with Mama Baba and your pretty girls. This is your home and tonight you will be happy—*muy contento*." She ladled the stew into wooden bowls and passed them to the men. "Tonight you will have no need of sleep for sleep is only for the old like me. Tomorrow at dawn when they lead you out to the cane fields, you will work willingly for you know you have your girls and Mama Baba to come home to."

It was a night of glory and wonder for Tamboura, and his blood boiled through his veins like liquid fire. It was a night of violent movement and quick spasms, of searching lips and seeking hands. It was all he had hoped for and dreamed about. It was the greatest night of his life and its bliss did not diminish until the first fingers of the sun strayed through the windows to touch the six bodies on the tumbled pile of grass and rags.

# chapter x

All Cuba was in a turmoil and many *Cubanos* were worried. Although a state of turmoil was quite acceptable and even enjoyed there, worry was not a natural state for *Cubanos*. They much preferred to live gaily and happily with no great concern for *mañana*, which, after all, never really comes. But now there were prospects of a most unpleasant and unprofitable *mañana* which would surely engulf them all in absolute ruin. *Madre de Dios! Que catástrofe!*

A little black cloud had appeared in the sky over England (may God condemn the stiff-necked heretics to eternal damnation!) and it had spread over the sea until it had reached the northern part of the *yanqui* United States (another country of heretics!). Like the little black cloud that presaged a hurricane, it could mean the end of everything in Cuba. It was all contained in one simple word—abolition! An end to slavery! As if the stupid money-pinching heretics cared about slavery—putting their own pale-as-milk children to work in their mills and factories and then condemning the God-ordained use of blacks on plantations. Why concern themselves about the *malditos negros? Dios sabe,* they were not human—not half as human as the poor little white children who toiled away to make money for those same English who now wept, wailed and wrung their thin white hands over the conditions of the slaves. Everyone admitted that the Negroes were much better off cutting cane in Cuba than cutting off the heads of their brethren in Africa and gobbling them up for dinner.

*Caramba!* The very economy of Cuba was based on slaves. Take them away and where would Cuba be? Who would raise sugar cane on the big *fincas?* Who would raise cattle on the big *estancias?* What would the rest of the world do for tobacco? For rum? Stop the traffic in slaves and all Cuba would be overgrown with weeds in one generation. Ay! That was the worry! That was the cause of the turmoil. Stop the traffic in slaves? Where then would be their stately palaces in Havana; the sumptuous jewels for their mistresses and the less sumptuous ones for their wives; the glittering *volantes* to ride in; the lavish balls and entertainments; the life of ease and comfort on the far-stretching plantations? What a prospect! *Ay, por Dios!* What would happen to them all without slaves?

But surely the rich slave traders in Bristol and Liverpool would put a stop to this nonsense. And surely the rich plantation owners in *los Estados Unidos* who needed slaves for their cotton would outweigh the opinions of their pinched northern brethren. Ay! The world was going crazy—*absolutamente loco. Abolicion?* Pah! It would never come. Light another cigar and forget about it.

But the rich fumes of Havana tobacco did not solve the problem. It just might happen. *Claro que si!* The movement was gaining ground all over the world. Altogether too many people in too many places were talking about it, not only in England and the United States but in France, in Holland, in Denmark, and like the little black cloud in the sky to which nobody pays any attention, the hurricane might be on its way. There was so much talk, so much pounding of fists on polished mahogany dining tables and buttonholing of men in the streets, so many quickly spoken Spanish words being spilled, and yet nobody was doing anything about it. In the meantime the price of slaves was going up with every shipment from Africa. The prices the planters were paying at don Solano's were fantastic. And nothing was being done about it. Not a thing.

Everyone looked to don César Montalvo to do something, and he finally did by inviting all the biggest planters on the island to a *banquet extraordinario* at the Finca Montalvo. Everyone came, for everyone in Cuba paid attention when don César Montalvo spoke. From the cattle *estancias* of Camaguey to the sugar *fincas* of Santa Clara to the tobacco fields of Pinar del Rio, there was no more respected name in all Cuba. He was the richest of all the Cuban planters, a Creole of distinguished ancestry who was even accepted by the Spanish. Let the *abolicionistas* do their damnedest, don César would have a solution.

It certainly wasn't a matter of buying up more slaves than they needed and raising the prices sky-high by bidding against each other. Oh no! Don César pointed out the fallacy of that. Slaves couldn't be packed away on a shelf and held in reserve. They grew old just like human beings. You couldn't store them like so many bottles of wine and know that they would improve with age. Don César was most astute and he gave them an entirely new notion of what they might do. Although his explanation had a certain amount of Andalusian circumlocution, it was sound and logical.

When Cuba was first settled by the Spaniards, there were neither horses nor cattle on the island. *Verdad?* And so all the horses and cattle, all the hogs and mules, all the donkeys and dogs and cats and doves and pigeons and hens and every other living thing that a man needed must be brought from Spain. *Verdad?* But now, if a man wanted a horse, did he have to send all the way to Spain for it? If he wished a cow or a mule, did it have to come to him across the ocean in a ship? No, no, no! Of course not. He either raised it himself or bought it from someone else who had raised it right here in Cuba. Today even the cattle were *creoles*—born and raised in Cuba. *Claro que si?*

Don César calmly lighted his cigar and let this bit of wisdom sink in. When he felt it had, he asked another question.

Were slaves different from other cattle? *Por Dios,* no!

If they could raise horses on their own *fincas,* then they could raise slaves. So let them start in right now and in twenty years, if the *malditos ingleses* should decide that the *malditos negros* were not cattle any more but human beings made in the image and likeness of God (may the good God pardon him for such impiety—a black man in the image of God Almighty?), let them and to hell with them. Cuba would have all the slaves it wanted or needed, bred and raised on Cuban soil. And—don César looked around at his distinguished guests and winked slowly and ominously—if any Cuban planter couldn't get enough slaves to do his breeding for him, *por Dios,* what was the matter with the planter himself and his sons? Although don César himself had never had a slave mistress for the simple reason that he could not stand the black stink of them, he knew that several bright-skinned children on his own *finca* were from the loins of his own son and some *fincas* had as many *mestizos,* all with a close family resemblance to the owner, as there were pure blacks.

So, let the Cuban planters get busy and either sire this next generation of slaves themselves or buy some upstanding young bucks and some young wenches to do it for them. Then, by merely placing one on top of the other in the manner in which nature had intended, *por consiguiente,* the island would be overrun with little black bastards. Because—and here don César winked again—if there was one thing these black fellows knew how to do without being told is was to *chingar.* No white man had ever had to tell them how to fornicate. This, then, was the way they could damn the stiff-necked English to the same hellfire to which they were now condemning the planters.

It was good advice and easy to follow. Heads nodded solemnly in agreement. Heretofore the slave population of the *fincas* had been ninety per cent masculine, for it was the men who worked and produced. Girl babies had often been thrown out on the dung heap to perish. Well, all that could be changed. Women could work too, and when they were not working they could be breeding children.

Then don César had a final word of caution.

"Breed your slaves as you would breed your horses. Choose only the best stock. Breed the strong, the handsome and the intelligent. Don't let the weak, the simple, the malformed or the stupid father the next generation. As you would not mate an Arabian stallion to a broken-down nag or a blooded mare to a common work horse, so guard your nigger studs and keep them from spurting their seed into some half-witted slut. Guard your fine nigger wenches as carefully as your own daughters so that no slant-faced, rubber-lipped African ape will perpetuate his likeness in them. Pick your breeders from the best tribes of Africa—the Dahomeys, the Nagos, the Hausas, the Mandingos, the Congos, the Aradas, the Fantis, the Fullahs and the Eboes. And then, *por Dios, Senores,* in twenty years or even less, Cuba can rub nigger shit in the lily-white faces of those psalm-singing *abolicionistas!*"

Thus—Tamboura!

And Omo and M'dong and the other young slaves don César and don Gregorio had so carefully hand-picked and purchased.

Thus—Pia!

And Maria Luz and Graciella and the fine-blooded Negro wenches don César had been guarding as closely as convent blossoms for his young studs.

Thus—Mama Baba and her close watchfulness over the six in her bohio to see that the right seed was planted in the right ground. And then, multiply Mama Baba's establishment by four, right on don César's plantation. In each of the three other bohios don César had established a wise old woman who knew how to cook stews properly spiced with aphrodisiacs (as if the young studs needed them), and to surround her charges with a sufficiently erotic atmosphere, designed to stimulate those desires which needed so very little stimulation. Wise Mama Baba! She knew that back in Africa a man's desire was heightened by what he heard and saw under the next bush. She was quite aware that while one couple would perform their functions admirably, they would perform even better when stimulated by another couple beside them and that both couples would be spurred on to even greater efforts by the presence of a third. Privacy was for white lovers who wished to indulge in the nuances of passion. But Mama Baba's charges were not white lovers who quoted poetry, indulged in sentimental serenades or swooned over roses in the moonlight. Mama Baba's charges wasted no time in fanciful preliminaries—they had a job to do and they did it and, *por consiguiente,* they enjoyed it.

During their residence with Mama Baba, Tamboura, Omo and M'dong picked up some Spanish. As the girls did not speak Hausa, the Spanish words were necessary to converse with them. In the cane fields they picked up other words, so the language was no longer as strange-sounding and as unintelligible as before. They learned the language of work in the fields and the language of love at night. What more was there for them to know?

The work in the fields was back-breaking and difficult. They swung their sharp machetes at the tall cane and watched it fall in giant windrows. They gathered it up in their strong arms and piled it in the high-wheeled oxcarts. They drove it to the *central,* slowly plodding along the palm-shaded roads. They unloaded it to be crushed and went back for more. It was hard work but it strengthened their muscles and toughened them. It added extra pounds to Tamboura and changed his figure from an adolescent youth's to a man's. Although the three didn't know it, they were picked men and they were given, by order of don César, some of the less strenuous work to do, but even that was difficult enough.

Like the other slaves, they were up at dawn with a hasty but abundant breakfast—food was always plentiful at Mama Baba's, even milk and eggs and meat. Then out into the fields in the cool of the morning and hard at work by the time the sun began to shed its heat. They worked steadily until noon, when the big bell atop the *central* started tolling. It was their signal to return to the slave quarters—a signal which all obeyed except those who were working in the *central* where the boiling vats must be under constant supervision. Then there was a three-hour respite from work in the cool shade of the bohio where they stripped off their sweaty breeches and lay naked on the pile of grass and rags, letting the breeze which came in the windows fan their bodies. The girls were apt to pester them at this time, lying beside them and starting little electric shocks in their bodies by the gentle movement of fingertips. But Mama Baba was adamant. There was a time for everything and this was a time for rest. If the wenches didn't get enough at night, they would just have to do without it in the daytime. She wasn't going to have any old busybody like Tia Chencha dropping into *her* bohio and seeing such goings-on—not on *her* floor in broad daylight. *No, señores!* And so they rested and the girls pouted alongside of them, hoping that Mama Baba would doze off, as she invariably did. Then the electric touch of the fingers quickly led to other things while Mama Baba snored.

They were back in the fields by mid-afternoon when the fury of the sun had lost its bite, and they worked steadily until after sundown. At night, don César imitated the custom of the curfew gun in Havana. Either he or don Gregorio applied a taper to the touchhole of a small brass cannon which, polished to look like gold, stood before the front steps at the entrance of the big house. Its welcome boom marked the end of their workday and they were free for a plunge in the river to clean themselves of the sweat and grime that had accumulated on their bodies, then to make their way slowly but contentedly to the welcome of Mama Baba's hut, her steaming stew, and the hour of sitting in peace and contentment outside her bohio when she lit the tallow dip inside and opened the door for the yellow light to shine out.

This was the social hour of the day, when the slaves strolled up and down the dusty street between the palm-thatched huts. It was a time for regaling each other with the latest gossip: the news of the big house, culled from that haughty and superior aristocracy of slaves, the house servants; and all the other little scandals and morsels of news in the slave community—who was flogged today, who was sold and why and where, who had been bought and who was sleeping with whom. Then, when the last straggler had sought his own bohio or the *dormitorio,* Mama Baba shepherded them all into the huts, the candle was snuffed, breeches and dresses were shucked onto the floor and the night began, a night of splendor and falling stars and crashing planets for Tamboura.

This was their life six days a week. On the seventh, *domingo,* they rested.

Came then the fateful day when Mama Baba announced to Tamboura that his little Pia was *embarazada* from his seed and that she was being taken from the bohio to a large building somewhat removed from the slave quarters and presided over by the plantation's mid-wife. Didn't Tamboura know that Pia was *embarazada?* Hadn't he noticed how her belly was swelling? *Ay de mi!* Tamboura had done his work well. M'dong and that lazy Mandingo, Omo, had not accomplished their task as yet. By rights, she should send Tamboura down to the men's *dormitorio* but she would keep him a little longer and if neither Omo nor M'dong produced any results, she would let Tamboura demonstrate his ability with Maria Luz and Graciella (as if he already hadn't). So, Tamboura remained in Mama Baba's bohio sleeping alongside the two couples and eating his heart out for Pia except when Omo or M'dong took pity on him and relinquished Maria Luz or Graciella to him temporarily. Within another month, Mama Baba proudly announced that both Maria Luz and Graciella were in the same condition as Pia and, much as she hated to have her big strong boys leave, they might just as well go down to the *dormitorio* and give her a much-needed rest from cooking.

"But," Mama Baba advised them with a waggling admonitory forefinger, "just as soon as don César find himself three more pretty girls, you come back to Mama Baba. You all three good boys and made no trouble for Mama Baba. You know your work and you do it fine. And," she added, shaking her head and drawing down the corners of her big mouth, "I sure hope don Gregorio don't send you to that old slattern, Tia Chencha. She don't know how to cook and her bohio! Whew! It stinks!" She was quite immune to the odor of her own hut.

They were far more homesick in the *dormitorio* for Mama Baba's bohio than they were for their homes in Africa. Nightly they paid her a visit, and she always had some choice tidbit saved for them, but it was almost more lonely to sit before her hut without the three girls than it was to remain sitting on the long wooden bench with the other men, outside the *dormitorio*. However, they were in the *dormitorio* less than a month before don Gregorio appeared with the welcome news that they were to return to Mama and when, that night after work, they ran up the street to her hut, they found not only the giggling old lady to welcome them but three new girls—a big Eboe for Omo, who spoke neither Spanish nor Hausa; a little bronze-skinned *mestizo* for M'dong, who bore a marked resemblance to the owner of the *finca* from whom don César had just purchased her, and a child of about fourteen for Tamboura. There was no doubt she was a virgin for she cried with pain the first night. But she soon forgot all about pain and became even more intoxicated with Tamboura than Pia had been.

And so they came to adjust their lives to the loneliness of nights spent on the dirt floor of the *dormitorio* or the erotic excitement of nights on the pile of grass and rags in Mama Baba's hut. Once, when Mama Baba was playing hostess to four other slaves and their companions, Tamboura, Omo and M'dong were billeted at Tia Chencha's, where they didn't enjoy themselves as much. She was a sour-faced old crone and, as Mama Baba had said, a miserable cook. Usually the three of them were together, although once Tamboura was sent with two slaves whom he had never been with before and, even if his bedmate left nothing to be desired, he missed the companionship of M'dong and Omo. However, they were seldom separated and don Gregorio came to regard them as a unit—*los trillizos mios* he called them—his triplets, and he was in the habit of thinking of them together. Maria Luz, Graciella and Pia came to their time and presented don César with a daughter and sons respectively, although the fathers were never able to pick out their own offspring from the litter of black babies that filled the nursery. Not long thereafter, the three girls returned to Mama Baba's and M'dong, Omo and Tamboura were off for a second round with them.

It was a happy homecoming for all six of them and Mama Baba made a little celebration out of it, decorating the inside of the hut with tuberoses which added their heavy scent to the already heavy odor. They stayed up late that night, for the next day was Sunday, the blessed *domingo*, which everyone on the plantation anticipated as a day of rest. In the morning they all donned the special clothing which was used only on Sundays—long white pantaloons, a white shirt and leather sandals for the men, and brightly colored frocks for the girls. This was the day they all went to Mass; they had not the slightest idea of what the gaudily dressed man in lace and brocade was doing before the flower-decorated altar in the plantation chapel, but they all enjoyed the color and the pageantry of the performance. It was enough just to sit still and look at the chapel, for it was the most beautiful thing that any of them had ever seen, with its gilded scrolls and white paint. It contained an almost life-size statue of a white woman with a pale blue robe whom Tamboura adored with a blind devotion. He was sure that nobody on this earth could ever be as beautiful, and throughout the mass he never took his eyes from the blue-painted plaster eyes. There was also a man, spread out on two pieces of wood with nails through his hands and feet and blood dripping from his wounds, but Tamboura never liked to look at him. He didn't want to be reminded of suffering. Every few days he saw a man strung up and whipped, and each time the whip cut into the man's back it reminded Tamboura of the streaks of fire that had crossed his own back on board the ship. Don César was neither unjust nor sadistically cruel, but discipline must be maintained and the whip was the most effective method.

No attempt was made to teach the slaves anything about the religion they witnessed, although some of the house slaves proudly mumbled their rosaries. Attendance at mass was compulsory once the priest had sprinkled a few drops of water on them. Going regularly was the extent of their religious duties, although, in truth, they did not connect their attendance there in any way with worship. Tamboura's own primitive religion lived in the little packet of African earth which he still wore and from which he refused to be separated. His sweat had rotted the plaited palm, and Mama Baba, who recognized that the amulet had some special significance for him, had coaxed it from his neck one night, to enclose it in a scrap of bright cloth which she had scrounged from one of the house servants. A year later, when that had become sodden and colorless, she added another layer of cloth and again, a year later, still another, but inside the windings of the cocoon, Tamboura knew that his spirit still dwelt. He regretted that there were no lions to slay in Cuba, for he remembered the fellow back in his village in Africa with the mat of black hair on his chest which had sprouted after he killed the lion. He would have liked the same adornment, but he was comforted by Mama

Baba's assertion that it would undoubtedly frighten the girls and that he was far handsomer without it.

Tamboura was happy. The work in the fields was hard and it seemed an eternity from dawn to dusk, but he was young, strong and healthy and there were compensations for his work. He enjoyed his clothes, particularly the white ones he wore on Sunday, for they seemed to link him to this new life; he enjoyed the time he spent in Mama Baba's bohio and the companionship of Omo and M'dong.

There was one other thing Tamboura enjoyed, on the rare occasions when it happened. Those were the times when he saw don César. His hatred of all white men strangely enough did not extend to don César. Don Gregorio he saw often and he had a certain amount of respect for the young man. But for some reason which he could not explain to himself, he loved the older man, despite his vow to hate all whites. Perhaps it was because don César was the only white man who had never fingered him as all other white men had done. Whenever he chanced to meet don César the *amo* always remembered him and spoke to him, calling him by name. At first Tamboura could not answer him because don César always spoke to him in Spanish, but now after hearing more Spanish than Hausa he was able to respond to the master's greetings with words, instead of merely standing still and digging his toes into the dirt in his embarrassment.

One morning, while working in the fields, the wooden handle became separated from the blade of his machete, and the foreman sent him back to the storeroom with instructions to the storekeeper to issue him a new one. He strode confidently along the dusty road, scuffing his sandals through the dust and avoiding the deep ruts made by the ox carts.

The sun on his back was warm like the sun of Africa, his belly was full, his body was strong, and now he was back in Mama Baba's hut where he felt at home and where, for the third time, he was bedded with Pia, who had now contributed two of his sons to the future prosperity of the Finca Montalvo.

Through the shimmer of heat waves, he saw a figure coming towards him on horseback, and as it came nearer he recognized don César, riding alone. This was strange, for the *amo* always had a groom with him—a middle-aged Negro who seemed to have become a permanent part of the horse he rode.

Tamboura stood in the weeds at the edge of the road to let don César pass, inclining his head as was the custom of slaves with the *amo* and mumbling the accepted phrase "*Amo bendido.*" He glanced up from under his long lashes as he saw don César stop.

"Lift up your head, *muchacho*. I would see who you are."

"I am Tamboura, *amo*."

"I thought as much. *Valgame Dios!* The broadest shoulders on the whole plantation! How many sons have you fathered for me so far?"

Tamboura ticked them off on his fingers and held up one hand with its fingers spread wide apart. The other hand was clenched with only two fingers upstanding.

"What, only seven? Nagao, the Fanti, has done better than you. He's given me thirteen."

Tamboura held up three more fingers.

"What are those for?" don César asked.

The seven fingers appeared again. "These boys—*muchachos!*" Tamboura closed his hands and then opened one to display only three fingers. "And these girls—*muchachas.*" He grinned and held up both hands with all fingers extended. "*Todo.*"

"Ten, eh?" don César laughed. "Well, Nagao has still beaten you. Must be you Hausas are not as good as the Fantis."

The patron's laugh encouraged Tamboura to speak. "Nagao been more busy than Tamboura. He get more girls. I sleep all-a time in *dormitorio*. No get chance to work like Nagao. He *siempre occupado* in hut of La Viejita. I go hut of Mama Baba but Mama Baba not always have girls, then I sleep alone in *dormitorio. Muy pocas muchachas!*" He made a long face at don César. "*Pobre* Tamboura! He like work more for *amo* but no can work alone."

"Well, I'm not complaining. You've done pretty well. That Arada I bought last year looked even better equipped than you but not a single pup out of him yet. Got to sell him—just no juice in him." Don César leaned over in his saddle and cupped his hand under Tamboura's chin, lifting his face up.

"You're a good boy, Tamboura. Gregorio says if we had another five hundred like you, we'd have nothing to worry about. You're a good worker, never complain, and you've never caused any trouble." He tipped back his big white straw hat and scratched his head. "I've got an idea, Tamboura. How'd you like to be my groom? Ever ridden a horse?"

Tamboura recalled the only time he had ever been on a horse, with his feet tied under the horse's belly and his hands tied to the saddle. That didn't count.

*"No, amo, nunca."*

"Time you learned. I'll have Ramon teach you. The blasted idiot managed to get *hemorroides*—bleeding ones—and he can't ride any more. You haven't got them, have you?"

*"No entiendo,"* Tamboura shook his head doubtfully.

"You'd damn well know if you had them, so I suppose you haven't." He looked straight down at Tamboura. "I'd like to show you off to my friends in Havana. You'll make an impression on them. All dressed up you'll be the finest-looking groom in Havana and I'll enjoy seeing my friends' eyes pop out when they see you. Go to the stables and ask for Ramon. Tell him I sent you. Tell him to take you to old Epifania and have her measure you for three suits of clothes, one of fine black *moer* and two of white cotton. Tell her to have the pants fit tight, like your own skin. Nothing worse than a wrinkle under your ass when you're riding all day. Then have Ramon take you to Carlos and have him make you a pair of boots and a pair of soft black slippers to wear with the black suit. *Entiendes?"*

*"Si, amo.* One black suit, two white suits with no wrinkles in the ass, one black boot and one black slipper for these." Tamboura held up one of his enormous feet.

"It'll take the hide of a whole steer to make a pair of boots for you! And tell Ramon to put you on a horse this afternoon—the black stallion—and teach you which is its head and which is its tail."

"And this?" Tamboura held up the machete.

"What's that for?"

"I take it to storehouse to get new one. Don Marco sent me. Told me hurry back."

"I'll explain to Marco that you're not cutting cane any more. *Vé te!"*

Tamboura lingered. He knew he should be overjoyed at becoming don César's groom. He would be the big man of the plantation—the most important of the slaves, outranking even the house servants. It was more than he had ever dreamed of. But one thing troubled him. He wanted to ask but he did not dare and yet he must ask. He must.

Don César noted his confusion.

"Well, what is it, boy? What's bothering you?"

*"Amo bendido. . . ."* Tamboura searched his Spanish for the right words. "Does this mean I no more sleep in bohio of Mama Baba when she need me?"

Don César slapped the smooth thigh-stretched cloth of his breeches.

"Olá! The young stallion already worries about his mares. No, Tamboura, your duties at Mama Baba's continue, only you'll be riding all day—and all night too." He roared out a mighty guffaw at his own joke. "Have no fear, Tamboura. You'll be at Mama Baba's as usual except for the nights that you accompany me to Havana, but Alix has a yellow girl and perhaps you can get a bright one out of her. *Ya vé te!*" He flicked his riding crop at Tamboura, who ran without knowing that his feet touched the ground.

Don César was still laughing over his own joke as he trotted along. Perhaps he could improve on it—make it into a riddle. "What rides a stallion all day and a mare all night?" Pretty good. When he went to Havana, he'd have to spring the joke on some of his friends. And to substantiate it, he'd have his groom along to prove it. One look at Tamboura would convince them.

He'd tell it to Alix, too, in the intimacy of their bed. The thought of Alix was comforting. To think that he had a real French *comtesse* for a mistress! *Aye de mi!* She was beautiful. A little inconvenient perhaps to have to make the journey into Havana every time he wanted to see her. He'd take Tamboura and bed him with Alix's Rachel. It might be another week before he could go. Sometimes he wished that he could bed himself with a black wench but he'd never been able to. He liked his women white and soft and blonde and intelligent—like Alix. He preferred the scent of Alix's *miñoneta* to Negro musk. *Caramba!* He couldn't wait a whole week to go. But then, she'd be all the happier to see him and, God knows, he'd be all the more anxious to see her.

## chapter xi

TAMBOURA COULD scarcely wait for his new clothes to be tailored or the boots to be cobbled. He fretted over the seeming delay and every moment he could spare from Ramon's instructions or from his duties at Mama Baba's found him hanging around Epifania's bohio, watching the nimble fingers of her three seamstresses as they progressed, with minute stitches, in the making of his new clothes. When old Epifania shooed him out, he went to the hut of Carlos to watch his boots being cobbled, but Carlos was as slow as Epifania. She had cut his clothes to the same pattern as don Gregorio's, but she had had to increase the measurements at every seam. Tamboura's big frame was something quite different from don Gregorio's slender body, although, much to Epifania's surprise, his waist was not much larger than his master's.

As the suits began to take shape and fittings became more frequent, Tamboura enjoyed standing on the wooden box in Epifania's bohio, accepting the admiring glances of the two old crones who sewed with her and the openly adoring looks of the young girl apprentice whose duty it was to keep the needles threaded and snip out bastings. There was a certain sensual joy to slipping on the sleek, smooth new materials and feeling them cool and snug against his legs. The suit of shiny black mohair was his special delight because this was a real suit, similar in cut and style to the Spanish suits that don César and don Gregorio wore. The trousers, so high of waistline that they nearly came up to his armpits, curved in to fit his waist and then curved out without a wrinkle to cover his round buttocks, slimming over his thighs like the skin of a sausage, only to flare out in wider bottoms around his ankles. With this suit, he was to wear a shirt of white lawn—without the lace or embroidery that decorated the *amo's* shirts—and a broad sash of dull black silk. Over the shirt went a short jacket, cut high in the back and wide in the shoulders with no buttons in front, although it did sport tasseled frogs of black braid. Tamboura was glad there were no buttons on his coat. Those devilish little circles of black bone on the trousers gave him sufficient trouble, for his big fingers were clumsy and the only pantaloons he had ever had previously had been cinched around the waist with a length of twine. Try as he might, he was forever getting the wrong button onto the wrong buttonhole, which made poor old Epifania cluck with distress, undo all the work he had so laboriously done and then wait patiently until his thick fingers maneuvered the right button into the right hole and progressed upwards until the closure was complete.

The white suits were quite different—instead of being Spanish they were Cuban—with breeches that slipped into canvas leggings. These were designed for riding when he accompanied don César to the city. Other suits, added as an afterthought, were of rough brown cotton which was quite good enough for riding on the *finca* and caring for the horses. The black suit, which was to be carefully creased and folded into a saddle bag, was only to wear after Tamboura arrived at don César's destination, when he exchanged his duties as a groom for a degree of personal attendance on his *amo*.

Then came the marvel of the boots which Carlos had made for him. They were beautiful to look at but, *ay de mi,* how they pinched his feet, which had never known anything more constricting than the thonged sandals of thick steerhide which all the slaves wore to protect their feet in the cane fields. *Ay, si!* They were beautiful to look at, so highly polished one could see one's face in them, but veritable *pendejos* to wear for even ten minutes. He couldn't move his toes in them and his feet felt more closely confined than they had ever been when he was shackled. The boots caused his feet to sweat and swell but Tamboura's pride in their possession conquered his discomfort. At first he hobbled around in them like a spavined horse, but he persevered until the leather stretched and he could go for several hours with them on his feet, and then for all day. But it was always a relief to get them off.

All the while the clothes were being tailored he was having dawn to dusk instruction from Ramon, who, although now unable to sit a horse himself, managed to instruct Tamboura sufficiently well from the ground. Tamboura rode around and around the corral, getting on and off until he was able to place one foot in the stirrup and with a leap accommodate himself to the saddle. He learned the use of the bridle and how to guide his horse by the pressure of his knees. He learned how to become one with the horse itself and to adjust his movements to that of the animal, until he became a veritable *centauro* and it was difficult to see where one big black stallion ended and another began.

In addition to his lessons in riding, Tamboura was instructed in the care of don César's person. He was taught how to lay out the *amo's* clothes and help him to dress, but he still had to learn the intricacies of shaving him and of tying his cravat. However, don César was willing to dispense with these services for the pride he took in Tamboura's attendance; it was something to have the finest slave in Cuba and a pleasure to show him off. He did as much credit to don César as the fine Arabian horse he rode, as the big diamond that sparkled on his finger, as the lush acres and the prosperous *finca* of Montalvo. The big black fingers would eventually master both the razor and the cravat. In the meantime, it would be enough just to have him along and have him admired. And don César did not lose sight of the fact that Tamboura's presence would be very good propaganda for his pet plan for self-propagation of the slave population of Cuba.

During the two years that Tamboura had been at the Finca Montalvo, he had never been away from the plantation. His world had shrunk to the immediate locale of the *finca* and even more narrowly to his days in the field and his nights at Mama Baba's. The world of Africa, the barracoons, Yendo Castle and the long voyage of the Middle Passage had receded in his memory and now seemed like experiences in a dream, although he still retained a vivid memory of his one brief glimpse of Havana, particularly the white girl whom he had noticed on the street. He had seen no other white woman, as don César was a widower and don Gregorio's wife a hypochondriacal invalid who rarely left her bed or room. Even those who had visited at Montalvo had remained invisible to him, as it was rarely that any but the house servants or the gardeners ever left the slave quarters to appear in front of the big house. The girl he had seen so long ago in Havana had become magnified in his dreams and was now somehow confused in his mind with the beautiful statue in the chapel. Whenever he thought of her, she appeared with the same china-blue eyes and the long golden hair of the image he worshiped each Sunday.

Before going to Havana with don César, Tamboura was taken along by his *amo* for an overnight visit at the Finca de las Delicias, owned by Raimundo Bustamonte, not far from the town of Cardenas.

Riding a length behind his master in the bright freshness of a Cuban morning, he marveled at the vista of the long road, the waving cane fields and the small pueblos through which they passed. In the villages he saw other white women but none of them compared with the image he cherished, for all those he saw were dark with olive skin. Most of them were elderly, their heads wrapped in black shawls, and the few that were young were far from the wonder he had imagined every white woman to be. Still, they were interesting to look at and he speculated on what the effect would be of his own black skin against the paleness of theirs. He even wondered if they were made the same as the black wenches with whom he was familiar and if they enjoyed men as much as the black ones did.

An hour or so before noon, they turned off the road between the tall white gateposts and the wrought-iron gates of Las Delicias, and cantered slowly up the long avenue of palms to the house.

Tamboura leaped from his horse and helped don César to dismount. He removed the saddle bags, and was about to take the two horses around to the stables when don César's restraining hand and a shake of his head stopped him.

"We are guests here, boy, so we have servants to wait on both of us. You come along with me. Their stable boy attends to our horses, then later, as they are our property, you must check to see that they are properly fed and stabled. A servant will meet you as we go in and he will show you where my room is. Take my things up there, unpack them and hang them up so they will not be wrinkled. Then ask the servant where you will sleep and go there, remove your white suit and boots and change to the black suit. Return to my room and await me there."

Tamboura followed out the *amo's* instructions. He found that he had been allotted a dark little cubbyhole on the ground floor, under the wide encircling verandah—a cell-like little room with a tiny barred window and a mattress on the floor. It seemed altogether too solid and too confining to Tamboura, accustomed as he was to the more primitive thatched bohios. But the joy of dressing in his new black clothes and the comfort of the soft slippers, after he managed to remove the boots, was welcome. He still had some trouble with the buttons but finally managed to get them all into the right holes. He found his way back through the high-ceilinged rooms, which contained so many wonderful things to look at and examine he was torn between his duty to report promptly to don César and a desire to examine everything he saw. Truly this house was as wonderful as the big house at Montalvo. Although not nearly so large it seemed brighter and more cheerful, for the blinds at Montalvo were always closed, causing a dim twilight even at midday. When he reached don César's room he found that the *amo* did not need him after all—he had already changed and was ready to go down to eat. He dismissed Tamboura and told him to go down to the kitchen for his meal.

This time Tamboura hurried through the big rooms, as they were now filling with men, although twice he was stopped by polished and glistening *Cubanos* who asked, "Whose man are you?" Each time he proudly answered, "Don César's."

Down in the kitchens he found everything in confusion as the household staff rushed madly about to get the elaborate meal with its wines up to the dining room. For the next two hours there was a constant flow of black-coated slaves with loaded trays going up the stairs and others coming down with equally heavy ones. Nobody pressed him into service, however, as they were all a bit awed by the presence of the great don César's handsome giant in his fashionable clothes. Many of the wenches cast inviting glances at him. Tamboura, his desires always near the surface, ogled them in return and replied to their inviting smiles with a grin of his own which promised much if the opportunity were available.

The hubbub died down after the tall yellow-skinned *mayordomo* ascended the stairs carrying a big silver tray with a steaming silver urn of coffee. Tamboura wondered when he, himself, was supposed to eat, for he had had nothing since early breakfast at Montalvo. He saw a number of slaves clearing the big table in the kitchen and when at last the condescending *mayordomo*—a *pendejo* who seemed to take himself very seriously and was not at all awed by Tamboura—returned from upstairs, he called to Tamboura to come in and eat. He had scarcely taken the first mouthful when a bell—one of a long series that lined a wall of the kitchen—jangled on its curved spring.

The *mayordomo* cursed all white masters in fluent Spanish, but jumped up as quickly as his dignity would permit and ran upstairs, only to return in a moment with a look of utter disgust to summon Tamboura to the dining room above. He followed the mestizo up the stairs and into the big room where a number of men were sitting around a big table. There were no ladies present and the air, despite the tall open windows, was blue with smoke. Everyone in the room was laughing and they were all looking at don César, who was puffing out volumes of smoke and laughing at the same time. He looked up to see Tamboura enter.

"And here, *señores*," he said with a flourish of his arm, making the diamond ring on his finger sparkle, "here, in the flesh, is the answer to the riddle that none of you could solve. This indeed is he who rides the stallion all day and the mare all night. *Hé aqui*, my slave Tamboura!"

His finger beckoned to Tamboura to come around to the side of the table and stand beside him.

"Yes, *señores*," he continued between sips of sherry, "some two years ago, I told you of my plan to make the Finca Montalvo entirely independent of Africa as a source of slaves. One of my first purchases after I embarked on that program was this man. I judged him to be about eighteen when I bought him, which makes him about twenty now, and I can tell you"—Don César brought his fist down on the table for greater emphasis—"in two years this fellow has produced ten *negritos* for me—seven boys and three girls—each one of them strong, healthy and vigorous. And there's probably another on the way. If I can find a supply of fine wenches, I'll stud him even more in the next twenty years and I figure that I'll get about two hundred slaves out of him—prime niggers, better than anything I can buy from Africa, for they'll all be hand-raised, civilized and able to speak Spanish."

"A magnificent specimen, don César." One of the younger men regarded Tamboura. "He reminds me of a fine *toro*—the same heavy shoulders and lean flanks. A regular beast of a man."

"But gentle as a kitten." Don César smiled and slapped Tamboura's buttocks under the shiny mohair. "Wouldn't harm a mosquito. He's never been housebroken. I'm just starting him in and I find him quick, intelligent and most docile."

Tamboura understood their Spanish and straightened up, spreading his shoulders under his coat.

"Handsome, too. Doesn't look like the usual run of niggers," another voice spoke up.

"No, *señores,* you may never have seen one like this before, as they are rare. This is Royal Hausa—the best blood in Africa. Notice the shape of the head, round and full without a sloping forehead; observe the fine straight nose and the smaller nostrils, the thinner lips and particularly the over-all bearing of the fellow. His ancestors have ruled for generations and it's quite apparent. There's not a mean streak in the boy, gentle all through and a real thoroughbred."

The younger man, who had compared Tamboura to a fighting bull, came over close to him and felt the muscles of his arms.

"As I said, a regular *toro bravo.* Did you ever think of matching him, don César?"

"He's a breeder, Raimundo," don César answered the owner of Las Delicias.

The other men crowded around Tamboura, some of them testing his strength as don Raimundo had done. Don César's pride in him was evident as he sat back and watched the others admire his slave.

"But that bulge in his pantaloons, don César?" Again it was don Raimundo speaking. "Surely you must have had it padded, the more to surprise us."

"Padding? *Merda!* That's the boy himself. Tamboura needs none of the padding that the young bloods of Havana use to cover their own deficiencies. If that boy had any more he'd be useless as a breeder, for no wench could take him."

Most of the men sauntered back to their chairs but don Raimundo remained standing beside Tamboura. He slapped him affectionately on the shoulder and turned to don César. *"César, amigo mio, un favor.* Sell him to me."

Don César shook his head in denial.

"Then promise me this." Don Raimundo was insistent. "If you should ever decide to sell him, give me the first refusal."

"Granted, Raimundo, but I have no desire to sell him."

Tamboura breathed deeply. The crucial moment had passed and he was safe. He had no desire to leave Montalvo; to leave M'dong and Omo, Mama Baba and the security of her dirty bohio; his splendid new clothes and his *amo bendido.*

But still don Raimundo persisted. "Then, if you will not sell him, loan him to me for a week."

"It's possible, *mi amigo.*" Don César flicked the long gray ash from his cigar onto the tiled floor. "But I have need of him. Besides his other duties, he's my groom, you know."

"Then today," don Raimundo importuned. "We approach the hour of the siesta. Grant me his services today. My wife's maid, sister of my *mayordomo,* who, as you may have guessed by the rather strong family resemblance, happens to be my half-brother, is beautiful as a picture." Don Raimundo kissed the tips of his fingers and tossed the kiss into the air. "A *mestiza,* yes, but truly a virgin as my wife has never let any buck touch her. What a union! What an offspring! Just a week ago I was telling my wife that Julita should be bred and my wife insisted that there was not a buck on the plantation good enough for her pet. I would be glad to do it myself, *señores,* but my wife is a very jealous woman. So, grant me this favor, César, and name your fee."

Don César dispensed with the matter of any fee with a wave of his hand. He turned to Tamboura.

"How are you feeling, boy?"

*"Muy bien, amo."*

"Think you could cover one of don Raimundo's wenches for him?"

*"Si, amo, con mucho gusto."*

"And do a good job?"

*"Seguramente, amo."*

Don César turned to his host. "The boy's yours, Raimundo, for the siesta hours and, to make doubly sure, for tonight if you so desire. He's willing and I'm damn sure he's able."

"It would be something to watch, don César." An old man with a ravaged face leaned across the table, his heavily ringed fingers drumming nervously on the polished wood. "I always keep close watch on my mares when they are being covered."

"I do not regard Tamboura as wholly a beast," don César answered courteously, although there was a trace of annoyance in the words. "He may be an animal but he walks upright like a man and he has the feelings of a man. I ask you, Señor Sanchez, could you perform effectively with the eyes of twenty men upon you?"

The old man recognized the rebuff of being addressed by his surname and the formal title. He withdrew his hand and sat back in his chair. Others, who had been hopeful of seeing what Sanchez alone had had the temerity to request, tried to conceal their disappointment. It would have been an interesting spectacle, particularly if the girl really was the virgin that don Raimundo claimed her to be.

Again Tamboura sighed with relief. He could not envisage himself performing with the eyes of all these men watching him.

"I'll call for the girl." Don Raimundo broke the awkward silence. "I'd like you gentlemen to see her, too." He walked to the wall and pulled at the embroidered bell cord. The bell jangled far off in the kitchen below. Soon the pompous *mayordomo* arrived.

*"A sus ordenes, amo,"* he bowed slightly to don Raimundo.

"Clemente, go to *la ama* and tell her that I crave her permission for Julita to be sent here. If she grants that permission, find Julita and bring her here at once."

"Julita, *amo?*" Clemente's eyes searched don Raimundo's face.

"You heard me, Clemente."

"But Julita, *amo,* what do you desire of her?"

Don Raimundo straightened like a Toledo blade that had been bent in a swordsman's hand and then suddenly released. Like the sharp blade, his voice had the edge of steel.

"You dare ask me a question, Clemente, about what I intend to do? Very well then, since the question is asked, I shall answer you. Your precious sister is going to be bedded with this man here"—he pointed to Tamboura—"and it matters not one whit whether you like it or she likes it or even if my wife likes it. Now, go, fetch her, and after you return with her, go immediately to the stables and seek Ayuba. Tell him to grease the big whip and you wait with him while he does it. I will come presently."

"Would you have me whipped, *amo?*" Clemente's face was contorted with fear.

"I would and I shall add ten more lashes for the second question, Clemente."

"Mercy, *amo.*" The man's knees were slowly collapsing and he knelt on the floor before don Raimundo.

"And ten more lashes for every second you remain here pleading."

The slave, his yellow face livid, struggled to his feet and stumbled to the door.

Don Raimundo smiled at his guests. "Although my good friend, César, in granting me the immense favor he has, does not think it apt for us to witness his stallion cover my mare, I think I can offer you an equally entertaining *pasatiempo*. My *mayordomo* has never been flogged before so his back should be sufficiently tender to warrant some squeals which may amuse you."

"I always string mine up by the heels." Sanchez, who had been so avid to witness Tamboura's exhibition, was smiling with anticipation.

"They swing too much that way," another spoke up. "Don't get the full bite of the whip."

"We have a set of irons on a brick wall," another contributed. "With something solid in front of them, they feel it right good."

Don Raimundo lifted his shoulders slightly in a little gesture of apology. "Sorry, *señores,* we are hopelessly old-fashioned here. We still use the same post my grandfather set up in the corral but with Ayuba at the whip, I think you will be well amused. He lays it on well as he has had much practice."

The door opened slowly and Clemente entered with a girl behind him. Her face was as pale as his and she was weeping. Don Raimundo called her to him.

"Wipe away your tears, Julita. Is that any way to greet your first man? See what I have found for you." He pointed to Tamboura.

Tamboura had heard and understood all that had happened. He was trembling inwardly, feeling the hot pain on his own back that he knew would soon be inflicted on Clemente. His fear had even conquered his anticipatory tumescence, but when he saw the girl, all pity for the cringing Clemente vanished. His desire revived with her beauty. She was a year or so younger than he and far whiter than any girl he had ever had before. Her long hair hung in curls to her shoulders and the dress that she wore was not the shapeless sack that covered the slave women back at Montalvo. It was white and belted in at the waist with a blue ribbon. Tiny gold earrings hung from her ears and a string of white beads around her neck set off her tawny skin. Don Raimundo took her arm and stood her beside Tamboura. She reached barely his shoulders.

The eyes in the room were contemplating the pair as the door of the dining room banged open. Tamboura transferred his eyes from the dainty morsel beside him to the white woman who entered. Even more than Julita he desired her, for despite her rage she was beautiful.

"Raimundo, what is the meaning of all this?" She looked around the room, conscious for the first time of the men sitting there, but their presence did not deter her.

Don Raimundo lifted his hands high over his head, his fists clenched.

"*Caramba!* Was ever a man so beset with problems? And now my wife! Questions, questions, questions, while I try to do a little business. What does she care if this plantation goes to ruin? If every slave dies off and we have none to replace them? Ay, ay, ay!" His voice rose in anger, then dropped suddenly, and he spoke calmly to his wife, spacing his words carefully so that no disrespect might be apparent.

"*Señora mia,* our good friend, don César, has made us a most generous offer—an offer which will be much to our advantage. He is lending me the services of his finest slave—probably the finest in all Cuba. The delicacy of the situation prohibits me from putting it into words, Señora."

She glared at the assemblage. "Delicacy of the situation! Bah!" She stamped her foot. "In other words, you would bed my Julita with that giant. He would kill her." Don Raimundo's wife was not one to mince words.

"If you prefer to put it that way, that is exactly what I intend to do. But have no fear, she will survive."

"*Ay, la pobrecita!*" The señora rushed across the room and put a protective arm around the girl. She looked up searchingly at Tamboura beside her. "But that is the lot of women! And just where do you intend to perpetrate this crime?"

The mechanics of the situation had never occurred to don Raimundo. Any place, he had supposed, would be good enough for a slave.

"The man has been allotted a space in the quarters for the house servants. He can take her there."

"My Julita on a pallet on the floor? *Dios mio!*" It was the señora's turn to throw up her hands in horror. "Never. Since she was a young girl she has slept in her bed in the little room beside my own. If you insist that this must happen, and I see that you fully mean to carry out your evil intentions, it will take place in her own room."

"That may be as you desire, señora. If you wish this musky buck in your quarters I cannot stop you but I assure you—"

"The room can be aired afterwards and the bedding

changed. Come Julita," the señora held out her hand, "and you too. What is your name?"

"Tamboura, *ama.*"

"Then come, Tamboura." She started for the doorway but turned to speak to her husband.

"Clemente informs me that you have ordered him whipped."

Don Raimundo bowed assent.

"Then add ten extra lashes on my account. A week ago he dropped a rare bowl of crystal and broke it. I had it in mind to have him punished then."

Don Raimundo and all the other gentlemen bowed deeply as the froth of her skirts swept out the door with Julita and Tamboura following.

As they walked through the big rooms, Tamboura reached out and clutched the girl's hand. It was small, soft, damp and trembling. With the other she brushed the tears from her eyes but lifted her face and smiled up at him. They followed the señora out into the patio and up the stairs to the wide balcony. She led them through a room all pink and blue and gold and into a smaller room, where she herself pulled the clean white embroidered cover from the bed. Her heels clicked over the tiles as she went out into her own room and returned with a bottle of scent which she liberally doused on Tamboura.

"There, Julita, he will smell like jasmine instead of a nigger. *Ay, mi querida,* I should have prepared you for this for in truth, you are like my own sister. My heart bleeds, Julita, actually bleeds for you but I must say my poor stupid Raimundo has done well by you. See, Julita, the brute is really handsome." She wet her fingers with the perfume and rubbed it on Tamboura's cheek. "Don Raimundo really knows best, my dear. We mustn't oppose him and now do be a good girl and do not scream for it would upset me dreadfully. Here, take this jar of ointment and have him use it. It may help you. I shall take my siesta in another room. And remember not to scream as it would awaken me." Her finger tapped Tamboura's cheek. "Do be gentle with her."

She left, closing the door behind her and they heard the click of a key in the lock.

It was Tamboura's first time in a bed. The soft mattress enchanted him. And the girl beneath him was far more beautiful than any he had ever had before. From far off they heard the panicked screams of a man, regularly spaced, scream following scream until there was finally silence. The girl was weeping and moaning in her own pain and the distant shrieks made her cry even more. But gradually everything became quiet as the whole household settled down for its daily siesta. The girl had stopped her moaning and she was resting, her head in the hollow of Tamboura's arm. He stretched comfortably, pulling her closer to him, and closed his eyes. The girl's hand crept up and rested lightly against the throbbing artery in his neck. He took her hand and lowered it, far down across his body, to where the moving fingers produced an ecstasy of perfect contentment.

## chapter xii

ALIX, COMTESSE DE VAUX, (the title was certainly *ci-devant* and its legitimacy doubtful) closed the slats of the *persianas* to keep out the glare of the noonday Havana sun and abate, if possible, the raucous noises which, day and night, arose continuously from the street below. *Mon Dieu!* These Cubans! For all their thin veneer of civilization, they were nothing but savages. Havana might boast of being larger than Cap François but Cuba would never achieve the cosmopolitan culture of St. Domingue. Well, that was the difference between the French and the Spanish. The culture of France was innate and born with them; what the Spanish managed to acquire they wore on their sleeve.

But, culture or not, it was far better to be here in Havana than back in Cap François where the blacks now had the upper hand. At least the Spanish knew how to keep them under control. Of course the French were more humane and what had happened in St. Domingue was entirely their own fault. All this silly talk about liberty, equality and fraternity had swept across the ocean to France's colony and there were always some crackpots who believed in it even in St. Domingue. The slaves had really had nothing to complain about. They had always been treated well on the plantation and she herself had been kind to them, indeed she had!

How kind she had been to her own dear Bonaventure. *Mais oui!* The fellow had been aptly named. It had been a "good adventure"—a thrilling adventure—for the fellow had been so savagely male and so superlatively handsome. Not particularly handsome of face, according to the accepted European standards, for his face was typically negroid. But what a superb body! No European possessed a body that could compare with his—a carved and polished statue of hard black ebony. And Bonaventure had been faithful, too. He had even sacrificed his life for her that last fateful night on the plantation when the slaves of Bouckmann's uprising had swept down out of the hills, burning the plantation and killing her husband, poor, simple, old Jean Albert. But Bonaventure had given her a chance to escape, at the cost of his life, and she had managed to flee from the plantation with only her maid Rachel. By hiding out in the cane fields by day and traveling along the roads infested with bands of wandering slaves at night, she and Rachel had made their way to Cap François with nothing but the clothes on her back and her precious jewels sewn inside them. How she had missed the strength of Bonaventure during those days and nights of horror on the road.

Her stay in fear-laden Cap François had been a brief one. For anyone who had been forced to flee the terror of the Revolution in France, there was no incentive to remain through what promised to be an even worse period in St. Domingue, so she had lost no time in quitting the island on the first ship that sailed. That it had brought her to Havana was immaterial. She might have preferred New Orleans where they spoke French, but she was here now and she was safe. Learning Spanish had not been difficult and perhaps Havana had been more generous than New Orleans might have been. At least here in Havana she had met don César Montalvo.

Her hand rested on the damask upholstery of the chair as she glanced around the room, dim now in its shuttered obscurity. To be sure it was his house, but through his generosity she had made it her own. César had been most willing for her to dispense with the stiff Spanish furniture and replace it with the more delicate and graceful Louis Seize which made a better background for her fragile beauty. Yes, César had been most generous in everything, but then, why shouldn't he be? God knows, she had been most generous, too. *Mais oui,* most generous! Every week when he came to Havana she must be an actress, playing the role of a woman madly in love, and each week she must repay him for what he had given her. It wasn't easy. César was at least twenty-five years older than she—well, actually if she admitted to her real age, which was thirty, he probably wasn't more than twenty years older—but it was not easy to feign a burning passion for a man whose fires had already started to die down and needed so much work on her part to rekindle.

*Mon Dieu!* What a difference between César's quickly satiated desires and the long nights of ecstasy she had spent with Bonaventure when Jean had been absent in Cap François. Fortunately he had had to go frequently and poor old

Jean was so abysmally stupid. He had never guessed and of course such a thought would never have entered his head. His wife bedded with a slave? Impossible! White men might bed with black wenches but no white woman ever bedded with a black man. Aie! What stupid fools they were not to! What joys they missed! She touched again in memory the smooth satin of Bonaventure's skin; felt the ripple of his muscles and yielded to the all-consuming animality of his fire which never needed to be rekindled. How she longed for it again.

*Damne!* She must put such thoughts from her mind. But . . . it had been wonderful! At least she would always have those nights to remember. Now she had this little house and, small though it was, it was in a good location, wedged between two big palaces on the Calle Colon; she had, too, a precarious toehold in Cuban society, for some few had been impressed with her title. She really did have a right to it. Cyprien, her first husband, would surely have been the Comte de Vaux as soon as his old uncle died, had he not been so careless as to have his head sliced off by Madame Guillotine.

With all its noise and dirt, Havana represented security, and she needed security, for her life had been a series of flights—first from Paris to escape the reign of terror of the Revolution and then from St. Domingue to escape another reign of terror of the slaves. Two husbands already dead and both by violence.

Thank God she would never have to flee again. The Spanish might be barbarians but they knew enough to maintain a stable government in Cuba with no talk of liberty, equality and fraternity. And they certainly knew how to control their slaves. She had passed the public whipping yard in Havana and heard the screams coming from behind the high walls. They said that half an hour under the whips would kill any slave. The Spanish had worked out an admirable system. If any slave, regardless of his ownership, jostled you in the street or displayed any rudeness, you had only to write your name on a slip of paper and hand it to him, with what you considered the requisite number of lashes he should receive written in the upper right hand corner. He was duty bound to carry it to his master and within a few days you received a delicately written note stating that the punishment had been carried out. Leave it to the Spanish to think of something like that—the French never would.

Soon she would be mistress of the big Montalvo plantation, with an assured place in Cuban society as the wife of the richest Creole on the island. How she would entertain! She'd insist that César buy an imposing palace in Havana because she had no intention of burying herself in the country. This little house might have been good enough for the first Señora Montalvo who, from all she could hear, was a meek little woman, entirely subservient to César. But it certainly wouldn't serve for the second Señora Montalvo, who, after all, was willing to trade her title of Comtesse de Vaux to become a simple Cuban señora. What a sacrifice!

And what jewels she would have! She loved jewels, but although their scintillating beauty appealed to her, she had a deeper reason for loving them. They represented security. Of what avail were the furnishings, the paintings, the gold plate and the rich tapestries of the Hôtel de Vaux in Paris when she had to leave so precipitately? Of what avail the vast fields, the slaves and the big house in St. Domingue when she had been forced to sneak out at night and hide in the cane fields? They had all been left behind, all lost forever. But each time the thought of the jewels stitched into her corset had been comforting. One diamond, weighing nothing at all, represented a whole bag of gold and it was certainly far easier to carry. Ah well, she needn't bother her head about such things any more.

The street outside seemed quieter. Now there was only a man shrieking at regular intervals about the mangoes he was trying so hard to sell. Perhaps if she rang for Rachel and had the slave bathe her with eau de cologne, she might sleep. An hour or so of sleep would erase any lines that thinking might have caused and she wanted to be looking her best tomorrow when César came. The mirror of her *table à toilette,* even in the dim light, assured her that there were no particular lines which needed to be erased. Her hair was still as palely gold as when she had married Cyprien twelve years ago; her skin was as white as the bisque statue of Eros which stood at the side of the table and a dab of rouge would quickly bring a faint pink flush to her cheeks. The shuttered light made her blue eyes a deep violet and although the blonde lashes caused them to appear rather weak and unimportant, a bit of *maquillage,* applied by Rachel's clever fingers, would rim her eyes with a darkness that would make them large and brilliant. She opened the filmy pinkness of her *robe de chambre* and lifted up her breasts with both hands.

What lovely round globes, so firm and beautiful! With the nipples reddened just a trifle with cochineal, they would send César into his usual short-lived ecstasy.

Yes, she would ring for Rachel. Rachel's deft fingers and the cool touch of eau de cologne would calm her. Then, with sprinkling of rice powder on the sheets to make them smooth and cool, she would sleep and perhaps if she were very fortunate she would dream of Bonaventure. Aie! His very name brought back that overpowering odor of musk which at first she had found so offensive and then, through its intimate association with his body, had stirred her as no other scent ever had. But she must not think about Bonaventure because if she did she would never sleep. No, never! It made her so restless, made her long for the days in St. Domingue when she could calm this restlessness merely by pulling the bell cord, bringing him on the run. Better to put him out of her mind now and hope that she might dream about him, for in her dreams he always seemed so real, so strong, so mightily enormous.

She rang, and waited for the answering tinkle down below, then anticipated the steps she knew she would hear on the outside staircase that led up from the little patio. Thank God she had her devoted Rachel! The tapping of heels came quickly, followed by a knock.

A mulatto entered—a tall, well-formed woman of about the same age as her mistress. What might have been beauty was marred by too high cheekbones and a narrow nose that gave an appearance of masculinity to the face. The woman's skin shone with a metallic glint, somewhere between copper and brass, and her hair was entirely hidden under a tightly wound turban of pale green and magenta madras.

"Rachel, *ma bonne,*" Alix sat down on the bed, "I am so nervous and upset I cannot sleep and you know how haggard I become if I miss my siesta."

*"Oui, madame,* but my fingers will put you to sleep."

The woman scanned the array of bottles on the dressing table and selected one. With a supporting arm, she lifted her mistress, removed the filmy robe and gently lowered her to the mattress. The pinkly white body stretched and the brown fingers touched it lovingly. It was quite apparent from the expression on the slave's face that this was no onerous task, but one which she enjoyed. The dark fingers played over the white skin, lingering, touching, patting and caressing.

"Aie, Rachel, I am already relaxed. Sometimes I wonder why you are so good to me."

"Madame took me from the slave cabins when I was a young girl. In another year I would have had to submit to any black buck that managed to grab me and throw me to the ground." Rachel shuddered. "I was spared all that, thanks to madame's goodness."

"But didn't you want them, Rachel?" Alix had heard the same words many times before and she always expressed the same baffled wonderment. It seemed quite inconceivable that any woman could refuse what she herself wanted so much.

"Never, madame. Men are such brutal creatures and so ugly too. When we were quite little girls on the plantation it was considered quite an adventure to hide in the bushes near the river where the men bathed on their way back from the fields. Most of the girls were quite excited and they all had their favorites among the men. Some were secretly in love with one or another and many were in love with one in particular."

"Could it have been Bonaventure?" The blue eyes opened wide in assumed innocence.

"Yes, it was Bonaventure."

"And was he your favorite too, Rachel?"

*"Mais non, madame!* I had no favorites. I detested them all and I only went because all the others went. Such ugly big creatures that men are and they do such horrible things. All men are alike, they want only one thing. Their gross black bodies repulse me—so different from yours. You are soft and white and beautiful."

"But some day, Rachel, you must have a man. Truly you would lose all your fear. When we move to Montalvo, I'll ask don César for some fine young buck for you and then you'll see."

Rachel sank to the floor, her arms outstretched on the bed, her face sunk in the sheets. Her voice was muffled by sobs.

"Oh, please, madame, never that. Let me serve you always. Have me flogged if I disobey you, but never, promise me, never make me lie with a stinking nigger."

"Then you aim for higher things, Rachel?" Alix propped herself up on her elbows to look down at the gaily colored turban. "Perhaps you want only a white man?"

"That least of all. Nobody! Nobody, madame. All I ask is to serve you."

Alix lay back on her pillow. "Well, Rachel, who am I to complain? I only wanted you to be happy, for indeed I do care for you. You have always been so devoted to me."

"And so I always shall be, madame."

"So, if you do not want a man, you need not have one."

*"Merci, madame.* Now I am happy again. Close your eyes and soon sleep will come to you."

Alix felt her muscles relax. She began to feel drowsy.

"Rachel." Alex felt herself drifting into oblivion.

*"Oui, madame?"*

"You mentioned Bonaventure."

*"Oui, madame."*

"Aie, but he was beautiful, Rachel."

"If being big like an ox and smelling like a goat makes a man beautiful."

Alix, Comtesse de Vaux—because it sounded so much better than plain Madame Albert—moved her head drowsily from side to side on the pillow in negation. Rachel flung the dressing gown into the air and let it settle over her mistress like a filmy pink cloud. She went to the window and made a further and entirely unnecessary adjustment of the *persianas*, straightened the array of bottles on the dressing table and tiptoed over to where her mistress was now sleeping soundly. One white hand was hanging over the edge of the bed. Rachel lifted it tenderly, gently so as not to awaken the sleeper, brought it to her lips and then replaced it on the bed. She tiptoed out, closing the door softly behind her.

## chapter xiii

DON CÉSAR and Tamboura were late in setting out from Montalvo. Don César's daughter-in-law, the ever ailing doña Beatriz, was dying again and a priest must be summoned to administer extreme unction. That this happened with unvarying regularity at intervals of about once a month did not mitigate the circumstances for, as don César argued with himself, one never knew which time might be the last and he could not have it upon his conscience that he was on his way to keep an amoral rendezvous in Havana while his only daughter-in-law was dying. There was the usual tension in the big house; the usual weeping and wringing of hands of the aged aunt who was doña Beatriz' companion; the usual hushed running to and fro of house slaves; and finally the arrival of the priest. After he had performed his ministrations and while the waxy odor of snuffed candles still hung heavy in the air of doña Beatriz' bedroom, she miraculously recovered, as she always did, sufficiently to be propped up in bed and to eat a hearty supper.

So it happened that instead of starting out for Havana early as he had planned, don César was not able to leave until midafternoon and did not arrive in Havana with Tamboura until the sunset gun boomed from the Morro. It was then necessary for don César to show Tamboura the entrance to the stables which, although connected with the house on Colon Street, had a separate entrance in the back on a narrow, weed-grown alley.

By the time the horses had been attended to under don César's direction, and he and Tamboura had been admitted by Rachel, the light was almost gone in the courtyard, one side of which was blankly bounded by the high wall of the Mendoza palace while the other side was a series of *balcons* and staircases, leading to the second and third floors.

Alix, who had been waiting all afternoon with increasing impatience, was torn between two different welcomes for her seemingly errant lover. Should she be haughty and offended over don César's tardiness and the lack of respect for her dignity shown by his keeping her waiting? Or should she play the part of the terror-stricken wife who, during her anxious waiting, had pictured her beloved in a variety of accidents which would bring him, bleeding on a stretcher, to her arms? In view of her anxiety to adopt the role of wife, she decided the latter approach would be the better and more sympathetic. When she heard the stable door open and the sound of don César's voice below, she contorted her features most convincingly into a display of grief, ran headlong down the stairs—taking care to lose one slipper in the anxiety of her haste—and flung herself, trembling and most solicitous of his welfare, into his arms.

During reassurances that he was safe and uninjured, while don César patted her shoulder and she recovered from a most convincing swoon, she took the opportunity to observe Tamboura standing silently like an oversized black watchdog behind his master. His white suit, damp with sweat and clinging to his body, outlined his proportions against the patio greenery, and she exulted in what she saw. Fate had seemingly played into her hands. Here indeed was another Bonaventure. No, this one far exceeded Bonaventure, for he had a handsome face as well as a most impressive physique. How different he was from the middle-aged, bow-legged Ramon who had always accompanied don César previously! She checked her enthusiasm. She must not, of course, notice the presence of a slave any more than she would the presence of a dog which had followed his master into the house. Although she might, in all propriety, have stopped to pat the dog's head, affectionately rumple his ears and speak an endearing word to him, even that was forbidden in the case of a slave.

Pretending to ignore Tamboura, she left it to don César to talk about him, which he did, once he had calmed her fears. But in her well-feigned distress, she seemed more desirable to him than ever before and the delay in arrival, coupled with the more than conjugal concern on her part, whetted his desire to be alone with her. Indeed, he was so anxious to get upstairs and accomplish the purpose for which he had come, he merely indicated Tamboura with a curt nod of his head.

"My new groom." He supported Alix, who limped most prettily and effectively from the loss of her shoe, across the patio. "Have Rachel show him the loft over the stables." And to Tamboura, he turned and said, "The señora's woman will show you where you are to sleep. She will tell you where to draw water, so bathe and change your clothes. When I need you, I will call you. Do not leave the house. I do not want you out on the streets of the city."

He turned to Alix, as he guided her up the stairs.

"Later, *mi alma,* I would have a conversation with you about my new groom but now. . . ."

Tamboura did not know where to go or what to do. He remained standing in the patio, without moving except to shift his weight from one foot to the other and curse his tight boots. Except for the discomfort he felt, he was quite unconscious of his immobility; his thoughts were completely involved in the heart-shaped face in its aura of gold curls, and the blue eyes which had appraised him so carefully over don César's shoulder.

The short twilight faded and night descended, dispersed only by the dancing light of candles from the floor above that glimmered on the foliage of the patio planting. The evening scent of jasmine permeated the courtyard and the little wall fountain in one corner dripped with a steady and monotonous cadence on the ferns below it. Still Tamboura stood in the spot where don César had left him until he saw a woman descending the steps. When she reached the bottom and beckoned to him, he followed her. She was a mestiza but Tamboura decided there was something about the woman he did not like and this puzzled him. There had never been any except the old and ugly that he did not immediately respond to and this woman was neither old nor ugly. Perhaps it was some instinctive feeling that she did not like him; perhaps it was her ability to look at him without seeing him. This indeed was a new experience for him, for he was far too accustomed to the inviting smiles of every colored woman he met and even the white *dueña* of Las Delicias had patted him most admiringly on his cheek. Quite unable to understand the woman's apparent hostility, he nevertheless welcomed her because it meant a release from his long period of waiting, pleasant though his thoughts had been during the interval.

"Come!" the mestiza beckoned again impatiently.

"Who are you, *perra?*" Tamboura resented her highhanded command, spoken with the authority of a white.

She met him halfway between the stairs and where he had

been standing and he was unprepared for the quickly raised hand and the stinging slap across his face.

"Call me a bitch, would you?" Her eyes were almost on a level with Tamboura's own. "Don't ever do it again. I'm no *perra* as you will find out. My name is Rachel and I am Madame's woman."

Tamboura had raised his own hand to slap her down but her unflinching defiance stopped him. Better perhaps not to start his new duties by quarreling with his *amo's* woman's slave.

"I am sorry, *dama*. Come, take me where I am supposed to go. I have become tired of standing here, rooted like a palm tree, and I have the instructions of my *amo* to carry out."

"That is better." Her animosity changed into a guarded indifference. "From now on you will treat me with respect although you need not call me *dama*. Rachel is sufficient. Follow me."

She led him into a dark room, lit only by the red glow of a charcoal stove, struck a light and applied it to a candle. He could see that the room was a kitchen and he could smell the aroma of food that was being kept warm on the stove. Hungry as he was, he realized he must first bathe and change his clothes as don César had ordered. While Rachel filled a wooden bucket with water and folded a towel over her arm, he watched her and then at the direction of her pointing finger, he picked up the bucket and followed her out through the patio and through the door which connected it with the stables, past the horses and up a ladder to a large loft above, where she placed the candle on the floor and indicated a soiled mattress spewing its straw out onto the rough planking.

"Here is where Ramon slept. Be careful of the candle and do not tip it over with your big feet. When you have washed and dressed, bring it with you to the kitchen and I will give you food."

"*Gracias,* Rachel." Tamboura was quite ready to forgive the woman even though her attitude toward him had not warmed. He was quite sure that she would eventually succumb to him although the necessity of wooing a woman with soft-talking was a new experience to him. He shucked off the white coat and shirt together but she, without pausing as much as a moment to admire his charms, had turned to leave. He felt that some word was necessary to make her turn around for he had a feeling that an appraisal, even by her cold eyes, of the swelling muscles of his chest would cause a change in her attitude. "I am hungry, Rachel"—now he really was soft-talking her—"and I think you are a good cook. I shall hurry."

She did turn around but her eyes were as coldly uninterested as before.

"You shall have enough to eat, *hombre,* but let us get one thing straight while we are yet quite new to each other. I am Madame's personal slave and you are don César's. Your status is equal to mine and you have an equal right to be here. I shall feed you well. If necessary I shall wash and iron your clothes. We shall say '*buenos días*' in the morning and '*buenas noches*' at night and that will be the end of our conversation. When you are ready to come to the kitchen, your food will be waiting." She turned abruptly and left, making her way in the darkness down the steep ladder.

"*Ay, que mujer!*" Tamboura sensed a dangerous lessening of his power over women. He had never been so completely rebuffed before. Even the little mestiza at Las Delicias had finally fallen under his attack. Despite her own pain and her sorrow at the shrieks of her brother under the whip, she had succumbed. And now this tall, bright-skinned woman had paid no more attention to him than she might have awarded to the black horse he had been riding. Ay! she would be a problem but one he was sure he could solve in time.

He undid the leggings, and removed the heavy boots after bumping his buttocks halfway around the loft. At one time he felt he must call Rachel to help him with the *pendejos* but to do so would reflect on his ability as a man, so he struggled until he freed himself from them and was able to shed his breeches. After washing himself from the bucket of water and drying himself on the rough towel, he dressed, feeling again the joy and assurance the black suit always gave him and welcoming the pliancy of the slippers after the imprisonment of his feet in the boots. Don César had given him a discarded red sash and this brightness appealed to his love of color. He wound it tightly around his waist, sucking in his belly to make it even slimmer, and admired the colorful contrast between the white shirt and the shiny black mohair of his pantaloons. Now that Rachel saw him dressed in all this elegance, she would certainly melt before his splendor. What *negrita* could resist him, cock-proud and rooster-elegant as he now looked?

But she didn't melt! The meal she served him was one of

the best he had ever eaten, but he had to eat it alone and in silence, for after putting the food on the table, she was gone. He sat solitary in the kitchen, feeling very sorry for himself, until he found the heat from the stove oppressive and decided to move his chair out into the dark patio behind a clump of greenery. It was fine to be don César's groom and dress in these nice clothes but he wished now he was back at Mama Baba's in his ragged old *pantalones,* sitting outside the bohio with Pia beside him and M'dong and Omo laughing and joking with him. He was troubled, too, at the thought of having to sleep alone in the big dark loft above the stables. Never in his life had he slept alone before. Even the crowded deck of the slave ship would be better than the phantom-peopled blackness of the lonely loft. On the ship he had had the warm assurance of Omo in front of him and M'dong behind him. Far better it seemed to him to remain sitting in the patio all night with the comfort of the lights on the floor above him and the reassuring sound of the far-off voices of don César and the woman who was with him.

Tamboura had been saving further thoughts about her for such a time as this when he was alone and could more thoroughly savor them. At long last he had finally seen the woman he had dreamed about. She was no longer the dimly remembered girl he had so briefly glimpsed in his passage through the city two years ago. Neither was she like the statue in the chapel at Montalvo. This flesh and blood reality was far greater than either of these. But she belonged to his *amo.* As such, she was sacred and he must never raise his eyes to look at her. Furthermore she was white and there was absolutely no bridge between black men and white women. Between black women and white men, yes! Even though his whole being cried out for her Tamboura knew if he even as much as looked at her, let alone touched her, don César would not hesitate a moment to have him flogged to death.

With his eyes fixed on the lighted windows above he relinquished all claim to the *amo's* white woman. But . . . if he could not have her, he could at least think about her. Don César might own his body but only Tamboura owned his thoughts. Nobody could punish him for his thoughts because nobody could know about them. Even the omnipotence of don César could not read the thoughts that spun in Tamboura's head. Let don César possess her once a week—Tamboura could possess her daily, even hourly.

The perfumed darkness, the canopy of vines which hid his chair and the steady drip of the fountain all contributed to his somnolent phantasy. Later, when the lights went out in the windows above, he sensed why they were extinguished. He pictured a bed, such as he had been on at Las Delicias, and on it a flesh far whiter and more beautiful than even the tawny curves of Julita. Although he knew that don César formed the other part of the picture, he banished him and substituted his own black body in the place of his *amo*. For all that don César might hold the actuality of that flesh in his arms, Tamboura held something more; the woman he held, albeit not substantial, was far lovelier, more pliant and yielding than any reality could ever be.

He closed his eyes, the better to visualize the picture, shutting out the shadowed patio, and the noises that came from the street through the grilled gate. From the kitchen, he heard snatches of a song in an unknown language. The words were strange, but the rhythm was barbaric and sensual, and stirred his blood. His fancied joy became greater than anything he had ever experienced in Mama Baba's hut or in the bedroom at Las Delicias. The cherished image had come to life and even though he might not satisfy himself with the reality, now there was an actual substance on which to base his dream. She was! She existed! His eyes had seen her! Something about the blue eyes, as they had regarded him over don César's shoulder, seemed to justify his right to dream of her. Now those eyes were looking at him again but they were closer this time for his own lips were pressed tightly against her lips and the paleness of that face gleamed whitely beneath the dark shadow of his own. His dream continued in a strange substance of reality.

"Tamboura!" The dream faded with the voice of don César.

"Rachel!" Tamboura stood up at the sound of the señora's voice.

Don César and the object of Tamboura's recent desires stood together in the patio, don César holding aloft a heavy silver candelabrum in which the flames of a dozen candles flickered in the soft night air.

Tamboura stood up and walked out into the circle of light, just as Rachel approached from the kitchen.

"Yes, *amo?*" Tamboura spread his big hands awkwardly in front of him for he realized he was in no condition to appear before a white lady. "I am here."

"And I, madame. You called me?" Rachel made a deep curtsey.

"I did, Rachel, but it is don César who would speak with you." Alix looked somewhat perturbed.

But not don César. There was a certain jovial condescension in his words, as when an adult talks to children, offering them a treat and assured beforehand of their joyous acceptance.

"The *Condesa* and I are retiring for the night and she will no longer need your services, Rachel, nor shall I need those of Tamboura. The *Condesa* agrees with me that it would be expedient if Tamboura shared your bed with you tonight. You are a fine-looking woman, quite worthy of Tamboura in every way, and as he will be here often from now on, it seems only right that you two should employ yourselves to add to your *ama's* prosperity."

Rachel's face contorted in startled agony as she stared at Alix, then with a quick glance she observed don César's unaffected joviality. She sensed there was no appeal but her words came spouting forth in a torrent of French which she knew don César did not understand.

"But, madame, you promised me."

Alix shrugged her shoulders, and replied in French.

"It is not for me to say. This is don César's idea and you must obey him." Then lapsing into Spanish, she continued. "You must speak Spanish, Rachel, out of courtesy to don César."

"And now both of you"—don César was going to award both his children—"we shall light you to your room. After all, it is not every night that we can celebrate a *luna de miel* here and we shall be your sponsors." He handed the candelabrum to Rachel. "You go ahead and light the way and Tamboura you follow. For once we shall yield precedence."

Rachel's hand trembled violently when she took the candelabrum and she spilled hot wax on don César's wrist, but in his jovial mood he did not upbraid her for her carelessness. Bearing the light, she led him across the tiles and around the flower beds through the kitchen door. With a backward glance as if to confirm the awful certainty that Tamboura and the others were behind her, she crossed the kitchen and lifted a cloth curtain that led to a smaller room. The candles illuminated its cleanness and simplicity. Tamboura saw a low bed with a smoothly stretched sheet over the mattress, an orderly line of cotton garments hanging from nails on the wall, a plain rush-seated chair, a small mirror and a niche in the wall with a collection of bottles and boxes. There was nothing else.

César looked at the narrow bed and laughed.

"Hardly wide enough for Tamboura's shoulders, is it? But you'll manage—this is a case where two will take up no more room than one. Work well tonight, Tamboura. If the *cachorrito* is a good one, we'll take it out to Montalvo and raise it." He pressed Alix's arm. "And I'll buy you the emerald ring you admired in the window on Obispo Street in exchange for the child."

Tamboura grinned. "It will be a good one, *amo*. Mine always are."

"You're a braggart, Tamboura, but you do speak the truth. And now we'll leave you. Light your candle, Rachel, and we'll light our own way back across the patio." He held up the curtain for Alix and they left with don César's laughter still ringing in the night. "Ay, Alix," he said, "your Rachel will bless me in the morning."

Rachel stood grimly in the middle of the floor and her look of intense hatred wiped the grin from Tamboura's face.

"Your *amo* has ordered that you stay here with me and my mistress has sanctioned it. So, you shall remain but you will not touch me. This is my bed and here I shall sleep but I shall sleep alone."

"You would be happier with me," Tamboura's grin returned. He felt confident. The *amo* had spoken and must the woman not obey? It was unthinkable that anyone should disobey the *amo*.

Rachel reached under the pillow and drew out a small knife whose sharp blade glinted in the candlelight.

"If you touch me, I shall use this," she threatened.

Tamboura laughed. "Your hands are weak, *mujer*." He spread out his fingers to show the enormity of his own hand. "Think you that I am afraid of that little knife?"

"I would wait until you are asleep."

"With you I would not sleep, *mujer*." Tamboura reached out his big arms to envelop her but she eluded him and slipped to the far side of the room. From the niche in the wall she took a small box and opened it. She withdrew something from it and threw it to the floor. The strange object fluttered from her hand as though it were alive, circled slowly in the air and landed softly on the floor at Tamboura's feet. He jumped back in terror. The little object did not move;

it was nothing but a few cock's feathers, red, white and black, tied together with a red string. But it struck fear in Tamboura's heart.

*"Nañigo!"* he exclaimed and he could feel his tongue dry against his lips.

"In St. Domingue we call it voodoo." Her thin lips made a straight line. She pointed to it with one slender bronze finger and as if obeying her direction, it caught an errant breeze and moved on the floor.

"Step across that, *hombre,* and you will die. The gods of Africa are powerful, as you know, and they obey my bidding. Remain on your own side and you will be safe. I shall not use the knife on you when you sleep as much as I would like to. You will find the floor hard but that is not my fault. Do we understand each other?"

Tamboura stepped away from the *ouanga* on the floor.

"I understand, Rachel."

*"Bien,* and when morning comes, you will tell don César, should he ask, that you passed a very happy night."

"As you wish, but it will be the first time I have ever lied to my *amo."*

"There is always a first time. The second time you will find it less difficult."

"You are a strange woman, Rachel." Tamboura spoke with deep respect. "Why do you hate me so much? I have never done anything bad to you."

"Because you are a man, Tamboura, and I hate all men. It is not you I hate, only that vile thing you possess."

"Others have not called it vile. Others have enjoyed it."

"But not I." She blew out the candle. "Take off your clothes or you will muss them and don César will suspect that you have not undressed. Here!" In the darkness she reached up and took a robe from one of the nails. She threw it at him and he felt the soft cloth enveloping his face. "Sleep on that, it will soften the hardness of the floor a little."

"Take away the *ouanga*, Rachel," he pleaded. "I fear that if I sleep I might roll on the floor and touch it."

"It will not harm you, unless you cross it. Now sleep and I shall wake you in the morning."

Tamboura removed his clothes and folded them carefully as he had been taught to do, placing them on the chair. He spread the thin robe as close to the wall as possible and lay down. The whisper of the bed rope and the rustle of straw in the mattress were the only sounds of another person in the room. Then there was silence, broken only by the hum of insects in the patio outside.

He sighed, wishing once again that he were back in the bohio of Mama Baba's with the delighted squeals, the harsh breathing, the raptured moaning, the smell of sweaty bodies near him. But he was not alone—for that he was grateful. For all the menace of the *ouanga* on the floor, Rachel was near and he was not alone. Now, lying naked in the darkness, he was again free to indulge in the dream that had so satisfied him in the patio—the dream of white skin and black skin. Ay! let Rachel sleep on her bed, the other was with him and she was true, right under the same roof with him. Why should he desire the skinny mestiza who didn't want him when in his dreams white arms enfolded him and pink lips touched his own. Ay, ay, ay! The vision mounted until it vanished in a long strangulated breath that drained his lungs. His hands fell to the floor. He slept.

In her narrow bed, protected only by the little bunch of chicken feathers tied with a red string, Rachel did not sleep. She lay still, scarcely moving all night until, in the first dim light of dawn, she looked across the room to where Tamboura sprawled on the floor. She closed her eyes and shuddered. He was even worse than she had imagined.

"Thank you, Maman Erzulie," her lips moved silently in impassioned gratitude, "for protecting me this night. Protect me from him always and I shall repay you well." She fell asleep and slept soundly after her long vigil.

Rachel was not the only one who found no rest that night. Alix waited until don César's sonorous snores assured her that he was sleeping soundly. She edged carefully away from his paunchy body, loathing it, and thinking only of the muscled ebony that Rachel must be enjoying, for surely with Tamboura beside her, she must have long since overcome her silly prejudices. Alix had a wild impulse to slip down the stairs and across the patio, into Rachel's room, order her to leave, and pre-empt her place beside Tamboura. But no, she must be careful and let her head not her heart rule her action.

She quit the bed slowly and noiselessly and sought the couch in the *sala*. Here she could think. She was certain her fertile brain would devise some plan whereby she could have don César and Tamboura too. She must consider it well and she did, from all possible angles.

When dawn came she went barefooted out onto the *balcon*, down the stairs and across the chilly tiles of the patio. Should she be seen, her excuse was already fabricated—she was ill and needed Rachel and Rachel had not answered the bell. But nobody saw her and she entered the kitchen and stopped to listen. In that moment of pause, she could identify Tamboura's powerful breathing and between his deep respirations, those of Rachel. Her hand, trembling with expectancy of what she might see, raised the curtain. Rachel was lying on her bed, her hands folded across her chest, sleeping peacefully. Tamboura was stretched out on the floor with Rachel's robe wadded beneath him.

Alix stood in the doorway, caressing his black body with her eyes. *Mon Dieu!* Did her eyes deceive her? Was this true? Could such a miracle be real? Her fingers itched to prove by touch the overwhelming evidence that her eyes saw. The man was sleeping soundly and he would never know. Her feet made no noise on the tiles as she advanced two steps into the room and stood over him. She knelt, reaching down one hand. And now, having touched, could she ever relinquish her hold? She must, she must, but she could not. Tamboura's eyes opened slowly and she quickly withdrew her hand. Her finger, laid across her lips, commanded silence. He understood and smiled back at her. Then, without glancing back, she left, hurrying across the patio and up the stairs, through the sala and into her room. Don César was still sleeping and she edged herself carefully back into the bed. Her plan was now fully formed, and she knew that nothing in heaven or hell, or on earth, could keep it from its eventual and, she hoped, quick fulfillment.

## chapter xiv

NEVER IN HER LIFE had Alix been more charming, possibly because she had never made so great an effort to please. Don César was doubly enamored. Once he had been somewhat doubtful—as all wealthy men are wont to be when a young and beautiful woman appears in their middle age. He had been afraid that Alix might be interested only in his money. But after her worry over his safety last night, and particularly after the unexpected fire and passion which she had so willingly volunteered this morning and which had left him quite breathless, his last doubts and fears were dispelled. Now, with her undeniable beauty facing him across the breakfast table in her bedroom, he was sure that her love for him was genuine. He was certain that she would grace the Finca Montalvo with all the dignity and beauty he might demand from a Señora Montalvo.

With Alix as his wife, he could even hope for another son which would make up to him for the lone granddaughter who was all that Gregorio and the priest-ridden Beatriz had produced for him. He knew there would never be any more, for if Gregorio came within ten feet of the marriage bed, Beatriz collapsed with one of her numerous ailments. With a son by Alix, the Montalvo name would be carried on and the Finca Montalvo would not have to be changed to some name like Hernandez, or Alvarez or Gonzales, by the marriage of his granddaughter. All Cuba would approve and marvel at his marriage with a French *condesa*. It would enrich the Montalvo blood and bring an authentic aristocracy to the Montalvo name which even the overbearing Spanish could not ignore. He must give the matter of marriage some very serious consideration. In the meantime and for this very present moment, he would enjoy Alix.

They were served by a rather sullen Rachel who, despite her long face, had assured don César with all politeness that Tamboura had quitted himself most admirably; she thanked him formally for his goodness in thinking of her. Alix tried hard to read some message in Rachel's impassive face. Had she enjoyed Tamboura or had she not? The question, however, would be answered when they were alone together. She was quite certain from the fact that Tamboura was on the floor when she had spied on them, that Rachel was still untouched. She hoped so. From now on, she was determined to share Tamboura with nobody. But first the foundations of her plan must be carefully laid.

The thin pink *robe de chambre* she was wearing was a most important part of her plan and she could sense that it was already producing the desired results on don César. For all the ardor that she had inspired in him an hour ago, she could see that another wave was beginning to rise. His eyes were curiously glazed and his tongue kept continuously making the circuit of his lips. With a graceful gesture, she poured him a steaming cup of coffee from the silver urn, taking care to let the thin sleeves fall away from her arms and bending just enough to give him a glimpse of her breasts. As though she had been serving him for many years, she added hot milk in the quantity she knew he favored with the three spoonfuls of sugar he liked, and handed the cup to him, realizing that it made a touching picture of domestic bliss. With a pretty little wrapping of the thin robe around her, she rose and took a pillow from the bed and placed it at his feet, only to sink down upon it, her head against his knees, her face looking up at him most demurely and her hand resting warm and provocative on his linen-clad leg.

*"Querido mio."* In any other woman it would have been a kitten-like purring but Alix was a more consummate actress. "Could any woman ask for more than this? You and I here together! I rich in my happiness and you—I hope—in yours. Ay, César, I wonder if you have any idea of just how much I really love you."

"I think you showed me this morning, *mi alma.* After that could I ever doubt you?"

"You shall never need to, César. But something is worrying me and I would hesitate to tell you if it were not. . . ." Her hand fluttered on his leg and she snuggled up even closer to him, sighing contentedly.

"If it were not for what, Alix?" He sipped the coffee, which was exactly to his taste. *Caramba!* Few women knew how a man liked his coffee. His first wife had always put in too much milk.

"If it were not for your generosity, *querido,* which is already too great, and if it were not for the fact that last night you promised me an emerald ring in return for Rachel's baby, if it comes—"

"Do not concern yourself about that, Alix," he smiled. "It's as good as yours in another nine or ten months. That Tamboura never fails."

The pink lips pursed themselves in a pretty little *moue* which Alix knew César would find most charming. "But I do not want or need the emerald, César. It is frightfully expensive. Oh, it is a pretty bauble and it would be most becoming on my finger but there is something I need far more and I need it so badly I cannot wait nine months for it. It costs much less than the emerald so I am emboldened to ask for it."

"And what does my Alix need that she doesn't already have?" His gratifying experience of the morning, so unanticipated and so freely given, had made him indulgent.

"A *volante,* dearest, and a slave to drive it. Have you any idea of how difficult it is always to have to ride in a hired carriage; to sit on greasy upholstery which perhaps some woman of the streets has sat on only five minutes before; to entrust myself to strange drivers? Whenever I go out it is the same story. Rachel must run down the street to find a stray vehicle and always, yes, always, César, it turns out to be a ramshackle affair with rope traces and some evil-visaged black *cochero* who frightens me nearly to death if we leave the city gates. Oh, César, since those terrible things in St. Domingue, all niggers frighten me." Her underlip started to tremble and she managed to squeeze out one large, perfectly formed tear which trickled slowly down her cheek.

"Hush, darling, I know, I know."

"But you cannot know, César. You did not see the brutish lust on those black faces. You did not see them hack at my husband with their machetes. You did not have to run from them in terror of your life and hide from them, expecting every minute to be discovered and used by one and another and another in their unbridled brutality."

"But darling, if you have a carriage, you will have to have somebody to drive it and although Rachel seems most capable, she could hardly do that." He had already decided in his own mind to give her the carriage. It was little enough to repay the joy she had so recently given him. "I do agree with you that a woman of your position does need her own carriage. It was stupid of me not to think of it before."

"No, César, for you already knew my aversion to having a male slave around the house and yet lately I have felt most insecure here while you were away—just Rachel and me, alone and unprotected. Why, darling, the other night a crowd of drunken young men came out of the Mendoza palace after the *verbena* on your aunt's saint day. They were roistering in the streets, shook the gates of the patio so that I thought they would part from the hinges, all the time shouting and demanding admittance. I was petrified, fearing that perhaps Rachel might have forgotten to lock the gates, but of course she had attended to them. Yet I could not help but think what might have happened had they been left unlocked. My position here in Havana is, to say the least, equivocal. Alone, a foreigner and unprotected."

"Poor dear." César's hand touched the blonde curls. "I have been stupid indeed."

"And last night"—Alix was quick to take advantage of his mood—"when I saw your slave Tamboura, I somehow felt that he was a slave I could trust and of whom I would not be afraid. Such an honest face, César. He does not look like an animal. I am sure he must be loyal and he certainly looks strong and capable. His very appearance leads me to trust him. He is the first and only slave I have seen in Cuba that has not terrified me."

Don César lay back in his chair, his eyes half closed, regarding her with indulgence. In his present mood he would have given her the moon, but Tamboura was something different.

"Tamboura is big as an ox and gentle as a kitten. I would feel perfectly safe about you with Tamboura here but, Alix, I have just trained him as my groom and in addition to those duties, he is most necessary at the *finca*. That boy's a breeder! Ten *cachorritos* already and more to come. But you shall have a carriage, and I could housebreak Omo for your coachman. Omo's a fine Mandingo boy."

Alix's caresses ceased. A shudder passed almost perceptibly over her and another tear, this one larger than the first, necessitated the application of a bit of lace. She sighed deeply, but she put a brave face on her disappointment. César must understand that she was not going to press the matter. It was merely the fancy of a silly, excitable woman and as usual she would defer to his superior judgment.

"Then, *querido,* let us entirely forget the matter of a carriage." Her hand resumed its caresses. "How silly I am. The hired *volantes* are quite good enough for me, for really, I go out very little and then only to the shops on Obispo and to church." Her hand became quiet and she rose slowly, not, however, forgetting to pat his cheek with a forgiving little gesture which so aptly implied that she was quite willing to sacrifice her needs. "And I myself shall make sure that the gates are locked at night and not leave it to Rachel. Do not let's speak about the matter again." And having resigned herself so bravely and touchingly, she managed to smile and took the cup from his hand. "Do have another cup of coffee, César, and if you'd like more *pan tostado,* I'll ring for Rachel."

He shook his head. "No more, Alix, but you are right, you do need a male slave here for protection and you do need your own *volante*. It's rather selfish of me to withhold Tamboura because, after all, with over five hundred slaves on the plantation, I can easily find another groom. Perhaps we could arrange for him to return to the *finca* from time to time, so his other duties won't be neglected. Also to keep him in good humor." Don César suddenly became very serious. "That, my dear, would be quite necessary for your protection."

She sank to the pillow again, quite confident that her point was nearly gained.

"For my protection? I don't understand, César."

"Of course not." His hand groped for hers and replaced it in its former position. "You know little about the handling of slaves or animals. Tamboura, like a stallion with his mares, is happy and contented and gentle when he finds a constant outlet for his animal urges. But take away his wenches from him and he would become mean and vicious, like a stallion kept in the stable and never allowed outside. You would see a different Tamboura after a few months. His pent-up desires would make him ugly and untractable, hard to manage, unreasoning, even dangerous. Of course, I could have him gelded, but I would hate to do it to him.

"And turn him into a fat, lazy eunuch, who would be no protection for me? Heavens, no! But you forget Rachel! She doesn't talk much, that one, but the few words she said this morning are sufficient to let me know that she will be quite able to keep Tamboura sufficiently drained so that he will be as contented with her as with a whole stable full of wenches at Montalvo."

Don César nodded in agreement. His last argument had been entirely swept away.

"And," Alix continued, certain now that she had won, "there is much here for him to do. The *balcons* need painting, the flower beds in the patio are running wild, the vines need pruning and oh, there will be plenty to keep him busy. It has been difficult for Rachel to do all the work—washing floors and cooking and caring for me. Not that I have complained," she added.

"Of course you haven't." His voice sank to a whisper and he closed his eyes, only to open them a moment later to look up at the little gilt clock on the wall.

"Ay, Alix, it has passed ten o'clock and I have a full morning of business to attend to. Aunt Maria"—he jerked his thumb in the direction of the Mendoza palace—"insists that she accompany me to Santa Clara to see Gregorio's daughter who has had a little trouble with the nuns. She's fifteen, you know, and should be out of school now, but with doña Beatriz in such poor health, it seems inadvisable to bring her home. Perhaps, Alix, the time will come when you can help with Gertrudis."

Alix had difficulty seeing herself in the role of grandmother to a lump of a girl, particularly one of fifteen years, but she rose to the occasion.

"Just the age when a girl needs an older woman for a *confidanta,*" she consented sweetly in her willingness to lift any care from her César's shoulders.

"And would you like to accompany Aunt Maria and me?"

Alix remembered the raddled old face, emerging from its folds of black taffeta like the head of an ancient turtle from its shell, the disapproving look in the faded eyes on the only occasion that César had presented her to his aunt. Old women were definitely not in Alix' program for the day.

"Just now, darling, as merely *une amie,*" she cautioned, "it would hardly be proper. Perhaps sometime later. . . ." Her words faded off in a vague promise.

"Then I must hurry." Don César disengaged Alix' hand and rose reluctantly. "I would much rather stay here with you but Aunt Maria's temper does not improve by waiting."

"Shall I ring for Rachel and have your man saddle the horses?" Alix was staking much on this last throw of her dice. She had won consistently this morning and she felt her winning streak would continue.

"No, I accompany Tia Maria in her coach and she will

remain at the convent for lunch, the better to soothe the Mother Superior over Gertrudis' naughtiness. As I would not be permitted to eat there, I shall borrow her coach to attend to my other affairs. I must see Miguel de Santiago about a matter of business, drop in at don Solano's to see if his new shipment of slaves has arrived from Africa. And, of course. . . ."

"The little matter of the *volante*," she reminded him, reaching up to pinch his cheek.

"And the little matter of the *volante*. Tell me, Alix, have you any choice in the color of the horses?"

She giggled. "They can be purple for all I care, just so they can take me places and as long as I have that fine strong—what is his name?" She had become suddenly forgetful.

"Tamboura."

"Oh yes, I can remember that for it is almost *drum* in French."

"And in Spanish, too."

"And with that fine strong Drum to drive me," she finished her sentence. "And now, if Tia Maria and your Gertrudis and the Señor de Santiago and all the rest are more important to you than I am, run along but you will of course be back for the siesta?" Her eyes promised much.

After the series of events of the morning, don César was doubtful if he could live up to that promise.

"*Querida mia,* how much I would like to, but there will be much to do today and it is my only day in Havana. I cannot possibly make it. But I shall have dinner here and stay all night because if I leave Tamboura here I do not wish to ride back to Montalvo alone at night. There are many escaped slaves on the roads after dark."

"Oh, you poor darling, how I am disrupting your life." She was properly penitent.

"And how much you have added to it." He was still in a daze from her outpouring of affection.

Alix waited for him, showing just the proper amount of disappointment, while he straightened the disarray of his clothing. She handed him his big white *paja de Panama* hat and then, as a last gesture of wifeliness, she stood on the *balcon,* waving to him as he left through the patio gate. As soon as he was gone, she shed her air of playful coquetry, and summoned Rachel with a peremptory tug of the bell cord.

"Where is Tamboura?" she asked.

"The lazy lout is sleeping on a chair in the corner of the patio under the *campanas de oro* vine. He never offered to help me with the work."

"Tell me the truth about last night," Alix demanded, her eyes gimlet sharp.

"There is nothing to tell, madame. The brute slept on the floor and I slept in my bed."

"So, you disobeyed don César."

"Oh, madame, do not tell him."

"I shall not. If he knew that you disobeyed him, he would have you sent to the whips. I could do nothing to protect you."

"Then you will not tell him?" Rachel reached for Alix' hand and kissed it.

"Of course not. I love you far too much, Rachel. I would not have you harmed."

"I owe you much, madame."

"You now have an opportunity to repay me."

"In any way I can."

"Then Rachel, send Tamboura to me, and take up your position at the patio gate. Do not leave it. If you see don César coming, run here to warn me."

The copper glow of Rachel's skin seemed to depart, leaving her face ashen as though a gray cobweb had been drawn over it.

*"Mais non, Madame!"* Rachel clutched at Alix' hand. "Not again! Not another Bonaventure?"

Alix snatched her hand away.

"Rachel, you must understand me. You must! Just as you, last night, were terrified over the prospect of being with Tamboura, today I am equally terrified over the prospect of *not* being with him. Just as every fiber of your body repulsed him last night, so today does every fiber of mine cry out for him. Since we left St. Domingue, I have spent all my nights, tossing and turning and wooing sleep on that bed," she pointed a disdainful finger at the rumpled sheets, "longing for those nights when I had only to ring the bell and Bonaventure would appear. Human flesh can stand it no longer. I would rather die. Tamboura is to be here from now on. He will not return to Montalvo with don César." She stepped to the mulatto and threw her arms around the woman. "Oh help me, Rachel, help me as you did before. Either help me, Rachel, or I swear I shall do away with myself. I can stand it no longer."

"It is what you most desire, madame?" Rachel was speaking with difficulty. "We have been so happy here, just you and me together, even though don César did come once in a while. But is it safe, madame? Don César?"

"I'll handle don César, Rachel. He is like all men—a fool where women are concerned. He is already entwined around my little finger, for see, he leaves Tamboura with me. Don't worry about him. Just go quickly and summon Tamboura."

Rachel shook her head sadly. "As you wish, madame. I shall be your accomplice now as I was with Bonaventure and I pray that no evil will come of this."

"None will, Rachel, I assure you. Oh, send him to me, send him to me now!"

"But he should bathe, madame. He has not bathed since last night."

"No, no, no," Alix wailed. "Now!"

She heard Rachel's steps growing fainter as they went down the stairs. She listened intently. Soon she heard the sluff of slippers on the stairs and she stood up, letting the rosy clouds of the *robe de chambre* settle around her in billowing folds.

Tamboura entered. He stopped suddenly in the doorway, scarcely able to believe his eyes. He had not known, when he finally awoke this morning, whether the vision he had seen beside his bed had been real or was only a continuation of his dream. He still didn't know but he knew that what he saw now was no dream. He remained standing as Alix slowly came to him.

"Tambour my big drum."

He had never heard his name so spoken before. It set every nerve in his body atingle.

"Tambour," she repeated, "can you only stand there? Can you only stand there and look at me?"

He advanced one step. Something inside him warned him to turn and run and not stop running until he reached the security of Mama Baba's hut. His hand crept between the buttons of his shirt and encountered the dampness of his precious amulet. His spirit was with him—it gave him strength. His arms reached out and caught her as she almost fainted. The same huge arms picked her up and held her. She pointed to the bed, as her fingers struggled with the buttons of his shirt to rest on the smooth skin beneath it. His skin felt cool and damp to her hot hands. There was a hardness under it so different from the flabby flesh of César.

Tamboura would have relinquished his burden on the bed but she shook her head and pointed to the windows. He carried her there and she reached for the cord that lowered the shutters. They rattled to the floor and the hot light of the sun vanished in a cool semidarkness.

"Now, Tambour," she cried. "Now! Hurry, Tambour, hurry!"

# chapter xv

THE TRIANGLE of love, hatred and jealousy—that geometric symbol of desire enflamed—sprouted a fourth and acutely sharper angle in the tangled relations of Tamboura, Alix and don César. Although recognized by nobody but herself, that angle was Rachel.

Don César, happy in his ignorance of what had developed between Alix and Tamboura, proposed marriage and was immediately and joyfully accepted, but using the prerogative of the bride-to-be, Alix would not yield to don César's importunings for an immediate marriage. She was far too happy the way things were to desire any change and now, secure in her knowledge that she would eventually become the Señora Montalvo, she wanted to enjoy her freedom a little longer, knowing that Tamboura would never be so easily accessible again. And don César himself, living in the nimbus of the joys another marriage would afford him, found some grounds of common sense in Alix' carefully made excuses and postponements. In one way, he was not a little pleased at her delay, for it proved to him, more forcibly than anything else, that she was not primarily interested in his money; otherwise she would certainly have hurried matters to completion. Her very willingness to postpone the marriage convinced him most emphatically that her love was for himself and not his wealth.

Alix was completely enraptured with her life! Tamboura had turned out to be even more than she had anticipated and his performances so far exceeded Bonaventure's that she could never regret her Dominican slave again. Her daylight hours were but a prelude to the night and each night she discovered new joys with Tamboura. Theirs was entirely a union of the flesh. Alix wanted it that way, accepted it for what it was and gloried in it.

Tamboura could have learned much from Alix and she from him, but they were too engrossed in exploring each other's bodies. The contact of black flesh and white was enough—the white mentality of Alix never searched the black mind of Tamboura, nor his hers. Their fierce appeal for each other lay in their polar extremes; had Alix inculcated Tamboura with any degree of her civilization, he would have lost some of his native savagery which was his strongest appeal for her. Similarly, it was the sophistication of Alix, in contrast to the primitive responses of the Negro wenches he had known, which appealed to Tamboura. His relations with them had been basic and fundamental. With Alix there was always some subtle nuance of passion which surprised amazed and sometimes even shocked him.

It was enough for them that hands touched, bodies touched, lips touched. Their desires were primitive and their satisfaction complete. Once their desires were satiated, they were content to lie in each other's arms without words until such time as desire was roused again. Their conversation rarely exceeded words of endearment, commands of love or such elemental things as hunger, thirst and sleep. Lacking conversation, they avoided all the pitfalls of disagreement and argument. They met on only one ground and on that they achieved perfect harmony.

One of the unused bedchambers with a huge old Spanish bed on the third floor had been cleaned and aired, ostensibly for Tamboura and Rachel. But on the rare occasions when Rachel used the room, to convince don César that she and Tamboura were still enjoying each other, Rachel slept on the bed, protected by the *ouanga,* and Tamboura on the floor. These nights became fewer and fewer after don César promoted both M'dong and Omo to grooms and had them accompany him to the city, for added protection against the runaway slaves who came down in bands from the mountain hideouts to rob and murder unprotected travelers at night. Then Tamboura moved out to the loft over the stables to share a mattress on the floor with his friends, glad of the opportunity for male companionship. He had found that even he was not always capable of satisfying Alix—the woman was insatiable—and his nights with M'dong and Omo became a welcome respite.

To Tamboura it did not seem inconsistent that he should share his *ama's* bed at night and arise in the morning to do the menial work of the household and stables during the day. The work around the house on Colon Street was far easier than chopping cane on the plantation and he knew that at any time he might be called from his duties as stable boy, floor scrubber or painter to satisfy Alix' whim of the moment. She delighted in the unusual. When he came to her, his black skin liberally bespattered with whitewash, he was all the more appealing. When he took her on the dirty mattress on the floor of the loft over the stable, she found it a welcome change from the big Spanish bed.

She made the discovery that rum released what few inhibitions he still possessed and made him more savagely amenable to her wishes. Drunk, Tamboura forgot his Spanish and lapsed into Hausa. He did not become angry or vicious. Rum merely stripped off the superficial gilding of his slight civilization so that Alix became for him merely a girl from his village and the civilized room a tamarisk bush under the African moon. She could not decide whether she enjoyed him more drunk or sober.

The bedroom on the third floor became their rendezvous because it was less subject to discovery than her bedroom, which opened off the main sala on the second floor. The danger of her own bed as a trysting place had been made most apparent one afternoon when don César's aunt, the superannuated Tia Maria of the Mendoza palace, came to call to offer her stuffily formal and most unwilling congratulations on her nephew's coming marriage. Tamboura had only had time to crouch among Alix' frothy laces in the big mahogany wardrobe and there he had remained during the entire stay of the aged aunt, while Alix excused her *déshabillé* on the grounds of a serious headache, which she hoped might speed the aunt on her way before poor Tamboura smothered in the Alençon flounces.

The days of entrancement slipped by into weeks and the weeks into months and there was no diminishing of ardor on the part of the lovers. Each found the other as responsive and entirely appealing as on the first afternoon they had discovered each other. Each meeting was an entirely new soaring of ecstatic wonder and joy. They never tired of each other and their capacity for repeated enjoyment was limited only by Tamboura's powers of recuperation.

Don César, ignorantly blissful, was never disappointed on his visits. Alix, fresh from the arms of Tamboura, could well afford to make César happy as a sop for all he was providing and about to provide. M'dong and Omo also anticipated these visits for to them it meant a change from the routine of the *finca*, a chance to see the city and an opportunity to visit with Tamboura. They were aware, through his prideful boasting to them, of his intrigue with his *ama* and although terrified at what he might suffer if discovered, they were proud of his ability to possess a white woman and not a little jealous of his success. They too had enjoyed admiring and appraising glances from Alix, but although she might admire them, her infatuation with Tamboura and her suspicion that neither of them could possibly exceed his capacity for satisfying her confined her to admiration only. Had Tamboura been absent and had either Omo or M'dong arrived without don César, she would not have hesitated to instigate further explorations, but the occasion never arose.

However as has been said, there was a fourth angle to the situation, an angle not of joy but of venomous jealousy, searing frustration and noxious virulence, all of which seethed inside the outwardly placid Rachel. She realized that the perverted love she had for Alix would never be requited and she had accepted the fact and grown to live with it. All she desired was to lavish her affection on her mistress and by so doing she felt amply rewarded in the joy of serving her. Rachel realized the economic security the marriage to Don César would bring her mistress and she was as anxious for it as Alix. She also knew that the only motive that impelled Alix was don César's money and position. As long as Alix did not love him, Rachel was willing to be a member of that freemasonry among women which prompts them to band together in fleecing the more stupid male.

But Tamboura was something else! That her adored mistress would give herself to this black savage was as repulsive to Rachel as if she were a white woman herself. That Alix would allow her lovely body to be pawed over by a black animal, only a few years out of the African jungle, was incomprehensible to the half-white Rachel with her predominantly white viewpoint. That Tamboura was a man as well as a slave, a Negro and a beast in Rachel's eyes, only contributed to her jealousy and her desire to rid herself and her mistress of him.

The fetish of cock's feathers had served to frighten Tamboura, but her secret prayers and incantations to the voodoo gods of St. Domingue to destroy Tamboura had brought no results. Losing faith in her own ability to bring the gods to wreak their vengeance on him, she had saved as many *centavos* as she could from the household money which Alix entrusted to her. When the *centavos* had mounted to a *peseta,* she visited the house of a *nañigo bruja* across the harbor in Regla, seeking her assistance to accomplish some horrible death for Tamboura. The *bruja* demanded certain things from Tamboura's body and this posed a difficult problem for Rachel. The fingernail paring she carefully picked from the floor one day after Tamboura had been trimming his nails in the kitchen with one of her sharp knives. The little tuft of pubic hair she saved one hair at a time, gleaned from a careful examination of the sheets before she laundered them. The small flask of urine had been drawn from the chamber pot he used and the dried semen scraped from a discarded towel.

Armed with these important ingredients, she returned to the *bruja's* house in Regla and watched the old crone while she, with many incantations, fashioned a clay image of an unmistakably masculine figure which contained the parts of Tamboura Rachel had collected. A long steel needle stood upright in a hole in the image's navel. Rachel was carefully instructed in the exact method whereby she could secure a particularly agonizing death for Tamboura. She was to remove the needle and plunge it deeply into the hole, reciting at the same time an incantation to Erzulie, the consort of Dambala, chief among the African gods. Rachel learned the precise words of the incantation in the bastard French which had come over from St. Domingue with the voodoo worship.

*Erzulie kalika elu*
*A la loa ki rèd.*
*Erzulie u madé kocho noir*
*M'apeé ba u li.*
*Erzulie madé kabrit noir de pyê*
*M'apeé ba u li.*

Erzuli kalika elu
You ask for a black pig
I will give you one
Erzuli you ask for a black two-footed goat
I will give you one.

Each night behind the closed shutters of her room, Rachel set the candle on the floor and spread a clean white cloth beside it with the clay image upon it. Again and again she stabbed with the needle, recited the words and prayed to Erzulie. But all her efforts were wasted. Tamboura continued as robust and healthy as ever. She passed the image through the flame of the candle but it only seemed to create a more intense fire within him. One night, in desperation, she smashed the little image to bits with a hammer, grinding the powdered clay into the floor with her heel. The next morning Tamboura greeted her with a leer that bespoke new heights of prowess during the past night and wolfed down a breakfast heartier than ever.

She consulted other *brujas* and *brujos,* stealing more and more until Alix started complaining about the high cost of food and prettily begged don César for more housekeeping money.

Rachel was convinced that had she been back in St. Domingue, she could have accomplished Tamboura's death as easily as she had managed the end of Bonaventure. The *bocor* in St. Domingue had effected that in a matter of weeks, although unfortunately Bonaventure's death in defense of Alix was so heroic as to enshrine him in Alix' memory. Certainly the *nañigo* of Cuba was not as powerful as its parent, the voodoo of St. Domingue. She abandoned Erzulie in favor of Baron Guede, the god of death, but he was as unmindful of her prayers as Erzulie. Even Dambala, the all-powerful, turned a deaf ear to her prayers. When she finally located a Dominican *bocor* who had fled from Port au Prince she felt she had solved the problem, but the powerful *ouanga* she had purchased from him and placed under the bed that Tamboura shared with Alix in the upper chamber produced no results. Rachel was so certain it would that she had spent the whole night crouched on the stairs listening for Tamboura's death rattle. All she heard were the sounds of violent lovemaking which sickened her so that she ran to her own room below to beat upon the rough walls with maniacal frenzy until her hands were torn and bleeding.

Well, there were other ways!

There was the religion of the whites—if neither voodoo nor *nañigo* could help, she would try that. Each morning on her trip to market, she stopped in the old cathedral and knelt before the holy images, pouring out her demands for vengeance in fervent silence and lighting a candle so that her supplication would not be forgotten. To no avail! The painted and gilded images in the cathedral were no more efficacious than the gods of Africa. Tamboura lived, sang, got drunk and sported with her beloved mistress with more verve and puissance than ever before.

She would gladly have killed him herself—stolen up behind him some day when he was eating in the kitchen and plunged her knife in his throat. But she realized that by so doing she would forever alienate Alix, and she herself would end up in the whip yard, that feared Gehenna which struck terror to the heart of every slave in Havana. She considered poison but she knew it would inevitably be traced to her as cook, and besides she feared that Alix might partake of the same dish as Tamboura, as they often ate together. In the hope of disaster she even encouraged the picnics in the country which Alix found so entertaining, when they would go to a deserted strip of beach near Mariano, Tamboura driving the *volante* with Alix and Rachel under the big black hood. While Rachel was spreading the food on a white cloth on the sand, Alix loved to have Tamboura shed his clothes and plunge into the ocean. The sight of his black body breasting the surf seemed to please her, although Tamboura was not a good swimmer and one day he had been sucked under by a heavy surf and nearly drowned. That it might happen again and this time disastrously, Rachel instigated more picnics and planned elaborate lunches to accompany them. But tragedy never struck and her only reward was to stand by and witness the disgusting servitude of her mistress, down on her knees, drying the salt-encrusted body of the big brute with a towel and then drawing him down onto the sand with her.

No, everything had failed! Tamboura still reigned, wielding his fleshly scepter in the little house on Colon Street, and Rachel could only beat her hands against the wall, or lie staring into the darkness of night which was no blacker than the jealousy that was consuming her.

Then one day, whether it was due to the gods of Africa or the saints in the cathedral or a combination of both, she had an inspiration. While wandering through the almost carnival hubbub of the Mercado de Colon, in search of just the right crayfish for her mistress' supper, she spied a young quadroon sidling up to a Cuban señor. Rachel was acquainted with the type this fellow represented—more white than black with carefully shaved *patillas*—sideburns that stenciled each cheek with sooty black, growing down from a head of carefully arranged hair that had been liberally greased to remove the kink. His mussed white suit aped in a shabby way the Cuban gentility and his furtive manner was a sure advertisement that he was a pimp. However, he was indulging in other business than pimping, for she saw the surreptitious spreading of white cards in his hand and the amused look of the Cuban who nodded for the fellow to follow him behind a pillar. Out of curiosity Rachel followed too and caught a quick glimpse of the pornography pictured on the cards. Although the plan did not come to her fully matured, she had the germ of it and she made a note of the fellow so that she would remember him, which would not be difficult as his flashy good looks made him conspicuous. When she arrived home, she counted the store of *pesetas* she had hoarded under a loose tile. They seemed ample.

During the several days that elapsed after she saw the quadroon, she completed her stratagem. It was a dangerous one for it involved her mistress and she knew it would forever put an end to Alix' relations with don César as well as with Tamboura. But her mania for vengeance completely overshadowed everything else. With both don César and Tamboura out of the way, she would have Alix to herself again, and if they faced poverty, so much the better. She would go out and work to support her mistress and thus demonstrate to an even higher degree her love and devotion. Better to be together in poverty than separated by Tamboura in affluence.

Having formulated her plan of action, she sought out the bright-skinned fellow one day in the market. He was not inclined to pay her any attention, as he saw no prospect for his wares in a decently dressed mestiza, but she halted him with the Cuban "p-sst." He stopped. After all, he could never be quite sure who might be a customer; he numbered among his patrons the Bishop's confessor, one of Havana's most pious dowagers, and the valet of the Governor General himself. Rachel sought shelter behind a barricade of wicker crates filled with clucking hens, and he followed her. Safe from passing eyes, he took a thin leather envelope from under his shirt and fanned out his wares in his hand. The pictures were revolting to Rachel but she recognized the effectiveness of the perverted poses. They were done in India ink and a few were colored, but all were lifelike.

She glanced through the spread-out fan without touching the cards and shook her head, refusing to accept for closer examination one or two particularly revolting masterpieces which the fellow pressed upon her.

"Do you do these yourself?" she inquired.

"No, *mujer*, I merely sell them. They are done by an old man. Once he was a great artist in Italy."

"Then you could have him draw something special for me—something done entirely to my order?"

"A request which many of my regular customers make." The fellow laughed to display a row of flashing teeth. "To many these ordinary representations do not appeal. They wish the different, the unusual, the more exciting. And what would you like, *mujer?* Do you care for whips, scenes of torture?" He appraised her carefully. "Or would you prefer a drawing in which only women appear?"

She discouraged his familiarity with a disapproving stare. "It is not for myself, *hombre*. I have no interest in your filth. I merely act as agent for someone very important in Havana, who, if I but say the word, could have you clapped in prison before night. However, if you are willing to do business, we shall talk business. And price," she added.

*"Sí, señorita."* The man's attitude changed abruptly and he appeared to lose some of his reptilian cunning. "You shall describe to me exactly what your patron wishes and I shall have it drawn for you in beautiful detail."

"And the price?"

"In ink or in colors?"

"There is a difference?"

*"Por supuesto."* He shrugged his shoulders at her ignorance. "The colored ones are far more artistic and," he smiled again, "much more realistic. These in black and white are only for the common trade."

"But the colored ones are more expensive?"

The Moorish ancestry of Spain held a heritage of bargaining in which both sides were prepared to indulge.

"For you, señorita, no! You and your patron are new customers, *si?*" He waited for her nod of agreement. "And I would have you for steady customers. Therefore on your first order I would make a low price, hoping you would find such satisfaction that you would want more and more and more."

"As I probably would," she agreed, knowing that she would never want to see this greasy-haired panderer again.

"Then, señorita, we shall make it very cheap, depending of course on the number of figures."

"Only two."

"Say five *pesetas* and in lifelike colors."

"Two *pesetas*," she countered.

"There is my commission to consider. So shall we say four?"

Rachel advanced her price.

"Three."

He spread the palms of his hands out in a gesture of defeat. "For you, I shall sacrifice my commission. Three it is."

"But there would be more than the mere sketch itself that I would require. It must be delivered and the delivery would take place in the country. It would necessitate the hire of a horse and a person of discretion, like yourself, to deliver it."

"How far from Havana?"

"Three hours to go—three to return," she answered.

"Ten *pesetas* for the hire of a horse and five for my time."

She made a rapid calculation on her fingers.

"Eighteen *pesetas*, all told?"

"And two more for my discretion." The ophidian gleam returned to his eyes.

She had twenty-one *pesetas* hidden in her room. She agreed. "And when will the sketch be finished?"

"Tomorrow at this hour."

"I would inspect it before it is delivered."

"Most certainly, señorita."

"Then I shall meet you here tomorrow with the money."

He concurred with another smile. "And now, señorita, the subject of the sketch."

"Your artist must visualize the most beautiful woman he has ever seen, blonde, with hair the color of spun gold, blue eyes and . . ."

". . . a figure like this?" The fellow's hands outlined a series of airy curves. "The artist is a master with women's figures, señorita."

"Yes, that will be one figure."

"And the other?"

"A Negro, an immense man, young, brutal but not necessarily ugly."

Despite his aplomb, the fellow was momentarily shocked. "A white woman and a Negro? That is a most unusual combination, señorita. I have never had such a request before."

"My patron is a most unusual person."

"Granted! And what position should these two be in?" With his index finger against the little finger of his other hand he was prepared to catalogue a number of various perversions.

Rachel was not interested. "I shall leave that to the artist. His imagination is more fertile than mine. However there must be no doubt but that the woman is white and the Negro strong, young and handsome. And then I would like an inscription lettered on the bottom. Can you remember it?"

*"Si, señorita."*

*"Cuando el gato va, entonces iran a jugar los ratoncitos."*

He replaced his sketches in the leather envelope and looked up at Rachel. The tip of his tongue protruded from his teeth and his eyes opened wide.

"The situation becomes apparent, señorita. When the cat is away, the mice most certainly do play. And such delightful little games they play—that big black rat and that pretty little white mouse. Ah, señorita, and can you blame them? What woman in her right mind would not rather have one of us instead of a white? If this beautiful blonde *dama* with the blue eyes should tire of her black boy, perhaps you could recommend me. I have been well trained, señorita, and I would know some tricks her black boy has not taught her."

"Undoubtedly you would, *hombre.*" Rachel was trying hard not to show her abhorrence because the fellow was necessary to her and she must insure his good will. "It is possible that I could recommend you after this one has been disposed of."

He closed one eye slowly. "And the address to which this work of art will be delivered?"

"Tomorrow," she said, "after I have seen the picture."

# chapter xvi

WHEN DON CÉSAR returned to the big house for his midday meal and siesta, he was met by an excited house slave with a packet in his hand, which he proudly handed to his *amo*. The arrival of any communication at Montalvo was quite an event and don César was puzzled by the shape and size of the packet. It was thin and square and stiff, much larger than a letter, and enveloped in a piece of white paper, now soiled by sweaty finger marks. Each end was sealed with blobs of red wax which bore no identifying crest. That he might give its contents his uninterrupted attention, he took it into his study, raised the *persianas* to flood the room with sunlight and sat down at his desk. With a sharp knife, he slit the wrappings to find another wrapping of thinner paper inside. *Caramba!* It must be something precious! Another slit of the knife and the picture was exposed. As he looked at it, his hands shook. He gasped—a quick indrawing and expulsion of breath—and he jumped up to carry it to the window for closer inspection.

The unknown artist had done a most professional piece of work. The pearly tinted body lay across the bed. The head with staring blue eyes dulled and blinded by sexual ecstasy, hung over the edge of the mattress, and the gold hair swept the floor. The woman's hands clutched with frantic urgency at the huge Negro above her whose head was thrown back in a rapturous agony of unbridled animal lust. The woman was far more beautiful than Alix and the Negro more of an idealized Hercules than Tamboura but don César immediately recognized what the drawing implied. His certainty was corroborated by the words at the bottom. So . . . the mice were playing while the cat was away! *Por Dios!* What a game they played.

The picture revolted him yet excited him. It was impossible to look at it without a surge of stimulation. Its voluptuously limned debauchery fascinated him even while his mind refused to accept what was so deliberately suggested. He carried the drawing back to his desk and propped it up before him to study it further. Could the message that it implied possibly be true? Who had sent it? A frantic examination of the wrappings revealed nothing and a hasty questioning of the slave who had received it gave no clue to the identity of the messenger who had delivered it.

No, it couldn't be true! He could never believe it of Alix; she was too fine, too wonderful, too loving. Why, she hated Negroes; feared them; could not even abide to have them near her. She had suffered so much from them in St. Domingue. His memory prompted him. Ah, but she had insisted that Tamboura was different. Tamboura, she had claimed, was the only male slave she would have in the house. She had even admitted that Tamboura was handsome. Well, he was! His male perfection was enough to negate his color. But it could not be true. *Caramba!* It just could not be true!

*Verdad,* there were some who did not want him to marry Alix. Among them, who could have sent this cursed thing? He ticked them off on his fingers. Gregorio? Yes, Gregorio stood to lose much by his coming marriage and had been bitter about it. But Gregorio had never been to the house on Colon Street. He could not possibly know what Alix had been doing. The Mendoza aunt? She lived next door to Alix and she might have seen something or heard about it from slaves' gossip. It would be like Tia Maria to do such a thing and even though her house presented a totally blank wall to Alix' she might have had a spying slave on the roof to observe Alix and Tamboura. But where would old Tia Maria, practically housebound these last few months, obtain a picture like this? Then who else? Who else might know about such a liaison? Alix' servant Rachel? No, according to Alix the woman was madly enamored of Tamboura and she would not want to destroy him. Omo and M'dong? Tamboura might have confided in them.

He rang for a slave and when the boy appeared, he sent him scurrying for M'dong and Omo. Don César questioned them closely regarding Tamboura, without trying to bring Alix into it. The boys preserved blank faces. Although they were trembling within, for they were quite aware of the trend of the *amo's* questioning, the very evasiveness of their answers convinced don César that they were stupid and knew nothing.

Like most men in his position, he had a few enemies in

Havana. It must be one of them who was aware of Alix' household and was merely trying to ruin her and don César's happiness at the same time. He told himself he was convinced of her innocence and that the picture was pure libel. But a serious charge like this demanded investigation. Certainly no greater calumny could be imagined against a white woman than to accuse her of relations with a slave.

He dispatched Omo and M'dong to saddle their horses, and clapped his big hat on his head to leave the house. As he reached the door of his study, he turned back to take a small pistol, scarcely larger than the palm of his hand, from the drawer of his desk and stuck it in his sash. There was a brace of pistols on his saddle but the smaller one was easier to hide. If there was nothing to the libel—as he was certain there wasn't—he would appear rather foolish, stalking into Alix' house with drawn pistols.

They did not stop to rest during the entire ride to Havana and they entered the gates before the siesta hours were over. The shops were still shuttered and the streets deserted. As they approached the corner of Colon Street, don César dismounted, handed the reins to Omo and bade the two of them follow quietly on foot with the horses, then wait inside the stable until he called them. As he turned into the alley behind the house he quickened his pace, and when he reached the stable door he took the key which Alix had given him from his pocket, unlocked the door and opened it stealthily, so that it would make no noise on its hinges.

Inside, he passed the two carriage horses in their stalls and the hooded *volante,* and crept over to the ladder that led to the second floor. As his head appeared above the floor, he could see that the loft was deserted. But he scarcely expected to find Tamboura here, now that he and Rachel shared the bedroom on the third floor. Alix had said she felt safer with the slaves in the house, within calling distance. Through the small barred window, he had a clear view of the patio. Its midday somnolence was undisturbed. Nothing moved except a brilliant blue butterfly which hovered over the roses.

Alix must be sleeping in her bedroom on the second floor. He hoped. He went down the ladder and out into the alleyway. M'dong and Omo were tying the horses and he summoned them inside to wait. With Omo's help, he divested himself of the heavy boots he had been wearing in the fields, and in his stocking feet he passed into the kitchen. Lifting the drapery, he noted that Rachel's room was vacant, the sheet smoothly stretched on the bed. Good! This indicated that she and Tamboura must be together on the third floor. His feet made no noise on the tiles of the patio or up the first flight of stairs. The door of the *sala* was open and he slipped in, avoiding the little tables filled with bibelots, until he came to Alix's bedroom. Much to his surprise, he saw Rachel, laying out a dress for her mistress on the bed. She looked up at him and her face blanched with fear, but he did not question her.

"Keep quiet," he warned her. "Do not move from this room. Make the slightest sound and I'll send you to the whips."

So, it was true! Instead of Rachel and Tamboura on the floor, it must be Alix and Tamboura. He raced up the stairs, along the *balcon* to the back and flung open the door of the rear chamber. For a long moment he stood there, transfixed in horror. Even though he was conscious of what his eyes saw, his mind refused to believe it. They were sleeping; Tamboura snoring flat on his back, his skin dewed with sweat, while Alix lay cuddled in the crook of his arm, her hand resting in bold whiteness against the black of his belly. How long he stood there he did not know, but each moment served to imprint the picture more indelibly on his mind in every startling detail. Now he knew who had sent the picture. It was Rachel, consumed by jealousy because Alix had taken Tamboura away from her. The shock that had swept over him when he first saw them gave way to a violent paroxysm of rage, but he managed to restrain himself.

Alix moved in her sleep, snuggled closer to Tamboura and her hand slid down his belly. She opened her eyes slowly, her lips seeking the purple paps of Tamboura's chest. She raised her head, shifting her position to shake her hair from her face and saw don César in the doorway. For a second that seemed like eternity, they looked at each other; then she was out of the bed and across the floor, on her knees before him, her arms wrapped around his legs.

"César, you have answered my prayers. You have come! Oh, *querido*, if you could but know what I have suffered, the agonies I have endured from that brute. He lured me up here, César, and then," she lost her words in hysterical sobs, "and then . . . he raped me."

"No, Alix." Don César spoke calmly though it cost him an effort to do so. "A woman who has been raped does not lie in her rapist's arms and try to excite him by further endearments to a second ravishment." He pushed her away from him but she still clung to him.

"I was out of my mind with fear, César! Mad! I was afraid. Fighting for time! I knew he would kill me if I didn't play up to him. He threatened me, César."

He ignored her.

"Tamboura!" His shout at the still sleeping Negro was heard by M'dong and Omo in the stables. "Tamboura!" He walked towards the bed, dragged the clinging Alix along the floor.

Tamboura jerked upright to a sitting position. He was too stunned to speak. He saw don César towering over him and Alix on the floor, her hands clutching like talons at don César's legs.

*"Amo."* Tamboura did not realize that he spoke.

"You are going to die, Tamboura. Do you know that?" An ominous tranquillity cloaked don César's anger. His words were no more impassioned than if he were telling Tamboura he was to go to the stable and saddle the horses.

Tamboura hung his head; he could not look in his *amo's* eyes.

"Must I, *amo?"*

"You must, but first I would know one thing and you must tell me the truth, Tamboura, for you do not want to die with a lie on your spirit."

"No, *amo."*

"Then tell me, how long has this been going on?"

"From the first day I came here, *amo."*

"Did you force your mistress to submit to you?"

"No, *amo."*

Don César shoved Alix away from him so violently that she fell back on the floor. He looked at her lying there, her hair spread out on the tiles, her face puffy from tears, and that white flesh which had once seemed so desirable now repulsed him. Her lips had tasted a Negro's lips. Her hands had caressed a Negro's flesh. During all these past months, the same lips had touched his, the same hands had fondled him.

"Get off the bed, Tamboura. Stand up!"

Slowly Tamboura rose. "What are you going to do to me, *amo?"*

"Eventually I am going to kill you, but not now." He whipped the pistol from his belt and fired at Tamboura. The sharp crack of the explosion brought a shriek from Alix.

A small hole appeared in Tamboura's belly and a red gush of blood spurted out onto the bed.

"You have hurt me, *amo.*" Tamboura gave Don César one anguished look, then clutched his belly and howled in pain.

"You will be hurt more. Walk!" Don César pointed to the door. Tamboura stumbled, crouched low, his hands encarmined from the wound in his stomach. He managed to reach the door, then fell across the threshold.

"Rachel!" Don César had caught sight of her face peering through the balustrade from the staircase below. "Summon M'dong and Omo. Quick!" He straddled the figure of Tamboura on the floor and reloaded his pistol. He turned to Alix.

"I shall not kill you. You are not worth the lead in this bullet and it would only be wasted. There are no words to describe what you are. The most disreputable white whore on the streets of the city, who spreads her legs for a couple of copper *centavos,* is better than you for even she would not take a nigger. You deserve to be shot more than this poor boy here for you knew what you were doing and the poor, stupid slave did not. But I shall have to make an example of him so that every other nigger in Havana will know what it means to lie with a white woman." He aimed the pistol slowly at Tamboura again. There was another shot and another spurt of blood came from a hole in Tamboura's arm.

M'dong and Omo had heard the shots and came running up the stairs. Rachel did not return with them. They stopped short at the sight of don César, astraddle Tamboura, calmly loading his pistol while Tamboura howled and the naked white woman on the floor shrieked and sobbed.

"Take him!" don César said. "Put him on a horse. Tie his hands to the pommel of the saddle. Prepare to ride with me."

"He has no clothes on, *amo.*" M'dong with one eye on the pistol stooped down to raise Tamboura.

"He is dying, *amo.*" Omo helped to lift the moaning Tamboura, who was writhing in pain.

"He will not need clothes where he is going and he will live until we get there. Take him!"

With Tamboura's arms over their shoulders, his feet dragging on the tiles, they supported him along the *balcon,* leaving a red trail behind them. Don César started after them.

"César!" Alix struggled to her knees. "César, César, believe me, he lied. Believe me, César, believe me! Do not take a slave's word against mine. Oh, what will become of me?"

"That, *puta,* is the least of my worries. I shall return here in an hour or so. Do not force your presence on me then. If I see you I shall surely kill you and I would not have it said that I murdered a woman, regardless of how low she was. Have your maid attend me when I return."

Step by step, Omo and M'dong, their own hearts heavy, carried Tamboura down the stairs. At the foot, they waited for don César. He preceded them across the patio, into the stable door and with merely a nod of his head, he indicated one of the stable horses. "Put a bridle on him, Omo, and ride him bareback."

He watched as they carried Tamboura outside and hoisted him into the saddle of Omo's horse. Don César tore one of the reins from the harness on the wall and handed the leather strap to them to bind Tamboura's wrists to the saddle. Tamboura, slumped over the horse's neck, had fainted. Don César picked up a bucket of water and sloshed it over him. He revived and resumed his howling. Don César mounted his horse, M'dong his, and Omo jumped up onto the unsaddled carriage horse.

They rode slowly down the alley, don César first, then the three abreast with Tamboura in the center. His screams continued and he had now reached a delirium of pain in which he reverted to Hausa.

"Oh my spirit, my spirit! Come to me and give me strength! Come to me and save me! My spirit that I left in Africa, join my spirit here and help me."

They turned from the alley into the street. Passersby stopped to look at the grim face of don César and the three Negroes behind him. Their attention was focused on the naked slave in the middle, tied to the saddle, blood pouring from the wounds in his body, his head slumped to his chest, his howls now losing their high-pitched intensity. Ay! here was a spectacle they did not see every day! They followed the procession and were soon joined by more of the curious, the idle, and the morbid thrill-seekers.

Tamboura's howls ceased. He had fainted again, and now his body slipped from the saddle, turning it with his weight. M'dong made to lift Tamboura back but don César would not allow it and for the rest of the way to the waterfront, his half-dead body dragged on the cobbles. The hours of the siesta were over and the crowd continued to grow until by the time the gruesome cavalcade had reached the public whipping yard, a line some two blocks long extended behind the four horses. Don César paused at the gates of the yard and turned in his saddle, raising himself high in the stirrups.

"Men of Havana, regard this slave," he pointed to the body of Tamboura, covered with blood and the filth of the streets. "And you slaves of Havana, regard him and remember him. He raped a white woman."

A slave inside the walls had heard the commotion outside and opened the gates. As don César, followed by the three horses, rode through, the slave would have closed the gate but don César stopped him.

"This is for the public," he said. "Go, tell the *azotador* to bring his heaviest whip. He is to whip this slave to death."

"He is not dead now, *amo?*" The slave regarded the battered form of Tamboura.

"I think not. Omo, M'dong, cut him free and carry him to the post."

Tamboura was not dead. He whimpered as they lifted him and his eyes opened.

"M'dong." Tamboura's voice was scarcely audible.

"*Adios,* Tamboura."

"*Adios,* Tamboura," Omo repeated.

They dragged him across the courtyard and with the help of the slave, they fastened his wrists in the manacles high up on the post and then stepped back. Another slave appeared, an enormous black, with both ears cut off close to his head. In one hand he carried a coil of black whip. He regarded the crowd and then don César.

"On whose orders do I whip this slave?"

"On the order of César Montalvo."

"He will not survive the whip, señor."

"He is not supposed to. Whip him until you are sure there is no life in him."

"And then?"

"Dispose of his body as you do others who die under the whip."

"There is a charge for disposing of the body, señor."

Don César reached in his pocket and flipped a piece of silver to the whip-master.

The big black strode to the platform where Tamboura hung from the post. His huge right arm was lifted high over his head. Then the coils of the whip snaked out to wrap around

Tamboura's back. He was alive but the scream that came from him was weak—a feeble falsetto.

Slowly Tamboura sank into a vast red cobweb of pain. The pain in his belly and the pain in his arm were as nothing compared to the pain that was eating into his back with slow, regular bites that were ripping his flesh away. Everything turned red—a brilliant flaming scarlet. He struggled to open his eyes and even the wooden post glowed like a piece of red-hot iron. He closed his eyes, never to open them again. The pain had become a living thing, tearing his flesh, penetrating his every fiber. He tried to scream but no sounds came. Again and again and again the whip caught him and in his pain, he saw the wide, sunburned savannahs of Africa, glowing red under a dying sun. A lion, vermilion bright against the red plains, stood poised. The lion leaped. Tamboura knew that the lion had seized his spirit and that he was dying. He welcomed death for he knew that his spirit had returned to the lion. There was no strength left in him to take another breath. He was dead.

Tamboura was dead but the blows on his back did not stop. They continued until don César lifted his hand.

"He is dead?" he asked the whip-master.

"He cannot be alive, but I will make sure." He coiled the whip and walked over to the bloody mass of meat that had once been Tamboura. His fingers clutched Tamboura's wool and pulled the head back. Tamboura's eyes were closed and the black fingers opened the eyelids. Then he wrapped one mighty arm around Tamboura's neck and twisted. When he released it, the head dangled awkwardly from the shoulders.

"He is surely dead now, señor."

Don César turned his horse and motioned to Omo and M'dong to follow him. The crowd parted silently to let them through and don César led M'dong and Omo along the waterfront. He dismounted in front of a cantina and went into the back of the wine shop where they could see him talking to a man inside. In a few moments, he reappeared.

Again M'dong and Omo followed him, back to the house on Colon Street. This time they halted their horses before the main entrance. Don César dismounted and spoke to Omo.

"Go to the stable and bring the other carriage horse here. We lead them both back to Montalvo." He entered the unlocked gate.

Rachel was waiting for him, standing stiff and straight in the middle of the patio.

"Madame craves a word with you." She looked directly at him.

"If she values her life, she will keep out of my sight." He looked up to see a billow of skirt retreat from the railing of the *balcon*. "You will both quit this house and this city before night. You are free to take your clothing. There are two ships sailing from Havana at sunset. One goes to Vera Cruz in Mexico, the other goes to New Orleans in Louisiana. It matters not which one you take, your passage is guaranteed on either one of them." He reached in his pocket and emptied it of all the money that was inside. There were several gold pieces, some silver, and a few copper coins. He handed them to Rachel.

"These are yours," he said and he looked at her searchingly. "You and I both know the little game the mice played while the cat was away. *Verdad?*"

She bowed her head.

"I am grateful to you." He turned and walked out of the patio, closing the iron-grilled gate behind him, put his foot into the stirrup and called for M'dong and Omo to follow him.

"Tamboura is dead," he said. "What a stupid waste of the best slave in Cuba."

"Tamboura is dead," M'dong repeated the words to Omo.

"Tamboura is dead," Omo echoed sadly.

## chapter xvii

ALIX WAITED in the shadows of the *balcon* until she heard the patio gate close. She ran down the stairs, dressed in her most elaborate gown. She could not believe that César was gone and would not see her again. She had been so certain she could patch matters up with a little acting—at first contrite and pathetic, then rising to a righteous indignation that he could so much as suspect her, and in the end forgiving him. Now he had left, without a word to her.

"What did he say," she demanded of Rachel.

"He said that we must leave Havana tonight. There are two ships—one leaves for Mexico and one for New Orleans. You have your choice."

"What does it matter?" Alix could weep now without thought of spoiling the elaborate maquillage she had used to hide the ravages of her earlier tears.

"They speak French in New Orleans," Rachel prompted her.

"And we must leave here?"

"We must."

"Then let us go to New Orleans. I am sick of these damned Spaniards. Aie, what more can happen to me?"

"Nothing, madame, I am here to protect you."

"But there is something you cannot protect me from. Something nobody can protect me from."

Rachel took her mistress in her arms and consoled her with soft pattings and sympathetic cluckings.

"Nothing can harm madame with me here."

"But oh, Rachel." Alix clung tightly to her. "You don't know the worst. All that has happened is as nothing. I'm going to have a baby, Rachel, a baby! Do you understand? A black bastard of a baby. I'm already nearly three months pregnant. I've visited three *abortistas,* but they have failed. The little black bastard grows inside me. Damn that Tamboura, damn him, damn him, damn him! When I was with him, he made me forget everything else. I took no precautions. Oh, Rachel, what shall I do?"

"Hush, madame," Rachel's moment had arrived. Alix was hers. "I will arrange everything. From the moment we step foot on the ship, you will become an invalid, keeping to your cabin. When we arrive in New Orleans, you will be carried off the ship on a litter and we shall seek some quiet boarding house or a little house of our own. As far as everyone else is concerned, you will be ill—bedridden—and I shall be your nurse. Gradually I shall pad my dresses until there will be no doubt in anyone's mind that I am *enceinte*. You will have to depend on me to be your midwife but I shall make the acquaintance of one in New Orleans and learn her methods from her. Then, when the child is born, you can pass it off as mine. I shall be its mother and you will miraculously recover." She clasped Alix tighter. "Aie! we shall be happy together, madame. What delicious little meals I shall prepare for you and we shall play *écarte* and *rouge et noir*. You will read books to me and I shall embroider for you."

"But what shall we use for money?"

"See, madame, don César gave me this." Rachel held out her hands with the coins.

"Bah! A paltry sum!" Alix looked at the meager gold and silver. "Is that all I earned in these many months?" She brightened. "But I have my jewels—the parure of diamonds, the necklace of opals. And I still have those I brought from St. Domingue."

"We shall make out, madame, never fear. And now I must attend to packing our clothes. Don César said we might take them."

"Well I should hope so! And more than our clothes. There are many valuables belonging to the Montalvo family in the house. Pack them with the rest of the things—the big silver coffee urn, the spoons, the amber and ivory crucifix, the silver statue of the Madonna. Strip the house of everything of value. César owes me that much. Come! Perhaps it is all for the best. At least one problem is solved. I shall not present him with a black child. Come, Rachel."

Alix started up the stairs. Halfway up she stopped to pick something up. It was a wad of cloth, still damp from Tamboura's sweat.

"He set great store by this," she said to herself. "He said that as long as he wore it, his spirit would never depart from him." She rolled the shapeless wad in her hand, then lifted it to her nose and sniffed it. For a second she was back in Tamboura's arms.

Perhaps for the first time in her life, Alix wept tears that were not for herself.

"Tamboura," she whispered, "Oh Tamboura. I think I loved you. I don't want your little black bastard, Tamboura. Already I hate it. But if it is a boy, I shall name him Drum and I shall give him this."

# book two

## chapter i

On the morning of April 22, 1820, the French-Spanish-American-Creole city of New Orleans was in a gala mood—a mood always easy for this mercurial city to adopt. The decorations left over from the recent Mardi Gras were once more tacked up on the house fronts, wound through the iron lace balconies and refurbished with leaves of palmetto, garlands of flowers and oleographs of General Andrew Jackson. The victor of the Battle of New Orleans, which had been fought only six years ago, was again passing through the city with his wife Rachel—en route to Florida, so recently a colony of Spain, to become the governor of that new addition to the United States. It was an occasion for celebration in all New Orleans and the city was ready to do homage to the lanky general and his rotund wife. That he had been hated by some and extolled by others made little difference now. New Orleans was no longer either French or Spanish—it was American, a part of the burgeoning United States—and General Jackson was a man high in favor with President Monroe in Washington.

New Orleans was ready to welcome him, although to the old Creole families it was a tongue-in-cheek welcome. Naturally no American, regardless of his position, could compare with their importance in the rigid social structure of New Orleans, but they were willing to do token welcome to any Johnny-come-lately if it meant a day of celebration.

And so the bands played, the militia marched in their fantastic uniforms, and the general and his lady progressed slowly up Orleans Street, turned right on Dauphine, down Dumaine, which was by no means as impressive as Orleans, to Conde and thence back to the Place d'Armes, which was later, had the general but known, to be named after him. The lace-curtained glass coach, which had come down the Mississippi along with the general and his wife, had all its windows open as it rolled slowly along over the cobbles, pelted with flowers and acclaimed by many a hearty *vive.* Some of the watching Creole ladies, of course, whispered the scandal about the general's plump lady who, 'twas said, had been careless about divorcing her first husband before she married Mr. Jackson. Others, glimpsing the plain stuff of her dress through the windows of the coach, waved their fans of Chantilly lace and sniffed at the *mode passée* in which the good lady was dressed. All of them had an invitation for the big ball that night on the upper floor of the French Exchange and each vowed to herself that her elaborate toilette would quite eclipse that of Madame Jackson.

Alix had decorated the long upper balconies of her house on Dumaine Street with a tasteful draping of red, white and blue bunting—how convenient that the Americans used the same colors as the French; and economical too—centered by a wreath of white *immortelles* around the oleograph of Jackson. She and her white girls, dressed in pale blue and pink to complement their unvarying pale-blonde prettiness, were lined up in chairs behind the convoluted grillework on the second floor while Rachel (honored today by having the same name as the general's lady) sat with the quadroon and octoroon girls on the third floor balcony, their olive beauty subtly enhanced by the pale yellow, peach and orange dresses they wore. Indeed, the whole combination made the prettiest of pictures from the street—the pistache-green stuccoed house, the elaborate black lace ironwork of its balconies, the colorful dresses of the girls—a most effective advertisement for Alix's prospering business. The girls were all beautiful, perhaps the most beautiful in New Orleans; it would be difficult to tell which were the loveliest, the pale beauties on the second floor or those of richer coloring on the third. But there could be no doubt in any man's mind that they were all superb. Alix had seen to that. *Par consequent!* They were her livelihood and the source of her many dollars.

*Vraiment,* neither Alix nor any of the girls in her house had received an invitation to the official ball at the French Exchange. Alix hardly expected one, for long ago she had dropped any pretension to being a French countess, since her profession excluded her from the possibility of taking a place in society. But although the Creole aristocracy of New Orleans might resent her appearance at the ball, she could take comfort from her knowledge that after midnight, when the gay beaux had dutifully escorted their dull wives and virginal sweethearts home, these same men would head straight for the *de Vaux Académie de Musique,* as Alix called her house—though the French referred to it as *Le Bordel de Madame Alix;* the Spanish as *La Casa de la gran Puta;* and the more matter-of-fact Americans simply as that whore-house on Dumaine Street. Alix cared not a picayune what others called her house as long as they came and brought their gold pieces with them. Yes, Gold Pieces! The tiny dollar gold piece was her entrance fee—to keep out the barbarous Kaintucks, she explained. Should a man desire to listen to the strains of the particular music for which the girls of the house were celebrated, he paid in twenty-dollar gold double-eagles. It was rarely that Alix extended credit. The music her girls made was never ordinary; it was worth every penny of the fee.

The sound of the military band down the street heralded the arrival of the parade and the girls leaned forward on the balcony as Alix had instructed; it gave those in the street below a better opportunity to appraise their beauty, not to mention the city's most voluptuous bosoms. On the arrival of the governor's coach, the girls tossed their bouquets down into the street, the multicolored ribbands which tied them flowing out in whirling streamers. It was indeed so pretty a sight that the naive Rachel—the general's wife, not the Rachel on the upper balcony, for she was certainly not naive—smiled and waved gaily to the assembled ladies, only to be reproved by a look from the general who knew from his former visit that the de Vaux Academy of Music was far more than its innocent name implied. But Alix was quite satisfied. She had been rewarded with a smile from Mrs. Jackson, which was more than many had received. She sank back in her chair, making a mental note of her clients as they passed—the young Armand du Plessis on horseback and following him, Jean Bellefleur of Bellefleur Plantation. Ah! there was Jacques Montpelier of Beauclair Plantation and there, that silvery-haired man in the carriage, the old Marquis de Thurville who, although now an American citizen, refused to give up his title. Mr. Edward Livingston passed on horseback and the fabulously wealthy Mr. Clark in a carriage. Pablo Hernandez, his adolescent face somewhat matured by long black sideburns, stole a glance at the third floor as he passed and Alix saw the adoring expression in his eyes as he looked up at her Renée-Rose on the top balcony. Lazare Le-Toscan, who was supposed to be the handsomest beau in the city, cared so little for convention that he looked up at Alix and waved gaily to her, and his companion, Bernard de Marigny, who had insisted on purchasing her octoroon girl, Clotilde, last year, acknowledged Alix' presence with a fillip of his riding whip. Most of her clients, however, passed the gaily decorated Academy of Music without even a glance in its direction, especially those who were riding in carriages with their wives. The girls were most discreet. Even though they might have released a man from their arms only a few hours ago that very morning, they permitted him to pass with no sign of recognition. One had only to compare their charms with those of the lady who sat beside her husband in the carriage to realize why he had sought their company.

One of the most elegant equipages in the procession belonged to Dominique You, the former lieutenant of the infamous Lafitte brothers. He, now turned eminently respectable in his elder years, was so impervious to the comments of his fellow citizens that he not only bowed and smiled to Alix but cupped his hands and shouted up to her.

"Must see you. Three o'clock?"

She glanced at her jeweled watch on its chain of diamonds and nodded acceptance. It was half after two now—evidently Dominique meant to come directly after the parade broke up. Kind of him, but then she and Dominique were old friends. They had been partners in many a shady deal in the old days when Jean Lafitte, from his blacksmith shop in New Orleans, and his brother Pierre from his Baratarian stronghold, controlled the commerce of the city while Alix pandered to its passions. Now Jean and Pierre had left New Orleans for the island of Campeche off the coast of Texas, and burly old Dominique had given up his pirating to run the prosperous blacksmith shop where much of New Orleans' elaborate ironwork was produced.

As for Alix, what cared she for respectability? She had buried all such claims when she left Havana with a black child in her womb. Now she was content to insist solely on the "Academy of Music" sign that hung over the banquette. *Damne!* Hers was not a whorehouse in the accepted sense of the word. Her elegant establishment was not to be compared with the broken-down cribs along the levee. On that one note of pseudo-respectability she insisted. To hell with the rest.

She relaxed in her chair. The parade was over and Onésime might as well remove the bunting and fold it up. She must tell him to save the picture of Jackson as the general might return sometime and it would save the expense of getting another. It hadn't been much of a parade after all. She had seen many in the twenty years that had elapsed since she arrived in New Orleans from Havana. There had been Spanish parades and French parades and American parades. Even the Duc d'Orléans had once ridden by in an open carriage and later had come to her Academy for a little concert by a quartet of her most beautiful quadroon girls. But the stingy duke had not left a centime in payment, although she could always point to an elaborate bed in one of her second-floor rooms and tell its occupant for the night that royal Bourbon flesh had once slept there, if sleep he could with four of her *filles de couleur* for company.

The girls would have lingered longer on the balcony, watching the passersby, for it was rarely that they were accorded such a privilege, but Alix herded her charges back into the house and sent a little slave girl—outside of Onésime there were only female slaves in the house—to tell Rachel to get hers back inside also. There was no reason for them to soil their dresses and besides it was high time they were all in bed resting. There would be little sleep tonight for any of them, with the holiday crowds in town from all the outlying plantations.

It was almost three o'clock and she prepared to hoist herself up from the chair with some difficulty. She had achieved enormous proportions—far too large for her tiny feet and ankles. Who would ever have dreamed that the slender Alix of Havana would ever become this fat tub of a woman? But it didn't matter now. She enjoyed her food. Devil take it, it was all she had to enjoy these days. That was one reason she was getting rid of Onésime. When a woman got as fat as she was, there was little pleasure in bedding oneself with a man. Moreover, Onésime was not the man he used to be, and that was the other reason for getting rid of him.

The door opened and Rachel came out on the balcony. Strange, Alix thought, how the years could have added pounds to her figure and drained them from Rachel's. Rachel was actually gaunt. Her high cheekboned face with its hollowed cheeks, raised on the thin post of her neck emerging from the black stuff of her gown, looked like a copper-colored skull stuck on a pike. Rachel seemed to have no breasts at all under the skimpy material, while she. . . . Alix looked down at the plump melons which overflowed her corsets. *Aie,* Nature had been far too generous.

But Rachel was strong, and she helped her mistress rise from her chair and guided her across the balcony and inside where the shuttered light scintillated in a rich pattern of reflected glints from crystal chandeliers, gold-leafed frames, damask upholsteries and a host of little shining bibelots.

"Should I touch up madame's hair a bit before she lies down?" Rachel reached up a bony hand to tuck a stray lock of the elaborate, brassy coiffure back into place. "The gray is beginning to show through."

Alix brushed the suggestion aside. "No time, *chérie*. Dominique You called up that he would be back here at three. No telling what he wants."

"Something about Drum?" Rachel's impassive face showed a trace of anxiety, her eyes questioning.

"Probably." Alix settled herself in the big chair where she spent most of her time and looked up at Rachel. "He's your son. I've completely forgotten that I ever gave birth to him."

"Well, I have always been a mother to him." The anxiety in Rachel's face disappeared and her features softened. "Except for you, madame, he is the only person I have ever loved. *Mais oui!* I was determined to hate him when I found out he was a boy. I had so hoped he would be a girl. But from the first moment I took him in my arms, so helpless, so little and so dependent on me for everything, I loved him."

"Poor Tamboura," Alix sighed. "*Mon Dieu,* but he was handsome, Rachel. I've never regretted those months I had him. I thought Hercule would take his place and then when I sold him and bought Onésime, I felt sure I had found a substitute for Tamboura, but they were both performers, Rachel, not lovers. And neither of them as handsome as Tamboura."

"Drum is handsomer." Rachel was quick to come to the boy's defense.

"He's lighter anyway," Alix admitted, "and no one could say he isn't handsome, but he lacks something that Tamboura had—his savage nobility."

"If you mean he isn't just an ignorant *bozal* like his fathere, you are right. Drum is far finer, far more sensitive, far more intelligent than that black ape ever was. What do you suppose Monsieur You wants to talk to you about?"

"I'll find out soon enough." A bell jangled below. "That must be Dominique. Don't bother to answer it. Let that lazy

Onésime stir himself. But Rachel, perhaps it would be better if you went upstairs and left Dominique and me to talk together."

Rachel reached the door that led to the narrow passageway overlooking the inside courtyard just as it opened to admit Dominique You. He was an enormous man, his shoulders stretching the seams of his coat. His thick, bushy beard was streaked with gray. Among Alix' dainty furniture and the little tables covered with porcelain bric-a-brac, he loomed even larger. Carefully, so as not to upset anything or to sweep anything off the tables with the skirts of his coat, he picked his way over to the chair where she was sitting.

"Alix, *chérie,*" he greeted her with the informality of an old friend. "You are more beautiful than ever."

"Liar," Alix smiled up at him. "But I love you for it, Dominique. It's nice to hear someone say it, even if it's not true, for my mirror tells me that I'm a fat old woman with nine chins."

"Once a beautiful woman, always a beautiful woman," Dominique replied gallantly. "There have been few in New Orleans to compare with you."

"Rubbish! But still I love you even if you are a liar. Tell me, Dominique, you didn't come all the way to Dumaine Street in the heat of the day to tell me that I am still beautiful." She picked up a little silver bell from the table beside her chair and allowed its tinkle to die away before she spoke again. "You must be thirsty."

"One of Onésime's *frappés* would fix that."

There was a scratch on the door and a little colored girl entered.

"Have Onésime prepare an absinthe frappé and bring it here . . . and hurry." Alix clapped her hands, sending the girl scurrying from the room.

"And now," she settled back in her immense chair, "we shall talk about the weather, about any engaging new scandal you happen to know, or destroy any reputation you wish, while we wait for your drink. Then, after you have been refreshed, we'll talk about the business that has brought you here. Did you hear about the duel Bernard de Marigny fought last night in St. Anthony's Garden with Polycarpe Rosiere?"

"The notices of Polycarpe's funeral were posted on the lamp-posts today but it has been postponed until tomorrow on account of the festivities."

"They'll have to close the coffin or he'll stink." Alix waved her fan languidly. "Bernard's killing off all my best customers. Penelope wept all the morning because she was madly in love with Polycarpe and he had promised her a *petite maison.*"

"Speaking of Marigny," Bernard laughed, "have you heard the latest about our New Orleans' darling? It seems that he challenged that seven-foot giant from Tennessee to a duel, just because the clumsy idiot spilled coffee on his trousers."

"Là, no!" Here at last was a bit of gossip that Alix didn't know and she was always an avid listener for something new.

"Seems the fellow from Tennessee doesn't believe in fighting duels, particularly not with Marigny who always wins, but his friend insisted that he fight. He reminded them that he had the choice of weapons, so he sent word to Marigny that he would fight him with axes, in six feet of water, in the Bayou St. John. Marigny's only five feet seven, you know. When he read the note he burst out laughing, jumped on his horse and rode to the Hotel Royale, found the Tennessean, jumped up on a chair and kissed him on both cheeks. They're the best of friends now."

Another scratching at the door announced the return of the slave and she entered, placed the tall milky drink on its silver tray beside Dominique You and left, again skipping out to the clap of Alix' hands.

"And now, Dominique, old friend, what do you want of me?"

"I'll not mince words, Alix. You sent Drum to me five years ago and had me apprentice him in Jean Lafitte's blacksmith shop. His five years are up—he's twenty today."

"Yes, I know. I've been thinking about it. A house such as mine was no place to bring up a young mulatto whose breeches stuck out straight in front of him every time he looked at one of my girls. And the girls were taking altogether too much interest in him. I caught him in bed with one of them. But perhaps most important of all I wanted him strong with muscles on his body and what better place to procure them than in a blacksmith shop. He certainly would never have had them here, being petted and spoiled by my girls. I had to make a man of him."

"Well, that's certainly been accomplished." Dominique You took a sip of his drink, smacked his lips and nodded with approval. "Nobody can mix drinks like your Onésime."

"He should know. I taught him."

"Yes, Drum's a fine young fellow." Dominique continued. savoring his drink. "An excellent blacksmith and he knows how to do good ironwork. But I'm afraid his breeches still stand straight out whenever he sees a girl."

"All the better for him," Alix smiled indulgently. "Well, you weren't going to mince words, Dominique, and I've side-tracked you onto ironwork and Drum's breeches. Just what did you want?"

"I want to buy him, Alix."

"He's not for sale. Sorry to be so blunt about it, *cher ami,* but there's not enough money in New Orleans to buy him. He's Rachel's son, as you know, and although Rachel is my slave, she is also my good right hand. I couldn't live or run this place without her. She could have had her freedom any day she asked for it these last twenty years, but she wouldn't take it. I've promised her that I'll never sell Drum and I've notarized her freedom papers and Drum's—they're with my will—so neither of them will ever be sold. Now you see why I was so abrupt with you. Drum is positively not for sale."

Dominique You replaced the glass on the silver tray and nodded his head in understanding. "I'm sorry, Alix. He's a fine boy and I like him. Also I need him. I'm working with Mayor Girod on a special project—one that will stun the world—and I need a strong, dependable slave like Drum."

Alix pointed her finger at him and laughed. "You mean the rescue of Napoleon from St. Hélène?" She had already heard of the secret plot. There was little in New Orleans that didn't eventually reach her ears.

"You know?"

" 'Tis common gossip that the big house now being built on the corner of Chartres and St. Louis is intended for Napoleon."

"Yes, that's what it's for. Jean is fitting up a ship in Campeche for the voyage. If anyone can rescue Napoleon, an old pirate like Jean can do it. And do you know about the tunnel, too?"

Alix was all attention. "The tunnel? No. Tell me?"

"There's going to be a tunnel, stone-lined to keep the water out, leading from the house to the levee. As soon as the emperor arrives, there'll be secret agents from England and France trying to do away with him. The tunnel will be a means of escape. We want nobody to know about it, that's why we are using only trusted slaves to dig it. *Voilà!* Drum! He can be trusted."

"But you'll need money too. I tell you what, Dominique. I'll contribute a thousand dollars to the cause and that will buy you two slaves to take the place of Drum. I need him here. I've sold Onésime."

"Sold Onésime? *Mon Dieu,* Alix! How will you get along without him? His drinks! To say nothing of his famous performances!"

"He *was* an attraction, Dominique. Merely *was!* You and I do not realize how fast time goes. When I sold Hercule and bought Onésime, that was ten years ago. There wasn't a handsomer buck in all Louisiana. He's light for a *griffe.* Whenever he was asked to perform, he did a wonderful job. But ten years, Dominique! Ten years, and Onésime is not as upstanding today as he used to be. Lately it's taken a diet of oysters spiced with Spanish fly to get him into condition for even an adequate performance. The other night, when Lazare LeToscan was entertaining a group of friends from upriver, he insisted that Onésime put on his famous act. . . ."

"The one you invented?"

"The same! It was my idea and every other brothel in New Orleans has copied it but they don't compare with the original."

"And what happened?"

"La!" Alix threw up her hands in mock horror. "Nothing, absolutely nothing! I was so embarrassed. All of the men started laughing and there was poor Onésime standing there at the most crucial moment, as limp as a wet rope. I had to return LeToscan's hundred dollars. Then and there I decided to sell Onésime to young Wurtzbourg whose only interest in life is liquor and. . . ." She shrugged her shoulders. "Onésime *can* mix wonderful drinks."

"He can, indeed." Dominique You drained the rest of his glass. "And you propose to use Drum in Onésime's place?"

"If he is adequate. I've not examined him since he was fifteen but at that time he seemed to show real promise."

"You won't be disappointed." He hesitated. "And will Drum take over all of Onésime's duties?" He lowered his head and looked at her out of the corner of his eyes, immediately regretting what he had said. His face suddenly turned a violent red. He could have bitten off his tongue for speaking.

Alix burst out laughing. "Why you old fool, Dominique. Blushing! At your age! If you mean the common gossip that's been going on for the last ten years that Onésime sleeps with me. Eh?"

He nodded his head sheepishly.

"Well—" Alix was laughing so hard she had to take her handkerchief to wipe her eyes. "I've never denied it. Never! On the other hand I've never admitted it. Never! You see, old friend," she leaned forward and put one heavily ringed hand on You's knee, "I have no reputation to lose. If New Orleans accused Madame de Marigny of sleeping with her mulatto slave, the very heavens themselves would fall. What a scandal! But if New Orleans accuses Madame Alix of sleeping with her mulatto, it only causes all of New Orleans to talk about me. And when a group of young bloods get together and start talking about me, the next thing they know is that they are all heading for my house. It's good business, you see. So I have never denied it or admitted it. But I'll tell you, in strictest confidence, that I do not intend to make a bedmate of Drum. When you get as old and as fat as I am, Dominique, the only satisfactory bed companions are a box of French chocolates, a book and one's memories." She sighed and patted his knee.

He sighed in agreement. "It's hell getting old, Alix. I remember back in the days when Jean and Pierre were at Barataria. Every likely wench on every ship we captured sooner or later came to my bed. Now. . . ." He patted her hand and stood up. "I'll leave, Alix. Don't bother to have me shown out. I know the way after these many years."

"Then you'll send Drum to me tomorrow?"

"He's nothing to wear except his work clothes. But he's done enough work for me during the last five years. I can dress him up for you."

"It is your suggestion, Dominique. I have not asked you, but if you are going to dress him, dress him as well as Bastille Croquère, the quadroon fencing master. They say he's the handsomest and best-dressed man in New Orleans. From now on, Drum should have that distinction."

"Agreed, but give me a week to have his clothes made. I'll guarantee you that he'll outshine Bastille." He offered her his big hand and she heaved herself up from her chair. Then with her arm around his waist, she walked with him to the door.

"I'll grant the week. Wurtzbourg will have to wait for

Onésime. You've been a good friend, Dominique, since those first difficult days when I arrived in New Orleans from Havana."

"I'd have married you then, Alix, if you'd have had me."

"And lucky for you I didn't. You'd have had one hell of a life with me as Madame You." She squeezed his hand and saw him out.

## chapter ii

ONÉSIME AWOKE with a start. The bright, mid-morning sun was flooding his tiny room in the *garconnière*—that two-story wooden structure which stood in every courtyard to house slaves below and bachelor sons above. He looked questioningly at the bell which was even now jangling faintly on its coiled spring. Who could be ringing madame's front door bell—the small bell in his room was hooked to the big bell in the porte-cochere—at the ungodly hour of ten o'clock in the morning? Tradesmen and slaves always came to the rear door and nobody, certainly nobody in all New Orleans, would be a customer at this hour. Not one of the girls would be up and madame would just now be having her morning chocolate. *Aie!* what a night last night! He was glad madame had sold him. He just couldn't satisfy any more, try as he might.

He rolled out of the narrow cot and grabbed the cotton trousers which were in a heap on the floor. Onésime was a big man, darkly negroid but handsome in a brutish way. His once flat belly was already showing a layer of fat and his years at the Academy of Music had creased his face with heavy lines and given him puffy bags under his eyes. Without waiting to put on shirt or shoes, he slipped out the door, down the narrow flight of wooden stairs, which he had to negotiate sideways, because of his wide shoulders, and across the courtyard, choosing the side where the sun had dried and warmed the flagging for his bare feet. Once again the bell pealed out and he saw Rachel's prim black dress, approaching the second-floor balcony.

"Answer that bell, you lazy nigger," she called down, her own curiosity making her voice petulant. "We're not getting rid of you any too soon. Hurry! Move! Shake the dead lice off'n you."

He glared up at Rachel with whom he had carried on a feud of long standing. "Shut up, you ol' black crow," he muttered, but quickened his step and passed into the cool shadows of the deep porte-cochere, the carriage entrance that led from the street to the courtyard. For a moment he fumbled with the bolts of the little door in the carriage gate. When he got it open, he was surprised to see an extremely handsome, young, bright-skinned mulatto, dressed in the height of fashion, standing outside.

"What yo' want, boy?" Onésime lapsed into Gombo—that colloquial French patois which the slaves had so bastardized that it had very little relation to its parent language.

"And what do you think I want, you goddamned *griffe?"* The answer came back in perfectly accented French. "When a man rings the bell, he usually desires admittance, *hein?* And stop speaking Gombo to me. You know French."

"Niggers like as yo' go roun to de back do'." Onésime cast a disparaging look at the young fellow, making a quick note of his light-bronze color. Onésime being a *griffe* with less white blood than a mulatto enjoyed any opportunity to insult one whiter than himself. *"Tapé couri,"* he continued in Gombo and jerked his thumb down the street while he made a motion to close the door. But the toe of a varnished boot made an entering wedge and a fist in a lemon-colored kid glove shot out, catching the unsuspecting Onésime just under the jaw. He fell, and the young mulatto stepped over him, inside the porte-cochere, and closed the door behind him. The varnished boot caught Onésime in the groin and he sat up, howling.

"Niggers like you better keep a civil tongue in their heads," the young fellow grinned, caressing his kid-gloved right hand with the left. "Now get up, stop your bawling and announce me to madame. Shame on you! Does she permit you to go around here half dressed?"

"Yes, man." Onésime wagged his head. "Sometimes I all dressed, sometimes I dressed like this, sometimes I buck nekkid. I 'nounce you." He struggled to his feet and took a closer look at the stranger. "I knows you, man! You Drum! How come you all dressed up so pretty like and what you mean hittin' Onésime? Man, I dandled you on my lap when you nothin' mo' dan a skinny li'l runt. How come yo' so damn uppity now? Yo' nothin' but a slave same's me. Yo' want to see yo' mama o' yo' wan' see Madame Alix?"

"Madame first, then my mother." Drum pulled a white linen handkerchief from his sleeve to flick the dust from his boot. But as it seemed this might soil the kerchief, he replaced it and calmly proceeded to rub his boots up and down Onésime's cotton-clad legs. "Whew! You're damn musky, man. Don't you ever take a bath?"

"Didn't get to bed till five this mornin', then you wakes me at ten. No time to wash me. *Tapé couri.* You knows de way here, you live here long 'nough when you's a boy. You allays was a mean bastard, Drum."

"And always will be, I reckon," Drum grinned.

The voices had brought Rachel down the stairs and into the courtyard. Now, as Drum stepped out from the obscurity of the passage into the full sunlight, she recognized him and ran across the flagging, her arms outstretched to welcome him. Tall as she was, she came only to his shoulders.

His air of bravado disappeared as he hugged her, lifting her feet from the stones and swinging her until she beat his chest with her hands.

"Drum! Drum boy!" Rachel proved that she could smile and even laugh. "Put me down, put me down! Whatever would the girls here think if they saw me being hugged by a handsome young fellow like you?"

"Not until I kiss you, *maman,*" which he proceeded to do, "and kiss you again. Oh, it's so good to see you, *maman,* and to know that I'm going to be with you now. Just seeing you for a few hours once a month hasn't been enough." He lowered her to her feet and leaned down to whisper in her ear, "How's the old hell-cat?"

"Sh-h-h," she cautioned, looking up at him, pleading with her eyes. "Oh, Drum boy, do try to get along with madame. She's good, really she is, and if you just try to get along with her, it will be much easier. You used to aggravate her so before she sent you to Dominique. I was always so afraid she would have you whipped."

"She's an old bitch and you know it, *maman.* She sits up there and gets fatter and richer all the time while you do all the work and what do you get out of it—one black dress a year."

Rachel laid one thin hand tenderly against his cheek. "Drum boy, remember one thing. I am her slave and so are you. She's a woman of many faults and a violent temper but you can handle her if you make it a point always to agree with her. Don't oppose her. She would as soon send you to the whips as look at you and"—she cautioned him to be quiet—"she can do it if she wants to and there's nothing in the world you can do about it. You shouldn't have come to the front door this morning; you shouldn't have hit Onésime; you shouldn't feel, because Dominique You has dressed you up, that you are a free man of color. You aren't, Drum boy, you're just a slave like your mama and if madame wants to, she can sell you tomorrow, just as she has already sold Onésime."

Drum turned to where Onésime was still standing.

"She's sold you, Onésime?"

"She sho has, Drum. I gettin' out jes' as soon as de new masta, M'sieur Wurtzbourg, come to town fur me."

Drum was all repentance. His gloved hand rested for a moment on Onésime's bare shoulder. He spoke softly without his usual bravado and to show his feelings, he spoke in Gombo.

"*Mo triste.* I'm sorry, Onésime. Do you hate to go?"

"*Oui,* Drum. Some ways. I bin here ten year and this my home, but maybe glad to go. Ev'y nigger buck in N'Orleans envious of me 'cause they thinks I lay de white whores ev'y night. M'sieur Wurtzbourg nice man, he is. I mix plenty drinks for him. He say, Onésime, you come by my plantation, you mix drinks, I get drunk all-a time."

"Rachel!" Alix' strident voice called down from the bedroom on the second floor. "What is all this fuss? Come here at once and tell me what's going on."

"We better go, Drum. Madame's all flittery and when she get flittery, all hell to pay." Onésime started back to his own quarters.

Rachel stood back the better to admire Drum. She straightened the heavy black silk stock, brushed a wisp of his hair back from his forehead and then motioned to him to follow her up the flight of wooden stairs along the balcony to the door of Alix' bedroom. They stepped from the brightness of the balcony to the darkness of the room.

"Who was making all that commotion?" Alix was propped up in bed, sipping her chocolate from a tall cup, the crumpled sheets of *L'Ami des Lois,* New Orleans' most scandalous newspaper, on the floor. She peered through the mosquito *baire* to see the two silhouettes in the doorway—the emaciated form of Rachel and the tall broad shoulders of a man behind her. "Who is it, Rachel? Whom are you bringing here? *Mon Dieu,* and me in bed with my hair in curlers."

"It does not matter, madame. It is only Drum."

"Drum? Since when does Drum come ringing my front door bell?"

"Since today, madame." Drum came into the room, a protective arm around Rachel. "The alley behind the house is a foot deep in dust and it hardly seemed fitting for the new clothes that Dominique You gave me to be soiled on the first day I wore them."

"Drum, is that you in all that elegance?" Alix parted the mosquito netting. "Rachel, open the shutters. I must see him."

Rachel crept out from under Drum's arm and ran to the other side of the room. As the shutters opened, Alix pulled back the *baire* entirely. The light of the sun fell full on Drum.

Alix had not seen her son in several months. The last time she had glimpsed him, sitting in the kitchen on one of his monthly Sunday afternoon calls on Rachel, she had hardly noticed him, occupied as she was in raging against the cook. She had been aware that he was a big fellow, with more than average good looks, but in his coarse cotton shirt and baggy breeches, he had failed to impress her. Now, *vraiment,* here was a different fellow. The picturesque raiment Dominique had chosen for him lifted him far above the ordinary.

He wore a bright green broadcloth coat, cut square across the waist, dropping in two long tails behind, almost to the backs of his knees. Its high rolled collar and broad reveres were of pale yellow satin, parting to show a spotless linen shirt. Around his neck was wound a high black silk cravat, tied in a bow in front and embellished with a cameo. Pale-yellow broadcloth trousers, enclosing his legs like the skin of a sausage, were strapped under the instep of high-heeled boots which lifted his height another two inches above the six feet two he stood in his stocking feet. A handkerchief protruded from the cuff of one sleeve and a bracelet of cameos, each the size of a silver dollar, showed on the other wrist. Despite the gay colors and feminine accouterments, there was no doubt of his masculinity. The broad shoulders of the coat had needed no padding, the black cravat was strained around the thick neck and the sash, pulled as tightly as it was, caused no bulge over its top.

Alix looked from the clothes to the face. Once again she saw Tamboura in the short nose, the wide black brows and the sensuous lips, but it was a refined Tamboura with smaller nostrils, narrower lips more prominently curved and, most noticeable of all, glowing skin which approached the color of amber instead of the darker hue of the father. Where Tamboura's kinky wool had separated into tiny peppercorns all over his head, Drum's hair was longer, straighter, and instead of a dull dead black it was lustrous and shining. It grew low on his forehead, and in accordance with the mode of the day he had allowed it to grow far down at the sides, shaving it precisely so that the sharp points extended out onto his cheeks. As Alix studied his face, she was appalled to see a ghost of herself mingled with Tamboura. The high cheekbones of the father were missing and in the contours of Drum's face there was a suggestion of hers. She wondered if anyone else would notice this almost hidden resemblance. It was not probable.

"Come closer, Drum." Alix signaled to Rachel to prop her up higher in the bed with pillows and handed the chocolate cup to her. "Come closer. Stand here where I can get a better look at you. Dominique has kept his word. You are better dressed than Bastille Croquère and, I vow, better looking."

"My clothes were made by Bastille's own tailor." Drum reached out his arm. "I've even got one of Bastille's bracelets and one of his pins. Dominique bought them for me."

"You're goddamned elegant." Alix nodded her head in approval, making a mental calculation of how much she had saved by letting Dominique dress him. "But don't get any notions into your head, Drum. You're here to work. Understand?"

*"Oui, madame."* Drum bowed correctly from the waist.

"And don't get big-headed just becuse you're dressed like Bastille Croquère and think you're a free man of color like him. You're not. You're not a fencing master and you're not free. Let's be perfectly clear about this, boy. You're a slave and you belong to me. Is that understood?"

*"Oui, madame."* Drum bowed again.

"Rachel." Alix pointed to the door. "Go to Onésime's room and get a clean pair of pants and a shirt. They ought to fit Drum even though he's bigger than Onésime. Bring them back here."

"Here, madame?" Rachel questioned.

"Here! You heard me. Now go, and on the way, go up and stop at Titine's room. Wake her and tell her to put on a *robe de chambre* and come here."

Rachel looked quickly from Alix to Drum. Her eyes begged him, pleaded with him. He caught her look and the lowering of his eyelids promised her that he would make an effort to be compliant, whatever was demanded of him.

"Close the door behind you, Rachel." Alix continued. "Tell Titine to knock before she enters. And when you return, don't come in. Leave the clothes on the floor outside the door." She waited for Rachel to go and for the door to close.

"Now, Drum." Alix was smiling and when she smiled she was always most charming. "We must save these beautiful clothes that Dominique gave you for very special occasions. We mustn't get them soiled. You had better take them off."

*"Oui, madame."* Drum recognized the wisdom of her words. "And where shall I go? Do I occupy Onésime's room?"

"Where shall you go, you idiot!" Alix' smile vanished. "Where shall you go? Take them off here."

"But, madame. . . ."

"You heard me. Shuck yourself out of those clothes, boy! If I were buying you at Maspero's exchange, do you think for one moment, I wouldn't have you shuck down? Nobody in his right mind ever buys a slave with clothes, and you've been away so long it's just like I was buying a new slave."

"But, madame. . . ."

"No more *buts*. Do as I say and quick! You might as well learn right now that when I speak, you jump. You may be Rachel's son but that won't stop me from sending you to the whips."

"I've never been whipped yet, madame. Dominique You never had reason to whip me."

"There's always a first time when a nigger gets uppity. Now shuck."

Drum's big fingers undid the cameo pin which he slipped into his pocket. They pulled on the knot of the cravat and loosened it. He unwound it from his neck and tossed it on a chair.

"Fold it and put it on the table," Alix commanded. "You've got to learn to take care of things that cost money."

He folded it and then removed the coat, standing before her in the full, long-sleeved shirt.

"Go on," Alix prompted him, "what are you waiting for?"

One by one he unbuttoned the tiny pearl buttons of the shirt, but before he could take it off, he had to unwind the sash around his waist. When it was removed, he remembered to fold it carefully and place it beside the cravat. Now he was able to slip the shirt off and he hung it over the coat on the chair.

"Boots!" Alix pointed down to his feet and he slipped

off his shoes, spreading his toes in comfort in his white socks.

"Stand them together under the chair. Be orderly. And now, your trousers."

"My trousers?"

"Yes, goddamn it, your trousers, pants, breeches, whatever you call them."

He hesitated but there was no avoiding her stare. The trousers presented some difficulty, for the broadcloth was now damp with his sweat and stuck to his legs, but he peeled them off, folded them carefully along the seams and laid them across the chair. He stood before her in his white linen drawers and his white socks, the white making a vivid contrast to his amber skin.

"Well?" she questioned, but she was interrupted by a knock at the door.

"Titine?" Alix called.

*"Oui, madame."*

"Come in."

The door opened to admit Alix' most beautiful and most provocative quadroon girl. Her skin, with the creamy texture of a magnolia petal, was a deep gold; her finely featured face devoid of make-up; no paint ever invented could have made her more beautiful. The long, lustrous black hair was carelessly wound in a knot on top of her head and skewered with a long gold pin. She was warm and living, but artificial in her beauty, like an exotic plant that has been grown under glass, almost too perfect. She clutched the filmy robe about her as she entered, lifting it so she would not trip on the froth of ruffles at the bottom, but instead of looking at Alix, she stared at the handsome stranger who was standing near the bed clad only in his drawers.

*"Bon jour,* Titine." Alix was all smiles again. "This is Drum, Rachel's son. He will be here now instead of Onésime. Titine, can you believe it, our poor Drum is a bit *pudique*. Imagine a big fellow like that being bashful in front of an old woman like me. He hesitates to remove his drawers, Titine. Perhaps you could help him."

"A pleasure, madame." Titine glided over to Drum, and lifting her hand from the robe she was holding together, she touched the hollow of Drum's throat, then, ever so lightly, her fingers slid slowly down the cleavage of his chest to manipulate the one button that held his drawers. With a pretty gesture, she popped the button out of its hole and the drawers fell to his ankles.

*"C'est un phénomène!"* she exclaimed.

Alix stared and clapped her pudgy hands gleefully together.

"I think our Drum deserves a reward. Give him a kiss, Titine—and let's see what happens."

The girl enveloped Drum in her arms, pressing her lips and her body against his. His hands, which had been hanging awkwardly at his sides, made a tentative movement, then suddenly seized her, slipping under the thin robe and pulling her to him. For a long moment they kissed, until interrupted by Alix.

"He's been rewarded quite enough, Titine. Step back!"

Again Alix regarded Drum and this time her hands clapped even more enthusiastically.

"I think he'll do, don't you, Titine?"

"Marvelously, madame, marvelously. He'll be so much more fun than Onésime. Mon Dieu! What a very monument of a man."

"That's why he's here. And now, Titine, you can go to your room. Oh yes, you'll find some clothes at the door. Hand them in to Drum."

"One more kiss, madame?" Titine opened her eyes wide and fluttered her lashes. *"S'il vous plaît?"*

"Get along with you! One more kiss like that first one and you'd ruin the poor boy." She pointed to Drum. *"Regardez!* At least we shall save money on oysters."

Titine swept out, albeit reluctantly. As she opened the door, she reached down and scooped up the rough cotton shirt and trousers which were lying on the floor and came back into the room and handed them to Drum. Defying her mistress, she kissed him quickly, then rushed out of the room.

"Working here will not be too bad, will it Drum?" Alix chuckled.

For the first time in their interview, he grinned.

*"Mais non, madame!* But it may be difficult in another way. A man can be tantalized to a certain point. . . ."

"You will find plenty of opportunities to go beyond that point." Her smile faded and she became serious. There was no longer any intimacy in her voice. "Now, Drum, let us understand each other well. You are Rachel's son and Rachel is a fine slave. Never once have I ever had to discipline her. I hope you take after her. But remember this." She pointed a finger at him. "Rachel's son or not, I'll stand no nonsense from you. You'll do as you're told, when you're told and without any back talk. You'll attend to the heavier work around here but you'll not find it too difficult. At night, you'll tend bar in the main salon. Onésime will teach you to mix drinks before he leaves. From time to time you'll assist my girls in putting on entertainments for my patrons. You'll probably enjoy that part of it—Onésime always has, at least until lately—but whether you enjoy it or not, you'll do it. Is that clear?"

"And may I ask of what the entertainments will consist?" Drum was most respectful, although he felt rather foolish, bowing without any clothes on. "I do not play the fiddle, madame, but I can do pretty well on the bones." He quite realized his position. No longer was he in the free and easy atmosphere of Dominique's shop. This woman was his mistess. She owned him and she meant every word she said. Her surface softness did not hide the iron will underneath.

"You'll not be required to play the fiddle here. Of that I can assure you, and as far as the entertainments are concerned, you'll know what to do when the time comes. However, there's one other thing that's very important."

*"Oui, madame."* Drum wished she would give him a chance to put on his clothes.

"You've got hot blood in your veins as you just demonstrated a few moments ago. From now on, you'll be living here among the most beautiful girls in the city. You'll be tempted, for they will go out of their way to tempt you, just as Titine did a few minutes ago. They'll find all sorts of excuses to get you into their rooms—the shutters will jam; the *baire* will fall down; the wardrobe door won't open. But keep your hands off them and keep their hands off you. At times you'll have full permission to touch them—the colored girls, never the white ones—but if I catch you fooling around with them without my permission, I'll raise such welts on your back you'll sleep on your belly for a month." She paused to let the full import of her words sink in. "If necessary and if you get too cocky around here, I'll have you ringed with a padlock and I'll hold the key. I don't want to do it if it isn't necessary because the holes spoil any man's appearance. But I'll do it if you don't behave yourself."

"Yes, madame." Drum reached anxiously for his pants feeling sure that if he were once covered, he could divert

Alix's talk about his being ringed. It made him nervous. As a blacksmith he had performed that humiliating function for many household slaves and he had no desire to go through it himself. He hastened to button the pants and hide the object of her threats.

"However"—Alix sank back in her pillows completely reversing her attitude and becoming friendly—"I'm in need of a new girl in the kitchen, so I'll buy one and you can have her for your own and perhaps she'll keep you satisfied. Maspero's expecting a new lot of slaves. I'll even take you along with me and let you help in picking one. She can sleep in the *garçonnière* with you."

"Thank you, madame."

Drum unfolded the shirt, shook it out and started to pull it over his head, but Alix stopped him.

"One minute, Drum, before you put your shirt on. Go over there to my secretaire. Here is the key." She slipped a gold chain over her head and handed it to him. "Now unlock that little top drawer. Inside you'll find something wrapped in white paper. Yes?"

Drum opened the drawer and found the object.

He carried it to the bed and placed it in Alix' hand.

She unwrapped the tissue and took out a small flat box of silver, about the size of the jeweled pomanders that women tucked inside their gloves. A long silver chain was attached to two corners. For a long moment, she held it in her hand, then pried open the cover of the box with her fingernail and looked at the wad of soiled cloth inside. As if it were a habit of long standing, she lifted it to her nose and sniffed. She shook her head sadly and closed the cover of the box.

"Kneel down, Drum." She beckoned him closer to the bed.

It seemed to him that her voice, usually so firmly decisive, quavered a bit as she slipped the chain over his head.

"That belonged to your father. He was my slave too. He brought it from Africa and he believed that as long as he wore it, it would give him strength and his spirit would never depart from him. It was true. While he wore it he was a veritable stallion and his spirit never departed from him until the day he lost it. Now it is yours. Wear it always."

He felt her hand clutch at his own.

He summoned up courage to ask a question that had long troubled him.

"Who was my father, madame? *Maman* never told me."

"She was forbidden. It is a subject we never discuss."

"But if he came from Africa, he was not white, madame?"

"No, he was not white—he was a full blooded Negro. He was a Royal Hausa and quite the handsomest Negro I have ever seen. He once told me that his father was a king in Africa."

"Then I am not really a mulatto? You always called me that." Drum's anxiety was apparent.

"The term is used loosely. But you know you could not be a mulatto. A mulatto is half white and half black," she paused a moment, "a white father and a black mother. Rachel is a mulatto. If your father had been white, you would be a quadroon."

"Then I am only a *griffe,* only one-quarter white?" Drum had suddenly descended in his own social scale. The exact percentage of white blood was so important and a *griffe,* being the child of a full-black and a half-black, was not as high as a mulatto.

"Yes, you are a *griffe,*" Alix agreed, "but you could pass for a mulatto or even a quadroon as you are so bright-skinned—brighter than most mulattos."

Then Alix did a very strange thing. She leaned over and kissed Drum on the forehead.

He was shocked. A white woman had kissed him, not in the heat of passion as he had heard in some fantastic, half-believed stories about white women kissing their slaves. This was a gentle kiss, almost a gesture of love. He stood up, fingering the silver charm which felt cold against his chest. He shivered with some strange fear, wishing that he was out of this room, out of this house and back in the comfortable security of Dominique's forge.

Alix already regretted her impulsive act. What an idiot she had been to yield to her emotions! "Rachel is so close to me that at times I feel like your own mother. Now, out with you! Go to Onésime and tell him to teach you to mix drinks. If you dare to sample one, I'll have you skinned alive. Hop to it and never forget, you're nothing but a slave."

She waited until he had closed the door, holding back her tears with difficulty.

"Tamboura!" She started to cry softly and privately so that no one would hear her. "Oh, Tamboura!"

## chapter iii

After Onésime had gone, Drum settled down easily into the routine at the Academy of Music, finding the work much to his liking and enjoying the novelty of sleeping through the morning, doing chores around the house in the afternoon and tending bar until dawn. In his starched white coat, his hair shining with pomade and his eyes sparkling, he deftly manipulated the bottles and glasses, using much more showmanship in his performance than the unimaginative Onésime had ever done. It added a certain fillip to the drinks, and seemed to enhance their flavor and popularity among the patrons of Alix' establishment. That he accomplished all this without tasting any of the liquor himself was quite phenomenal. But Alix was determined she would have no drunken sot around her place. He had to judge the effect of his skill by the expressions on the faces of the drinkers. Having learned the basic recipes from Onésime, he added little touches of his own, watching carefully to see how they were accepted.

His absinthe frappés, made with costly ice which came, packed in sawdust, down the long stretches of the Mississippi, were veritable masterpieces. After a week, his fame began to spread, and soon men were coming to Alix' not primarily to indulge in the carnal delights she offered but to have one of Drum's drinks. That the liquor put them in a mood to taste other delights was entirely to Alix' profit.

Usually about eleven o'clock, there came a hiatus in Drum's activities. The crowd that had come in the evening after dinner had found their companions and drifted off to the girls' rooms. Those who had dropped in merely for a few drinks and a round of gossip had left. Not until the opera or the ball of the evening was over would the second crowd arrive. For this quiet hour, provided he had no customers, Alix had given Drum permission to leave the bar, but had resistricted him to the courtyard where he would be on call. He had, over the course of a few weeks, chosen a seat on the far side of the courtyard under the shadow of the *garçonnière,* where his room was. Here he could observe without being seen. Sometimes one of the girls would forget to close her shutters, knowing that the windows faced only on the courtyard, and then, from his vantage point below, he could watch an interesting *tableau vivant* in the rooms above. These were gala nights for Drum but the scenes he witnessed were as disturbing as they were interesting. Except for the kiss he had received from Titine the first day he arrived, he had had no feminine contact, despite the fact that he was surrounded with nothing but women—the only cock in a pen of chickens.

*Damne!* It kindled an unquenchable fire in a man! He cursed Madame Alix softly under his breath. She had forgotten her promise to supply him with a wench. What did she think he was made of? In a few days more even the fear of being ringed would not deter him. He'd tumble one of the girls on her bed, *hein?* No man, especially not himself, could sit in the courtyard, knowing full well what was going on in over a dozen rooms above him. At Dominique's he had had more liberty than this. There he was free to go to Congo Square for the Sunday afternoon promenade and dances. With his good looks, he was never alone for long. After it was dark there were many alleyways and dim corners around the old square where the slave girls entertained their friends of the evening. But here! Madame never allowed him to get away from the house.

He shuffled his feet nervously, rubbed his hands together, pulled at his knuckles, adjusted the stretched cloth of his trousers. He could not sit any longer. He stood up, stretched himself and danced on his toes. Aie! He was restless. He knew exactly what every one of those men upstairs was getting. It must be wonderful to be white! To be rich! To be like M. Bernard de Marigny who everyone said was the richest man in the United States. Even being a blacksmith was a lot better than this. At least one's body became tired and with fatigue desire vanished. And there were the Sundays in Congo Square.

Someone was rapping on the door that led out into the back alley. Glad of an excuse for something to do, Drum trotted the length of the courtyard and opened the door. A veritable behemoth of a black man stood there, his long coat, his tall hat and the whip in his hand announcing to the world that he was a coachman.

"I Pompey," he announced. "M'sieur Brulatour he don' tol' me to call fur him 'zactly at midnight." He regarded Drum pompously. "He tol' me to come in and wait fer him. Ain' yo' new here, boy?"

"What yo' wan'?" The coachman was black and Drum condescendingly spoke to him in Gombo.

"What I wan'?" Pompey from his exalted position as the Brulatour coachman sneered at Drum as a mere house servant. "Better git to know who I am, boy. Ain' you knowin' that I Pompey? Ain' yo' knowin' I'se de Brulatour *cocher?"* He started to step inside the door but Drum barred his way.

"Out of my way, nigguh." Pompey brushed Drum aside. "M'sieur Brulatour say fer me come inside and wait fur him and I'se comin'."

"Whom are you shoving?" Drum no longer spoke Gombo but had switch to his French which was pure and perfectly accented. "Madame Alix allows no slaves in here. If you wait, you wait outside."

Pompey, sure in his exalted position as coachman, paid no attention. He lumbered to the center of the courtyard, pulled up a chair, placed his top hat on the ground and sat down with the permanence of a mountain.

Drum's taut nerves after the weeks of enforced continence, and his temper, like his mother's, always close to the surface, were both strained to the breaking point. He had dogged Pompey's footsteps and now stood before him, feet far apart, hands on hips.

"You heard me, you *brut!* Madame Alix allows no slaves here."

"You here," Pompey snickered. "You here and you nothin' but a nigger slave even tho' you's a little bit bright-skinned."

"I'm Madame Alix' slave."

"Ho, ho." Pompey rocked back and forth on the chair in laughter. "Ho, ho. Yo' braggin' cause you slave to de biggest goddam who' in New Orleans. Ho, ho! Maybe dat big fat ol' who', Madame Alix, makes yo' sleep wid her like she did po' Onésime. She sho' drain that black boy all out." He looked up at Drum. "Ain' yo' shamed, slaving in a who'house. Me, I'se a Brulatour slave. Brulatours quality, they is. Ain' no cheap who'house dirt."

Drum leaped.

With both feet he struck the coachman in the chest, toppling over the chair and throwing the big black on the ground. In a moment Drum was upon him, kicking, punching, jumping on the recumbent figure, but not for long.

Pompey struggled up, dragging Drum with him and flung him away, much as a baited bear shakes off a dog. With the whip still in his hand, he lifted his arm and brought it down on Drum's shoulders. It bit through the thin cotton coat that Drum was wearing and he let out a shriek of pain. Once again the whip bit into him but he backed up, ducked low, and ran, ramming his head into the belly of the big black. Pompey dodged sufficiently to escape the full force of the blow, but Drum, unable to stop his headlong rush, stumbled on the flags and fell. Again the whip lashed him and again he cried out but he was up on his feet and his fist crashed into the big black's face.

Howling, snarling and shrieking at each other, they fought. They fought like a couple of mad bulls. Nothing was barred, no effort was too great or too little if it yielded an advantage. Pompey grabbed the chair he had been sitting on and splintered it over Drum's head. Drum's light coat was ripped off and he in turn clawed at the heavy coat the coachman wore, until it parted in shreds. Drum's arms, strengthened by his days at the forge, were as hard as the iron that had molded them and although the other man was bigger and heavier, Drum was the stronger and more agile. Fist beat against flesh, accompanied by curses which the smithy and the stables had taught them.

In his utter concentration on either maiming or killing his opponent, Drum had not noticed that the balconies were now filled with men and that a party of latecomers, who had just entered the front door, were standing only a few feet away. Suddenly the courtyard became lighter, as lanterns were brought in and held aloft, but still the fight continued.

Alix appeared on the second floor balcony, wringing her hands, a distraught Rachel behind her.

"Stop this! Stop it immediately! I'll not have it!" Alix saw the reputation of her house ruined. "Gentlemen, gentlemen, I appeal to you. Stop it! Call the police! Drum!"

His nose was spurting blood and one eye was partially closed but Drum heard his mistress. Didn't she know he couldn't stop? If he stopped for one second, Pompey would kill him.

"Drum!" she shrieked again, "Stop, or I'll have you flogged within an inch of your life. Oh, somebody do something. Rachel, Rachel, go down and stop your son."

"Madame," young de Marigny called up from the flagstones below, "for the love of God, do not stop them. This is the most exciting sight I've seen in years. Let them go! A thousand dollars to the owner of the winner."

"The man's mine," Brulatour shouted. "Let them go on."

"A hundred dollars on madame's Drum." Another waved a fistful of bills in the air.

"Taken!" The beaux of New Orleans dearly loved to gamble on anything.

"Two hundred on Brulatour's Pompey! He's a real *brut*."

"But not as strong as Drum. Five hundred says so."

"Madame, will you hold the money?"

Alix sank back into a chair as her lap was flooded with bills and gold. Still the money came—a hundred dollars, fifty dollars, three hundred dollars, a thousand. New Orleans had found something more exciting than cards or dice to gamble on.

Now the cries that Drum heard were different. He heard his name shouted over and over again, coupled with Pompey's. He was getting tired but he sensed that the other man was more exhausted than he. Hitting Pompey was like pounding a feather bed. His blows had no effect on the *brut*. They clinched and for a moment they hung together, each gasping for air to ease his strained lungs. It was Drum's opportunity and in a flash he brought his knee up with all the strength he possessed, straight imto Pompey's groin.

The big Negro screamed and fell back on the pavement, his hands clutching at his pain, his body writhing on the flagstones. It was the advantage that Drum had wanted. He leaped for the man's chest and when he landed, he heard the crunch of ribs beneath him. His hands sought the screaming throat and the screams choked into silence. He looked up to see the circle of men close around him and recognized Bernard de Marigny, who was a nightly patron.

Drum could hardly speak but he managed to gasp out a few words.

"Do I kill him, monsieur?"

"Heavens no, Drum, Jean Brulatour would never be able to explain to his wife that her favorite coachman was killed at Madame Alix'. Let the bastard go. You've won!" He stepped over to Drum and lifted him off the other's chest, raising Drum's hand high in victory.

"Gentlemen, I proclaim Madame Alix' Drum the winner."

"Why did you stop it?" someone asked.

"This is not Rome." Marigny bowed in the direction of the voice. "We are not watching a battle of gladiators to the death. One gentleman has the right to kill another in a duel but one slave cannot ruin another man's property in a fight."

"He should have killed the *brut*."

Marigny addressed the speaker again. "And would you have recompensed Brulatour for the death of his slave? No, messieurs, it was a fair fight and Drum has won. Collect your bets and be sure to give Madame Alix a generous *lagniappe* for staging this interesting spectacle for us. Dr. Roberts, are you here?"

"Here, Bernard," said a voice from the edge of the crowd.

"Come over here and see if Drum is all right."

"I'm no nigger doctor, Bernard."

"And Drum's no ordinary nigger. Any man who can fight like that is not ordinary. Tomorrow he'll be the toast of New Orleans. Think of the honor, Roberts. Someday you can tell your grandchildren that you attended the famous Drum after his first fight."

"I'm all right, m'sieur." Drum had got his breath. "Better see about the other man."

"He's Brulatour's worry. Hey, Jean, come over here and arrange to get this carcass out of here. He's still alive but something tells me he'll never breed any more pickaninnies. He's still hanging onto his balls."

A middle-aged man pushed through the crowd and came to where Pompey was stretched out on the flags. He prodded the black with his toe. "Of all the cowards," he spat on the groaning man. "Get up! Tomorrow I'll sell you at auction. I'll not even sell you at Maspero's. He wouldn't handle *merde* like you."

Marigny called for a bucket of water and with his own hands sponged Drum's face and torso. Drum was not badly hurt. Once the coagulated blood was washed away from his face, he had suffered little except a closed eye which was already purple and some bruises on his body. Then Marigny led him triumphantly through the crowd of men and up the stairs to where Alix was sitting, busily occupied in counting the bills and gold in her lap.

Marigny bowed low to Alix.

"*Chérie*, tonight you have accomplished a miracle! Your Bernard is no longer bored. Only this evening, I said to myself, 'Bernard, shall we go to Madame Alix' or shall we stay home and quietly cut our own throat from sheer ennui?'

Fortunately, *chérie,* I argued myself into coming and I wouldn't have missed it for anything in the world." He drew his *porte-monnaie* from his inside pocket, opened it and drew out a thousand-dollar bill which he tossed among the others in Alix' lap. "To the owner of the winner! We must have a similar performance again, madame. Something tells me that you have started a new vogue in this old city. Tomorrow I shall go to my plantation early and line up my slaves. If I can find one big enough and strong enough, I shall bring him to the city and we'll stage another fight with Drum."

Alix looked up at him. Things had been happening much too rapidly for her to comprehend but the pile of money in her lap was sufficient evidence that whatever had happened was to her advantage. It had come through Drum and now Drum, in his tatters, was standing before her. She remembered that she had threatened to have him flogged. Have him flogged? *Mon Dieu!* She fingered the thousand-dollar bill that Marigny had tossed in her lap. Le beau Drum had earned her more money tonight than all her girls together. She gathered up the money, wadding the bills and the coins into a little bundle, and stuffed them into her bodice. Once again, Alix was mistress of the situation. She reached out her hand to Marigny and hoisted herself up.

*"Cher ami,"* she tapped Bernard on the cheek lightly with the tip of her fan. "How could you ever believe that the Academy of Music would not allay your ennui? To entertain my beaux has always been my greatest ambition and tonight I have done well, *hein?"* She turned to Drum and her fan gave him an equally affectionate tap.

"You were quite wonderful, Drum. I shall most certainly reward you tomorrow."

*"Merci, madame."* Drum was enjoying his position in the spotlight, his mistress' commendation, and the admiring stares of the men around him. He squared his shoulders, flexed the muscles of his arms and in sheer exuberance danced a few steps on the balls of his feet. At this moment he would have welcomed another fight. His blood coursed through his throbbing arteries, demanding some sort of action. More than anything else, he wanted a woman.

"Reward him tonight, madame," Marigny spoke up. "What do you have in mind for him tomorrow?"

Alix hedged. She had no intention of doing anything at

all for Drum tomorrow but she could afford to be magnanimous with promises.

"Tomorrow I had planned to visit Maspero's. I had intended buying a wench for the kitchen and letting Drum have her for his own. You know how it is with these young bucks—it's hard to control them unless they're ringed and 'twould be a shame to ring Drum, *hein?*"

Marigny looked down at Drum.

" 'Twould be a sacrilege, madame, *Vraiment,* a crime." Hand on chin, lips pursed, regarding Drum with wide-open eyes, Marigny pondered. The fist of one hand smashed into the palm of the other with sudden inspiration.

"Messieurs!" He walked to the rail of the balcony the better to be overheard by those below in the courtyard. "We have a most important mission to perform—now and immediately. We leave Madame Alix' en masse on a mission of charity."

"Charity?" someone shouted up. "Since when have you been interested in charity, Bernard?"

"For the space of two whole seconds," Marigny shouted back. "But, messieurs, this is a most worthy charity. *Voilà!*" He pushed Drum to the rail in full sight of those below. "Behold our Drum! Has ever a man battled more gloriously without hope of any reward? *Jamais, messieurs, jamais!* Never! So the brave Drum shall be rewarded, *hein?* We shall go as a delegation to Maspero's, taking the victorious Drum with us. There, we shall awaken the good Maspero from his well-earned slumbers. We shall demand admittance and Maspero will not refuse for we are all good customers of his. And, once inside, we shall enthrone our Drum in the place of honor. We shall have Maspero parade his entire stock of wenches before our Drum. He shall have his choice and whatever one he desires, we shall purchase her for him—share and share alike the expense."

*"Vive le bon Bernard!"* they shouted. Leave it to the fertile mind of Bernard de Marigny to think of the unusual, the different, the titillating.

"With your permission, of course, madame." Bernard bowed to Alix.

Veritably this Drum was making her fortune tonight. Alix was conscious of the wad of bills in her bodice and now these dear boys were going to buy the slave she had considered—only considered—spending her money for.

"My permission is granted. But you must allow Drum time

to dress. Attired as he is, he certainly could not appear on the streets."

"We bow to your wisdom, madame." Marigny regarded Drum with a smile. "I vow if *le bon Dieu* had been as generous with me as with Drum, I would like nothing better than to parade the streets of New Orleans bare-assed for all to see. But, come, Drum, get ready!"

"And while you wait, messieurs,"—Alix could well afford to be generous—"champagne on the house. Rachel, attend to my wonderful boys."

## chapter iv

THE COLORFUL old city of New Orleans had seen many parades marching through her narrow streets, but never one more fantastic than that which set out from Madame Alix' Academy of Music shortly after midnight. Two slaves with *flambeaux* led the procession of nearly thirty men—the majority of them representing the oldest and wealthiest Creole families in the city. Immediately behind the slaves marched Drum, attired in all his green and yellow finery, flanked on one side by Bernard de Marigny and on the other by Marigny's constant companion, Lazare LeToscan, over both of whom Drum towered. In the excitement of the moment, distinctions of color had been forgotten. Drum was temporarily as important as a horse which had just won a race, and as the owner's arm might have encircled the neck of his horse, so now did de Marigny's arm circle Drum's waist and LeToscan's arm his neck. Drum was a conquering hero and several magnums of Alix' finest champagne had raised the spirits of the crowd to a point where white blood sportingly acknowledged the superiority of colored. Drum, with his first two glasses of champagne—at LeToscan's insistence—already producing a floating lightness in his head, walked along with his varnished boots scarcely touching the cobbles, so intoxicated was he with victory, flattery and . . . the unaccustomed taste of wine.

As they marched along they sang the popular Gombo song . . .

*Danse, Calinda, bou-djoumb! bou-djoumb!*
*Danse, Calinda, bou-djoumb! bou-djoumb!*

. . . keeping in step to its rhythmic beat, entirely oblivious of the fact that they were waking the good citizens of the city. But then these citizens were accustomed to being awakened by the antics of the young bloods. They merely rolled over in their beds, more than a few among them wishing their own young days were not already passed and they were with the group outside, participating in whatever exciting deviltry was afoot.

Flambeaux leading and the singing pacing their steps, they arrived at the corner of St. Louis, where the tall arches of Maspero's Exchange presented a bleak and shuttered appearance. A dim light burned in one of the upper windows of the old building, once the property of Jean and Pierre Lafitte, and the site, along with Dominique You's blacksmith shop, of many of the off-color deals those three worthies hatched—deals that had resulted in piracy on the high seas, sunken ships, men and women walking the plank, and the capture of entire slave settlements on the African coast. But Maspero, like Dominique You, had eschewed piracy after Louisiana became a part of the United States and now his establishment was the city's most popular auction mart, where the choicest slaves—the exotic, the unusual, the erotic and the perverted were offered for sale to ready bidders. Once arrived, the crowd halted on the banquette, all eyes raised to the second story where the light burned.

"Hey there, M. Maspero." De Marigny led the shouting. "Wake up! A delegation of New Orleans' most distinguished citizens awaits you below."

"Up, Maspero!" LeToscan joined in with his shouts. "We honor you this night by doing business with you."

The others echoed similarly loud-voiced demands until they were rewarded by the appearance, on the balcony above, of Maspero himself, a candlestick with a dripping candle in one hand and a pistol in the other.

"What in hell's going on down there?" He peered down at the mass of faces below. "Can't an honest citizen enjoy a night's rest?"

"Whoever claimed you were honest, Maspero?" de Marigny laughed. "Nobody ever expected you to be honest or even wanted you to be honest. We love you because you're a rascal. But, dear Maspero, be careful with that goddamned pistol. You wouldn't want to shoot your best customers."

The sound of French words and aristocratic voices convinced Maspero that this was no roving band of Kaintucks from the levee. He leaned over the iron railing, trying to identify the faces below him. "Who are you and what do you want?"

De Marigny, always the leader and spokesman, called

back. "Your good friend, Bernard de Marigny, Maspero, and here beside me is another good friend and patron of yours, Lazare LeToscan, and I could name many more. That's who we are and as to our business, we have come to buy a slave—a wench to be specific—and we want only the best that you have."

"But my slaves are not here," Maspero remonstrated. "I only sell them here. They are all down in the slave pens."

"As we well know. But come, M. Maspero. Dress and take us there and stop brandishing that pistol. We can see your slaves there as well as here and as our time is valuable, hurry. You'll be well paid for your trouble."

Maspero hesitated, but to offend Bernard de Marigny would be fatal to his business. Just as all New Orleans imitated Bernard's new way of tying a cravat, so did they follow him in everything he did. Maspero well knew that if Marigny chose to buy his slaves elsewhere, not a single customer would turn up for his auctions.

"*Mon cher* Bernard," he shouted back, "if you and the gentlemen can wait but five minutes until I draw on my trousers and my shoes, I shall accompany you. Five minutes, *messieurs, à tout à l'heure!*" He disappeared back into the window and in less than the allotted time, he was down on the street, his nightgown billowing out over the top of his trousers, his tasseled nightcap still askew on his head.

Once again the procession started, this time down St. Louis and along the levee to the edge of the canal where a low stuccoed building, with grated windows, stretched out dismally alongside the stagnant water. Maspero fitted a huge iron key into the iron-bossed wooden door and let them in. His shouts awakened the sleeping slave guards and soon there were more flambeaux lighted. In their flickering light, rough benches were hurriedly placed in front of a low wooden stand. From the cages around the central courtyard came a low wailing and moaning; the awakened slaves were frightened. They could not imagine what might be about to happen to them as they saw the finely dressed white men take their seats on the benches. However, they finally deduced from the lighted auction block that they were to be sold and their cries of fright turned to pleadings to be purchased.

"Buy me, masta' buy me! I'se strong, I is. I'se a good boy. Ask 'em for Grosjean."

"Buy me, masta'! I'se trained houseman, fitten for to serve you yo' dinner, masta'."

"Don' buy no slave 'til yo' sees me, masta'. I'se de best. I cuts cane all day and jumps de wenches all night fo' yo'."

"Quiet!" Maspero's voice commanded silence. "One more yip out of any of you and you'll taste the whip." In the sudden silence that ensued, he mounted the platform, took his place on a straight-backed chair and looked down on his audience.

"And now, messieurs, what can I do for you at this unusual hour and under these most unusual circumstances?"

De Marigny pushed Drum forward.

"Do you want this man sold?" Maspero inventoried Drum in his green coat and pale yellow trousers.

"Hell no, Maspero!" Le Toscan answered. "There's not enough money in all New Orleans tonight to buy this buck. He's Madame Alix' Drum, the best goddamned fighter in the city. We're buying the slave for him, Maspero, and Drum is picking her out. Show us your best wenches, Maspero, and shuck them down before you bring them in. Only the best is good enough for Drum and the one he wants will be the one we buy."

Maspero conferred with his white overseer, who had tumbled out of bed on hearing the noise. The man left, running in his bare feet to a cage at the end of the courtyard. In a few moments he was back, leading some twenty female slaves, who were pulling their rough osnaburg dresses off over their heads as they walked along.

They lined up in the shadows behind the platform and after a few more whispered words of consultation with the white man Maspero turned to his audience.

"Here, messieurs, are the best females I have. I've been culling the good ones out for a special auction next week. I warn you, they are not cheap."

"We don't want a cheap one." De Marigny pushed Drum forward. "Up on the platform with you. You'll want a good look at them as they come along. The decision's up to you."

Drum jumped up on the platform and stood alongside the seated Maspero, who motioned for the first woman in the line to come up. She ascended the steps slowly, a brazen wench of some twenty years, probably an *os rouge,* a cross between an Indian and a Negro, because her skin was copper colored and her hair straight and long. Her lips parted in a professional smile of invitation and she lifted both breasts with her hands as she sidled up to Maspero and then turned and faced the audience.

"Turn around and face him." Maspero pointed to Drum. "You're picking her, fellow, so you have my leave to finger her if you want."

Taking her cue from Maspero's words, the girl, with an over-exaggerated movement of her hips, hands still lifting her breasts, strutted over to Drum.

"I don't min' havin' a nigguh masta', seeing as how's he's a pretty man like yo'." Her hands slipped down from her breast to glide provocatively over her flanks. "Yo' likes me, pretty man?"

In his present condition Drum was quite willing to settle for the first one that came along, but even though this one's superb body enticed him, he found her face ugly with its high cheekbones and thin nose. He hesitated and then shook his head slowly.

"Mayhap I'll come back to you," he promised.

" 'Member my name, pretty man. My name Alix."

"Hell no, Drum! Pass her by! Never do to have two by the same name in the same house," LeToscan shouted. "Bring on another, Maspero."

The next was more to Drum's liking. She was bright of skin, dainty and delicate, with short curls which danced all over her head and little breasts no bigger than oranges. With modesty she spread her hands in front of her and walked demurely, her head cast down.

"A pretty wench," Maspero said. "Only sixteen and good blood on her father's side. A mulatto from Teneriffe Plantation."

She walked over to Drum and had he raised his arm, she could have passed under it without stooping, so tiny she was. His fingers itched to touch her bright skin and he drew her closer, cupping one breast in his hand and letting the other slide slowly down her back. She seemed emotionless, devoid of any response, but he liked her and he hesitated. His mind was made up for him by de Marigny.

"Too small for you, Drum. She'd never be able to take you. You'd kill her the first night."

And so they passed before him—African black, mulattos, quadroons, octoroons, tiercerons, *griffes* and *marabous*—some with a sprinkling of white blood which gave a glowing brightness to their skins and some the unadulterated ebon black of Africa. He was confused by the multiplicity of choices. Each was warm and provocative and each possessed that which he desired more than anything else. Some he called closer to him that he might pass his hands over them and let his fingers linger on their soft flesh. Some he hesitated to touch for fear the slightest contact might prove climactic. Their very nearness, their odor, their warmth and their womanhood inflamed him and in desperation he would have settled for any one at hand if only he could be back with her in the little room of the *garçonnière* at Madame's. But his audience insisted that he see them all.

And see them all he did until the very last one, who caused such a commotion before she was forcibly lifted up the steps that Drum's desire was cooled by his curiosity to see what was happening. The girl struggled like an eel in the arms of the slaves who held her, a maelstrom of black arms and legs, snarling, kicking, biting and thrashing, screaming with vehemence and hatred. Once she eluded her captors and only by grabbing her legs and throwing her to the ground did they succeed in recapturing her. Even the little whip of the overseer, wrapping around her legs, did nothing to subdue her; she only shrieked the louder. Finally she was carried up onto the platform where one of the slaves held her, her wrists securely anchored behind her back in his big hands. Her chest heaving, she glared at Drum and spat at him, but her very defiance made him certain he desired her more than all the others who had submitted so meekly.

"A guaranteed Jaloff, messieurs." Maspero leaned forward in his chair to run his hands over her flanks. "Pure blooded! First one I've had in over a year. Rare, you know. Most beautiful niggers that ever came out of Africa. Grandmothers of most of the quadroons you gentlemen find so exciting." He slapped her round buttocks. "Yes, messieurs, a real Jaloff."

"A real vixen," someone from the audience spoke.

"Spirited as a fine horse but she can be broken. A spitfire now but she'll give any man a run for his money."

Drum gasped and he heard the same sharp intake of breath from several of the seated men. This was no bright-skinned hybrid with a superficial veneer of white beauty. This was African—a resplendent young animal, with a skin of burnished sheen that resembled blue-black steel in the shadows and polished copper where the light of the flambeaux gilded it. Her head was covered with a close cap of smooth black velours; her face was an delicately profiled as a Greek coin and its angry contortion seemed to add to its beauty, for the eyes were wide set, the nose straight and finely nostriled, the lips full and beautifully formed. Her breasts were round, not pointed and pear-shaped as with so many of her black sisters, and the nipples stood high in dark violet bosses. There was a suggestion of felinity about her long clean limbs, the grace and power of a black leopard in the twitching muscles under the velvet skin.

With a sudden twist, she freed herself from her captor and sprang at Drum, threatening him with her teeth, her eyes rolling in frenzy. Talon-like, her hands reached up to rip his face but he caught them and forced them down with one strong arm, pinioning her motionless. His free hand roved over her body. She stood, panting, enduring Drum's hand as it lifted her face that he might see its perfection more clearly; stroked the throbbing column of her throat; lifted the orbs of her breasts, weighing their opulence, relinquishing them to wander over the globe of her belly and then seek the dark sanctuary between her legs. He bent over slightly, the better to accommodate the investigations of his hand and as his head lowered past her face, she pounced, fastening her teeth in the lobe of his ear. Drum let out a yelp of pain. His hand left the warm softness where it so greatly desired to linger and came up swiftly with a cuff that knocked her head to one side. Surprised, it was her turn to yelp in pain, and she stood still, quivering before him.

"Our Drum's got another fight on his hands," someone shouted. "Don't use your knee this time because if you don't want her, I do."

Drum looked down at the shining face so close to his own. With a last gesture of defiance, she darted her tongue out at him. Again he cuffed her with such force that her head jolted sideways. He could feel the tenseness passing out of her body and when she looked up at him again, the blazing enmity of her eyes had died down to a smoldering fire.

"Why are you fighting me, girl?" he whispered to her.

Surprisingly, she answered in good French, not in Gombo.

"No colored man is going to pester me. I've been raised for a white master."

"No white man could ever love you like I will. Trust me, girl." Aloud he asked, "What's your name?"

"Calinda," she answered, biting off the word as though she hated it.

It was enough to set the audience singing again and they stomped their feet to keep time to the music.

*Danse, Calinda, danse avec Drum*

*Danse, Calinda, sous tu homme.*
*Danse, Calinda, bou-djoumb!*

"He'll be dancing on top of her soon. Aie! Calinda! Wait till you see what Drum has waiting for you."

Drum's arm still held her tight although he sensed it was no longer necessary. Her brief rebellion was over. She was as ripe for mating as he was himself. She saw how handsome he was, despite the purple eye which was now completely closed, and the sting of his slap on her cheek was now sweet to her.

"I want this one." Drum appealed to the faces below him.

"She's yours," de Marigny answered as spokesman. "And there's not a man here who doesn't envy you."

"She's expensive, that one." Maspero grinned, figuring how much extra he could get from this group of young hotheads.

"How much?" de Marigny countered.

"Seven hundred dollars and that's rock-bottom. On the block she might fetch a thousand."

De Marigny seldom thought twice about money. He stood up and counted the men. "Each man here is assessed twenty-five dollars. Cheap enough for an evening's entertainment. Pay Maspero, and you, Maspero, write out a bill of sale to Madame Alix de Vaux for this girl Calinda. Drum's a slave himself so he can't own her."

The men rose and made their way to the platform, each withdrawing his *porte-monnaie*. Drum relaxed his hold on the girl but instead of moving away, she snuggled closer to him.

"Calinda," he whispered again, "you're mine now."

"They call you Drum?" she asked.

"I am Drum."

"I've never had a man, Drum. My old master was saving me for his son up north. When the young master came back, I was to be his but old master died and young master never came so now you're my master."

Drum shook his head. "Not master, Calinda. I'm a slave too."

"Then how could you buy me?"

"I'm not buying you, these men are. You'll belong to my mistress, Madame Alix."

"Who's she?" Calinda bristled. "Will she let me be yours, Drum?"

"She will." De Marigny was standing on the platform and he had overheard the last of the conversation. "She will, no doubt about that. And now, put on your dress, Calinda, and we'll start." He handed Drum a piece of paper. "Give this to Madame Alix."

Once again the procession started through the streets but this time de Marigny and LeToscan walked behind Drum and Calinda, watching Drum's arm about the girl and his fingers feeling the warmth of her flesh through the rough fabric. When they reached the Academy of Music, Rachel was waiting anxiously at the open door and the whole company would have entered again, had not de Marigny blocked their passage through the little door that opened in the big double doors of the gate.

"We disperse now, messieurs," he said.

"Oh no, Bernard." Young Pablo Hernandez wet his lips with his tongue. "Now comes the most exciting part. We're going to watch her and Drum get together."

"Sure, Bernard."

"That's what we've been waiting for."

"That will be the *pièce de résistance* of the evening."

"Surely having bought her, we can see her broken in."

"We've seen how Drum handled his man, now we want to see how he handles his woman."

De Marigny, his arms still across the door with Drum and Calinda inside beside Rachel, looked out on the faces of his friends.

"It would be a most interesting spectacle, I agree with you. But impromptu and *impropre*. It would be lacking in finesse. We would merely see a fumbling man mounting what looks to be an unwilling woman. There might be a certain spiciness in seeing him master her but let us wait, *mes amis*. Later, in another week, perhaps, we can petition Madame for a real performance, such as Madame alone can stage. We shall all appreciate it more, for with rehearsals, the act will be smoother, more interesting, much more professional and much more to your liking."

"But she won't be a virgin then."

"Chances are she's not a virgin now," Marigny smiled. "All wenches claim to be on the block, but virgins are a rarity which I have never encountered except on my own plantation."

"Bernard's right," LeToscan agreed. "Let Madame Alix handle this and you'll not be disappointed. Besides, I'm tired." He yawned to prove it. "So let us wish our Drum good luck tonight and leave him."

Although some grumbled their disappointment, they all started to leave. De Marigny was the last and he turned to Drum behind him.

"Plow the ground well tonight, Drum," he smiled. "Plow it and harrow it and prepare it for seed. Learn how to do it well. My friends and I shall be here soon to witness a special performance for which tonight will be only a rehearsal. Can we count on that?"

"With a little practice, m'sieur, I should be well able to repay you for all you have done for me tonight. May I thank you for your goodness?"

"You may and shall, Drum. I shall return before the others, alone, and you and Calinda can both thank me, together and separately." He turned and left.

Rachel shepherded the two through the empty courtyard. There were no lights for there had been no further music in the Academy after the men had left. Alix appeared on the upper balcony, her nightgown a blur of pale white in the darkness.

"Did they buy one, Rachel?"

"Yes, madame."

"And what kind of a wench did they get?"

"A fine one, madame, as far as I can see in this light. She's black."

"Black? Didn't you want a bright one, Drum?"

"I'm satisfied," he answered.

"Bring her here in the morning and I will examine her. Oh, Drum, be sure to fold your clothes when you take them off. You might be in too much of a hurry to think of it."

Rachel led them across the courtyard to the narrow stairs that ascended to the *garçonnière*. A candle in a brass stick was in readiness on one of the lower steps and she struck the flint in her pocket tinderbox, waited for a flame to appear, and lit the candle. She held it up to Calinda's face.

"She's pure black, Drum. I hoped you'd get a quadroon."

"Black or white, she's the girl I wanted, *maman*."

Rachel kissed the girl gently, put the candle in her hand and pushed them both up the first narrow step. As she watched them go up, she called out to Drum.

"I've put clean sheets on your bed and there's a pan of water with towels. You'll find leaves of bergamot, vervain and verbena to rub yourselves with and a jar of scented tallow to make it easier for her. *Bonne nuit.*"

*"Bonne nuit, maman,"* Drum answered, his hand caressing the ascending legs of the girl before him on the stairs.

They entered the little room and Drum snuffed the candle. In the darkness he stripped off his clothes and they fell on the floor in hasty forgetfulness of Madame's instructions. The rough osnaburg dress followed. Not for them were the leaves of bergamot—the warm smell of flesh was a far sweeter perfume. Not for them the pan of water and the towels—the smooth slipperiness of sweaty skin was far more lubricous. Step by step, so closely joined together that they cast only one pale shadow on the moonlit floor, they neared the bed and then were upon it.

For a few moments there was a spasmodic movement as lips sought lips. The movements increased and there was a little scream of terror from the girl. Drum put a hand over her mouth and she did not scream a second time, but only moaned softly. Eventually the movements on the bed ceased, only to start again a short time later. Throughout the hours of darkness that followed, until the moonlight had fled and the stronger light of dawn crept into the little room, the movements started and stopped again at intervals. Some time after the full force of the sun had flooded the room, Drum got up and closed the shutters. In the sun-streaked darkness, they both slept, tightly embracing on the narrow bed.

## chapter v

ALIX ENTIRELY approved of Calinda from a business point of view, for there was no denying that she was a most valuable slave. But from the moment of their first meeting, each felt a deep-rooted hatred of the other. Calinda resented the fact that she had to relinquish Drum to the authority of another woman and Alix did not approve of his affection for a woman blacker than himself. She had eventually intended to get some valuable light-skinned progeny from Drum's loins that she could dispose of at a profit. Bright-skinned fancies were becoming more and more in demand but anything this girl produced would be only a *griffe*.

Calinda, of course, obeyed Alix in the household and kitchen duties allotted her, but did everything perfunctorily and sulkily. Her attitude barely stopped short of being disrespectful. Alix threatened several times to have her disciplined, once even going so far as to summon the police to take her to the public whips, but Rachel intervened and managed to convince her that the girl was scarcely housebroken and would in time be more amenable. Alix doubted that but she agreed to give her another chance.

In private with Drum, in the hours they shared together in the little room of the *garçonnière,* Calinda railed and ranted against Alix. Drum himself had no particularly deep affection for his mistress, but he tried his best to quiet Calinda's resentment. Like Rachel, he lived in terror of the time when Calinda might go too far, when it would be too late to save her from the whips.

Yet Calinda was capable of deep affection, as she showed plainly in her relations with Drum. She was his, body and soul, and there was no demand he could make she would not try to gratify. But she sensed that she could never possess him as completely as he possessed her, and she was maniacally jealous. If her man so much as looked twice at one of Madame Alix' girls, or regarded overlong an admiring wench on the rare occasions when they were permitted to visit Congo Square on a Sunday afternoon, she either brooded and sulked or stormed at him. Drum had only one remedy for her moods. When she was sulky he cajoled her into bed, and when she screamed with jealous rage he knocked her down and carried her to bed. Making love to Calinda was the only way he knew to bring her around.

When his duties as barman, fighter or exhibitionist for the evening were over, she would be waiting for him to subdue her and thus reassure her. The white man's civilization had failed to change her primitive nature, or soften her fierce pride and possessiveness. Drum's body, she felt, belonged to her and she resented even the thought of another's touching it. But also her own body was utterly and completely his, and he could use it as he wished, even offer it to another man if he chose to do so.

One afternoon Marigny came to the Academy of Music and asked permission of Alix to go to Drum's room in the *garçonnière*. There he found Drum and Calinda in their hour of siesta and announced that he had come to claim the thanks that were due him for bringing them together. With Drum's assent, Calinda readily accommodated herself to Marigny's demands, but when he turned from her and laid his hands on Drum, she lay stiffly incensed beside them, bitterly resenting their intimacies. Had not Drum been anxious to remain in the good graces of Marigny, he might at least have made some token show of resistance; as a slave he could do no more than that. But Marigny's influence was too important to him, and he warned Calinda with a meaningful look not to interfere. That her man was willing to submit to Marigny was something quite beyond her comprehension. It was not a matter of moral outrage; Calinda knew nothing of morality. All she could see was that another person was usurping the place she felt was rightfully hers.

Later, at the more elaborate performance which she and Drum staged in the Orléans four-poster, for the benefit of the group of men who had purchased her, she was quite at ease and entirely unembarrassed. Despite the thirty pairs of eyes watching them, she had her man entirely to herself and the applauding audience made no difference. However, when, as often happened, Drum was commanded to assist in one of Madame's *tableaux vivants*—for which Alix was famous from Boston to New Orleans—and Drum's co-performers were the lovely quadroons of the third floor instead of herself, Calinda would be in such a state they had to lock her in the little room of the *garçonnière*. It took all of Rachel's and Drum's best efforts for several days after that to render her tractable again.

If the *tableaux vivants* consumed her with insane jealousy, the fights which Madame's patrons demanded affected her even more. When Drum fought she was so worried for fear he would receive some lasting bodily injury that she would become actually ill. As painful as it was to her, she insisted on watching, and during the fight she would cower under Rachel's protective arm, feeling each one of the blows, suffering from each thud of the other man's fist on Drum's flesh until, at the end of the fight, she was physically and emotionally exhausted. She was never too ill, however, to bathe him, tend to his cuts and bruises and spend the night beside him, listening to every breath he drew and praying blindly to her pantheon of African gods that he would never have to fight again.

But fight again he did, with increasing regularity. It had become quite the fashion for masculine Creole New Orleans to repair to Madame's one night a week to see Drum fight and wager money on the outcome. Marigny had brought in a big black from his cane fields and pitted him against Drum. Pablo Hernandez of the loose wet lips, not to be out of fashion, recruited a big *bozal* he had just purchased, for the same purpose. LeToscan was about to send a strong young *marabou* to the plantation whips for punishment, but instead decided to match him against the champion. De Marigny's big buck was strong and husky but slow witted and no match for his competitor's strength and sagacity. The Hernandez' *bozal* was equally strong but even more stupid; Drum had him pinned to the ground in less than ten minutes.

However, LeToscan's *marabou* proved much more formidable, driven as he was by the knowledge that he was literally fighting for his life. LeToscan had told the fellow that if he won over Drum, his entire punishment would be waived, but if he lost it would be tripled. No man could take one hundred and fifty lashes and live.

The *marabou* was indeed a fierce antagonist. At first he was canny and careful, slipping away from Drum and dancing outside the reach of his powerful arms. Indeed, he showed too much care for his own safety to please his master. LeToscan called for a poker to be heated and rammed the red-hot iron against the slave's buttocks. With a yelp of pain the *marabou* grappled with Drum until they fell to the floor. As Drum struggled to get up, the fellow grabbed his ankles and he fell again. Drum seized the *marabou's* hands and managed to pinion them behind his back, but as he did this he felt his opponent's teeth sink into the calf of his leg. It required a gigantic effort to raise himself sufficiently to get his hands over the fellow's head. Locking his fingers in the *marabou's* eye socket, he pulled the head back sufficiently to free his leg from the savage teeth. With his eyes gouged out, Drum's antagonist was helpless. A final clout on the head knocked him into insensibility. The fight was over.

Drum was not to know until several weeks later that LeToscan had led the blind, stumbling, half-conscious wretch down to the levee. There he had stood the fellow up with his back to the river and fired three shots into him. The body had rolled down the incline of the levee to the Mississippi and been carried away.

A couple of days after the fight, the bite in Drum's leg became badly infected. At the insistence of Marigny, Dr. Roberts, who had been educated in New England, was persuaded to bring his medical knowledge to aid in Drum's recovery. But in spite of all the doctor could do, the infection grew worse, until Drum's condition grew so grave that Roberts decided the leg would have to be amputated, and he so informed Alix.

"If I amputate, madame, you'll have a one-legged nigger on your hands—a practically worthless slave. After all when a horse breaks a leg we shoot it."

"I'm not going to have Drum shot." Alix was emphatic. "Is there nothing you can do but cut off his leg?"

Roberts shrugged. "I don't know, madame, I just don't know. But it looks like it. I've never treated a nigger before and I never thought I would. I'm no veterinarian. But I've come to like this black boy of yours. He's been in intense pain but he has never complained. Instead of letting him suffer like an animal, I've given him opium to reduce the pain. I've done everything that I would for a human being and I'm not so damned sure but that he is a human being and a pretty good one at that. I'll save him if he can be saved, even if I have to cut off his leg."

After he had gone, Alix descended the stairs to the courtyard, made her way across it and up the narrow steps to Drum's room in the *garçonnière*. Calinda was with him, kneeling on the floor beside the bed, fanning his fevered body. She looked up at Alix and the malevolence in her glance said plainly that she held her mistress accountable for Drum's suffering. Alix ignored her. She walked to the bed, pulled down the sheet and looked at the puffed, discolored and swollen leg. She saw the suppurating pus and she recoiled. To her it looked hopeless—this misshapen lump of flesh could never be a leg again. Drum's eyes opened and he looked up at her. He knew that his life depended on her decision. Although it was illegal to kill a slave, it was a law which was frequently broken without compunction by slave owners. On the plantations, aged and maimed slaves were taken out into the field and shot. City slaves were treated with a little more finesse: they were poisoned.

Drum's eyes pleaded with her mutely.

"Don't worry, boy." There was an odd tenderness in Alix' voice—something which Drum had heard only once before and Calinda never. "Nothing's going to happen to you. You have my word for it. Calinda, call Rachel."

"I'm here, madame." Rachel had spied Alix going to Drum's room and had followed, standing just outside the door. She realized that Alix' decision meant life or death for Drum.

"Rachel,"—all sentimentality had departed from Alix and she had once again become impersonal and efficient—"how long has Dr. Roberts been treating Drum?"

"Two weeks, madame."

"And is he better or worse than when Roberts started?"

"Worse, madame."

Alix looked down at Drum, moving closer so that her hand rested on his forehead. It was dry and hot.

"Does that old nigger woman still sell simples at the corner of St. Claude and the Place Publique?"

"As far as I know, madame."

"Then go and see if she is still there and if she is, give her a dollar and bring her here. Dr. Roberts' northern medicines may cure those white-livered people in Boston but it takes old-fashioned black medicine to cure a nigger. Hurry, Rachel! I'm not going to have Drum lose a leg. He's going to get well to fight again."

"Oh, madame." Calinda was down on her knees before Alix. "Don't let him fight again."

"Shut your mouth, girl! We're either going to have a one-legged Drum or a fighting Drum."

"Oh, don't let them cut off his leg," Calinda sobbed. "Don't, madame, don't."

"Then let me handle this." Alix motioned for Calinda to place the one chair in the room beside Drum's bed. She looked around at the bare room, the narrow bed, at Drum's gaudy suit hanging from a nail on the wall and Calinda's dress hanging limply beside it. The room was clean—she gave the girl credit for that—but lacking in every comfort. Well, that was the way it should be! Slaves didn't need luxury and Drum had a bed, which was more than most slaves had. But the bed lacked a mosquito *baire* and that was one thing a sick man needed. He shouldn't be subjected to the swarms of mosquitoes which made the hot nights a misery. Alix had a fear of insects which bordered on a phobia.

"When Rachel returns," she instructed Calinda, "Tell her to have a *baire* fitted over this bed. "And you, Calinda, keep on fanning him."

Alix sat watching Calinda fan Drum, stopping only to soak a cloth in water, wring it out and apply it to his forehead, then resume the fanning again until it was time to freshen the cloth once more. Only once did Alix move and that was to pull the sheet down over Drum's shoulders. She saw the little silver box, rising and falling on his amber chest with his labored breathing. She leaned over and tapped it with her forefinger. Drum opened his eyes and focused them on her.

"Do you remember what I told you about this?" Alix asked him.

"Yes, madame," he replied with difficulty.

"Your father once said that it contained his spirit. He told me that nothing could happen to him while he wore this. Perhaps it will help you. I only know that when he lost it, he died. You have it and you still live."

A commotion on the stairs outside announced the arrival of Rachel and the herb woman. They came into the room, Rachel gaunt and distressed, the old woman even more obese than Alix. A black face, huge, round and sagging with pendulous cheeks, rose from an assortment of evil-smelling rags that caused Alix to pinch her nostrils together with her fingers. From one ham-sized arm hung a wicker basket filled with wilted leaves, scrubbed white roots, short lengths of bark-covered withes, and an assortment of little bundles of dried herbs, tied together with string. In the other hand she carried a live red rooster by his tied feet. In contrast to

Rachel, the old crone was in exuberant spirits. The rich Gombo she spoke was barely intelligible.

"Dis yeah de sick *homme?*" She cackled in a series of words that ascended pitch by pitch. "Waa-for dis whoppin' big buckeroo sick?"

At a motion from Alix, Calinda drew back the sheet and the old woman stared first at Drum's naked body, clucking in unfeigned admiration, and then at the suppurating leg. She leaned over to examine the wound, touching the swollen flesh with her black fingers.

"Him's bad. *Très malade.* Meybe he a-gonna die. Wha-fer you want Mère Angelique to do? *Aie, mo connai!* You wants Mère Angelique make him well again, *hein?*" Somehow her high-pitched cackle created confidence.

"Yes." Although Alix resented the old woman's good humor, she felt encouraged by it.

*"Bien! li kalle mait'non!* Soon him sleep. When wake up, feel better. Mère Angelique fix 'im good." She laid the squawking rooster aside and rummaged in her basket, picking out a bunch of leaves here, a few roots there, some more leaves which she considered carefully only to throw them back in the basket, then more leaves and some bark which she stripped from the withes, until she had a sizeable bundle in her lap. These she handed to Rachel with orders to go into the kitchen and boil them. While Rachel was gone, Mère Angelique managed to lower herself to the floor. A search in the pile of rags which covered her produced a long rosary, crudely made of large black seeds, strung on dirty twine with a crucifix of white bone at the end. At each bead she mumbled an unintelligible prayer:

*Heru mandé, heru mandé, heru mandé*
*Tigi li papa*
*Heru mandé*
*Tigi li papa*
*Heru mandé*
*Do se dans godo*
*Heru mandé.*

When she reached an occasional larger bead she lapsed into a fairly intelligible Gombo version of the Our Father, to which she affixed a long roster of saints' names. By the time she had accomplished the long process, Rachel was back in the room with the steaming pot of herbs. Mère Angelique shook the rosary over them, clicking the beads together, and then doused them in the steaming mess. She snatched the sheet that had covered Drum and tore a square from it. Dumping the pottage into it, she passed it gingerly back and forth from one hand to the other until it reached the right temperature, then placed it on Drum's leg. He winced from the heat but she held it in place until he became accustomed to it. Then her hands reached for the red cock, and she laid it on its back on the floor. Taking a long knife from her basket, she held it over the bird while she mumbled another series of unintelligible words. The rooster, evidently sensing that his last moment had arrived, emitted a forlorn crow which seemed to please the old hag, for she laughed again at what seemed to be a good omen. With one slash of the knife, she laid the fowl open, neatly cleaving it from neck to tail. Spreading open its severed body, she laid it over the steaming poultice, then tore the remainder of the sheet into strips and bandaged the whole agglomeration tightly to Drum's leg.

"Six days,"—she counted them off on her fingers—"six days no touch. Bile this." She handed a tied bundle of herbs to Rachel. "Make him drink it. Keep him shittin' all-a time. Make him drink lots water. Keep him pissin' all-a time." She pointed to the bulging bandage on Drum's leg. "Pretty soon big stink. Phew! but no take off. One day God de father, one day, Holy Virgin, one day Jesus Christ, three day, conjur' spirits, much betta, goddam strong. Two dollar please."

Alix paid her and she gathered up her basket, tucked the rosary in her hidden pocket and signaled to Rachel to show her out. Rachel returned and the three women remained with Drum—Alix on the chair, Rachel standing behind her and Calinda kneeling on the floor beside the bed.

"You're going to be all right, Drum," Alix tried to encourage him.

"Pain's eased, madame." Drum attempted a weak smile.

"You needn't fight any more if you get well."

"Like to fight, madame." Drum's smile waxed a little stronger.

"As you wish." Alix silenced Calinda, who was about to protest, with a look that caused the girl to sink back on her knees.

Within an hour, beads of perspiration appeared on Drum's forehead and he slept. Throughout the long afternoon he continued to sleep and his breathing became slow and regular. Even the erection of the mosquito *baire* did not disturb his deep sleep and when the *baire* was in place, a fresh sheet found to cover him, the shutters closed to keep out the sun and the room straightened, Alix left, arguing with herself that the death of a slave, outside of the monetary loss it would cause her, made very little difference, yet knowing in her heart that it did. For the first time, she felt that Drum was hers—her son. Yes, her son and Tamboura's.

Later that evening, when Dr. Roberts dropped in for his usual round of drinks—inferior now that Drum was not mixing them—he went across to the courtyard to see the sick man. He found him sleeping comfortably, with Calinda beside him on the floor, still plying the fan. He felt of Drum's forehead, then pulled down the sheet to see the misshapen bulge of the poultice on Drum's leg.

"Mère Angelique?" he asked of Calinda.

She bowed her head.

"Then leave it on." He bit his underlip. "A dead rooster, I suppose, and some of her herbs. It's worked before and there's no denying he's more comfortable. Yale could do worse than to send down for the old woman and let her teach a class. Beats me how she does it, but at times I think the old hag knows more than I do." He drew the sheet back up and left the room.

Drum slept throughout the night and intermittently throughout the next day except when Calinda woke him to pour the bitter brew from Mère Angelique's steeped herbs down his throat. His face lost the dry, ashen, lifeless look and some of the sheen reappeared on his skin. Calinda never left him and Alix wisely did not insist on her doing the work around the house, quite content to let her devote her time to Drum. As each day passed, Mère Angelique's prophecy that the poultice would stink became overpoweringly apparent. By the third day, its odor was so bad that even Calinda was nauseated and Rachel could scarcely enter the room. Its stench floated out the window and settled in the courtyard and by the fifth day it had permeated the front of the house. But each day Drum improved and on the sixth day he was propped up in bed and heartily enjoyed his food, quite oblivious of the horrible smell.

That same afternoon Mère Angelique arrived again, took a long satisfied look at her patient, and then, with the same knife that had split the cock, she proceeded to cut off the putrid poultice attached to Drum's leg. It came off in a mass of crawling maggots, but after Mère Angelique had washed the leg with warm water, there was nothing but a clean, nearly healed wound in the midst of an expanse of pale, lavender-colored flesh. She clucked happily and applied another clean bandage.

*"Maint'non,* you be usin' that thing agin." She pointed to Drum's naked body and giggled. "If'n pore old Mère Angelique once again young, she no charge yo' nuttin'. She take her money a-lettin' you pester her. Hiy, yi," she turned to Calinda, "you's lucky, gal. Goddam few women so lucky as yo'. Enjoy it, gal, enjoy it long's you kin. But don' tucker him out now. Don' heat 'im up. Whure'all I gits me my money? Whure's de madam what keeps dis who'house. She owin' me two dollars more." She turned to leave, only to meet Dr. Roberts and Dominique You coming into the room.

"Here's your two dollars, Mère Angelique." Dominique You reached into his pocket and took out two silver dollars.

"And here's two more." Dr. Roberts handed her another pair. "But I'll give you five if you'll tell me what leaves and herbs you used to cure Drum."

The old woman looked at him suspiciously. She had no intention of disclosing her secrets but she had no desire to incur the white man's enmity.

*"La, m'sieur,* old Mère Angelique *pas connai.* Jes' don' know. Fust I tells de prayer and den after de prayer, de spirits tells me what to use. Each time diff'rent. No can tell yo'. Be much obliged if'n I could 'cause sure would like them five dollars but jes' cain't remember."

She left and Dr. Roberts and Dominique You came over to stand by Drum's bed.

"How you feeling, Drum?" Roberts asked. "Let me look at your leg." He studied the healing wound carefully. "Looks good to me, how does it feel?"

"Feels good now that that stinking mess's off," Drum laughed. "I feel good too. Feel so good that tonight Calinda is going to sleep alongside me instead of on the floor. About time, *hein?"* He looked up at Calinda who hung her head, embarrassed by the white man.

"Alix tells me you want to keep on fighting, Drum," Dominique You said.

"Oh no!" Calinda finally found words.

"Shut your mouth, gal. If I want to fight, I'll fight."

"You like fightin', Drum?"

"Sure do, Doctor, sir. Like to push my fist into another man's guts and feel him crumble up."

"All right then, fight, you stubborn bastard." You cuffed him gently. "But if you're going to fight, you're going to learn how to do it. A good fighter's like a good swordsman. He's got to *know*. Look at Bernard de Marigny! The best man with a rapier in the city but he practices at it. Spends a couple of hours a day with Bastille Croquère. That's what makes him good."

"Fighting with your fists is different from fighting with a sword." Drum's conceit would not admit that there was anything about fighting he didn't already know.

"No!" You bellowed. "It's just the same and, dammit, you're going to learn to fight. There's a man down on the levee, an Englishman, used to be a champion in London and he knows as much about fist fighting as Croquère does about dueling. Just as soon as you're up and about, we're going to see him. No more fights for a couple of months anyway—not until you learn something—and then, we'll make you a champion, maybe send you to England like they did Tom Molyneux. I'll foot the bill for the lessons and Alix will damned well give you the time off. Agreed?"

"If you say so, m'sieur."

"I do say so." You turned to Roberts. "Doctor, when will this buck be up and rarin' to go?"

Dr. Roberts looked down at Drum and winked.

"Looks as though he's up and rarin' to go now."

"Sure am, Doctor," Drum winked back.

"I'd say in about another week. He's got to exercise that leg some before he can start. Have the woman massage it and as soon as he can, have him walk on it. Soon as he gets the stiffness out of it, he'll be as good as ever, thanks to old Mother Angelique."

"I'll be back in a week," Dominique promised, "and now we'll leave you."

Drum waited for the diminishing sound of their footsteps on the stairs. He turned and pushed the piled-up pillows onto the floor and threw the sheet back.

"Calinda." His voice was thick with impatience and desire. "Get out of that dress and come over here. There's just one thing I need now to make me feel like a man again."

"I know, Drum." Calinda closed the door with one hand and stripped the dress over her head with the other.

She looked at the bright body lying on the bed and as always, when she looked at it she marveled at it. "And I'll feel like a woman again." One step took her to the bed and to the arms that were waiting for her.

# chapter vi

DRUM HAD ALWAYS loved the levee, but since coming to Madame's Academy of Music he had had few opportunities to go there and enjoy the excitement. Now once again, seated up beside the coachman, with Dominique You behind on the velvet cushions of his open barouche, he thrilled to the life of the levee.

Vessels of all rigs, shapes and sizes were tied up, sometimes three deep, along the big crescent curve the Mississippi made around the city. There were ocean-going ships, sails furled and their gangplanks spewing forth sailors of a dozen different nationalities to add to the turbulence of the levee. Further up the river, bordering on the American town, huddled a conglomeration of flatboats, keelboats and smaller river craft, with here and there a floating store, presided over by some tobacco-chewing Kaintuck. Over all hovered an aroma of raw hides, salted meats, rum, tar and coffee, all intermingled with the damp smell of river mud. Dark-skinned Cubans jostled brisk Yankees from New Hampshire; red-faced Englishmen spouted cockney phrases to uncomprehending Portuguese *bravas;* Carolinians talked of horses, Kentuckians of liquor, Georgians of women; and supercilious Creoles regarded them all with disdainful curiosity. Throughout the long day and far into the night, burly Negro stevedores scurried back and forth unloading and loading ships to the never-ending din of hawkers, blind fiddlers, beggars, pickaninnies jigging for pennies, flower sellers, importuning drabs and enormous Negro women who waddled by, steaming coffee pots on their heads, ready to pour a cup for a penny.

Grogshops did a thriving business, with here and there a tin-roofed shanty where a man shucked oysters, offering them with a peppery sauce which scalded the tongue but gave a delicious flavor. Further back were lines of miserable cribs where two-bit prostitutes did a thriving business, sometimes unable to get off their backs for hours at a time when the lines of sailors who had made this their first destination on quitting ship grew block-long.

Dominique You's carriage moved slowly through the confusion of traffic, halting frequently for the passing of huge drays or of another shiny Creole carriage. Drum, high up on the box, dressed in his plain white cotton shirt and pantaloons, had a vantage point to view the life that ebbed and flowed around him. With difficulty the coachman squeezed the horses through the crowd and over the canal which separated the Vieux Carré from the American part of the city. Turning at the levee, they proceeded a short way up Gravier Street where, at Dominique's order, they paused before a narrow frame house a block up from the levee, which displayed a small, crudely lettered sign: GENTEEL ACCOMMODATIONS FOR ENGLISH SEAMEN ONLY.

Drum held the reins while the coachman jumped down and knocked on the door, which opened immediately to frame an immense white man, somewhat stooped now, but still a commanding figure in height and breadth. His battered face looked like a mass of putty which some amateur sculptor had tried to fashion into a human likeness but had given up soon after starting. The broken nose, the single eye, the scarred cheeks and the swollen ears were crowned by a shock of graying ginger hair that had the appearance of a much-used doormat carelessly thrown on a bald skull. The man looked beyond the slave on the doorstep and, under a sheltering hand, focused his one pale-blue eye on the carriage.

"Mister You!" He motioned to Dominique to come in. "A pleasure, Mister You! A pleasure and a great honor."

"Hop down, Drum." Dominique climbed out of the carriage and went up the steps of the house, extending his hand to the man in the door. "How are you, Sailor Jem?"

"Fine, Mister You! Fine! And will you step over my threshold? And your servant, Mister You?"

Drum followed Dominique inside and saw that the interior was neat and clean as a ship's cabin. The floors of the small front room were holystoned as white as any ship's deck, and a row of identical chairs stood at attention around the walls. The long, straight hallway beyond had a number of doors leading off it on either side and here, presumably, were the "genteel accommodations for English seamen only."

"Jemmy," Dominique said, still nursing an aching hand

rescued from the grip of the big man, "they tell me you used to be the fightingest man in all England."

"Champion, Mister You, champion! Champion of England, sir!" The scarred lips twisted into a smile. "Yes, sir! This hand was shook by the Prince Regent, hisself. Lost me championship (nobody can keep a championship forever, now, can they?)—lost me championship to the Game Chicken, what everybody calls 'im, though his real name was Pierce, Hen Pierce. You knows about 'im, sir. Never lost a fight. If I had to lose me championship, the Chicken was the man to lose it to. Yes, sir!"

"Then you retired from the prize ring?"

"Yes, sir, Mister You. Went to sea, and wound up here in New Orleans. Purtiest place I'd ever seen. Decided to drop anchor and settle down. Bought this house and went into business. Every decent English seaman what comes to New Orleans and wants a clean bed in an honest house comes here. Known from Bristol to Calcutta, I am, from Singapore to Rio. Now, what can I do for you? Honored I am to have you here."

"Can you teach a man to fight?"

"Well, now, Mister You." Jemmy appraised Dominique's figure. "I reckon I can. But, Mister You, ain't you a bit on the elderly side to be a-thinkin' of taking up the art of pugilism?"

Dominique roared. "Too damned old, Jemmy. But I've had fights aplenty in my day—fists, cutlasses, grappling hooks, even horseshoes. Do you know that a horseshoe in a man's fist is a gallant weapon? No, Jemmy, it's not me." His thumb indicated Drum. "It's this young varmint here. Name's Drum and thinks he's a fighter. Good too, but unschooled. With a little scientific knowledge like you can give him, he'd be as good as any boxer you have in England."

Jemmy transferred his gaze from Dominique to Drum who had been standing in the background.

"Nigger, eh?"

"No, not a nigger—only a half-nigger—colored. Part human. But if you object to training a colored boy . . . ?"

"Object? Me obect? Look, Mister You! Tom Molyneux was me idol. Grandest fighter he was that ever lived. He was black, black as the ace of spades." He put his hand out to Drum. "Glad to make your acquaintance, lad. Shake. Your color ain't a-goin' to rub off."

Drum extended his hand slowly after embarrassedly wiping

it on his breeches. He was confused. White men did not shake hands with Negroes. It just wasn't done. As long as he had known Dominique You, he couldn't imagine shaking hands with him.

"So you want to fight?" Jemmy said. "What did Mister You say your name was?"

"Drum, m'sieur."

"Well, Drum, never mind the Monsewer. Call me Jemmy or Jem."

"Yes, m'sieur." Drum grinned and shook his head in apology for his error. "Yes, Jemmy, sir."

Dominique lowered one eyelid and Jemmy understood that it was inherently impossible for a Negro to address a white man as an equal.

"And you want to learn how to fight, Drum?"

"Yes, Jemmy, sir."

"Looks like you got a fightin' build. Take your shirt off."

"And shuck your nether togs, too," Dominique added. "Wait till you see how this buck's hung, Jemmy."

"Colossal, Mister You, colossal." Jemmy squinted his one eye. "But damned dangerous for a fighter. Damned dangerous. Of course, in England we protects a man's privates with a heavy leather strap, like what jockeys use in ridin' horseback. Protects a man, it does."

Dominique shook his head. "Wouldn't do in New Orleans, Jemmy. Nigger bucks fight naked, stark naked. White men like to see 'em stripped to their skin. Grabbin' each other's balls is part of the sport. When one buck can get ahold of the other's knockers and squeeze 'em, you'll hear hollerin' such as you never heard. Finishes him off quick. No man can fight with his knockers squeezed. So far, Drum's been lucky."

Jemmy shook his head and clucked dolefully. "Broughton wouldn't never've approved. Never. No more hittin' below the belt, ever since Broughton. Fight like gentlemen, says Broughton's rules. No gougin' eyes, no bitin', no wrestlin'. Scientific pugilism, that's all what's allowed these times. But let me tell you this, Mister You. I can learn this boy to do two things—fight his opponent and defend hisself so that, naked or clothed, them glorious parts of his will never be in no danger." He came over to Drum. "May I?" he asked.

Drum looked puzzled, but Jemmy accepted his silence as consent. With a practiced hand he went over Drum's body, expertly gauged his musculature—its good points and bad. When he had finished, he stood back.

"From the waist up, the fellow's fine. Good chest, good back, fine arms—though wanting some in biceps development. Strong back, fairly good hands, though a little small. Good thick skin that won't never break too easy. But from the waist down, he's too puny. Legs not developed and too spindly. "Legs"—Jemmy looked at Dominique as though seeking confirmation—"are as important as arms. Arms are offensive, legs defensive, and defense is as important as offense in pugilism. Got to build 'em up."

"How are you going to do that, sir?" Drum surveyed his legs. They had always seemed satisfactory to him.

"Three ways—runnin', skippin' and liftin'. Two months ought to do it. Now, lad, slip on your breeches and come out in the garden behind the house."

Drum followed the two white men out into a small walled area whose one struggling live-oak sapling and a small plot of scraggly flowers were its only claim to horticultural distinction. Big Jemmy indicated a plank bench along one wall for Dominique You, while he and Drum faced each other in the center of the clean-swept flagging.

"Now, fight!" Jemmy said.

And Drum fought. But he did not fight Jemmy—he fought only the thin air. When he drove a punch to Jemmy's head, it missed by an inch. When he grabbed for Jemmy's hulking body, he couldn't touch it. Jemmy was able to stand in one place and by merely swaying slightly keep out of reach of his opponent. Drum turned, lowered his head like a bull, and charged, but he met only a cushion of air. He swung massive rights and lefts to Jemmy's body. But Jemmy, big a target as he was, just seemed to float away. At the end of ten minutes Drum was dripping sweat, panting and feeling his knees like water under him. Jemmy, however, was as cool, calm and collected as before. There wasn't even a bead of sweat on his forehead. As Drum wound himself up for another blow, Jemmy casually swung first his right, then jabbed with his left and Drum sprawled on the ground, unable to get up.

"He'll be all right in a minute," Jemmy assured Dominique as he splashed a bucket of water over Drum. When Drum opened his eyes, Jemmy gave him a hand up and supported him as he walked over to the bench on legs that buckled under him.

As a matter of truth, Drum had expended more of his skill in avoiding hitting Jemmy than in his effort to hit him. It was a major crime for a Negro to strike a white man and Drum knew it. He had been commanded to fight with Jemmy and he had pretended to obey that command, but with every blow he had deliberately missed his target. Which is not to say that Jemmy's avoidance of Drum's blows was not skillful; the skill was simply unnecessary and wasted. Nevertheless, the instruction was not lost on Drum. He saw its value. But it seemed to him that Jemmy's scientific boxing would not always be effective in the rough-and-tumble combat he was used to.

"Now you see what I mean about fightin', lad," Jemmy was saying. "You think you're a fighter, but you don't know one damned thing about the noble art of fisticuffs. Flailin' your arms around like a windmill ain't a-goin' to do you no good. Just tires you out. I could've stood there for an hour and let you punch circles around me till you dropped to the ground exhausted. Hope I didn't hurt you, but your lesson for today was just to show you how easy it is to knock a man cold."

"I didn't know what hit me," Drum confessed.

"Tomorrow morn, ten o' the clock," Jemmy said. "Two hours in the morning. Afternoon you box with your own shadow. Then you run for five miles, out in the country. And here"—he reached for a short length of rope under the bench. "Take this with you and learn how to skip the rope. Like this." Big Jemmy took one end in each hand and threw it over his head, skipping it as it touched the ground. He went so fast that Drum was unable even to see the rope.

"This boy got a wife?" Jemmy asked Dominique as he stopped his skipping.

"Nigger slaves don't have wives." Dominique shook his head. "He's got a wench he sleeps with—a hot little bitch she is, too."

"Well, then, keep him away from her. Once a week if he has to, but that's all. Can't build him up daytimes if a wench drains it out of him nights." He looked at Drum and asked, "Still want to make a fighter?"

Drum shook his head. "Not if I have to give up Calinda, sir."

"Don't matter if you want to or not. If you're going to make a fighter, you got to get along without women. Others have. I had to when I was a-fightin'. Kind of hard, getting used to living without it after you've been having it regular, but I'll see to it that you're so damned tired when you get back home you'll not even be interested. You Dominique's boy?"

"No, sir. I belong to Madame Alix."

"Jemmy raised his brows. "The bawdy house on Dumaine Street?"

Drum nodded.

Jemmy's breath whistled through his teeth and he let out a roar. "Here I'm going to make a fighter out of a man, try to keep him away from the female sex, and the lucky bastard lives in the finest whorehouse in the city. Hell and damnation, boy, what do you want to be a fighter for?"

"Reckon I don't know, sir." Drum grinned sheepishly. "Maybe because Madame craves me to be one."

"Shut up, Drum!" Dominique got up from the bench. "Don't matter one way or the other what you want. Madame says you're going to fight and you fight. Jemmy says you're going to sleep alone and you'll sleep alone. I say if you're going to fight, you're going to learn how. Come on, Drum." He went inside the house and down the long straight hall, Drum and Jemmy following. As he opened the front door, he turned to Jemmy.

"Ten o'clock tomorrow morning," he said. "I'll be here with him but tomorrow Drum won't ride with the coachman —he'll run alongside."

When they returned and Dominique delivered Jemmy's fiat, all hell broke loose in the Academy of Music. Alix laughed at the idea while she condemed Jemmy to eternal damnation. A big strong buck like Drum! As if he couldn't accommodate ten women one night and fight the next! She would be losing a good profit on him and that she wouldn't consider. Not for a second! He was just getting so he could participate in her *tableaux* with some degree of professional skill and gaining a reputation for a good performance. The very idea. He'd fight and he'd also. . . .

Dominique held up a restraining hand.

"And how much do you make out of your little dramatic sketches?" Dominique asked.

"For Drum and one girl, twenty-five dollars. With two, fifty dollars and for a real melee, with four girls fighting to rip the clothes off Drum, one hundred dollars, plus ten dollars for new shirts and pants for Drum."

"One hundred dollars—say one hundred and ten because instead of buying new clothes, you mend the old ones." Dominique wagged his head at her. "One hundred and ten paltry dollars and on Drum's first fight, you took in more than two thousand, yes?"

Alix grudgingly agreed.

"Which leads me to believe that you're a hell of a business woman, *chérie*. You can't see beyond the end of your nose. Any mulatto stud that you can pick up at Maspero's for five hundred dollars can put on as good a show as Drum."

"Not many as good as Drum." Alix shook her head.

"Hell! I'll find you one that's better equipped. Maspero's dealing in fancies now and he'll be on the lookout for you. He'll get you a real freak. But we're going to make a fighting bull out of Drum, not an exhibition stallion. I'm willing to pay for his learning because I'll win far more back on him than I'll pay out. Your job is to keep him out of your beds and keep that wild cat, Calinda, away from him. Lock him up if you have to or lock her up. Let him at her once a week—on Saturday nights—and he can rest on Sundays. I'll do my part, you do yours and we'll both make money on Drum—more in one night than you'd make on your stable of fillies in a week. Agreed?"

Dominique's words had wisdom and Alix consented. Drum would have six nights of continence imposed upon him. *Bien!* Lock him up in his room and lock Calinda up in another. That was a simple solution.

But Alix figured without Calinda. When the last male guest of the Academy of Music had departed, and Drum had shed his white bartender's coat and was about to climb the narrow stairs to his room with Calinda, Rachel broke the news to her. She refused to believe it, but Drum confirmed Rachel's statement—he had been hoping that the regime would not start until the next night, however—and now Calinda faced the awful truth that she would not have Drum until Saturday. Until Saturday! Today was only Wednesday! Tonight, Thursday night and Friday night without Drum!

*Damne!*

Calinda exploded!

But Drum dragged her off, although his heart was not in his work. He locked her in a little room off the kitchen and allowed Rachel to follow him up the stairs and bolt his door on the outside. For some ten minutes, the house was quiet and then Calinda started shrieking, calling Alix all the foul epithets she had learned in her brief stay at the Academy of Music. Rachel tried in vain to calm her through the bolted door but to no avail. She hammered on the door with her fists, then grabbed the one chair in the room, broke it apart, and used one of the legs to pry the door open. Brandishing the chair leg, she burst out into the courtyard and headed straight for the stairs that led to Alix' room. Had she succeeded in reaching it, she would undoubtedly have pounded Alix to a pulp. Her rage was homicidal. Alix had taken Drum away from her and nothing else mattered. Rachel, followed by the female slaves of the house, tried to stop her but she turned and clobbered Rachel over the head, knocking her unconscious, and would have done the same with the others if they had not fled, cowering under the stairs that led to the *garçonnière*.

Drum, locked in his room, knew that if the girl laid hands on Alix nothing in the world would save her. He eased himself out of the window, hung by his fingers from the ledge and dropped to the flagging below. His legs withstood the shock and he ran to Calinda. In her frenzy she would not listen to him. Brandishing the stick, with threats to kill Alix, she tried to keep him off, but Drum made a dive, caught her around the ankles and threw her to the ground. Grabbing the chair leg from her hand he sat on her chest, trying to quiet her.

Alix, about to settle herself in bed for the night, had heard the commotion. She came out on the balcony, her face white, her hands trembling.

"Get rid of that little bitch," she shouted. "Shoot her! I heard her threaten me. She was going to kill me."

"No, madame, no!" Drum was pleading for Calinda. "She didn't mean it. She was just upset because we were separated. She'll be good now." He slapped Calinda across the face. "Shut up, gal," he whispered, "if you want to live."

"Call the police, Rachel! Call the police!" Alix was quite unaware that Rachel was beyond calling. "Have them take this murderess to the whips. Fifty lashes, no a hundred! That will teach her."

"Please, madame." Drum held his hand over Calinda's mouth. "She's all right now. She'll be a good girl. I'll take her back to her room now. Please, madame."

Alix disappeared from the railing and Drum saw the white

blob of her nightdress descending the stairs. He whispered to Calinda. "Don't say a word. Let me talk her out of this. For the love of God, shut up!" He removed his hand from her mouth and stood up, pulling her up with him.

"Where's Rachel?" Alix demanded. Then she saw the dark mass of Rachel's dress on the stones and it set her off again.

"She's killed Rachel. Oh my God! Rachel! You'll suffer for this, girl. Rachel!" Alix' screams not only brought out the girls from the second- and third-floor rooms to hang over the balconies but penetrated Rachel's unconsciousness to rouse her. She struggled to her feet and managed to get to Alix's side.

"I'm all right, madame! Quite all right. Do go upstairs and get the girls back into their rooms. Drum and I will attend to Calinda." She laid a reassuring hand on Alix' arm.

But Alix was not to be reassured. She had long itched to punish Calinda for her insolence and independent airs. Now was the time to punish her, now and right here on the spot. No use sending her tomorrow to the public whipping post next to the stocks in the Place d'Armes. Right now and right here! She looked up at the rows of faces dimly seen above the railings.

"Toinette, Roselle, Titine, Renée-Rose!" Alix called the strongest and tallest girls in her house. "Down here!" She waited for them to come tripping down the stairs.

"Toinette, Renée-Rose, take hold of one of the bitch's arms. Titine, Roselle, take the other." She waited until they grabbed Calinda, and managed to hold her. "Rachel, get my whip."

Drum relinquished Calinda unwillingly to Alix' authority. Now that the inevitability of punishment had become a reality, the girl ceased to struggle and dumbly accepted her captivity. In a moment Rachel appeared with a light coachman's whip which she handed to Alix but Alix merely indicated Drum with a nod of her head in his direction.

"Fifty lashes," she said. "It's not a heavy whip but lay it on well, Drum."

"I can't, madame." Drum could not scar the flesh he loved so much.

"You'd better"—Alix was grim—"because if you don't she'll go to the Place d'Armes tomorrow and you along with her. She'll find the lash of Olympe a lot stronger than this plaything and so will you, Drum. I've pampered you two niggers long enough. Time you both learned that you're slaves. Lay it on, Drum, and don't hold it back."

He didn't dare to disobey her. He knew that Calinda would suffer far more from the heavy lash of the public whip wielded by the *brut*, Olympe. He waited till the four girls got a more secure hold on Calinda's wrists, and spread her arms straight out. He raised the whip. It cut through the air and although he had tried not to put the full force of his strength into it, it stung Calinda's back and she screamed.

"One," Alix counted, "and put more force into it than that, Drum."

One by one, with a short respite after each ten, Drum brought down the whip fifty times. The black skin of Calinda's back turned red, then broke. When Drum had finished, the whip was slippery with blood.

After the last stroke, Alix commanded the girls to release Calinda and the girl fell to the flagging. Like a mother hen with her flock, Alix sent them upstairs ahead of her. Rachel and Drum were left alone with the sobbing Calinda, for the other female slaves had hidden in their rooms, fearful that Alix' anger would include them in the punishment.

Drum gathered the whimpering girl in his arms and carried her up to the room they had always shared and laid her gently on the bed. Rachel appeared with a candle, warm water and soft cloths and washed the blood from Calinda's back. Gently she spread a healing ointment over the lacerated skin and bandaged it.

"Carry her downstairs, Drum."

"Not tonight, *maman*. Tonight will not matter. Madame need never know."

"No, Drum, tonight will not matter, and if necessary I shall lie for you in the morning." She leaned over and touched Calinda on the shoulder where the black skin gleamed above the white bandage. "I think you have learned one thing tonight, Calinda. Madame is your mistress and you are her slave. And so are you, Drum, and so am I. Nothing we have is our own, not even our bodies. Love is not for slaves. From now on remember that. Tonight you can stay together. But after tonight do not cross Madame again. You, Drum, become the fighting man that Madame wants and you, Calinda, relinquish Drum for six nights and be glad that you can have him on the seventh." She walked out and closed the door behind her, but she did not slip the bolt in place.

Drum gathered Calinda into his arms, tenderly and without urgency. They both needed comfort. Before this night, they had been two exuberant young animals, glorying in each other. Tonight they were fully aware that they were mere chattels—slaves. Tonight they needed the physical contact of each other in order to share each other's suffering. The bodily suffering of Calinda was no greater than the mental suffering of Drum. It was a suffering that drew them closer together than ever before and it was during those hours that Drum's son was conceived—not in the wild frenzy of animal lust which they had formerly enjoyed but in a quiet soothing consolation that released their minds and bodies and let them feel they were not animals but human beings.

The *sereno*, the lone watchman who paraded the night streets of New Orleans, was announcing the hour. He called out the morning hour of five. Exhausted, satiated and sorrowing, Drum gathered Calinda up like a child and deposited her, sleeping, on the pallet on the floor in the little room off the kitchen. Then he climbed the steps back to his room and stretched out alone on the sheets that were still warm from her body.

His thoughts were bitter. He was Madame's slave. She wanted him to fight. He would learn more about fighting than any other man in New Orleans. He'd be better than Big Jemmy. He'd vanquish every man pitted against him. Outwardly he would be a model slave, obedient and cheerful and uncomplaining. In that way he could protect himself and Calinda. But inside he would be ruled by one abiding and overpowering passion. He would hate the big, soft, white woman sleeping in her big, soft, white bed. *Mon Dieu,* how he would hate her! But, he would be smart. She would never know how much he hated her until that one supreme moment when—just how it would happen he did not know—he would tell her. Aie! He would tell her.

## chapter vii

AT TEN O'CLOCK the next morning, with no traces—at least none which were apparent—of the sleepless night he had spent, Drum was again at Sailor Jem's, having run all the way alongside Dominique You's carriage instead of riding up with the coachman. He arrived panting and dripping with sweat but Jemmy gave him only time to strip off his wet shirt before they started to work, using, as before, the walled garden behind the house. Dominique sat on the bench and watched, absorbing the theories that Drum learned by action and storing them in his mind so that he himself could coach Drum.

And so, for many mornings, Drum came to Jemmy's house and for many afternoons he drove outside the city with Dominique. When they reached the outskirts, he got down from the carriage and ran beside it along the country roads. If they were seen by any of Dominique's acquaintances, he told them that he was exercising Drum's wounded leg but gave no hint he was being trained as a fighter. To supplement his runs in the country, Drum jumped rope and lifted heavy weights until the calves of his legs rounded out and his thighs swelled with strength.

In the weeks that followed, he learned many things. He learned how to stand with his left foot forward, angled to give him greater resistance to another man's blows, anchoring his huge body to the floor so that he could not be easily toppled over. He learned a complicated system of footwork, more involved and more intricate than any jigging dance. He practiced to be always in balance, his feet planted firmly on the ground, braced against the blow he might unexpectedly receive at any minute. Even when his two feet seemed to be dancing, there was always one big foot whose sole was firmly braced so that he would not be knocked down.

He learned to protect his head with his left shoulder, keeping it always below the muscular protection of that shoulder, for, as Jemmy explained, the head was the most vulnerable spot. It was the one part of his anatomy which was not protected by a heavy padding of muscles. Where the skin was stretched tautly over the bone the blows were not cushioned by a layer of flesh, and took effect immediately. Jemmy stressed the fact that he must protect his eyes above all else, and always watch his opponent. He must learn to anticipate his opponent's next move by such small signs as the glance of the other man's eyes, or a tensing of a muscle preparatory to striking a blow.

Drum learned the power of a straight quick jab with his powerful left, either to the body or to a vulnerable part of the face, such as between the eyes, on the nose or landing on the lips to split them open like a ripe tomato. He sensed the psychological advantage of making his adversary bleed, for it not only frightened him and produced visible evidence that he was hurt but gave the audience something to cheer about. Then, it was advantageous if he could land a blow so that the other's forehead would be cut and the blood would run down into his eyes to blind him. When using his right, Drum learned to put the full force of his shoulder and back muscles behind it, striking his opponent's body, whenever possible, directly over the heart with such a force that it would cause that already overworked organ to deviate in its mathematical regularity and possibly stop beating entirely.

At the same time, Drum learned to defend himself, never overreachng himself, so that he would lose his balance, and always endeavoring to keep his own body away from the blows of his opponent. He developed a flexibility of body so that no matter how tightly he was clutched in the viselike grip of another's arms, he could wiggle out of the grasp, expanding and contracting his muscles so that he could slither out of any hold like a snake. To aid him in doing this more effectively, he kept his body oiled so that even after washing himself, a residue of oil would remain in his pores, keeping his skin glossy and slippery.

Finally, from Jemmy who had learned to fight before the Marquis of Queensberry, then not yet born, had turned pugilism into a gentleman's sport—in those brutal days when two men faced each other, bare-knuckled and stripped to the waist, with nothing barred, to fight until one was a battered corpse or well might be—Drum learned to kill his opponent if he could win by no other method. The noble Marquis of

Queensberry did not rule the slave fights in New Orleans and they were far more savage than fights had ever been in England. For one slave to kill another in a fight was not murder, so Drum learned lethal techniques. He was taught the spots on the body where pressure could be exerted to kill a man—a finger driven like a steel nail through the eye; the edge of a hand slammed against a man's windpipe; a blow with all his enormous strength to the solar plexus; and the gripping, pulling, tearing motion that would strip off a man's genitals and leave a gaping, bleeding hole in his groin.

All these things Drum learned in those long weeks of work, sweat and exhaustion until he finally felt himself become a fighting machine—a highly complex instrument whose mind had become devoid of almost every thought except that of the ability to use his whole body to destroy another's. Trained to this peak, it became increasingly necessary for him to fight and test his new ability, for Jemmy was aware that nothing proved a man's own superiority more than a complete victory over another. It engendered confidence, inflated his ego and added a strut of self-importance to his walk.

So Dominique You announced to the young bloods of New Orleans that Madame's Drum was ready to fight again and that his leg was completely healed. Immediately Lazare LeToscan, whose man had lost the last fight to Drum, brought forth another, whom he had been keeping in reserve for just this announcement. Lazare's man was a powerful young Fullah somewhere between eighteen and twenty. He was a big fellow, tall but a bit on the rangy side. Until the day Lazare had purchased him—having seen him working in the fields of a neighboring plantation and being immediately impressed by his enormous physique—he had been nothing but a canefield worker. LeToscan had matched him with several of the slaves on his plantation and the fellow had won mainly through an instinctive use of brute force. He had a gentle disposition, but if his master commanded him to fight, he fought, obeying the order as unquestioningly as he would if he were told to cut cane.

The night came when Drum and the Fullah boy faced each other, their bodies gleaming like bronze statues in the flambeaux-lighted courtyard of Alix' house. Once again. Alix, from her vantage point on the second-floor balcony, held the bets, her lap overflowing with banknotes, gold and silver.

Betting had been heavy this night and although nobody discounted Drum's ability to fight, several had bet on the Fullah because of his longer reach and LeToscan's claims of his prowess and past successes.

In a breathless silence, the whole gathering stared at the two motionless gladiators who seemed frozen and sculptural as the flambeaux gilded their naked bodies with flickering tongues of light. Dominique You seconding Drum, and Lazare LeToscan his Fullah, pushed their two fighters into the middle of the open space in the center of the court. For a moment neither Drum nor the Fullah moved, and in that moment Drum sized up his adversary. His eyes made a quick survey of the lithe body, appraising its weak and strong points, and he immediately spotted a weakness in the legs, a lack of rotundity in the chest and arms that were too finely muscled. In that moment, while he studied the other's physique, the germ of a plan, entirely divorced from the fight he was about to start, entered his mind. It was only half formed but to bring it to fruition he must win the fight. He felt pretty certain that he would.

The Fullah, tired of waiting for Drum to begin, sparred and struck for the stomach but Drum danced sideways, pivoting just enough to let the blow swing past him, and countered swiftly with a short jab with his left to the Fullah's face. He followed this by a slower right hook to the body as the fellow instinctively raised his arms to ward off another blow to his face. The Fullah rocked on his heels, stunned for a moment. Smack! Drum's fist crashed between the Fullah's eyes. Then, with a rapidity which made his arms seem like crashing pistons, he hammered blow after blow on the staggering Fullah. Each one took effect. Blood streamed from the fellow's nose, lips and cheek. He staggered and Drum was upon him, pounding unmercifully on his body until there was scarcely an inch which was not bruised or bleeding. Then, concentrating all his strength in one hammer-like blow which had the whole leverage of his powerful body behind it, Drum drove a blow to the fellow's heart, and saw him crumple. He did not fall at once, but seemed to melt, like a pewter image left on a hot stove, until he sprawled in a welter of arms and legs at Drum's feet. Drum placed one bare foot on the Fullah's chest, reached down and lifted one of his arms, releasing it. It fell limply to the floor. The fight had lasted less then ten minutes, during which time the

Fullah had not scored one hit. Drum was uninjured except for his bleeding knuckles.

A roar of shouted acclamations burst loose from a hundred throats. Even those who had bet on the Fullah cheered Drum, for it was the neatest, cleanest, quickest fight they had ever seen. Not that they wanted a neat, clean, quick fight. Oh, no! They had hoped for something more gory, far more brutal and even deadly. But the very speed and efficiency with which Drum had dispatched his man won their admiration. They had never seen such fighting before—it was as clean-cut as surgery, as economical as the motion of a machine and as deadly as hitting a man with an axe.

Lazare LeToscan, oblivious to the needs or suffering of his own man, stepped across the Fullah's prostrate form and lifted Drum's arm high.

"*Voilà* Our Drum! The best fighter in New Orleans!"

Again the crowd roared and the cheers sounded sweet in Drum's ears. He had fought and won and the primitive sense of the brute—victory over his opponent—lifted him from the position of slave. For a moment he was a man among men. Now the plan that had germinated when he first saw the naked Fullah facing him grew in Drum's mind until it blossomed and bore fruit. He knew that at this moment, regardless of his colored skin and his slave status, nothing he could ask would be denied him in the prevailing excitement.

LeToscan kicked the Fullah with the sharp toe of his varnished boot. The man did not move.

LeToscan shrugged his shoulders. "Did you kill the no-good bastard, Drum? If I keep on fighting my niggers against you, I'll not have one left."

"No, I didn't kill him, M'sieur LeToscan. See, he still breathes."

"Too goddamned bad you didn't. I bought the clumsy *lourdaud* for a fighting nigger and see how he turned out. Now he's worthless as a fighter—everyone has seen him whipped without even landing a blow. I'll send him back to the canefields tomorrow."

"M'sieur LeToscan, sir." Drum had embarked on a strange request. "Will you sell this boy?"

"Sell him, Drum? Hell, I'll give him away if anyone wants a worthless heap of *merde* like that. Paid a thousand dollars for him a month ago. He's not worth three hundred as a field hand now."

"Did you say you would give him away?" Drum was quick to follow up the lead LeToscan had given him.

"Sure, Drum, do you want the bastard? Save me the trouble of carting him back to the plantation and having to look at his smashed face."

"I'd be very happy if you'd present him to Madame Alix, M'sieur LeToscan. We could use him around here."

"Here, Lazare." Bernard de Marigny stepped forward with a clutch of banknotes in his hand. "Give him to Drum and I'll pay you for him. I won nearly two thousand on Drum tonight and you lost. I can afford to be generous."

"Keep your money, Bernard!" LeToscan waved de Marigny back. "What do you want him for, Drum?"

"Well, he can tend bar for Madame and I can teach him to mix drinks."

"Don't forget to teach him to mix my special," a voice called down from the balcony.

Drum recognized the speaker.

"A special Planter's Punch, made with double cognac?" Drum called back and then turned to LeToscan again. "I can use him as a training partner,"—he grinned—"and he can do some other things for Madame that I am not able to do any more."

"Not able, Drum?" another voice called out. "You seemed pretty capable the last time I saw you perform here."

"More able than ever before," Drum shouted back, "but Madame wants me to be a fighter, not a performing stud. Can't do both and this fellow looks like he might put on a good stiff performance."

"I'll send Madame the papers in the morning," LeToscan laughed. "Mayhap the fellow can stand up for the women if he can't stand up for you. Get him out of here, Drum, and come back and mix us some drinks."

Drum reached down and got the limp Fullah to his feet. He shook him vigorously but the boy did not open his eyes. Drum spied the bucket of water nearby, placed there by the seconds. He knelt on the flagging, letting the Fullah's body slump to the ground and reached out for the bucket, splashing the contents over the fellow's head. Slowly the Fullah opened his eyes to see Drum bending over him.

"Don' hit me no mo', big boy," he mumbled in thick Gombo. "Don' hit me no mo'."

"I'll not hit you. Get up on your feet. Can you walk?"

"Mo' bettah you help me, big boy. Laigs don' seem to hold up no mo'."

Drum got him to his feet.

*"Messieurs,"* he turned to the crowd. "Monsieur LeToscan asked me to clean this heap of *merde* out and then come back and mix some drinks for you."

"On the house." Alix' triumphant voice floated down from the balcony.

"And so, with your permission." Drum walked away bearing the weight of the Fullah on his shoulders, dragging the man's bare feet on the stones behind him.

He got him through the kitchen and into the little room that Calinda had occupied alone of late—at least for six nights out of seven—where he fell in a sprawl to the pallet on the floor. Drum straightened out his legs and made him more comfortable.

"Don' hit me no mo'," the Fullah begged.

"I'll not hit you, man. What's your name?"

*"Mo 'pelle Blaise."*

"Then, Blaise, you stay here. Rest yourself. I'll send someone to clean you up. We're going to be friends, Blaise. *Mais oui!* I nearly killed you but I've nothing against you. You're going to stay here with me. We'll be friends, *amis, comprend'?"*

"What's your name?"

"Drum."

"We be frens, Drum." Blaise closed his eyes.

Drum went out and closed the door. On his way through the kitchen, he met Calinda who had been waiting for him. She had a pair of freshly ironed pants and a shirt on her arm but they dropped to the floor as she threw herself into his arms.

*"Aie, mon massacreur!"* She was sobbing and laughing at the same time. "You all right?"

He held up his skinned knuckles. "Just this! Not another scratch on me. Let me wash my face, *mignon,* and get into those clothes. There's a couple of hundred thirsty men out there, all wanting a drink and I owe them a lot tonight."

"Who's he?" Calinda pointed to the closed door while Drum dashed water on his face.

"Name's Blaise. I won him for Madame tonight. Now he can stay up till morning mixing drinks and I can sleep nights. And he can stand up in Madame's salon while her pretty little bitches rip the clothes off him. Let him work them over. I'm no fancy man. From now on I'm a fighter and I'll use him to spar with me. May even teach him how to fight."

"He's a pretty boy," Calinda smiled. "I saw him fighting."

"You keep your eyes off him and your hands too. Catch you fooling around with him, I'll give you fifty lashes myself."

"I don't want him Drum, not as long as I can have you."

"You don't get me much lately, *chérie.*"

"Not enough, Drum."

"Then don't figure on Blaise being in the saddle when I'm out of it. That's mine!" He let his hand slide slowly down over her belly. "Mon Dieu! You're getting fat, Calinda."

"That's your son, Drum." She grabbed his hand and held it over the round swelling of her stomach. "I was going to tell you tonight if Madame let us be together. You didn't even notice last Saturday night."

"*Poupée,* I didn't notice anything. I wanted you so much I wouldn't have noticed if your skin had turned white. You really mean you're . . . ?" He drew her to him and kissed her long and tenderly. "Oh, *poupée.*"

"Careful now." He pushed her away. "Don't get me excited or those men will never get their drinks. Look, get some warm water and go in your room and wash the blood off that poor bastard. Put some of *maman's* ointment on him and give him a pair of my pants to put on." He shook a warning finger at her. "If you touch more than his face, you'll be sorry." Drum smiled. "You saw him. He's even more of a man than I am."

"He'll never be the man you are." Calinda fastened the last button of his shirt. "Now go, but remember, you've got another tussle on your hands tonight and one that you won't win in ten minutes either."

"Is it safe for my son?" Drum patted the bulge affectionately.

"*Maman* says it won't matter."

"After tonight, chérie, I'll make doubly sure that nothing happens to my son. When you're sleeping where Blaise is he'll be sleeping with me in my room. Then I'll know where he is and I'll know where you are and I'll know I can trust you."

"And I'll know where you are and I'll know where he is but perhaps I won't trust you." Calinda remembered the afternoon when de Marigny and Drum were both beside her.

"That's something you'll never need to worry about." He was out of the door and across the courtyard. Calinda could hear the shouts that acclaimed him as he walked to the bar. She was happy. Her Drum was safe. Slowly she gathered up some clean linen rags, dipped out some still warm water from the kettle into a basin, lit another candle and went into her room where Blaise was stretched out on her pallet. The candle she placed on the floor, and knelt down beside him. Carefully she washed the blood from his face. But try as she would, she could not keep her eyes from wandering.

## chapter viii

THE BILL OF SALE for the Negro slave Blaise, which Lazare LeToscan's attorney delivered to Madame Alix, recorded the sale—for the sum of one dollar and other valuable considerations—to Madame Alix de Vaux. Thus he became her property and she was legally his mistress. But Blaise never really belonged to her. He was Drum's own boy, and he felt he belonged to Drum body and soul. Drum had fought him and punished him severely in the fight but Blaise gloried in the remembrance of the pain he had suffered; he saw in Drum all the things he longed to be himself. To him the dashing Drum represented the apex of perfection and the few years' difference in their ages was just enough to bring about the hero worship which Blaise accorded the handsome mulatto.

Drum was light-skinned, Blaise was black, and the difference in pigmentation alone was enough to make Blaise grateful that Drum would even so much as notice him. Drum's rakish good looks were something for Blaise to marvel at and admire. But he was not jealous of Drum's good looks—he gloried in them. Drum, having lived in the city all his life, had acquired a cosmopolitan dash and a superficial elegance which poor Blaise, a mere *brut* from the canefields, might never hope to attain. His idol's elegant clothes, which hung from the nail in his room, were venerated objects to Blaise, whose rough cotton pants and shirts did nothing but cover his nakedness. Often he stroked Drum's lustrous garments, letting his fingers linger lovingly on the smooth broadcloth and the shiny satin.

The finely accented French that Drum spoke was a marked contrast to Blaise's roughly mouthed Gombo. Drum's feet fitted snugly into his varnished boots—Blaise's overgrown, calloused feet had never known shoes. In contrast to Drum's superbly muscled body, Blaise felt his own to be thin and scrawny.

In short, Drum was everything that poor Blaise desired to be and he determined to pattern himself after his idol in every way. Some things of course would be impossible to achieve, such as Drum's good looks and his beautiful suit, but at least Blaise could learn French, which he set out to do, copying Drum's inflection and accent. Although he could never have Drum's long hair, he brushed his own wiry mop to a semblance of order and flattened it with grease, carefully cultivating the few hairs that grew on his cheeks into a semblance of Drum's sidewhiskers. There was, however, one way in which he could excel his idol, although he was not aware of it and would not have believed it had it been suggested to him. He was larger than Drum and his physique, although immature and untrained, possessed a greater potential than Drum's; Blaise was taller by an inch, with longer arms and legs. He begged to be allowed to train with Drum, but Blaise, his eyes completely blinded by hero worship, never came to realize that he was beginning to surpass Drum after a few months. Constantly striving to improve himself, he accomplished much. He lost his stooped shuffle and began to walk erect, lifting up his feet with the same nervous step that Drum employed. In time he came to relinquish his thick Gombo; he learned to eat with knife and fork, sitting at a table; he pared his fingernails and toenails evenly and kept the rim of black grime from showing under them. Within a few months, he had changed from a field-hand *brut* to a smart young man, clean, immaculate in freshly laundered white pants and shirt and a face far more handsome than he imagined it to be.

As for Drum, he accepted Blaise's worship as a matter of course. He was never consciously unkind to the Fullah boy who was constantly at his elbow, but he treated him exactly as he had seen white masters treat their slaves—as a thing, not a person. Blaise was kept running to wait on him; only too anxious to be of service, he jumped at the chance to perform the most menial services. Blaise bathed him, rubbed him down, anointed him with the oil which Drum always used to keep his skin in condition, helped him to dress on the rare occasions when Drum wore his good clothes, and would willingly have lain down on the floor and thanked his idol for kicking him, if Drum had so much as expressed such a wish. Drum accepted all Blaise's services without comment or thanks. When he scolded him for being a stupid *brut*, Blaise accepted the censure meekly. As long as he could be with his master he was happy, and to him Drum was truly his master. As for Alix, he rarely saw her and when he did he became awkward and tongue-tied to think that he was in the presence of a white woman.

Blaise was quick to learn and soon caught on to the tricks in mixing drinks. Although he could never do it with the flair and showmanship Drum displayed, he soon achieved a share of the popularity which the master had enjoyed at the bar. Lacking, however, were the quick and the ingratiating repartee which endeared Drum to Madame Alix' customers. Blaise could never think of anything to say when some Creole elegant started chaffing him, but his grin was so wide and so startling white-toothed, his eyes so softly brown and honest and his dependability so apparent that these qualities soon endeared him to all, quite as much as Drum's flashy mannerisms.

There was one possession of Drum's which Blaise admired most of all. Calinda! Without even admitting the fact to himself, he had been in love with her since the first night she had come to him and washed the blood from his face. She had been so tender with him, even washing parts of his body where there was no blood, it had been a new experience for him. He had never known affection from the time he had been torn from his mother's arms as a child of seven and watched her mount the auction block to be sold. Later he had been knocked down in a miscellaneous lot of twelve children and sold to the famous Falconhurst Plantation in Alabama. Here he had grown up with enough to eat and the impersonal kindness which Warren Maxwell always accorded his slaves. He had never been starved, gone naked, slept without a roof over his head or been whipped—but neither had he ever had any love or affection. When he had been brought into New Orleans with the Maxwell caffle and sold to Lazare LeToscan, he had been horribly homesick for the carefree days at Falconhurst. His had been a rough, masculine existence in which love had had no place and into which tenderness had never entered.

He had longed for love as a homeless dog longs for a master. Now he found himself in a place where people treated him kindly. Drum accepted his worship and returned it with a casual friendship of sorts. Calinda accepted it more graciously and returned it with occasional evidences of affection, each one of which Blaise remembered and treasured. Actually he saw more of Calinda than Drum did, for Drum's hours of waking and sleeping were at variance with the rest of the household's. Drum went to bed early each night except Saturday, and alone except for Blaise's joint occupancy of his room.

Although Blaise managed to accommodate most of his hours to coincide with Drum's, during the long nights when Drum was asleep and Blaise was on duty at the bar, he and Calinda saw much of each other. Calinda was now performing most of the maid's duties which Rachel had done previously, and part of those duties was to bring drinks to the various rooms, which necessitated her waiting behind the bar while Blaise prepared them. During these moments they always talked and then, when the house became quieter after midnight, they drew their chairs up beside each other in the courtyard and whispered together. Later, when the last guest had departed, they treated themselves to bread and coffee in the kitchen, lingering over it and yawning until Calinda went to her little room and Blaise climbed the stairs on tiptoe so as not to waken Drum. On Saturday nights, however, Blaise never went up those stairs, but crept into the lonely pallet on the floor of Calinda's cubbyhole, reveling in the fact that the very mattress he slept on was hers, that the sheet under him was redolent of her body and that the thin pillow under his head had been hollowed by hers.

Blaise had never had a woman when he arrived at the Academy of Music but he did not retain his chastity for long. Alix had had him brought to her room, examined him with enthusiasm and pridefully pronounced him more than adequate for a coming performance of one of her famous melees ordered in advance by young Pablo Hernandez as an evening's entertainment for a visiting *Cubano* cousin from Havana. That night Hernandez and his cousin received an unexpected double portion of entertainment for their money; Alix had demanded that Drum be present to initiate Blaise into the intricacies of his duties.

"That black *brut* won't even know what to do unless you tell him," she said. "The lying bastard claims he's never been with a woman and if he's telling the truth, which I doubt, what kind of a performance could he put on?" She waggled an authoritative finger at Drum. "Fighting or not fighting, it won't do you any harm for one night. Besides"—she relaxed her authority enough to smile at Drum—"you'll enjoy it, damn you, as you always have and don't tell me you won't. One night a week with Calinda will never be enough for you. How are you managing these days anyway? You and Blaise playing with each other?"

"Me and that black monster? Pfft!" Drum was properly outraged. *"Regardez,* madame! At seven in the morning I get up. I run five miles. I go to Masta' Jemmy's at ten and practice until noon. In the afternoon I work out for four hours, then I am ready for bed again. But. . . ."—he grinned at her, quite overjoyed at the prospect, for he had always enjoyed the melees despite the difficult time they meant with Calinda afterwards—"perhaps one night would not be harmful."

"Then be on hand this evening."

And Drum was. Along with Blaise and six of Alix' charming quadroons! Hernandez and his Cuban cousin had an entertainment such as they had never seen before. Indeed Blaise's performance, even without coaching, was entirely professional and compared favorably with that of Drum. Nobody could have imagined that it was his first experience. The audience was most enthusiastic.

*"Que hombres!"* the Cuban was heard to exclaim. *"Como dos fuentes de agua!"*

*"Fontaines?"* Hernandez lisped in French which he considered more elegant than Spanish. *"Fontaines, mon cher cousin? Comme deux cataractes d'eau! Un veritable déluge! Un torrent! Un flux!"*

The cousin nodded his head and agreed. *"Una inundacion verdadera."*

After that performance, which Alix had watched from behind a screen in the salon, she knew she could rely on Blaise's proficiency, and did not call on Drum again. Calinda was supremely happy. Drum, however, relinquished his duties with some regret. When Blaise, always willing to surrender to his idol, offered to turn over his tips, Drum accepted them without compunction for, as he argued with himself, what would a *brut* like Blaise do with money anyway? As for himself, he was saving the tips for new and more resplendent clothes. He also had in mind that eventually—after he had his own new suit of course—he would buy Calinda a dress for their occasional promenades in Congo Square. It was only fitting that she should be well dressed, seeing that he had become a celebrity in New Orleans. He was known all over the city, up the river as far as Natchez, and even in Mobile and Pensacola. People pointed him out as Madame Alix' fighting black or that mulatto who fights in the whorehouse on Dumaine Street. Or, more simply, as the old bawd's fighter.

*Mais oui!* Drum was really a fighter and through Blaise's importunings to be allowed to emulate him, he taught him how to fight well too. Blaise was an apt pupil and he soon became more than a sparring partner for Drum. He became a formidable opponent, except that he himself did not realize his proficiency and always pulled his punches so that he would not hit Drum with full force. But Drum pummeled him unmercifully.

Every morning he kicked Blaise awake, even though the poor fellow had had only a few hours of sleep, and together they crept out of the sleeping house in the cool hours before the real heat of the sun began, jogging along through the city and out into the more rural part of the new development where Bernard de Marigny was converting the family plantation lands into city blocks. Here they would run along the dusty, vacant streets with such fanciful names as the Rue de Craps, the Rue d' Amour and the Rue De Grand Homme—which Marigny told Drum he had named in his honor. Returning to the house they would have a hearty breakfast and Drum would take Blaise with him to Jemmy's. Dominique had not offered to pay for Blaise's instruction, but Jemmy became so interested in the big fellow and his earnest desire to learn that he taught him without charge. Blaise did manage a few hours sleep in the afternoon and some sparring with Drum later before it was necessary for him to take up his duties at the bar.

With training, Blaise's spindly legs swelled with muscles, his chest rounded, his long arms grew stronger, his neck thickened out and, without actually realizing it, he too became a fighter, albeit a fighter who never fought. His first engagement with Drum was his last and although at times he wished he might take the master's place within the open circle of spectators, especially if Drum seemed to be having a difficult time, Blaise was willing to allow him all the honors, content merely to stand by in his white jacket and be prepared to serve drinks after the fight was over, and Drum had won.

And Drum always won. He fought at least once a month, sometimes twice, and on one occasion he had two fights in one week, for this kind of fighting was becoming the most exciting method of gambling in the city, far more thrilling than playing cards or fighting cocks or baiting bears. Indeed, what more interesting spectacle than to watch two handsome young animals trying to massacre each other?

Although Drum had always been a prime favorite of Marigny's, who boasted that he had discovered him and thus inaugurated the fashion of fighting slaves in New Orleans, there was no man in the city more anxious to own a slave who could beat him. Marigny had to be first in everything. If he could have had Drum he would have been happy but, failing that, he must find a champion of his own. His supreme moment would come when he could hold up his man's hand as the victor. Just once he hoped to see Drum's handsome face bloodied, his nose crushed, his lips smashed so that he, Marigny, might have the distinction of having accomplished it. It was a challenge to his superiority which he must meet and master.

Failing to find a man himself, Marigny had given Maspero orders to look around for a fighter, price to be no object. Scenting a handsome profit, Maspero found a man, the slave of a tavern owner in Savannah, who had gained a certain reputation as a bouncer. Marigny took one look at the fellow, whose name was Babouin—a most appropriate name as he looked like a baboon—and bought him. Immediately he summoned Dominique You to arrange a match between the baboon and Drum.

Babouin was an ill-formed beast of a man with the preposterous claim that he had been fathered by a gorilla in Africa. However, when one looked at him, the claim did not seem so unlikely, for the fellow looked enough like an ape to have been the offspring of one. It would have been impossible to say what African tribe had spawned him. Short, immensely muscled legs seemed altogether inadequate to hold up his huge upper body with its enormous dangling arms and apelike hands. His head was small and mongoloid with a low forehead and huge prognathous jaws. Small yellow eyes squinted out from under overhanging brows and the fact that both ears had been chewed off added nothing to his appearance.

Stripped and facing Drum, he was an awesome sight, actually lacking only fur to transform him into a beast. Drum immediately recognized him as a dangerous opponent. Babouin had only one method of fighting—to wrap his huge arms around his opponent and crush his chest, squeezing the breath out of him. Twice Drum was caught in the beast's arms and only by a superhuman effort was he able to dislodge himself each time. He dared not get near enough to be caught again and his blows on the creature's body seemed to have no more effect than hitting a stone.

The third time that Babouin caught him, he felt that he was done for. He ached from the pressure of the huge arms and felt himself helpless as he was lifted from the ground. He tried to knee the man as he had done with the coachman in his first fight but it was impossible. The breath was fast leaving his lungs but his months of training directed his brain and he was able to extricate his right arm sufficiently so that his forearm came between his body and that of Babouin. As Babouin continued to press, Drum inched his arm up until he got his hand free. He clutched the man's throat, his fingers seeking the hard cartilage of the larynx deep in the muscles. When they located it, he squeezed and although he could not exert all the pressure he wanted, owing to the constriction of his arm, it was enough to shut off the man's wind. Slowly the apelike arms relaxed but Drum kept his hold, choking Babouin until the fellow sank to the floor. Then with his foot on Babouin's neck, Drum was again master of the situation. He allowed just enough air to pass into the tortured lungs to keep the man alive. Dominique You came forward and lifted Drum's hand as the winner but when Drum stepped back to receive the acclamations, Babouin struggled to his feet and would have continued the fight.

"Get back," Dominique shouted. "The fight is over."

"Not fo' me," Babouin muttered.

"Oh yes it is." Dominique pushed him away and as Babouin once again moved toward Drum, Dominique threatened him. "Back, I tell you the fight is over."

"Let them go on! Let them finish it!" De Marigny rushed up in support of his man.

"No, Bernard." Dominique shook his head. "Drum won fairly." He turned to the men, now pressing close to the two fighters. "What say you men, did Drum win?"

As the majority had placed their money on Drum, they were loud in their support of Dominique, but it was most evident that Marigny did not agree with them. He had planned much and bet heavily on Babouin. Far more than the loss of the money, he regretted the thrill of that long anticipated moment of victory and the boasting pride he could take in owning New Orleans' champion.

"The fight is *not* over." Marigny tried hard to control his rage. "Both men are able to fight. I insist that it go on."

A chorus of "no"s silenced him.

"It seems to be agreed among those present that Drum is the victor." Dominique You placed an arm around Drum's shoulder. "Therefore, Bernard, we shall fight no more tonight but if you wish, we can make arrangements for a return engagement—say two weeks from tonight."

"Unless the fight is finished tonight, there will be no return engagement." Bernard could no longer control himself. "I had thought I was dealing with gentlemen. It seems that I am not. You're not a person I shall challenge, Dominique You. A Marigny does not soil his sword with the blood of a Lafitte pirate." He turned his back on Dominique You and called to Babouin, "Get your pants, you goddamned baboon and follow me. Fifty lashes for you tomorrow for letting yourself get choked." He did not wait to see if Babouin was behind him but turned and strode across the court to the porte-cochere. Someone handed Babouin his trousers and he slipped into them, running after Marigny.

At the entrance to the porte-cochere, Marigny halted and turned. Babouin was immediately behind him and he brushed him aside.

"Lazare," he called, "aren't you coming with me?" Lazare and Bernard were inseparable. Where one went the other always followed.

"Not tonight, Bernard!" Lazare had no desire to leave. "I am staying to celebrate Drum's victory. I'll meet you later."

"Indeed you shall!" Marigny's voice was hot with anger. "You'll meet me later in St. Anthony's gardens, at five in the morning."

Lazare LeToscan ran across the courtyard to Marigny and laid a restraining hand on his shoulder.

"Good God, Bernard, are you challenging me?"

"Most certainly! Tonight is a test of our friendship."

"As if our friendship needed to be tested, Bernard."

"Any man who is not with me is my enemy. Our seconds will attend us at five."

"Think, Bernard, think what you are doing. Do not let this momentary pique over losing a stupid fight destroy our friendship. You are acting ridiculously."

Marigny advanced one step which brought him close to LeToscan. Slowly and deliberately, without taking his eyes from LeToscan's, he reached behind, his hand searching for something in the tail pockets of his coat. He drew forth a lemon-colored kid glove, regarded it a second, then stared again at LeToscan. Deliberately he raised his hand with the glove and slapped LeToscan across the cheek.

"Unless you are a coward, you will fight me."

"Very well, Bernard." LeToscan shook his head and sighed. "If you insist that I kill you, I regret that I must." LeToscan bowed formally. "At five?"

"At five! Pistols or rapiers, Lazare?"

"Rapiers, Bernard."

"Then do me the favor to bring the set your father sent you from Spain. You are more accustomed to them." Marigny stepped from behind Lazare LeToscan so that he could see the circle of faces in the courtyard, all of whom were aghast at what had happened. He nodded briefly.

"Messieurs, the question as to who has the better fighter, Madame de Vaux or Bernard de Marigny, has already been settled in my own mind. I am convinced that my ugly monster is the better fighter. I shall, however, honor all my bets without protest. Good night, messieurs."

At five-twenty the next morning, Lazare LeToscan died with one of his own rapiers through his heart. He was twenty-four years old, popular, supremely handsome and enormously wealthy, but he was dead. All New Orleans mourned him but nobody more than his best friend, Bernard de Marigny, who had killed him. It was said that Marigny wept as he walked away from the duel, leaving Lazare LeToscan's corpse on the ground behind him.

## chapter ix

SOME TWO MILES out of the city, in the newly developed Faubourg Marigny, Drum and Blaise passed daily, on their morning workout run, a little spring which bubbled up between two large stones to form a limpid cress-rimmed pool. Over it spread the wide branches of an ancient live oak, bearded with long gray streamers of Spanish moss. Behind the tree, growing in almost tropical lushness, was a thicket of palmettos, interlaced with a jungle of wild *lantanier*. Because of the clear water of the spring, this had become a stopping place for Drum and Blaise, marking as it did nearly the middle of their course. It had become such a well-established habit to stop there that they had filched a couple of tin cups from Alix' kitchen, which were kept hidden in a crotch of the tree, and every day they drank deeply of the cool water and threw themselves down on the patch of grass under the shade to catch their breath for the return to town.

As always, they had stopped this morning, their shirts plastered to their backs with sweat, out of breath and dog tired. Blaise filled the cups and brought them to where Drum was sitting. Together they gulped the water greedily and then flung themselves, belly down, onto the soft grass under the big oak. For some moments they remained motionless, eyes closed, breathing hard and fast to regain their wind. Each knew that it was time to start back but he procrastinated, savoring the sweetness of relaxation a little longer. Aie! it was good to do nothing; to erase all reality from one's thoughts; to be neither black nor white; to be neither slave nor free. For these few moments they had no responsibilities, no fights, no demanding mistress, no Rachel with work to be done, no white men waiting for drinks, no melee that demanded their attention. Here they were devoid of any personality and became merely breathing organisms, luxuriating in the filtered sunshine that was drying their backs and the cool grass that was smooth against their cheeks.

Blaise stretched out his long arm across the grass to shake Drum's shoulder. Just as he was about to speak, he heard the cracking of a stick back in the tangle of shrubbery. In the stillness, the sound was magnified to a pistol shot.

"Whas-sat?" Blaise propped himself up on his elbow and gazed into the thicket of *lantanier*.

"Somebody's goat," Drum yawned. "Lie down, nigger, let's take five minutes more to. . . ."

His words were not finished. Three men leaped out of the shrubbery and flung themselves down on Drum and Blaise. The very suddenness of the attack stunned them and their struggles were useless. Strong arms pinned them to the ground, muscular legs straddled them.

"Turn 'em ovah." The words had a thick, Georgian accent. "Turn 'em two bah-sta'ds ovah and let 'em see who's gonna beat the livin' shit outa that theah high yello' fancy boy."

The pinioning arms relaxed just enough to flop Drum and Blaise over onto their backs but each found a burly slave astride his chest with his knees pinning down their arms, his hand clutching at their throats. A pair of thick, bandy legs, like sawed-off trunks of trees, wedged their way in between the shoulders of the big blacks. Drum had no need to look up to recognize who it was. The malformed legs told him it was Babouin and when he confirmed it, by letting his eyes wander up the soiled, grease-blotched pantaloons to the huge chest which showed through the unbuttoned shirt, he saw the malevolent face of Marigny's fighter.

"Ain' no white mens heah now to pertect yo' fancy boys. Jes' me, Babouin! Tha's all! An' you know what I'm a-goin to do to you? I'm a-goin' to beat hell out o' yo', yo' goddam Drum. And then,"—Babouin drew a short, stubby knife from his belt—"I'm a-goin' to carve my name on yo' belly, so's all the world will know that Babouin whupped you."

Drum tried to wriggle out of the grasp of the slave who was on his chest, but he was helpless.

"Might be yo' think I'se ignor'nt," Babouin continued. "Might be yo' think I cain't spell, might be," Babouin leered. "Spell my name good, I kin. Listen! B-a-b-o-u-i-n. How's 'at? Kin write it good, too. Gonna write in on your yellow belly. How you likes dat, huh?" He breathd on the knife, wiped it on his pants and tested the edge with this thumb. "Sharp's a razor, boy. Shave yo' hair right off. Sure cuts good. What yo'all's got to say, who'house boy?"

"I say let me up and let me fight you." The hand on

Drum's windpipe relaxed enough for him to speak. "I fought you fair the other night. Now you fight me fair."

"Sho' I let you up. I let's you fight fair. Ho, ho!" Hands on hips, Babouin looked down at Drum and roared. "I fights yo' fair, fancy boy, 'cause I likes to fight but I fights yo' wid de knife and you fights me wid yo' bare hands. Tha's fair! Let 'im up!" Babouin nudged the slave who was sitting on Drum. "Let's see how he kin fight 'thout no big white mens to pertect him."

The slave slid off Drum and he jumped to his feet.

"Keep a-hold of that other fancy boy, Bouc-noir," Babouin cautioned the slave sitting on Blaise, "and yo', Michel, yo' run down to Masta Marigny's and tell him and he's frens that Babouin done caught dis heah Drum. Tell him I waits to carve my name on him till he's comin'."

The slave called Michel started off on a run. Drum knew that the Marigny *pavillon* was about a quarter of a mile away. Allowing perhaps ten minutes for the slave to run there and another ten minutes for Marigny and his friends to return on their horses, he had about twenty minutes. But it made little difference if Marigny were there, for Marigny's presence would not necessarily guarantee a fair fight. Marigny was out to get him. He shifted his eyes long enough from Babouin to glance down at Blaise, still struggling but held on the ground. Drum was tempted to run, for he knew that Babouin's short legs would never catch him, but he couldn't leave Blaise behind for he knew that Babouin would wreak his vengeance on him. After all, Blaise was his own nigger. He couldn't desert him.

Warily Drum circled around, keeping his distance from Babouin who crouched with arms outspread to gather Drum into his gorilla embrace. The sunlight glinted on the short blade of the knife, and its reflection seemed to be an evil eye which followed Drum wherever he went. The space in which they fought, however, was limited—only the little patch of greensward under the tree, and as Drum retreated, he found himself up against the tangle of shrubs and vines. Carefully he circled, hoping to get out into the open space of the road, but before he could maneuver it, Babouin made a grab for him and caught him. For a few moments, Drum struggled and managed to get in a few telling blows, but, although he could see Babouin wince from the force with which the blows struck him, they were as ineffective as the sting of a mosquito. The big arms closed around him. Drum filled his chest with air, knowing that when he expelled it, he would achieve a tiny shrinkage which might allow him to slip out, for the residue of oil and the recent sweat on his body made him slippery as an eel. Yet, although he forced out every breath of air in his chest and wriggled as much as he could, he could not loosen the other's hold.

"Fifty lashes I took on my back 'cause of yo', fancy boy," Babouin muttered. "Fifty lashes, and I'd of tooken fifty more if'n Masta Marigny hadn't made me promise to carve yo' up."

Drum tried for the hold that had been successful in his previous fight with Babouin, struggling to extricate his arm and reach the other's throat but Babouin had learned the trick.

"No, you don', who'house boy. And don't think you kin knee me neither. Got 'em well wrapped up today so's you can't hurt 'em. Come prepared I did. Think I'll put my name on yo' back too. Look pretty there."

Drum felt the pressure of one of the huge arms relax slightly and the warmth of a hand creeping up under his shirt. A sting of pain slashed at his shoulder. The pain caused him to cry out and he redoubled his efforts to free himself. Suddenly, much to his surprise, he saw Blaise's face over Babouin's shoulder. He saw Blaise raise his arms, saw a huge branch of wood in his hands. Swiftly the cudgel descended, and he heard the dull thud as it came in contact with Babouin's head, and felt the immense arms slowly relax. As he stood, free, straining to fill his lungs with air, he saw Blaise reach down to the recumbent Babouin, take the knife from the inert fingers and plunge it in the man's throat. The blood gushed out and Blaise laughed, raising his foot to kick the carmined face.

Blaise brought his heel down once more, then stopped.

"Hurry," he pushed Drum ahead of him to the road. "Marigny'll be here any minute. Don' want him to find us here with his two dead slaves. No tellin' what he'd do to us."

Drum came to his senses. He hurried along beside Blaise. As he passed the slave who had been sitting on Blaise's chest, he noticed him stretched out on the ground, a splotch of blood on his dirty pants. Where his face had been there was only a yawning, bloody mass on which the flies were already settling.

"Better hide." Blaise had suddenly taken command of the situation. "Marigny'll follow us if we keep to the road. Can't get back to the city now. They have horses and they'll ride us down."

"Over there," Drum pointed as he ran. "Ditch!"

They ran faster now, keeping off the road and taking advantage of any cover they could find. Once Blaise became entangled in a web of ground-spreading bindweed that snared his feet and caused him to stumble. He still had Babouin's knife in his hand, and he reached down and slashed at the vines to extricate himself.

Drum pointed to a straight line of green shrubs and when they reached it, they plunged down the steep bank into the water. The tall reeds that grew in the muddy ditch provided a good covering and they sank their bodies into the water, keeping only their heads free.

Drum broke off one of the reeds and handed the hollow section to Blaise. "If they come, put this in your mouth and keep your head under water. You can breathe through it. I don't think Marigny'll chase us. He'd have let Babouin kill the both of us sure 'nough but now he's got two dead niggers on his hands and it won't look too good for him to have two more."

Blaise ducked under the water to try the reed, then surfaced again.

"Sure, he'd let his baboon carve us up and then send us back to N'Orleans with Babouin's name on us just to prove we'd been beaten. Nothing we could say would of made any difference. Marigny would have made up some story and his friends would have stuck with him. It would be their word against ours."

"And our word wouldn't be worth a goddam because we're slaves," Drum added.

"So Babouin would have been champion and Marigny'd crow all over that his nigger had licked you."

"If he hadn't killed me. Chances are now that if we don't say anything about it, Marigny won't, because he won't want to be laughed at. But I'm going to tell Dominique You just the same."

Off in the distance, they heard the sound of horses and of horsemen calling to each other as they galloped by. Drum looked at Blaise and winked.

"They've gone," he breathed more deeply, "but we'll stay here a little longer. Look at my back—is it cut badly?" Drum hoisted himself out of the water and Blaise pulled up his shirt and looked at the wound, washed clean now by the water but still oozing blood.

"About as long as your hand but only skin deep. Hurt?"

"Not much," Drum sank down into the water again to ease the smart of the cut. "Tell me, *mon ami,* how'd you get loose from that big nigger on your chest?"

"What you say, Drum?" Blaise looked at him as though unable to believe what he had heard.

"You deaf?" Drum grinned. "I said what did you do to that big buck astride you?"

"You said mor'n that," Blaise insisted. "You called me your friend."

"Well, goddamn it, you are. Didn't you just save me from getting carved up?"

"You meant it, Drum? You meant that I am your friend?" Blaise had never felt so happy before. The homeless dog had found more than a master.

"Sure I meant it. We're friends. Now tell me what happened. You kill that nigger?"

"Sure did, killed both of them."

"How'd you manage the first one?"

"Well that fellow named Bouc-noir that was sitting atop me, he got so interested in what Babouin was doing to you that he turned a little so's his leg came right across my mouth. I bit. Chawed right through his pants and bit a hunk out'n his leg. Phew! he sure tasted like a goat. He rolled off me and I got up, grabbed that branch of wood and pounded his ugly face in while he a-yelling. Then I clobbered Babouin with it. That's all. How long we goin' to stay here in this water, Drum?"

Drum waded to the shore and crawled up the steep bank. Parting the branches of the thicket that grew at the top, he peered out. For several minutes he continued to look, but seeing nobody he turned and motioned for Blaise to follow. Taking their time, keeping as much under cover as possible, they made their way back to the city by a roundabout way, but instead of going to the Academy of Music they called first at Dominique You's. Dominique's slave let them in the back door and they waited for You inside in the court.

When Dominique talked with them, he corroborated Drum's opinion. With Babouin and Bouc-noir both dead, Marigny would probably not make another move. A new scandal, coming on top of Marigny's senseless killing of his best friend, would be unforgivable.

To assure their safe arrival at the Academy of Music, You was about to order his own carriage but Drum pointed out their wet muddy and bloody clothing, so You compromised by walking with them and offering to explain the matter to Madame Alix.

She, of course, was horrified to think that the great Bernard de Marigny—who had always been one of her best customers—would stoop so low. But even more she feared that if Marigny should alienate himself from her establishment, the fashionable young bloods would also stay away to the detriment of her business. Dominique however, allayed her fears. Since the death of LeToscan, he said, Bernard had lost most of his fashionable pre-eminence in the city. Alix was only partly convinced. She was inclined in some obscure way to blame both Drum and Blaise, until Dominique convinced her that the fault certainly was not theirs. To prove it, he stripped off Drum's bloody shirt and showed her the knife wound on his back.

Fortunately, as Blaise had diagnosed, the wound was superficial. Rachel sent Calinda scurrying for cobwebs which she applied to stop the bleeding, then bound up the wound. Drum went up to his room and Calinda followed, heaving her swollen body up the stairs one at a time by grasping the handrail.

As the months had progressed and her body had become more and more misshapen, resembling so little her former lithe grace, Drum had fought a growing revulsion. He wanted the slender, panther-like Calinda, not this blowsy woman whose ponderous belly seemed far too big for her slender legs. She was ugly enough when her bulging deformity was hidden by her rough dress, hiked up in front and dragging in the back, but when she removed her garment and stood before him in her naked pregnancy, the very sight of her repelled him. He knew that it was his child she carried, but he could not bear to have her misshapen flesh beside him on the bed.

Gently, so as not to betray his feelings, he placed his hands on her shoulders and turned her to face the doorway of his room.

"I'm all right, *poupée*. Don't worry, just let me sleep. Much has happened this morning but a few hours' sleep will put me to rights. I'm tired as a plantation mule."

"Then let me come and sit beside you and fan you. It will cool you and make you sleep."

"With you beside me, *poupée,* I'd get hotter than ever and you know I would not sleep."

"I am no good for you any more, Drum," she sighed, sensing his desire to be rid of her.

"No good?" He saw that she was hurt. "Silly *poupée!* You are to be the mother of my son, and once the squalling little brat appears, I'll show you how much good you are for me. I'm looking forward to it as much as you are. But just figure, Calinda. This morning I have run, I have fought, I have been slashed, I've walked all over New Orleans and now all I want is to sleep."

"But you have not eaten," she insisted. "I will go and prepare food for you and bring it up."

Drum shook his head, "The stairs, *poupée!* I will not risk my son again on those stairs. But you are right, I am hungry. Fix something good for me and send it up by Blaise."

She looked at him suspiciously.

"You like Blaise?"

"Sure I do. He probably saved my life this morning."

"But not better'n me?" Her jealousy needed reassurance.

"That big black *colosse?* If he falls down the stairs it will not injure my son."

She edged out of the door reluctantly, hoping he would call her back. Drum realized that he had hurt her by dismissing her but it was something he could not help. Soon things would be the way they were before and he could make it all up to her. *Mon Dieu!* how he would make it up to her. He dismissed the matter. Women were stupid, brainless things anyway. What did it matter. She'd get over it—she'd have to. He slipped out of his muddy trousers and stretched out on the bed. His hunger possessed him. He was ravenous. If that goddamned Blaise forgot to bring him his food, he'd. . . .

That goddamned Blaise! That same Blaise had saved his life only this morning. If it hadn't been for him he wouldn't be here now, for he knew that with the knife in Babouin's hands it would have been a fight to the death and he would have been the one to die. Yes, Blaise had saved his life. Blaise was a pretty good boy—not much like the stupid, gombo-talking bastard he had once been. Perhaps, Drum thought, he had ridden the boy a bit too much in the past. It had been "Blaise, hop to it! Blaise do this! Blaise do that!" And he was becoming a damned good fighter too. Damned good! Suddenly he saw Blaise in a new light. He remembered the months of devotion he had so carelessly taken for granted.

*Damne!* The fellow had proved his worth.

The door was pushed open by one of Blaise's big feet and he came in, bearing a tray covered with a napkin. He walked over to the bed, laid the tray down beside Drum and whisked away the cloth.

Drum looked at the food, then up at Blaise.

"How you feelin', Drum?"

"Pretty good, *mon ami*."

Blaise seemed to straighten up and his big lips parted in a white-toothed smile.

"Damned good teeth you got, boy," Drum smiled back.

"Good enough to chaw a piece out of that black goat's leg. Phew! I can taste that nigger meat yet."

"And you saved me from getting cut up," Drum added.

"Didn't save you," Blaise shook his head, "got cut up anyway."

"Well at least I haven't got B-a-b-o-u-i-n carved across my belly."

Blaise giggled. "Sure wouldn't look very pretty in one of Madame's melees."

"That part's your business now." Drum studied the plate of food. He was starved but he did not touch it. He was thinking. Serious thoughts they were. Suddenly he made up his mind.

"Well, you ignorant nigger," he reverted to the commanding tone he had used so often with Blaise. "What you standing there a-gawking at me for? Nothing else to do?"

"No, Drum." Blaise's smile of happiness faded at the harsh words.

"Well, I got something for you to do, and when I speak, you jump. Understand?"

Blaise nodded his head. Something wonderful had disappeared in his world. For a few moments Drum had treated him as an equal. Once more he was nothing but a slave.

"Go over there and take down my yellow pants," Drum ordered. "Hands clean?"

"Yes, masta, washed them afore I came up."

"Don't masta me, you black son of a bitch."

"Yes, Drum."

"Then hop to it. When I tell you something, do it. Don't just stand there like a hump on a log."

"You gonna wear them pants today, Drum?"

"Don't ask questions. None of your business if I wear those pants or not. Jump!"

Blaise took down the pants from the nail and handed them to Drum, who reached into the back pocket and drew out a little cloth bag. He emptied it onto the bed, beside the tray and counted out the silver, gold and bills it contained. He nodded his head.

"More'n enough, Blaise."

"More'n enough for what, Drum?'"

"More'n enough to take you down to Labatut's and order you the best suit of clothes in New Orleans—better than Bastille Croquère wears, and shoes for those big clodhoppers of yours, and a frilly shirt and a black silk stock."

"You means me?" Blaise's big mouth dropped open.

"I mean you, you ignorant nigger son of a bitch, you clumsy bastard, you goddamned good-for-nothing hunk of black meat. Come Sunday, you and I are going tail chasing in Congo Square and I'll be damned if I'll be seen on the street with any barefoot buck in a pair of cotton pants. Wake me up at four and I'll take you down to Labatut's. He'll have to measure that hulking frame of yours with a furlong rope instead of a yard measure but I guess he can do it. And if we can't get shoes for you, I'll take you to Dominique's blacksmith shop and have you shod like a mule. Now, get to hell out of here and let me sleep but be sure to wake me up at four."

For the first time in his life, big Blaise wept. He stood like a gangling boy, his big feet toed in, while he blubbered. Tears ran down his cheeks but while he sobbed he was grinning. He came over to the bed and bent down, taking Drum's hand in his big, pink-lined paw.

Between his sobs, he was laughing.

"Go to sleep you goddamned good-for-nothing hunk of yellow meat," he laughed and cried at the same time, squeezing Drum's hand. "*Mon ami,* I'll wake you at four."

"You'd better, Blaise boy." Drum hoisted himself up on one elbow. "But remember this, you no-good whorehouse stud. I can still lick you fighting."

"You sure can," Blaise ducked out the door to avoid Drum's worn leather shoe which came hurtling across the room. It hit the door jamb with a thud and Blaise's head reappeared in the door.

"You're always right, Drum, but one thing you sure got wrong. You called me a no-good whorehouse stud. People around this town think I'm a pretty damned good one."

Drum lifted a leg of chicken to his mouth and winked. "We'll find that out Sunday night when you're doing it for fun rather than for money." Drum ripped the meat from the bone and sent the bone flying after Blaise. Blaise caught it, stuck it in his mouth and ran down the stairs, his bare feet clumping on the boards.

# chapter x

DRUM'S SUNDAY promenade with Blaise, in all his new sartorial glory, had to be deferred for a week because M. Labatut, the tailor, could not, of course, give precedence to Blaise's suit over those of his white patrons. Even though, as Drum had the temerity to argue—and with a white man too—their money was just as good as white money. It was, however, finished by the middle of the following week and delivered to the Academy of Music by a cocksure little colored boy. The arrival of the big box, splendidly covered with a remnant of wallpaper and tied around with green tape, was almost too much for the long-expectant Blaise. He carried it up to Drum's room as he might a crate of eggs, where he found his idol stretched out on the bed.

"Open it up!" Drum was impatient to see the suit but Blaise's hands lingered lovingly and long over the gaudy paper box. His big fingers struggled to unknot the tape and he was deaf to Drum's "Cut it!" Finally he managed to untie the knot, and carefully wound the tape around his fingers to save it. Even the worthless length of tape was a valued possession, and possessions had been missing in Blaise's life. Then came the moment of lifting the cover and removing the layer of tissue paper. Blaise took a long breath and took the suit out of the box. He was speechless in open-mouthed awe.

"Put it on!" Drum yawned elaborately to show that he was not impressed with fine apparel, although he was quite as excited as Blaise. "You'll need drawers. Cain't put those fine pants on over your bare ass. You sweaty and stinkin'?" he asked.

"Washed myself clean this mornin'," Blaise assured him.

"You still sweaty and stinkin' and always will be," Drum laughed. He knew now that Blaise would not take every word seriously.

"Ain't got no drawers, never had none," Blaise said. "What's a nigger like me doing with drawers?"

"Let you wear mine then. Wear them, not keep them for your own, un'erstand?" Drum got up and rummaged in the pile of clothes on the floor until he found his own drawers which he threw at Blaise. "Ain't too dirty—only worn them a week."

Blaise stripped off the rough cotton pants and the mended cotton shirt which, with an identical outfit now hanging on the clothesline in the courtyard, were the only garments he possessed. He pulled on the drawers Drum had tossed to him. Then came the almost unbearable joy of dressing.

M. Labatut had pointed out that to duplicate the green and yellow splendor of Drum's suit would lessen the effect of both. Blaise had indeed set his heart on a suit identical with Drum's but when he saw the wealth of other colors and materials which M. Labatut spread before them he was quite willing to change. After much deliberation, Drum and Blaise had finally settled on a coat of deep-purple broadcloth with reveres of pale-lavender satin, identical in cut with Drum's—short in front, cut in a straight line around the midriff, but long in tail behind with coattails lined with the same delicate lavender satin. The trousers were to be of the same shade of lavender, fastened like Drum's with straps that held them taut under the instep of the shoes.

Blaise was so excited and so confounded by the intricacies of buttons and straps that he would never have been able to accomplish dressing himself, had it not been for Drum's expert valeting. First, after the drawers, came the ruffled shirt of fine lawn with its small buttonholes and tiny pearl buttons—far too complicated for Blaise's big fingers. Then there were socks of white French lisle to be drawn over his big feet, all preparatory for the big event, the trousers. To avoid soiling them, Drum made Blaise stand on the one wooden chair in the room and ease the sausage-tight pants slowly up over his bulging calves and over his thighs, then fasten them around the tucked-in shirt with a complexity of buttons and straps, all of which were as bewildering to Blaise as a cat's-cradle of string.

Getting the shoes on, big as they were, over Blaise's feet was something of an accomplishment. Once on, he was scarcely able to stand in them but Drum insisted, in spite of his moans, that he wear them. Blaise managed, although his feet, horny, calloused and spread out as they were from a lifetime of freedom, were scarcely suited for shoes. But the imprisonment of his feet was quickly forgotten in the glory of the purple broadcloth coat whose rich plum color was particularly becoming to the deep sepia of his skin. Everything fitted to perfection, for old M. Labatut was a master tailor and had seldom had such an impressive model on which to display his artistry.

The lavender trousers were as Blaise's own skin; there was a snowy whiteness to the ruffled shirt and a perky jauntiness to the tied cravat; an over-all glossiness in the rich broadcloth and the shiny satin of the coat; a polished blackness to the shoes which quite transformed the former field hand. Added to the sophistication of the new clothes was a cosmopolitan poise which Blaise had learned—a result of his careful aping of Drum—that made it quite impossible to recognize the clumsy *brut* who had formerly wielded a cane knife, in this sartorially perfect young buck.

When Sunday afternoon finally arrived and Blaise again donned his clothes to walk with Drum to Congo Square, had it not been for the color of his skin, his excessive height and the way the plum-colored broadcloth stretched tightly over his shoulders, he might have been mistaken for any of the young Creole *hommes du haut monde*. The purple and lavender were an excellent foil for Drum's green and gold, sufficient to bedazzle the eyes of any wench, and if both strutted a little too arrogantly and turned up their noses at their less fortunate brethren whose only claim to Sunday elegance was the same shirts and breeches they wore every day—although carefully laundered—these two were to be forgiven for their snobbishness. Even though they were both slaves, they were now aristocrats among their fellows.

But even slavery could be forgotten on a Sunday afternoon in early spring, with all the excitement of Congo Square spread out before them. This was the day that all slaves longed for and this was their own particular domain. Here, for one brief afternoon and evening, the household slaves of the city and nearby plantations were permitted to meet in a social whirl of their own. It almost rivaled carnival. Booths, covered with a tatterdemalion patchwork of ragged awnings, were set up crazily along the banquettes that bordered the square, and here free men and women of color attended to their own little businesses. There were a variety of refreshments, most of which could be bought for a copper penny. Pigs' knuckles, ham hocks, spareribs and crisply fried bacon rind mingled their odors with messes of boiled peas, collard greens and turnip. Flaky brioches were waiting to be filled with shucked pink shrimps; piles of fruit invited strong white teeth to savor their juices; crusty French bread could be dipped in *sirop de batterie;* and sections of pale green cane could be chewed for their delicious sweetness. Here, also, the outer as well as the inner man could be satisfied, for there was scarcely a slave present who did not have at least a two-bits lagniappe, solemnly presented to him every Saturday night by his master. For all there was something to tempt the coins from their pockets—booths of cheap brass jewelry, with enormous hoop earrings; gold-washed, glass-stoned brooches; cheap filigreed bouquet holders which dangled on a chain from a wench's black finger; and gaudy cuff links and cravat pins for the young bucks who had neither cuffs nor cravats.

One of the most popular booths of all had an awning that cast a purple shadow over big Hyacinthe, the conjure man from Haiti, who sat with his young, gazelle-eyed assistant, Lucifer, behind a wooden board on which were spread a number of red- and blue-wrapped paper packets. The red contained a love potion which would bring the most diffident swain panting after the girl who desired him, while the blue were guaranteed to send any girl a-running to a man's bed. Big Hyacinthe sat back in the shade, certain that many of the packets were purchased by women who had their eyes on him, while others yearned for the pretty Lucifer, whose assignations, accomplished under the board counter of the booth, further added to Hyacinthe's income.

Drum and Blaise promenaded slowly and magnificently as befitted two peacocks among the lesser barnyard fowl. Many there were who knew Drum and his reputation as Madame's fighting boy but few had ever seen Blaise before; his magnificence created quite a stir. Wide-hipped, big-bosomed black girls in starched white cottons with their madras tignons of vivid blues, greens, scarlets and purples, passed the two with a high-pitched cackle to attract attention and a hopeful backward glance to see if it had been effective. A number of the girls who eyed them carried a small roll of rag carpet under one arm, advertising themselves as two-bit prostitutes who were only too willing to spread their bit of carpet in the dust of some dark alley or under a bush for the quick gratification of any man who had the necessary money. But Drum and Blaise were looking for neither black girls nor two-bit whores. They were seeking at least a mulatto or, if possible, a quadroon—some girl whose bright skin would be a fitting complement to their obviously high station. Bright-skinned girls were, however, hard to find in Congo Square. Most quadroon and octoroon girls were trained for higher game than the slaves who congregated there on a Sunday afternoon. They were the carefully nurtured hothouse plants which were raised apart from both blacks and whites to make their demure debuts at the famous quadroon balls, where it was hoped they would attract a rich white man who would set them up in style. Only those who were employed as household slaves ever appeared in Congo Square. Yet Drum had found them there before and he was most certain that he and Blaise would encounter them again.

They wandered off the banquette, over into the square itself, where an impromptu orchestra of banjos, guitars, drums and bones was playing. Some couples were dancing with abandon to the African rhythms and Drum and Blaise stopped to watch them. One girl, dancing with closed-eyed ecstasy, excited Blaise with her gyrating hips, and he would have approached her when she finished dancing, but Drum held him back.

"Nigger slut!" Drum spat in the dust. "You wants something better than that musky wench. You let me do the picking. Don't get too anxious! Keep your pants buttoned till it gets dark. And don't think we're going with any carpet slut either. No, man, tonight we're aiming for the best."

"Got no money to pay for the best, Drum," Blaise complained. "Just have to take one of them two-bit carpet wenches or nothing."

"Pay?" Drum was incensed. "Who said anything about us paying? I never paid for anything yet. We'll pay nothing, *mon ami,* nothing! Plenty girls here willing to go out with boys like us for nothing. Plenty others willing even to pay us. Don't stretch your breeches, man. Leave it to Drum—he'll find something for both of us."

By the time night had fallen, they had made the circuit of the square many times. Poor Blaise's feet were torturing him and Drum left him on a bench, with strict instructions not to leave, while he went to the booths for food. He returned shortly with a paper of fried yams and another of boiled shrimp. They sat and ate, shucking the shrimps and watching the procession pass by. By now the crowd was begining to thin out. The older people and the children had left for their homes and the promenade was made up mostly of young people, all with watchful eyes for a partner.

Drum dropped the paper of shrimp that they were eating from and nudged Blaise. Two late arrivals, whom they had not seen before, fresh and cool looking, sauntered by.

"Come, man." Drum cocked his head in the direction of the two girls who had just passed. "That's for us." He stood up, wiping his hands on the kerchief in his sleeve and handed it to Blaise who did not possess one. They walked quickly for a few steps to catch up with the girls. It was evident that the quarry was as anxious to be caught as the hunters were to catch, for the girls slowed their steps. Although they did not look around, Drum knew they were conscious that they were being followed.

They were both slender, *café au lait* in color, and dressed in what might have been hand-me-downs from their mistresses, for their dresses had a certain richness of cut and material that placed them, albeit somewhat shabbily, on a par with the clothes worn by Drum and Blaise. But what had caught Drum's attention was the fact that neither wore the madras tignon—that gaudy headdress whose main purpose was to conceal the short, kinky, negroid hair. These girls had long black hair which curled down to their shoulders and which they would not hide beneath a tignon. Drum had also had a look at their faces when they passed and he had seen that they were both pretty with a certain air of good breeding.

Appearing entirely oblivious of the two men behind them, the girls chatted with a self-conscious *hauteur*, gesturing with a lofty gentility and laughing with low-keyed little chuckles that ascended and descended the scale in imitation of their Creole mistresses. After a few more steps, a handkerchief fluttered to the ground, making a pool of whiteness on the dusty banquette. Drum swooped down to pick it up, lifted it to his nose and smelled the odor of eau de cologne, probably filched from some mistress' dressing table. He quickened his step to draw abreast of the two, motioning with his elbow for Blaise to step up on the other side.

"A thousand pardons, mademoiselle." Drum bowed formally from the waist. "May I return this precious kerchief which one of you just dropped?"

The girl nearest Drum lifted her pretty heart-shaped face and without smiling showed him the kerchief in her hand.

"You err, monsieur," she said, shaking the kerchief out to its full length. "It could not possibly be mine, unless. . . ." She glanced at her companion. "Veronique, did you by chance drop your kerchief?"

"La," the other cried, "I do believe I did, Jeanneton."

"Then allow me." Drum proferred the wisp of perfumed cambric. "Could this be it?"

*"Merci."* The girl fluttered her eyes at Drum. "How very kind you are. It is indeed mine and I should have been desolated at its loss. It was embroidered by the good sisters in the convent."

"And I return it with regrets, mademoiselle, for with such a delicious odor, I would like to keep it as a souvenir of a very charming young lady." Drum was not to be outdone in gentility although the allusion to the convent embroidery was difficult for him to top.

She took it from him. For a moment there was a strained silence. The formalities had passed—the gentilities had been observed. Now, if formality and gentility were still to be the order of the evening, there was nothing more to say or do except for the two men to bow and pass on and the two girls to curtsey and walk away in another direction. But none wanted that. The proprieties had served their purpose. Contact had been made and a lowering of barriers could now take place.

"Might we accompany you girls wherever you are going?" Drum essayed one more propriety.

"My sister and I are only returning to our home after a visit to friends. It is unfortunate that our way led through Congo Square for it is hardly safe for two girls to walk alone here," Veronique responded.

"And we would welcome your company, but, *hélas,* messieurs, we are not acquainted," Jeanneton answered.

"I am Drum," he slipped his arm inside Veronique's elbow. "And this is my very good friend, Blaise." He nodded at Blaise but looked at the girl, Jeanneton.

"And I am Veronique," the girl on Drum's elbow added, "and this is my sister, Jeanneton. We are of the household of old Madame Mercier. We would welcome your escort and your protection, messieurs."

Drum and Veronique walked on ahead, Blaise and Jeanneton following. They walked slowly, arm in arm through the now almost deserted streets, illuminated only at the corners by the dull gleam of a lantern and occasionally by a circle of light from an opened porte-cochere. On the grilled upper balconies, cigars glowed and dresses made smudges of white as the occupants of the houses sought the cool of the evening air.

Drum's arm slipped out of Veronique's arm and circled her waist. Her hand reached for his and rested inside its moist warmth.

"You are Drum, the famous fighter?" She leaned her head against his coat. "He of the house of Madame Alix in Dumaine Street?"

"I am he," Drum answered, proud to think the girl had heard of him.

"They say no man can whip you."

"That is true." Drum held her more tightly. "But what a man cannot accomplish a woman can. I would not like to lose to another man but I am always happy to surrender to a woman."

"We shall see." Her arm encircled his waist under the green coattails and she felt the warmth of his body through the thin shirt.

They sauntered slowly through the dark, quiet streets, and by the time they had reached the block where the Mercier house stood, their hands had explored and discovered mutually entertaining delights. These explorations were but a prelude to a more intense gratification. That both Blaise and Jeanneton had been similarly employed Drum could see when he looked at them.

At the corner of the block of the Mercier house, they halted and the two sisters drew apart for a whispered conversation. Drum looked at Blaise.

"Doing all right, boy?"

"Just following you. When I sees you do something, I do it. Figure if you can do it, I can. So far have figured right."

The whispering between the girls stopped and they returned to Drum and Blaise.

"Can you be very quiet?" Veronique asked.

Drum nodded.

"Then come, but do not speak and perhaps it would be better if you removed your shoes when we arrive."

That was welcome news to Blaise, whose new shoes were inflicting tortures on his poor feet. He immediately leaned up against the wall and slipped off his shoes and stockings.

The girls led them down through the dusty alley that led

to the back of the house. With her finger to her lips, cautioning quiet, Veronique pointed to Drum's shoes, then bidding the two fellows to wait, she and Jeanneton quietly opened the door. Veronique stepped inside and they could hear her footsteps on the flagging. In a moment she returned with her finger on her lips and they followed her through a paved corner of the inside court, along a narrow wooden balcony to another closed door which Veronique opened. Once inside, no candle was lighted and the light from the window gave only the vague outlines of a double pallet on the floor. Jeanneton closed the shutters which made the room dark and unbearably hot but gave them added security.

Now the prelude was over! Gentility and propriety were shed as hastily as the clothing which was stripped off in the darkness. Flesh touched flesh. The only sounds were the ecstatic moans of the girls and the heavy breathing of the men which combined with the movements of bodies. At times, in the darkness, Drum was not sure whether it was Veronique or Jeanneton who was in his arms but he did not care. One was as avid as the other.

The minutes leaped into hours. Once they all lay frozen in immobility as a step was heard outside on the balcony. It dragged along slowly while they all held their breath.

"My father," Veronique, or it might have been Jeanneton, whispered in Drum's ear.

"Veronique! Jeanneton!" They heard the hoarse whisper through the shutters. "Are you home?"

*"Oui, mon père."* Veronique's words were fraught with mock slumber.

"And Jeanneton?"

*"Ici."* Jeanneton also feigned sleepiness.

"Good night, my darlings." The steps continued to drag along the balcony. A door opened and closed and again there was silence.

Drum breathed deeply again. Although lips pressed and hands caressed it was impossible to establish the rapport that had previously existed. Drum and Blaise had fully accomplished what they had come for and now, with gratification, there was no urgent need for rekindling dead fires. Drum felt himself drifting off to sleep. But daylight must not find them there, and he shook Blaise awake. Together they dressed hurriedly in the dark, not bothering with such complexities as tying cravats, putting on socks and shoes and buttoning shirts. Quietly, Veronique opened the door and stepped out on the balcony, then beckoned to them to follow. Drum brushed her lips in passing and felt her fingers linger on the throbbing artery in his throat. Then, following her, stepping carefully so as to avoid creaking boards, they descended from the balcony to the firmer stones of the courtyard and out into the alley.

The door closed and Drum and Blaise were alone in the alley. The dust felt good to their bare feet, the cool air fanned the sweat from their bodies and they strode along, arm in arm—two cocks of the barnyard who had demonstrated their ability to rule the roost.

As they walked they started to sing, at first softly and then more loudly. One song led to another until Blaise started in to sing the ever popular . . .

*Danse, Calinda, bou-djoumb! bou-djoumb!*
*Danse, Calinda, bou-djoumb! bou-djoumb!*

Drum's thoughts returned to Calinda. Suddenly he wanted her—not as she was, big with child, but as she had been. The joy that he had had that evening evaporated with the knowledge that nobody could give him the pleasure Calinda could. He had wanted what he had sought, he had obtained it and he had reveled in it; now he regretted it. Suppose, oh just suppose that Calinda had done to him what he had done to her—that she had gone out, found another man and spent the night with him. *Mon Dieu!* He would kill any man she had been with. Now he began to understand her intense jealousy of him. The very thought of another man touching Calinda caused a cold sweat to break out on his forehead. He looked at Blaise beside him, happily singing in his unattached innocence. He looked at Blaise's suit and realized how much Calinda would have treasured a new dress. Aie! he should have thought of her before Blaise. But he owed Blaise something for saving his life and so did Calinda. Surely he could not begrudge the gift, for Blaise was a good friend. Blaise was his only friend. He shrugged his shoulders. Why should he regret these few hours with Veronique and Jeanneton? After all, Calinda would never know and what she didn't know would not hurt her. But the song Blaise was singing still disturbed him.

"Sh-h-h, you braying donkey, we'll wake up the whole city. And keep your big mouth shut and walk softly on those big feet of yours. *Maman* said she'd leave the back door unlocked so be quiet when you go up the stairs. Wonder what time it is."

As if to answer him, the *sereno* called out in the next block.

"Four o'clock on a warm, dry, spring morning."

"And we get up at six," Blaise sighed.

"Come on." Drum quickened his steps and when they neared the alley that ran behind the Academy of Music, they walked softly on their bare feet. Drum pushed open the door, but instead of the quiet darkness they anticipated, the kitchen was lighted and Rachel stood in the doorway. "It's about time." She was stern and disapproving. "An afternoon in Congo Square does not last till four in the morning."

"Is it Drum?" Calinda's voice from the little closet off the kitchen was strangely weak.

"Yes, it is, and high time it was." Rachel grabbed Drum's shoulder and pulled him into the kitchen, then pushed him towards the door of Calinda's room.

Halfway across the kitchen Drum heard a sound he had never heard before or which, if he ever had, he had paid no attention to. It was the cry of a newborn baby. He looked at Rachel, his eyes wide with a question. She nodded her head. He tiptoed to the door.

A tallow dip in a tin candlestick on the floor shed its light on the pallet where Calinda lay. Her face was pale—almost the color of Blaise's pants, Drum thought—but she managed a wan smile and with one hand she drew down a corner of the sheet that covered her. Drum came closer and saw the little head that nestled in the crook of her arm. He took another step towards Calinda and the little mouth opened in a wail. Calinda moved slightly and offered her full breast to the open mouth. The wailing ceased. Drum knelt reverently beside them. His finger hesitated, then touched the little head ever so lightly, and he leaned down to kiss Calinda's hand supporting the baby's head.

"My son?" Drum whispered.

"Your son," she answered, drawing down the sheet further to expose the naked child.

"Indeed he is a wonderful son." Drum's finger traced the wrinkled forehead, the button of a nose and the softness of the cheek to the chin. "He is beautiful, Calinda."

"He is lighter than I am, Drum, but not as light as you."

"It doesn't matter. He will be bigger and stronger and I hope better than I am."

"I would not want him bigger, Drum, and he could not be better than you."

"I am not good, Calinda. I am not good. . . ."

Her fingers closed his lips. "You might tell me something I do not want to hear. I am happy now and if I heard it I would be unhappy. Do not tell me."

"There is nothing to tell." Drum's finger lingered on the little head. "Can Blaise see him?"

"Yes, I want Blaise to see him."

Drum walked to the door of Calinda's room and called Blaise in. Rachel followed.

Blaise studied the little head. He saw nothing particularly wonderful about the wizened, old-man features but he could not tell Drum that. He groped for words.

"He'll grow up to beat you, Drum."

"Beat me? Sure he'll beat me. He'll be the fightingest fighter of all."

The baby's mouth slipped from the nipple. His eyes closed in repletion and he slept. Calinda looked down at him.

"He's Drum's son," she murmured.

"And that's what we'll call him," Drum smiled at her—

"What?" Calinda asked.

"Drumson." Drum's finger rested lightly on the baby's cheek.

# chapter xi

DESPITE HIS HAPPINESS at the birth of his son, Drum's thoughts often returned to his night with Veronique and Jeanneton. Even though he had Calinda again, he still desired the two light-skinned sisters. But his desire seemed as nothing compared with his pride of parenthood.

To him it was a scarcely comprehended miracle that some chance moment of his ecstasy had, without any conscious determination of his own, produced this new life. Somehow he felt that there must be some power beyond himself that had performed this miracle, for certainly the ecstatic moment of his orgasm could not be the contributing factor. There must be something else! Outside of the expression *"Mon Dieu"* which Drum repeated parrot-wise, he had no knowledge of religion, no understanding of God, no cognizance of any greater meaning to life than the satisfaction of his desires of the moment. A man ate when he was hungry; he slept when he was tired; he fought when he was opposed; and he took a woman when his blood was hot. Of all the demands of his body, the last was what dominated him most, but that this mere yearning of the flesh could result in his siring of a man-child was the supreme miracle he could not comprehend. And yet, through the chance meeting of his mother, Rachel, with some other man, he himself had received life. He thought about this unknown man who had sired him, and wondered about him. Who was he, what had become of him, what was he like? He would have asked Rachel about him, but she had never been willing to speak about this unknown man, this father to her child. He must have had a face; what had he looked like? Was his body big and strong? Was he tall and well formed? Was he more of a man, Drum wondered, than he himself was? It was difficult for him to imagine Rachel in any man's embrace. Had his father received as much joy from her as *he* did from

Calinda? And when he was born was his father happy? Was he as proud of his son as he himself was of Drumson?

He would take his son up in his big hands as gingerly as he might have picked up one of Madame's Dresden bibelots, fearful lest he break one of the child's tiny arms or legs. Then he would study the baby carefully, discerning in him certain traces of himself and certain of Calinda. The shape of the ears was hers; the shape of the lips was his as was the downy hair on his head and the well formed nose and the narrow nostrils. The color of its skin bothered him a bit for this Drumson was neither as light as his father nor as dark as his mother. Of course any child of Calinda's could not be as bright-skinned as himself. He, Drum, was a *griffe*, but his son, being the offspring of a *griffe* and a Negress, was a *sacatron*, only one-eighth white. Yet it seemed to Drum that the child was far lighter than any *sacatron* he had ever seen before. Its down of hair was soft and straight, its nostrils not flattened and its lips not thick. Perhaps, he thought, it was because Calinda was a Jaloff, whose blood had contributed much to the famous beauty of the New Orleans quadroons.

But the color of his son did not worry him too much. The child was not pure black and would have a certain standing in the slave aristocracy. Sufficient to Drum was the miracle that had produced him. He wished he could know on what particular occasion Drumson had been conceived and if at that moment of conception any unusual thought had crossed his mind. Had it? He could not remember. Surely an event of such importance must have presaged itself in his mind. But he could recall nothing. Nothing . . . except the usual feeling of pride he always had when he acquitted himself like a man. Yes, pride, and now he was proud of his son, proud even of his son's name for he felt it to be a good omen that as the drumstick beats the drum, so would this Drumson beat this Drum. He wanted his son to be better than himself. He hoped that Drumson would be something more than a fighter. He hoped. . . . He didn't know what he hoped. Perhaps being a fighter wasn't too bad after all. It was a hell of a lot better than being a canefield worker. To be champion of New Orleans was something. Man! The women sure turned around to look at him. See how easy it had been to get Veronique and Jeanneton. He was champion!

Indeed, Drum was champion and his championship stood.

Although it was becoming increasingly difficult, Dominique You still managed to schedule matches for him. Every young blood in New Orleans and every plantation owner up river wanted to own the fighter that would lick Drum. The odds were high, fifty to one, and the long odds were tempting. But even more of an inducement was the prestige that would come from owning the fighter who could lick Drum. What Marigny had tried, others attempted, some from a purely mercenary motive, others for prestige. But Jemmy's training was sound, Drum had been a faithful student and in a day of catch-as-catch-can, no-rules, nothing-barred fighting, Drum's scientific knowledge stood him in good stead against a procession of black brutes who were out to best him.

Sometimes Drum attributed his success to the little silver box he always wore around his neck. Once he had opened it, prying the cover off with his fingernail, and was disappointed to find nothing inside but a soiled rag. He had remembered Madame Alix sniffing at it, but when he placed it to his nose, he could smell only his own sweat. The bit of rag had been sewn up with tiny stitches. Drum's curiosity impelled him to rip it open. Inside he found only a caked bit of dirt, nothing more, but although it seemed a worthless nothing, he had Calinda sew it back into the soiled rag which he replaced in the silver case. It had never been separated from him since the day Alix had given it to him. Gradually he came to think of it as his protector.

It remained for Pablo Hernandez to produce Drum's most formidable contender. Pablo Hernandez—he of the long black *patillos,* the slack mouth and the moist red lips—had discovered his man in the *Calabozo,* or as it was more familiarly called, now that New Orleans was American, the calaboose—the old Spanish-built prison. A friend of Pablo's, one Othon St. Denis, of a prominent but impoverished Creole family, searched all of New Orleans late one night in a humid downpour to find Pablo and finally when he located him at the Academy of Music, he managed to convince Alix with his last ten-dollar bill that his message for Pablo was of sufficient importance to warrant his breaking in on him.

Othon dashed up the stairs to the third floor, where he knocked on the door behind which Pablo was supposed to be. He was rewarded by hearing Pablo's voice through the closed door.

"What in hell do you want?" Pablo was in no mood to be disturbed.

"It's Othon, Pablo, Othon St. Denis, and I have most important news for you."

"Nothing is more important than what I am doing now. Can't it wait another half-hour?"

"Another half-hour would be ruinous." Othon tried the door but it was locked. "Soon all of New Orleans will be at the calaboose and I want you to get there first."

"Go away." Pablo was disgusted. "The calaboose! What do I want with that hell-hole? If all New Orleans wants to go there, that's their business. I'll stay here in bed." His voice lowered, "Turn over, *chérie*."

"But let me talk with you, Pablo. I swear, if you do not, you'll regret it the rest of your life."

There was a movement inside the room and a key grated in the lock. The door swung open and Othon entered. By the light of a single candle on the stand beside the white mosquito-*baire*-draped bed, he saw a girl, sheet hastily thrown around her, scuttle back into the transparent tent, and then saw Pablo's face emerge, the black sidewhiskers strangely masculine in contrast to the diaphanous fabric.

"What is this, a joke or something?" Pablo was not pleased at being interrupted.

"No, Pablo, no! I've just seen the best fighter that ever landed in New Orleans. Better even than Drum."

"Better than Drum? Go away! There's no one better than Drum."

"This one is, I swear it. I just saw him lay out six men and it took another six to get him to the calaboose. In another hour it will be all over town. If you get there first you can get him."

"Six men, you said?" Pablo parted the mosquito *baire* and thrust his legs out.

"Six men," Othon nodded.

Deaf to the entreaties of Titine, for it was she who was the other occupant of the bed, Pablo leaped out, reached for his pants and with Othon's help dressed himself hurriedly.

Pablo stopped in the salon only long enough to toss a gold eagle into Alix' lap and together the two of them were down the stairs and out into the street. It had stopped raining but the steamy heat, rising from the accumulated dirt and offal in the street, enveloped them with a miasmic putrescence. New Orleans was a dirty city and a rainstorm, instead of cleaning it, only seemed to make it dirtier. Pablo whistled for his coachman and the light barouche drove up. Without waiting for the coachman to get down to open the door, Pablo opened it himself and jumped in, pulling Othon in beside him.

"The *Calabozo,* and quick." Pablo turned to Othon. "Unless this is true, *amigo mio,* I'm going to challenge you to a duel, come morning. One does not leave the arms of Titine on a fool's errand."

"It's true, Pablo. Listen—" and to corroborate his claims, Othon related the events of his evening.

For several weeks, he had been madly enamored of a *placée,* a celebrated quadroon, whose aging white lover had set her up in a little cottage on the Rue des Ramparts. On the nights when her lover was unable to come, she lighted a candlestick and placed it in the window at the left of the door, in anxious expectation of the young and virile Othon. If the old man was there, she placed the candle in the window at the right. This night, it happened that as Othon was passing, as he did regularly each night, the candle was in the right-hand window. Knowing, however, that the protector of the pretty quadroon was a man of limited capabilities and that his visits seldom lasted long, Othon decided to return later and wandered down Rampart Street to Congo Square. There the sudden downpour had forced him to seek shelter in a tavern frequented mainly by free men of color and Negroes. There he had waited for the rain to let up so that he might stroll past the house of his *bien-aimeé* again to see if the candle had been shifted. The rain became worse so he stayed in the tavern, where he was treated with considerable deference, being given a table and chair and receiving the welcome attentions of an attractive mulatto wench.

While he was sitting there, an enormous Negro, decently dressed in the wide-bottomed trousers and striped jersey of a sailor, came in and took his place at the rough bar. He was already drunk but desirous of becoming more so. He spoke English with a West Indian accent and when the bartender, who spoke only French and Gombo, failed to understand him, he became argumentative and quarrelsome. In their desire to quiet him, one or two of the men in the tavern approached him, speaking to him in English, but the man was now drunkenly belligerent. He grabbed a bottle from the bar and broke it over one man's head, whereupon a free-for-all started. Othon managed to get out the door with his girl, and from the vantage point of a dark doorway across the street, shielded from the rain, they indulged in making love while they watched the carnage on the banquette in front of the tavern. The huge Negro, his back to the wall, fought off all comers, felling them one by one. According to Othon, he could have kept on winning had not a policeman —still called by the old Spanish name of *sereno*—happened along. Witnessing the battle, he left hurriedly, soon to return with another *sereno*. By this time the burly black was completely out of control, and as the *serenos* were not armed it would have been suicidal for them to try to arrest him. However they enlisted the services of some of the free men of color who were there and six of them managed to overpower the black, but not until, according to Othon, six others had been laid out cold on the sidewalk. The *serenos* managed to tie the black's hands behind him and march him off to the jail. Othon, having completed his dalliance with the mulatto girl in the doorway, was now in no mood to care which window the quadroon's candle might be in. The prowess of the black had impressed him and he followed the procession to the calaboose to see the big Negro safely locked up.

Othon St. Denis desired a fighter of his own more than any other young blood in the city but he knew he would never be able to afford one. If he could get Pablo to purchase this man, he thought he might wangle a share of him, for Pablo not only greatly wanted a fighter who could whip Drum, but he was also notoriously rich and generous. It was this combination of Pablo's sporting blood, his wealth and his generosity, plus their friendship, which had impelled Othon to tramp the streets of the city in the driving rain in search of him.

Now the Hernandez carriage arrived at the *Calabozo* and the two men jumped out. The door of the prison was closed but the chain which hung beside it rang a bell inside and after it had clanged dismally several times, the door opened. An obese, bald man, his naked suet-white shoulders gleaming in the light of the lantern he held aloft, peered out.

"I am Pablo Hernandez of Veinte Robles plantation."

"And what if ye are?" The man was not impressed.

"Perhaps this will help you to recognize me." Pablo held up a silver dollar.

The man's manner changed. He became instantly obsequious.

"Not *the* great Pablo Hernandez?"

"The same."

"And what can I do for sich a fine gentleman?"

"You have a prisoner here."

"By the saints, we have many, y'r honor."

"But one particular one who was admitted only an hour or so ago—a big black who was in a fracas up at Congo Square."

"That black devil?"

"We would see him."

"Ay, y'r honor, 'tis hardly safe. We've got him chained up."

"Then he could scarcely harm us." Pablo passed the silver through the bars and the man winked, unlocked the gate and let them through.

"The bastard's a Jamaican," the jailer explained. "Says he's owned by the captain of a Jamaican ship that put into port today. We got that much out o' him and we've sent for his master. Thought you might be him when ye rang the bell. Can't keep the bastard here, we can't. Got to rid ourselves of him quick." Carrying the lantern, he led Pablo and Othon across a dirty courtyard surrounded by barred cells. On the opposite side, he stopped before a heavy grille and thrust the lantern inside.

"He's the one," Othon cried.

He was answered by a rattle of chains. Pablo looked in. The man was sitting on the floor of the cell. Most of his clothes had been ripped off. His arms were stretched out sideways, chained to hooks in the wall, and his feet were in heavy leg irons. The light of the lantern was reflected in the eyes which glared back at them.

"Open the lock," Pablo told the jailer.

"He's a wicked un," the jailer cautioned.

"I'll take my chance. He's chained."

The jailer fumbled with a big ring of keys at his belt, selected one and turned the lock, and the door swung open. Pablo took a step inside, straddled the chained legs and, reaching down, grabbed the Negro's face in both hands.

"They tell me you're a fighter," he said.

"I fights when I gets drunk, suh. Fights like a hellion, suh. But never fights when I'se sober, suh." Evidently the effects of the rum were passing off for the man seemed coherent.

"How'd you like to be my fighter?" Pablo asked.

"What yo' mean fighter, suh?"

"Just what I said. Fight for me. Fight another man for me. Whip him and I'll set you free."

"Gotta buy me fust, suh. Cap'n Jenkins he don' want to sell Big'un."

"Is that your name?" Othon asked.

"Yes, suh! I'se Big'un. 'Cause I'se bigger'n anyone else. Cap'n Jenkins allays take me to sea wid 'im."

The outside bell rang again and the jailer, torn between his duty to remain with the white men and to answer the bell, hesitated. Pablo pointed in the direction of the door and the fat man lumbered away, to return in a few minutes with a dandified little man, who minced across the courtyard, two steps to the jailer's one. He disregarded Pablo and Othon and looked into the cell.

"Big'un, you drunk again. Oh, Big'un, whatever am I going to do with you?" he squeaked in a high falsetto.

"Bloody drunk and fightin', Cap'n masta."

"You're naughty, Big'un, naughty, naughty, naughty! I'll have to punish you."

"Whup me, Cap'n masta, whup me good and I'll not get drunk again."

Pablo took a step towards the little man.

"This fellow your slave?" he asked.

The captain suddenly became aware of Pablo's presence.

"He is, sir."

"Want to sell him?"

"Sell Big'un? Heavens, no!" The captain seemed shocked at the idea. "Couldn't get along without him. Keeps discipline for me aboard ship. Any man gets out of line, Big'un clobbers him. No, couldn't sell Big'un." The captain shook his head, then carefully fingered his long hair which the movement of his head had disarranged.

One advantage of being as rich as Pablo was that he never had to take "no" for an answer.

"Tell you what I'll do. An ordinary slave like this Big'un would fetch around three hundred and fifty dollars at auction here and that's more than he'd bring in Jamaica. I'll double the amount. Seven hundred dollars for him." Pablo saw the captain hesitate.

"Don' sell me, Cap'n masta," Big'un pleaded. "Won' git drunk no more, suh, never."

The captain took another look at Hernandez, making note of the richness of his clothes, the enormous diamond ring on his finger, the other diamond in his cravat, the elaborate watch chain and the ornate gold fobs that hung from it. He shook his head slowly.

"I'll make it an even thousand." Pablo was determined to have Big'un. "And I'll go even better than that. I've got a herd of *bozals* up at my plantation—fine young bucks all of them, and some almost as big as this one. I'll throw one of them in along with the thousand. Any one of them's big enough to keep your sailors in line."

"I wuth more'n thousand dollars to you, Cap'n masta." Big'un was almost crying.

"Shut up!" Jenkins shook a tiny fist at Big'un. "Worthless, impudent nigger! Drunkard, fighter!" He turned to Pablo. "Can't sell this man to you under false conditions. I must tell you he's a wicked man when he's drunk. I cannot guarantee him. He killed a man in a fight in Barbados and another in Grenada. But when he isn't drinking he's very gentle."

"That's why I'm buying him—'cause he's a fighter."

"Then, I'll accept your offer. But on one condition."

"Name it," Pablo countered.

"You pay them to let Big'un out of here. He'll be tractable now. Rum's all scared out of him. Then we'll go to your plantation and you let me pick out the slave you are going to give me. Line them all up and strip them down and let me take my choice. Yes?"

In his present anxiety to buy Big'un, Pablo would have let the little captain pick out five slaves. He agreed eagerly and held out his hand.

"Gentleman's agreement," he said.

"And accepted as such," the captain answered.

Othon felt that this would be an opportune time for him to speak.

"I'd appreciate it, Pablo, if you'd let me buy a share in this fighter." Othon was well aware that Pablo was fully acquainted with his financial condition but he was trusting in his generosity.

Pablo slapped Othon on the back.

*"Mi amigo,"*—when he was excited Pablo always lapsed into Spanish—"he's half yours, if you'll take over his training, and if he's half as good as you say he is, you'll be rolling in money after his first match with Drum."

# chapter xii

RAINSTORMS LIKE the one which had dogged the footsteps of Othon St. Denis in his search for Pablo Hernandez came to be a daily occurrence in New Orleans that summer. The deluge combined with the hottest summer the south had ever known to turn the city into a steaming pesthole. Lying saucer-like in the wide embrace of the Mississippi, the city collected and conserved the rains in her sordid embrace. The water lay stagnant in the streets, putrefied by rotting vegetables, ordure, and accumulated filth, until it scummed over with a poisonous verdigris of thick green velvet. New Orleans has never pretended to be a clean city. Now it seemed as though the accumulated corruption of centuries was seeping out like festering pus from the ground beneath it; vomiting up between the slimy cobbles; oozing from the very sogginess on which the city rested and trickling in from the levees. It seemed as though the river itself had gathered together the sewage of the continent and deposited it on the city. To cross the streets at midday was an excursion into hell, for either one was drenched in the descending torrents or, when the rain ceased, the sun boiled up a miasmic steam which enveloped one with a noxious exhalation of poisonous vapors.

Summer had always suspended many of the activities of the city. The balls and the soirees were over, the opera house was dark, and business took a lethargic holiday. It was even too hot to make love. With many of Alix' best-paying clients in the north, where they sought the healing waters of White Sulphur or Saratoga or rocked on the big-piazza'd wooden hostelries of the Adirondacks or the White Mountains, business at the Academy dragged. Alix herself could well have afforded to close the place for the summer months. But it seemed easier to stay on rather than to disband the white girls, farm out the slaves, and then have to start all over again in the fall, which would have meant recruiting new white girls and would involve far more work than the comfort gained by closing up for the season. So, life at the Academy of Music paced itself slowly, catering to an occasional old customer who returned to the city on business or to escape from boredom with his wife, and entertaining those from other cities who had heard of Madame's famous melees. And, of course, there were always those few reliables who had rather be hot and uncomfortable in New Orleans than be at ease in any other place on earth.

Some evenings, however, there were no customers at all and Blaise, Drum, Calinda and Rachel with the two adolescent slave girls, Marie and Yvette, congregated in a corner of the courtyard. Both Drum and Blaise had been watching the growing nubility of Yvette, whose breasts, just within the past year, had begun to stretch the thin cotton of her dress. But Rachel watched the girls and guarded them like a mother hen with two lone chicks, keeping them out of reach of the men's wandering hands, and even sleeping between them in the kitchen. As for Marie, she was still in the gangling stage of adolescence and lacked any attraction for the men. On the evenings that they sat together, Rachel saw to it that the two young slaves were carefully sequestered while she, Calinda, Blaise and Drum talked, hummed songs, or merely fanned themselves around a smudge fire of corncobs which helped somewhat to discourage the mosquitoes.

Indeed, mosquitoes were no novelty to New Orleans, but this year they quite took possession of the city. The continuous rains multiplied their reproductive haunts and caused them to breed by the millions. That these were the deadly genus Aedes which transmitted yellow fever was a fact about which the inhabitants of the steaming city were woefully ignorant. Alix, of course, had no conception of their death-dealing potential, but she had a healthy fear of them. Not only did she fear them for the ravages they made on her own tender skin—of which they seemed to be particularly fond —but they were bad for her business. The satin skins of her young ladies were certainly not made more delectable when covered with ugly red bumps, and no man could fully appreciate the delights of her establishment when his pleasures were interrupted by the necessity of slapping his own backside. Consequently the Academy of Music was as wholly mosquito-proof as any house in New Orleans could be.

Every one of Alix' beds was tented in a beruffled and embroidered mosquito *baire,* outside of which the incessant droning of the impotent pests could be tolerated without fear.

Her own bed was equally well protected and her favorite chair was surmounted by a framework of thin bamboo over which was draped another wraithlike *baire*. Although the mosquito *baires* were hot, confining and smothering, their discomfort was as nothing compared to the stinging bites of the scourge.

It was a well-accepted fact that mosquitoes would not bite Negroes. Of course not! The whites were certain that no mosquito could possibly plunge his proboscis into their tough, black, animal hides and all agreed that black blood was far too thick to be siphoned off. Therefore, *baires* were unknown in the slave quarters of the city and the fact that Alix, in a sudden burst of pity and generosity, had once ordered one for Drum and then completely forgotten that he had it, made him probably the only slave in the city to be so protected. Blaise also! For despite the common belief that mosquitoes would not bite black flesh, Blaise's continual slappings and his accompanying grunts as he lay stretched out naked on his pallet on the floor, so disturbed Drum that he invited him to share his bed.

The little closet off the kitchen, where Calinda slept with Drumson six nights out of the week, was so tiny and so secluded she had little trouble from the swarms, but Rachel, who bedded down in the kitchen between her two young protégées, was unprotected. She and the girls rubbed themselves with citronella oil until the whole kitchen stank and Drum complained that even the food tasted of the stuff. As an added precaution, Rachel kept a smudge pot burning in the kitchen doorway which discouraged a few of the pests but only a few.

And so the Academy of Music dozed in the steamy heat, as did the whole city, while disaster headed for it aboard the barque *Guadelupe* out of Panama via Merida and Havana. Sickness had broken out on the *Guadelupe* and she had already had three burials at sea when she arrived in New Orleans with two of the sailors' faces yellow with jaundice, their bodies burning with fever and their mouths spewing the black vomit. The health authorities—politicians who knew nothing about health or sanitation—rushed them from the ship to the hospital where they promptly died and everyone heaved a sigh of relief. But by the end of the week there were twenty-four cases of yellow fever, commonly known as Bronze John, in the city. "Nothing to worry about," the authorities said. "Keep it quiet. Bad for business if it gets noised about." And life in New Orleans went on in its usual summer lethargy. The rains fell, the city steamed, the citizens slapped wildly at mosquitoes and the deaths increased. But few persons—outside of the authorities, who vainly tried to keep the matter quiet; the doctors, whose nostrums were powerless to save the victims; and the mourners of the dead, who fortunately were the ragtag and bobtail of the city—were even aware that Bronze John was a visitor, and business went on as always. Consequently Dominique You accepted Pablo Hernandez' challenge, conveyed to him through Othon St. Denis, and the fight between Drum and Big'un was set up, with odds fifty to one.

Othon had been remarkably efficient in his subtle propaganda. To claim too much prowess for Big'un would have been to lower the odds, but not to create the impression that he was a worthy adversary would cause people to lose interest in the fight. He managed by certain innuendoes and meaningful glances to let it be known that his man was a well-known fighter—champion of Jamaica, in fact—and to substantiate his claims, he brought Big'un in from the Hernandez plantation a week before the event and exhibited him to a selected few in the slave quarters of the St. Denis home. Here he invited friends and acquaintances to come to see Big'un work out, neglecting to mention that he was only co-owner of Big'un with Hernandez and referring to him as "my fighting nigger." One glance at the ebon giant convinced all who saw him that here was such an opponent as Drum had never met before, and the odds rose somewhat, although there was still a comfortable margin to make plenty of money. Othon also sent out letters to many of his friends who had left the city for their plantations, hinting at a most unusual event which might take place at Drum's next fight, and painting such a mysteriously exciting picture of his fighter that many planned to come back to the city, if only for that night.

On the night of the bout, there was a goodly crowd at the Academy of Music, despite the heat, the rains and the mosquitoes. Seated under her transparent white canopy which had been carried out onto the balcony, Alix, as usual, held the bets. For a wonder, the rain held off. It was a clear evening with only an occasional rumble of thunder in the distance and streaks of heat lightning in the sultry skies that promised more rain to come.

Drum himself had seen Big'un. Dressed in their best, he

and Blaise had gone uninvited and unaccompanied to the St. Denis house and rapped on the back door. The ancient slave in his threadbare livery who opened the door looked up in astonishment at the two young Negroes, dressed far more richly than his young master. Their appearance caused him to be surlier than was his wont.

"Whaffor you niggers ringin' dis heah do' bell? Who'n you wants to see heah? We ain' buying no catfish from no peddlahs today."

"Not selling catfish," Blaise answered. "Selling good manners, we are. Figured you could use a-plenty."

"And we're not wasting words with you, old man." Drum could be surly too. "We are here to see Monsieur St. Denis. Please ask him if he would kindly see Drum."

The old slave straightened himself up till his eyes came nearly to Drum's chin.

"Monsieur Othon St. Denis he don' truck wi' fancy niggers all dress up in dey mastah's cas' off clotheses, even if they name' Drum or Banjo or Gee-tah. Monsieur St. Denis, he ain' to hum to no Drum-nigger today, he ain'."

"Who wants to see me, Louis Phillipe?" Othon, in shirt sleeves, walked across the courtyard.

"Some picayune nigger name Drum, suh, I tells him yo' cain't be bothered."

"Drum? Tell him to come in and mind whom you turn away after this."

"And de oddah popinjay wid him?"

"All right."

Drum did not forget his manners. Othon St. Denis was a familiar sight around the Academy of Music, at least when he had five or ten dollars to spare. He clicked his heels together smartly, bowed from the waist and addressed Othon very respectfully.

"Monsieur St. Denis, sir, I hope we're not intruding. I've heard a lot about your new fighter and I wondered if I might have a look at him."

Othon sensed a little additional advertising value in having Drum see Big'un. It could be spread around most carefully that Drum had seen him and been impressed, perhaps could even be embroidered with the suggestion that he was somewhat fearful. It might bring more people. Othon was so convinced that Big'un would win he had borrowed as much money as possible, even putting up his share in Big'un as security. The more people, the more chance of betting and the great prestige to himself when Big'un won.

"And why not?" he said agreeably. "Come this way. Big'un's just finished working out. Kind of hot and sweaty but you won't mind." Othon led them up a short flight of stairs to the *garçonnière* and into a small room where Big'un was stretched out full length on a pallet on the floor. Hearing Othon enter, he stood up, wavered a little, then straightened up.

Drum appraised him. *Mon Dieu! Quel homme!* A veritable giant! This didn't look too easy. And in addition to his size, the fellow looked intelligent, too. There was always some weak point—always something the practiced eye could find in an opponent—but as Drum surveyed his man there seemed to be no weak point. He was strong, he was tall, he was intelligent. His legs were like tree trunks, his chest like a barrel, his neck like a black marble column and the muscles in his arm stood out like knotted hawsers. To make matters even worse, the colossus' mouth turned up in an engagingly friendly smile.

"Shake hands," Othon said to Drum, "with the man you are going to fight tomorrow night."

Drum stepped closer and took Big'un's hand. It seemed strangely hot and dry and now that he was closer, he saw an unusual yellow cast in the whites of Big'un's eyes. There was a smell of rum on his breath.

"Ain' got no grudge gainst this-yere fellah, Masta Othon, suh," Big'un said. "Don' much care to fight man I ain't mad at. Fine upstanding buck, this Drum. Likes him for a fren."

"You'll fight him, never fear. Once Drum slugs you in the face, you'll forget you wanted him for a friend." Othon stroked Big'un's arm affectionately.

"Fight him an' you says so, Masta Othon, suh."

Drum returned Big'un's smile but his was a smile of gratification more than greeting. His trained eye had just discovered the weak point he had been looking for. Again Big'un wavered on his feet. His hand passed to his forehead as though to wipe away a film before his eyes.

"Then we fights, Mista Drum. Sure do admire them pretty clotheses you and your fren wears. Admire 'em, I do."

"Lick Drum tomorrow night and you'll have a suit better than that." Othon was all encouragement.

"And if I lick you," Drum continued to smile, "I'm going to get myself a new suit too." He turned to Othon. *"Merci,*

Monsieur St. Denis, *merci*. See you tomorrow night, Big'un."

"Tomorrow night, Drum. Sure am tired. Been a-punchin' a big sack of dirt all mornin'. Sure am tired." Again his hand brushed across his eyes.

Drum and Blaise followed Othon St. Denis down the stairs and took leave of him at the door, not forgetting the proper obsequious ceremonials whereby a slave took leave of a white man. But once outside the door, Drum was jubilant.

"How come you so happified?" Blaise asked. "Don't that goddam big *monstruosité* scare hell out of you?"

"Because I'm goin' to lick the shit out of that black son of a bitch, that's why."

"Looks mighty big to me." Blaise was skeptical.

"No bigger than you and I can lick you." Drum was confident. "Listen, Blaise boy! That Big'un's a toss pot. Stank of rum. Othon gives him rum to make him fight. Now, remember this, a man who's drunk fights viciously. He's mean and nasty and when he's as big as this Big'un bastard, he's dangerous. But when a man drinks, he can't think straight. Pretty soon he gets confused. That's when I step in and hammer the living shit out of him." Drum fingered the silver box under the ruffles of his shirt. "He's as good as licked now, Blaise boy. Just wait and you'll see. Watch *papa* Drum."

But, on the night of the fight, with Big'un standing before him in his awesome black nakedness, Drum was not quite as confident. However, if Big'un's wavering had been only momentary yesterday it was certainly in evidence today. The fellow's big feet seemed hardly to support him, his eyes were yellow and bloodshot and his whole skin, despite its blackness, had a brassy, metallic tinge. Drum smelled the reek of rum and knew that Big'un was drunk, bolstered up to fighting pitch by rum. Yet Drum sensed that there was something more to it than mere drunkenness. Big'un's grinning friendliness of yesterday had departed. Now he glared with malevolence and Drum noticed that his surliness extended even to Othon St. Denis, and to Pablo Hernandez when the latter came up to run his hands over him. Pablo looked even more slack-mouthed and dissipated than ever. Instead of taking an active part, as the owner of a fighter, even a part-owner, naturally would, he delegated everything to St. Denis and sat apathetically in a chair on the edge of the cleared circle, seemingly taking little interest in anything that was happening. Drum noticed how he slumped down in his chair, his eyes closed, his hand occasionally pressed to his forehead.

Pablo had never been much of a drinker—women were his only vice—and Drum was surprised to see him drunk, for drunk he certainly seemed to be.

Dominique You conferred with Othon. They advanced together to the center of the cleared space and at a nod from Dominique, Othon raised his hands as a signal for quiet. Gradually the voices lulled. Even Pablo Hernandez opened his eyes and sat up in his chair.

"Messieurs,"—Othon lowered his hands and bowed in several directions—"and Madame,"—and he waved up at Alix in her white tent on the balcony. "Tonight, through the kindness of New Orleans' patroness of sport, Madame Alix de Vaux, we are privileged to witness another memorable battle between her slave, Drum, undisputed champion of New Orleans, and a slave, belonging"—he paused for a moment to allow the full significance of his words to sink in, for indeed it was the proudest moment of his life—"to M. Pablo Hernandez, the popular owner of Veinte Robles plantation, and . . . myself. Our fighter's name is Big'un. He's champion of the island of Jamaica, having won many fights in the course of which he has killed two opponents. We therefore offer you tonight the greatest exhibition of fighting the city has ever seen." A shift in the wind sent the smoke from the smudge fire of corncobs into Othon's face and he retired coughing, to the accompaniment of good natured applause, as he and Dominique You backed out of the open space.

"I shall count three," Dominique You said. "Then go at each other. One . . . Two . . . Three! Fight!"

Big'un stumbled as he advanced towards Drum but caught himself. Drum, dancing on the balls of his feet, backed away a step and as Big'un came on, crouching, with both arms outstretched, Drum found his opening and swung low with his right, catching Big'un on the side of the face. The force of the blow staggered him and he stopped, shook his head and then advanced again. Drum tried the same tactics a second time but this time Big'un straightened up just as the blow would have landed and his right reached out and met Drum's chin, hitting him with a force that caused Drum to stagger backwards, lose his balance and fall. He was not able to get up before his opponent had thrown himself across him and now, with Big'un's face close to his, Drum got the full force of the reeking, rum-soaked breath. With difficulty, he arched his body, but Big'un's flesh, strangely hot and exuding heat like a stove, rested on him like a mountain and could not be dislodged. Big'un's enormous fist came down on Drum's face like the blow of a sledge hammer. Drum felt the spurt of his own blood on his face and he felt that his nose was broken. Again the fist descended, but this time Drum saw it coming and was able to move his head slightly to one side, enough so that the fist merely grazed his temple. Even so, the force of it almost knocked him unconscious. He struggled to slip out from under, but Big'un was now sprawling with his whole body on top of him, his weight crushing him against the flagging. Drum squirmed but it was no use. Suddenly he screamed, as Big'un's teeth sank into the lobe of his ear, tearing it off. The huge black hand closed around his throat, choking off the scream. Big'un laughed.

"Tastes good, yo' do. Thinks I'll take another bite out of yo'. Eats yo' other ear. Chaws it right down. Maybe chaws yo' balls off too. How you likes that, fancy boy?"

Drum had managed to slip one arm free. With all the force he could command from his supine position, he drove it into his tormentor's groin, catching him in his tenderest spot. Now it was Big'un's turn to scream as he released Drum's throat and shifted his weight. It was the opportunity Drum had been waiting for. He heaved, arching his body with its heavy burden, and sent Big'un off onto his back. With a leap, Drum was on his feet. He jumped, landing with the full force of both feet on his opponent's stomach. Big'un's legs stretched out with a jerk. In an instant Drum was astraddle him, feet spread wide apart with Big'un's heaving chest between them. He raised one foot to bring it crashing down into Big'un's face but Big'un was not through fighting. He grabbed Drum's foot, twisting it as he jackknifed up, throwing Drum off balance but far enough away so that both men could scramble to their feet. Once again Big'un rushed, grabbing Drum around the hips and pulling him down.

For the second time, Big'un had the advantage and he used his hamlike fists on Drum's face and chest, pummeling him until he could not raise a hand to defend himself. Dimly Drum heard the cheers of the spectators. As the blows continued to land, he knew for the first time that he was licked. Pain had become so much a part of him that he was conscious of nothing else. Big'un was killing him. And as the blows continued, he hoped death would come soon for it would mean an end to the horrible torture that was being inflicted on him. But now the blows no longer hurt him. Big'un was still pounding away but it seemed there was no strength left in the blows. Drum's courage returned, dragged up from the limbo of pain. Perhaps he was not beaten yet. Somewhere, floating down and penetrating his consciousness, he heard a voice.

"Separate them, Dominique, separate them. I'll yield the fight. Separate them or Drum will be killed."

Madame—Drum's thoughts were confused—Madame didn't want him killed.

With a last surge of strength he grabbed one of Big'un's hands with both his own. His left encircled the wrist and with his right, he slowly bent the fist back until the fingers opened, increasing the pressure as he forced the hand back until at last he heard the bones of the wrist snap. Big'un howled, rolled off Drum onto the floor, screamed once and was quiet. Only his body twitched.

"Fight, Big'un!" Othon St. Denis was yelling. "Fight! Get up, you goddamned black bastard and fight."

Drum struggled to his knees, collapsed, then pulled himself up again, but when he tried to raise himself from his knees, he was unable to stand. He knelt, swaying from side to side. He could see out of only one eye and that through a film of blood and sweat, but he saw St. Denis run to the big brazier which had been lit to dispel the mosquitoes. Othon snatched a half-burned corncob from the fire and applied the glowing coal to Big'un's cheek, holding it there. Drum could hear St. Denis' curses and could smell the sickly odor of burning flesh. But Big'un did not move.

Drum managed to hoist himself to his feet and saw Dominique You come toward him, but he waved him back. Slowly, like an earthquake moving a mountain, the black bulk of Big-'un twitched in a spasm of convulsions. He rolled over on his side, his stomach heaving and a stream of vomit came from his mouth—heavy dark blood that, in the light of the flambeaux, stained the stones black. Dominique You was about to raise Drum's hand in victory when he saw the puke pouring from Big-un's mouth. He dropped Drum's hand and took a step nearer the supine figure, hesitated, then came close enough so that he could stoop down and put a trembling hand on the Negro's forehead. He recoiled from the burning fever.

"Bronze John!" he jumped up and cried out the dreaded name.

Othon St. Denis rushed forward but Dominique You's restraining hand held him back.

"Don't touch him!"

"But I just did touch him. My God, will I have it?"

The circle started to widen, leaving Dominique You, Drum, Othon St. Denis and the stricken Big'un in the center of an ever growing circumference. Only Pablo Hernandez remained, slumped on his chair, his head sunk on his chest, a string of bloody saliva oozing from the corner of his mouth down onto his waistcoat. Suddenly, as if the idea of flight had been simultaneous in everyone's mind, there was a stampede for the door, and the porte-cochere became a milling mass of men, clawing their way out. Dominique You walked over to where Pablo was sitting.

"Pablo, have your coachman get your slave out of here." He shook Hernandez by the shoulder but Pablo only slumped lower in his chair. Dominique's hand sought his forehead.

"*Mon Dieu!* It's struck him too."

"And me next," Othon was wailing.

Dominique You disregarded Othon. "Blaise, where are you?" he called out.

"Here, M'sieur You, suh," Blaise came running up.

"Go outside, call the Hernandez carriage and tell the coachman to drive up on the banquette directly in front of the door."

Rachel came running down the stairs from the balcony.

"Madame's fainted."

"Well, loosen her stays, burn some feathers under her nose or do whatever people usually do. Is she sick or just fainted?"

"She's got no fever," Rachel answered. "I felt her, she's not feverish."

"Then she'll be all right." Dominique looked up to see Blaise returning.

"Come over here and help Monsieur St. Denis get his nigger out of here."

"He isn't mine," Othon said, denying any ownership, "he's Pablo's."

"You were turkey-cocking around here a little while ago, claiming he was half yours. He still is. He's not going to die here—not if we can help it. Get him out. Blaise, carry Pablo out and put him in his carriage, then come back and help Monsieur St. Denis get his fighter out of here."

Blaise picked up Hernandez and started for the door. Othon gazed wildly about. He reached down and grabbing one of Big'un's arms started to pull the black body across the flagstones, but made little progress. Blaise returned and took hold of the other arm whose broken hand dangled awkwardly. Together they dragged the black carcass across the stones and out the porte-cochere and lifted it up into the carriage beside the slumped figure of Pablo Hernandez. Once more the unconscious figure of Big'un heaved, and the black vomit from his mouth spurted over the immaculate white pantaloons of Pablo Hernandez.

"Take them back to the plantation," Othon cried out to the coachman, and started to run down the street.

Blaise walked back into the courtyard, shutting and bolting the street door behind him.

Dominique You was still standing beside Drum. With only Blaise for an audience, he raised Drum's right hand.

*"Voilà, le champion!"* he said. "Take him upstairs and tend to him."

## chapter xiii

UNABLE TO SLEEP, notwithstanding the careful ministrations of Blaise and the loving care of Calinda, Drum lay stiffly beside the sleeping woman, listening to her breathing, the occasional whimper of little Drumson and the stentorian snores of Blaise. Every muscle in his body felt the effects of the pounding he had received and his nose and ear throbbed with pain. As soon as the weak sun, strained through the lowering clouds which presaged another rainy day, had lightened the room sufficiently, he forced himself out of bed, stepping with difficulty across the floor.

He hesitated, fearful. It took courage for him to look at himself in the shard of mirror which he had salvaged for his room. His first forced glance caused him to recoil in horror. Surely that battered visage regarding him through puffed and purple slits of eyes could not be his own. His nose, which had always descended in a broad Grecian line, straight down from his forehead, was now smashed flat, spreading over his face like an overripe tomato. A ragged fringe of bloody flesh dangled where his right ear lobe should have been, and all his features seemed to have melted together in a bruised, swollen mass. His body, such as he could see of it in the mirror, was covered with bruises and blotches of extravasated blood.

Drum was disheartened. Always vain, he had been proud of his comeliness for he realized that his good looks had been his entree to popularity with women and almost equally so with men. Now, with a face like this one that stared back at him, who would ever want to look at him again? No amount of elaborate clothes could ever change him now. The swelling of his face would disappear, the clear color would return, the eyes would again appear normal and the bruises on his body would scab over and heal. But nothing, no, nothing could ever replace the ragged tatter of his ear or reshape his broken nose.

He touched the malformed nose gingerly with his finger, hoping to mold it back into a semblance of its former shape, but the pain was too great. Suddenly his proud young world had collapsed. Aie, Veronique! Strange that the thought of her should trouble him at this time. Surely she would never want to see him again, nor Jeanneton. He glanced down at his body. Thank God, it had been only his ear that Bigger had chewed off and that he had not been able to carry out his further threat! Drum managed a wan smile through his cracked lips. *Damne!* He was still a man and he could still satisfy any wench, if she did not look at his face. But then, what woman was ever interested in a man's face when he was with her in a dark room? As for Calinda, she would still worship him even though he were faceless. No need to worry about Calinda! And what about the little wench Yvette, whom *maman* guarded so jealously? Some night when *maman* was getting Madame ready for bed. . . . *Aie!* Things were not so bad after all. He was still *très mâle*. Even Madame had not wanted him killed. *Aie!* He had heard her call out for him to be spared. Could that mean that he really meant something to her? Of course not! The old bitch only wanted him to keep on fighting and make money for her. Then he remembered how she had looked at him that day she had hung the silver chain around his neck. She had been almost human then—not like a white mistress with a black slave. Well, things were not so bad after all. Now he had a face like a fighter. Sure! Why not? That's what he goddamned well was. His flattened nose and missing ear would advertise his profession. Now all the world would know that the big *griffe* with the broken nose and the fancy clothes was none other than Drum, the champion. He stumbled back to bed, feeling better. So much better, in fact, that he allowed his hand to stray along the satin smoothness of Calinda's breasts before he dozed off to a dreamless sleep, which continued all that day and through the next night. He was secure and safe in his own little world under the white mosquito *baire* while grim Bronze John flitted relentlessly through the city on tiny, transparent, humming wings.

It could no longer be kept a secret that New Orleans was seized by an epidemic that was claiming victims without distinction of class, position or color. Slaves were dying alongside their white masters. The proud Creole lady who went to bed one night, carefully attended by her slave, might awaken the next morning in a delirium of fever, her face darkened and blood oozing from lips, gums and nose. The Creole dandy whose valet helped him into bed might awaken in the morning to ring in vain for the slave whose corpse was already stinking in the *garçonnière*. Deaths were increasing. Two hundred and four one week, 559 the next, then leaping to 947.

The entire city was panic-stricken. Crowds milled on the levees, seeking accommodations on boats that would carry them away—anywhere, it didn't matter as long as it was away from the stricken city. But there were no boats, for all traffic by sea and river now shunned the city. Boats from New Orleans were flagged away from the ports of the country. Those who had horses had long since departed and the roads leading out of the city were choked with pedestrians, sinking beside the road and dying in their tracks, leaving behind a trail of abandoned valises, hat boxes and other impedimenta which they had thought so necessary and which had suddenly become so worthless. Death stalked the steaming squares of the city, unobstructed and unmolested, because nobody knew the cure. The best medical minds of the country, although certainly not admitting their inability to cope with yellow fever, had no idea what to do.

Fantastic explanations were offered and equally fantastic cures advocated. As soon as one cure had proved useless, another was promulgated and quickly became the fashion. Doctors ordered cold treatments, hot treatments; open windows, closed windows. It was believed that there was some mystical curative power in the juice of fresh oysters and the total supply of the city was exhausted in a single hour. People guzzled limewater, swallowed sulphur and purged themselves with violent cathartics. One school advocated quinine while another swore by opium. Bleeding was popular either by cups or leeches and many a poor soul who might possibly have recovered was so drained of blood he died anyway.

What caused Bronze John? Learned heads conferred with solemn waggings. It originated in rotting wood. Ridiculous! It came from tiny specks in the air. Of course not! Any but the most abysmally ignorant knew that it was pestilential effluvia—a nice long name that sounded sufficiently awesome and professionally Latin to have an authoritative ring. Yes, they finally agreed, undoubtedly it was pestilential effluvia, arising from river bank, canal and swamp. They sniffed. They could smell it. The decision was made, notwithstanding the self-evident fact that New Orleans always stank of one kind of effluvium or another—putrefying animals, rotting vegetables, sweating, unwashed bodies, stagnant water, human excretions and offal. And so, it was officially pronounced by the learned faculties of the medical schools, many of whom had never stepped foot in New Orleans, that the cause of Bronze John, yellow fever, yellow jack—call it what one might—was pestilential effluvia. It sounded so damned nice, so tongue-rolling, so Aesculapian.

Thus, having discovered the cause, naturally there could be but one remedy. If Bronze John was in the air, then its infection must be taken into the body through the mouth or nose. Consequently anything that could purify the air, or pollute it with a stench sufficient to overcome its inherent poison, would, of course, be the sovereign panacea. It was a well-known scientific fact that thunder purified the air but as man was not Immortal Jove, with thunderbolts in his hand, he could only avail himself of the next best thing—cannons. So cannons boomed at street corners at regular intervals and the successive booming of the big guns caused the wretched fever victims to fall into convulsions and cover their eyes from the chips of plaster that fell from the ceilings. And tar! That could be burned and everyone knew that burning tar sweetened the air. After considerable scientific pondering, one learned physician decided that lime would sweeten the air and no sooner had he uttered his pronouncement than banquettes and courtyards took on the pristine whiteness of a New England winter. Alas, to no avail! Think again! Surely smudge fires would purify the air, and now everybody—at least those who were out on the streets—wandered around in a dense fog of smoke. (It is quite possible that the incessant booming of the cannons frightened a few of the mosquitoes and perhaps the smudge fires and the burning tar discouraged others, but the main cause of the yellow fever continued to bite and infect the people. Who could ever imagine a buzzing little insect to be the cause? Incredible!)

Necklaces of garlic buds were declared a sure protection and the belles of New Orleans, such as remained in the city, became as pungent as a Neapolitan housewife. Camphor gum would certainly banish the effluvium, so men and women sniffed the aromatic gum through their nostrils. Eating onions! Ah, that would pile effluvium upon effluvium and prevent the poison from entering one's lungs. Now half of New Orleans was suffering heartburn along with the fever.

Hardly more fantastic and equally inefficient were the remedies of the conjure men—a live frog boiled in water and the liquor therefrom flavored with red pepper and drunk exactly at the stroke of midnight; poultices of goat dung, mixed with human urine; the tail feathers of a black, white and red rooster under the pillows of the stricken. The rooster feathers of the conjure men were as efficacious as the cannon shots recommended by the medical profession. The rains fell daily and the mosquitoes continued to breed, undeterred by asafetida bags, crossed sticks at the doorways of houses, sprinklings of holy water from the cathedral and innumerable novenas. The mosquitoes gorged themselves on infected blood and flew away to spread the infection. But to the worried New Orleanians, the mosquitoes were only a lesser plague—nothing could be done about them and it would be ridiculous to try.

There were no longer coffins in which to bury the dead; no longer even pine boards to make rough boxes; no longer priests to administer last rites, or sextons to dig graves, or hearses to carry the dead to the cemetery. The corpses, stark in their horrible corruption, were carried out of doors and laid on the banquettes where they awaited the arrival of pest carts, driven through the streets at night by frightened slaves who loaded the dead like cordwood and gave them a hasty burial in muddy ditches, unblessed and often unmourned.

The only businesses that flourished in the city were the saloons and the whorehouses. Drink and fornicate today for tomorrow you die! Cram as much sensual pleasure into the fleeting hour as possible because you'll be a long time dead and there was damn little fun awaiting you in a muddy ditch. Have another Sazerac, *mon ami,* and don't worry if the bartender collapses while he serves you the drink. Get yourself an octoroon wench, *mon brave,* and if she is dead when you achieve your climax, well, *c'est la vie* or rather *c'est la mort.* Live today, *mon frère,* because tomorrow you'll be a stinking corpse.

Brothel madams collected money with one grasping hand while the other fell in the inertia of death. All but Alix! For once her avarice was outmatched by her fear. No one was to leave the house! Lock the front doors and nail them shut! Only Rachel could leave by the back door and that only for a daily trip to the market. Yes, the two young slaveys could go with her to carry things if she needed them. But no one else! Alix dispatched all her white girls from the house, turning them out into the streets to shift for themselves. Her octoroon and quadroon girls, which were naturally her own property, could not be disposed of so summarily, but these she put to manual labor, hemming new sheets, mending old ones and doing a multitude of household tasks while they longed for the old days when they were above all menial work.

Drum and Blaise were forbidden to leave the house under pain of punishment at the public whips. Drum knew that Madame was frightened and in her fright she was quite capable of carrying out her threats. Calinda must keep Drumson—it was felt that infants were particularly susceptible to the disease—away from all the rest of the household.

There was not much use in Rachel's taking the two young slaves to market with her for practically everything had disappeared from the stalls. Fortunately the Academy of Music did not suffer too much from lack of food, owing to Rachel's acumen. There was a large supply of hams and bacons hanging from the rafters in the kitchen, along with braided strips of onion and garlic. Rachel had purchased live hens, whenever she could find them in the market, and instead of killing them for food, she kept them in the courtyard until she had a sizable flock which supplied eggs while they bespattered the flagging. A milch goat, who had already eaten all the flowers and herbage in the court, produced milk, and the visits to the markets usually yielded a few yams, turnip greens or collards and occasionally a fish. When everything else failed, they could always have beans and rice, with pone, so they managed to live although their diet was neither rich nor varied.

Alix moved only from her *baire*-draped bed to her *baire*-tented chair and back again. Titine and the other girls sewed, gossiped, told and retold stories of their patrons, and managed—quite successfully while Rachel was out—to entice both Drum and Blaise into the shelter of their protected beds. But Drum was not as easily influenced as Blaise; Calinda was sleeping regularly in his bed now. Fearing the poisonous effluvium which was supposed to exude from the ground, he brought Calinda and Drumson up from the closet off the kitchen to his room, and he refused to let Blaise sleep on the pallet on the ground floor. Now all four—Drum, Calinda, the baby and Blaise—occupied the tiny upstairs room in the *garçonnière* with the door and window tightly closed. Drum and Calinda had the protection of the mosquito *baire* which Alix had left there, while little Drumson, who slept beside Blaise on the floor, shared with him a tattered *baire* which Alix had discarded and Calinda had patiently mended. Rachel, disdaining the protection of a *baire* for herself or her two girls, claimed that no mosquito had ever bitten her yet, but she did keep a smudge fire burning in an iron pot in the doorway of the kitchen.

Life at the Academy of Music had lost all its carnival gaiety. Days and nights had become a furtive defense against the entry of death, eked out with scanty rations, marred by petulant clashes of temper, and punctuated by plenty of hard work for all. Except of course Alix, who, like a lump of white, unbaked dough, luxuriated in the shelter of her bed, sipping her rich chocolate and eating the delectable omelets and the caramel *flans* which Rachel prepared for her alone.

After a few days of rest for his bruised limbs, Drum was up and about as usual. The swelling of his face had gone down and the broken nose, although flattened and far from the adornment that it had previously been, did not disfigure him too badly. The chewed ear, to be sure, could never be repaired, but at least the tattered ear and the flattened nose branded him as a fighter, and with these identifying marks of his profession he added a bit of swagger to his walk. He was still champion and now, *mon Dieu,* the world would not mistake him for a fancy man. But he must keep in training. Fortunately he had Blaise to work out with. Morning runs were out of the question, so they worked out in the courtyard, skipping rope among the hens and cursing their foul droppings when they stepped in them.

It was pleasant working in the cool of the morning, when the *garçonnière* side of the courtyard was in shadow. They were up before the rest of the house was astir, and down the narrow stairs to the courtyard, damp from the continuous rains, where they fought, wrestled, boxed and pummeled each other until the sweat ran down their backs in rivulets. Then they doused each other with bucketfuls of water and scrubbed themselves with Rachel's homemade soap. After a rubdown with one of Alix' old towels, they were ready to go into the smoky kitchen for Rachel's breakfast—there was always plenty to eat even though it might be nothing but strong black coffee to wash down hot cornbread and blackstrap molasses. Always before they reached the end of their practice, they could smell the tantalizing aroma of coffee being boiled and hot breads being baked. To be sure, there might not be ham or bacon but coffee and bread made a good breakfast and it was a lot more than many in the city had.

"That's enough, Blaise boy." Drum stood still, panting from the spirited opposition Blaise had been giving him. "But you've got to keep your head down. If you come sailing in with your head all cockalorum, you'll get the goddam thing knocked off. Could have done it two or three times this mornin'. But keep on and you'll make a pretty good fighter some day. Might even whip me," he said with a wink, cuffing Blaise.

"Don't want to be a champion, Drum. Like to fight with you, but doin' want to fight anybody else. Don't likes hurting people."

"Didn't mind killing Babouin or Bouc-noir that day," Drum reminded him.

Blaise reached down furtively, rippling the muscles in his arms like a cat. Before Drum could see what he was doing, he had picked up one of the buckets of water and splashed the contents over him. The cold water made Drum yelp and he dived for Blaise, catching him around the neck. Slowly, and mainly because Blaise did not resist too much, Drum forced him to his knees and pushed his head down into the other full bucket. He held it there for nearly a minute, then released him, and as the snorting Blaise straightened up, Drum grabbed the bucket and flung the contents over him.

"Didn't mind killing those varmints." Blaise shook himself like a spaniel. "Had a hard time keeping my hands off that Big'un nigger t'other night. Knew you'd whop him, though."

"I knew it, too, but almost didn't." Drum threw the soggy towel to Blaise. "Come on, boy, let's eat. Hope *Maman's* got something besides pone and coffee this morning. I'm hungry."

Blaise mopped himself as dry as he could with the wet towel and slipped into his pants as Drum tied his own single garment around his waist. "Goddam those hens," he cursed, as some fresh droppings squeezed between his clean toes. "I'll wring their goddam necks some day."

But when they reached the kitchen, there was no welcome aroma of coffee, no smell of freshly baked croissants. The kitchen was dark and cool inside. The charcoal fire was out in the stove, and there was no sign of life, except a quiet sobbing from the corner of the room.

*"Maman!"* Drum cried out as he ran over to the pallet where Rachel was still stretched out. *"Maman!"*

Yvette, who was kneeling on the floor beside Rachel, looked up with eyes reddened from crying. She struggled to her feet, wiping her eyes with the back of her hand.

"She's sick, she is, M'sieur Drum. Awful sick, Rachel is. Cain't wake she up. She won' talk, neither'll Marie."

Drum took a step backward, treading on Blaise's toes.

"You mean. . . ." He was afraid to ask.

"Bronze John done come heah." Yvette, now that she had an appreciative audience, was wailing loudly. "Bronze John done come heah and tooken our Rachel an' Marie."

"She's not dead?" Drum's momentary fear of the disease had departed.

"Dunno, M'sieur Drum. I jest woken. She's eyes closed and she out'n her haid and she fearful hot. She been a-raving. So's Marie, only she worsen Rachel. She a-pukin' blood all ovah de floah."

Rachel and Marie were stretched out on the pallet, Rachel decently clothed in a long white nightgown, Marie as naked as the wailing Yvette. Drum cursed himself inwardly. Even in his fear and anxiety, he could not but notice how Yvette's young breasts hung down and he ached to touch them even before he laid a hand on his mother's forehead. He dismissed the temptation. *Maman* was sick! What a cur he was, even to think of playing with a wench's titties when his own mother was dying. Yes, his mother was dying! He knew it. Suddenly the whole bottom dropped out of his world.

*"Maman."* He flung himself on the floor beside her, pushing Yvette back. Her body had the same stovelike heat that Big 'un's had had. Her eyes were closed and there was a drool of bloody saliva at the corner of her mouth. The skin of her face was blotched with large red stains, the veins distended as if about to break. Each breath was painfully drawn through gaping purple lips as though it were an ordeal of heavy labor. The girl beside her was in the same condition, lying senseless in her own vomit.

"Get busy," Drum jumped to his feet and slapped the wailing Yvette to bring her to her senses. "Call Calinda!" Then he wondered why he wanted the girl to get busy. There was nothing she could do. But surely someone could do something to save his mother. "Start the fire and get something for breakfast. Make coffee! And you, Blaise, go to one of the empty rooms on the second floor and take down the bed.

Bring bed and mattress down here and set it up over in the corner. I'll not have my mother die on the floor."

"Madame?" Blaise questioned.

"To hell with Madame!" Drum was impatient. "It's my mother that's sick."

"Cain't cook nothin'." Yvette was trying to kindle a fire with Rachel's tinder box. "She's allays a-done it. Don' know how."

"Well, goddam it, learn, and put on some clothes."

"Madame want she's breakfus'." Yvette's hands managed a flame which caught onto the charcoal. "Chocolate she's a-wantin'."

"Then let the old bitch come down and get it herself. Let her keep on ringing till her goddam hand falls off. Go up to my room and wake Calinda. She knows how to cook."

Yvette and Blaise collided in the door, bent on their separate errands. As they met, Blaise, no longer fearful of Rachel, lifted her in his arms, swung her around and kissed her before he set her down. She squealed and tried to fight him off but Drum did not notice. With the fire burning, he put a kettle of water on to heat. From the line which hung over the stove he grabbed a dish towel, soaked it in cold water and tenderly sponged Rachel's face, wringing out the towel and dipping it in the water again and laying it across her forehead. Slowly she opened her eyes.

"Tamboura!" She gazed at Drum with eyes that mingled hatred and fear.

"What you say, *maman?*" Drum bent low to hear her. "Yes, Tamboura—Drum, that's me, *maman.* Oh, *maman,* you're going to be all right. You've got to be!"

Her words were hard to understand and her language was so garbled that half of her sentences were unintelligible. She was somewhere far away, certainly not on the floor in Alix' kitchen. It dawned on Drum that the reason he could not understand some of the things she was saying was that she was talking in a foreign language. From the few words he knew, he thought it might be Spanish.

"Don't talk, *maman,* save your strength." Drum raised her head a bit to smooth the pillow beneath it. As he did, he noticed that the girl beside her was no longer breathing. She was dead. As Drum raised Rachel's head, she retched, the vomit staining her nightgown. Drum heard a footstep behind him and looked up over his shoulder to see Calinda. He motioned to her to come to him and pointed to the dead girl beside Rachel.

"She's dead." His voice was noncommital, "Cover her up and see if you can get that stupid Yvette to make some coffee. Might do *maman* good."

"Nothin' gonna do her no good, *mon cher*. Bronze John taken her." Calinda had never been overfond of Rachel. She pretended no grief. "But I am not afraid. I'll nurse her."

Blaise lumbered through the doorway with the heavy mahogany headboard of a bed.

"Madame sure is raising holy hell. She says what's going on in this house of hers."

"Tell her Rachel's sick with yellow fever. That'll shut her up."

Blaise left with the message and to get the remainder of the bed. By the time he had carried it all downstairs, and set it up, Alix, still in her nightgown, appeared in the kitchen.

"Who told that ignoramus to burst into one of my rooms and take down the bed?" she demanded.

"I did." Drum matched his tone to hers.

"Don't get too biggity," Alix reminded him. "I can have you stripped down, remember that."

"Strip me down if you want to." Drum pointed to Rachel. "*Maman's* sick. She's slept on a pallet on the floor all her life and if she's going to die, she's going to die in a bed, even if it's a whore's bed."

"Hold your tongue! Don't sass me." Alix came hesitatingly across the floor. "Rachel, oh, Rachel!"

The familiar voice penetrated the dark eddies of Rachel's unconsciousness. She opened her eyes and this time Drum knew that she recognized them. She was back in New Orleans.

"Madame." She was speaking French and her words came with difficulty, "Your breakfast will be late this morning. I will get it soon. Please go back to bed and I will bring it up to you."

"It's all right, Rachel," Alix said tenderly. "You just stay there. Calinda'll get it for me."

Drum and Blaise lifted Rachel from the pallet and placed her on the bed. Alix followed them and with a peremptory nod of her head she dismissed Blaise, who went over to the far side of the kitchen to stand beside the stove with Calinda and Yvette.

Rachel closed her eyes wearily.

*"Maman,"* Drum cried out, *"maman,* don' leave me."

Slowly the sick woman's eyes opened. Her hand struggled to move. She could not lift it more than a few inches.

"Not . . . your . . . mother, Drum." The words came slowly. The hand resolved itself into a pointing finger. "She's . . . your . . . mother." The finger pointed to Alix.

Drum turned quickly to stare at Alix.

"You?"

Alix came and stood beside him, and reaching down, lifted Rachel's hand.

"Rachel's dead, Drum." Alix was crying. He had never seen her weep before. He had not thought it possible.

"But she said you were my mother."

"Dying people often say strange things, Drum."

"But they do not lie. Tell me, madame, tell me the truth, or by God, I'll choke you." He jumped toward her, hands outstretched.

Her brief sobbing was over and she cowed him with a glance.

"Don't threaten me. Don't touch me. Don't forget what you are—a slave. Your father forgot and he was whipped to death."

"Whipped to death? Because of you?" Drum lost all fear of the fat white woman and her threats. He stared straight at her. The widespread fingers of his hands were trembling.

Alix was frightened. She sensed that his underlying hatred of her was inflamed by his sorrow. Her hand went up but instead of brushing his away, she laid it tenderly on his cheek.

"If you kill me now, Drum, the whole world will say that Alix de Vaux was murdered by her nigger slave. Yes, that's what the world will say, but only you and I will know that Alix de Vaux was murdered by her own mulatto son."

Drum's hands dropped to his sides.

"Then it's true! You are my mother!"

"Yes." She took refuge in tears, hoping to gain his sympathy, although she sensed that the moment of danger had passed.

"And my father?"

"Tamboura. Your father would have been a king in Africa and he was the handsomest man, black or white, that ever lived."

Drum dropped to his knees beside the bed. His hand sought that of Rachel's, still warm.

*"Maman."* His own tears started. He felt a hand lightly on his head, and looking up his eyes met Alix'.

"Mother?" The word was a question.

"Yes, Drum," Alix spoke slowly. "You may call me 'mother' but only this once. Never again. The world must not know for your sake as much as mine. Rachel gave you all the love and affection you ever had, yet do not think, Drum, there have not been times when I longed to hold you in my arms. Do not think when I have seen you fighting I have not felt proud of you. I have looked at you and I saw all the glory of your father in you. And let me tell you this: black or white, he was the only man I ever loved. But there was nothing I could do to save him. I have not given you the love a mother gives her son. I could not. I had to harden my heart against you. And now, you have called me 'mother' and I shall call you 'son'. And I shall kiss you as a mother kisses her son." She leaned down and brushed her lips on his forehead.

*"Voilà!* For a brief moment, we have been mother and son. We shall never mention it again. New Orleans has never known and must never know that I gave birth to a Negro's child. In repayment for my having given you life, you must help me keep the secret. If it were discovered, we would both be hounded out of the city. I would be thought too low even to keep a whorehouse and you would be persecuted as my nigger bastard. Shall we keep silent?"

Drum nodded grimly. "And I am still your slave, even if you are my mother."

She nodded in agreement.

He stood up, and his fingers rested lightly on Rachel's cheek.

"I have just learned something, *maman,"* he said softly and his pride gave a new ring to his voice. He turned and called Calinda and Blaise to the bed. They came over and stood beside him.

*"Maman* spoke to me before she died. She told me that my father was a white man, not a Negro. Do you understand what that means? I am not a *griffe,* nor am I a mulatto. My father was white and *maman* was half white. That makes me a quadroon." He looked to Alix for confirmation.

"Yes, Drum is right." Alix clutched his hand and her fingers closed around his in appreciation. He would keep her secret and if he wanted her to lie a little she would. The lie would cost her nothing and it would buy his silence forever. "Drum's father was white. Rachel wanted it kept a secret because she hated white men." Alix decided to embroider her lie. "And Drum's father,"—she paused for the effect her words would make—"was a grandee of Spain."

His chest swelled and he gathered Calinda to him but over her shoulder he saw the naked form of Yvette, still standing by the stove. Her breasts were round and full and he wanted to touch them. No woman would refuse him now. Even with his broken nose and his torn ear. He knew that he was a mulatto and all the rest of the world would think him a quadroon. The knowledge of his new social status had quite dispelled his grief. Again his eyes sought the round dark globes. Some day soon he would touch them. Some day soon!

# chapter xiv

THE RAINS ceased, the sun shone and dried the stagnant pools and Bronze John reluctantly terminated his visit to the stricken city. True, he did not depart at once, but each week the number of deaths lessened and the city slowly returned to normal. Those who had fled started to come back, and with the advent of autumn, except for the plethora of mourning veils and crêpe armbands, life in New Orleans began to glide along as gracefully as ever. Although there were fewer balls and a larger number of the boxes at the opera were covered with latticework so that their black-clad occupants could not be seen by the audience, business picked up at the Academy of Music. Widowers who had been summarily deprived of their conjugal rights found temporary forgetfulness in the Academy, where every attempt was made to assuage their sorrow with the new white girls Alix had managed to lure to New Orleans from as far away as Richmond by offers of better pay and steady employment. Maspero had found two new octoroon girls for her whom she immediately purchased, along with two small slaveys to fill the places of Marie and Yvette, who had died five days after Marie.

Drum's short grief at Rachel's passing was quite swallowed up in the awareness of his new position on the ladder of color. He knew he could expect neither love nor affection from Alix, not that he particularly wanted or needed it. The gulf between them was far too great—there was no bridging the immensity between mistress and slave. His father had evidently tried to do it and been flogged to death for the attempt. To hell with her! She had served her purpose.

Despite his knowledge, Drum's position at the Academy of Music remained the same as before. There was little change in the running of the household. Calinda grudgingly assumed Rachel's duties although without the dead woman's devotion or experience. The management of much of the household fell on her unwilling shoulders. She was by nature a slack housekeeper, indifferent to dirt and disorder, but under Alix' constant nagging and threats, she eventually achieved some efficiency. Calinda delighted in the fact that she had two new girls to slave for her, and with the desire of a bondwoman to wreak her vengeance on someone more unfortunate than herself she made their life a hell on earth for them. Her favorite method of discipline was to pinch them, and this she did so viciously that their scrawny bodies were a mass of black and blue marks. Blaise resumed his duties as bartender. Titine, who was losing the soft freshness of youth, was demoted to Alix' personal maid, which nevertheless gave her an opportunity to lord it over Calinda.

Dominique You had returned to New Orleans and was again seeking matches for Drum but finding it more and more difficult to secure them. Drum had been relieved of all menial work in the house that he might continue to keep himself in trim, and so Blaise had more work than he could do, especially as Drum insisted that they continue to work out together daily. It never occurred to Drum to help him. After all, Blaise was his slave; he had won him. The only duty he was willing to assume occasionally was to do the marketing, because it gave him a chance to mingle with the market crowds and ogle the many women who were there.

Women, all women in fact, were beginning to interest Drum more than ever before. His feelings toward Calinda had cooled since the birth of Drumson and more immediately since she had assumed Rachel's duties. Unconsciously, too, he was jealous of her devotion to the child. Between being a mother and a housekeeper, she had little time for Drum and when she crawled in beside him in the early hours of the morning, her only desire was to sleep. When her movements woke him and he demanded that she accommodate him, she often did so unwillingly and even more often refused him. The first fire of their passion had burned out—both were aware of it, yet it angered Drum that she did not respond as before.

The big bed which had been removed to the kitchen during Rachel's dying moments still remained there. Alix was superstitious and she would not consider a bed that had witnessed a death as being appropriate for joy. Drum and Calinda continued to share it, at least for the present, although it was mutually conceded that when he started to fight again in earnest, she would move into the little closet off the kitchen and Blaise would share Drum's bed.

At times, Drum even looked forward to exchanging Calinda as a bedfellow for Blaise. At least, Blaise did not tempt him as Calinda did. On the few occasions when he had been able to arouse her to a semblance of her former ardor for him, it almost invariably happened that Drumson began to cry. Regardless of Drum's passion, Calinda would be up and out of bed, comforting the child, while he scalded her with invectives. Such moments led to violent quarrels between them. On the last occasion when Drumson's whimpering had taken Calinda away at a most crucial moment, Drum refused to allow her to return. To punish her, he forbade her his bed for two weeks.

Not that he didn't still care for her. He supposed he really cared more for her than anyone else. Sure . . . he loved her. But, he had to teach her a lesson. She had to know that he came first. *Mon Dieu!* Why shouldn't he? He'd won her by fighting just as he had won Blaise. She belonged to him and she ought to put him before Drumson. His vanity as a male animal could not possibly relinquish her to another male animal even though his competitor was an infant and his own child. Therefore, she must be brought to heel and must be made to know that he was her master. *Damne!* Give her time and she'd get such an itch for him she'd come crawling back to him on her hands and knees. Let her crawl! It would do her good.

But Calinda had a mind of her own and having been kicked out of Drum's bed she was determined to have him seek her rather than to seek him. If any crawling was to be done, he'd be the one to do it. Conversation between them ceased. When it became necessary for one to address the other, it was done through a third person—Blaise or even little Drumson.

"Blaise, tell that lazy Drum I needs a bucket of water."

"Blaise, tell that good for nothing Calinda that if she wants a bucket of water, she can damn well get it for herself."

Drum managed to get through the first week without Calinda fairly well by tiring himself with such unremitting and continuous exercise that he was asleep before he reached his bed. However, Saturday night came and he retired early as was his custom; he felt certain that she would relent and sleep beside him. He forced himself to keep awake until Calinda and Blaise returned, sometime during the early morning hours after the last guest had gone. When they came in he pretended to be asleep while he waited for Calinda to slip into bed beside him. He had quite forgiven her and his first words would be ones of endearment. He'd call her by his old name for her—*poupée,* little doll. That would put her in a good mood.

But Calinda had no intention of coming to him. Methodically she made up her own bed on the floor, cooed over the sleeping Drumson and then went into Blaise's cubbyhole where she stayed several minutes. Drum was unable to see inside the door but he heard the hum of voices and Calinda's giggles. Had there been no voices, he would have been suspicious but soon she came out, took off her single garment and stretched out on the pallet.

*"Bonne nuit, Blaise,"* she called softly

*"Bonne nuit, Calinda,"* he answered her.

She blew out the candle.

Drum writhed on the bed. His first reaction was to go to her and either drag her into bed with him or force her on the floor. His need was great but his pride was even greater. She'd come to him. She'd come to him or else she'd sleep alone the rest of her life. Damn her! Damn them both! She could play up to Blaise. She could go in his room and talk and giggle with him. How did he know what they were doing in there? Go to her? Like hell he would. He lay on his back, staring into the dim whiteness of the mosquito *baire*. There were other women! He'd find them! *Mon Dieu,* he could find plenty. There was Veronique and her sister Jeanneton. He wove a phantasy around them, far more brilliantly painted then any actuality, and in so doing he relieved himself and slept.

Drum did not relent. Neither did Calinda, who seemed to take a perverse pleasure now in playing up to Blaise, especially in front of Drum. Obviously she was doing this to make him jealous and, forewarned by this knowledge, he ignored as much as possible her arch glances, her little attentions and her coy smiles, all of which Blaise accepted willingly but with a certain amount of guilt, keeping an eye on Drum to see what his reaction might be. To prove that he didn't care and that he was quite aware of Calinda's tricks, Drum went out of his way to leave them together. When the time came for the next Saturday morning's marketing, he informed Calinda—through Blaise, of course—that she was to remain at home and that he would attend to it alone. To his surprise, she showed no disappointment and her ready acceptance of the fact caused Drum to fear that he might have overplayed his hand.

But once in the market, after poking the breasts of chickens with an exploratory finger, seeking out the freshest vegetables and testing the coffee with experimental sips, he did not regret that he had planned this venture alone. Over the coffee cup, with its enticing aroma, he saw a longed-for sight that had been occupying his thoughts for many weeks. It was Veronique, and the very sight of her light-skinned loveliness entirely dispelled his annoyance with Calinda. The suppressed longing of weeks caused him to tremble and his coffee cup clattered in the thick saucer as he put it down on the table. Like a man in a dream, fearful lest he wake up and dispel such a vision, he dashed after Veronique, catching up to her behind a pile of empty barrels. Her back was to him and he laid a hand gently on her shoulder, feeling the warmth of her flesh through the thin material of her dress. She turned around, startled, and for a brief second, owing to his changed appearance, she did not recognize him, but when she spoke Drum was certain that she was quite as glad to see him as he was to see her.

For a long moment they looked at each other and Drum tried to read in her eyes the effect his broken nose might have on her, but he could see only one thing—her eyes burned with the same bright desire as his own. If she had noticed the misshapen nose or the missing ear lobe, it had been only momentarily. He looked around quickly to make sure they were unobserved. Without the preliminary of a word, he pulled her to him and she hung heavy in his arms.

"You are not dead," she whispered. "I was so worried. Seeing you again has made me happy."

"I have dreamed about you." Drum kissed her.

"Let me go, *mon cher*." She disengaged herself, albeit unwillingly, from his arms. "I have only a moment. Madame Mercier is waiting for me. Quickly, Drum, and let's not waste words. Can you see me again?"

"Yes, when?" He was already excited at the prospect.

"Saturday, a week from tonight. At eleven o'clock. Madame plans to spend the night with Madame Hernandez at Veinte Robles Plantation to condole with her on the death of her son. My father drives her. Besides the other servants who will all be in bed, we shall be alone. I'll be waiting at the back door to let you in. You'll bring Blaise for Jeanneton?"

"Jeanneton will not need Blaise."

"But mayhap I shall not want to share you."

Drum smiled. "Think you not that a share of me is better than Blaise? Blaise cannot come so you will have to share me," Drum lied. This could not be shared with Blaise. This must be for himself alone.

"Then eleven, a week from tonight."

"At eleven," he called softly after her, and left the market, his feet scarcely touching the banquettes. To hell with Calinda! Let her carry on her pique with him. He couldn't care less. Why should he want her blackness when this brightness beckoned to him? He was damned if he'd ask Blaise to go along with him. With Blaise busy at the bar and Calinda serving the rooms, he'd slip out and nobody would know about it. He wouldn't even bother to dress in his best clothes. Too many buttons and things—better the cotton trousers and the plain shirt which could be slipped off in a moment. He was jubilant as he returned to the Academy.

Although Calinda could not possibly have had any suspicion about his coming rendezvous with Veronique, she seemed disposed to end their differences. She took special pains to cook the dishes he most favored, and when she served him, she stood close to him so that her hips rubbed against his elbows. It would have been so easy for him to take her then, but he remained adamant. One night he awoke to find her standing inside the *baire* beside the bed, her hands lightly touching him. For a moment he was tempted to yield to their gentle stroking, but he thought of Veronique and turned away from her.

"Get away!" he said. "You can't smooth things over so easily. Get back where you belong, on the floor. I don't need no goddam black wench."

"Oh Drum, I'm sorry." She was trying to restrain her tears. "I want you so much. You'll never know how much."

"There's others who want me—lighter-skinned than you. So keep on wanting me till I get ready for you. I'm not one that you can put on and take off like an old shoe. Go on! Go sweet-talk Blaise like you've been doing! Go tend to Drumson! Time comes I want you, I'll goddam well let you know."

She still stood there, hoping that he might relent, but he sat up in bed and slapped her so violently that she stumbled backward and fell. He heard her get up a moment later, and then he lay awake, listening to her sobbing, half tempted to get up and take her in his arms and kiss her tears away. In the morning she was more hostile than ever, slamming his tin plate of breakfast down on the table before him, but serving Blaise with a cajoling nicety. He shrugged his shoulders. He knew now that he had the upper hand. She would come back to him whenever he wanted her. He had only to crook his little finger and she would come a-begging. Well then, let her beg. If she wanted him badly enough she'd get down on her knees to him.

As the week passed, she relented and he knew, when Saturday arrived, she was ready to surrender. It had always been their night and Drum could sense that she was hopeful, but he ignored her and went to bed early, soon after it was dark. He heard her moving about the room, and once she came and stood near the bed, parting the *baire* and looking down at him while he feigned sleep. With a sigh, she let the netting fall and went out in the courtyard about her duties. When he was sure that both she and Blaise were occupied, he got up, slipped into his two garments and the rough sandals that he wore every day and tiptoed out.

He ran most of the way to the Mercier house. He was early; the *sereno* was just calling ten o'clock as he turned the corner of the square. Notwithstanding his premature arrival, Drum ventured a light tap on the Mercier back door. Evidently Veronique had been anticipating him, for the door opened quickly and she was there waiting for him, finger to lips with the same caution to silence. She bade him take off the sandals he was wearing and follow her barefooted. He made the remembered journey through the court and up the wooden stairs to the same room in the *garçonnière* but this time she did not close either the door or the window.

Warm flesh pressed against him and he knew it was Jeanneton. Her fingers, or perhaps Veronique's, found the fastenings of his clothing and they fell to the floor. He was glad now that he had not yielded to the temptation of Calinda's hands for with both Veronique and Jeanneton importuning him, he needed all the vigor he was capable of. Darkness covered them like a warm dark cloak and the hours passed in a cycle of frenzied movements and quiet relaxations. He heard the call of the *sereno* as he passed, calling two, three and finally four o'clock. He was ready to leave. Completely satiated, he could not rouse himself again but he had to promise that he would return the next night.

"And bring Blaise with you," Jeanneton begged.

Drum laughed softly, "Why do you want that Blaise boy when you can have me?"

"Don't want him," Jeanneton giggled. "But there are two of us and only one of you."

## chapter xv

DRUM HURRIED home from the Mercier mansion. He was completely satisfied. He had proved to himself that despite his deformity of face, he was still desired by women. The evening had been all he had anticipated, and yet . . . something was lacking. In all those wild, fantastic moments with Veronique and Jeanneton there was something missing. It was the quiet surrender, the overwhelming peace that he had always found afterwards in Calinda's arms. It was the time when, having proved himself, it was not necessary to prove himself any more. It was a calm drifting in utter contentment. Despite their frequent quarrels and bickering, and the past weeks of feuding, he knew that Calinda held something that no other person had for him. Now he longed for the quiet refuge of her arms, her fingers twined in his hair, the sound of her heart beating against his own and her almost inaudible murmurs of affection. The passions of Veronique and Jeanneton had overwhelmed him with a torrent of violence. Now all he wanted was the comfort and solace of Calinda and the security of her nearness. He hurried his steps. He'd pick her up bodily from the pallet on the floor and carry her to the bed. He'd make it all up to her.

She deserved far more than he had ever given her. She had borne his child; her patient hands had nursed him; she was the one person whom he could trust. He started to run through the deserted streets, longing for the familiar sight of his own back door, the cool passageway that led to the courtyard, the warmth of her body as he picked her up and carried her to the bed. One kiss and he could attest that all had been forgotten and that once more he was hers. He would sleep in her arms. *Mon Dieu!* He would sleep like a baby.

His running footsteps brought him to the door, which he found unlocked. In the darkness, he breathed in the cool air of the passageway as he came out into the dark courtyard.

The door of the kitchen was open and he took off his sandals before entering, shedding his trousers and shirt as he walked across the floor to the pallet where he knew she would be sleeping. Scarcely breathing, so as not to awaken her, he knelt down and stretched out his hands but they encountered only the rough blanket on the floor. Puzzled, he stood up. Naturally, she was in his bed, waiting for him, and this time he would not push her out. No! He tiptoed across the floor to the ghostly draped bed and paused for a moment. There was a rustle inside it as someone shifted on the straw tick. He parted the thin netting and reached down with his hands, groping for the warm flesh he knew to be there. His hands touched the flesh and it was warm but it was not the soft flesh of Calinda. He felt the firm, hard muscles of a man's chest and over it, the soft flesh of a woman's arm. The breath from the two on the bed reeked of rum.

There was a movement of the two—a shifting of bodies, a satisfied grunt, a long sigh. Drum stood for a moment too shocked to think. He knew the man to be Blaise, even in the darkness. And he knew the woman was Calinda. He was stunned. Calinda would never do such a thing to him. She was his woman and Blaise was his friend. In a manner of speaking, he owned them both. But it *was* Calinda and it *was* Blaise. Then goddamn them to hell, he'd kill them. He raised his arm, his fist tightly clenched and brought it down, not knowing where it would strike, with the force of a hammer. He heard the dull thud it made and he did not know which one he had hit, but he did not care. The blackness of the kitchen turned to a brilliant fiery scarlet in his eyes. He had been tricked—he struck again! He had been duped—again his fist descended! He had been . . . !

He heard the cry from the bed, a mingled cry of woman's pain and man's hurt. With it there was a quick contortion of a black form against the white sheet and Blaise catapulted from the bed, catching Drum around the waist and knocking him to the floor. Calinda was sobbing.

Drum felt the weight of Blaise's body across him but he was out from under it and on his feet in an instant. He could not see but he sensed that Blaise was on his feet also. Carefully Drum circled, feeling any moment that he might be grabbed again. His hands encountered the broad top of the kitchen table and he clutched the side of it, knowing that for the moment it was a bulwark against any surprise attack. As his hands slid along the smooth boards, they encountered a knife. The feel of the handle told him it was one of the long butcher knives and he weighed it carefully in his hand, clutching it tightly to fortify his grip on it. Slowly he inched around the table, so that he might be facing the door and the half-light that came from the courtyard. He saw a figure circling the table, the naked figure of a man, and although he could distinguish neither face nor features, he recognized Blaise's monumental body.

"Don't fight me, Drum." Blaise's words had neither anger nor rancor. "Don't fight me."

"Not going to fight you. Going to kill you. No man creeps into my bed. No man takes my woman away from me."

"He didn't! He didn't, Drum. Don't blame Blaise." Calinda was beside Drum, her hands clutching at him. She flung her arms around his neck and her fingers caught in the silver chain. He pushed her away and as she fell, the chain broke and he heard the little silver box clatter to the floor.

"Get away from me, you bitch. Going to kill you too, soon's I finish with this bastard. Called himself my friend, he did. And I called you my woman. But my woman's got to be a one-man woman. I don't share her with nobody."

"An' I don' share my man with anybody either. Where you been tonight? Who you been sleepin' with?"

"Someone better than you. You're nothing but a common slut, worse than those white girls upstairs. You and Blaise! Bah!"

"Don' blame Blaise. I made him. He wouldn't, only I got him drunk so's he'd do it. I only wanted to learn you a lesson, Drum. You're all I ever wanted but you won't give yourself to me. I thought maybe if you'd see someone else wanted me, you'd want me too."

Drum ignored her, speaking to the man across the table.

"If you didn't want to, Blaise, why'd you do it?"

"Didn't want to, but I did it anyway. Feeling happy with the rum in my stomach. Couldn't stop once I got started. Why didn't you take me with you tonight, Drum?"

Drum leaped upon the table, knife in hand. He felt Calinda clutching at his ankles and he saw Blaise crouching below him. Then he jumped, feet foremost, and caught Blaise in the chest. Blaise hit the floor but, before Drum could catch him, he was out of the door and in the courtyard. It was getting lighter now and Drum could see him. Blaise had something in his hand. It was a saw which had been hanging on a nail since the day they had sawed the boards to make Rachel's coffin.

Blaise was half sobbing, half shouting.

"Don't fight me, Drum. Don't come near me. I'll use this on you and I don't want to do it. I don't hate you, Drum. Being a friend to you means more than loving Calinda. Don't fight me, Drum, please don't. I don't want to hurt you, Drum."

"Shut up!" Drum circled with the knife poised. He saw an opening and closed in. Blaise's hand reached up and grabbed his. For a long moment it was a contest of brute strength but Drum's hand slipped out of Blaise's grip and the knife came down only to ring against the blade of the saw. The sound was a bright, whining musical note that lingered in the stillness. Blaise retreated, until his back was to the wall. Again Drum lunged; the knife struck flesh and he heard Blaise howl.

"Don't Drum. Oh, don't!"

"I'm going to kill you. Going to cut you up. Going to chop you into little pieces. Then after I get you chopped up, going to chop Calinda too."

Drum saw Blaise's left arm hanging helpless at his side. The blow aimed at his heart had gone wild but the arm was ripped from shoulder to elbow. It would be easier to finish him off now—a man with only one arm was not a serious opponent.

"Don't do it again, Drum. Don't!" Blaise was pleading. He remained motionless against the wall, the blood streaming from his arm, forming a red pool on the flagging. "Oh, Drum, don't le's kill each other."

The first faint rays of the sun broke through the morning mist and lighted the courtyard with a pale, unearthly light which silhouetted Blaise's blackness against the white wall. The fingers of his left hand dripped blood but his right hand was raised and Drum saw the bright reflection of the light caught in the polished steel of the saw. The saw moved and the light with it. Drum saw it descending and he ducked, bringing his hand with the knife up from underneath and striking with all his strength. But in that infinitesimal second with the glancing light of the saw blade over him, he felt the knife snap as it struck the hard stucco wall, and a sharp cleavage of pain in his throat. Slowly he sank to his knees, his eyes still open, staring at Blaise above him, so well known and so familiar. He wanted to speak and his hands came up slowly to tear the jagged blade from his neck but there was no strength in him to raise his hands. There were words he wanted to say to Blaise but he could not remember what they were nor could he translate them into sound. He slumped from his knees to the flagstone and the blood spurted from the gash in his throat to mingle with that of Blaise on the pavement. His legs crumpled under his body. Somewhere, far off in another world, there was the sound of a woman screaming and a man's voice calling his name over and over again. The fingers that held the stub of knife relaxed and opened their hold. His eyes closed and they were no longer suffused with the redness of anger. In its place was a whiteness, blinding and brilliant, penetrating from his eyes to his brain. He seemed to see the outline of a man, towering tall and straight. He heard a voice calling his name. It was necessary to follow that voice and he followed it. He did not know where he was going but there was only one way to go. He departed, leaving the bleeding hulk of what had once been himself.

"You've killed him." Calinda was down on the flagging, trying to lift Drum's body.

"We both killed him," Blaise answered. "And now I'm going to kill you. Drum was going to do it. I'll do it for him."

Calinda looked up at Blaise.

"Yes. 'Thout Drum I don't want to live no more. Here." She pulled at the saw which was still deeply embedded in Drum's neck and handed it to Blaise, unmindful of the fountain of crimson spurting out. "You killed Drum with this. Let me die the same way."

"Stop it! Stop it at once!"

They both looked up. Alix was teetering on her bare feet beside them.

"Is he dead?" she pointed to Drum.

"He's dead," Blaise answered. "I killed him. He was going to kill me so I killed him first."

Alix' tiny white hand descended in a vicious slap on Calinda's cheek.

"Get away from him! I suspect you're to blame for all this."

Calinda inched away on her knees and Alix knelt beside Drum's dead body. Her hand lingered on his hair, combing it back from his eyes. Slowly she heaved herself to her feet. Her moment of emotion had passed. She was now in command of the situation.

"There'll be no more killing here." The authority in her

voice was not to be denied. "Drum was killed in a street fight, managed to make his way home and died here. Understand? That's your story and you'll stick to it. I should have you both sent to the *Calabozo* and flogged to death but I won't. I'm not losing two valuable slaves to avenge the death of one. But remember, one word of what has really happened and I'll send you both. You, Blaise, heard a noise at the back door. You got up to investigate. You found Drum with his throat cut. You dragged him in here and he died. Repeat it."

"Yes, madame." Blaise hesitated. "I was sleeping. I heard a noise at the back door. I got up, found Drum with his throat cut. I pulled him in and called Calinda, but he was dead when we got to him."

"You won't be called on to testify anyway, but if other slaves ask you, that's your story. From now on, Blaise, you'll fight in Drum's stead. And you, Calinda, you'll be his woman."

"Yes, madame." Blaise bowed his head.

"Calinda?" Alix was peremptory.

"Yes, madame."

"Tend to your child, he's crying. And you, Blaise, prepare a coffin for Drum." She turned and walked across the courtyard to the stairs that led to her room. Halfway across, she collapsed and fell. Blaise and Calinda rushed to her, thinking that she was dead, but Alix had only fainted. Between the two of them, they carried her upstairs to bed.

When she came to and had regained possession of her senses, she dispatched Titine with a message to Blaise and Calinda.

"The silver chain that was around Drum's neck is not to be buried with him. It is to be brought to me."

# book three

## chapter i

THE DROWSY SUMMER afternoon droned on at the Academy of Music, whose modest sign, now almost illegible with peeling paint and tarnished gold leaf, still hung before the house on Dumaine Street. Everyone in the house was asleep, except Drumson. Blaise and Calinda slept on the bed in the kitchen with their numerous progeny sprawled about on the floor. Madame Alix, her liver-splotched bloodless hands clutching the linen sheet like talons, slept in her big draped bed upstairs, her mouth open, her crude false teeth on the table beside the bed. The white girls slept on the second floor, and on the third floor, the octoroon and quadroon girls.

In the little room in the *garçonnière,* formerly occupied by Drum, a flashily handsome quadroon, with long black curly hair, was prostrate on the floor, and the narrow bed which Drum had once occupied held his son, Drumson, who was fully awake. He looked up at the same blotched ceiling and had similar thoughts to those his father had had before him. Uppermost in his mind just now was the fact that sleeping was a waste of time for a hot-blooded young man of eighteen years. There were far more interesting things he might be doing. For instance, he might, if he dared, creep across the courtyard and up to the third floor. One or two of the girls there had eyed him lately and he might . . . he might. . . . He wondered if his father had ever done just that. He'd bet he had!

He knew his father hadn't stuck around the place day and night, seeing other men enjoying themselves and having only the solace of his own right hand. Bah! He was sick of the place; sick of his life here; sick of taking drinks to rooms and seeing the pleasures that other men could purchase, which were denied him. Yes, he was sick of it all. He was sick of the swarm of half-brothers and sisters who were all blacker than he was. Sometimes he wished that old Madame would sell him off as she had sold his two oldest half-brothers, Tom-Ned and Blazes, when they got to be fifteen. He even envied Firefly who was next to be sold. Madame had even threatened to sell that no-good quadroon bastard who was snoring on the floor. He wished she would. Then perhaps she would let him take part in her melees. He was old enough now and he knew he could do a better job than Anatole. He'd peeked through the keyhole several times. Damn! If old Madame would let him do that, it would be almost as good as being a stud on a big plantation, which had lately been his prime ambition.

Being an old woman's slave sure was hell. What did she know of the sap that was rising in him? What fellow wanted to belong to an old woman who spent all her time in bed and almost never let him leave the house. He'd rather have a master—some young Creole gentleman who would treat him like a man. That's what he'd like. Man! That would be living, to have a young master and get out of this goddam house. He'd sure earn his keep for any master. He'd get him a hundred new suckers every year. A hundred? He'd get him a thousand. He'd be like his pappy. He'd be like Drum.

His hand wandered up to the thin silver chain with the pendant silver box attached to it which hung about his neck. As long as he could remember he had always worn it. Twice during his lifetime the chain had worn so thin that it had broken and old Madame, stingy as she was, had had it repaired for him. She sure was stingy. Wouldn't get him a suit of clothes like his pappy's—all *he* had was just a plain old black suit. Uncle Blaise had told him about those clothes and how his pappy had looked in them, and said his pappy had been buried in them. Uncle Blaise's suit had long since worn out but he still kept it, ragged though it was, and he let Drumson look at it once in a while.

He stretched out on the narrow bed, his eyes searching the stained spot on the ceiling. With a little imagination the two round spots could resolve themselves into a pair of women's breasts and Drumson often pictured them as such. That damned Anatole! What a bastard he was—always bragging. Madame let him out on Sundays and he went to Congo Square. When he came home he'd always tell Drumson tall tales of what had happened and how because he was so good-looking, so light-skinned and had such a reputation as stud-boy at Madame's, all the women chased after him and even offered him money to go with them. Of course, Anatole was good-looking and upstanding—that's why Madame had bought him—but secretly Drumson thought himself better looking than the brighter Anatole. Uncle Blaise had said that he was bigger than his father, taller and broader shouldered, and once Madame Alix had said that he was like his grandfather, only lighter. He lacked the long curly hair his father had had, his lips were thicker though well bowed, but he had the same straight, almost Grecian, nose, the same well-formed chin, and the same velvet-soft eyes.

He was tired but he wasn't sleepy. Uncle Blaise had given him a stiff workout this morning and all the muscles in his body ached from fatigue. Tired he was, but his mind kept going to the third floor on the other side of the courtyard. He'd like to try going across but Uncle Blaise would probably catch him. Uncle Blaise was a regular plantation overseer when it came to making him work. Said he was going to make a fighter out of him. That's why Madame didn't sell him. She needed a fighter now because Uncle Blaise hadn't fought for several years. He'd been champion of the city, so he said, for three years after Drum had gotten himself killed. Until he lost three fights in a row and had his arm chawed so badly in the last one the vet had to cut it off at the elbow. Now he was determined that Drumson would be as good a fighter as his pappy had been. Drumson knew his father had been the best fighter New Orleans had ever had. When ever men got together in Madame's salon and the talk turned to fighting instead of women, someone always started talking about the wonderful Drum who had never been beaten. Nobody had ever been able to understand how he could have been killed in a street brawl. Must have been ambushed by a gang. Had his jugular vein cut, so they said. Uncle Blaise said it was women who had ruined him. Bah! Drumson wished some woman would ruin him. Uncle Blaise said if he wanted a happy life, he should keep away from women, but how could a man be happy without them? Just thinking about them set his blood on fire.

"Who in hell's ringing that bell?"

Drumson sat up reluctantly, cursing the loud jangling that had intruded on his thoughts. He pulled on his trousers with some difficulty and with one hand pressed down in front of him, ran down the stairs and across the courtyard. He hoped it was no woman ringing the bell, but then women never rang the bell at the Academy of Music except on those rare occasions when a white girl came to apply for work. He stepped into the cool dampness of the porte-cochere and loosened the bar on the small door that was set in the big wooden ones. It creaked slowly on its hinges. Outside, standing on the banquette, he saw a smartly dressed but extremely untidy-looking young Negro coachman, and behind him a shiny new barouche with a white man sitting in it.

"Dis heah am de A-cademy of Music?"

"It is, but it's closed till evening." Drumson was disgusted with the fellow's appearance. The livery, obviously new, was stained, spotted and rumpled. It looked as though he had slept in it.

Drumson was about to close the door when the man in the carriage called out.

"Ain' here fer that kin' of business, boy. The lady what keeps this place here?"

"The Madame is in." Drumson bowed respectfully.

"Here, Ajax, help me down."

Ajax ran to the carriage, and placed his shoulder so that the white man could get a good grip on it as he eased himself down onto the frail step and out onto the sidewalk. He limped across the banquette and over to the door where Drumson effectively barred his entrance.

"But Madame is resting."

"You got pretty damn poor manners fer a nigger. Don' you know the proper way to 'dress a white man? If'n you don' I'll learn you, right now."

"Madame is resting, master, sir." Drumson didn't need to be told a second time.

"Tha's better. Now, git yo'self in and present Mistah Hammond Maxwell's compliments to your mistress. Say that he craves a word with her about important business, if'n she so favor him." The words, spoken slowly and with an obvious attempt at gentility, betokened the man's unfamiliarity with formal language. He was a gentleman. Drumson could see that. A gentleman . . . but not a Creole gentleman for he lacked the urbanity of the Creole, either city-dweller or plantation owner. He was about thirty, give or take a year, with a face that was still handsome although furrowed by deep lines of dissipation. The face was browned by the sun, and its darkness made the blue eyes seem strangely light. Blond chin whiskers, cropped close, crept halfway down his cheeks, terminating in a straight line where the razor had stopped them. He was not tall but he was well built, with the appearance of strength under his clothes, which were obviously expensive—a white linen suit, somewhat rumpled;

a ruffled white shirt; a string tie, carelessly knotted, and a wide-brimmed, finely woven Panama hat. He was obviously not a city man and Drumson placed him as a plantation owner of considerable wealth. Instinctively, he liked him. Although the man had an air of authority about him, it was not hard to want to do his bidding.

"Will you please enter, master, sir. Come in out of the hot sun. Cooler in here."

The man placed one foot over the high threshold and drew the other stiffly after him, waited for Drumson to close the door and then preceded him into the brilliantly lit courtyard. Drumson motioned to a bench under a decorative banana tree, pulled his shirttail out from his pants and crouched down, carefully dusting it off.

"Sit down, master, sir. I'll go see if'n Madame will receive you." He turned to walk away but the man called him back.

"What yo' name, boy?"

"My name's Drumson, sir."

"Tell me, boy. You Mandingo?" Maxwell was studying Drumson carefully, a look of curious unbelief on his face.

"Mandingo, master, sir? Don't know about any Mandingo. Never had a nigger here named Mandingo. Why do you ask me if my name's Mandingo?"

"Whaffor you ask me whaffor?"

"No offense, please, master, sir. I just don't understand. My name is Drumson."

Hammond Maxwell continued to look at him long and searchingly. He shook his head and sighed. When he spoke it was more as though he were speaking to himself—thinking out loud—rather than speaking to Drumson.

"Mandingo's a blood line, not a name, boy. Had me a Mandingo once. Named Mede. Finest goddamned nigger I ever owned. You look like him. Jesus Christ! You the spittin' image of that Mede. Never saw two niggers look so much alike, 'though you considerable brighter'n him. Was sure you was Mandingo. Mighty scarce they are. Like to get me another to breed to a Mandingo wench I got back home." His eyes seemed to penetrate Drumson's thin cotton garments to the flesh underneath. "Tell me, you like it here, boy?"

"I like it fine here, master, sir, but sure hope Madame sells me soon to some nice master like you. Don't like belonging to an old woman. I'd like to belong to a man."

He grinned up at Hammond, showing a white, even row of teeth.

"Run along!" Hammond was himself again, his voice brusque, his manner commanding.

"The name again, master, sir?"

"Mister Hammond Maxwell of Falconhurst Plantation."

Drumson kept repeating it over and over as he bounded up the steps two at a time. He ran along the balcony and rapped on Alix' door. She answered him with senile petulance and he let himself in. She was sitting up in bed, bolstered with a mound of pillows behind the white mosquito *baire*.

"Who's been ringing the bell?" she asked, adjusting the clumsy, badly fitting false teeth. "Answer me! Who's been ringing the bell?"

"Gentleman by the name of Mister Hammond Maxwell. Says he comes from Falconhurst Plantation. Craves to see you, madame."

She pulled back the transparent drapery. Alix at seventy had lost much of the flesh she had formerly had and her skin hung in loose folds from her chin. When she raised her arms, pendulous white bags of skin drooped down from the bones. Sagging breasts were outlined under her thin nightgown. But her hair was as brassily blonde as ever; red circles of rouge dotted her raddled cheeks and her eyebrows were blackly penciled over eyes outlined in mascara, streaked by the tears from her rheumy eyes. She shifted her mouth, trying to ease her teeth.

"Hammond Maxwell! Falconhurst Plantation? I know the name. Rich as all getout! Raises the finest slaves in the South. All the other plantations mortgaged to the hilt but not Falconhurst. Has the good sense to raise niggers instead of cotton and Falconhurst niggers all prime stock. Bring the highest prices. Scandal there some eight or nine years ago; I disremember what it was. But rich!" Alix was thinking out loud, quite unmindful of Drumson who was listening attentively. "Never been here before as far's I know. What brings him now? Funny time to come. Why didn't he wait till evening? Lives in Alabama, so probably doesn't know any better. What does he look like?"

"Young man, madame. Got a game leg. Drinking man too. Smell it on his breath. Asks me if I'm Mandingo. Am I Mandingo, madame?"

"No, you're better than Mandingo. You're Royal Hausa."

She sank back on the pillows. "Young man, you say? Must be the son. Seems to me I heard the old man died last year. Maspero called on me. Said he had a buck he thought I might want. Came from Falconhurst and Maspero wanted two thousand dollars for him. Said he would be a sensation here. Maspero said he'd heard the old man died rich. Now the son must have all the money. Probably wants me to put on a melee especially for him." She lifted her head. "That no-good Anatole still sleeping?"

"Yes, madame."

"Go down and tell Mr. Maxwell to come up. Then go rout Anatole out of bed." Alix was already planning how much she would charge this rich young man and how much extra she would add to it for disturbing the routine of her home.

Married or single? Now she remembered. His wife had died in childbirth, baby stillborn too, which in itself had not been too unusual, but there were some ugly rumors about it. Seems she had had a lover and he suspected the child was not his. At the same time there had been the strange disappearance of a Negro slave, quite a noted fighter. She looked up at Drumson who was still standing there, awaiting her word of dismissal. "Get going, hurry." She clapped her hands weakly together. "Don't stand there gawking at me."

Drumson backed out of the door and ran down the stairs. Hammond was still sitting on the bench. Drumson helped him up. They went upstairs slowly. Drumson rapped on Alix' door and she called to them to come in.

"Mr. Hammond Maxwell?" Alix reached out a tiny hand, to be held briefly by the big sunburned hand of Hammond Maxwell. She withdrew it quickly, aware of the calloused palm—most men's hands which had held hers had been soft and pliant. Her thin reedy voice quavered in an aged tremolo but even its feebleness had an accent of authority. "Mr. Hammond Maxwell of Falconhurst, yes?"

"The same, Miz. . . ?" Hammond was embarrassed by the fact that he did not know the old woman's name; embarrassed also by the fact that he was addressing a woman of such advanced years—one almost senile. Although he despised white women, he retained an inherent respect for them, particularly elderly ones. He doubted now that he would ever be able to tell this superannuated old crone his reason for coming here. Doc Redfield must be crazy. He had steered him to the wrong place.

"Call me Madame Alix." She smiled with an attempt at coquetry. "Everyone in New Orleans does. I have heard of you and your father, Mr. Maxwell. Everyone in the South knows that a Maxwell slave is the finest money can buy. But I have never had the pleasure of meeting either you or your father."

"Papa's dead." Hammond's expression changed momentarily and the wooden mask of his features showed a fleeting expression of sadness. "He never was much a one for the city. Crippled by rheumatiz, he was, these last years and never left home. I've been in Texas nigh on to eight years. Just came back to Falconhurst 'bout a year ago. I've been tryin' to get things organized there, 'tho papa left ever'thing passin' well. Jes' arrived in New Orleans with a caffle of slaves, and an ol' frien' of mine, Doc Redfield, told me to come here. Said you might be able to help me."

"And how can I serve you, Mr. Maxwell?" Alix scented a customer who, being a bit out of the usual, might pay more money for the unusual. "Tell me frankly what you have in mind. I've been catering to the young men of the South for many years—too many." She essayed a little *moue*. "But I assure you, whatever you want, I can supply."

"You have white women here?" Hammond had decided to break the ice.

"But naturally." Alix now felt on safer grounds. "And a beautiful selection if I do say so. The prettiest girls in New Orleans and all real ladies. My girls could take their places anywhere in the world."

"That's jes' what I'm a-lookin' for." Hammond seemed relieved. "Wants me a good-looking one, good dresser, and one that's got a few brains in her head. But," he paused to give particular emphasis to his words, "don' want none that drinks. Cain't stand a likkered up woman. If'n you have what I wants, willin' to pay your price, if'n it's fair."

Alix was puzzled. Certainly any woman, for a few hours in the afternoon, need not meet such exacting specifications. That she must be good-looking was readily understandable; but what difference would it make if she were a good dresser when her appearance in clothes would be only momentary? As for having brains—the conversational ability of her girls was certainly not what her clients came for. And although she might understand an aversion to liquor, it hardly seemed in keeping with the man whose very breath proclaimed his indulgence.

"And I wants me a yella-haired one too." Hammond was most emphatic. "Don' wan' me no black-haired girls. Light complected is what I wants."

Alix took the last specifications as a subtle compliment to her own golden hair. "I think I can satisfy you, Mr. Maxwell. Do let me call my girls in and you can take your pick. There are several blondes and I'm sure you will like one of them. It's a rather unusual hour and they may not have completed their toilettes. But it can be arranged, yes, it can be arranged. Will you be staying the rest of the afternoon or all night? I could suggest an intimate little champagne supper *à deux*, and then after that perhaps you would like to see one of my famous melees."

"Ain' a-staying' at all, Miz Alecks. Stayin' at the HO-tel, so don't need to stay here. Eatin' there too so don't require none of your malays." Hammond was certain that the unknown word betokened something to eat.

Again Alix was nonplussed. Just as things had been progressing nicely, he had thrown her off the track. Obviously the man was drunk. Perhaps she had better ask him to leave. If he made any trouble, she could summon Blaise and Anatole and even Drumson.

Hammond sensed her confusion.

"Les' get down to business, Miz Alecks. I came here for you to help me. Need somebody's help and Doc Redfield, he tol' me you might be able to help me git a white woman like Maspero might help me, was I lookin' fer a fancy."

Calloused by years in the business, Alix was not easily shocked; but she was now. Her words were touched with anger.

"Mr. Maxwell, this is no slave market. My girls are for hire not for sale."

"Knows that, Miz Alecks, but cravin' yo' to help me jes' the same. If'n you cain't help me, p'raps you know who kin. Willin' to pay fer that, too. Man like me 'custom'd to buying what he wants, that's me. I wants a nigger wench to sleep with, I goes out and buys me one. Wants me a fancy like a quadroon, goes to Maspero's and buys me one. Got the money to buy 'em. But this is different, Miz Alecks. Needs me a white woman now. Not to wife! Ain't gonna marry her but needs one to run my house. Built me a new house and needs a white woman to dress it up. Cain't have no fancy yella wench a-sittin' at my table. Wants one with manners, good dresser, good talker."

Alix regarded him. He was a fine-looking man, young and attractive. Outside of the slight limp he was sound and hearty. His face was coarsened by drink but he was clean shaven and well dressed. More important still, there was something about him which women were sure to like. Perhaps it was his blondness, or his limp, or his very ingenuousness, or it might have been the combination of all of them but he was a man whom women would instinctively mother.

The man was not drunk. Alix realized that now, although his request was most unusual.

"You should get married, Mr. Maxwell."

He shook his head and smiled as though sharing a secret with her. "That's easy, Miz Alecks. Sence I come back from Texas, all the mamas 'thin two days' ride of Falconhurst been invitin' me to frolics and dancin's and partyin's. Others been a-droppin' by Falconhurst, with their gals all prettied up. 'Jes' a-passin' by, Mr. Maxwell, jes' a-passin' by an' dropped in to condole with you on the death of yo' father.' None of them would-a known papa from a mule had they met him on the road. No more marryin' for me, Miz Alecks. Don' wan' none of these high family gals, all prettified outside and rotten inside. A-wavin' their fans and a-battin' their eyes, whilst their mamas set back and grin as much as to say 'how much you offerin' fer my little gal, Mr. Maxwell?' Wouldn't let one of 'em into my house."

Alix was beginning to understand. Evidently the man had been cuckolded once and was unwilling to try marrying a second time.

"But you could get an older woman for a housekeeper," she insisted.

"Don' want no old hens a-eartrumpetin' aroun'." He was beginning to like the old woman and his smile was followed by a wink.

"Then, do I understand you have come here with the idea of taking one of my girls home with you?"

"Pays you well if'n you got what I wants."

Alix leaned forward. "But . . . do you know what my girls are?"

"Whores." He nodded. "Knows exactly what they are. At least they's honest about it. But all white ladies is whores, barrin' present comp'ny of course. I knows. But cain't live on a plantation like Falconhurst with a big new house 'thout having me a white lady. 'Druther get me a white lady that I knows is a whore than to get me some young quality miss and find it out later. I wants one I kin buy, jes' like I buy me a nigger wench, altho' she'd be no slave, of course. Got me a daughter to bring up in the new house. Leavin' a passel of colored brats behind me in the ol' house. This new house jest a show place for my daughter when she grows up."

"How old is your daughter?" Alix had become interested in this man and his proposition. It intrigued her and she scented a good fee. "Do you really think a woman from my house would be a fit companion for a young girl?"

"She's twelve," Hammond answered, "an' I figures a woman who's a-been a-whorin' probably wouldn't want a young girl to go that a-way. She'd be a lot better than one of these hoity-toity misses who'd been a-spreadin' her legs even fer her brothers."

"Your opinion of white women is not very high," Alix said, "and perhaps you are right."

"Know damn well I'm right." Hammond nodded emphatically. "Doc Redfield says your girls are all ladies even if'n they do be whores. Figured out in my own mind a girl from here, given a chance to be a real lady, might do a lot better than a real lady given a chance to be a whore. You're right about my 'pinion of white women. Don' trust 'em. But gotta have me one. Cain't let my daughter come up by herse'f with jes' Lucretia Borgia and Ellen over her. Runnin' wild she is. No better'n a nigger wench. Only place I knows to git me a woman is here and only way I know to git one is to buy one."

"Believe me, Mr. Maxwell, your problem is one I have never encountered before. Had you come here this afternoon, desiring one of my girls, I could have supplied you. But to provide you with a housekeeper, a preceptress for your daughter and possibly also a companion for yourself. . . ." Alix threw up her hands. "I'd like to help you, but frankly there is not a white girl in my house I would recommend. . . ." She paused, and suddenly snapped her brittle fingers. "I think I have an idea. But I can't tell you now. You must give me time to think it over."

Hammond thanked her with a smile. "Didn't 'spect to walk in here and walk out with one, Miz Alecks. Don' even buy me a slave that way. Kin I come back tomorrow?"

"Do! Even then I may not be able to help you, but I do have someone in mind."

"Thank you, ma'am."

"Then tomorrow. Tomorrow evening, if possible." The tone of her voice dismissed him and she sank back among the pillows, her mind already busy with prospects and the price she intended to charge.

Hammond made no move to leave. Instead he settled back in his chair.

"And now, Miz Alecks, I'd like to talk about another matter about which I've more 'sperience. When I came in here, your servant opened the door for me. Does that boy have Mandingo blood?"

"You mean Drumson?" Alix shook her head. "Before we discuss him, let me say, Mr. Maxwell, he is not for sale if that is what you have in mind."

"That's 'zactly what I had in mind, Miz Alecks. But don' say he's not for sale. Every slave is for sale, if'n the price is high 'nuf."

"But not Drumson." Alix continued to shake her head. "And besides, he has no Mandingo blood, and I should know because his father and his grandfather were my slaves. His grandfather was Hausa—direct from Africa."

"Hausas are good," Hammond acknowledged. "Practically as good as Mandingos."

"His grandfather was Royal Hausa, which is better than any Mandingo."

"Rare," Hammond agreed

"Drumson's good on both sides but he's not for sale."

"Taken me a great notion to him." Hammond pressed his case. "Offerin' you good price, say two thousand dollars."

"Two thousand dollars?" In spite of her refusal to sell Drumson, Alix was interested. She had estimated his worth at around fifteen hundred. Two thousand was a tempting offer, but she sensed that Hammond might go higher.

"Would want to look him over again 'fore I decided."

"No, Mr. Maxwell, Drumson's not for sale." Her words, however, did not have the finality they implied.

"Falconhurst a good home fer him. Like to breed him. Good blood lines runnin' out in niggers today. Hard to git anything good any more. Mos' slaves today nothin' but mongrels. I'll make it twenty-five hundred."

Alix was weakening. "He's not been brought up for plantation work. He's a city nigger. Couldn't work on a plantation—house-born, house-broken and house-trained."

"Don' mean to make him no field hand, Miz Alecks. We don't raise crops. Raises only niggers—they's the best cash crop. I'll put him in charge of the new house."

"And then, after you'd kept him a few years and bred him out, you'd sell him."

"Don't sell our house slaves. Had Lucretia Borgia afore I was born. Had Memnon for years too. This boy turn out well, I won't sell him. Turn out mean and ornery, I'll git rid of him. Cain't have a mean nigger 'round the house."

"Nothing mean about Drumson."

Hammond started to answer but a wave of Alix' hand stopped him. For a long moment she did not speak.

"You have come to me today, Mr. Maxwell with two very unusual propositions. I am a business woman and I try not to be sentimental. I shall try to help you on your first proposition . . . for a price." She looked up at him and he nodded his head. "As to your second, I hesitate. I am an old woman, Mr. Maxwell. Older than you might think to look at me. When I die I do not know what will happen here. I've nobody in the world to leave my money to so I shall leave it to the church in the hope that the masses said for me will expiate my sins. My slaves and my girls who are not white will probably be sold at auction. Drumson might be a lot worse off than with you. I'll sell him to you at the price you mention. I'll know he'll not be sold as a field hand after my death and I have heard enough about Falconhurst to know it will be a good place for him."

"Agreed," Hammond nodded, "but I'd like to look him over again."

"Certainly, I'll have him come here."

Hammond's face flushed an even deeper red, he hesitated, then stammered. "But I want him to strip down so's I can go over him."

"Naturally," she smiled as she reached for the bell cord. "Mr. Maxwell, I've kept a brothel for many years. There is little about the anatomy of man or woman I am not acquainted with. When I buy myself a buck, I go over him exactly as you intend to do." She pulled on the bell cord and sat up among her pillows.

## chapter ii

ALMOST BEFORE the last notes of the bell had ceased their tinny echoing in the courtyard below, Drumson was again knocking on Alix' door. At her mumbled permission, he entered, slowly and with fear. He wondered what she and the white man had been talking about. He sensed that he had been an important part of their conversation.

"You rang for me, Madame?"

"Come in here and close the door behind you. Step over there in front of Mr. Maxwell and shuck yourself down, boy. Mr. Maxwell wants to look you over."

Drumson's fingers trembled as he undid the buttons of his shirt and dropped it to the floor. He had no hesitancy about undressing in front of Madame—she had seen him and Blaise working out naked many times in the courtyard—but the trembling in his fingers increased as he untied the drawstring that held up his pants. They fell to the floor and he stepped out of their limp folds. He was well aware that such an examination as this was the prelude to a sale—the sale of his own body to a prospective customer. True, he had bragged to himself that he wanted to be sold. Now, faced with it, he was frightened. This was his home, the only home he had ever known. As Madame's slave, with Blaise and his mother and his own room in the *garçonnière,* he had been secure. This unknown man before him was a stranger. Suddenly the outside world seemed big and unfriendly.

Hammond motioned for Drumson to come closer to him and with expert fingers made a thorough examination of the boy's body. Drumson's thin cotton clothes had not concealed his physique. Only once before in a lifetime of buying, breeding and selling slaves had Hammond beheld such physical perfection, and now his thoughts went back to that day some nine years ago in old Mr. Wilson's library when he had first seen Mede, the Mandingo. That was perfection, too.

He had known the instant he had seen Mede standing before him that he must have him at any price, and he had bought him. Now he was equally sure he must own Drumson. The boy was not as heavy, not as massive as Mede had been, but he was as perfect. Where Mede's perfection had been in his savage magnificence, this boy's excellence was heightened by intelligence. His features were finer, more classically chiseled than Mede's had been. His eyes were keener, brighter and showed a depth of emotion which Mede's had never shown.

Hammond's hands pulled Drumson down to his knees before him and then wandered over his head. Phrenology was in vogue at that time and Hammond, purely for business purposes, had laboriously digested a book on the subject. About the only thing he remembered was that the bump of amativeness was located at the base of the cranium and his fingers now informed him that this boy was well endowed in that respect. So much the better. He needed an excess of amativeness to make him a good breeder. Hammond's fingers spread open Drumson's eyelids and noted the clear bluish white of the eyeballs; they opened the wide mouth and entered it to feel the formation of the strong even teeth; then wandered down the thick column of the neck with its pulsating veins to the broad shoulders.

Carefully he examined the flawless surface, the satin smoothness of the copper-colored skin, for wens, moles, pimples or welts left by a whip, but found none. A few rudimentary hairs in the cleavage between the pectoral muscles caused him to frown. He had a desire to pull them out—a Negro's body should be smooth. Well, what were a few hairs? His hands proceeded and found Drumson's belly to be flat and well muscled with the navel deep and well formed, not protruding in a lump as it did on so many Negroes. He lifted the genitals with one hand, weighing them and testing their solid heaviness. With the other hand he drew back the foreskin and released it, letting it roll back in place.

Ignoring Drumson, Hammond addressed Alix.

"Ever bred this boy, Miz Alecks?"

She shook her head.

"Looks like he has good sap in him," Hammond considered, "but never kin tell. Sometimes these big bucks ain't no good 'tall when it comes to gittin' suckers. Lotsa beef but no sap." Hammond's hands turned Drumson around and signaled for him to bend over. He spread the cheeks of the boy's buttocks and then slapped his rump gently as a signal for him to stand up. His hands glided over Drumson's calves and then down to his toes. Having completed his thorough examination, he pushed Drumson aside, the better to talk with Alix.

"Waz-zat doodad he's a-wearin'?" He pursed his lips and pointed to the silver pendant.

"His grandfather's and it belongs to him. He must always wear it." Alix was emphatic.

"Ain't never bo't me no nigger before a-wearin' jewelry but if'n it's his'n, it's his'n." Hammond could not keep his eyes off Drumson. He was envisioning another generation of tall young slaves like this one. Big Pearl, his Mandingo wench, was young enough to have a lot of suckers in her yet. She was only about twenty-five or so, and with this fellow siring her progeny, he would have slaves that would be fancies in any market. Also, with Drumson he'd not have to worry about inbreeding as he had with Mede. Mede's son out of Big Pearl, who was Mede's own sister, was already big and strong for his eleven years, but stupid—damn stupid in fact; could hardly make himself understood.

"I wants this boy, Miz Alecks. Wants to take him with me right now. Les' see now. We agreed at twenty-five hundred. Right?"

She faltered. "Oh I really . . . Doesn't seem as though . . . I don't know. . . ."

Hammond reached into his coat pocket and took out a thick wallet. He opened it and took out the bills and slowly counted off twenty hundreds and ten fifties. Carefully he smoothed them, aligned them, and proferred them to Alix.

Drumson's eyes followed his movements. He could count and he realized that he was bringing a high price. Pride in his value made him stand even straighter.

Alix counted the bills slowly and wet her lips with the tip of her tongue.

"Your bill of sale, Mr. Maxwell?"

"Gets it when I comes back tomorrow." He turned to Drumson. "You got any other clothes than these?" He pointed to the shapeless heap of garments on the floor.

"Go and change into your black suit, Drumson, and then come back here." Alix clapped her hands together. *"Allons!"*

"You sold me, madame?" Now that it had actually happened, he was aware of the enormity of the transaction. He pulled on his clothes, looking at her reproachfully.

"Go along now! Perhaps Mr. Maxwell will allow me five minutes with you when you return."

"Sure thing, ma'am." Hammond rose awkwardly, not knowing just how to take leave of the woman on the bed. He bowed stiffly. "I'll go with him and wait for him downstairs and I'll come back tomorrow."

They left and Alix sank back on the pillows. She looked at the bills in her hand and counted them over again. These pieces of paper for her grandson? Yes, he was really her grandson. She . . . grandmother to a black slave! Ridiculous, but it was true. Surely she didn't need the money and it would only be more for the fat priests to gloat over. She could have given the boy his freedom but manumission was a long and costly process and besides he was far too young to be free. Better to sell him to a man like Hammond Maxwell than to have him running around the city as a freedman or have him standing on the auction block under the rotunda of the St. Louis Hotel, being knocked down to some planter. She had heard enough about the Maxwells and their plantation to know that he would be well off there and he needed some sort of discipline.

The door opened and Drumson entered, dressed in a plain but well-tailored suit of black alpaca. Its short, waist-length jacket covered a white linen shirt and the long trousers reached to decent black shoes which glistened with polish.

"Come over here," Alix beckoned. "Kneel down." She waited for him to kneel beside the bed and her hand went under his chin to untie the string tie and undo the button of his neckband. The dry, aged fingers crep along the warm dark flesh until they encountered the silver chain. For the first time since that long-ago day in Havana when she had picked up the sodden little bag Tamboura had worn around his neck. it was passing out of her possession. It was her last link with Tamboura. She fingered the warm metal, moist from Drumson's sweat. Her fingers left it reluctantly.

"Don't ever part with this, Drumson, and if you have a son, give it to him. Your grandfather brought it from Africa. Never forget that he was the son of a king. You are Royal Hausa. Remember it."

"Why are you selling me, madame?"

"Why did I sell Tom-Ned and Blazes? I am selling you for the same reason. There's not enough work here to keep you busy. And besides, I might die tomorrow. Then where would you be? You might end up in the cane fields. Now I'll at least know where you are. It's better, Drumson, better this way."

"Don't want to leave Blaise and mammy. Don't want to leave you, madame."

"Be good for you to get away from here. This isn't a very good place for a healthy young buck like you. Be a good boy and mind Mr. Maxwell. Do as he tells you and never argue with him. You'll be coming back tomorrow and probably Mr. Maxwell will be coming to New Orleans again and maybe he'll bring you with him. You'll see Calinda and Blaise often. Now go, boy, I'm tired." She seemed anxious to be rid of him.

Slowly Drumson rose from his knees. He was trying hard to feel bad about being sold, but he knew that deep inside he was really happy to leave. He liked Hammond Maxwell better than old Madame. Now he could get out in the world and see things. There would be wenches at the Maxwell plantation. Ee-yuh! And he had plenty of sap in him. Yes sir! He turned from the bed and backed out the door, keeping his eyes on Alix, but once outside on the balcony he raced down the stairs to where Hammond Maxwell was waiting in the courtyard. Together they walked out the front door and onto the banquette. The shiny new barouche was waiting. Hammond signaled for Drumson to open the door and help him in, then motioned for him to get up beside the coachman.

"The St. Louis Hotel, Ajax," Hammond Maxwell said.

From his lofty perch, Drumson looked back at the Academy of Music. In an upstairs window, he saw Calinda, waving a large white napkin. Blaise was behind her. He could see that Calinda was weeping and he felt like crying, too, but he looked down at his new master, saw him smile, and grinned back instead. As suddenly as he had felt sad, he felt happy again.

Ajax drove up to the main entrance of the St. Louis Hotel with a flourish, and before Drumson had time to get down and open the carriage door for his master, a gorgeously uniformed black fellow had the door open and was helping Hammond down with many a "Yes, suh, masta." Hammond spoke to Ajax and told him to stable the horses, then beckoned for Drumson to get down and follow him. Drumson hesitated at the door of the hotel but Hammond brusquely ordered him to follow.

"When you're with me, boy, you follows me in this way. When you're alone, you goes around to the back."

Drumson had never seen anything like the splendor of the lofty domed room inside with the light streaming through the opening in the top. The marble floor under his feet, the marble pilasters that supported the dome and the marble-topped bar that went halfway around the room seemed like something out of another world. There was a modicum of quiet under the great dome for the slave auction, with its attendant bustle and crowds, was over for the day. Now the men were lined up at the big circular bar and as Hammond passed a few of them greeted him. One, a distinguished-looking elderly man, put out his hand, grasped Hammond's and pumped it.

"Mr. Maxwell! Didn't know you were in the city. Want to tell you about those six boys I bought from you last year. Finest boys I ever had. Got any more like them?"

Hammond shook the man's hand.

"Mister. . . ?"

"Meadows, sir, Meadows of Olneybrook Plantation above Natchez. Bought my boys from you at the Forks-in-the-Road. Like to get me some more just like them."

"Maspero's got some he's offering at private sale—eighteen bucks and six wenches. My best stock. Beard's having a *vendue* here tomorrow. Some sixty bucks and about twenty wenches—all prime stock but not real fancies like Maspero has."

"Shall attend, Mr. Maxwell, shall most certainly attend." Meadows glanced at Drumson. "Likely-looking boy you got there. He for sale?"

Drumson felt his heart sink to his shoes but he perked up when he heard Hammond say, "Sorry, Mista Meadows, this boy's not for sale. Just bo't him and takin' him home to breed 'im. Royal Hausa blood, mixed up with a little human."

"First one's a buck, save him for me." The man looked longingly at Drumson as they walked away.

From the bar they entered the parlors, filled with elaborately dressed and coiffured women. The air was heavy with perfume and there was a twittering of strange birds in gilded cages. They went up a deeply carpeted staircase to a long, carpeted corridor with seemingly hundreds of doors, all looking exactly alike. Hammond stopped at one and pointed to the number.

"Remember this, boy! This'n's our room. One hunnert and sixteen. You read numbers?"

Drumson reached up and traced the brass numbers with

his finger. "One, one, six," he said and was pleased when Hammond approved with a nod.

Inside, the room was darkly cool, with the shutters closed. Drumson saw a big bed of some dark and richly carved wood, spread over with white; a carpet flowered with roses the size of cabbages, and a clutter of marble-topped bureaus, washstands, and tables. Elaborate oil lamps with dangling crystals took the place of candlesticks and there were heavy damask draperies, gold cornices and sentimental chromos of languishing maidens.

Hammond went across the room to a small door that opened on a dark and windowless little room with marble tiles instead of a carpeted floor. Along one wall was a narrow wooden bed. The room also contained a big double-doored wardrobe, a high-backed tin tub and a tall copper pitcher of water on the floor beside it.

"You sleep here." Hammond pointed to the cot. "In the morning, I'll call and you better be up and on yo' toes." Hammond led the way back to the big room and dropped down into a chair. "You'n me gonna have a talk. First, you he'ps me off with my boots. I'se crippled a little and al'ays needs help. Know how to take off a gen'mun's boots?"

"No, Master Maxwell, sir."

"Time you larned. Turn 'round. You grabs my foot 'tween your laigs. Then I puts my other foot on yo' ass. I pushes and yo' pulls. Un'erstand?"

Drumson did as directed and between Hammond's pushing and his pulling he eased the boot off gently. The other came off more quickly.

"Socks now." Hammond stuck out his foot. "Peel 'em off. Mah feet's sweaty. You dries 'em off good with yo' han's. Rub yo' fingers 'tween my toes."

Drumson was repelled by the white pulpiness of Hammond's feet, the malformed toes and the dampness of the flesh. White flesh, he decided, was ugly. He rubbed Hammond's feet briskly, manipulating each toe separately, and after the operation Hammond stretched his feet out luxuriously on the soft carpet.

"Now we talk, boy. I bo't you today. Know what that means?" He waved away any answer that Drumson might have given him. "Mean's you're mine, lock, stock and barr'l. I speak, you jumps. Makes no diff'rence what I says, you does it. No argument. White man talks, you jumps. Al'ays 'bey a white man, even if'n he not yo' master. Howsomever, if'n I'm not around and some other white man tell you to do somep'n you don' think right, you just tells him 'yes, masta suh, I does it jes' as soon's I speak to my master.' But no argyments! Never!"

"No, sir, Master Maxwell, sir."

"I'se Masta Hammond to you. Yo' my body servant. You calls me Masta Hammond. House servants all call dere masta by his firs' name. Fiel' hands by de las' name. And always say 'suh.' Tha's proper respect."

"Yes, Master Hammond, sir."

"Now we don't whup much at Falconhurst but we sure can whup when needful. Got me a big buck by the name of Clees which do de whuppin'. You gets sassy, you gets lazy, you gets out o' han', I'll have you stripped down 'fore you knows it. Catch you sneaking 'round de quarters at night, pesterin' them wenches 'thout my say-so, I take the meat right off'n yo' back. You'll git plenty of chance to pester the wenches when I tells you."

"You mean. . . ?"

"Shut yo' mouth, boy! Don't int'rupt me. Don't ask me no questions. I talk, you listen. Don't look right for a nigger to int'rupt his masta."

Drumson bowed his head in acknowledgment but raised it to look at the man who was talking to him. Somehow, Drumson did not fear him. He realized there was a certain man-to-man attitude in Hammond's talk to him.

"You 'beys me, boy, and we gits along fine. 'Druther have you like me than hate me. Cain't do nothin' with a sullen slave but sell him. Course you got some human blood in you —ain't full nigger—so's you'll probably hate me at times. Tha's the human part of yo' a-coming out. Times I'll hate you and you'll know it. Diff'rence is I kin show it, you cain't. But we'll get along. Got me a new house back at Falconhurst. Just built. Fine as any house in Alabama. My papa always wanted to be quality and now, by God, I got the money and we're goin' to be quality. Goin' to leave old Lucretia Borgia in the old house with my fam'ly. New house all goin' to be for yo' li'l mistress, Miss Sophie. Think you kin ac' as houseman alongst being my body servant whilst I'm in the new house?"

Drumson nodded his head. "Housemanned for Madame Alix this last year."

Hammond grunted an acknowledgment. "Jes' one thing I don' like about you, Drumson. You talks so precise-like.

Hard to understan'. See if'n you can't talk mo' like the niggers at Falconhurst when you gets there and not be so uppity. Now, you gets me a clean pair of socks out'n that wardrobe there and puts them on and 'nother pair of boots." Hammond punched him good-naturedly in the ribs and limped across the room in his bare feet to pour a glass of corn whiskey from the bottle that stood on the table beside his bed. "And bring me 'nother bottle of corn from the wardrobe, too," he called.

Drumson brought it and put it on the table, waited for Hammond to sit down and then knelt in front of him with the clean socks.

"Have to learn to make me toddies, boy. Al'ays drinks 'em hot at home but too much bother here. There'll be no likker in the new house, 'cept fer what I use. Stric'ly temp'rance for Miss Sophie. Ain't a-goin' to have her learn 'bout likker. Jes' let me ketch you in my likker once and I'll have Clees strip you down, Un'erstan'?"

"Yes, Master Hammond, sir. Always a lot of likker 'round the Academy but never touched it."

"Better not!" Hammond drained the glass and wiped his lips with the back of his hand, waiting for Drumson to put on his boots. "Yes, siree, boy, you touches one drop o' likker and I'll have Clees skin you alive. Ever see a nigger with the skin all off'n his back?"

Drumson shook his head. The subject frightened him.

"Ain't purty, boy. Sure ain't purty. Happens though. Selling me a nigger tomorrow, right here in this HO-tel. Mustee boy, white's I am almost, but tricky. Too much human blood. Found him a-pesterin' one of the wenches one night, so had him stripped down. He won't bring much with his back all scarred, but had to make a 'zample of him." He waited for Drumson to rub his hands over the boots to remove any dust that might be on them. "You should have heard that boy howl. That Clees lays 'em on good." Hammond seemed satisfied with Drumson's services. "I'm a-goin' out. You'd better come with me. Ain' no use yo' hangin' 'round here. Lessee how smart you are. Go and find the back stairs, boy. Go out to the livery stable back of the hotel. Tell my coachman, boy named Ajax, to get my carriage ready and be 'round front in 'bout half an hour. You be sittin' up beside him. No runnin' back to Miz Alecks', un'erstand?"

"Yes sir, Master Hammond, sir." Drumson had no desire to run back to the Academy. Life seemed far more interesting here. He was out of the door and down the long corridor of the hotel. He saw the wide carpeted stairs where they had come up but he knew he was forbidden to use them without Hammond beside him. At length he spied a door with letters printed on it. Although he could not read, he sensed that this door was different from the others and opened it with some trepidation. But he was right—it was the way out. A flight of uncarpeted stairs led down to a long narrow hall with an open door at the end.

Once outside he crossed the street to a low building with a wide-open door, in which several white men and slaves were lounging. By the smell he recognized it as the stables and once at the door, he spied Ajax, whom he had ridden beside on the carriage. He delivered Hammond's message and listened to Ajax grumble as he harnessed the team.

He waited for Ajax to finish harnessing and when it was done and the boy started to climb up on the box, Drumson stopped him.

"Come here." Drumson yanked him to one side. "You're just about the dirtiest nigger I ever saw." He unbuttoned Ajax' coat, took it off and shook it to snap off the bits of straw and hay which clung to it. His hands brushed off Ajax' breeches. "And you stink. Stink like a horse and stink like a nigger. Go wash yourself." He pointed to a bucket of water one of the horses had been drinking from. "Wash under your stinking arms," he directed.

When Ajax was finished, Drumson slipped the coat back on him, buttoned it correctly, picked some straws from his kinky wool hair and looked him over. "Now you look some better." He climbed up beside Ajax and they rounded the corner. Drumson had seen footmen riding on carriages that stopped at the Academy and he now aped them by crossing his arms and holding them at a smart angle in front of him. He noted the look of surprise on Hammond's face when they drove up and as soon as they stopped, he was down over the wheel, opening the door of the carriage, bowing low for his master to enter.

Hammond placed his hand on Drumson's shoulder and got in.

"Take me to Beard's," Hammond said. "They're on Magazine Street, number thirty-eight."

Noticing Drumson's spruceness, Ajax straightened up, held the whip at a smarter angle and the horses clip-clopped over the cobbles. He made one wrong turn but Hammond corrected him and when they arrived at the slave trader's place of business, Drumson was once more on the ground, helping Hammond out.

"You come along with me. Ever seen a slave jail before?"

"No, Master Hammond, sir."

"Time you did. Mayhap you'll be in one some day so's you better git yo'self a good idea."

They entered a dusty, cluttered room, where a red-bearded man, who looked more like a saloon-keeper than a prosperous slave merchant, sat behind a plain deal table, on which the most conspicuous object was a bottle of corn. He rose as Hammond entered with Drumson behind him.

"A very good afternoon to you, Mista Hammond." Beard was the leading slave dealer in New Orleans at that time and much appreciated Hammond's business. "You got 'nother slave fer me to sell? Likely young buck, this'n. Fetch you a good price."

"Just bo't him and not sellin' him. Goin' to breed him." Hammond's voice suddenly became serious. "Well, Mista Beard, did you find out anything? Any news?"

"Always aim to satisfy, Mista Hammond. Everything's signed, sealed and delivered. Yassuh! Called on that Monsewer Roche yisterday. Queer duck he is. He'd a nekked mustee boy 'bout fifteen a-sittin' on his lap, so white you'd never known he was a nigger. Nekkid—buck, starin' stark nekkid with nothin' on but di'mond earbobs. Asked Monsewer about them twins of your'n you sold him—Meg and Alph—and he says he sold them four year ago—got too old fer him. 'Pears he don' like 'em after they's grown up. Sold 'em to a family name of Chauvet over on Gravier Street, for house servants. Called on the Chauvets and they was willin' to part with 'em. That one, named Alph, he got some welts on his back. Drinks if'n he can steal it, Mista Chauvet says. A-stealin' likker alla time. One named Meg, he's all right. So, I bought 'em like you tol' me. Got the pair of 'em for two thousand. That all right?"

Hammond was visibly pleased. "Deduct it from my 'count. Where you a-keeping 'em?"

"Locked up in a cell upstairs by theyselves, 'way from the rest of your lot. Didn't think you'd a-want them a-talking to your boys."

"Tha's right. Now, you put them up tomorrow and remember, you stop the biddin' at two thousan' and sell them to me. You gets your commission on the purchase and on the sale but don' let 'em go to anyone else."

"Right." Beard poured out a glass of corn for Hammond and pushed it along the table to him with a finger whose black-encrusted nail tapped on the glass as it inched it along.

Hammond accepted the corn and drank it.

"And now, Mista Beard, I'll take a last look at my lot, jes' to see if'n they be al'right. Sure that Meg 'n' Alph can't see me nor hear me?"

"They's sep'rate—all by theyselves upstairs. Can't see nor hear nuthin'." He got up, drew a big bunch of keys from the drawer of the table and opened a door in the back of the room. Behind its wooden panels was an iron grille which he unlocked and swung open. Drumson followed the two men out into the open courtyard around which were rows of cells. The doors were all open and a large number of slaves were milling about or sitting on the ground. As soon as they saw Hammond, they all came rushing up to him.

"Masta Maxwell, suh, Masta Maxwell."

They were all delighted to see a familiar face and it was plain to see that they all liked him. They clustered around him, laughing, whooping and grinning.

"You all right, boys?" Hammond grinned back at them.

"We's fine, Masta Maxwell, jes' fine. We's all waiting for tomorrer. Waitin' fer us to find a new masta."

"Never fin' one so good's you, Masta Maxwell."

"You shore they's a-gonna buy me for a stud, suh?"

"When you gits back, 'member me to Miz Lucretia Borgia, masta suh."

Hammond clapped first one and then the other on the back, assuring them, joking with them and keeping their spirits up. Each felt he was going to be a stud on some breeding farm and was delighted over the prospect. Hammond had encouraged their fantasies, knowing however that most of them would be sold to the cane fields for a brief five or six years of killing labor. For a moment he wanted to gather all these familiar slaves, whom he had seen growing up from children to young manhood, about him and take them all back to Falconhurst. They were his. Inwardly he cursed himself for a sentimental idiot. Dammit! This was what he had raised them for. Whatever would he do with all these fellows, eating their heads off back at Falconhurst, with another crop coming on next year, and another the year after and the year after that? He sighed. Slaves were his business and a damned good business it was—better'n cotton, even if it wasn't so genteel. Better money in slaves than anything else, but this was the one part he disliked—selling them. He signaled to Drumson to follow him out.

Drumson felt he was going to be sick. There was a sour taste of vomit in his mouth and he had to swallow hard to keep it down. He had always known he was a slave but now for the first time in his life he was supremely conscious of it. He could be one of those fellows back in there. Tomorrow, like them, he might be standing on the block. Tomorrow, like them, he might have to listen to voices bidding for him, with one voice in the end claiming him. He shivered and swallowed his puke. As they passed out onto the banquette and he helped Hammond into the carriage, he gained assurance from the solid feel of white flesh under the thin linen of the coat sleeve. He had already been sold and now he belonged to this man. This man was his master. There was comfort in the thought. He closed the door of the carriage and hopped up beside Ajax.

"Back to the hotel, Ajax," Hammond called out.

Drumson closed his eyes and envisioned the big, elaborately furnished room at the hotel and the little room off it. That was where he would be staying tonight, not in one of the barred cells at Beard's slave jail. He was Master Hammond's slave. He was content.

## chapter iii

THAT FIRST NIGHT was far from being the glamorous experience Drumson had anticipated. It was, in fact, less interesting and exciting than an evening in the Academy where there was always something happening. After they returned to the hotel room from Beard's, Hammond pulled a bell cord, and soon a most elegant young Negro appeared at the door, resplendent in a uniform of sky blue with many rows of bright brass buttons. Drumson could only stare at the splendid suit while his master ordered dinner. Hammond spurned the exotic Creole dishes on the printed menu. He ordered the same food he was accustomed to at home—fried ham, fried potatoes and fried eggs, along with coffee and bread, and asked that the order be duplicated for Drumson. When the boy returned, bearing two napkin-covered trays, he deftly set up the table for one, with snowy white napery, fine china and silver—the water in a crystal carafe and the coffee in a silver pot. The other tray he carried into the small room and placed on the floor beside the bed.

A little self-consciously, as though not quite accustomed to the finery, Hammond seated himself at the table with Drumson standing behind him and told him to pour the coffee. When he had bolted his own dinner, he told Drumson to go eat his in his dark cubbyhole. Drumson found that his food was identical with his master's but instead of being served on fine china, it was on a clean-scrubbed tin plate, with wooden-handled steel knives and forks. The coffee was in a tin pot and the mug from which he drank was of thick earthware. When he had wiped the last bit of ham grease up from his plate, he came to the doorway. Hammond was reading a copy of the *Picayune*.

"Master Hammond, sir?" Drumson was in a quandary as to how to proceed. Hammond had told him not to ask questions but now there was a necessity for asking. "Can I ask you a question?"

"Shore kin, boy, if'n you wants information." Hammond looked up from the newspaper. "Al'ays ask me questions if'n you not sure about somethin'. Better to ask questions than to make mistakes. Jes' don' never int'rupt me whilst I'm a-talkin'."

"Yes sir, master, sir. How am I to go about washing these here plates and thing?"

Hammond laughed. "You don' bother yo' head 'bout washin' these thin's. Tha's all 'tended to fo' you. You jes' ring de bell like I done. Boy comes up and totes away the dirty dishes." His thumb jerked in the direction of the bell. "Go ahead, pull it. He come soon."

"Another question, Master Hammond, sir, but I don' know how to ask it. Something I want to do—something I have to do."

Hammond's good nature changed to a frown. "If'n you wants to go out, no! Ain't goin' to have no nigger of mine goin' 'bout the streets a-raisin' hell at night. Wants you here where I knows where you is. Ain' havin' valible property out carousin' round. Where you wants to go? Back to Miz Alecks? You homesick?"

"No sir, Master Hammond, sir. Don't want to go out." Drumson's face twisted and beads of perspiration stood out on his forehead. "Ain't that at all, Master, sir. I need. . . ." He was at a loss how to put his emergency into words.

"Needs what?" Hammond was becoming exasperated.

"Need to make water, sir. Need to mighty bad. Can't hold it much longer, Master Hammond, sir."

Hammond's frown broke into a grin. "Gotta piss? Then hurry, boy! They's a privy fer niggers out in the livery stable. Run along and come back quick. Cain't have you holdin' yo' water."

"Thank you, master, sir. Can't hold it much longer." Drumson was out the door. He ran down the hall, took the stairs two at a time and dashed across the street. He found Ajax sitting on his haunches in the doorway and blurted out his need. Ajax pointed to a privy in the rear of the stable. It was nothing more than a long bench with a series of round holes cut in it, entirely unpartitioned from the main part of the stable although partially hidden behind one of the stalls.

An elegantly dressed Negro woman, arrogant in her black silk gown and little cap of lace was squatting on one of the holes but Drumson paid no attention to her. His need was far too great to worry about the amenities. She, however, was definitely interested in him and watched the process with great concentration.

"I'se Mist'ess Belcour's servant." She smiled up an invitation from her sitting position. "We's in Room One-Three-Eight. My mist'ess she's a-going to de ball tonight. Po' li'l me! I be all 'lone. Like mighty well to entertain nice-lookin' young boy like you if'n you could come to my room. You're shore a mighty powerful boy. Inviting you, I am, if'n you not too busy." Her small hand came up, grasping warmly and with urgency.

The temptation was great but Drumson knew that it would be impossible. It was his first night with Hammond and he did not dare to make any plans of his own.

"Thank you, ma'am." Drumson felt he should bow but he was not able to manage it.

"My name's Poppit." The caress of her hand detained him.

"I'd like to mighty well, Miss Poppit, but my master needs me tonight." Hypnotized by her fondling, he was reluctant to leave.

Her disappointment was evident. She snatched her hand away and Drumson buttoned his fly with difficulty. To pacify her, he jerked his head in the direction of Ajax who was standing behind him, eyes bugged wide open. "Maybe you'd like this boy, Ajax, here. He's our coachman."

Ajax stepped forward grinning but she disdained his presence. "He's too black." She shook her head and smoothed down her dress. "I'se quality and don' take up wid no fiel' hands nor no stinkin' stableboys." With a flounce of her skirts she was off and Drumson followed her into the back door of the hotel and up the stairs. Halfway up the stairs she stopped and waited for him to catch up with her. In an instant her arms were around him and she had planted a kiss on his mouth. For a long minute they stood there, bodies straining against each other, until he wrenched himself away and not daring to look behind him fled up the stairs, raced down the hall and, breathless, knocked at the door of Hammond's room.

"You didn't need to race yo'self." Hammond was impressed by his evident haste in returning. "Now, set yo'self down and wait here till I gets back. Don' know what time I comes back but wan' you here when I does. Don' leave this room. Un'erstan'?"

Drumson nodded. He had hoped to accompany his master wherever he went.

"If'n you wants, you kin set yo'self out on the balcony," Hammond continued. "Mayhap the HO-tel don' permit it but if'n anyone ast you, say you Masta Hammond Maxwell's servant and he give you leave." He waited a second expectantly. "Ain't you goin' to pass me my hat?"

Drumson jumped. He took the white Panama, blew on it to remove any possible dust and handed it to him. After Hammond left, Drumson made a tour of the room, opening wardrobe doors and bureau drawers, investigating every item, but taking pains to put everything back in its proper place. When it started to get dark, he had no idea of how to light the lamps or even if he were permitted to do so. Soon after he had completed his inspection of the room, there came a rap on the door. He jumped to answer it, thinking Hammond had returned, but it was only the boy in the blue livery.

"Come to get yo' plates and things," he said. "Ain't yo' gonna hand me them?"

Drumson ignored his loftiness. With a sweep of his hand, he indicated the empty plates on the table and those of his own in the other room.

"Master Hammond Maxwell's servant don't wait on hotel trash," he said loftily. "If you want the plates, take 'em, but don't expect Master Hammond Maxwell's servant to wait on you." The boy gathered up the dishes meekly and departed.

Drumson was left alone with nobody to talk to, nowhere to go and nothing to do. It was a new experience for him because all his life he had been surrounded by people. But the novelty of his surroundings kept him from being lonely. He went out through the tall French window onto the balcony and sat primly in an iron chair, looking down at the crowds below. The street lanterns illuminated the scene and he was enthralled by the arrival of carriages and coaches, the elaborate toilettes of the women and the clothes and manners of the men. He envisaged the men who would be coming to Alix' now and he wondered if Hammond Maxwell would be among them.

But Hammond wasn't. He had started out from his room with no idea as to where he might be going and he had gone only as far as the hotel bar under the big dome. The bar was equipped to serve hot toddies and the warm drinks were much more to his liking than the cold liquor he drank in his room. Acquaintances and strangers soon formed a small group around him and the hours passed in conviviality.

He felt no intimacy with his drinking companions, but their talk, which alternated between cotton and slaves, interested him, particularly the latter subject on which he was an authority.

Since his father's death and his return to Falconhurst, Hammond had given up all pretense to raising cotton, which had hitherto given the plantation a modicum of gentility. Now his business was slaves. He was not ashamed of it. Slaves did not have the respectability of cotton—slave dealers were looked down upon—but he was not a slave dealer, he was a slave breeder. Let the cotton planters mortgage their worn-out soil, mortgage their land, their houses, their slaves, even their daughters' pianos and their wives' diamonds. Each year saw the cotton aristocracy deeper in the debtor's slough while he continued to prosper with his slaves. His sales this year in New Orleans would be at least $100,000 and probably a great deal more. Cotton! Bah! It was impossible to supply the ever increasing market for slaves. Planters were even mortgaging slaves to buy more slaves. Let the cotton planters look down their aristocratic noses at Falconhurst as a slave-breeding plantation. He could look down his nose at them with the iron kettles of gold that were buried at Falconhurst and the money that he was now entrusting to the banks in New Orleans, Natchez and Mobile.

Yes, his business was slaves and he enjoyed it, all except the selling off of his stock as it matured. His entire plantation was given over to raising them and the barren soil which had been depleted by cotton was now turned over to the grazing of cattle and the raising of produce for the slaves' sustenance. The plantation had become practically self-supporting and his slaves grew strong and healthy on a diet which included milk and pork and eggs. Not for them was the diet of corn pone and sow belly, which was the standard feed on many plantations. That was why Falconhurst slaves were such prime specimens compared to the scrawny runts that other owners produced. Falconhurst bred them and Falconhurst fed them. Outside of the yards of osnaburg and tow linen he bought for the slaves' clothes and the rough shoes he had cobbled for their feet, Hammond made few other purchases except medicines—purges for their stomachs, arnica for their sprains and laudanum for everything else—a hogshead of blackstrap molasses now and then and such tools as were necessary for cultivation.

To the talk of cotton and the superiority of Petit Gulf

Seed over Tennessee Brown he lent a deaf ear but when the conversation turned to slaves, as it always did when the subject of cotton was exhausted, his opinion was sought. Everyone in the South, from Richmond to Charleston, from Natchez to Mobile and perhaps most of all in New Orleans, recognized the Falconhurst breed as the finest. Falconhurst bucks were strong, clean-limbed and healthy, without blemish, brought up to be docile, obedient and hard workers. Their backs were unscarred by lashes; their eyes were not crazed with fear; they did not cringe in terror before a white man. Falconhurst wenches were lithesome, with skins plumply gleaming like polished ebony, fecund, and usually pregnant at time of sale, which was a positive guarantee of their ability to add to their new master's wealth. Ownership of a Falconhurst slave was something to brag about; ownership of a dozen conferred a patent of nobility.

Around eleven the meeting broke up and Hammond, after a steady succession of hot toddies, was able slowly but successfully to negotiate the lobby, the stairs and the corridor to his room. He knocked on the door and Drumson, who had been sitting on the dark balcony because he had not been able to light the lamps, rushed to open the door. Hammond pitched forward and fell into Drumson's arms. The boy half dragged, half carried his master across the room and lowered him gently to the bed.

Hammond roused himself, staring into the darkness.

"You Mede." It was not a question but a statement.

"Yes sir, Master Hammond, sir." Drumson was so glad to have him back he would have agreed to being Lucifer.

"Yo're Mede! Yes you are. Damn glad to have you back, boy. Shouldn't never have kilt you. Never wanted to. Un'erstan', boy? Un'erstan'?" Hammond was weeping maudlin tears. "Didn't wan' to do it. Knowed it wasn't yo' fault but had to. Jes' had to. Nigger shouldn't ought to touch a white lady. White ladies ain't for pesterin'."

Drumson was struggling to remove Hammond's boots. It was not easy because of Hammond's supine position but he managed, with some tugging, to get them off. He eased Hammond's legs up onto the bed.

Remembering his master's instructions, he carefully wiped his feet, massaging them with his hands. With one arm under Hammond's shoulders, he lifted him and slipped off the rumpled linen coat, then untied the stock and managed to get the shirt off. He hung them up carefully as he had been taught to do.

"No light here, Mede." Hammond raised himself up on his elbow. "Why in hell don' you light the lamps?"

"Don't know how, Master Hammond, sir."

"My coat pocket."

Drumson searched the pockets of the coat and found a small metal box which contained the new type of matches he had seen men light their cigars with. He scratched one on the side of the box and by its light he located the single candle in his own little room and lit it. Its flickering yellow flame dispelled the darkness and he carried it out to the table beside the big bed. Hammond's fingers were ineffectually fumbling with the buckle of his belt. Drumson noticed and unbuckled it.

"Take 'em off." Hammond raised one hand and pointed to the chest of drawers. "Nightshirt."

By lifting and pulling, Drumson managed to get the trousers and drawers off. His master lay naked on the bed. Drumson was astonished to see that his body was covered with a fine furring of hair which glowed in the candlelight with a golden aura. He marveled at the beauty of it—so different from his own dark body. He had a desire to stroke it for it had the same sensual attraction to his fingers as the fur of a kitten, but he restrained his hands. After opening several drawers, he located what he thought might be a nightshirt, although he was quite unacquainted with such a garment. Those white men whom he had seen in bed at Alix' had never worn anything. It was not easy to slip the long white garment on over Hammond's head, but by lifting him he managed to get it properly adjusted at last.

"Gotta piss." Hammond heaved himself over on his side and indicated the chamber pot under the bed. Drumson held it for him, although during the operation Hammond managed to wet one side of the bed. He rolled back, his eyes open, focused on Drumson.

"Wants to talk, I do. Wants to talk to you, Mede. Come here!"

Drumson approached the bed and found Hammond's hand clasping his wrist—clasping it so tightly the fingers dug into his flesh.

"You Mede?" This time it was a question.

Again Drumson humored him. "I'm Mede, Master Hammond, sir." He had no idea of who the person called Mede might be but he sensed Hammond's need for such a person.

"You sho'? Many nights I see you, Mede. See you a-sufferin' in that bilin' water I put you in. Hear you a-screamin', Mede. See that pitchfork a-goin' into you. Then I wakes up a-screamin' too and Ellen tells me it all a dream. You ain' no dream, Mede, you real." Hammond's hand tightened on Drumson's wrist. "You real 'cause I kin feel you."

"Yes, Master Hammond, sir," Drumson spoke softly. "I'm real, I'm Mede. No dream, master, sir."

"You're a good boy, Mede. Best fightin' nigger I ever had—on'y one I ever had. You sho' fit that Topaz, Mede. You good fighter. Thought you was a goner then. Mighty happy you whupped him. Always sorry I kilt you. Didn't want to but all Blanche's fault. She an awful whore, Mede. She let her brother lay her long 'fore she married me but t'weren't Charles' fault no more'n it were your'n. He tol' me she was pizen. Warned me a-fore I married her. She jes' a no-good whore, Mede. She make you come to bed with her? Did she, Mede?"

Hammond seemed to expect an answer in the affirmative so Drumson gave him one.

"Yes, sir, Master Hammond, she sure did. Didn't want to but she made me. You say always obey white folks."

"You did right to 'bey her but wrong to rape her. White women crazy sometimes, Mede. Jes' plumb crazy a-wantin' a man. Blanche crazy—all likkered up probably. Tha's why she made you do it. But she didn't make them goddam twins do it. They did it 'cause they wanted to. Them twins horney li'l bastards and that Meg boy, he hung heavy. He and Alph look jes' alike with clothes on but when they shucked down, al'ays tell which one is Meg 'cause he hung twice as heavy as Alph. Never could understand how Blanche could take you'n Meg, specially you. Ain' goin' to punish you no more, Mede, 'cause I wants to sleep nights and now you back you lets me sleep. But got to punish them twins fer what they did. Goin' to buy 'em back tomorrer and then goin' to punish them so they never want to touch no white lady, never 'gain. Never you rape no white lady 'gain, Mede. You hear me? If'n any white lady want you again, you says, 'Yes ma'am, mist'ess, I glad to 'blige you and do as you wants but firs' I gotta ask my masta.' You 'grees with 'em, Mede, only you doesn't rape 'em. Un'erstan'?"

"No, Master Hammond, sir." Drumson was beginning to be fearful of the direction the conversation was taking, "I'll never touch a white lady, never." Although he knew that Hammond was drunk and raving, the talk was on dangerous ground. Anything that had to do with a black man raping a white woman was dangerous.

"Didn't crave to kill you, Mede. Didn't wan' to. You de finest nigger I ever had. Finest nigger anyone ever had. Come closer, Mede. Wants to know you're real." Hammond's clutch on Drumson's wrist was like a band of steel. He pulled Drumson closer and reached up, patting Drumson's stomach and letting his hands slide down over his rump.

"Mighty glad you back, boy. Knowed when I saw you in that whorehouse I'd a-found you 'gain. Knowed in the minute I laid eyes on you. Happy to get you back. Ain' never goin' to fight you 'gain, Mede. Ain' gonna take no chances on losin' you like when you fought Topaz. Goin' to stud you. Goin' to turn you out to the wenches, boy. How you like that? Goin' to put you to Big Pearl 'gain, o'ly this time, you gets me a better sucker than Ol' Mista Wilson 'cause you not Big Pearl's brother no more. How you likes that?"

"Like it fine, Master Hammond, like it fine."

"You forgot the 'suh', Mede. Al'ays use the 'suh' for proper respe't to yo' masta, boy."

"Yes sir, Master Hammond, sir."

"Got me three or four good young wenches back at Falconhurst. Jes' ripe for you, Mede. Thinks now that you come back I better buy me some more. We go to Maspero's tomorrer, no, cain't go tomorrer 'cause Beard a-selling my lot, but we go. Buys us half a dozen nice wenches, 'bout fifteen, sixteen. Mayhap I gets me a nice quadroon for myself. Keep her in the new house fer when I sleeps there. That Ellen gittin' mighty fat but she a good woman. Man likes a change once in a while but never did like black wenches. Gets me a quadroon one but buys black ones for you. Don' want none with human blood for you. Maybe I do though. Maybe I let you breed me some bright skins. Fancies bring more money these days. But you too black to breed bright skins. Better stick to black ones for you—nice shiny black wenches."

"I'm a *griffe,* So Madame says, Master Hammond, sir. She says my pappy, Drum, was half white. I can get you bright ones, master, sir." Drumson was proud of his copper skin.

"That's Miz Alecks, she's a liar. You're all black, Mede. You're pure Mandingo. Mandingo bes' of all 'cept Royal Hausa and ain't never had no Royal Hausa."

"Yes sir, Master Hammond, sir. I'm pure black. I'm Mandingo." Drumson knew he must agree with Hammond in everything.

"No you ain't. Whaffor you a-lyin', Mede? You're Royal Hausa now. You're better'n Mandingo. First one ever I had. Papa say there ain't none no mo'. Mighty rare. He never heard tell of but one in his life. Say they better'n Mandingo but not so big. You're Royal Hausa now, Mede, but you're sho' big boy."

"Yes sir, Master Hammond, sir. I'm a big boy, bigger'n anyone else."

"But don' never trust no white woman, Mede. All prettied up on the outside they are. Yella hair a-curlin', pretty dresses with li'l rosebuds all over 'em. Pretty as a picture but rotten inside, Mede. Rotten! I know. I married Blanche and she pizen jes' like her brother said. Pizen! She slept with her brother, slept with you, slept with Meg, slept with Alph. Now she dead, Mede. I kilt her after she borned her black baby you fathered. Kilt her jes' like I kilt you but kilt her easy like with Doc Redfield's pizen. Pizen for pizen. She never knowed she a-dyin' so's she never came back to ha'nt me like you did. I kilt you the hard way. Boiled you up I did in the big kettle. Made soup out-a you. Held you down in with the pitchfork 'til you dead. Now I sorry. Don't come back no more to ha'nt me at night. Won't do it again, Mede. You promise you don't ha'nt me no more?"

"I promise, Master, sir."

Hammond's hand relaxed its hold on Drumson's wrist. His arm fell back onto the bed and his head sank down into the pillows. His words drifted off into an unintelligible mumble of which Drumson could understand only a few names—Blanche—Mede—Charles—Meg—Alph—Lucretia Borgia—Ellen and, most of all—Papa.

Drumson recalled the conversation of that afternoon at Beard's. He remembered the names of Alph and Meg. They must be the same two that Hammond meant to buy back. He felt a twinge of jealousy. If Hammond could forgive Mede for what he had done to his wife, perhaps he had also forgiven Alph and Meg. Perhaps they would take his place as Hammond's body servant and he would be sent out to the fields.

But no! In his drunken stupor, Hammond had thought he was Mede and it was Mede that he wanted with him. He had said something about punishing Meg and Alph. So he didn't care for them, after all.

Hammond was now asleep. His breathing was slow and

regular. Drumson tiptoed away from the bed, closed the shutters of the room so the morning light would not enter and took the candle into his own dark, hot, little room. He decided to leave the door open in case Hammond should call him during the night. He removed his clothes, which had not been off since he had left Alix', taking care to fold them carefully. The coolness of the marble tiles chilled his feet as he walked across them to his narrow bed. He blew out the candle and placed it on the floor beside the bed. The sheets were clean and smooth and he stretched out on them. A little breeze wandered into the room and fanned his sweaty skin.

Hammond was snoring now. Far off, Drumson could hear the familiar bonging of the cathedral bell. He counted the strokes and then listened. Soon he heard the *sereno's* voice calling out from the banquette below:

"Twelve o'clock of a fine summer night with the promise of another nice day tomorrow."

*The promise of another nice day tomorrow. . . .* Drumson removed the hot pillow from under his head and laid it on the floor—he was not accustomed to pillows. He stretched his long legs, turned over on his side and closed his eyes. He was content. It would be another nice day tomorrow and he was glad he was not back in the Academy of Music. What was it Hammond had said? He was going to buy half a dozen wenches to take back to Falconhurst with him. Half a dozen! All of them for Drumson! He wished it might be a dozen, twenty, fifty, a hundred. EE-yuh! It would be another nice day tomorrow and the day after and the day after that. EE-yuh! He went to sleep with the raucous snores of his master ringing in his ears.

# chapter iv

DRUMSON AWOKE early the next morning. He found it difficult, even after forcing his eyes open, to orient himself in the hot, dark, windowless room. With the realization that he was in the St. Louis Hotel and not on Dumaine Street, he jumped out of bed, totally unconscious of the time, not knowing even if it was daylight. But it must be morning, he realized, for the sun was streaming through the shutters of the big room. Hammond was lying sprawled across the bed, his nightshirt wound around his chest, his body bare and shining golden in the half-light.

Slipping back the bolt on the outside door carefully so that it made no noise, he ran down the corridor and down the stairs to the stable. To his relief, no woman, especially not that Poppit wench with her caressing fingers, was enthroned in the privy, so he could attend to his needs and find water to wash in. An all-over wash was out of the question, but he splashed his face and hands, then decided to take off his shirt and wash his upper body. His white shirt, which had been clean only yesterday, was now creased and rumpled and clung damply to his wet back. But he remembered that Calinda had put his one other shirt in his bundle and as soon as he was back in his room—noting gratefully that Hammond was still asleep—he changed.

Not daring to do anything else, Drumson sat on the edge of his cot from where he could see Hammond's figure on the bed. After a hungry hour, he was rewarded by a movement and heard a shifting of weight on the mattress. He was up and out in the other room, standing beside the bed as Hammond opened one eye slowly and then the other. With some difficulty, he managed to focus them both on Drumson.

"Who're you, boy?" There was a belligerent gruffness in his voice.

"Drumson, Master Hammond, sir. Your boy, Drumson, the one you bought from Madame Alix yesterday."

"Sho' nuff." Hammond pulled the nightshirt down over his nakedness. "Remember now. Thought for a moment you someone else. Musta been a-dreamin'."

"Last night you called me Mede, Master Hammond, sir. But I'm Drumson."

"What else did I say to you? Anything?" Hammond sat up in bed, staring intently at Drumson.

"Nothing, Master Hammond, sir, just nothing. Called me Mede, that's all. Didn't disabuse you of it, Master Hammond, sir. Just pretended I was Mede. What can I do for you, master, sir? Can I help you?"

"Jes' a 'semblance, boy, jes' a 'semblance to a slave I once had. Nice boy, name of Mede. Best nigger I ever had."

*But you killed him!* The words ran through Drumson's mind but were never spoken. Aloud he repeated his question. "What can I do for you, Master Hammond, sir?"

Hammond seemed to be scarcely the worse for wear for his last night's drunkenness. He hung his legs over the edge of the bed, rubbing the soles of his feet on the carpet, and pointed to the bell cord.

"Give it a tug," he said, and almost as soon as Drumson had finished ringing the same boy in the sky-blue uniform appeared at the door.

Hammond ordered breakfast for them both, deviating not at all from the menu he had ordered for dinner on the previous night but instructing the boy to bring, in addition to the breakfast, a copper pitcher of hot water. He ate from the tray on his knees, while still sitting on the side of his bed, and told Drumson to prepare a bath for him in the big tin tub. When he had finished eating, he shed his nightshirt and squatted in the tub, letting Drumson soap his back, scrub it and then pour water over it to rinse the lather off. When he had finished, he bade Drumson take his own clothes off and use the same water to bathe himself.

What with bathing, breakfasting and dressing, the remainder of the morning passed. Drumson spent most of his time in his own dark little room, polishing Hammond's other boots and his own shoes, then puttered around, putting the big room to rights, seeing that his master's clothes were in order and gathering up the soiled linen. The hotel's laundress was summoned. She rustled in noisily in stiffly starched white, mumbling a string of pleasantries, gathered up the pile of soiled linen, which included Drumson's shirt, and departed, promising the lot back by evening.

Hammond took a large, leather-bound ledger out of one of the drawers in the bureau and started making entries in it, slowly and painstakingly, with a sputtering pen.

"Can I go out on the balcony, Master Hammond, sir?"

"Look first to see if'n they's any white ladies a-sittin' out there." Hammond didn't look up from his work.

"Ain't nary a one, Master Hammond, sir."

"Then you kin go but don't set down, keep standin'. Mayhap the HO-tel don' like niggers a-sittin' on the balcony. Don' know myself if'n they do or not, so keep standin'."

The streets of New Orleans at noon were practically deserted and did not afford the colorful spectacle of the night before, but Drumson found plenty to interest him in the itinerant vendors who paced up and down calling out their wares in lilting cadences.

But all these everyday sights were nothing compared to the procession of Negroes which turned the corner onto the street of the hotel. The straggling procession was headed by the red-bearded man whom Drumson recognized as Beard, the slave dealer. He was followed by a banjo-strumming Negro and he in turn by two others who bore between them a crudely lettered sign. Had Drumson been able to read, he would have seen that it advertised a sale of slaves.

VENTE Á L'ENCAN
EXTRAORDINAIRE
SALE BY AUCTION
67 MALE NEGROES, ALL YOUNG AND VERY LIKELY
23 FEMALE NEGROES, SOME WITH CHILD
ALL OF THE FAMOUS FALCONHURST BREED,
NEVER SOLD BEFORE TODAY,
ST. LOUIS HOTEL, PROMPTLY AT TWO O'CLOCK
MAJOR JAMES BEARD, AUCTIONEER.

Behind these followed a straggling, shuffling line of slaves, two by two, some of them jigging in time to the crackling of the banjo, but all smiling, laughing, talking, bantering, knowing that they were the center of attraction.

The music seemed to attract spectators from nowhere and by the time the procession reached the hotel, the banquettes were lined with people. Hammond had heard it and came out on the balcony to stand beside Drumson.

"Them's my bucks and wenches," he said proudly as he looked down on the marching column. They were all dressed neatly in black trousers and clean white shirts with a strip of red cotton cloth wound around their waists. The women had long black dresses, white aprons and white turbans, with a fichu of some thin white material at their throats. "Beard's having his vendue here at two o'clock. Been marching them bucks and wenches all over the city this mornin'. Hope he ain' got them all tuckered out. Hope he's fed and watered 'em. Can't trust these damn dealers—cut costs at every corner." He leaned over the railing, just as Beard had halted before the entrance of the hotel.

"Major Beard," Hammond called down and waited for the red-bearded man to look up. "Major Beard, did my niggers get fed and watered this noon?"

"Feed and water waitin' fer 'em at the stable out in back," Beard shouted up. "Feedin' em good, I am—spare-ribs and pone."

"And see that they gits sweetnin' on their pone," Hammond shouted back. Then Hammond re-entered the room and instructed Drumson to help him on with his boots, straighten his stock and hand him his hat.

"You might's well go with me," he said, sensing Drumson's reluctance to be left alone. "Might need you for errands or somethin'. Put on yo' coat and look smart, boy. You's my servant and wants you to be a credit to me." He waited for Drumson to get ready and together they descended the wide front stairs to the lobby below, then through its maze of potted palms, heavy furniture and fanning ladies to the bar beyond. There was a milling crowd under the high dome and men were lined up three-deep at the marble bar. Feverish activity on one side of the room attended the hauling out and placing of a wooden stand which had two steps on one side, a platform on top and two steps down on the other side. Behind this, in a permanent rostrum, set into one of the niches between the marble pilasters, Major Beard was seated, directing the frenzied comings and goings of two of his white assistants and a number of his own slaves. When the hands of the big clock over the bar pointed exactly to two, he stood up, rapped sharply on the desk with his gavel and waited for the men standing at the bar to turn around and face him. Gradually the hum of conversation ceased and all eyes were directed to Beard. Noticing a group of three ladies at the door, he gallantly invited them in, caused chairs to be placed for them and saw to it that they were comfortably settled and supplied with large palm-leaf fans and tall glasses of iced raspberry shrub.

"Ladies and gentlemen." He cleared his throat and bowed deeply to the seated women. "Today I have the honor and the great distinction of presentin' you all with some most superyor stock—the famous Falconhurst breed of slaves—sold by my good friend and valued patron, Mista Hammond Maxwell of Falconhurst Plantation who is here hisself to guarantee his stock and answer any questions you might want to ask." He gestured to where Hammond was standing and all eyes turned to him. Many of the men bowed and the ladies applauded prettily with their lace-mitted hands. "You-all know the great superyority of the Falconhurst breed 'thout my a-tellin' you. Falconhurst slaves is carefully bred and raised from dams and sires personally selected by Mista Hammond Maxwell hisself who is carryin' on the same scientific breedin' methods his father, Mista Warren Maxwell, 'naugurated many years ago. None of these slaves has ever bin sold afore, 'cept possibly as young 'uns, when they was purchased by Mista Hammond Maxwell after most careful 'samination 'cause he's mighty perticular 'bout his stock. Most of the stock here, however, was bred, borned and raised right there at Falconhurst from Falconhurst sires and dams. Conditions for sale as always—one-third down and remainder to be paid on delivery. Temp'rary 'commodations, awaitin' time of delivery, can be obtained at my slave jail on Magazine Street where stock will be well fed and cared for at the rate of two bits a day. Ev'ry precaution will be taken to restrain slaves remanded to my care after the sale but will not be personally responsible for any slaves unless spancelled." He leaned forward, lowered his voice and addressed the three women seated below him. "For the convenience of the ladies assembled here, I'll ask if there is anythin' special they have in mind. If so, shall sell sech stock as they wishes fust, so that they will not be forced to wait through the entire sale."

A black lace-mitted hand was delicately raised.

"Madame Duchamps." Beard bowed low, acknowledging the elderly lady.

"Would you be offering a wet nurse, Major Beard? We have a new grandchild, with not a slave in the city or on the plantation to nurse him."

"Several." Beard lowered his voice confidentially. "And one I can particularly recommend. She's one of the Falconhurst lot that's just birthed a healthy male child. Full of milk, strong and healthy. Young'un being sold with her at no extry charge." He laughed at his own attempt at witticism, turned and addressed one of his assistants. "Bring out that Judith wench and her young'un."

Drumson, standing behind Hammond, saw a door at the rear of the circular room open and a young woman step out. She was carrying a baby in her arms, wrapped in a length of white cloth. Two of the slave assistants helped her up the steps.

"Now here's Judith," Beard announced. "A clean, healthy, well-spoken, well-trained wench of . . ."—he referred to a paper on his desk—"approximately twenty years. She has already birthed three children and this is her fourth which shows her to be a good investment for any owner. She's been housebroken and trained as a seamstress. Young'un is male, 'bout a week old, sound and perfect in every way. Judith, hold up your child."

She uncovered the face of the baby and held him forward for all to see. She seemed nervous but not frightened.

"Five hundred dollars." It was a man's voice bidding from the bar.

"And fifty." Madame Duchamps raised her hand.

"Six hundred," the male voice was quick to respond.

"And fifty." The lace-mitted hand was raised again.

The bidding continued, through the seven hundreds and the eight hundreds until it reached the sum of $950 with the bid on Madame Duchamps. For several minutes Beard exhorted his audience, finally being rewarded for his exertions by another bid for $975 which was quickly topped by the lace-mitted hand with $1,000. Sensing that the bidding had reached its peak, Beard brought his gavel down.

"Sold! To Madame Duchamps, the slave Judith and young'un for the sum of one thousand dollars."

The lady stood up, fumbled in her reticule for a roll of bills from which she carefully counted a certain number, walked over to Beard and handed them up to him.

"Will you accept this as a deposit, Major Beard, and let my husband's office attend to the balance tomorrow? They will also collect the bill of sale, but I would like to take the wench with me now as we need her badly."

"Quite all right," Beard assured her and motioned for Judith to get down off the platform. She followed the woman back to where the other two ladies were still sitting, whereupon they abandoned their chairs and fans and swept out of the room, Judith following. An audible sigh of relief escaped from the male spectators as soon as the women had departed. Now the sale could proceed in its proper manner. Women at a sale were a damned nuisance.

Drumson saw Hammond fish a stub of pencil out of his pocket, flip through the pages of a small notebook and enter the amount opposite a name.

Beard rustled the papers on his desk.

"Next, gentlemen, the male slave Apollon, nineteen years old. Bred, borned and raised at Falconhurst under the personal supervision of the late Mr. Warren Maxwell and his son Mr. Hammond Maxwell. Has already had apprentice training as a blacksmith, knows how to shoe horses and do simple ironwork. 'Cordin' to Mr. Maxwell's carefully kept records, has already sired three suckers so's there's good sap in him." Beard peered at the door until it opened to admit a superb young Negro, who strode with confident steps to the platform and mounted it.

Beard scanned the audience carefully, shading his eyes with his hand.

"Is Mista Raoul Duplessis present this afternoon?"

A foppishly dressed young man with dark curling side-whiskers raised his hand languidly.

"This is the buck I wrote you about, Mista Duplessis." Beard spoke in the direction of the raised hand.

"Examination permitted, Major Beard?" Duplessis asked. "I have but just arrived back in the city and was unable to come to your jail."

"Most certainly, suh." Beard bowed ingratiatingly, "All Falconhurst slaves can be privately inspected in the small room." He directed his assistant to lead the fellow down from the platform and take him out the door where he entered. Duplessis squeezed through the crowd and followed.

"And while we are waiting, we'll proceed with the sale," Beard continued. "Next the male slave, Seneca, experienced dairy hand. Already sired two suckers at Falconhurst and"—he winked at the audience—"rarin' to go to sire more for some lucky owner."

Seneca, a husky young man, entered, walked arrogantly to the platform and produced a storm of bidding, finally being knocked down for $1575. By this time, Duplessis had reappeared, having conducted his examination of Apollon.

The slave was about to ascend the block but Duplessis restrained him with a hand on his shirtsleeve.

"Major Beard." Duplessis spoke low as he was directly below the rostrum. "To save your time and mine, I offer two thousand for this slave. Will you ask if there are any higher bids?"

"Two thousand dollars has been offered for the slave Apollon. Are there any further bids, gentlemen?" Beard waited for a moment although he realized that nobody would be willing to top this figure. He brought his gavel down three times. "Sold to Mista Duplessis."

Duplessis carelessly counted out the money and passed it up to Beard.

"You can send the bill of sale to my New Orleans house," he said, then added for Beard's ears only, "and thank you for advising me. The extra fifty dollars is for you." His hand on Apollon's shoulder guided him out of the room through the press of bidders.

Drumson heard a man laugh in front of him, and his words as he addressed his companion.

"What in hell does Duplessis want of a blacksmith?"

His companion's only answer was a slowly closed eyelid and a knowing smile.

Hammond made another entry in his little book and Drumson thought he looked rather surprised. Drumson knew that two thousand dollars was an unusual price, even for a prime slave.

The sale was resumed. One by one the Falconhurst slaves —men first, then the wenches—came out through the small door, walked the few paces to the block, ascended the two steps and stood there for a brief interval. They were all young, in their late teens and early twenties—most of them with a record of successful sirings, for although the labor potential of the slaves was fully recognized, Falconhurst stock was primarily for breeding. There was Scorpio, a huge black, slim-hipped and big-chested; Juniper, with a grinning face and a mouth overflowing with white teeth; Regal, whose white blood showed in his long, black, curly hair; Saint, whose lewd eyes looked anything but saintlike; Jeremiah, with thick lips and a small skull; Johnny Little, with bulging arms that strained the cloth of his white shirt; Jupiter, with mincing step and long dark locks and eyelashes; Beau, scowling and unfriendly; Jackanapes, all giggling lips and dancing feet. And so they proceeded, each for his brief moment of glory, while hands were raised and prices were shouted. Some were taken off to be stripped and examined, and others were extolled and praised.

They were a fine group of males—prize stock—and most of them were purchased to be the progenitors of more prize stock. Some of them, however, were destined for the cane fields where their strength would be exhausted after a few years and their young blood would move ever more sluggishly in their veins until it ceased to flow. Yes, they were all animals in the eyes of their purchasers; animals who heard, spoke and saw—but also animals who thought, reasoned and knew anguish. Were they human? Of course not, weren't they black? Only whites were human beings. Only whites possessed their own bodies.

Drumson, standing behind Hammond, shivered. He felt the sweat on his back turn cold as it gathered drop by drop and coursed down the channel of his spine. This went on every day, not only here under the soaring dome of the St. Louis Hotel but in some twenty other slave markets in the city. In the secluded backwash of Alix' courtyard, Drumson had never fully realized what it meant to be a slave. Now it was beginning to dawn on him and he was frightened. This man in front of him, this superior being, this god, this immortal from another world, this white man owned him—owned his very flesh. Again Drumson shivered but a look at Hammond's face calmed him. Since he had to belong to some man he preferred to belong to Hammond Maxwell.

There was a lull in the sale. Beard called for a pitcher of ice water, poured some in a glass and gulped it down, making a wry face. One of his white assistants stepped up to the rostrum and whispered a few words. The slave dealer listened attentively, nodded his head several times, shoved his papers back and rapped on the rostrum with his gavel.

"Gentlemen, I'm a-going to interrupt the sale of the Falconhurst stock long enough to sell two slaves for Mista Antoine Chauvet of this city. I must explain that these two slaves which are coming up are not from Mr. Hammond Maxwell's consignment. Mista Chauvet is anxious to sell them but insists that as they are twins, they must not be separated. Therefore bids will be considered for the pair only." He sat back in his chair and waited for the door to open. As two male slaves entered and walked to the platform, standing side by side on the narrow top, Beard continued:

"Alph and Meg—short for Alpha and Omega—twin slaves, age around twenty-five or twenty-six, both sound in wind and limb, housebroken and employed as house servants by their present owner. To be sold as a pair only, so remember, gentlemen, you are bidding on the pair."

It was the first time Hammond Maxwell had seen the twins in nearly ten years. They had been born at Falconhurst and raised in the house, sired by the Maxwell house servant Agamemnon on the cook, Lucretia Borgia. When Hammond had sold them they had been adolescents, engagingly youthful in their first flush of manhood, twin boys who were so similar in appearance it was impossible to tell them apart.

Hammond had sold them unwillingly, before he had been aware of their complicity with his wife, to a wealthy man in New Orleans by the name of Roche, a hunchbacked Frenchman whose tastes were as perverted as his body was twisted. He had offered an unheard-of price for them, so intrigued was he by the fact that he had never had minions in duplicate before. To insure their purchase, he had even bought their mother Lucretia Borgia, who was not only the cook at Falconhurst but Hammond's second mother and the actual overseer of the plantation. Lucretia Borgia, however, a strong-minded, domineering woman, had been unable to stand the scented luxury of Roche's New Orleans home. She had run away and returned to Falconhurst, utterly disgusted with her twin sons, and abandoned them to the senile sensuality and strange embraces of their new owner.

Since his return to Falconhurst, Hammond had desired not only to repurchase the twins but also to pay Roche for the run-away Lucretia Borgia. To this end, he had deputized Beard to find them.

Beard, however, had been diligent in his search and he had discovered that Roche had kept the boys only a couple of years until the novelty of their identical adolescence had worn off. Then he had sold them to a wealthy widow in Baton Rouge. She, in turn, after another couple of years had disposed of them to the elderly couple in New Orleans, the Chauvets, where Beard had located them, and purchased them on Maxwell's orders.

Hammond regarded them closely, scrutinizing them to find some traces of the boys he had been so fond of and had sold so many years ago. There was little to remind him of the youths who had been born and bred in the old house at Falconhurst. Now they were gross and coarsened, their faces ravaged with drink and lechery, their bodies soft from lack of exercise, their expressions surly. Hammond guessed that the better-looking one of the two might be Meg for even in the dissipated face he could still see a resemblance to the boy who had been his body servant. He had guessed correctly. Meg still retained enough sensibility to be visibly nervous but Alph accepted his position with stoic impassivity. Meg was aware of what might happen to him should he be sold as a field hand. He was far too accustomed to the easy life of a house servant to be able to endure the rigors of plantation work. His head turned nervously from side to side, scanning the audience, while Alph gazed straight ahead.

Drumson saw how Hammond lowered his head so that his hat brim hid his face.

Bidding was slow and desultory. Many resented the interposition of these two outsiders. They had come to buy Falconhurst slaves and figured that old Chauvet was taking advantage of the popularity of the sale to get a better price for his slaves. Hammond did not bid and when the price had finally climbed by bids of twenty-five and fifty dollars to the sum of $850 for the pair, one of the interested bidders interrupted the sale.

"Seein 'as how these ain't Falconhurst slaves, how 'bout havin' 'em shuck off their shirts. Want to see if they's scarred up by whoppin's."

Beard leaned over the rostrum.

"Off with your shirts, boys."

Meg and Alpha responded slowly. Their shirts dropped to the floor and they turned around. Although Meg's back was unscarred, Alph's showed the criss-crossed welts of former whippings. The bidder who had asked to see them sat back in his chair. He shook his head in denial of any further interest.

"Might consider the one on the right," he said to his neighbor, "but the other's a bad 'un and if'n I have to buy 'em both together, I don' want that whopped one. He's wild, he is."

Once again the bidding started but it was now slower than before. It stopped at an even $1500 for the pair and all of Beard's pleadings and exhortations could not raise it a penny more. Without looking at Hammond, he lifted the gavel.

"Goin'," he brought it down once; "goin'," he brought it down a second time, and raised it for the third.

"Sixteen hundred for the pair." Hammond spoke for the first time.

Both Meg and Alph looked in the direction from which the voice came. It was Meg who recognized Hammond.

"Masta Hammond suh, Masta Hammond." He slumped to his knees and spread his hands in supplication. "Buy us, Masta Hammond, suh, and take us back wid you."

"Thought you said these wasn't Falconhurst slaves," the man who had been bidding on them called out.

"Didn't say they weren't," Beard answered him. "Said they was bein' sold by Chauvet and they is. Didn't know he'd bought them from the Maxwells. Did he, Mr. Maxwell?"

"No," Hammond answered. "Sold them a long time ago when they's about fifteen or so. Had some trouble with 'em and thought I'd better get rid of them. One on the left stole likker and couldn't break him of it. Break him of it now if'n I buys him back. Good blood in 'em and might still use 'em."

With the knowledge that these were Falconhurst slaves bidding started again a little more briskly. Hammond bid in at $1900 and was topped by a bid of $1950 which he again raised to $2000. For a moment there was no further bidding and Beard took advantage of the lull by knocking them down to Hammond. They were taken down off the platform. Meg was all smiles and even the sullen Alph seemed to find some consolation in the fact that they were once again Maxwell slaves.

"We a-goin' with you now, Masta Hammond, suh?" Meg called out.

"Have your men keep that boy quiet, Mr. Beard."

"Yes, suh, Mr. Maxwell. Do you want to take possession of them now?" Beard called down from the rostrum.

"No, Mr. Beard. Yo' 'tain them in your jail until time fer me to leave. Be obliged if you'd keep them in spancels till I calls fer 'em, and keep them away from your other slaves."

"Take us now, Masta Hammond, take us now," Meg was sobbing as he was pushed out the door. His sobs were cut short by a blow from a small whip in the hands of one of Beard's assistants across his naked back. The door closed behind him.

With the resumption of the Falconhurst sale the audience came to attention again, and Hammond and Drumson remained until the last slave was sold. Then, telling Drumson to follow him, he went back upstairs to his room, had Drumson help him off with his boots and clothes and close the shutters. Soothed and fortified by a couple of tumblers of corn, he fell back on the bed and slept.

Drumson, with nothing else to do, repaired to his own airless cubbyhole but he did not sleep. Instead he lived vicariously the lives of the slaves he had seen sold that afternoon. With them, he stood on the block; through their ears he listened to the bidding on his own body; with their eyes he envisaged their first meeting with their new masters. He thought of their transportation to some distant plantation, and their induction into the new life there, rising in the chilly dawn in some hovel of a cabin, and working in the fields all day.

Although he himself had felt neither loneliness nor homesickness for his former home, he now experienced all the pangs he imagined those bartered minds must now be suffering. But, in the end, he realized their sufferings had not touched him. He was securely safe here in the St. Louis Hotel with his master snoring only a few feet away. He forgot the sufferings of the others and fell asleep. Yet even in his dreams, he was sold over and over again, mounting the block time after time until he was awakened by Hammond's call.

## chapter V

HAMMOND SAT ON the very edge of the delicate Louis Seize chair in Alix' apartment. He felt awkward and did not know what to do with his hands or feet, which suddenly seemed too large. Alix, in bed, had seemed far less formidable than this elaborately dressed, emphatic woman with her worldly-wise eyes who now sat before him, half reclining on a chaise longue, propped up with a multitude of lacy pillows. Her skillful maquillage hid many of the marks of senility which had shown when she was lying in bed. Now the glittering jewels, the aigrettes sprouting from her hair, the stiff damask gown and the heavily ringed fingers, coupled with the air of authority with which she addressed him, caused him to feel like a little boy apprehended in some secret, forbidden pleasure and called to account on the carpet.

"Mr. Maxwell,"—even her smile did not make him feel at ease—"Frankly, the request you made of me yesterday afternoon has been one of the most difficult I have ever tried to fulfill."

"Yes, Miz Alecks!" Hammond nodded in agreement, not knowing what else to say.

"You came to me for a woman—a white woman—"

"Yes, ma'am." Hammond dimly remembered a scolding he had once received from his mother. Alix' tone reminded him of it.

"But why, Mr. Maxwell, why?"

Hammond swallowed hard. This worldly woman did not invite confidence and yet he felt he must confide in her. "Because, ma'am, I didn't know where else to go."

"Then why didn't you go out and find one for yourself? You are a man—young, good-looking, wealthy. Certainly it would not be difficult for you to find another wife. You married once, why not again?"

"Because, Miz Alecks, ma'am," Hammond blurted it out

quickly so as to rid himself it, "I'm scairt of white women. Don' know how to talk to them." He lowered his head so that he would avoid her eyes. "Cain't bed 'em. Can't stand the sight of 'em." It was a confession which he would never make to anyone else, a shame which had burned inside him.

Alix, who had attuned herself to every nuance of a man's feelings, sensed the effort it had caused him to make this declaration. Suddenly she became more sympathetic, even a trifle tender. Alix, too, had memories. . . .

"I think I know how you feel, and believe me, it is not unusual. A marble statue may be beautiful but its frigid whiteness is cold and lifeless, whereas the statue of bronze is warm and full of life."

Hammond looked up at her, surprised at her understanding. "Guess I ain't the only one then?"

"Of course not! Why do you think our leading citizens marry a white woman, yet spend their time and squander their love on some quadroon *placée?* Their wife is to bear them children—their pretty quadroon is for love, companionship and pleasure. But come, let us get back to our subject."

"Yes, ma'am, such as fer instance, kin you help me?"

"It is possible." Alix' small venture into sympathy had ended. "But before we speak about that, perhaps we should make some financial arrangements."

" 'Spects to, Miz Alecks, 'spects to pay you for your services."

"Which will be a round sum, Mr. Maxwell—a round sum of, say, five hundred dollars." She waved him to silence as he started to answer. "For me, and then there will be another five hundred for the lady in question, provided, of course, she is satisfactory to you and that you meet with her approval. Do you agree?"

The sum of a thousand dollars to a man who had just sold a hundred thousand dollars worth of slaves that same afternoon did not pose any particularly important problem. He accepted by merely nodding and reached in his pocket for his wallet, but again Alix stopped him.

"We are not traders down on the levee, Mr. Maxwell. It doesn't have to be on the barrelhead. Now, let us discuss the matter a little more in detail." She leaned back among the frothy little pillows that filled the space in the chaise longue. Hammond replaced his wallet and listened.

Alix had a sincere desire to please him. She realized he

might become an influential friend, and the prospect of such easy money, without stirring from her room, appealed to her. Neither Alix nor Hammond believed too thoroughly in the much-vaunted virginal innocence of most of the Southern belles. Their lives were not as sheltered as the painstakingly built-up traditions of the times would have the world believe.

A young girl on a plantation was trained with one object in view—to marry and become the mistress of another plantation. She was to follow in her mother's footsteps and one of the most important duties of a successful plantation mistress was the care of her slaves. It was she who looked after the slaves in sickness and in childbirth. There was little about the sexual relations of the plantation slaves she did not know, from insemination to childbirth, through sickness, old age and death. Then too, Southern homes of the period were little more than superior hostels for wayfaring gentry and were always filled with distant relatives, friends and even strangers, who accepted the proffered hospitality for a day, a week or a month. The youths of the period were hot-blooded and impetuous; the maidens, despite their magnolia-petaled purity, were at least curious. If the slaves enjoyed the sexual act, why should not they? And they did, with the result that many a visiting maiden departed with an intimate knowledge of the prowess of her host's sons and many a week-ending young man-cousin carried away the memory of having deflowered the plantation's resident charmer. Just as Hammond had discovered that his bride had already been initiated by her own brother, so had many another Southern bridegroom discovered that the supposed virginal little missy whom he had married was most practiced from having "played house" with her brothers, cousins and friends and, occasionally, from having encouraged the advances of some handsome mulatto house slave.

All this Alix understood, and with it Hammond's unwillingness to attempt marriage a second time, especially after having found that his first wife's nymphomania had enveloped his Negro slave, Mede, and the twins, Meg and Alph.

But, Alix informed him, women seldom entered into a life of prostitution without some very good reason and the reason that impelled most of them was the simple fact that they enjoyed it. None of these, and she wagged her finger at him in a knowing way, would consider living out her years on an outlying plantation, being chatelaine of a house and taking on the responsibility of molding a young girl's character. No!

That would be out of the question and she could not and would not recommend such a one. Yet occasionally there had been an occupant of her house who had come there not because she enjoyed the work or loved it but purely through force of circumstances. Yes, it had happened.

Such a one was Augusta Devereaux.

And who was Augusta Devereaux?

Alix explained. Some five years ago, young Hercule LeSieur had arrived at her house shortly before dawn with a young lady, enveloped in a long black cloak and carefully veiled. Hercule was one of Alix' favorites—young, darkly handsome and rich, heir to the big LeSieur plantation, husband to a charming young woman and father to two young children. But, on that night, the young lady with him was most certainly not his wife—most assuredly not for he would never bring her to Alix' house where he himself had been such a frequent visitor. Instead the young lady in question was the daughter of old Major Devereaux whose crumbling mansion had, only a few months before, sheltered young Hercule LeSieur returning from a visit to Baton Rouge. Augusta, at that time in her early twenties, and forced to remain in the isolated plantation house because there was not enough money for a New Orleans debut, had attracted the attention of young Hercule. He had found it expedient to visit the Devereaux plantation several times after that. The result, as Alix could plainly see from the bulging figure of the young woman, was a pregnancy already considerably advanced. Old Major Devereaux had not minded his daughter's being an unpaid and unappreciated workhorse on his worn-out plantation, but when she had reached out to find some meaning for her barren life and found it in young Hercule, she had been forced to flee from her father's wrath.

Augusta had come to New Orleans, seeking help from the only person who could help her—Hercule himself who was responsible for her condition. And he had succored her in the only way he knew, by bringing her to Alix'; there she had remained the few months before the stillbirth of her child. Thereupon, Hercule, not unmindful of his obligations, had set her up as a *coiffeuse*, a trade which she had learned by dressing the girls' hair at Alix'. As Alix and her girls were the only people in New Orleans with whom she was acquainted, it was natural that they should become her first patrons and through them she had gained entree into all the other "respectable" brothels of the city. After the sudden death of Hercule, she had continued on in her business, scarcely, however, making both ends meet.

Although Augusta had never been actively engaged in that profession which Hammond thought might be a qualification, she had transgressed the mores of Southern womanhood sufficiently to be a woman of experience. She was well born—the Devereaux family, although fairly scratching the bottom of the barrel, were aristocrats—well educated, and withal a woman of taste and refinement. Although young, she had a head on her shoulders. She was a woman who could take her place among his friends; a woman who, regardless of her one misstep, could well chaperone Hammond's daughter and one whom he might eventually love and marry.

This last suggestion Hammond waved aside. But he would be willing to see this Miss Devereaux.

"Not Miss Devereaux," Alix corrected him. It would not be fitting for her to be an unmarried woman, living under the same roof with himself. For propriety's sake, she must be a Mrs. As a widow, it would be quite proper for her to take charge of his house, and the Devereaux clan being large, with many branches, it seemed perfectly safe for her to change her identity to Mrs. Devereaux. That point settled, Alex leaned forward in her chair and placed one of her heavily ringed hands on Hammond's linen-clad knee.

"You recommend her?" Hammond had come to respect Alix' judgment.

"Most highly."

"Then trot her out," Hammond grinned.

"But you must remember"—Alix returned his smile—"you are not buying a slave. For heaven's sake, do not ask her to shuck down. She is a lady and in spite of her past, she is still a lady. You must treat her as such. Promise?"

He nodded his agreement as she reached for the bell cord. Much to Hammond's surprise, Drumson answered the bell.

"You?" Alix looked at him in amazement.

"Thinkin' perhaps Masta Hammond might be requirin' me." The impressionable Drumson was already losing the precise accent Hammond had objected to, and coming to talk more and more like his Master. He had been anxious to penetrate the closed door to find out what was transpiring between Hammond and Alix. The only reason that they could be together, he thought, must be something that concerned him and he had been consumed with curiosity to know what it was all about. Consequently when the bell jangled in the kitchen he had run to answer it.

"Well, as long as you are here," Alix' look shared her pride in Drumson with Hammond, "go to the next room and tell Mrs. Devereaux that I would like to see her."

"You mean Miz 'Gusta, the *coiffeuse?*" Drumson had admitted her to the house many times.

"The same." Alix' voice became stern, "But you had better forget that you ever saw her before. If not, and should you ever mention it in the future, I'm instructing Mr. Maxwell to touch you up with the whip. Understand?"

"I've never seen her before, madame, never." Drumson backed out of the room.

Within seconds there was a knock on the door, and at Alix' invitation the door opened.

Hammond, remembering his manners, rose from his chair as the woman entered. Her appearance left nothing to be desired. She was blonde, as Hammond had requested, but hers was not the vapid yellow and white blondness of his former wife. Where Blanche's hair had been a dirty yellow, this woman's was a pale ash blond. Instead of Blanche's dumpy figure, Hammond saw a tall, slender woman with pale skin heightened, he thought, by a little rouge, but so skilfully applied that it was impossible to detect. Her long hair, dropping in a waterfall of curls in the back, was partly hidden by a bonnet of black straw, ornamented most modestly by one small pink velvet rose. A dress of gray sateen, printed with tiny pink and white roses, belled out around her ankles only to be nipped in at the waist above which her breasts rounded out, catching the light on little steel buttons and setting them aflicker.

Hammond judged her to be still in her twenties, with an appearance that was almost girlish, if one did not look at her green eyes, which had a calculating stare that took in everything they saw. Yes, Hammond was able to understand why young Hercule had found her attractive. Her eyes were shaded by long, lustrous lashes, and her nose—engagingly tilted and just a trifle retroussé—gave her, even in her severe gown and staid demeanor, the slightest appearance of a hoyden. He noticed that her mouth was small but her lips full, and when she smiled at him, as she did on entering the room, the lips parted to disclose white, even teeth.

Alix introduced them.

"Mrs. Devereaux, Mr. Hammond Maxwell of Falconhurst Plantation."

Hammond took the proffered hand in its black lace mit, not knowing exactly what to do with it. It felt cool and relaxed in his own hot, sweaty palm. He dropped it.

"Your servant, ma'am."

"And now," Alix stood for the first time, "I shall leave you two alone to become acquainted."

" 'Tain't necessary, Miz Alecks." Hammond was frightened at the prospect of being left alone with this strange young woman. " 'Tain't necessary 'tall. I'm shore Miss Devereaux will do. You've talked me over with her no doubt and you've talked her over with me. She's a mighty fine lookin' lady and I'll be proud to have her at Falconhurst. If'n she accepts me after seein' me, I'll 'cept her. Tha's all, Miz Alecks. Ain't no need for us talk about nothin' now. Plenty of time for that when we gets to Falconhurst."

"Are you quite sure, Mr. Maxwell?" Augusta Devereaux regarded him coolly. "Are you quite sure I shall be satisfactory?"

Hammond liked her voice—it was positive and assertive. The whine which had always accompanied Blanche's words was missing.

"Quite shore, ma'am."

"Then when do we leave for Falconhurst?"

"Got me 'nother day's business here in New Orleans. Needs to buy me some fancy stock at Maspero's and should be able to leave day after tomorrow. Like to leave's early's possible as we've got a middlin' long journey ahead of us. Suppose you got boxes and sich to tote with you?"

"Indeed I have." Augusta smiled at him. "I'm afraid you'll think I'm a vain woman, Mr. Maxwell, but I'll take as little as possible."

"Take all you wants to. Plenty o' room. We got a kerridge fer you. Got us two wagons for the new slaves and sich. Plenty o' room for yo' boxes. Send my boy Ajax to get 'em early. Could you be ready 'round seven in the mornin'?"

"I could and shall. My house is on Bourbon Street, the third house from the canal."

"We'll be startin' then." He bowed awkwardly to her and then to Alix.

"Thank you, Miz Alecks. Reckon I'll be goin' now. Reckon you done a good job, Miz Alecks. Be happy to welcome you to Falconhurst, Miz Devereaux." He looked around for his hat, forgetting that he had left it downstairs.

"There remains, however, one very little thing more," Alix reminded him.

Hammond looked at her blankly.

"Your inside pocket," Alix smiled.

Hammond fumbled in his pocket and drew out the wallet. Something seemed wrong to him. He had purchased many slaves in his lifetime, both male and female, and had never had any compunctions about paying for them. A loan of money to his wife's father had, in a way, purchased Blanche, although it had not been a downright cash payment. But this woman, so coolly indifferent to him, so patently well bred, should not be purchased with money. And yet she was. Five hundred dollars! It was less than he would pay for an inferior Negro wench. Well, if that was the way she valued herself, he'd pay it, although somehow it didn't seem right. He counted out the money and placed it in her hand with an equal amount in Alix'.

"Thank you, Mr. Maxwell." Augusta placed the money in her reticule without counting it. "We shall understand that this is my salary for a year. Next year, if you decide to retain my services, I shall expect a like amount."

"Granted." Hammond was glad that the woman was business-like.

"And I hope I may serve you well, Mr. Maxwell. As Madame may have told you, I am not untrained in the duties of a mistress. Although my father's plantation was small and we had only some thirty slaves, I did look out for them."

"At Falconhurst we gotten 'bout four hundred, ma'am," Hammond stated rather proudly. Once more he bowed his leave-taking and opened the door, nearly colliding with Drumson who was waiting outside, straining to listen to what was happening. Drumson's dark skin was a welcome relief after the surfeit of white to which Hammond had just been exposed.

"Come on, boy, le's get the hell out of here."

"Yes suh, Mr. Hammond, yes suh." Drumson too was willing to leave. After his short glimpse of the outside world, the close restriction of the Academy oppressed him.

Alix waited until she heard their footsteps descending the stairs and turned to Augusta who was still standing before her.

"Well, Gussie, what do you think of him?"

"He's handsomer than I had imagined. He's young. He's rich." She clutched Alix' hand and patted it. "It will not be difficult. I might even fall in love with him."

"And when you get to be Mrs. Hammond Maxwell of Falconhurst. . . ."

"I shall not forget who made it possible for me to become that." Augusta patted Alix' hand again and the two women exchanged glances.

# chapter vi

IT HAD BEEN such a long ride—such a tiresome, plodding, dusty journey over rutted roads which at times were little more than weed-grown cart paths; through small, poverty-stricken, slab-sided villages; past unpainted, decrepit farmhouses. Only occasionally was there a prosperous-looking plantation where the big house gleamed white through the long avenue of live oaks that bordered the entrance drive. It had been such a hot ride—three days of blinding sun, rising dust and streaming sweat. It seemed to stretch into eternity as mile after weary mile of fields, woods and grubby countryside rolled by, all looking so depressingly familiar that one day became identical with the one that preceded it and the one that followed it. The journey was so long that Drumson despaired of ever reaching Falconhurst. The farther they progressed, the more it seemed to recede into the distance.

He had left New Orleans in high spirits, feeling that he was on the very edge of some new and great adventure which would transport him from his old familiar, uneventful life into another which promised something much more colorful and exciting. Their departure from the city had been early in the morning when New Orleans was just awakening and the streets nearly deserted. Their three vehicles made quite an impressive caravan. First came the new barouche, shiny with varnish, bright with paint and impressive with its gray broadcloth cushions and its raised top of smooth black leather. Ajax, his uniform carefully brushed and cleaned by Drumson, sat on the high box, driving Mrs. Devereaux and Regine, the quadroon girl Hammond had purchased at Maspero's. Regine, far more beautiful than any girl Drumson had ever seen before, with a tea-rose complexion and long, curling black hair, sat primly, as befitted her role of servant to Mrs. Devereaux. She was dressed quietly in black, with little bands of white at the high neck and long cuffs, her face nearly hidden in a black poke bonnet. Augusta, properly garbed for traveling in shiny gray alpaca, wore the same rose-trimmed bonnet she had worn the first day Hammond had seen her. They were the only occupants of the barouche and Drumson felt proud of Miz Augusta, as he had been taught to call her, for her good looks and her modish clothes.

Hammond had instructed him that he was to obey her in all things and that, just as he was his master and owner, Miz Augusta would be his mistress. Although his pride and respect were already given to Augusta, his eyes were only for the beautiful Regine, who sat beside her. She, however, scarcely noticed him. Her eyes were only for Hammond. And, Drumson observed, so were those of Miz Augusta. Just let Hammond approach the carriage and both were all smiles and fluttery compliance. When Drumson came near them he was treated kindly but impersonally. Yet he had caught Regine looking at him and he knew that she was aware of him.

Following the carriage with its varnished elegance, Hammond drove a team of mules, hitched to a long farm wagon in which rode his six new purchases—four lithesome, dark-skinned wenches, Phronia, Lesbia, Ann-Mary and Balsam, whom he had purchased along with Regine from Maspero. In truth, the four had cost him only a little more than he had paid for the beauteous Regine. He had purchased her for the clarity of her skin and the beauty of her face, but these four had been bought for their strength and their potential ability to bear children. That they were good-looking, too, was important, for Hammond had no desire to produce ugly slaves. They ranged in age from a possible fourteen to perhaps sixteen, but all were nubile, approaching the time when they would, Hammond hoped, produce a sucker a year for him until he sold them in their early twenties.

His other two purchases were two young brothers, one eight, the other ten. He had picked them up cheap. In bone structure and physique they promised to be healthy, valuable properties in another eight or ten years.

Although Drumson had never had any experience as a driver, he was given charge of the last team of mules and the big wagon they drew. This was piled high with luggage—Miz Augusta's numerous boxes, Regine's modest one, Drumson's own neat package, Hammond's valises, and the meager bundles the slaves had brought with them. In the back of the wagon, separated from Drumson by the pile of luggage, rode Meg and Alph, completely isolated from the rest of the party, their legs chained with spancels, their hands manacled and themselves chained to the wagon. They sprawled on the floor, their legs hanging down over the tailboard, utterly miserable in their isolation. Hammond had never spoken a word to them since the day he purchased them. He had turned a deaf ear to all their pleadings, not even looking at them and completely ignoring them whenever he chanced to come near. What few orders he gave were passed on to them through Drumson who had strict orders to have no other communication with them. From his position up front he could hear but not always distinguish their mumbled conversation; much of the time Meg was sobbing and Alph cursing.

The first night en route they all spent at a large cotton plantation not far from the Louisiana-Mississippi line. Although the house had, at one time, possessed considerable grandeur, it was now only shabbily genteel, with evidences of approaching poverty in the threadbare carpets, the worn upholsteries and the faded curtains. It was evident by the reception they received that Hammond had been here before. Much ado was made over him by the master and mistress, and the two unmarried daughters of the household were charmingly in evidence, dressed in their best, fluttering their fans and never missing an opportunity to exclaim "la, Mr. Maxwell." Augusta was treated as coldly as was compatible with good manners for it was evident that she presented a threat to the hopeful aspirations of the two daughters. That night Drumson slept on a trundle bed in Hammond's room, and Regine with Augusta. The female slaves were quartered in a hastily vacated cabin to which Hammond held the key. Meg and Alph were securely spancelled in the horse barn along with Shoat and Jackson, although the two young boys were not restrained. They showed no disposition to run away, and were plainly grateful for the three plentiful meals a day Hammond provided and for the mothering and companionship of the four girls.

The second night was spent at an ordinary on the Tombigbee River, whose course they were to follow north until they arrived at Falconhurst. Here there was only one large room available and there had been some problem in deciding how they were to sleep. The proprietress of the tavern, a tall, gaunt woman in a torn calico dress, taking it for granted that Hammond and Augusta were man and wife, had shown them to the room, which contained a large bedstead, spread over with a soiled coverlet. But on being informed by Hammond that he and Augusta were not married, the woman had grudgingly allowed Augusta to share her bed. The slaves, she insisted, must be quartered in the barn, which Hammond felt was safe enough; with Meg and Alph secured, the wenches would be in no particular danger either from the aged stableman or from Shoat and Jackson. This left only the disposal of Regine and Drumson, neither of whom Hammond would allow to stay in the barn, stating that he needed Drumson's services and that Regine was obviously too good to sleep in the hay. As there was no room for her in the restricted quarters which Augusta shared with the lady owner, Hammond solved the problem by ordering a shuck mattress placed in front of his door for Regine and a blanket spread on the floor of his room for Drumson.

When, however, Drumson had undressed his master and then himself and was about to blow out the candle, Hammond restrained him.

"Let that Regine girl come in here with me and you sleep out in the hallway."

Drumson opened the door and signaled to her to come in. She looked at him, wondering just what was required of her, but Hammond called to her softly from the bed and she ran across the floor. Heavy in heart, Drumson went out and closed the door. But he could not sleep. He could hear the movements inside—the rustle of the shuck mattress, the creak of the bed cords and all the little moans and sighs, the meaning of which he knew too well. Every fiber ached to be in Hammond's place. His anguish mounted until it seemed unendurable, and even his self-inflicted release, accompanied by those same little moans, brought him no respite. Finally there was a stillness and not long after, the door opened quietly and Regine came out. Drumson heard Hammond's voice.

"Come in here, boy, and go to bed."

He slept fitfully, and awakened early in the morning while Hammond was still sleeping. His roving eyes caught a splotch of rumpled white on the floor which he was certain had not been there the night before. He rose and picked up the garment; it was Regine's shift. He buried his face in it, smelling the faint odor of her, which again excited him, but he knew he must dispose of it. He tiptoed to the door to return it to her, but as he opened the door to drop it on her bed, Augusta, fully dressed, passed by. She looked at the telltale garment in his hand and then at him. It was sufficient to tell her exactly what had happened. The color mounted to her face, then drained, leaving it curiously white.

"Good morning, Drumson," she said. "I hope your master slept well last night."

"Yes ma'am, Miz 'Gusta, he shore did." Drumson dropped the offending garment on the still sleeping Regine and closed the door.

All the next day Drumson noticed that there was a decided coolness between Augusta and Hammond and an even more decided coolness between her and Regine. She answered Hammond's questions civilly and abruptly with a clipped measurement to her words which Drumson noted but Hammond completely disregarded.

The third night, they were quartered at a splendid plantation where Hammond once again was a welcome guest and where every provision was made for their comfort. As there were no marriageable daughters here, Augusta was received with as much warmth by the mistress as Hammond was by the master, and here, as on the first night, Drumson occupied a room alone with Hammond, and Regine had a closet off Augusta's room. The next morning Augusta was once again treating Regine with kindness and her pique with Hammond seemed to have disappeared.

When they stopped at noon on their fourth day, Hammond pointed out familiar landmarks, with the assurance that they would be at Falconhurst in another hour or so. A short time later, they passed through a dismal little village which wandered down two sides of a dusty street. It boasted the usual tavern and livery stable with loungers in the door; a general store whose porch was crowded with a motley collection of farm tools, washtubs and barrels; several tired-looking shops and a few residences upon which the dust of the road had settled, giving them a dull gray appearance. As they passed through the village, Drumson noticed that the men in the doorway of the livery stable hailed Hammond, and two women, passing in the street, bowed to him. Drumson could see that his master was well known here.

"Thinkin' we'se at Benson," Drumson heard Meg say. "Not fur now to Falconhurst. Be glad to git there."

"And git rid o' these goddam spancels," Alph answered.

"And see mammy."

"And get me a drink of corn."

About three miles the other side of the town, Drumson saw Ajax turn the carriage off the road into a weed-grown, rutted lane which led straight up a rather steep knoll to an imposing house, which stood, painfully exposed in barren grandeur, about a quarter of a mile away. The pure lines of its pseudo-Greek elegance rose starkly over the dusty fields where rows of blackened stubble testified mutely to abandoned cotton fields. It reared itself to an imposing height of three stories over a barn and carriage house behind it, the third story having dormer windows under a sloping roof. In the front, four soaring white pillars, Ionic crowned, which reached from the foundation to the roofline, held up a semicircular porch and stood out with startling clarity against the pinkish-red bricks. No tree, bush nor shrub softened the raw newness of the house, only the green of rampant weeds.

Seeing Ajax and the carriage turn into this lane, Drumson had expected that Hammond and his wagon would follow them. To his surprise, Hammond continued along the main road and signaled, by standing up and waving, that Drumson was to follow him. Hammond continued, however, only a short distance, turning in at a much more traveled lane, between two wooden fence posts, to where a weatherbeaten two-story house, with a sweeping roof which hooded an upstairs and downstairs gallery, sat somnolently and a bit sway-backed a few hundred feet from the main road. Where the new house had risen starkly from the rough, raw fields, this one was shaded by trees and nestled comfortably to the earth in a bed of tangled greenery—tall sunflowers, unpruned rose bushes, crepe myrtle, rank weeds and matted flowers, among which hens, guinea fowl and turkeys scratched, cackled and gobbled. The only sign of life was a group of naked pickaninnies, playing in the dust by the worn wooden steps that led up to the house. These, however, provided the alarum which turned the sleepy house into a frenzy of activity.

"Masta Hammond, Masta Hammond." A boy of about ten started jumping up and down, unable to contain his excitement. "I seen you first, I seen you first."

The shrill voices of the other children, echoing the words of the boy, dispersed the chickens and fowl while the self-constituted herald who had first spied Hammond rushed up the canted wooden steps.

"Miz Ellen, Miz Ellen, Miss 'Cretia Borgia! Masta Hammond done come home! He's here, Masta Hammond is."

Hammond's wagon had stopped before the steps but before he could get down over the wheel a light mulatto woman, short in stature but heavy breasted and with wide hips, came running down the steps, followed by three children, all of whom were dressed. She wore a tattered brown sateen which at one time might have had some pretentions to modishness but which was now so spotted, soiled and draggle-hemmed that it seemed hardly fit for the ragbag. The children, several shades whiter than the woman, were also clothed with some pretense of gentility, but their clothing, like hers, was soiled, stained and ragged. The brood gathered about her by the front wheel of the wagon and Hammond reached down, patted the woman gently on the head and let his fingers slide down over her cheek.

"It's good to see you, Ellen." His smile included the children. "Everything all right?"

"I'se been a good boy, papa." The youngest of the children started climbing over the wheel.

"Course you have, Johnny." Hammond leaned down and lifted him up into the wagon while the others climbed up. "And have Tom and Eddy been good boys too?"

"Eddy hit me"—Johnny pointed an accusing finger at the oldest—"but I'se been good."

"Sh-h-h," Ellen quieted him. "Yes suh, Masta Hammond, suh, everything's all right. 'Cretia Borgia'll be here in a minute, suh. She jes' a-puttin' on a clean wrapper. Tryin' out leaf lard today, we are, and she gits hersel' all spattered with grease. Miz Sophie, she a-playing down by the creek. You, Eddy, git yoursel' down from the wagon and go find Miz Sophie. Tell her her papa's done come."

Suddenly, as though exploding from a cannon, an enormous Negro woman catapulted out of the doorway and down the steps, her wide arms outstretched, her calico wrapper half buttoned and her head hastily bound in a strip of violently green cotton.

"Masta Hammond, suh. Bless de Lawd you's home safe 'n soun'. We sure missed you 'roun heah."

The group at the wheel deferentially parted to let her through and she flung both arms up, catching Hammond around the calves of his legs. He jumped down, to be smothered in her embrace which he returned affectionately.

"You been behavin' yourself, Lucretia Borgia?" Hammond grinned and slapped her broad rump.

"Cain't help behavin' myse'f these days, Masta Hammond, suh. Dat Memnon, he gittin' too old to misbehave any mo'. Forgettin' dat a woman need a bit of pesterin' once in a while. Wishin' you sell him nex' time yo' go to N'Orleans and git me a nice young buck with plenty o' sap in him. Maybe I gives yo' couple mo' twins."

Drumson's mules had reached the tailboard of Hammond's wagon and halted of their own accord. He jumped to the ground and stood alongside Hammond.

"Mammy." A sorrowful wail came from the back of Drumson's wagon, echoed by another and even louder one. "Mammy, it's Meg, it's Alph."

Lucretia Borgia looked up at Hammond beside her.

"Wha't that noise? What that mean, Masta Hammond, suh? Who-all a-sayin' mammy to me? Who sayin' they's Meg and Alph?"

"It's them." Hammond jerked his thumb towards the back of the second wagon. "They's behind them boxes. You takes a look at 'em now if'n you wishes, 'cause you ain't goin' see much of them afterwards."

With the familiarity of an old servant, she laid a trembling hand on Hammond's arm. Her round, shiny face was drawn in sudden panic and the bounding aplomb which had marked her appearance disappeared.

"Masta Hammond suh, if'n them's my twins back there, you ain't gonna do to them boys what yo' did to Mede, is you? Ain't seen them twins for 'bout ten years, almost forgotten 'bout them I had but they's my flesh and blood. Cain't bear to see you bile 'em up in no kittle like you done biled Mede. You a-goin' to kill 'em?"

"Masta Hammond, no." Ellen, too, put her hand on Hammond's arm. "Don't! You've felt bad 'nough 'bout Mede dying. You kills 'em, you never sleep again."

He shook off both hands. "What yo' wimmen talkin' 'bout? Ain't nobody said nothing 'bout killin' nobody. Jes' said you won't be seeing much of 'em any mo' cause they ain't goin' to be no house servants. Bo't 'em back again, I did, and goin' to use 'em but don't need no mo' house servants. Got me a smart boy in New Orleans"—he pointed to Drumson—"and goin' to put him in charge of Miz Sophie's new house."

Lucretia Borgia was only half convinced.

"Whyn't them twins get theyselves down and come 'round here and see they mammy?" she questioned.

"Cause they spancelled," Hammond explained. "Cain't take no chances on they runnin'."

Again Lucretia Borgia looked at him with a question in her eyes, but he looked away.

"If'n you wants to see 'em, go 'round and take a look at 'em. Guess after all these years, they be glad to see you and mayhap you glad to see 'em. Whure that Memnon? He's they pappy and mayhap he likes to see 'em, too."

"Memnon down in the quarters a-dolin' out corn rations for the week." Lucretia Borgia was already edging away from Hammond and as she passed Drumson she surveyed him carefully.

"You the spittin' image of that Mede boy we had here onct." It was plain to see that she was full of memories of the dead Mandingo. She hurried around to the back of the wagon. Hammond, Ellen and the children accompanied her and Drumson sidled up to the wagon wheel where he could peer around the piled-up luggage.

Lucretia Borgia stood, her hands on her ample hips, regarding the two dust-covered men chained in the back of the wagon.

"Mammy, wha'fer Masta Hammond done keep us chained up? We ain' done nuffin'. We ain' a-goin' ter run. We'se too glad to git oursel's back to Falconhurst." Meg's tears rolled down over his dust-encrusted cheeks, making wet black tracks on his face.

"Mammy, could you get me jes' a little drap of corn? Achin' all over I is. Rheumatiz I cotched from ol' masta. Hurtin' me powerful it is."

Lucretia Borgia continued to stare at these two grown men. The last time she had seen them, they had been boys. Now she hardly recognized them. Their births had been a long time ago and her affection and love for them had long died. But . . . they were hers.

"Dunno why Masta Hammond got yo'uns spancelled," she spoke slowly, "but reckon he's got good reason. But you's back at Falconhurst. Glad to see you both here onct mo'." Suddenly the maternal love which she had thought forgotten was rekindled. She turned to Hammond.

"Kin I unloose 'em and take 'em into de house? Knows you says they ain' house servants no mo', but kin I give 'em somep'n to eat? Kin I, Masta Hammond suh? Long time since these yere boys tasted they's mammy's cookin'."

Hammond shook his head as he mounted the wagon again. "You'll see 'em again, Lucretia Borgia. Promise you that. Ain't a-goin' to sell 'em. Now I'm a-takin' 'em down to the slave pen. Ellen, you 'n Lucretia Borgia bed them wenches in the women's shed and see that they's fed. And a-fore you go,

Lucretia Borgia, give me the key to the slave pen. Take those two little bucks and put them in the barn with the other boys. Don' forget to lock the door of the girls' shed—gotta keep the bucks away from these new girls till I decides which ones goin' to get 'em." He motioned to Drumson. "Git up here," he said and as Drumson took his seat beside him, Hammond picked up the reins. They turned the corner of the house, just in time to see the wet and bedraggled figure of a white girl about twelve years old come running up the road between the long line of slave cabins and sheds.

"Poppa," she was screaming, waving her arms and running, then stopping to gather up the long wet skirts as she came through the dust. "Poppa, you home? What you brung me, poppa?"

Hammond stopped the mules and reached a hand down over the wheel to hoist her up. She leaped up, threw her arms around his neck and smothered his face with kisses, her long, snarled blond curls covering his face.

"Papa's home, Sophie." Hammond managed to extricate himself from her damp embrace. "Wha'for you all wet?"

"Been a-playin' wid Lou-Emma. Been a-sailin' boats. What you brung me, Poppa?"

"Go back to the house, change your clothes and get yourself all prettied up. Goin' over to the new house to live. Want you should look nice to meet Miz Augusta. Tha's whut I brought you from the city—nice lady—white lady who's a-goin' to be like a mama to you. Brung you somethin' else, too. Now, scamper. Get yo'self clean 'cause soon's I gets back to the house, we're a-goin' over."

"Who's he?" Sophie pointed to Drumson.

Drumson turned to look at the girl. He was shocked to see her pale blue eyes so badly crossed that he was unable to tell whether she was looking at him or not. He bobbed his head in acknowledgment of her inquiry.

"He's yo' new boy. Goin' to be yo' house servant over to the new house. He named Drumson."

Sophie giggled. "Shore is a funny name but shore is a pretty nigger boy. He's mine?"

"He's yours."

"Kin I have him whupped if'n he's naughty?"

Hammond shook his head. "Any whuppin' to be done 'round here, I does it. No one else. Now run!" He eased her down over the wheel and started the mules.

The wagon left the house behind and turned into a dusty

road which ran between the slave quarters. Drumson saw clean, well-built cabins, neatly whitewashed, lining each side of the road. Orderly vegetable gardens surrounded each one and before some of them young women were down on their knees, weeding or gathering produce for the evening meal. As Hammond passed, they all stood up and greeted him. Drumson noticed that they were all big-bellied with pregnancy. After the cabins, they passed a number of long sheds, each with barred windows and massive wooden doors. The doors now stood wide open and the barracks were deserted. Drumson guessed, rightly, that the slaves were out in the fields working. At the very end of the street, separated from all the other buildings, stood a small structure of heavy planks, whitewashed and clean, with tiny barred windows, so high that one could not look inside. The door, also of heavy planks, was closed, fastened with a ponderous padlock, and further secured by two wide planks fastened into iron hasps. Hammond lifted them out, took the key that Lucretia Borgia had given him and opened the padlock, letting the door swing open. He picked up the light mule whip from the wagon seat. Then taking another key from his pocket, he walked around to the back of the wagon.

"Please, Masta Hammond suh." Meg was still weeping. "We's home now, Masta Hammond suh. We's home 'gain. Why'n you let us loose? Wha' for you keepin' us spancelled?" We ain' goin' ter run. Al'ays loved you, Masta Hammond. 'Member how you used ter say I'se de bes' boy you ever had? 'Member how I ate from yo' own plate an' slept in yo' room? 'Member how Alph dreened the rheumatiz from yo' pappy? 'Member how I used ter fix toddies fo' you jes' like you wanted 'em?"

Hammond maintained a stony silence. He undid the padlock that held the running chain between the handcuffs and pulled it out. It rattled to the ground.

The mention of toddies had started the more stolid Alph. "Let me fix yo' toddies, Masta Hammond suh. Ain't never forgotten how yo' pappy liked 'em. Cain't I have jes' a drap o' corn for myself? I'se turrible miz-rable, Masta Hammond suh, and you 'members how yo' pappy said only corn'll fix rheumatiz. Achin' all over, I am."

"Jump down!" They were the first words that Hammond had spoken to them since he purchased them.

"Wha's this li'l house?" Meg regarded the building with the high barred windows. "Ain' never seen this place 'fore.

Somepin new? Why you puttin' us in here, Masta Hammond suh? We bin locked up since de day we lef' our old masta, Mista Chauvet."

The horsewhip snaked around their bare calves, then bit into their backs. Both boys yelped with pain.

"Git inside," Hammond said. "Jest in case you wants to know, this yere's the slave pen. This whure we keeps runners and other bad 'uns. This goin' to be yo' home fer some time so better git used to it."

"Wha' we done, Masta Hammond suh, wha' we done? We never don' nuthin' bad. Them things we done with Masta Roche we hadda do, Masta Hammond suh. You cain't blame them on us. He made us do 'em. Didn't want to but he made us." Meg eyed the whip in Hammond's hand. "You goin' to whup us, Masta Hammond suh?"

"Whuppin' too good for you varmints. As to what you done. Better think back a long ways to when you livin' here afore. You remembers Mede?"

"Yas suh, Masta Hammond suh, remembers that big Mede," Alph, who was slower witted than Meg, answered. Meg's teeth were chattering so with fear that his lips could not frame the words.

Hammond's mouth was a grim line.

"Mede done learned his lesson. He'll never rape no white woman 'gain. Neither'll you when I gits through with you." Hammond pushed them both inside the door, closed it with a bang, snapped the padlock and put the planks back in place. He slipped the key in his pocket.

The two pairs of hands encircled the bars. The voices echoed strangely inside the empty room.

"Masta Hammond, 'tweren't our fault. 'Tweren't Mede's fault nuther." The words became inaudible with sobbing.

Hammond turned his back on the slave pen.

"Better drive over to the other house, Drumson, and get this stuff unloaded. See to it that Miz Augusta and Regine gits settled in. Needs a lot to be done—beds to be put up and ever'thing. Miz Augusta'll know whut to do. You step right lively and help her."

"Yas suh, Masta Hammond, suh." Drumson reached out to take the whip that Hammond handed to him. It was the same whip he had held in his hands for four days. Now it felt strangely different. It had cut into flesh—it had given pain. He hated to touch it. He turned the mules and left Hammond standing beside the slave pen. The noise of the mules and the sound of the wheels served to muffle the cries that came from the pen. Drumson felt glad that he was on his way to the new house. Stark and ugly as it had seemed, rising in its nakedness from the raw fields, it did not have the mysterious air of tragedy that seemed to hover over the old house.

## chapter vii

When Drumson arrived back at the new house, he was confronted by a stormy Augusta, whose quick nervous steps as she strode back and forth across the portico betrayed her anger. She was followed by a weeping Regine who seemed on the verge of hysterics. Before Drumson was able to stop the mules, Augusta came running down the steps to the wagon wheel, her eyes blazing, her words rushing forth in a torrent.

"Where's that Hammond Maxwell?" she demanded, as though it was Drumson's fault that he was not there.

Drumson looked at her blankly. He could appear stupid when he wished or when the occasion seemed to demand it.

"He's back over to the other house, Miz 'Gusta, ma'am."

"Then go back immediately and fetch him. Tell him he must come here at once, do you understand, at once. And have him send back some servants—intelligent ones if he has any—and a lot of them. I want wenches with brooms and pails and brushes; I want men with hammers and nails and saws. If I had ever known this place was in such a horrible mess, I would never have left New Orleans. Now go, and hurry! There is much to be done before night."

Without waiting to unload the boxes or staying to expose himself longer to Augusta's ire, Drumson turned around and headed back for the old house. Hammond, sitting on the gallery, surrounded by his nearly white children, did not seem surprised to see him return, and at Drumson's repetition of Augusta's demand that he come back to the new house at once, Hammond merely laughed.

"Kinda put out, ain't she? Thought she might be. So, I'm not a-goin'. You jes' tells her I'm busy—got a plantation to tend to that's a damn sight more important than a house. I'll be over later. Memnon," he half turned to call into the house. "Memnon, round up 'bout six boys and four or five wenches wit' some cleanin' things 'n tools. Better get that

Brute boy and them wenches I jes' brought from the city. Pile 'em all in the wagon and let Drumson take 'em back." He looked down at Drumson and laughed again.

"Bet she's madder'n a wet hen and don't knows as how I blame her. But I'm a-keepin' away from her 'til she gets herself cooled down. Want some advice, Drumson?"

"Yes suh, Masta Hammond, suh." Hammond's way of talking made Drumson feel they were almost on equal footing—men banded together against women.

"When a white woman gets a hair across they ass, you jes' keeps out o' the way 'til they gets rid o' it. Pretty soon they calms down. When you gets back, tell Miz Augusta I'll be over 'fore nightfall and I'll have Lucretia Borgia send over supper fer you-all. Tell her to go ahead and do anythin' she damn pleases over there 'ceptin' the lower room on the ell in back is to be my bedroom and the room over it Regine's. Room over the kitchen is fo' you. Ask her kindly to get the beds set up. We sleeps over there tonight."

"Yes suh, Masta Hammond, suh. Downstairs room in back for you, upstairs for Miz Regine, room over kitchen for me. Yes suh!" He looked up as a straggling procession of slaves shuffled up. Memnon herded them into the back of the wagon. One, an engaging fellow of about Drumson's age and coloring with a saw and a carpenter's box, jumped up on the seat beside him.

"I'se Brutus," he grinned as the mules started. "Who're you, new boy?"

"Drumson. Jes' got here today. Goin' to be the house servant over to the new house."

"You lucky. Tha's whut I hankerin' fer. House servant. Craves to git me inside the big house. Carpenter now and I don' like it. Perhaps you can work me in. We be frens, huh?"

Drumson had never had a friend of his own age. Something about the fellow appealed to him—his humor, his good looks, his light coloring. Perhaps it was the fact that they were both young, both ripe for adventure.

"Ain' got me no frens here," Drumson admitted. "Shore likes to have me one. Shore we be frens."

"Wants to stay here," Brutus admitted, "but thinks they goin' to sell me, come next year. Don' sell house servants here. That Memnon bin here all his life. If'n you says a good word fo' me, I yo' fren for life."

Drumson nodded. It was a *fait accompli*—they were friends.

Augusta exploded again when she saw that Hammond had not returned but she seemed somewhat mollified when she saw the small army of servants Drumson had brought with him. She ordered him out of the wagon and into the house and he, sensing the propaganda value of Brutus' inclusion in whatever project was under way, pulled at the fellow's shirt-sleeve and brought him along.

"This yere's Brutus, Miz Augusta, ma'am. He right smart boy. He'n I git things goin' fer you."

Once inside the door, Drumson could well understand Augusta's anger.

The house was a scene of utter confusion. Crates, boxes, bales and bundles were piled high in the hall and in the adjoining rooms. In order to pass from one room to another, it was necessary to push the crates aside or climb over them. He had a fleeting impression of a wide, white-paneled, high-ceilinged hall, with a fan-lighted back door corresponding to the front door. Under tall, open archways, supported by fluted white columns, they progressed through two large rooms on one side of the hall, out through a shelved pantry into a smaller room at the rear which was evidently a kitchen for it held a large black, cast-iron stove—the first that Drumson had ever seen. A narrow stairway led from this room to a room above which Drumson figured must be the one Hammond had designated for him. He went back down again and out through the pantry into the big room which Augusta said would be the dining room, then into the front room which she called the parlor. They crossed the hall into two large corresponding rooms on the other side, and then into the ell, where a wood-paneled room with a richly carved mantelpiece occupied a position corresponding to the kitchen. The staircase that led from this room, however, instead of being plain and utilitarian like the one in the kitchen, was fitted with ornately carved railings, and curved instead of leading straight up. An outside door opened in the rear so that a person could enter or leave without going through the rest of the house.

"This yere's Masta Hammond's room, Miz 'Gusta, ma'am." Drumson's arm included the room and his finger pointed to the stairs. "That one up there's Miz Regine's. My room's over the kitchen."

Augusta turned to him.

"Who said so?" she demanded.

"Masta Hammond, ma'am. He says to tell you the downstairs room in the back is his'n. The room over it to be her'n and mine over the kitchen, ma'am. Them's his words, ma'am. Miz Regine. . . ."

"Don't call her Miss Regine," Augusta snapped. "What do you think she is . . . white? Well, she isn't. She's just as much a nigger as you are. Just a slave, that's all. So, Maxwell wants her to have the room over his. With a staircase between! We'll see about that. Now, let's get to work. What's that boy's name with you?"

"Brutus, ma'am. What kin he do to help you?"

"What can he do? My God, look at this mess! Four miserable days on the road and when I arrive here . . . what? Not a bed to lie down on, not a washstand where I can wash my face, not a place to make a cup of coffee. Get those others in here. First we've got to get beds up to sleep in if we can find them." She noticed the tools in Brutus' hands. "Can you open those crates?"

"Yes ma'am, sure kin." Brutus was only too anxious to be useful. He was willing to do anything to ingratiate himself. This was his opportunity.

"Then see if you can find some crates that contain beds. Know what beds look like? No? Then I'll go with you."

Brutus and Drumson ripped the boards off crate after crate. They found chairs, tables and a sideboard. One huge crate held an ebony pianoforte; another was filled with folded damasks and still another with silver candelabra and a silver coffee service. At length, the ripped-off boards disclosed the high mahogany posts of a bed and Augusta directed that they carry it upstairs to the big room at the left of the portico.

"This will be my room," she stated. "Mr. Maxwell's daughter will have the room behind it and"—her lip curled—"the small one in the rear will be for Regine. Where is she? What's she doing?"

"She downstairs, ma'am, a-sittin' on the porch," Drumson replied.

"Sniveling, I suppose."

"Yes, Miz Augusta ma'am, she kind-a cryin' like."

"Has been, ever since that night at the tavern. Doesn't she know why Maxwell bought her? Then she'd better find out. Give her a broom and tell her to start working."

Drumson left and went downstairs. He discovered Regine sitting on a box in the hall, and delivered Augusta's message. She reached up a hand for him to help her up and he could see his own desire for her, reflected in her eyes.

Augusta and Brutus were upstairs, the other slaves were dispersed about the house. Drumson gathered her into his arms, pressed her to him and found her lips warm and soft against his own. Neither of them spoke but when they separated and he led her upstairs, he knew that she belonged to him, even though Hammond owned her.

Augusta marshaled all the slaves upstairs and set them at various tasks of cleaning, while Drumson and Brutus located more beds and set them up. They found ropes to cord them and mattresses to place on them and eventually a large case the contained linens. One by one the big beds were made, all except the testers that went on the high frames, but Augusta decided that this final touch could be postponed until later.

She was an efficient manager and skilled at getting work out of the slaves. She seemed to be everywhere. No sooner was a crate opened than its contents were toted off by strong black hands to its proper destination. It was she who planned the rooms. Hammond had been overgenerous and there was more than enough furniture, all of it new, for the whole house. He had contracted for the furnishings for the entire house in New Orleans and had chosen none of it himself, merely stipulating the number of rooms. Most of the furniture was ornate, sprawling and ugly, but its very bigness fitted the huge rooms and its ugliness was dwarfed by the architectural elegance of the house.

The heavy, damask-upholstered Empire chairs and sofas, Augusta decided, were destined for the parlor. Here too, she had laid the big roll of carpeting with its florid design of pink and yellow roses, and here she had hung the long rose damask draperies under their bright metal cornices. One of the last boxes to be opened disclosed the metal frame of a big chandelier with box after box of cut crystals which nobody but Augusta knew how to put together. She had them hang the chandelier frame but put the boxes of crystals aside to await her greater leisure.

The big ormulu-encrusted sideboard and the wide expanse of mahogany table went into the dining room. Barrels, which disclosed china and glassware nestled in the straw packing, were placed in the pantry.

The large room across the hall from the parlor Augusta designated as the ladies' sitting room and here she placed the pale green French furniture with its yellow upholstery and hung the yellow brocaded draperies. The big room behind it, which led into Hammond's bedroom, she decided to call the gentlemen's sitting room and relegated to it all the bastard chairs and tables which seemed unrelated to anything else. As order evolved under her fingers, she began to feel a proprietary interest in the big house and the too plentiful and too ornate furniture. It had taken form under her hands—it was hers.

By late afternoon the place began to look like a home. The servants were exhausted, but Augusta kept pushing them on. Plain wooden bedsteads were set up in Regine's room and Drumson's. When it came to furnishing the latter, Drumson surprised even himself by daring to approach Augusta.

"That Brutus boy, he's a smart boy, Miz 'Gusta. He takes hol' and do the work hisse'f 'thout nobody a-tellin' him whut to do. We goin' to need 'nother boy 'round this house 'sides me. Brutus' a nice-lookin' boy too—not too black. Whyn't you keep him here with us? Kin if you asks Masta Hammond. Set up 'nother bed fo' him in my room."

Augusta paused in her directions to the girls who were making up a bed in the big back room which she had designated as a guest room.

"Perhaps you are right, Drumson." She gave further directions for the making of the bed and walked over to one of the windows where a rosewood chair had been left, temporarily awaiting placement. She sank down into it gratefully, welcoming the breeze that entered at the window, and motioned to Drumson to sit on the floor in front of her. "Sit down, Drumson. Perhaps it's time you and I became acquainted. We can both do with a few moments of rest."

"Yes, Miz 'Gusta, ma'am." Drumson too welcomed the respite.

"You're the only connection I have with New Orleans. I always liked you in the days when I used to come to Madame's and I like you now. You're a smart boy, Drumson, and I'm glad I've got you. Between us, we'll have to manage this house and I think you're right. We're going to need more than one house boy. I've been told that I should manage this house as though it were my own. Very well, then, I'm going to make you our butler."

"Butler, Miz 'Gusta ma'am? Wha's that?" Drumson had never heard the word before and he didn't know whether it boded good or ill for him.

"Well, it's something new that some of the English families in New Orleans have. It means the head servant of the house. It's like being the overseer on a plantation. All the slaves in the house will be under you. I'll give you your orders and you'll pass them on and be responsible."

"An' they calls me 'butler.' Tha's good."

"Now about this boy Brutus. What makes you think he's a good boy to have around the house?"

"We're frens, Brutus and me. I likes him, what little I've seen him, Miz 'Gusta, ma'am."

"Very well then, I'll take your word for it and give him a trial. I'll tell Mr. Maxwell I want Brutus for a footman. That means he'll help you, Drumson, work along with you. Then we'll have Ajax for a coachman. Mr. Maxwell will have to give us two boys for gardeners—the outside of this place needs a lot of work. Then we'll need a young boy—maybe that Jackson boy who came along with us—to work in the kitchen. Guess that takes care of our men servants. So, if you can find another bed, you can put it up in your room for Brutus and I'll have the girls make them up. Now, let's see what we're going to need for female help. First we'll have to have a cook. Wonder if Mr. Maxwell has one over at the other house. By the way, Drumson, what is the other house like?"

"Old house, Miz 'Gusta. Kinda fallen-down lookin' 'thout paint and not so much. Lady over there by the name of Ellen with some mustee kids which look as though Masta Hammond might be they poppa. Big fat woman, name of 'Cretia Borgia seems to run the place. Man named Memnon, he butler." Drumson was proud of his ability to use the word correctly.

"This Ellen woman—is she white?"

"No, ma'am, she quadroon . . . mebbe octoroon. She mos' white but she's a-gettin' awful fat too. Seemed mighty familiar with Masta Hammond."

Augusta sat still for a moment, not bothering to reply. She sighed deeply, then brought herself back to the problem at hand. "All the slaves but you, Brutus and Regine can sleep on the third floor. If Hammond does not have a cook, we'll have to buy one. Regine can be my maid and Miss Sophie's, too. Then, we'll need a girl for downstairs and one for upstairs. That Balsam wench that came with us is not too bad and rather pretty, too. She could do for downstairs and we could use Phronia up here for chambermaid. I feel a little more acquainted with those girls who came with us than I would with strangers. I wonder if we need anyone else. A girl for the kitchen? No, we'll have Jackson for vegetables and washing up. But we shall need a laundress. You and Brutus can wait on table and that reminds me, I must get new clothes for you both."

"Pretty blue ones with shiny buttons like they got in the hotel?" Drumson had not forgotten the resplendent boy who had answered the bell.

Augusta shook her head. "Nice white coats while you're serving dinner. Gray coats the rest of the time and black trousers all the time. I'll have to teach you to take care of your clothes."

"Knows how, Miz 'Gusta, ma'am, but don't think that Brutus boy ever had real clothes. Ain't got nothin' but tow linen. Teaches him myself, I will."

Augusta nodded but it was apparent she had not been listening. She sat silent a few minutes, seeming to enjoy the breeze as it rippled the curls on her forehead. At length she turned and regarded Drumson, not as she would a slave but almost as another person. She started to speak and then stopped. When she did speak, although she looked directly at Drumson, she seemed to be speaking to herself.

"I must get clothes for Regine, too. Black dresses with white aprons." Her voice lowered and became confidential. "How do you like Regine, Drumson?"

He hardly dared to answer her, remembering as he did the hidden kiss behind the packing cases. How did he like Regine? But he must be careful. Did Miss Augusta suspect? Would she tell Hammond?

"She is beautiful, Miz 'Gusta ma'am. Shore is. Most beautiful girl I ever seen, that is, colored girl."

Augusta smiled. "That's nice because she thinks you're the handsomest boy in the world. Told me so, she did. Said she wished you were her man."

"It won' do her no good wishin', ma'am. She's Masta Hammond's wench, she is. She gotta do like he says."

Augusta was indulgent. She reached down and patted Drumson's head. "Patience, boy! White masters tire quickly of their wenches."

"Don't know 'bout Masta Hammond, ma'am. That Ellen woman over to the other house look like she been Masta Hammond's wench good many years. Them mustee kids shore look like him."

Augusta's fingers reached down and pulled the lobe of his

ear. "Didn't I tell you that you and I are friends, Drumson? You and I'll have to work together in many things. Maybe I can help you to have Regine. Maybe you can help me in some other things. Rome wasn't built in a day," she sighed, "nor was Falconhurst settled in a day either. We'd better get to work. But remember this, Drumson. You may be Hammond Maxwell's slave but I can make or break you. Be loyal to me and I'll see to it that you have it easy—a good job here in the house, and perhaps Regine, too. But, work against me and I'll have you out chopping cotton or whatever it is that they do here. Understand?"

"Guess I do, Miz 'Gusta ma'am." Drumson was willing to give her his entire loyalty, provided it did not interfere with his loyalty to Hammond. Regine was a big prize.

"Then we'd better get to work, and you forget all about our little talk, eh? Call Brutus and tell him to find another bed and mattress like yours and set it up in your room."

They heard the noise and commotion of a horse and carriage stopping outside and Augusta dispatched Drumson to find out who it was. He was just in time to open the front door for Hammond and his daughter. Sophie, primped and curled, was somewhat more attractive than Sophie bedraggled and wet, although her finery was far too elaborate for a girl of her age, and fanciful as it was, it was soiled and worn. The white satin dress, lavishly trimmed with cheap cotton lace around the belled-out skirt, was spotted and creased, the artificial roses at the shoulder crushed and tired-looking, as was the matching wreath which she wore in her hair. The first thing Drumson looked at was her eyes; they still wandered in different directions. Otherwise, she was not unattractive. Her adolescent body was plump under the restricting bodice; her neck and forearms tanned in contrast to the milky whiteness of her upper arms. Drumson judged her to be about twelve or thirteen years old, seeing there was already a promise of breasts under her dress.

"Miz Augusta feeling better?" Hammond whispered to Drumson. "Gotten over her mad?"

Drumson nodded and held the door open.

"Ain' it purty, poppa?" Sophie ran the length of the hall, peering into the downstairs rooms. "We goin' to live here, poppa?"

"Yes, birdie." Hammond looked around the hall, surprised at the amount of work which had already been accomplished.

What had only a few hours before been a nondescript pile of crates and bales now had the semblance of a home. It was not complete—far from it—but it had progressed sufficiently to impress him. He looked up to see Augusta slowly descending the stairs. She had brushed her hair and wiped the traces of grime from her face. She came down, cool and unhurried, hesitating a moment on each step.

The house, which she had entered only a few hours before and had rescued from complete confusion, had become her own home. Her slow progress down the winding staircase expertly conveyed her ownership. She greeted Hammond pleasantly, almost formally.

"We have made some progress, Mr. Maxwell," she said, approaching him. Kneeling down, she took Sophie's hand in hers. "And this, I presume, is Sophie. I'm going to be your. . . . What shall I be, Mr. Maxwell? Mrs. Devereaux seems far too formal. How would you like me to be your Aunt Augusta, Sophie? And now, may I kiss you?"

"If'n you wants to." Sophie displayed no enthusiasm. "But you ain' my aunt. Ain' got no aunts. Got me Ellen and 'Cretia Borgia. An' if'n I don' want to live over here, I ain' goin' to. It's purty here, but ain' no one to play with over here. 'Ceptin' him." She pointed to Drumson. "He's shore a purty boy. Likes him to play with me."

"You kin have yore Juno over here. She cain't sleep here though." Hammond was evidently trying to placate her. "Drumson, you go out in the kerridge and git them hampers. Lucretia Borgia cooked supper fer you-all. We a-goin' to eat here with you. Eat my suppers here after this. Noons I eat over to the old house."

"Put the hampers in the kitchen, Drumson." Augusta led the way into the parlor and indicated chairs for Hammond and Sophie, but Sophie dashed away. They could hear her racing up the stairs.

"There are a few arrangements I'd like to make, Mr. Maxwell, about staffing this house. I've talked some of this over with Drumson, who seems to be a smart boy."

"Ought to be, paid enough fer him. But you do as you wants to, Miz Augusta. You're in charge here. Full charge. Got plenty slaves fer you to choose frum."

"Then I'm going to make Drumson our butler."

"Wha's that?" Sophie had made her tour of the upstairs and popped into the room again.

Fortunately Hammond had heard the word and explained to her.

"And I'd like this Brutus boy that's been here today for Drumson's assistant."

Hammond shook his head in indecision. "He's a pretty good carpenter, ma'am. Trainin' him to sell next year. Should get round two thousand fer him, trained as he is." He stopped shaking his head. "All right, if'n you wants him, you kin have him."

"And I'd like that Jackson boy who came with us. He's a smart little fellow and I can train him for kitchen work. I hope you can provide us with a cook."

"Lucretia Borgia been a-trainin' one fer you. She called Clytie. Makes fine biscuits."

Augusta nodded her acceptance, making the mental reservation that she would soon teach the new girl how to do more than fry ham and eggs, which she had discovered to be Hammond's favorite dish.

"The girl Regine can be servant for Miss Sophie and myself. Her room"—she scrutinized Hammond carefully—"opens into your daughter's so it will be convenient. Then we'll need two more girls. I had thought of Balsam and Phronia. They are untrained but I'll make them competent."

"That Phronia? She the one who come with us from New Orleans?"

"The same."

"She too young. Ain' mor'n fourteen. Too young fer breedin'. Better get an older one. That Balsam, she 'bout sixteen so she's all right. Bed her with Drumson, but Phronia too young to bed with Brute."

Augusta looked quickly at Sophie, who sat dumpily in her chair, listening to the conversation but quite evidently unimpressed.

"Mr. Maxwell, you seem to forget. . . ."

" 'Bout Sophie. Sophie's 'quainted with these things. Been brought up on a breedin' farm. Knows whut's a-going on s'well as I do."

"From now on we shall avoid such subjects." Augusta was firm.

Sophie roused herself from her lethargy. "Ain' you goin' to put this Drumson to Big Pearl? 'Pears to me he'd git some good suckers out'n her."

"Later." Hammond evidently regretted her participation in the conversation. "Later, Sophie."

"Then how 'bout Elvira," Sophie persisted. "She's a purty wench—awful purty. Said you was a-savin' her for a nice buck. Let Brute have the other 'n let Drumson have Elvira."

Hammond's face turned red.

"All right, I'll send for Elvira. Supposin' you go upstairs and see your room Aunt Augusta fixed up fer you." He waited for Sophie to leave but she remained in her chair.

"Seen it onct. Don't want to see it 'gain."

"Then go anyway."

"Won't."

Augusta came to the rescue.

"If you'll go upstairs to the big room in front which is my room, and look on the table beside my bed, you'll find my reticule. In it, you'll find a little bottle of perfume. It's from Paris. Why don't you try it?"

"Kin Drumson go with me?"

"No," Hammond said, "now scoot." He waited to hear her footsteps die away on the upper floor and turned to Augusta.

"You're right, Miz Augusta. Shouldn't talk such things afore Sophie. But this yere's a breedin' farm and she's heard a lot, specially whilst I was away in Texas. Mayhap you kin change her. Want you should make a lady outa her. Think you kin?"

"I'll try, Mr. Maxwell. But do you think such things should go on here in the house—such as wenches sleeping with our boys? Is it necessary to turn the house into a stud farm?"

"Cain't help it, Miz Augusta. Cain't be wastin' these boys just a-waiting on table." Hammond seemed to have made up his mind. "And besides, when the saps a-risin' in 'em, if you keeps 'em away from the wenches you're sure goin' to have trouble. These yere boys are men now, strong men with strong yearnin's. If'n we don't give 'em wenches to dreen off their sap, they'll have to be gelded. Never gelded a nigger yet." He paused a moment. "Always a first time, though."

"Heavens no!" Augusta was shocked. "Let them have the wenches. Their rooms are over the kitchen so it's away from the rest of the house."

"Better that way, Miz Augusta. You nor Miss Sophie nor Regine not safe in this house less'n those boys have wenches or less'n they gelded. We got to use a lot of wenches here at Falconhurst and them boys goin't to come in useful. That Brute boy, he's already gotten me four fine suckers. And this boy Drumson. Bo't him fer breedin' not ans'ering the do'bell. Buttles for you daytimes and works for me nights. Keep him happy that-a way too."

Augusta bowed her head. "Very well, Mr. Maxwell," she sighed, resigned. "It's your business. Naturally you can run it as you choose."

"And this is yo' house. Do with it as you please. I'll not bother you."

"Thank you, Mr. Maxwell."

Drumson, who had been standing by the door listening to the conversation, was thinking only of the Elvira who had been awarded to him as his companion. His thoughts were wandering but he was called back to reality by Hammond's question to him.

"Did you git my room ready so's I kin sleep here tonight?"

"Yas suh, Masta Hammond, suh."

"And Regine's?"

"Yas suh, Masta Hammond, suh."

Augusta got up suddenly.

"I shall see about getting supper on the table," she said. She disappeared through the dining room into the kitchen.

Hammond winked at Drumson.

"That Elvira wench, she purty. 'Spects you goin' to like her. She not black, neither. But she small. Fear maybe you too big for her, so you be careful. Better you get some bacon rind from Lucretia Borgia and go slow, boy, go slow."

Drumson yearned for Regine but this Elvira sounded promising. He had no idea why he might want bacon rind or what it might have to do with Elvira but he'd ask Brutus about that. He'd also ask Brutus what *gelded* meant. He'd never heard the word before.

"Thank you, Masta Hammond, suh. 'Preciates all you done fo' me."

"Then you git busy for me. Tell you what I'll do. You and Brute, you both git busy. First one gits his wench knocked up, I gives him a silver dollar."

"Shore be glad of that silver dollar, Masta Hammond, suh." Drumson felt sure it was his already.

## chapter viii

THE DAYS ROLLED by into weeks and gradually the big house at Falconhurst developed from a raw, untenanted building into a gracious home, both inside and out, under Augusta's excellent management and Drumson's willing co-operation. He had learned some things at Madame's and Augusta taught him the rest. Although he had had no experience in handling slaves, he quickly became adept at getting the most possible out of them by a combination of good-humored cajolery and stern discipline. If the first did not work, he tried the second, and with Augusta backing him, he applied the whip when necessary, although it was only the same light mule whip he had seen Hammond use on the twins. This he kept beside his bed in his room with strict orders that it never be touched. His strokes were always few in number and light ones at that but the very threat of them was usually sufficient.

The first slave he had been forced to punish was Ajax, who disappeared early one afternoon, making it impossible for Augusta to take a drive she had planned into Benson. When he reappeared just before the evening meal, Drumson accosted him. The fellow said that Miss Sophie had ordered him to go to the river with her, to stand by while she waded in the water, and he thought he must obey her. Drumson agreed with him but told him that whenever he went out, regardless of who ordered him to go, he must report first to Miss Augusta and never leave if there was a possibility he might be wanted. To remind him of this fact and impress it on his mind so that he would not easily forget it, Drumson had Brutus hold him while he stung the calves of his legs with the whip until his howls attracted Sophie herself. She came running to the barn and watched the process with excited enthusiasm, denying vehemently that he had been with her. Drumson felt that Ajax had been punished enough, but now Sophie picked up the whip and started to lash him. Her strokes were much more vicious than Drumson's, and it was Ajax' louder howls that saved him. Hammond, attracted by the screaming, came into the barn and grabbed the whip from Sophie. For a moment, Drumson thought he was going to use it on her, but Hammond merely handed it back to him and walked away.

When he returned to the kitchen a few moments later, having delivered Sophie to Augusta, Hammond forbade Drumson ever to let her have a whip in her hands again.

"Even if'n she orders me to give it to her?" Drumson asked.

"Even if'n she does. 'Tain't fittin' for no gal to whip niggers. And yo', boy, you take care how you use that whip. Don' never let me hear of you doin' it on yo' own 'cord, 'ceptin' Miz Augusta gives you leave."

Clytie, the cook Lucretia Borgia had trained, was the only one Drumson experienced any serious difficulties with. She had expected that she was to wield exactly the same authority in the new house that Lucretia Borgia had exercised in the old—the supreme factotum of the house servants—and when she discovered that she was subservient to Drumson and through him to Augusta, she became rebellious and disagreeable. She was one of the few older hands, somewhere in her late twenties, and had already produced eight children, all fathered by Clees, who was the self-appointed bully-boy of the plantation, owing to his length of residence there and his position as whipper. Clytie resented her present separation from him and was always running off to meet him outside or else providing him with special little dainties in the kitchen. Whenever Drumson entered the kitchen and found them together, he was treated to surly looks and derogatory remarks. That these remarks were always made in the third person prevented him from taking open umbrage at them, although he knew they were intended for him.

Clytie and her man Clees were Drumson's only problems. All the rest of the servants showed him proper respect and he had few difficulties with them. Balsam, who was in charge of the second floor, was secretly enamored of Drumson even though she was Brutus' bedmate, so she was always compliant. She was, however, a lazy girl, doing only what was expected of her and that indifferently. As for Elvira, she was so devoted to Drumson she worked overtime to gain his approbation.

Sophie had been right. Elvira was a pretty girl with a head of short curls. She was agreeable, clean, charming and naturally a coquette. Regine was the only one of the servants not directly under his supervision, spending all her time on the second floor, caring for Augusta's and Sophie's clothes and their personal needs. It was rarely indeed that she and Drumson ever had a moment together and when they did, neither of them dared repeat the intimacy of the embrace they had stolen the first day. But Drumson knew that she was as anxious for it to be repeated as he was.

However, the demands that Elvira made on him each night kept him physically satisfied. Although he responded with the proper amount of ardor, he realized that his own passion was always much more quickly appeased than that of Brutus. Elvira was demanding and convenient and he was ready to comply, but his mental image, even in his most ecstatic moments, was always that of Regine. It was her body that he held, her lips that he kissed, her warmth that he entered. Elvira sensed that she did not possess him entirely and redoubled her efforts to please him. But always, when he had reached the point of satiation and she was no longer desirable to him, he moved to the other side of the bed, not wanting even the touch of her body.

On the whole, however, he was content with Elvira. But, even in his contentment, he was beset by fears. Brutus' explanation of the word *gelding* had struck terror in him. He tried in vain to think what it might be like to experience the horror of emasculation, but it was beyond the scope of his imagination. The only thing that calmed his fears was Brutus' assertion that no slave on the Maxwell plantation had ever been gelded. But he recalled Hammond's final words, "there's always a first time," and the words brought back his fear.

While Drumson was having his difficulties with Clytie in the kitchen, Augusta was experiencing hers with Sophie. During the first years of her life, while Hammond was away from Falconhurst, Sophie had been indulged in her every whim and notion by an aging grandfather and a fawning Lucretia Borgia, both of whom had doted on her. She had always been a precocious child, far more accustomed to the conversation of adults than that of children. The only ones of her own age she had ever known were the slave children on the plantation and she had queened it over them, exacting complete obedience. In this she was upheld both by her grandfather and Lucretia Borgia. In their eyes, she could do no wrong. Whenever she was at fault, she laid the blame on some small slave, partly to defend herself but perhaps even more because she enjoyed the punishment she knew would be inflicted on her victim. More often than not, she maneuvered them into some compromising position, just to see her grandfather's or the cook's wrath descend upon them.

After her grandfather's death she had been even more spoiled by her father, not because he loved her so much—actually he had very little affection for his daughter—but through a sense of duty to her as a white child and the future mistress of the plantation. Any attempt that Ellen might have made to discipline Sophie was, of course, nullified by Ellen's position as a slave.

It was only natural that the child should resent Augusta's authority. The first few days Sophie refused to abandon her own way of life, treating Augusta merely as though she were another slave. Augusta, not daring to go too far in the way of discipline, merely spoke of her naughtiness to Hammond, who shrugged his shoulders and ignored it. Finally, however, matters came to a head. It was Drumson—all unknowingly—who precipitated matters by the most agonizing confession he had ever been forced to make. He had first sought out Brutus, begging for advice on what he should do. Brutus, on learning of his dilemma, had considered it of such importance that he had called in Elvira and Balsam and together they had discussed the matter. All had urged him to go to Augusta and tell her exactly what had happened, admitting that although it was a most dangerous thing to do, it might be better in the end. Certainly it would be better than for Hammond to find it out. That would mean the end of Drumson.

"Ain' a buck on this plantation but what afeared of that Miz Sophie," Brutus had affirmed. "She a bad 'un. Likes to play 'round wid de boys and ain' no one kin stop her. No boy dast to go to Masta Hammond an' tell him. All scairt for fear he kill 'em."

"Praps he kill me." Drumson was more frightened than ever. "Or wors'n killin' me, perhaps he geld me."

"Not if'n you goes to Miz 'Gusta first. She yo' fren. She understand. She know you're not a-lyin' to her."

Brutus tried to give Drumson courage. "Ev'y boy at Falconhurst scairt of Miz Sophie 'cept that Clees bastard. He al'ays a-lettin' her sit on his lap when he come to de kitchen. Thinks he started her, I do."

"You better go to Miz 'Gusta, Drumson." Balsam put a protective arm over his shoulder. "Praps you feels better if'n we all goes wid you."

Bolstered by Brutus, Balsam and Elvira, Drumson approached Augusta, who was hemming damask napkins by an open window in the ladies' sitting room. She looked up, surprised to see almost the entire household staff approaching her en masse, but she laid down her sewing, sat back in her chair and invited their confidence with a smile. The look of terror on Drumson's face forewarned her.

"Miz 'Gusta, ma'am, might I have a word with you?" He halted a few steps from her.

"Why of course. Why are you trembling, Drumson?" She was trying to put him to ease. "Has something terrible happened? If so, I am glad you came to me. I don't want you ever to be afraid to come to me with anything. Never."

"Mighty scairt now, Miz 'Gusta, ma'am," he admitted.

"Well don't be. Whatever it is, your coming to me is sure to mitigate the offense. Is it something you did?"

"No ma'am, Miz 'Gusta. Ain't nothin' I done did."

"Then something Brutus did, or Balsam, or Elvira?"

"No, ma'am, nothin' they done neither. Nothin' none of us done did. Nothin' Ajax did, nor Jackson, nor Merc, nor Jupe. But we all scairt, Miz 'Gusta. Scairt of Miz Sophie, we are."

"Oh for pity's sake! Of Miss Sophie? Why, she's nothing but a little girl."

"Not so little, Miz 'Gusta, ma'am, and she white. What she say, Masta Hammond believe. What we niggers say, he think jes' lies. She white, Miz 'Gusta, ma'am, but she bad."

Augusta laughed. "Naughty at times, I agree, but I hardly believe she's bad. Now, supposing you tell me exactly what this awful thing is that frightens you all so. You've never lied to me before and I shall believe you."

"Yes ma'am, Miz 'Gusta. I honest. But what I got to say's a hard thing. Miz Sophie's Masta Hammond's chile. He'll believe her afore he will me."

"But you are not talking to Master Hammond now. You are talking to me. Master Hammond has told me that I am the head of this house. You are doing right to report anything to me first. I'll judge the matter and if I deem it necessary, I'll pass it on to him. Now, Drumson, what is all this about Miss Sophie? Go right ahead and tell me. Just tell the truth and don't be frightened."

"Hard for me to tell a lady, Miz 'Gusta, ma'am, but got to tell you. Ain't fittin' to talk about to a lady neither."

Augusta looked at the four pairs of eyes facing her. In her intuitive woman's way, she had an idea of what might be forthcoming.

"Go ahead, Drumson, and take your time. I'll listen. Just be sure you are telling me the truth."

There were no further preliminaries. He knew he must blurt it out now, regardless of the circumstances.

"Yesterday," he began, "I was in the pantry, unpacking them barrels o' dishes. I was a-taking the plates and sich out-a the barrels and the straw and a-carryin' them into the kitchen fer Elvira to wash 'em. Then I carries the clean ones back to the pantry. Didn't want that Jackson boy a-washing them—feared he break 'em. Clytie, she a-setting at the table and Clees, he a-setting there too, drinkin' a cup of coffee and a-eatin' a piece of that there poun' cake you learned Clytie to make. Miss Sophie, she a-settin' on Clees' lap, kinda lovin' him up like as how she shouldn't and he a-lettin' her. Had his arms 'round her, feedin' her pieces o' cake and a-lettin' her drink outa his cup. Clytie she awful mad but she not speakin' a word."

"What's Clees doing in our kitchen?" Augusta demanded.

"He's Clytie's man, Miz 'Gusta ma'am. He there a lot. She al'ays a-feedin' him."

"Well that's going to stop." Augusta was firm. "We're certainly not going to have that behemoth cluttering up the kitchen and keeping Clytie from her work."

"Yes ma'am, Miz 'Gusta, he shore is what yo' calls him." Drumson had no idea of what the word meant but he was sure it was not complimentary. "So purty soon, Miz Sophie, she slide down outa Clees' lap and she come in the pantry with me. Jes' then I a-standin' up on the li'l ladder, a-puttin' some of the clean dishes up'n the top shelf.

" 'You shore a purty boy, Drumson,' she a-saying to me. 'Whyn't you never play with me?'

"I laughed, Miz 'Gusta ma'am, sayin' to her I too big to play with her. She better play with Jackson or that Juno wench what come over to play with her.

"She say she don' want to play with Jackson—he too li'l and she sick of playin' with wenches. Say she like mo' playin' with me. Say she know nice game to play with me."

"And then, Drumson?" Augusta bit her lip but her voice remained calm.

"And then, ma'am. . . ." He hesitated, unable to speak. "Jes' cain't tell you no mo', ma'am. Ain' a-fittin' fo' me." He hung his head.

Elvira stepped forward.

"No, it ain' a-fittin' fo' Drumson to say, Miz 'Gusta, ma'am. But if'n you wants to know, I'll tell you, ma'am. She a-doin' the same thing with Drumson, that I ketched her a-doin' wid Ajax out'n the stable. She done it with Merc and with Jupe and she all-a time a-doin' it wid Clees. She a-goin' 'round all-a time unbuttonin' the boys' pants she is and a-playin' wid 'em. That's what she-a-doin', Miz 'Gusta, ma'am. Ain't only de boys here at the house but she a-going out'n de fiel's. She a-doin' it to all de boys what's here."

"Yes ma'am, Miz 'Gusta, ma'am." Brutus found courage to confirm Elvira's words. "Ain' a boy on de place but what wants to run when he see Miz Sophie a-comin'. She mo' bold than de nigger wenches. Boys don' min' de wenches a-lovin' 'em up onct in a while but they's mighty scairt of white gal. She plague 'em all. They's fear'd not to let her and fear'd to let her. She say if'n they don' she run tell Masta Hammond they a-goin' to rape her so's they gotten to let her. Ev'y one fear'd Masta Hammond goin' fin' him and her some day."

Augusta's lips set in a firm line. Balsam started to speak but Augusta waved her to silence. For a long moment she sat there, looking from one to the other.

"Is this true, Drumson?" She looked straight at him. "Tell me, is that what Miss Sophie did to you?"

" 'Tis true, Miz 'Gusta. Don' know what Miz Sophie done to them others. Didn' see nothin' with Ajax nor Merc nor Jupe. Brutus, he been here long time and he know. I only seen her with Clees in the kitchen."

"You should have told me then."

"Yes ma'am, Miz 'Gusta. Should of, but a servant don' go a-telling things he sees white folks do. Ain' up to him to carry tales 'bout white folks."

"In this case it was. But I think I understand. And you, Brutus, this ever happen to you?"

"Yes ma'am, Miz 'Gusta. Onct 'fore I come over here. Buildin' a chicken coop, I was, and Miz Sophie she done come down a-sayin' she a-goin' to he'p me. She start in kinda pushin' me, kinda playin', then a-pettin' then she start a-foolin' roun'. Then she get mad. She say I no good. Say I no bigger'n dat Ol' Man Wilson and he no older'n she is. Say I too small to bother with. Shore glad fer onct I so small."

Augusta's hand silenced him. She turned to Elvira.

"And you say you saw this happen with Ajax?"

"Yas ma'am, Miz 'Gusta, in de coach house."

Augusta stood up.

"We'll say no more about this matter. I am sure all of you are telling the truth but you must not blame Miss Sophie. She did not realize that she was doing wrong. I do not want the matter ever mentioned again, not among yourselves or among the other servants. Drumson, you go out and get Ajax and bring him in here. Then, when I dismiss him, I want you to bring the two yard boys in. Hurry, because I want to talk with all of them before Mr. Maxwell and Miss Sophie return from Benson." She was about to dismiss them when she remembered something. "Drumson, before you call Ajax, tell Clytie I want to see her. Now, go, all of you. Go about your work as though nothing had happened. It will not happen again and I can assure you, you need have nothing to fear for I shall not mention your names in any discussion I have with Mr. Maxwell."

They filed out, through the parlor and the dining room, into the pantry and the kitchen. Clytie was chopping something in a huge wooden bowl. Drumson informed her that Augusta wanted her.

"Who she think she is, a-orderin' me 'roun', a-tellin' me whut to do." She delivered a few more vicious blows to the bowl with the chopping knife. "Don' she know I'se busy a-gittin' Masta Hammond's supper?"

"Better go, Clytie." Drumson was emphatic, and, still spluttering, she flounced out.

They waited, huddled together in the kitchen, until Clytie returned. It was plain to see she had been crying. She was quite aware that the others knew why she had been summoned, but anger and resentment had been drained out of her by fear.

"You folkses a-wantin' a cup-a coffee?" she asked meekly. "Got it all het up here fer Clees but he ain' a-comin' here no mo'. Miz 'Gusta say he gotta keep 'way. So's we might's well drink it while it hot."

She poured it out into the cups without waiting for an answer and put the stoneware jug of molasses on the table.

Meanwhile Drumson had summoned Ajax from the coach house. Again they waited, this time five instead of four, bound together by their common fear. When Ajax returned, his face drawn, biting his broad lips, Clytie drew out another of the kitchen chairs and poured him a cup of coffee.

"Guess we all gotta stick together now," she said. "Hopes they don' do nothin' to Clees."

And so they waited, sitting in silence while Merc was called in and after him Jupe. Even young Jackson had his turn on the carpet. The only one of the servants who was not questioned was Regine.

Soon after Jackson reappeared, taking his place along with the rest at the kitchen table, Augusta entered through the pantry door. She looked at the assembly—Drumson, Brutus, Ajax, Merc, Jupe and Jackson sitting on one side of the long bare wooden table, facing Clytie, Balsam and Elvira. Augusta clapped her hands together smartly.

"Has all work stopped here for the day? This is not Christmas. No reason for you to stop your work. You, Ajax, get back to the barn. Jupe and Merc, there's plenty of weed-pulling and grading to be done. Upstairs with you, Balsam. I want the floor of the guest room waxed so you can see your face in it. Clytie, get on with the supper and make that hot slaw like I told you to. And you, Elvira, set the table in the dining room. We're using the pink china tonight with the silver candlesticks. Drumson, I'll talk with you."

He followed her out into the hall and up the stairs to her room. She sat down and motioned to him to come near her.

"I once told you, Drumson, that I was your friend. I hope I have proved it to you today. Do you know what would have happened to you, had Mr. Maxwell caught you and Sophie in the pantry? Do you know? Even though it was not your fault, you would have been flogged within an inch of your life and probably sold."

"Yes ma'am, Miz 'Gusta, I knows."

"So, I have shown you that you can depend on me." For the first time she smiled at him. "The time will come, Drumson, when I shall need you to do a favor for me. Will you do it?"

"Shore will, Miz 'Gusta."

"It might be a difficult one."

"Don' make no diff'rence, Miz 'Gusta, ma'am. You my mist'ess. You pertected me today. I'm yo' boy, Miz 'Gusta, ma'am."

"Then remember that, Drumson. Now go, see that things go on here as though nothing had happened. You'll never be bothered by Miss Sophie again. What that child needs is a mother, someone to make her toe the line."

"Pity she ain' got none, Miz 'Gusta, ma'am."

"She may have one sooner than she thinks. Now go, Drumson."

He walked out of the door feeling that a great weight had slipped from his shoulders. Replacing it was an overwhelming love for Augusta. He might be Masta Hammond's slave but he sure was Miss Augusta's boy.

# chapter ix

ALTHOUGH HE WAS calmed by Augusta's assurances, Drumson was, nevertheless, fearful of what Hammond might already know or soon discover. He stood, in his starched white coat, behind Hammond's chair at dinner, facing Brutus across the length of white damask, pink china and burning candles, as Brutus took his place behind Augusta's chair. Their eyes met and he knew that underneath the carefully composed impassivity of Brutus' features, there lurked the same fear. However, dinner passed smoothly without any untoward incident. Hammond ate and enjoyed the hot slaw which was one of the many new foods which Augusta was introducing. There were, Hammond had already discovered, other foods besides fried ham and eggs.

Sophie, who usually ate with Hammond and Augusta, was not present and Augusta excused her absence by saying that she had a headache and was a bit feverish. Hammond displayed some surprise but no concern. Sophie had always been as healthy as a young mule and had never had any ailments, but he accepted Augusta's explanation without questions. Drumson noticed that the conversation was desultory, carried on by both Hammond and Augusta without animation and merely to cover up an otherwise awkward silence. Hammond really had only one topic of conversation—slaves. He was little interested in any talk that did not have some bearing on them, and was not adept at social chitchat. After Drumson had served the dessert and brought in the big silver tray with the shining new coffee service, Augusta rose from the table with the suggestion that Drumson serve their coffee in the ladies' sitting room across the hall. Hammond followed her, telling Drumson to bring him his regular after-dinner toddy, instead of coffee.

Once seated uncomfortably on a fragile French chair in the front room, Hammond was forced to listen to Augusta. Drumson was able to hear very little of the conversation, only those words that were spoken as he entered with new toddies and removed the empty glasses. He knew they were talking about Sophie, and he could tell from the expression on Hammond's face that he was giving the matter serious attention. From the fragments that he could overhear and piece together, he was able to inform the others who were anxiously awaiting his reports in the kitchen that Augusta had managed to give Hammond some of the facts without attaching any blame to Sophie. It was merely that the child had been allowed to run wild, she said. She completely exonerated the male slaves with whom Sophie had been amusing herself. She insisted that Sophie was unaware she had been doing anything wrong, and that the male slaves were unwilling participants. It would serve no purpose to punish them, Augusta maintained, and it certainly would do Sophie no good. Hammond finally allowed himself to be convinced, although with reluctance. After the flare of his first anger had died, he agreed with Augusta. To scar every slave with lashes would certainly put a stigma on the Falconhurst breed. To kill them would be useless, for although slaves were essentially cattle, unlike steers they were worthless when dead for neither their flesh nor their hides were marketable. So what then would Augusta suggest? Hammond, it seemed, was open to suggestions.

Bringing in the third toddy Drumson overheard further information to be relayed to the expectant ears in the kitchen. Augusta was discussing the merits of sending Sophie away to school. Hammond, Drumson reported, was not entirely agreeable.

The fourth toddy however brought the news of Hammond's acceptance; Sophie was to be sent to a certain Miss Pentecost's school for young females in Mobile. Everybody felt relieved when Hammond himself brought his empty glass to the kitchen for his sixth drink and treated them all with drunken conviviality. Evidently they had nothing more to fear. Clytie slipped out the back door to keep a rendezvous with Clees; Merc and Jupe climbed the stairs to their rooms on the attic floor; Ajax went out to attend to some forgotten chore in the barn, taking Jackson with him. Balsam and Brutus went up to the room above the kitchen and Elvira followed them reluctantly, hoping that Hammond would release Drumson quickly after the removal of his boots. After bedding Hammond, Drumson would have little more to do except make a tour of the lower floor to see that all doors were locked, candles extinguished and the windows closed lest a sudden shower during the night spot the damask draperies.

Hammond was still sober enough to walk to his own room without Drumson's assistance. When Drumson opened the door, he found Regine sitting up in Hammond's bed, and her eyes followed him as he went about making his master ready for the night. As he was drawing off the boots, he noticed they were new and stiff, and he proceeded cautiously, anticipating Hammond's curses.

"Goddam boots too stiff." Hammond extended his feet for Drumson to remove the socks. "Been a-hurtin' like hell all the time I been a-listenin' to that woman shootin' off her mouth 'bout Sophie a-goin' 'way to school. Hell, she sure a long-winded bitch. If'n she go or not don' make no neverminds and she probably needs a little polishin'. Went away to school myself onct. Sophie comin' up jes' like a nigger wench. Purty soon she makin' eyes at the white boys and ain' none of 'em goin' to marry her with her gooch eyes, 'specially if she acts like a varmint, less'n some no-good, goddam son of a bitch marries her fer her money." He waited for Drumson to bring the china wash bowl and then placed his feet gratefully in the warm water, wiggling his toes in relief. "Look, boy! Scoot over to the old house and go up in my room. Aside the chest you'll see my old boots. Fetch 'em back so's I can use 'em tomorrow. Ain' no use in killin' myself 'nother day."

Drumson knelt before his master, holding a towel to dry his feet, but Hammond waved him away.

"Regine dries 'em fo' me when I'se finished. Goin' to set here awhile. Got to think 'bout some things. Skedaddle now and get them boots. When you comes back, leave 'em outside the do'."

"Yas suh, Masta Hammond, suh." Drumson was half out the door. He dreaded the trip over to the old house—down the hill, through the thickly wooded glade at the bottom where the creek was bridged by a single plank, up the rise that led to the old house, past the burying ground where white marble slabs glowed ghostly in the night. But if he ran, he'd get over there and back in a hurry, and there was the pleasant anticipation of Elvira's warm flesh to welcome him when he returned. It would be pleasanter if it were Regine's but he realized that what belonged to his master could never be his. He wondered if, in his drunken stupor, Hammond could fully appreciate Regine and he was certain that he couldn't. Hammond was incapable of giving her the full fire of passion that he could. No white man could! But what good did it do him to think about it?

Fortunately there was a moon which dispelled the darkness, but when he entered the thick patch of woods at the bottom of the hill, the moon's light was hidden by the leaves and the tattered hangings of moss. It was so dark he could not even see his own hand. He thought he heard something stir alongside the path and the sudden rustling in the bushes startled him so that he ran even faster. There was a pool of moonlight in the still water of the creek and he heard his feet hit the plank bridge, and the hollow sound that they made echoed back to him from the water below. Now, faced with the uphill path, he had to slow down, but when he reached the crest and saw the white gravestones, like dancing wraiths suddenly struck still, he once again hurried his steps, more confident now as he saw the sway-backed silhouette of the old house. It was dark—there were no lights in any of the windows—and he ran around to the back and entered through the kitchen door.

The remnants of a fire in the fireplace showed the lumpy outlines of Memnon and Lucretia Borgia, sleeping on a pallet on the floor. He tiptoed past them, not however without waking the woman.

"Who in hell dat?" She sat up quickly. "Memnon, wake up —dere's someone here in de kitchen."

"It's me—Drumson." He was quick to identify himself, for he did not want any poker-wielding Lucretia Borgia after him. "Masta Hammond send me over to git his boots. Wants a candle, I do. Got to go up to his room 'n fin' 'em."

Still grumbling, she heaved herself up from the floor, fumbled in the darkness for the kitchen tinderbox, struck a light and applied it to a candle stub.

"What you mean a-rampagin' through here this time o' night? Ain' you got no manners, boy? Cain't you knock on de do'? How'n you don' know ol' Memnon he ain' a-pesterin' me o' somepin? Nex' time you knocks and waits. Git up and git dem boots and git t'hell outa here."

"Yes'm, yes'm." Drumson reached for the candle but Lucretia Borgia held it away from him.

"You uppity city niggers ain' got no manners. No bringin' up! Lived in N'Orleans myself I did onct. Never did see sech goin's on as I saw there." She held the flickering candle up close to Drumson's face. "But yo' shore a purty buck. Whyn't you take off yo' shoes and stop here a few minutes? That Memnon, he 'sleep and he don' min' even if'n he wakes up. How 'bout it, purty boy?"

Her hand pulled Drumson over to her but he grabbed the candle from her, dashed up the stairs and found the boots. Lucretia Borgia was waiting hopefully for him in the kitchen when he returned but he did not stop to speak to her. He handed her the candle and was out the door.

"You uppity li'l som-of-a-bitch," Lucretia Borgia called after him.

His running feet carried him past the burying ground and down the hill. His feet touched the plank bridge and once across it he hurried his steps through the pitch darkness. Without warning he collided with something in the path—something big and warm and immovable. There was a sudden male yelp of surprise, followed by an indrawn feminine cry. Drumson had nearly had his breath knocked out of him by the unexpected impact. He stood still, gasping, smelling the sweaty body of another man near him.

"Who t'hell is you?" a bull voice bellowed.

Drumson recognized the voice as that of Clees.

"Drumson from the new house."

"Spyin' on us, huh? You're the goddam sneakin' bahst'd whut done wen' and tol' Miz 'Gusta 'bout me. Whut you tells her? You tells her I a-lettin' that Miz Sophie diddle me in de kitchen? You a-tellin' her dat? Dat why she tell me I cain't come no' mo'? Dat why, huh, you pipe-stem li'l city nigger, you?"

"Ain' said nothin' bout you and Miz Sophie. Nothin'!" Drumson was getting his breath and started to move around Clees.

"Drumson ain' said nothin'." It was Clytie's voice trying to pacify Clees.

"Ain' so shore." Clees' hand reached out of the darkness and grabbed the front of Drumson's shirt. "Don't trust this li'l rat. Goin' to give um a lesson."

The fist that hit Drumson's face had risen quickly and entirely invisibly but it hit with a sledge-hammer force that would have knocked Drumson down had not the other hand been holding him up by his shirt. Again it hit, numbing the side of Drumson's face and making his head reel.

"Tha's 'nough, Clees, don' hit um no mo'. Masta Hammond won' like it if you messes up his pretty boy." Drumson could feel Clytie's hands pawing at Clees' arm.

It had been a long time since he had worked out regularly every morning with Uncle Blaise in Madame's courtyard, but now almost automatically he raised his right arm, swinging from the shoulder as much as he could with the grip on his chest. He felt his fist crash into the softness of Clees' belly and he heard the big fellow grunt. The boots slipped from his left hand as he raised it to crash it into the face before him. He felt the satisfaction of hearing the blow land and the yelp from Clees, then once again he felt the hammering blows on his face. They hammered him down until he was flat on the ground. Rough shoes were stomping on him until he slipped into a blacker darkness in which there was no pain, nor any thought.

How long he remained there he did not know, but eventually he felt the warm touch of soft fingers on his cheek and kept hearing his name spoken over and over again. He tried hard to answer but found it impossible until, with a final effort at concentration, he opened his eyes. The darkness had disappeared in the dim half-light of dawn which grayed the trees and silvered the festoons of hanging moss. Now he could see Elvira kneeling beside him, repeating his name over and over again.

"Wha's happened, oh wha's happened, Drum-boy?"

He tried to reply but he couldn't remember. His head ached with a relentless throbbing and his face felt as though it had been pounded into a pulp.

"Kin you git up?" Elvira was trying to raise his head.

With difficulty, Drumson made the effort, first raising himself on his elbows, then to his knees and finally to his feet. He swayed, holding onto Elvira for support and then, her arm supporting him, walked painfully to the house with her. It was fully light and the sun was shining when they finally got there. Elvira helped him into the kitchen. Clytie was up and had a fire already started in the big iron stove and was putting a pot of water on to heat. She looked up, surveyed the ravages to Drumson's face, her own livid with fear.

"Somepin' happen to he?" She helped Elvira, taking hold of one of Drumson's arms and guiding him to a chair.

"Don' know what. Kin you talk now, Drumson?"

He looked up at Clytie.

"You knows what happened. You was there with Clees. You heard."

"Ain' been nowhere, ain' seen nuthin'." Clytie was vehement in her denials. "Ain' seen Clees since Miz 'Gusta put 'im out yestiday." She walked over to the stove, tested the temperature of the water in the pot with her finger and poured out some in a basin. "Better git some of that blood off'n his face 'fore Masta Hammond call him. Better git him washed up, Elviry." She rummaged in a closet under the sink and found a clean cloth. "Here, wash him up so's Masta Hammond won' known he been a-fightin'. Won' stan' for no nigger fightin', Masta Hammond won't."

"Who been a-fightin'?" They all turned to look at the pantry door. Hammond was standing there, dressed in his shirt and trousers but barefooted. "Where's my boots I sent you for las' night, Drumson? Ain' in front o' my do'."

Drumson struggled to rise to his feet.

"No suh, Masta Hammond, suh. Don' jes' know where them boots is at. Los' em I did, down in the woods by the creek."

Hammond walked across the kitchen floor to stand directly in front of Drumson.

"Plain to see you been a-fightin'. You sure look as though you tangled with a wil' cat. Who you fightin' wid?"

"Don' jes' rightly know, Masta Hammond, suh. Ain' a-seen him. Was a-comin' home las' night, taking the short cut like you tol' me and jes' after I cross the bridge, wham, somepin' hit me on the head. Knew'd it was another man but jes' ain' certain who it was."

An audible sigh escaped from Clytie who covered it up by exaggerated display of busy motions.

"I knows who done it, Masta Hammond." Elvira was waiting patiently, cloth in hand, to wash Drumson's face. "I know who done it. Clees."

"Shet yo' mouth 'til you asked." The toddies of the night before and his annoyance at not finding the boots waiting for him, together with the evidence of Drumson's fighting, were all combining to rouse Hammond's anger.

"She don' know. She don' know nuthin'." Clytie knew she should keep her own mouth shut but she was too anxious to protect Clees.

"An' who tol' you to open yo' trap?" Hammond swung around only to see Clytie's back while she spun the handle on the coffee grinder. "Goddam wimmen talk too goddam much! Now, what is all this? Drumson lookin' like he been gored by a bull; Elvira shootin' her mouth off that Clees done it; and Clytie a-puttin' her oar in that he didn't." He turned back to Drumson, leaned over and examined his face. One eye was badly puffed, the under lip was cracked open and there was a patch of skin missing from the cheek. A lump as big as a goose egg decorated Drumson's forehead and through his torn shirt, there were bruises on his chest.

"Come on now! Either we gets the truth easy-like or all of you gets whupped and I means it." Hammond was in no mood for trifling. "Drumson, who you been fightin' with?"

Drumson tried to steady himself on his feet. "Jes' like I said, Masta Hammond, suh. Ain' shore. Pretty dark in them there woods at night. But I guess Elvira's right. Thinks it was Clees."

"What you'n Clees been argifying 'bout? Ain' goin' ter have no feudin' on the place. Ain' goin' to have no fightin' neither. Fightin' marks up a slave worse'n whuppin'. Whuppin' don' hurt they faces."

"Ain' had no trouble with Clees." Drumson was telling the truth. "Leastwise not afore now. He mad 'cause Miz 'Gusta say he cain't sit here in the kitchen no mo'. He say I tol' her he been here."

"So it was Clees?"

"Thinks so, Masta Hammond, but didn't see him. Couldn't see him in the dark."

Hammond looked down at his bare feet. "Elvira, you runs down and see if'n you kin find my boots. Clytie, you gits me some breakfast here in the kitchen. Drumson, git yo' face washed and eat somepin'. Soon's we finish we's a-goin' over to the ol' house. Goin' to find that Clees. Ain' goin' to have no fightin' at Falconhurst. Goin' to make a 'zample."

"You going to whup Clees?" Clytie nearly dropped the cup of ground coffee. Her hands were trembling so she had to set it down on the table.

"Whups him if'n I wants to. Takes the skin clear off'n his back if I wants to. Whup you if'n you don't go 'bout gitting my breakfast and keep yo' goddam mouth shet."

Elvira returned with the boots, and Clytie managed to get some sort of breakfast on the table while Elvira cleaned off Drumson's face as best she could. Brutus and Balsam came down the stairs; Merc and Jupe descended from the attic, carrying their shoes in their hands, followed by Jackson. Ajax entered, bringing with him the odor of fresh horse manure. All sat in silence, waiting for Hammond to finish his breakfast. When he was through, he indicated the eggs and ham left on the platter.

"Eat it," he said to Drumson. "You shore goin' to need it."

Afterwards Hammond and Drumson walked in silence over to the old house, past it and down the dusty road that went through the slave quarters, where cabin doors were being opened, slops being emptied, fires being started. What few slaves were out greeted Hammond, but they were aware, from the look on his face, that something of importance was about to happen. When he reached the long shed that housed the men, Hammond saw that Memnon had already unlocked the door and he entered, Drumson behind him. The slaves were just getting up, some dressed, some still sitting on their pallets on the floor, yawning, stretching and trying to force their consciousness to the recognition of a new day after a night of oblivion.

"Whar Clees?" Hammond demanded.

"Ain' here, Masta Maxwell, suh." One of the boys pointed to an empty pallet with a neatly folded blanket that had not been disturbed.

"Then fin' him. All o' you start lookin' fer him. First boy that fin's him gits two bits."

They tumbled out of the house, running in different directions while Drumson waited beside Hammond. His head was throbbing, the cut on his face pained him and every breath he took was difficult. Although he was distressed with the bodily pain, he was more disturbed over the fact that Hammond was angry with him. He knew he was innocent of any wrongdoing but he had had no opportunity to justify himself and he doubted if Hammond would listen to him if he tried.

One of the slaves came running in, followed by Clees.

"I foun' him, Masta Maxwell. Foun' him a-sleepin' in de hay in de hoss barn. Here he is, Masta Maxwell, suh. Does I git de two bits?"

Hammond reached in his pocket, found the piece of silver and flipped it to the boy. He looked at Clees. It was impossible not to see the swollen and discolored eye where Drumson's fist had landed.

"Where you bin las' night? Why'n't you sleepin' here?" Hammond demanded.

Clees was truculent, big with bravado.

"Gets back from de barn too late. Foun' de do' here locked. So's I sleep in de barn."

"You knows 'nuff to be here at closin' time. You knows. Whure you bin las' night?"

"Ain' been no place, Masta Maxwell, suh. Jes' been a-sittin' in de barn, a-puttin' neatsfoot oil on de paddle. Kinda gettin' dry 'cause we ain' had no whuppin' here fur a long time. Oilin' it up good, I was, case it needed fur them two you got in de pen."

"You bin a-fightin' wid Drumson las' night?"

Clees shook his head more positively than necessary.

"Ain' never a-fightin', Masta Hammond, suh. You knows I never fight. Knows you don' 'low it here. Ain' never a fightin' man, I ain'."

"Then were did you get that black eye?"

Clees' fingers slipped up to his eye. He had felt the pain but he was unaware that it showed.

"Runs into a rake a-settin' on de flo'. Pops us and hits me in de eye. Da's all, Masta Maxwell, suh."

"You're a goddam liar, Clees. You were out a-pesterin' Clytie last night, down by the crick. And you was fightin' with Drumson."

"Oh no, Masta Maxwell, suh. If'n he say so, he's a-lyin'. He couldn't see me, he couldn't. So dark there he couldn't see who a-hittin' him."

Clees was not very quick-witted but now it suddenly occurred to him that his words were even more incriminating than a confession. For the first time that morning Hammond smiled.

"Yo' ain' a-goin' to whup me, Masta Maxwell? Ain' a-goin' to whup me fer takin' a li'l poke at that Drumson boy? We jes' a-foolin', Masta Maxwell, suh. Didn' hurt him, did I, Drumson? We wasn't mad—jes' a-fightin' fur fun tha's all. Him and me good frens, Masta Maxwell, suh."

Clees towered a head over Hammond, but Hammond reached up and slapped him across the face.

"Shet up! Take a-hol' of his arms, boys." Hammond called the slaves to him. "Take him down to the barn." He waited until six of them grabbed hold of Clees. "And take this un too." He pointed to Drumson. "Goin' to whup both of 'em. Ain' goin' ter have no mo' fightin' here. Wants ev'y slave, man and boy, down to the barn. Any of you feels like fightin' you jes' remember what you a-seein' today." He waited until they had secured Drumson, then looked around as though trying to identify one particular person amidst the sea of black faces which confronted him.

"Whure's that Hannibal boy?" he demanded.

"Here I is, Masta Maxwell, suh." A big fellow, lacking perhaps an inch of Clees' height but even more heavily muscled, stepped forward.

"Think you can put some beef into that paddle? Think you kin made the blood spurt out o' Clees' ass?"

"Sure think I kin, Masta Hammond, suh."

"Then go, git 'em ready. Five strokes for Drumson and do him first. Then, let him down and hist that Clees up. Give him thirty strokes and if'n he still squealin' after thirty strokes, give him five more for lyin' to me."

"No, Masta Maxwell, suh, no please suh." Clees struggled to turn toward Hammond. "Not thirty strokes suh. Never fight 'gain suh. Never lift a hand to nobody. Jes' trust me, Masta Maxwell, suh. But don' give me thirty. Jes' give me five like you a-givin' Drumson."

"You've whupped 'nough otherns. You kin take it. If'n they took it, so kin you. Take 'em both away boys."

Drumson felt the iron grip of hands around his arms as they propelled him up to the barn. He knew it was useless to plead with Hammond. When they reached the big wide barn doorway, he was led inside, stripped of his clothes and thrown down flat on his back on the floor. He could not see exactly what they were doing, but he felt straps being tightened around each ankle. One of the fellows, a mustee by the name of Rex and and a great friend of Clees', stood on a box in the doorway and pulled down a rope that led through a pulley block. A similar rope on the other side was pulled down and Drumson realized that the ropes were being fastened to the ankle straps.

"Pull 'im up!" Hammond was standing just outside the doorway. Rex and the other man yanked viciously at the rope.

Drumson felt his back scrape along the rough wooden floor. There were twinges of pain as his flesh picked up the splinters. Then his feet were up in the air, his legs being spread-eagled out. Up he went, his head dangling down, his arms falling below. At first he was able to support his weight by his hands but he was yanked up so high even the tips of his fingers did not touch the floor. He swung helplessly.

"Careful now, Hannibal." Hammond was talking. "Don' hit 'im on his back. Don' wan' any scars on his back.. An' don' hit his knockers. Just on the fat part of his rump. 'Member now, only five strokes, only lay 'em on good.

He'll swing after the first one so let him stop swingin' 'fore you lay on the second. Mayhap you won' bring blood in five strokes and all right if'n you don'."

Drumson saw the sun shining on the floor, lighting a patch of the dirty boards with brightness. He saw the tips of Hammond's boots and noticed that there was mud on them. He could see the bare black feet of the slaves and he could even see a small, red-backed ladybug walking sedately along a crack in the floor, trying in vain to cross it. It was very quiet. His head ached and he thought he would split open from the spread-apart position of his legs.

Then it landed. It was as though a thousand hornets had stung him at once—as though a building had fallen on him. His body swung forward and the breakfast he had so recently eaten descended from his stomach to his mouth and spewed out on the boards. His body stopped swinging and it came again. This time he screamed.

"Masta Hammond," he tried to call out but he choked on the vomit in his throat.

"Three," someone was counting. Drumson did not need anyone to count—he knew how many there were.

"Four." This one seemed worse than all the other three combined. He couldn't take another. He couldn't. But he did.

"Five." It was over. The arc of his swinging body slowly diminished. Once again his hands were on the floor. He welcomed the feeling of the rough boards under his fingers. He sank lower, resting on his elbows. His chin touched, then his chest and finally his whole body, wrapped in fire, sank onto the boards. The ankle straps were removed. Hands reached down to help him up. He stood naked and tortured before Hammond, feeling Hammond's eyes upon him but seeing only pity and compassion there. Now he realized there had been a motive in his punishment. It was necessary that both he and Clees be whipped. When two men fought there was blame on both sides. But Drumson realized that Hammond accepted his innocence. Five strokes, although they caused a hellish amount of suffering, were only a token punishment. It was Clees who was to receive the full amount.

Drumson reached his hands around back to feel of his smarting rump. They came away dry. There was no blood.

Clees was up in the air now. Although he was to blame for this, Drumson felt sorry for him. Clees was hollering, writhing from the ropes, trying to lift himself up to face Hammond while he begged for mercy, promising in one breath that he would never do such a thing again and in the next protesting that he had never done anything. His mouthings were cut short by the smack of the thick, perforated cowhide paddle against his flesh. What had been words were now only incoherent screams. Again the paddle descended. Again there was a scream. It continued. Now there was blood running down Clees's back. It trickled down his neck into his hair and dripped off onto the floor. As he swung from the force of the blows the blood spattered far out, making a line of shiny crimson on the floor.

The blows continued. Rex, Clees' mustee friend, was scowling, mumbling to Big Archer, another of Clees' friends, but Hammond did not notice them. Someone said twenty-three. Then it was twenty-four. Clees had ceased to scream. The only sound that came from him was a low moaning. Twenty-five, twenty-six, twenty-seven. Even the moaning stopped. Thirty. The swinging body slowly came to rest. The ropes were lowered at a signal from Hammond and Clees slumped onto the floor. He was unconscious and they rolled him over onto his stomach. From the waist down he was a mass of blood and pulpy shreads of meat, and the paddle in Hannibal's hands was as gory as Clees' backside.

"Now, you all see what happens to fighters?" Hammond reached down and picked up Drumson's clothes and threw them at him. "Guess there'll be no more fightin' from now on. Never mind rubbing the pimentade into Clees. He's had 'nuff now. Throw a bucket of water over him. Carry him down to the shed and lay him on his bed. He don' have to work today. And you, Drumson, git yo'self dressed. You ain' bleedin'."

Drumson found it almost impossible to bend over sufficiently to draw on his trousers but he managed. He stuck his arms into the shirtsleeves and managed to get the shirt on, then the thin gray alpaca coat over it. He forgot about the string tie in his pocket.

"Kin you walk?" Hammond asked him.

"Guess so, Masta Hammond, suh."

As they passed the cemetery, Hammond halted for a moment to look at one of the tombstones. Drumson could not read the words on it, but he noticed that it stood quite a distance from the others. Then he saw Hammond do a strange thing. He reached down, picked up a handful of the raw dirt and approached Drumson.

"Hol' out yo' hand, boy."

Drumson held out his hand and Hammond dropped the raw dirt into it.

"Tha's Mede there," Hammond said, pointing to the dirt in Drumson's hand. "Best nigger I ever had."

## chapter x

DRUMSON'S WOUNDS were quick to heal and left no damaging scars or disfiguring welts on his body. Fortunately they left no scars on his spirit either. The five strokes of the steerhide paddle which he had received at Hammond's orders, although excruciatingly painful at the time, had served to bring him even closer to his master. A new rapport now seemed to exist between them, a greater intimacy than before. Although their status as master and slave had never been more clearly established, each now felt a bond of mutual ownership. Hammond possessed Drumson as a slave but, equally important, Drumson possessed him as a master. It increased his desire to serve and he came to anticipate Hammond's wishes even before they were spoken.

Although he still desired Regine, the fact that she belonged to Hammond and was therefore sacrosanct negated any animosity. The slave mind was conditioned to accept without questioning that which was permitted and that which was not possible. It made it easier for a slave to exist if he could sublimate his desires to those of his master. If he could do this through affection he found it much easier. Rebellion made life more difficult for any slave. Drumson was learning the philosophy of slavery. Why beat his head against a stone wall, only to bloody it and accomplish nothing? Things were as they were—it was impossible to change them. By accepting Hammond as his master, by loving him, by making a veritable god of him, he was able to get through his days easily and avoid punishment.

He knew his lot was far better than most. While other slaves toiled day after day without respite in the hot sun, he was inside in the shadowed coolness of the big house. Where other slaves walked barefoot in the dust of the fields, his feet, shod in shoes of soft leather, walked over polished floors and thick carpets. Not for him were the corn-husk pallets or the folded blanket on the hard floor of the slave barracks; his bed was as soft and as comfortable as Hammond's own and he had Elvira to share it. If he behaved himself and minded his manners, he would never have to suffer the indignity of having strange men poke at his body, nor would he have to mount the block for men to buy him. Although he was subservient to Hammond and also to Augusta, he himself had his own little kingdom and his subjects were Brutus, Ajax, Merc, Jupe, Elvira, Balsam and now even a grudging Clytie. Since Clees' punishment she had become more tractable and her hostility to Drumson was less marked.

When Clees recovered, Clytie continued to slip away from the house at night to meet him, but Drumson did not feel it necessary to report her absence. She, in gratitude for his forbearance, entered into an unspoken truce with him and as a result conditions in the kitchen were far more harmonious.

There had been an exchange of letters between Augusta and various correspondents whose identities were unknown to Drumson for, although he was often sent into Benson to mail letters and bring back others, his inability to read kept him from deciphering the addresses. He suspected, however, that the letters had something to do with Sophie's departure for school, as did also the frequent visits of the dressmaker from Benson and the packages of cloth and trimmings which arrived by post from New Orleans and Mobile.

Sophie resented Augusta's suggestion that she go away to school and her father's approval of the idea. It meant an end to her uninhibited life and her carefree comings and goings on the plantation. But Augusta had painted a most attractive picture of the life of a young lady at school—a minimum of study, and new friends, new dresses and, most important of all, an opportunity to meet the many brothers, cousins and young uncles of her schoolmates during holiday visits to other plantations. In the end she was won over despite the continuous battle between her and Augusta over the latter's choice of dresses. Sophie favored flamboyant silks and satins, gussied up with all the superfluity of laces, artificial flowers and passementerie which she saw illustrated in the steel engravings in *Godey's Ladies' Book*. It was useless for Augusta to point out that these were not fitting for a young girl. Sophie insisted. Finally a compromise was reached. Sophie was allowed her choice of two ball gowns for formal events at the school. The other dresses, however, were to be chosen by Augusta. The net result was a collection of simple cottons and calicos, quite fitting for a schoolgirl, together with two elaborate gowns which would have done justice to a New Orleans quadroon ball.

Drumson knew in advance when Sophie was leaving, for he had to supervise the hauling of the trunks and boxes to her room. When the day came for her to depart, there was a carriage full—Augusta, of course, was to accompany Sophie. But Sophie must have a slave to wait on her at school so Juno was chosen for that position. Then, Augusta herself must have a slave with her; it would not be fitting for her to return alone and she would require the services of a maid en route. She insisted on Regine and Hammond gave his grumbling assent. Ajax was to drive them in the new carriage, followed by Merc in the spring wagon to carry the luggage. Arrangements had been made by letter to various plantations along the way for overnight stops, so the women would not have to stay in ordinaries or taverns along the route.

When, at last, they were all piled into the new carriage, with the attendant confusion of loading the baggage and a hundred other last-minute errands and emergencies. Drumson was exhausted. Hammond, fortified by several extra toddies, seemed glad to be rid of them. Watching the carriage roll down the dusty drive, he informed Drumson that he would be staying at the old house until Augusta returned and ordered him to carry over his clothes, razors and such personal belongings as he might need for the fortnight.

As Augusta had instructed, Drumson lowered the shades in the main part of the house, closed the shutters, shrouded the furniture in sheets and stripped the beds. He wondered, as he took the sheets from Regine's bed, how often she had slept in them if at all. He also made an important discovery.

For several days after his fight with Clees and his subsequent punishment, he was unaware that the silver chain and its medallion were missing from around his neck. It had become so much a part of him that he did not notice its loss until one night Elvira called its absence to his attention. He worried about it for it was his only possession, and according to his old mistress it gave him some sort of protection. Together he and Elvira had searched the spot where the fight had taken place but to no avail. He had also gone over the barn floor where he had been hoisted up and whipped but it yielded not a trace. Now, to his surprise, as he stripped the sheets off Regine's bed, he found it under her pillow. His joy in recovering it was doubled by the knowledge that she had found and treasured it.

With everyone away, there was little work or responsibility for what was left of the household staff. Hammond came over once a day and took Drumson away with him, mounting him on a horse to make the rounds of the plantation.

Under Hammond's careful supervision, the entire farm was practically self-supporting—a self-contained community under the reign of an exacting but benevolent dictator. Unlike other plantations, which depended on cotton, rice or cane for a cash crop and used slaves to produce it, Falconhurst had its cash crop in slaves and used them only to produce their own sustenance. Hammond believed in feeding his slaves well. Theirs was not a monotonous diet of coarse corn pone with an occasional hunk of fat meat. They were well fed and they showed it in their sleek skins, their strong, well-muscled bodies and their strong bones. Slaves were his cash crop—everything else was merely subsidiary.

The male slaves who worked in the fields were in training to be sold as field hands; the others, whom Hammond considered of superior intelligence, were learning trades and would command higher prices as artisans. Male slaves outnumbered females two to one. The females were used principally for breeding for they never fetched such high prices as males. They were lodged two, three, four, and even six in the new cabins, along with the temporary males whom Hammond had chosen for them. Once they became pregnant they were transferred to the long women's shed and their male companions dismissed to go back to the male shed. If a woman did not achieve pregnancy within a certain period of time with one man who had a known fertility record, she was slated to be sold at the next sale. Males who were unable to prove their virility were also quickly sold.

Newborn children were allowed to stay with their mothers for about two weeks after birth. After that they were merely unidentified children in the communal nursery where women nursed their own babies only by chance. As soon as a woman gave birth to a child, she was sent to the women's shed until such time as she was once again assigned a male companion and sent back to the cabins. Wenches were exposed to their first pregnancy when they were about thirteen. From thirteen to twenty-two or -three they were in production, after which they were ready to be sold in the New

Orleans market, along with a recently born child or a prospective one.

The children, entirely ignorant of their parents' identity, ran naked and barefoot for some nine months of the year, wearing shapeless osnaburg pinafores during the cold months. While they were still very young they were all housed together, regardless of sex, in an old building known as "The Chapel," named for its use during Hammond's mother's lifetime. At the age of eight or ten, the sexes were separated and the boys sent to the hayloft of the barn, the girls to a community house to be closely guarded until they were sufficiently nubile to procreate. Babies were named at birth by Hammond and their records were kept in his ledgers; somehow the names managed to stick to them.

By a careful selection of mates—no wench being allowed the same mate a second time except in unusual cases—Hammond avoided any sentimental attachment between male and female. There was never any form of marriage, not even the simple "jumpin' the stick" ceremony. The women had no choice in their mates, neither were the men allowed any preference. On rare occasions, with three or four couples occupying one cabin, some male would become desirous of another wench, whereupon quarrels would ensue. These were quickly settled when they came to Hammond's attention, either by punishment of the man or wench involved or by the two being separated and sent back to the sheds. On the whole, however, there was little difficulty.

In one respect, Falconhurst differed from most of the other plantations. Hammond insisted on cleanliness in all the slave quarters and among the slaves themselves. He held periodic inspections. Although he knew nothing about sanitary conditions, he was aware that clean surroundings bred healthier slaves. They bathed daily in the river during the warm weather and at least once a week in their cabins during the chilly months. Bedding was aired, floors scrubbed, interiors whitewashed, clothing laundered and latrines disinfected with ashes. In cases of sickness Doc Redfield, the veterinarian, was called in and the ailing slaves were isolated. Sickness, however, was practically unknown. Hammond's slaves were free from ringworm, rickets, deformities, scars and other disfigurements.

They were undoubtedly the happiest slaves in the South. They were prize cattle, fed, pampered and treated as such. None was ever overworked—as a matter of fact, it was difficult to find enough work to keep them all employed. Punishment was at a minimum. Minor infractions were punished by short rations, a temporary confinement to the slave pen, or a withholding of women. Whipping was the exception rather than the rule. Slaves born on Falconhurst never became runners although occasionally when Hammond purchased young adults they took off for their former home. When they were captured, as they usually were, real punishment was inflicted on them; but this happened only rarely. Even when the time came for them to be sold, Falconhurst slaves were not unhappy. Most of them regretted leaving the familiar surroundings where they had been born and spent all their lives, but any change was welcome and the prospects of the trip to the city and being sold were painted in such glowing pictures that it became something to anticipate rather than dread.

The Falconhurst slaves had achieved distinction. This was a period when slaves were a man's proudest possession and the criterion of his wealth. They had become a luxury which the impoverished Southern plantations could ill afford, yet more and more slaves were purchased every year. Falconhurst slaves, like the decorative peacocks on the lawn of the big house, were something to point out with pride —a status symbol of prosperity, even though the plantation itself might be mortgaged for its whole worth.

Drumson saw all the workings of the plantation as he rode about with Hammond. He saw the rows of kneeling figures in the fields, weeding and harvesting. He saw the shavings curl under the carpenters' planes; the sparks fly from the red-hot iron on the blacksmith's anvil; heard the rhythmic tapping of the cobblers' hammers as they made shoes for the plantation; listened to the soft humming of songs as the women spun and wove cotton, linen and wool and stitched it into clothes. He saw the communal nursery where women, big with child, sat awaiting their own delivery, tending to the children of others and knowing that soon they would be abandoning the child in their womb to the impersonal care of other women.

Of Meg and Alph, still imprisoned in the slave pen, Drumson heard and saw little. Once a day they were led out by Hannibal, securely spancelled, allowed to remain in the sunshine for an hour or so and then returned. Hammond had given strict orders that none of the other slaves were to converse with them and he himself still ignored them whenever he chanced to see them. Of late, they had given up their pleading for release and their protestations of innocence. They knew why they were being punished. They remembered back to that time some ten years ago when they had discovered that Mede, the Mandingo, was being forced by Hammond's wife to share her bed. Emboldened by her acceptance of a slave paramour, they had blackmailed her into acceptance of themselves. Meg and Alph knew there was more punishment in store for them than being kept in the slave pen, but of what it might be they were ignorant. The very uncertainty made the threat more terrifying.

On one of Hammond's daily trips around the plantation, followed by Drumson, he stopped at a small slave cabin, quite some distance from the others. Older than the other cabins, unpainted like the old house itself, it seemed to belong to another era. The new cabins, standing straight and four square, well built, resting firmly on good foundations, were floored, securely roofed, whitewashed and weatherproof. This one, seemingly a relic of the past, was made of logs, with only a door and no windows. It canted crazily to one side as if ready to topple over at a touch. A sway-backed roof of shakes appeared to give scant protection. A wattle-and-daub fireplace and soot-blackened chimney climbed erratically up one side. Altogether it seemed an incongruous note in the otherwise snug and well-constructed street of new cabins.

On the worn doorstep, half hidden by the tall sunflowers that grew on each side, a boy was sitting. His superb body had promise of great strength. It was impossible to judge his age for although the body was that of a youth in height and musculature, the face, blankly handsome and completely devoid of expression, was that of a child. A torn pair of breeches was his only covering, and where the sun hit the skin of his back and shoulders it lighted the pure darkness with reddish brown patches. He was amusing himself with a piece of string, winding it slowly around one finger with intense concentration, then unwinding it with equal seriousness. He looked up as Hammond dismounted, and slowly rose to his feet.

"Mas'r, 'mun," he murmured.

"How'r you, Ol' Mista Wilson?" Hammond ran an appraising hand down the smooth ebony of his arm. "Still growin', huh?"

A woman, equally gigantic, appeared in the doorway.

"He still a-growin', Masta Maxwell, suh. Jes' don' know whar he a-goin' to end up. He mos' big he's father now and he only thirteen summer."

An older woman, tall and regal-looking, appeared behind the other.

"He good boy, Masta Maxwell. Ol' Mista Wilson never done give us no trouble. Strong too and a-goin' to be handsome like Mede. You a-comin' in, Masta Maxwell, suh? You a-comin' in ter set fer a spell?"

Hammond laughed. "Knows what you wan' to talk to me 'bout, Lucy—'bout Big Pearl here."

"Cain hol' 'er down much longer, Masta Maxwell. Gittin' mighty rambunctious, she is. Some night she a-goin' a-traipsin' down to de men's shed, rip off dat padlock from de do' and go rampagin' in. Den Gawd he'p dose boys in dere when Big Pearl gets started on 'em."

The younger woman giggled at the mention of her name. "Jes' goin' to do dat some night, Mista Maxwell, suh. Jes' like Lucy says. Goin' to rip off dat lock and pleasure me wid ev'y boy in de shed. Goin' to tire 'em all out come mornin'."

"You do and I'll strip you down," Hammond threatened, but it was plain to see that he didn't mean it, nor was Big Pearl afraid of him.

Drumson thought she was the most impressive woman he had ever seen. Although she was enormous in size, she was so perfectly proportioned that she was beautiful. She loomed over him like a colossus carved out of polished ebony and it was plain to see that Ol' Mista Wilson had inherited his mother's size and good looks. His father, Mede, had been Big Pearl's own brother, both of them children of Lucy. Through the intermingling of relationship, Big Pearl was her son's aunt as well as his mother and Lucy a double grandmother.

"Tha's what I come down to see you for today, Lucy. How you like this boy, Big Pearl?" He called to Drumson to dismount. "Come over here, boy! Thinkin' of havin' you cover Big Pearl. She pure Mandingo, she is. Thinkin' she the only pure Mandingo o' breedin' age in the whole South. That her boy, that Ol' Mista Wilson. Goin' to make me a fighter out o' that boy," Hammond said, "but gotta get me someone to train him."

"Kin I say somepin', Masta Hammond, suh?" Drumson was down off his horse. "My pappy Drum, he was champion fighter of New Orleans and he learned my Uncle Blaise how to fight. Uncle Blaise learned me."

"Why'n you tell me this before?"

"You never asked me, Masta Hammond, suh."

"You sure goin' to be busy, boy, studdin' Big Pearl and teachin' Ol' Mista Wilson be a fighter. How you like this boy, Big Pearl? Name's Drumson. He part Royal Hausa—jes' as good if not better'n Mandingo. You and him gets together and makes me a good sucker, huh?"

"Sho' likes to try, Masta Maxwell, suh." Big Pearl was appraising Drumson. "He pretty boy and he shore looks like Mede but 'pears like he mighty li'l. Not even so big like that Trooper boy you guv me las' time."

Hammond grinned back at her and slapped her heartily on the rump.

"You goin' to get a big surprise, Big Pearl. Done fingered this boy 'fore I bought him. Promise you he's jes' as big as Mede—mayhap bigger. Said to myself when I bought him—this boy jes' right fer Big Pearl."

"When he goin' ter git started, Masta Hammond, suh?"

"When you wants him."

"Wants him right now. Lucy she kin run ovah to de spinnin' house. Ol' Mista Wilson, he go out play somewheres. Kin he come in now? Kin he, Masta Maxwell, suh?" Big Pearl was eyeing Drumson more favorably now.

Hammond looked at Drumson speculatively.

"Don' know if'n he kin do it now, Big Pearl. He been a-workin' pretty hard on that Elvira wench. Ain' 'complished nothin' yet with her. P'haps better wait and let him rest up a week or so 'fore he tackles you. He got plenty o' sap in him but don' think he gotten 'nough fer you and Elvira too. What you think, Drumson? Think you kin tackle both?"

"Thinks I kin, Masta Hammond, suh. Shore thinks I kin. Elvira she got news fer you. She thinks she knocked up. She talk wid Clytie yestiday mornin', Masta Hammond, suh, and Clytie tell her she shore think so. Was a-waitin' to tell you when she shore, 'n that Balsam wench, she think she's a-knocked too. Brute he's a-braggin' that she is and says he's goin' to get that silver dollar fust." His eyes wandered to the enormous breasts that showed under the thin fabric of Big Pearl's dress. "Shore like to try this Big Pearl, Masta Hammond, suh. She a-comin' over to the new house to stay?"

"Hell no! Cain't have no gyrascutus like Big Pearl a-stalkin' through the new house, knockin' down all the furniture. Elvira stay there till Miz 'Gusta get back and we see 'bout gettin' two new girls. Now on, you comes over here every afternoon when you finished yo' work in the new house. First you takes on Big Pearl and then you learns Ol' Mista Wilson to fight, if'n you able to move a finger after Big Pearl get through with you. You craves startin' now?"

Drumson was as anxious to begin as Big Pearl was. The anticipation of being enveloped in that voluminous flesh aroused him. The effect was patently visible and he was embarrassed in front of Hammond.

"If'n she wan's, Masta Hammond, suh."

Big Pearl's eyes had not deceived her. She lost no time in replying. "Shore does, shore does! You come in here, boy. Lucy, go fin' somepin' to do. Mista Wilson, you go play. Thank'ee Masta Maxwell, suh, thank'ee." She gently nudged Lucy out of the door, gave Ol' Mista Wilson a well-placed kick in the rump which started him running, grabbed Drumson by one hand and pulled him inside and closed the door.

The inside of the cabin, notwithstanding its crazy sideways cant, was immaculately clean. Light filtered in through the cracks in the logs—bright streaks of sunlight with golden motes floating in them. One side of the room was occupied by an enormous bed with thick round wooden posts to support it and covered by a red and white patchwork quilt. Opposite it was the fireplace, a yawning black void, above which, on a narrow ledge, was one of the most unusual sights Drumson had ever seen. It was a curious decoration of a grinning white human skull, surrounded by radiating, curved rib-bones and two enormous femurs.

"Tha's Mede." Big Pearl noticed Drumson's fascinated gaze.

"Mede, Mede, Mede!" Drumson walked over to the fireplace and touched the bones gingerly. "Tha's all I hear. Ev'y one a-talkin' 'bout that Mede. Masta Hammond say he bought me 'cause I looks like Mede. I look like Mede, Big Pearl?"

"You shore do, Drumson, but you don' 'pear so big as Mede. He taller'n you. He bigger'n ev'y way. But you purty as he and he the purtiest boy I ever saw. Tha's all we got of po' Mede now—them bones—'ceptin' Ol' Masta Wilson which I birthed. Mede his pappy, he was." She pulled impatiently at Drumson's sleeve. "How come we talkin' 'bout Mede? Tha's long 'go. Mede all fergotten now."

Drumson shivered as his fingers stroked the white bones once again. Strange things had happened here at Falconhurst and he was apprehensive. For the first time he wished he were back in the sunny courtyard of Madame Alix' house with his mother and Uncle Blaise. Even his love for Hammond seemed insecure for he knew that Hammond had loved Mede and yet look what he had done to him. He felt Big Pearl's fingers pulling at his string tie. It came loose and fell to the floor. Her big fingers—strangely gentle now—clumsily undid the buttons of his shirt. She reached down and slipped off his shoes and with an abandoned gesture swept back the coverlet of the bed.

"Ain' no use in messin' it up," she said, looking at him under narrowed lids as she pulled the shapeless osnaburg dress off over her head. "How long you a-goin' to stan' there wid yore pants on?"

Drumson's trousers slipped to the floor in a rumpled pile alongside his white shirt. He felt strong arms tugging at him as he half stumbled, half fell on the bed. No longer was he a man—an aggressor. He was devoured, consumed, swallowed and shattered. He was lifted to insurmountable heights and plunged to unplumbed depths. Breathless, he struggled to survive the onslaught of flesh which ravaged him, until he fell shattered in a sunburst of explosions that left him spent and exhausted.

Big Pearl heaved herself up from the bed and walked across the floor to fill a gourd dipper with water from a bucket. She brought it back to him, lifted his head in the crook of her arm and held the dipper to his lips. He drank greedily and she released him.

"You shore are like Mede." She lowered his head. "Never knowed 'nother boy could do it like Mede. Le's do it 'gain now."

"Cain't Big Pearl."

"That Mede he could."

"Mede better'n me, I guess." Drumson reached for his clothes and put them on slowly, sitting on the edge of the bed and finding it an effort to lift his arms.

"But you be back tomorrer. Masta Hammond say you mus' come back ev'y day to pleasure me 'til you gits me in foal. You gotta learn Ol' Mista Wilson how to fight too."

"I'll learn O' Mista Wilson first. Never be able to learn im after I gits through with you."

Drumson opened the door and stepped outside in the linding sunlight. Hammond had led his horse away and e had to walk back to the new house. His legs felt weak s water but he had a strange floating sensation that was finitely pleasant. Ol' Mista Wilson had moved a few feet way from the doorstep and was now sitting on an up-rned washtub, still winding and rewinding the string 'ound his finger. His vacant face had become animated. e looked up at Drumson and grinned.

"Peeked through the crack I did. You better at pesterin' y mama than that Trooper. He not much good."

Drumson cuffed him, not ungently.

"You goin' to learn me how to fight?" Ol' Mista Wil-n doubled up his fist and presented it to Drumson.

"Shore am."

"You teaches me ter pester de wenches, too?"

"Won' need to teach you that," Drumson answered. Vhen the time comes you knows how."

He walked down the road between the cabins, conscious the admiring glances of the wenches as he passed. Al-ady the plantation grapevine had carried the news that had been with Big Pearl. But Drumson had eyes for ne of them. He even dreaded going back to the big use and meeting Elvira. For once the thought of Regine iled to arouse him. More than anything else he wanted crawl up the kitchen stairs, fall on his bed and pull the vers up over his head. It would be good to sleep and plenish his drained body.

His hand reached up under his shirt and he felt the tle silver box. All his fear and insecurity had left him. adame was right—the little silver box had brought him od luck. He stopped at the burying ground and regarded e marble slabs. Mede might be dead, but he, Drumson, rtainly wasn't.

# chapter xi

HAMMOND MAXWELL rarely displayed his feelings, but Drumson could see how elated he was the day Augusta and Regine returned. With Augusta and Regine back, he actually beamed. He had met them on the road to Benson, and had ridden back alongside the barouche, quite forgetting his errand in town at his joy in seeing them again. When they neared the driveway that turned off to the new house, he had galloped ahead to alert the servants to their arrival, with the result that when the carriage drew up at the door Drumson, Brutus, Elvira, Balsam, Clytie and even Jupe and Jackson were all lined up on the front steps awaiting them. Hammond was most gallant—bowing and smiling and handing Augusta down from the carriage with a flourish, even taking her arm as he escorted her up the steps, but he paid no attention to Regine. Drumson was holding the big front door open when he heard his master say, "It's shore good to have you back again, Miz Augusta. Missed you here at Falconhurst, we have. Ain' seemed like home 'thout you."

"And it's good to be back again, Mr. Maxwell." Augusta answered his welcoming smile with one of her own.

Followed then a frantic scurrying about the house by all the servants—a hurried pulling up of shades and opening of shutters with a whisking off of sheets and covers. The new house emerged from its sepulchral gloom to take on a lived-in radiance once again. Augusta was the catalyst which had brought it all to life.

The bell in the pantry jingled merrily and Drumson looked upon the numbered board to find that the summons came from Augusta's room. He took the polished stairs two at a time, anxious to have a word with her alone and put into words his own joy at having her back again. Although he knew it was impossible, he wished she would take him in her arms as he remembered Calinda doing when he w ı small boy. Actually, when he entered the room, Augusta lid come over to him and pat his cheek, which was almost ıs good.

"Have you been a good boy, Drumson?" she asked. "Have ʼou behaved yourself while I was away?"

"Yes'm, Miz 'Gusta, ma'am, bin good 'n ain' bin whupped ince you gone."

"I should hope not, Drumson."

"Ain' never going to get whupped 'gain, Miz 'Gusta nam, but didn' hurt me much," he boasted. Now that the vhipping was over he rather treasured its memory.

Augusta sighed, then lifted her head and smiled as though he were talking with a small child and wished to dismiss he subject.

"Well, I am home and now things will go on as before. wish you would tell all the servants to come here—all xcept Regine. Children always expect presents you know nd, after all, you are my children. Now go, and bring hem all back with you, even Ajax and Merc and Jupe."

Drumson lost no time in rounding them up and they led up to Augusta's room. Hammond, hearing the noise, ame in and stood behind Augusta.

She opened the lid of the trunk to disclose a number of arcels, all wrapped in paper and each labeled with a tag vhich she read before she picked up the parcel.

"We'll start with Jackson," she said, "because he's the oungest." The parcel which she handed to him was heavy nd bulky.

He accepted with open hands and stood holding it, looking dumbly at Augusta. A present was something which he ʼas quite unable to comprehend. He was even a little fearful f the package and completely at a loss what to do with it.

"Well, open it!" Augusta waited impatiently.

Slowly, and with eyes on her rather than on the package, ackson carefully unknotted the length of red string and ulled off the paper, taking care not to tear it. The present merged from the wrappings—a mechanical bank. Truly it ʼas a most wonderful metal contraption which showed two rightly painted Negro boys, one of whom had an inordinately wide mouth. Jackson regarded it, reveling in the right colors but not knowing what it was for except that was wonderful to look at.

"It's a bank," Augusta explained. "A place to keep ıoney."

"Ain' got no money, Miz 'Gusta." Jackson had little idea of what money meant except that he had seen coins.

"Well, you shall have from now on. Every week, if you are a good boy, I shall give you a penny. Here's the first one. Now bring your bank over here and let's put it on the table."

Jackson was loath to let it out of his hands but, with eyes staring wide, he carried it over and gingerly placed it on the table. His hands lingered on it as he watched Augusta open the chatelaine purse which hung at her belt and take out a penny. She inserted this in the hand of one of the gaily painted Negroes.

"Now watch carefully, all of you."

She pressed a button somewhere in the bottom of the contraption and the mechanical Negro's arm drew back, then whipped forward, releasing the penny which was fired straight to the other figure's mouth, and disappeared. There was a long drawn "oh" of wonderment from all, even Hammond.

"How that thing work?" he questioned, pulling a penny from his own pocket. He inserted it just as Augusta had done and she showed him where to press the button. With unerring aim, the arm drew back, fired the penny and landed it in the open mouth. Hammond was so intrigued that he fished out all the change in his pocket and one by one he fired the coins into the open mouth.

"No more," he said as he relinquished it to Jackson. "You got all of fifty cents in there now."

The boy reached for it and his eyes filled with tears.

"Thank your mistress," Hammond prompted him.

"Grateful, Miz 'Gusta, mighty grateful," Jackson mumbled, holding the bank tightly with one hand and wiping the tears from his eyes with another. He had not yet fully comprehended the marvel that he held but he did know that this was by far the most wonderful thing that had ever happened in his whole life.

Starting now with Drumson, Augusta handed out the other packages. Opening each was a surprise and a miracle. It gave each one of them a possession of his or her own. Drumson received a ruffled white shirt with an elaborate cravat of glossy black satin that wound around his throat and tied in a bow in front.

"To wear when we have special guests for dinner," Augusta explained, "and the first time you wear it, I'll show you how to tie it."

Brutus drew a pair of gaily embroidered galluses.

Augusta laughed as she handed them to him. "I sit in fear and trembling every night at dinner, Brutus, for fear you are going to lose your trousers. They keep slipping down and down and down. Regine will sew some buttons on for you and with you wearing these, I shall be able to eat in peace."

Clytie, Elvira and Balsam all had large squares of brilliantly colored silk to use as headcloths. Merc and Jupe each received a jackknife such as nobody had ever seen before, with three blades which could be pulled out and snapped back. Ajax was overjoyed with a small, silver-mounted whip. And then . . . after they were all quite overwhelmed with their riches, Augusta lifted the tray of the trunk and brought out another package, this one wrapped in tissue paper, which she handed to Hammond.

"By rights," she said, "I should have given this to you first but I could not wait to see the expressions on the servants' faces, so do forgive me."

Hammond acted even more surprised and pleased than the slaves. He took the tissue-wrapped package and just as carefully as any one of the others, he undid the string and unwrapped it. Slowly he held up a dark jacket of black and gold brocade, his eyes questioning Augusta as he did so.

"You wear it," Augusta explained, "when you are at home in the evening. It's far more soft and comfortable than a regular jacket. They call it a smoking jacket but as you do not smoke very often, we'll call it a toddy jacket."

Drumson thought for a moment that Hammond was going to kiss her. He made a move in her direction as if to do so, but instead he extended both hands and grasped one of hers.

"Mighty good of you, Miz 'Gusta. Never had me a present since I was 'bout that Jackson's boy's size. Why, this is better'n Christmas, Miz 'Gusta. All these things from you. What kin we do? Yo' jes' 'spress the wish and we'll do it for you."

Augusta withdrew her hand slowly from Hammond's grasp. She looked at him thoughtfully.

"Yes, you can do something for me—something I'd really

like to have—something that would make me very happy."

"You jes' name it." Hammond was all enthusiasm.

Augusta walked to one of the windows which looked out on the front of the house. Much work had already been done —grading and weeding—and grass had been seeded and come up, covering the big lawn with green. But the house still stood, starkling gaunt in the vacant fields. She pointed out the window to the long lane that led down to the main road.

"I'd like to see an avenue of trees planted there, all the way from the house to the road. It will take years for them to grow and probably I'll not be here to see them when they are grown, but it's what this house needs."

"We'll start tomorrow." Hammond caught her enthusiasm. "What kin' of trees you aimin' at havin', Miz 'Gusta?"

"Live oaks would be nice but they take so long to grow. Willows grow faster but they don't last so long."

"Tell you what we'll do." Hammond felt that he had the right solution. "First we'll plant an oak and then a willow, then 'nother oak and 'nother willow all the way down. Willows grow up fast while oaks a-comin' 'long slow. Then, when the oaks grow up, we'll cut down the willows." He regarded her with a trace of amusement. "But, Miz 'Gusta, them trees ain' fer you—they's for Falconhurst. We'd like to do somethin' fer you personal."

"But just now, Mr. Maxwell, Falconhurst is my home and anything you do for Falconhurst, you do for me. Believe me, nothing would please me more. It would be a pleasure to watch them grow."

Hammond kept his word. The next day a work detail of some hundred slaves from the old house started combing the plantation for willow and oak saplings. They were dug up, transported in farm carts and planted, equidistant, down the long length of the avenue. Only a few of them died—most of them lived and flourished. Augusta had chosen well.

A few days after her return, she announced at dinner, which she and Hammond always ate in the big dining room, that it was time they did some entertaining. There was no use, she reminded him, in having a big house like Falconhurst unless there were some opportunity to show it off. Surely, she suggested, he must have some friends on surrounding plantations whom they could entertain.

"Ain' many." Hammond laid down his knife and fork to think. "Plantations done run down after so many years of cotton and mortgages done et them up. Thar's Doc Redfield and his wife. They's slave owners but guess you wouldn't call 'em quality. Then, o'course, thar's Lewis Gasaway and his wife. Gasaway's still got money tho' they's a-losin' it ev'y year. Lewis's an old friend of mine and his wife was a St. Clair. Lewis married quality though she's as plain as a stump fence. Then there's the Holcombs—new family 'round here which bo't 'The Coign,' Old Mista Wilson's place, what died. Bo't us our Mandingos from Ol' Mista Wilson when he still alive."

Drumson became interested in the conversation. Ol' Mista Wilson was Big Pearl's boy. Evidently he was named after Big Pearl's former master. But the Maxwell Ol' Mista Wilson, stupid as he was in most things, was really learning to fight.

The mention of Wilson's name had started the same train of thought in Hammond's mind. He turned around in his chair to face Drumson, who was standing behind him.

"How you comin' with our Ol' Mista Wilson? That boy able to larn anythin' o' his head all muscles?"

"He's a-larning, Masta Hammond, suh. Larns him ev'y day 'fore I goes in to see Big Pearl."

"How you comin' wit' her? She a-wearin' you out?"

"She shore a powerful woman, Masta Hammond, suh. She able to take ten men 'stead of one, ev'y day."

"Drumson!" Augusta rapped sharply on the table. "We'll have no more of that talk in the dining room."

"Boy ain' a-doin' no harm, Miz 'Gusta." Hammond looked surprised and annoyed at her interruption. "He jes' a-answer-in' my questions. I tol' you, I cain't waste this fine buck jes' a-totin' a silver tray 'round. Goin' to get me a prime sucker outa Big Pearl an' him. Half Mandingo and part Royal Hausa with a dash o' human blood to lighten it up. Come it's a male and give it sixteen, seventeen years, should fetch more'n three thousand in New Orleans, less'n I keeps it my own self. Won't be no mo' certified Mandingo blood, come 'nother twenty years."

Augusta's lip quivered. She deliberately laid down her fork, dabbed at her mouth with a napkin and addressed Hammond. Her words came slowly and without a trace of anger but there was no mistaking their meaning.

"Mr. Maxwell, I agree that you have every right to run your plantation as you see fit. That is your business. But while I am here and you have told me that I am mistress of this house. If so, I forbid any further mention of the various sordid details of your business when I am present. Yes, Mr. Maxwell, I forbid it." She signaled to Brutus to pull back her chair and started to rise.

"Set down!" Hammond's knife clattered to his plate.

Almost automatically Augusta resumed her seat.

"Yes, Mr. Maxwell, but please remember one thing. I happen to be white, not black. Command me if you will, but please do not use that tone of voice to me again."

"I'll use whatever goddam tone o' voice I wanna use. I'll say any goddam thing I wan' to." Hammond had never had anyone, man or woman, cross him before. His face flushed; his fingers closed into a fist so convulsively that the knuckles became white under the tan.

"Then you are at liberty to do so, Mr. Maxwell." Augusta leaned forward, looking directly through the flickering candle at Hammond. "But you will be saying them to someone else besides myself. There are many things which go on in this house of which I do not approve. I have said nothing heretofore and I shall not mention the matter again. Now, with your daughter safely away in school, I see no reason for me to stay here any longer. Therefore, if you will excuse me, I shall go up to my room and pack."

"You ain' leaving!" Hammond's fist came down so hard on the table that it upset his goblet of water. With an angry sweep of his hand, he swept the glass to the floor. Drumson sopped up the water on the table with a napkin, his hand trembling. He could see that Brutus also was frightened.

"And I suppose you will put me in spancels and chain me to the bedpost to keep me here. It's time you learned, Mr. Maxwell, that there are two classes of people in the world—free and slave—black and white. I happen to be free. And, I happen to be white. It would be well if you learned a few manners and conducted yourself as a white man rather than a Negro."

"Who you callin' a nigger?" Hammond rose so quickly that the heavy chair went over backward. "And who are you? Don' fergit one thin'—even if you ain't a whore, I got you in a whorehouse. Plenty of coverin' goin' on there and 'twan't good honest business like breedin' slaves, either. You ain' so much. I know all 'bout you and that LeSieur fellow. You shore wan't so finicky with him." He had talked himself out of breath. He stood for a moment, glaring at her. "Go if'n you wants to. Falconhurst got 'long 'fore you come—Falconhurst still be here after you go." His fingers drummed on the table. "Git me a toddy, Drumson."

Augusta did not answer him. She bowed her head. Her hand raised the napkin to her face but this time she was not dabbing at her lips. She was crying.

Hammond reached behind him and picked up his chair, pushed it up to the table and sat down slowly. The flush had disappeared from his face. Under his tan he was strangely pale. One hand reached out, hesitatingly to her, across the table.

"Miz 'Gusta, will you accept my apologies? I've said things I didn't mean to say and things I hadn't ought to've said. I don' want you to go."

She did not answer him, nor did she lift her head to look at him. He waited expectantly for her to speak. Drumson set the toddy down beside Hammond and he sipped at it to test the temperature, then drank it in one gulp.

"I had no business talkin' 'bout such things 'fore a lady and you are a lady, Miz 'Gusta. I'm not used to talking with ladies. I'm not used to all this"—his gesture indicated the dining room, the silver candlesticks, the fine linen, the polished mahogany. "Should have stayed over to the old house. What fer I'm tryin' to be anythin' else 'sides a slave trader? Tha's all I am, Miz 'Gusta, and a slave trader's 'bout the lowest thing there is. You've seen 'em—trampin' the roads with a caffle of miz'able slaves taggin' on behind. Well, that's me, 'ceptin' I got a house to live in and don' needs to go traipsin' 'bout the country a-buyin' and a-tradin' my cattle. Miz 'Gusta, ma'am, you onct said this is yo' home. You're right. You made it and it needs you to keep it." He hesitated a long moment. "I needs you too, Miz 'Gusta."

She raised her head and looked at him. The napkin had not wiped all the traces of tears away. She managed a smile —not a very convincing one.

"Thank you, Mr. Maxwell. We have both, I fear, acted rather stupidly and said many things we regret. I cannot accept your apologies unless you accept mine. This is your house and you have a perfect right to discuss your business as you see fit. However, I still think it better that I leave."

"You're not happy here?" His anxiety betrayed itself in his question. "Look, Miz 'Gusta. If'n you says the word, I'll take Drumson away from Big Pearl. I'll take Elvira and Balsam out o' the boys' room."

Drumson caught Brutus' eye. The conversation was not going too well for them.

"No, Mr. Maxwell, I can quite understand why you would want the good blood in Drumson perpetuated. No, let them continue as they are and definitely—most definitely—that is not the reason that impels me to leave. But I cannot stay here any longer under false pretenses. I am not what you think I am. I have imposed upon you."

"No?"

"Yes, I have. The story which Madame Alix told you about me, although it contained certain elements of truth, was not entirely true. I am not Augusta Devereaux—I never was."

"Then who are you?"

"Gussie Delavan—not that the name will mean anything to you. I was born in New Hampshire. One year the Devereaux family came to the White Mountains for the summer. My mother was a chambermaid at the Flume House, a hotel where the Devereaux family were staying. My mother had permission to keep me with her and as Cecile Devereaux and I were about the same age and the only young children at the hotel, we played together every day. That summer my mother ran off with a man and abandoned me. The Devereaux family kindly offered to take care of me as Cecile and I were so fond of each other. When they returned to New Orleans in August, I went with them. Cecile and I were like sisters. Although she had a Negro servant, it was I who took all the care of her, dressed her hair, mended her clothes and waited on her, although my position in the family was not that of a servant. When Mrs. Devereaux was taken ill, I took over the management of the house and after she died, I was in complete charge both of the house in town and the plantation house. It was Cecile who fell in love with Hercule LeSieur. When she could no longer conceal her condition, her father ordered her out of the house. Hercule could not marry her and in desperation he took her to Madame Alix' and naturally I went with her. Cecile died. Having left the Devereaux home with her, I could not return. Madame Alix was very kind to me. She offered me a place in her house but I could not bring myself to accept it. I had always been adept at hairdressing so I took it up as a profession. It is true that I did the hair of all the girls in Madame Alix' and in some other places of like repute."

"Then you ain' . . . ?" Hammond seemed relieved rather than distressed at her deception.

"I never was. But let me continue, Mr. Maxwell. When Madame Alix heard that you were looking for a woman for your plantation and to help with your daughter, she thought of me. She even furnished me with the clothes that I have with the understanding that I would repay her from the money I was to receive from you. Knowing that you had requested a woman with a 'background,' she invented one for me which seemed to satisfy you. That is why I am telling you now that it is not true. I have entered your house under false pretenses and that is why I now feel I should leave."

Very slowly Hammond stood up and walked around behind her chair. He shoved Brutus away and pulled back her chair for her himself and offered her his arm.

"It is not dark outside yet, Miz 'Gusta. Supposin' we take a stroll down the road to look at the new trees which you wanted set out. An' I was a-thinkin' 'bout somethin' else, ma'am. I kin remember back to the days when my mama was a-livin' at the ol' house. Had a flower garden, she did, and right pretty it was. Guess it's time I tho't 'bout plantin' somethin' else 'sides yams and sorghum. If'n I'm a-goin to be a gentleman, a-livin' like a white man, guess a few posies would help matters out." He looked at her and smiled.

"I've always wanted a flower garden." Augusta felt more tears coming but tried to hold them back. "But perhaps more than a flower garden, I've wanted a home."

"Falconhurst's yourn, ma'am, jes' so long as you wants to stay here."

"Thank you, Mr. Maxwell." Augusta adjusted her step to his as they passed out into the hall. He held the front door open for her.

"You've made a right purty place out of it. Proud of it, I am. Proud to have my friends at dinner here when you gets ready to serve 'em. P'rhaps, Miz 'Gusta, havin' done so much with the house you might do somepin' with the master."

She had controlled the tears but still she did not dare to speak.

"Spen' most o' my life with slaves, Miz 'Gusta. Got so I talk and act like one o' them. Perhaps you kin change that."

Drumson heard the big front door close. With Brutus following him, he ran to the big windows of the parlor that looked down the lane to the road, now lined with saplings. The sun had set, leaving an afterglow of pink, purple and rose in the sky. He saw Hammond and Augusta walking down the lane, stopping from time to time to discuss some particular tree which had been set out and was flourishing.

Brutus stepped up beside him to peer out the window.

"Looks mighty lak you soon going to be pleasurin' that Regine wench," he said. "Don' reckon Masta Hammond goin' to be a-needin' her much longer."

## chapter xii

FORMAL INVITATIONS to the dinner, written out in Augusta's copperplate hand in purple ink on fancy gilt-edged notepaper, were mailed. Of late years guests at the old house had been a rare occurrence. Occasionally a trader would arrive with his caffle and be invited to remain overnight, while his slaves were bedded down in the barn. Otherwise, Falconhurst was not known for its hospitality. This was not so when Hammond's mother was still alive. Then there had been considerable entertaining but, of course, at that time Falconhurst had been a cotton plantation and as such had occupied a certain respectability in the social hierarchy of the South. After old Warren Maxwell had abandoned the raising of cotton and substituted the more profitable breeding of slaves, the Maxwells, although attaining an envious place financially, had lost the modicum of social prestige they held through his wife's family. Now Augusta's remark that there was little use in having a fine house if nobody but Hammond and herself were ever to see it had awakened his dormant desire to be accepted socially. The new intimacy he felt between himself and Augusta made him anxious to show off the house, of which he had become very proud, and also Augusta, of whom he felt even prouder. She was, he admitted, a fine-looking woman, an excellent housekeeper, a most efficient manager and, perhaps most important of all, a charming companion. Certainly she was like no other white woman he had ever met before.

And so, the invitations were sent out—to the Holcombs of The Coign, to the Gasaways of Burnt Hill and to the Redfields of Three Oaks, which was the name Doc Redfield had just given to his small plantation. With prosperity the Redfields had acquired a certain amount of respectability, and a recent extended visit to Richmond, where Redfield had gone to purchase slaves, had given them a veneer of social graces. At the last moment, Hammond decided to ask the Rowe sisters—the Misses Ellybee and Abbie Ruth—maiden ladies of eminent respectability who, although impecunious, managed to exist almost entirely on the past glories of their worn-out plantation and their aging slaves. Years ago they had snubbed the socially inferior Maxwells, but with Hammond's widower status and his return from Texas to prosperity their attitude had changed.

There was the problem of putting up the guests, for of course guests for dinner must remain overnight, even the Redfields who lived less than an hour's drive away. The new house had, in addition to Hammond's bedroom on the ground floor, only four large bedrooms on the second floor, not including the small one Regine occupied. In her perplexity as to where to put the guests, Augusta consulted Hammond. She volunteered to move up to the servant's quarters on the third floor for one night but he would not hear of it. He suggested instead that she send Regine up there and use the room herself, thus relinquishing her own room to the Misses Ellybee and Abbie Ruth. Augusta agreed that it would be a good solution, secretly happy that Hammond was willing to forego Regine for at least one night and pleased that the suggestion had come from him without any prompting on her part.

Never before in its short life had the new house been so thoroughly scrubbed, waxed, polished and shined. The household staff was not large enough and some of the field hands were brought in to apply their vigorous muscles to rubbing beeswax and turpentine into the floors and polishing them with powerful arms. Furniture was rubbed with lemon oil until it shone. Carpets were spread with wet sawdust and swept; the crystals of the chandeliers were washed in ammonia water and dried with tissue paper to make them sparkle; silver was polished with whiting; linen was washed and bleached and scented with lavender. Two new girls, Cassandra and Berenice, recommended by Lucretia Borgia, were drilled to replace Balsam and Elvira, whose pregnancies were now apparent, and Lucretia Borgia herself lumbered over from the old house to superintend activities in the kitchen. Ellen, with Hammond's brood by her, was left alone in the old house with only Memnon to look after them. Ellen, who had once charmed Hammond by her fragile octoroon beauty, had ceased to be important to him any more. He suspected that Augusta knew about their relationship but he was not certain. Augusta had never visited the old place and there was a sort of unspoken agreement between them that she would not. The new house was a new way of life for Hammond. He was already regretting much of the old and he did not want to mingle the two.

The day of the dinner dawned crisp and clear with a hint of autumn coolness in the air. Drumson arose early. Because of Augusta's sensitivity about the use of household servants for breeding, Hammond had not as yet assigned Cassie and Berenice to Brutus and Drumson, so Drumson crept out of a lonely bed. During the last week he had been too occupied at the new house to visit Big Pearl, and this morning, as he slipped out from the covers and stood up to put on his clothes, he was aware of the demands of his body. Over a week! Masta Hammond jes' better do somethin' 'bout it pretty soon. Whoo-ee! 'Nother night alone, 'n he wouldn't be able to get his breeches on. He'd jes' have to crawl up the back stairs and give it to that Cassie wench who was always a-switchin' her fat little rump every time she passed him. She was a-wantin' it jes' as bad as he was. He shook Brutus awake and noticed that Brutus was in the same condition. Each time Drumson thought about it during the morning, the same condition appeared, much to his embarrassment.

The guests began to arrive during the afternoon. First came the Holcombs in their shiny new coach with a liveried coachman named Caleb and a valet for Mr. Holcomb, a snobbish young mulatto named Bruno. Caleb was relegated to sharing Ajax' quarters and Bruno, Hammond said, could bed himself down with Drumson, to be on hand to serve Mr. Holcomb night and morning. The Holcombs were a fine-looking couple in their twenties and Mr. Holcomb was not only handsome but most affable. When Drumson took his hat, he laid an appraising hand on Drumson's shoulder. He squeezed his fingers over the firm muscles and remarked what a fine-looking boy he was, inquiring if Hammond had any at Falconhurst for sale, as handsome and as well set up as Drumson.

"Not house servants," Hammond had answered, "but I've got some pretty fine boys. Line 'em up fer you tomorrow if'n you likes."

"Most certainly would. Always interested in getting good boys. Getting harder and harder to find. Like to take about three or four fine Falconhurst boys back with me."

Augusta's introduction and greetings stopped any further discussion of business between Hammond and his guest.

Soon after the Holcombs came the Redfields. Although he was still called "Doc" from his days as a veterinarian when he had treated cattle and slaves, Redfield was now, through marriage, the owner of Three Oaks and his dealings in slaves had increased the Redfield finances to an eminently respectable level. Mrs. Redfield, a gross but motherly woman who had formerly been the community's midwife, was now hardly recognizable in rustling magenta taffeta and a recently acquired Richmond accent. They were both rather awed by the invitation but quite determined to live up to it.

Almost before the Redfields were seated with the Holcombs in the ladies' drawing room, the Rowe sisters arrived in their lumbering old coach. Miss Ellybee, tall, gaunt and dressed in rusty black, was a decided contrast to Miss Abbie Ruth, her younger sister, who twittered up the steps in a froth of laces, ribbands, beads and passementerie, quite ignoring Augusta and having eyes only for Hammond. They were in the midst of their greetings when Lewis Gasaway arrived with his wife Lou-ella, a plain little woman with a tired face and her hair so tightly pulled into a shiny bun that it seemed impossible for her to smile.

It was a strangely assorted, though most convivial company that sat down to dinner in the big dining room that night. The old traditions of gentility of the South were passing, for the Rowe sisters were condescending to sit at the same table with a former veterinarian and his wife; and the haughty Holcombs were breaking bread with Hammond Maxwell, who, as he himself admitted, was little more than a slave trader. But the magnificent table, stretched to its full length, was gleaming with silver, and the big cut-glass epergne in the center was filled with fragrant white roses and lacy fern. The massive silver candelabra sprouted tall wax tapers and the silver champagne buckets contained precious ice which had come overland, packed in sawdust, from Natchez. Each woman's plate was marked with a nosegay of flowers, prettied up with a paper frill, and each man had a boutonniere of a white rose. It was all most elegant, most proper, and altogether in the tradition of gracious hospitality.

Drumson ladled the steaming chicken okra soup from the big silver tureen and Brutus placed the plates before the guests. Lucretia Borgia's roast turkey steamed with succulent fragrance and the roasted hams gave off the spicy aroma of cloves and caramel. There was a plethora of corn ıddings and delicate soufflés, of spiced pickles and jewel-like lies and a seemingly never-ending procession of fruit cakes ıd pound cakes, of Lady Baltimore cakes and pecan pies, ıtil, everyone agreed, nobody could possibly eat another orsel and the ladies arose heavily from their chairs to be epherded across the hall into the ladies' drawing room for eir thimble-sized cups of coffee. The men remained at the ble for their port, although with the exception of Mr. Hol-ımb, they preferred corn. As usual, Hammond was served s toddy.

With the departure of the ladies, the conversation im-ediately turned to the favorite male topic of conversation—aves—and once again Holcomb eyed Drumson appraisingly.

"Mighty fine boy you got there, Mista Maxwell. Well set p, handsome face and nice manners. Sure like to have him."

Hammond smiled to take the edge off his refusal.

"Breedin' him, I am. He's part Royal Hausa with a little ıman blood. Breedin' him to a pure Mandingo I got from ld Mista Wilson who used to live at yo' place onct."

"Make you a good offer on him," Holcomb persisted, while rumson could feel the beads of cold sweat breaking out on s forehead. "Might even throw in my boy Bruno to boot. amned good-looking boy he is, too."

Hammond shook his head and Drumson experienced a elcome respite from fear. "Got some mighty fine boys over the other place to offer you, Mr. Holcomb. Line 'em up fer ıu tomorrow, I will, and you takes yo' pick if'n any interests ıu."

"Even if I can't buy him, I certainly would like to see this ıy here without his clothes. Just a matter of curiosity 'cause e don't see many such fine specimens any more."

"Drumson glad to 'blige you tomorrow. He'll shuck down r you. Huh, Drumson?"

"Yas suh, Masta Hammond, suh." Drumson resented the ct that he would have to undress before Holcomb's prying es.

Holcomb accepted his defeat gracefully and restated his sire to take a number of Falconhurst boys back with him. e too, he said, had become interested in breeding slaves, and it seemed were both Lewis Gasaway and Doc Redfield. All e South had become interested in only one thing—slaves ıd more slaves, breeding them, raising them, selling them ıd buying them.

Redfield signaled to Drumson to fill his glass, and lean across the table to Hammond.

"Knows you won't sell this boy, Ham, but likes migh well to have the loan of him fer a few days. Got me thr wenches gettin' fresh and could use him for studdin'."

"Any time, Doc, any time that Missus Devereaux ca spare him." Hammond looked up and smiled indulgently Drumson, "He purty busy jes' now coverin' my Manding wench but think she catches right soon. Should! He bee a-workin' mighty hard on her. He already got one wenc knocked up so's there's good sap in him." Hammond hes tated and regarded Redfield through narrowed eyelids. H fingers drummed on the table nervously as though he we unwilling to speak the words he was thinking. A sip of h toddy seemed to make up his mind for him.

"Say, Doc, you done any doctorin' lately?"

"Jes' my own critters. Don' do much outside any mo'."

"Used ter do some geldin' didn't you?"

Redfield looked at him in surprise but nodded his affi mation.

"Still got yo' hand in? Think you could nut a boy?"

"Never fergits. Jes' grab his balls in one hand, razor in th other—one swoop and he's nutted. Bleeds a lot but cobwe will stop it. Younger they are, the better."

"Never seen it done." Holcomb was interested.

"Nor I, but shore likes to," Gasaway added.

"Mos' house servants used ter be gelded." Redfield spok with the authority of his profession. "Couldn't have b bucks rampaging through the house, all horny. Don't do so much now 'cause everyone want to breed. Seems though the whole South breedin' niggers today, so they ai a-wastin' their bucks by geldin' 'em." He looked up qui zically at Hammond. "How come you asking, Han Heard you say a hundred times, ain' no buck from Falco hurst ever been gelded. Heard yo' papa say he no use f gelded boys nor gelded horses. Al'ays bragged 'bout it, did."

"Never had one nutted," Hammond added. "Don' believe it. Them boys got little 'nuff to pleasure themselves 'cepti they gets their fun from the wenches. No suh, never believ in it and still don' but I got me a couple of boys here- twins they are—and family up in Tuscaloosa interested buyin' 'em for house servants. Got a lot of daughters in th family and won't consider these boys less'n they gelde

Thinkin' I just might do it. Thinkin' you might do it fer me, Doc."

Redfield's hand shook a little as he lifted his glass.

"Twins you say? 'Members you had twins once before."

"Same ones," Hammond nodded, "older now though. Jes' o't 'em back last time I was in New Orleans." Again his yes narrowed as he looked at Redfield and this time Red-eld gave an almost imperceptible nod of understanding.

"Meg and Alph?" he asked.

"The same," Hammond confirmed.

"Be glad to help you out. If'n you wants, I'll drive over the house tomorrow mornin' whilst you showing yo' boys Mr. Holcomb and get me my instruments. Needs to hone nat razor of mine up sharp. These boys kinda old and 'spects ney carries on a lot. Have to tie 'em up good and have a igger set on they heads. P'rhaps Mista Gasaway and Mista Holcomb'd set some store a-seein' it. Mayhap be in-erestin' to 'em if'n they never seen it before. Kinda amusin' ometimes."

It was Drumson's hands that were shaking now. He looked cross at Brutus, who had returned from serving the ladies, nd their eyes met, poignant with hidden meaning. It was uddenly brought home to them that here, in the midst of ll this elegance and luxury, they were still slaves, chattels, omething to be used or abused, something to be petted or uffed, something to be smiled at one minute and lashed the ext, even to have their manhood stripped from them with a troke of a sharp razor to satisfy an owner's whim.

Drumson regarded the men seated at the table. Holcomb, legant and poised, twirled the stem of the wineglass in his ong, slim fingers with their polished nails. His straw-olored hair was carefully curled and pomaded and the ouge on his cheeks was scarcely perceptible unless one eaned over his shoulder to fill his wineglass. Across the olished mahogany which mirrored the twinkling candle-lames in its red-brown depths, Lewis Gasaway clutched his lass of corn with stubby, broken-nailed fingers, calloused y hard work. His big Adam's apple rose and fell in his hroat as he swallowed, and the deep creases in his face from ose to mouth betokened a life, short as it had been, of self-ndulgence and self-will. He was tall and thin and ugly in is sunburned whiteness. Drumson wondered how he might ook, stripped of his clothes, and marveled at how Mrs. Gas-away could bear his scrawny limbs alongside her in bed.

Doc Redfield's hands were gnarled and liver-spotted with a thin line of black at the edge of his nails. Prosperity had added an expansive pot belly to his narrow-shouldered frame and now, replete from his enormous dinner, he had unfastened the top button of his breeches, so that a roll of fat protruded from under the bottom of his flowered waistcoat. His sparse red whiskers, streaked with gray, were dribbled with corn from one side of his mouth and his few teeth were only blackened stubs. His breath, as Drumson leaned over to refill his glass, was foul.

Drumson regarded his own master, this all-powerful demigod who, by a word or a whim, could condemn two men to a life of miserable impotency. Of all the four at the table, Hammond was by far the finest looking with his crisp blond hair, his clear tanned skin and his wide shoulders, but again Drumson wondered if Regine had ever shuddered because of the malformed leg which was now hidden by his trousers.

These men! These all-powerful white-skinned men! What were they? Ugly, malformed, narrow-shouldered, big-stomached, their scrawny legs covered with long black hairs, and their bulging bellies with the unhealthy whiteness of bullfrogs—all of them puny in their manhood for all their boastful pretensions! Could it be that they were jealous of the strong clean limbs, the satin-smooth skins, the deep muscled chests and the abundant virility of the black men? So jealous of their robust manhood that they had reduced the black man to the status of an animal because they feared him, because they were jealous of him! Could it be that they desired to rob him of his virility because they possessed so little in comparison to his? For the first time since he had come to Falconhurst Drumson was beset by doubts. He almost hated his master—hated him for the words that condemned the luckless Meg and Alph to needless suffering.

Hate his master? Hate this man who gave him a home? And yet by a word this man could deprive him of his home and sell him tomorrow. This man had given him Elvira and Big Pearl, yet he had withheld the one person he wanted, Regine. He gave him food—the same food that he and his guests were eating—yet by a nod of his head he could condemn him to bread and water. But, Drumson consoled himself, Hammond had not deprived him or sold him and there was no indication that he might. After all, why should he worry about what might happen to Meg and Alph tomorrow? It would not make him suffer. No, he couldn't hate this man for there was a bond of loyalty between them. His fingers itched to touch him and he leaned over, prompted by an indistinct sound of knocking on the front door that was almost drowned in the conversation, letting his hand graze ever so slightly Hammond's elbow.

"Hears a knockin' on the front do', Masta Hammond, suh. You a-wishin' me to answer it?"

Hammond lifted his head and listened. He could hear the light tapping of the heavy knocker.

"Better go see."

Drumson walked through the parlor and out into the hall, hearing the hum of the ladies' conversation in the drawing room. As he neared the door, the knocking grew louder and more insistent. He opened it and peered out into the darkness. A tall man, dressed in a rusty black frock coat, soiled gray trousers strapped under scuffed boots and a black felt slouch hat which shaded his face, stood on the threshold.

"Evenin', suh," Drumson greeted him.

"Mista Hammond Maxwell ter home?" The voice was nasal and rasping.

"Mista Maxwell's at dinner, suh."

"Then you kindly begs Mista Maxwell's pardon and asks him if'n he be willin' to spare a moment for a word with Mista 'Zekiel Montgomery, who he knows."

Drumson was undecided whether to permit the man inside or not. He peered beyond him into the darkness and saw the dim outlines of a buckboard with two horses and a group of black faces, visible more through their white teeth and the reflections of light in their eyes than by recognizable outlines. His moment of hesitation was brief, for this was a white man and therefore must be treated with courtesy.

"If'n you please to come inside the do', I'll 'nounce you to Masta Maxwell."

The man sidled in, fumbled with his hat and removed it as Drumson closed the door behind him. A two days' growth of gray stubble cast a shadow over the lower part of the narrow, pockmarked face, and the eyes, small, narrow and deep sunk, glittered like buttons. A dirty finger straightened the soiled shirt collar and adjusted the greasy cravat. The eyes quickly surveyed Drumson.

"Mista Maxwell got himself a new boy 'long with his new house, huh? Ain' seen you the last time I's here. Mighty well set up. Likes to have you myse'f. Step lively and tell yo' master Mista 'Zekiel Montgomery's here."

"Yas suh." Drumson turned on his heel and walked back to the dining room. He defied the man's "step lively" by the slowness of his steps. Once back in the dining room, he hesitated to disturb Hammond. He waited for a lull in the conversation, not daring to interrupt, and when Lewis Gasaway had finished with some anecdote about his plantation—naturally the conversation was still about slaves—Drumson leaned over Hammond's shoulder and whispered the announcement.

"Zeke Montgomery, the slave trader?" Hammond looked to Drumson for confirmation which Drumson was unable to furnish. "Never did care for that man," he addressed the others, "but suppose he wants to bed down for the night. I'll speak to him." He excused himself from his guests and followed Drumson out into the hall where Montgomery was still standing by the door, hat in hand.

"Evenin', Mista Montgomery." Hammond did not extend his hand but attempted to inject some note of cordiality into his greeting.

"Evenin', Mista Maxwell, evenin'. Just a-passin' through and wondered if by chance you might have a couple of boys you wanted to part with. Got me a caffle of 'bout thirty boys—mos' prime stock and'd like to add a few more. Could be you'd like to do some tradin' 'fore I takes 'em to the Forks in the Road."

The "no" which was on the tip of Hammond's tongue was never spoken. He bethought himself of Clees, whose badly scarred rump would add little luster to the Falconhurst reputation were he to be sold at the next sale in New Orleans. Selling him to Montgomery would be a good way to rid himself of the brute. But with his guests demanding his attention, and the lateness of the hour, it was scarcely the time or place to go into the complicated mechanics of selling a slave. Hammond knew that Montgomery's opening gambit of his willingness to buy was only an excuse. The man's main reason for presenting himself was to obtain accommodations for the night. The sale could be concluded in the morning before Redfield returned from his trip to his house to get his instruments.

"Got a man I'm thinkin' 'bout selling, Mista Montgomery. Glad you happened 'long. You jes' might be int'rested. Tell you what. Whyn't you stay overnight and we'll talk 'bout it in the mornin'? Filled up here, we are, with a houseful of company, but they's plenty of room over to the old house. You bin there before."

Montgomery nodded.

"Then take yo' caffle over there for the night. Rouse Memnon and have him bed yo' boys down in the barn and he'll 'commodate you in the house. Yo' boys been fed?"

"Yas suh, Mista Maxwell. Fed 'em 'fore dark come on. Been lookin' for a place to keep 'em overnight and 'preciate yo' offer mightily. Don' like leading a caffle 'long the road at night. Got me some runners in this bunch o' thirty bucks and can't take no chances. They's all spancelled, howsomever, so's they'll be safe in yo' barn. Thanks you mightily I do and will be pleased to git me a Falconhurst nigger come mornin'. Remembers yo' courtesy when I dickers with you. Offers you a good price I will."

"Askin' one. This boy Clees a powerful boy—'bout the biggest and strongest I ever had. Need to get me a good price for him, if'n you're int'rested."

"Shore am and thank you, Mista Maxwell. Ask for Memnon, you say?"

Drumson held the door open for Montgomery to leave. So Clees was to be sold! He had wondered what slave Hammond had in mind and, as always, had been a little fearful that it might be himself. Any mention of a sale was enough to send a chill of fear into a slave's heart. Masters were capricious. One never knew what they had in mind. Now he was not only relieved but happy. Although he had seen little of Clees since their flogging, he knew that the big buck was his enemy. With Clees out of the way, he would feel better at Falconhurst. That goddam Clees would get his comeuppance tomorrow.

Tomorrow! Who-ee! It would be a busy day. First all the plantation slaves would be lined up for Mista Holcomb's inspection and Drumson hoped he'd be on hand to see them. Then Meg and Alph would have their knockers cut off, and Drumson was looking forward to seeing that too. As long as it was not his own which would be severed by the razor. . . . And then that goddam Clees was to be sold and again Drumson hoped he'd be on hand, just to see the expression on Clees' ugly face when he knew that he was going. Who-ee! It would be an exciting day. He had a big parcel of news to relay to the servants in the kitchen. He followed Hammond back to the dining room, only to find that the group was breaking up and the men were coming out to join the ladies. He and Brutus busied themselves setting the dining room to rights, discussing the events of the morrow in whispers. When they entered the kitchen with their trays full of glasses, they were both primed with the news they had to tell.

Clytie was kneading dough at one end of the table; Regine, Cassie and Berenice were still on duty in the upstairs rooms to help the ladies; Bruno, Holcomb's man, was examining his face in a pocket mirror near one of the candles; Ajax was entertaining the visiting coachmen with cups of coffee. Lucretia Borgia had gone up to her temporary room on the third floor.

"Big day here tomorrow," Brutus announced, important with his news.

"Big day any day when we's got company," Clytie grumbled. "Ain' used ter takin' orders no more from that 'Cretia Borgia. She think she mo' mistress than Miz 'Gusta."

"More'n company tomorrow." Drumson too was bursting with news.

"What a-happenin'?" Ajax leaned back in his chair, his fingers in the armholes of his waistcoat which he was wearing to impress the other coachmen.

"Yo' masta," Drumson pointed to Bruno, "he's a-wantin' to see all the Falconhurst boys tomorrow. Says he's goin' to buy hisself some."

"Hopin' he takes me with him," Bruno's face lit up with anticipatory pleasure. "Al'ays likes to see my masta finger new niggers. Pleasures me, it does."

"And then," Brutus was waiting for his chance to contribute, "Masta Hammond he a-goin' to nut them two boys he been a-keepin' in the pen—that Meg and Alph. Says he's a-goin' to sell 'em fer house servants. Whaffor they's got to have they's nuts cut off fer if'n they's going to be house servants?"

"My masta sure never has cut mine off," Bruno simpered. "Pleasures him too much they does."

"What you mean?" Drumson looked at the smoothly rounded, almost girlish face of the yellow boy across the table.

"Keep yo' goddam mouth shet." Caleb, the Holcomb coachman who was sitting beside Ajax, half rose from the table. "Don' pay no 'tention to that biggity yella boy," he said to Drumson. "He new up at de Coign. Masta jes' bo't him down in New Orleans."

"Tells masta on you, you threatenin' me," Bruno bristled. " 'Sides, you jealous cause I won't pleasure you. You stinks, tha's why."

"I tells masta 'bout yo' foolish talk and you gets yo' ass whipped."

Bruno decided it was better to keep still. He drew out a comb and ran it through his long hair, curling his lips at Caleb.

In the awkward silence that followed, Drumson decided to drop another bombshell.

"And . . ." he paused for a second so that his words would have added emphasis, "come mornin', Masta Hammond he a-sellin' Clees. Slave trader done come tonight and stayin' over to the old house. Got himself a caffle of thirty boys in the barn. Masta Hammond says he a-gettin' shet of that Clees tomorrow."

Clytie poised both flour-laden hands in the air. Silently she lowered them, hastily scrubbing her fingers together to remove the bits of dough, then wiping them on her apron. She gathered up the big pan and with a mumbled something about putting it behind the stove to rise, left the group. A moment later Drumson heard the back door close. His first impulse was to run after Clytie but just then there was a series of rings in the pantry. The Holcombs' room was registered on the board, as was Hammond's. Drumson sent the still pouting Bruno upstairs and went himself to Hammond's room. Although Clytie's absence was on his mind, he did not dare mention it to Hammond for he knew he would be punished for discussing plantation business before the other servants. He went through the long preparations of getting his master ready for sleep, helping him off with his boots, massaging his feet and spreading down the bed. As he was hanging Hammond's clothes up in the wardrobe, Regine came into the room. She started to unpin the plain gold brooch which held the fichu around her neck but Hammond stopped her.

"Not tonight, girl. Too many people in the house and yo' mistress she a-sleepin' upstairs. Better go to yo' room up on the third floor."

# chapter xiii

CLYTIE HAD BEEN stunned when she heard Drumson's announcement that Clees was going to be sold the next day. Each year, when the caffle of slaves was made up to go to New Orleans, she had tortured herself with the possibility that either Clees or she herself might be included and that they would be sold separately. Without Clees she would kill herself. Through her intimacy with Lucretia Borgia, she had wheedled her into getting Hammond to let Clees be her man and her infatuation for him had increased over the years. After her training as a cook for the new house, and with Clees managing to ingratiate himself with Hammond, Clytie had been lulled into a false sense of security. As each year's caffle departed without them, she began to feel that neither of them would ever go. Their nights together had been a little more difficult for her to manage after she had moved to the new house, as she and Clees no longer shared a cabin with the other couples. But he knew his way around the plantation and had succeeded, night after night, in not being locked up in the dormitory. Since his whipping, however, things had changed and he was under closer surveillance. That she did not have nightly access to him had been torture for Clytie.

Clees must know the awful news. Yes, he must, if for no other reason than that they might spend this night, which might possibly be their last, together. Clytie felt she must have him once more, one last remembrance to treasure if she were to see him being led off in a caffle come morning, chained in a long black line that stumbled down the lane and out onto the main road behind the slave dealer's buckboard, never to be seen again.

Without any definite plan, she had put the bread dough down behind the stove, glanced nervously at the group of servants still talking at the long table, then had opened the kitchen door as noiselessly as possible and run out. She had plunged headlong down the path, running through the woods and over the bridge to the old house.

The buildings loomed gray out of the darkness, enveloped in a ghostly quiet. Keeping in the shadows, she skirted the corner of the old house and ran down the street of cabins. Now she was glad she remembered where Clees slept in the dormitory, for he had always bragged that he had the coveted top bunk, directly under the barred window at the end of the slave barracks. This position had been a mark of his authority and she hoped he had not been forced to change since his punishment. The side of the barracks was in deep shadow and she groped her way along it, keeping track of the black rectangles that marked the small barred windows. From the inside, she could hear the snores and the rasping breathing of the men. When she reached the window which she felt still marked Clees's bunk she found that, stretch as she might, she could not reach up to it. Then she remembered stumbling over a bench which the men used to sit on in the early evening before they were locked up, and she returned to get it. Of heavy planks, it was so big that she could not lift it, but she managed to drag it along the ground until she had maneuvered it beneath the last window. Then, by holding on to one of the bars with her left hand, and pulling herself up, she could get her elbows on the window sill and stretch her right hand inside. Her fingers groped in the darkness, first touching the rough husk mattress and then, by stretching them to their very limit, the warmth of bare flesh. It was a knee, and as her fingers closed around it, the man inside moved, bringing his body closer. Her hands slid up along the thigh.

"Oh, let it be Clees," she thought.

Her experienced fingers told her that it was, and even in her anxiety to waken him, her fingers were loath to leave their familiar locale. She heard Clees sigh in his sleep. But she must resist the temptation, and her fingers moved to his chest.

"Clees," the fingers tweaked one of his nipples. "Clees, is that you?"

A hand inside clutched hers and as Clees jumped up, her hand slipped down to the hard muscles of his belly. A face appeared between the bars and although she could not distinguish his features in the darkness, she knew it was Clees.

"That you, Clytie?" He was surprised and pleased but shocked to see her. "What you a-doin' here? Wants to get yo'sel' whupped? Cain' get out to pleasure you tonight, Sugar, but don' go. You pleasures me tonight, Sugar, through the window."

"Sh-h-h!" Her fingers extricated themselves from his grip and closed his lips. "Clees man, lissen to me! Jes' now, I heard over to de new house that you's a-goin' to be sold tomorrer."

"Me sold?" Clees was incredulous. "You ain' a-heard right, Sugar. Masta Maxwell not a-sellin' me. I'se his best nigger."

"No you ain'. That uppity Drumson his best nigger now. Shore goin' to sell you tomorrow. Slave dealer comed here tonight. He's a-sleepin' over to the old house. He's got a caffle o' slaves wid him. Masta Hammond done tol' him he sell you to him tomorrer. Wants to get shet of you cause yo' welted."

"Knows 'bout de slave dealer." Clees's head was close to the bars. "Bedded down his caffle in de barn. Got a lot of boys . . . mean bastards, too! They's all spancelled down 'cause they's runners."

"An' somepin' else, Clees man. 'Members those two boys in de pen? Them that Masta Hammond done fotched from N'Orleans? Knows who I mean?"

"That Meg and Alph?"

"Guess so." Clytie had never heard their names.

"He a-sellin' 'em too?"

"No, ain' a-sellin' 'em. Worse'n that. Tomorrow that ol' Doc Redfield, the veternary, he a-cuttin' they's balls off. Druther you be sol', Clees man, than have that happen to you." Her hand went back through the bars once again to confirm Clees' wholeness.

"You sure Masta Maxwell say he a-goin' to sell me?"

"That Drumson say so and he tellin' de truf, I think. That Brute boy, he say so too. Tha's whaffor I come. Want you onct mo' 'fore you goes, Clees man. Can' bear to have you leave 'thouten I have you onct mo'."

"If'n I goes, you goes wid me." Clees had forgotten to whisper.

Clytie put her fingers to his lips again.

"What you mean? Masta ain' a-goin' ter sell me."

"Takes you and runs, I do. We runs together."

"Cain' run. You knows no nigger ever runned and got away. Cain' run 'thouten no pass and besides, how you think you can run? You locked up in here."

"Got to git out. Got me a notion. Got to think. Lissen,

Clytie! Falconhurst slaves no good to help us. Only a few here help us. Mos' o' the res' jes' ignernt niggers that don' know what 'tis to be free an' don' care. Ain' got no guts. Jes' willin' to stay here and be sold, come fall. But tonight we got us 'bout thirty boys down in de barn. Big fellers too 'n mean bastards. Mos' of 'em runners afore. Clytie, sugar, you gets me outa here."

"How'm I gonna do that, Clees. Cain' break dese bars."

"Don' needs to. Lissen! Run down to the carpentry shop. Tain't locked. Inside right behin' de do' when you opens it, you fin' a crowbar. You knows what a crowbar is?"

"Don' rightly."

"Long bar, iron. You gits it. Don' let anyone see you. Bring it back to me. While you gone, I wakes some o' the other boys I think runs wid me. Rex, he go in a minute. He a mustee, whiter'n Masta Maxwell hisself. Lazarus he go, too, and Cobalt. Thinks Big Archer he come along, p'rhaps Dobbin and Amos Jesse. Mebbe Maresfoot. And I kin get that Meg and Alph. If'n they knows they goin' to get nutted tomorrow, they shore run, too."

His face came close to the bars and their lips met.

"Loves you, Clytie sugar." His hand pushed her gently. "You run now. When you comes back, you raps on de bars here quiet like." He waited until he saw her run off into the shadows, then jumped down and walked on silent feet to several bunks, shaking the occupants and waking them, whispering so as not to wake the others.

"You wants to be free?" he asked each one. "Tonight we a-goin' to run but we ain' skulkin' out 'lone. We goin' regular like so's they won' ketch us. We goin' to fix it so nobody follers us. Rex here, he a-goin' to be a slave dealer, a-drivin' he's horses, and we goin' to be his caffle, walkin' long behind he's wagon."

"But Masta Maxwell!"

"Come tomorrer, ain' goin' ter be no Masta Maxwell. We kills him and all de rest. We got thirty men down in de barn and we got them two in de pen. Ain' more'n four men over to the new house 'n a few slaves. We kill de whites and ain' nobody left ter send out no 'larm."

It was no great matter for Clees to convince them. In every group there are malcontents and Clees well knew whom he was talking to. Some of them, at Hammond's orders, he had punished for running. Rex, the big mustee, had always resented his slavery. Tall, white and blond, a typical Teuton despite his colored blood, he had always known that once he could manage his escape, the way would be easy for him. Clees' plan sounded like a good one.

There was a faint tapping on the iron barred window and Clees ran over to it. Clytie pushed the end of the crowbar between the bars and Clees clutched at it.

"You go down de road out to where the lane goes up to de new house. Purty soon Rex, the mustee, come along with a wagon. You waits wid him 'til I comes."

Clytie left and Clees slipped into his clothes and found those he had awakened all dressed and huddled at the door. He had to work by touch only, as it was so dark inside the dormitory he could not see, but he inserted the point of the crowbar in the crack of the door and pried it slowly open. They could hear the hasp of the padlock on the outside slowly tearing out of the wood. With the door open a crack, he was able to lift the heavy wooden bars that were placed there to reinforce the padlock. Some of the slaves were awakened by the noise.

"Wha's a-goin' on?" a voice asked out of the darkness.

Clees brought the heavy crowbar down on the floor.

"Any man what speaks gits his head bashed in. If'n you-all stays in yo' beds, nothin' happens to you. If'n you starts to make trouble, you gits yo'self kilt. We a-leavin'. Them boys who stay in bed and keep they's mouth shut ain' a-goin' git hurt. Won' get whupped, come tomorrow neither."

"I'se a-sleepin'," the voice said. "Ain' heard nothin'. Ain' seen nothin' neither."

Another heave on the crowbar and the door opened. Clees led them all outside and they placed the wooden bars in their iron stanchions, barring the door once again.

They stood in a circle in the shadows, arms around each others' shoulders, heads together while Clees developed his plan.

"Fust off, we goes to the ol' house. That ol' she-goat, 'Cretia Borgia, she over to de new house. Ain' nobody there 'cept ol' Memnon, Miz Ellen and her kids and that slave dealer man. Rex, he a-goin' wid me. We takes care of the slave trader. Rex takes his clothes and dresses up in 'em, so don' tackle him when he come out, all dressed up like a white man. You, Dobbin, you comes along wid us. We do in ol' Memnon. He ol' and he won' put up no fight. Kill de ol' bastard. Archer, you 'n Cobalt ten' to Miz Ellen and the kids. Don' kill 'em. Jes' tie 'em up good. Simeon, you 'n Maresfoot take de crowbar and go over to de pen and loosens them two there. Tell 'em if'n they don' come wid us, they goin' get they's balls cut off'n 'em tomorrow. Pip 'n Dode you go over to de tool house and git all the scythes you kin find. Loosen 'em from the snathes, if'n you has time. Git pitchforks too. Git crowbars, git anything you-all kin kill wid. Micah, you 'n Plutarch go down to de barn 'n harness up de slave man's wagon. Tell them boys down in de barn we'se all a-runnin' and that I come soon with the keys to take off'n they's spancels. Keep in the shadows. Anybody see you, just pop him on de head."

They all separated. Big Archer, Clees' best friend, walked along with him and Rex, Dobbin, Amos Jesse and Cobalt followed. Archer was a big man, small of head but wide of shoulders.

"Whaffor you wants me jes' to tie up that Miz Ellen? Ties her up 'n come mornin', she works hersel' loose and puts the 'larm on us. She a white nigger, all fur de white folks."

"You thinks you better kill her too?"

"Kill her I goin' ter, but fust I'se going to have her. She mos' white. Al'ays hankered fur a white woman. Now goin' to have me one."

"Take too much time."

"Won't take me long. Ain' had no woman fur three months. Masta Hammond ain' give me none."

"Don' make me no diff'rence what you do, jes' so long you ready to leave when we are."

"Kills them kids too. They Masta Maxwell's. They git away and run a-screamin' to the new house. Got to surprise the new house. Cain't have nobody a-runnin' there."

"Jes' you say, Archer." In his desperation, Clees was not particularly concerned with murder. The punishments he had inflicted at Hammond's order had inured him to pain and the flogging he had received had further calloused him. Catlike and stealthy, he crept up the steps of the old house and moved along the gallery without even a board creaking under him. The open kitchen door yawned, showing its gullet of blackness, and he turned and waited for Rex and the others.

"Memnon a-sleepin' in thar." He pointed into the blackness from which issued Memnon's stentorian snores. His lifted hand froze the others into immobility as he entered, slow step after slow step. He could see the dark heap on the pallet and he sensed that Memnon would be lying with his head to the wall. Cautiously he raised the heavy crowbar, then brought it down with all the strength of his arms. The sound of contact was dull and hollow with only the sharp crack of bone and a hiss of air from emptied lungs. Clees waited, anticipating a move from the mound, but none came. His fingers, fumbling in the darkness, encountered the woolly skull and came away with the warm wetness of blood. He had aimed well in the darkness. Memnon's head was cracked open like a watermelon.

"He done fer," Clees whispered. "Whar's Archer?"

"I'se here."

"Miz Ellen, she sleep in the front room cause I's watched her undress some nights. Kids sleep in the next room. Cobalt and Dobbin, you tends to de kids. Archer, you takes Miz Ellen. Rex and me, we find the slave trader." Clees was familiar with the downstairs and he led the way through the dining room into the parlor and opened the door that led upstairs. He paused at the door leading up and grabbed Archer's arm.

"What you goin' to do, do it goddam quick and make no noise. Don' let 'er scream. An' you, Cobalt and Dobbin, make sure them kids don' squawk." He left them at Ellen's door and then, together with Rex, crept down the dark hall. One by one they opened the doors, peering into the half-darkness, listening for a man's breathing. At the end of the hall, a door which opened into a small room disclosed the sounds of an occupant—a regular, hoarse breathing. Clees entered, the crowbar raised, but he had no sooner crossed the threshold when the man sat up in the bed.

"Who there?" he asked. He did not seem to be particularly frightened and his voice did not quaver. He probably thought that it was Memnon. Clees stopped, holding Rex back with one hand. He kept quiet, not answering Montgomery's question.

They could see Montgomery moving on the bed and the dim motions of his hand as he reached out to the small table beside the bed. Suddenly there was a flicker of light from a tinder box and Montgomery applied it to the candle which stood on the table. As the flame caught, he blinked, then opened his eyes to see the two men standing just inside the door.

"What you niggers want?" There was fear in his voice now.

Clees advanced with the crowbar and Montgomery knew what they wanted. He knew they were going to kill him. His mouth opened, showing the snags of teeth in his lower jaw. He tried to scream but with a sudden lunge, Clees was upon him, belaboring him with the heavy bar. With the full strength of his arms he brought it down again and again and again. The white sheets became encrimsoned and the mass on the bed that had been a man lost all human resemblance.

Clees reached under the bloody pillow and found what he had expected to be there, a long-barreled pistol. He pointed to the worn valise on the floor.

"If'n he got this, mus' be powder and bullets thar." Rex rummaged in the valise and found them.

"Shuck yo'self down, boy, and git yo'self in them clothes." Clees indicated the rusty black suit that hung over the back of a chair. "Reach in de pockets and see if'n you kin find de key for de spancels that locks up dem boys in de stable."

Rex shed his pants on the floor and reached for the suit. Before he put it on, he felt in the pockets and produced a bunch of keys which he handed to Clees. "These them?"

From the front of the house came a muted scream. Then silence again.

"Archer a-gettin' his, I reckon," Clees laughed.

Rex dressed as quickly as possible in the unaccustomed clothes, experiencing some difficulty in pulling on the boots. When he had dressed, even to the slouch hat, Clees pulled him back beside the door. Steps were coming down the hall but it was only Big Archer with Cobalt and Dobbin.

"They gone," Archer said.

" 'n Archer, he didn't give us no chance. Pleasured her his-self and then killed her while we a-doin' in de kids. Wanted her myself, I did." Cobalt glared at Archer.

"Ain' got no time. You-all gits plenty of pleasurin' onct we free. White women over to de new house, too. Takes 'em if'n you wants 'fore we kills 'em." Clees herded them out into the hall. He turned to look at the shapeless mass on the bed, leaned over and spat on it.

"Go ahead, white man! Go ahead and buy me tomorrow if'n you wants." He picked up the burning candle and threw it in the midst of the bloody sheets. He waited a moment to see that it caught. When the cornhusk mattress was blazing, he backed out of the room. Together the four of them ran down the hall and out of the house.

Now they were bolder. There was nobody nearer than the

new house to see them, and there was only one light in the new house across the little valley. That was high up on the third floor. The moon had come up and although it was only a last quarter-moon, it shed sufficient light for them to see where they were going. As they passed Lucy's cabin, the door opened. Big Pearl stuck her head out and quickly withdrew it.

Clees found the doors of the barn open. Montgomery's slaves were all awake, milling around, restive at their spancelled restraint. When Clees entered, they besieged him with questions.

"We a-goin' to get outa here?"

"Wha's happening, nigger? Whar's that old bastard, Masta Montgomery?"

"You men wants free?" Clees asked them.

"Sho' wan's it, nigger."

"Then you-all do like I says. I'm de overseer here now." Clees was leaving no doubt about his authority.

"We follows you."

In the wan light the moon let in through the open door they could see Rex, and the sight of a white man in white man's clothes silenced them.

"He a nigger, jes' like you-all, but he a mustee. He a-goin' to be yo' new masta 'cause he looks white and whilst we on de road, he's a-goin' to be de slave trader. You pertends to min' him but don' forgit, he's a-takin' he's orders from me. I rides wid him on de wagon and you-all come 'long, spancelled behind. That way nobody thinks we's a-runnin'. Thinks we jes' 'nother slave trader 'n he's caffle on de road. Unnerstand?"

They all voiced their assent.

Four more figures appeared in the doorway. Simeon and Maresfoot led Meg and Alph into the circle of light. Meg stepped up, facing Clees.

"Who're you, big boy? Tell me what's a-happenin' here. Wha's all this talk 'bout me and Alph gettin' gelded tomorrow?"

"I'se Clees. Masta Maxwell done goin' ter sell me tomorrow, he says, and says too he goin' have that vet come over ter cut yo' balls off. Knows it's true. My wench Clytie she cook over to the new house. She tells me. You wants to run wid us o' you wants to stay here 'n get yo'sel's nutted. But," Clees lifted the crowbar, "if'n you stays, you stays a dead men. Ain' havin' nobody a-runnin' to the new house, tellin' on us."

"We goes wid you." Meg answered for himself and Alph. "You a-knowin' how to shoot that gun?" He pointed to the pistol in Clees' belt.

"Kin shoot it but don' know how to load it," Clees answered.

"I do," Meg asserted, "if'n you wants to let me have it."

Clees handed the pistol over.

"Any corn here?" Alph questioned.

Clees pointed to a rough cupboard, locked with a padlock. His crowbar quickly wrenched it off and it disclosed a line of jugs on the shelves. He handed one to Alph who drank long and then passed it to the row of Montgomery's slaves who were standing in line, waiting for Rex to remove their spancels. All drank deeply. Pip and Dode arrived at the barn, wheeling a handcart, piled high with farm tools. Clees gathered up the spancels from the floor and threw them in the back of the covered wagon which had already been harnessed with Montgomery's horses. His mind had gone far beyond the present. He envisioned himself and Rex and Clytie in the wagon, with the long line of spancelled slaves behind. When he got far enough away from Falconhurst, he'd start selling off the slaves.

As each man was unchained he moved out from the barn and grabbed a scythe blade, a crowbar, a pitchfork, a sickle, a sledge-hammer or some other weapon. When they were all loose, Clees held up his hand for silence.

"Now, we goes to de new house. Got to git us rid of all of 'em over there, white folks and niggers too. Goin' to be harder but we's got 'bout forty men and not more'n ten of 'em, white and niggers together. Likely they got guns and we got only one so we'll have to rush 'em."

The last jug of corn was passing down the line and as it was handed up to Rex, on the wagon seat, Clees knocked it to the ground.

"Ain' havin' you drunk. Aims to have you keepin' yo' wits 'bout you. Drive dis wagon down to whure the lane comes down from de new house. My wench waitin' for you there. We comes soon. Soon's we arrive, we spancel all dese boys 'hind de wagon and start out. Heads north. Hear tell they's free country up there. Mayhap we gets there in a day or two. Nobody goin' to pay no 'tention to a slave trader and his caffle goin' 'long the roads. Come on boys."

They started for the new house. The last gleam of light on the third floor was now out. No longer did they move slowly and furtively, seeking the shadows. Instead they marched with heads held high and backs straight. The flames from the old house were now mounting, and the bright light gilded the blades of the scythes. The slaves from the cabins were standing in little knots on their doorsteps. There was nobody to tell them what to do and they were unable to think for themselves. They merely stood, huddled together dumbly like sheep. A shout arose from the men's barracks and they could hear the men inside, frightened of the fire, beating on the door. The long line plunged from the moonlight into the darkness of the woods by the creek. A figure glided from Lucy's cabin, and crept along seeking cover under the trees, running with long determined steps but keeping out of sight of the men.

# chapter xiv

When Drumson had finished his chores for Hammond, he made his customary rounds of the house, snuffing the candles, bolting the outside doors, closing the windows on the ground floor and doing a superficial tidying-up. He, along with Brutus and the rest of the household servants, would be up again at dawn, giving the entire house a final polish so that when the white folks arose, everything would once again be clean, sparkling and in order. He was fatigued—it had been a long day—but he was not sleepy. He wondered if he dared skip out of the house and leg it down the path to Big Pearl. The idea excited him and he was half tempted to try it until he returned to the kitchen and realized that Clytie had already skipped out. He wondered if she had returned. Already he was regretting his rashness in spilling the news about Clees. He knew he was never supposed to divulge any of the plantation business he might overhear to the other servants but it was a rule seldom observed. The life of the white people in the big house was always the principal item of conversation in the kitchen.

But in this matter of Clees, he realized, he should have kept his mouth shut. Naturally Clytie had gone as fast as her legs would carry her to tell Clees. Well, there was nothing he could do about it now except to hope that neither would be found out and place the blame on him. He consoled himself that there was nothing either Clytie or Clees could do about the matter. If Hammond had decided to sell the big buck, he would be sold regardless of Clytie's warnings. Her telling Clees would make little difference. Still, Drumson decided, it would not be wise for him to be absent from the house, too. Big Pearl would have to wait until some other time.

Soft footsteps were approaching through the pantry and although he was not expecting Clytie from that direction, he stood waiting, holding the one candle which he had not extinguished. But it was not Clytie. It was the fellow Bruno, Holcomb's body servant, smirking and looking mighty pleased with himself.

Drumson had felt an instinctive dislike for Bruno from the moment he first saw him, and he had resented Hammond's directing that the boy bed down with him. This Bruno boy was far too pretty to be a man. His face had the rounded cheeks, the bee-stung mouth and the long lashes of a girl, veiling deep brown eyes as lambently luminous as those of a cow. His pale ivory skin glowed with an underlying pinkness that made him appear to be continually blushing. Long black hair, falling in curling locks to cover his ears and banged straight across his brow, gave him the appearance of wearing a curious sort of a cap. His body was as lithe as an adder's and he crossed the kitchen floor as though his feet barely touched the scrubbed boards.

"I'se a-sleepin' wid you tonight, man." His smile to Drumson was as inviting as though he himself were playing the host. "Where we-all a-sleepin', man?"

"Upstairs." Drumson pointed to the stairs which led up from the kitchen. "Not much time for sleepin' tonight. Got to git ourse'ves up early in the morning, come four o'clock. Mos' midnight now." He lifted the candlestick to light Bruno up the stairs. Brutus was sleeping, sprawled across the bed which he had so recently shared with Balsam. Neither the light nor the entrance of the two fellows disturbed him and he did not awake even when Bruno tiptoed to the edge of his bed and looked him over carefully.

"Glad I'se a-sleepin' wid you, man, 'stead of him," Bruno snickered, holding his hand in front of his face and moving his shoulders as though it were some little joke he and Drumson shared together.

Drumson did not answer him but pointed to the side of his bed towards the wall.

"You sleeps on the inside," he said as he started to undress.

Bruno made short work of his own undressing. He shucked off his shirt, pants, socks and slippers in an untidy pile on the floor and jumped up on the bed, staring at Drumson as he slowly removed his clothes, folding them carefully and placing them over a chair. Drumson caught Bruno's eyes appraising his body and he suddenly felt embarrassed. There was something about this boy he could not understand. Brutus had never looked at him this way and neither had any other male.

Quickly he blew out the candle and sank down on the bed. A reek of perfume, mingled with musk from his companion's body, lay heavy on the air, permeating the room with an odor that was sensuous and at the same time repellent. Drumson felt awkward and ill at ease but he punched his thin pillow into shape, stretched his long legs down straight and then turned over on his side with his back to Bruno, his body balanced on the edge of the mattress. The sleep he sought did not come and the silence in the room seemed pregnant with unspoken words and disturbing desires. The strangeness of having another person's body, warm and odorous, in his bed, and to know it was a body he could not touch, kept him from slipping off into sleep. He had a strange desire to reach out and touch this man beside him, yet the thought of touching his flesh was repugnant. The rustle of the husks as Bruno edged closer, the warmth of his breathing on Drumson's back, the overpowering scent of his body, the very nearness of him which promised so much and yet denied the very release Drumson was seeking, kept him awake, staring wide-eyed into the darkness. He was missing Elvira; he was missing his afternoon excursions to Lucy's cabin and the frantic wrestling with Big Pearl in the sun-striped darkness. Who-ee! The next time he saw Big Pearl she would have nothing to complain of.

His side ached from the cord that pressed through the edge of the mattress and he yearned to turn over onto his other side, but he did not want to face Bruno who he knew was not sleeping. For so long he had slept on his other side, with Elvira in his arms, it seemed unnatural to be facing the outside of the bed, listening to Brutus' snores and the soft breathing of Bruno. Perhaps if he were to change beds and go over with Brutus he would feel more comfortable. He could see, in the dim light, the black form of Brutus sprawled diagonally across the bed. If he were to wake him now, it would be difficult to explain, on the morrow, his reason for changing and his inexplicable dislike of this Bruno fellow. Evidently his tension was transferred to Bruno for he could feel a certain rhythmical movement from the other and feel his breath even closer on his back. Bruno's movements quieted and his breath came more naturally and Drumson, unable to stay longer on his side, eased himself over on his back, staring at the ceiling, wide awake.

Then he felt the warmth of Bruno's fingers as they slid along under the sheet and came to rest on his side, barely touching, yet evident. For a moment the fingers remained still, as if they feared to be brushed off, then, gathering courage, they advanced, creeping up his thigh. Drumson stiffened, his muscles taut, his mind wary, but the fingers continued their slow advance. Without having been rebuffed, they became bolder and abandoned their furtive timidity. They clutched, and although their grasp was unwelcome, at the same time it was strangely satisfying. Drumson took a long breath. The warm grasp of the hand was so rapturous, yet unwanted. He resented the motion that hand was making but he was powerless to stop it for it produced the very ecstasy he had been seeking. And yet the ecstasy itself was odious. He suffered it to continue another long minute then, fearful of results, he reached down and grabbed the supple hand and flung it away.

"What you think you doin'?" His whisper was not loud enough to wake Brutus and strangely enough, he was unable to put into it the anger he thought he felt.

Bruno's lips nuzzled his ear, and Drumson felt the warm wet tip of Bruno's tongue trace a quivering path across his cheek. He moved his head slightly so it would not touch his mouth.

"Don' yo' want me to pleasure yo', man?" The lisping words came softly, "Kin do it fine. Masta says I better'n any wench. Been hopin' all day to pleasure yo'. Don' get de chance to pleasure black boys much. Masta don' 'low me."

Drumson struggled to find courage to push the boy away. He did not know whether he wanted to throttle him or clasp him tightly in his arms.

"Go to sleep, boy. You gettin' me all 'cited."

The hand returned and for another small moment, Drumson suffered it, through sheer inability to push it away.

"See, you likes it. You goin' to like me too. You goin' to 'joy ever'thin'." Bruno's soft words were insistent.

Drumson knew the moment had come. If he remained another second he would succumb and something inside himself fought against his surrender. His hand pushed the soft fingers away and with a leap he was out of bed and onto the floor.

"Whar you a-goin'?" Bruno whimpered. "Come back."

"Don' know whar I a-goin' but ain' a-stayin' here. Ain' a-lettin' you slobber over me. Ain' a-lettin' no man do those thin's. Girl is all right but man's different. Howsomever," he smiled into the darkness, "if'n I was a-goin' to let a man do sech thin's, think I'd let you." Drumson reached out in the darkness and found his pants. He drew them on and sought with his feet to locate his slippers. A glance at Brutus' bed showed that he was still sleeping.

"Come back, man. Come back," Bruno was pleading.

"Ain' comin'." Drumson could laugh now that he had escaped from Bruno's embraces. A plan had already formulated in his mind which offered far more than Bruno's synthetic pleasuring. He could afford to offer a palliative to the boy he was leaving.

"Look, Bruno, try Brute here. He's a-sleepin' and he think you his li'l Balsam come back."

"Don' like him so much's you. Come back, man?"

"Ain' a-trustin' myse'f 'gain," Drumson laughed as he stepped out on the stairs and closed the door.

"Regine!" Without knowing it, he spoke her name out loud. She was what he needed—not Elvira and not Big Pearl and certainly not the unnatural embraces of Bruno which had already excited him to the point where he had to find someone. Regine! Tonight of all nights he could have her. Why had he wasted time on Bruno? She was alone, on the floor above him. He slipped off his shoes and took the stairs two at a time.

It was hot and breathless in the long corridor that ran the length of the third floor. All the doors along it were closed. Hammond's orders were strict ones. It was he who chose his slaves' bed companions, not they themselves, and few dared to disobey him. Drumson realized the punishment he would receive were it to become known he had been with Regine, Hammond's own bed woman, would be far more brutal than it would be for taking any other wench. But no threats of future punishment could deter him now from quenching that desire which his own thoughts and Bruno's soft fingers had engendered.

His hand, in the darkness, counted the doors as he went along the hall. Clytie and Lucretia Borgia were in this room. Had Clytie returned? He opened the door a crack and could see in the moonlight from the window that her bed was still whitely spread and unoccupied. Lucretia was flat on her back, a shapeless black mass, snoring loudly. Drumson backed away and closed the door. He knew that Clytie and Clees must be together somewhere and the mental image of what they might be doing further inflamed him. He passed the room of Cassie and Berenice. There was another place where he would be welcome but neither of them were what he desired. Jackson's room! He should have put Bruno in with Jackson.

The next door was Regine's. He lifted the latch so that it made only a faint sound as the metal scraped against the wood. The door pushed inward with a sharp creak of the hinges and he stood breathless for a moment, frozen into immobility. Nothing stirred and he entered, closing the door behind him and latching it. The window of the room was open wide and he could hear the noise of night insects outside and the booming of a bullfrog down in the creek. But the sound he listened for was the regular breathing of the girl on the bed. The light from the window showed her black hair, spread out in a wide circle over the pillow. The privacy and the heat had prompted her to dispense with any nightgown, and as Drumson took two soundless steps across the room, he could see her body, shadowed and darker against the sheet. She was sleeping soundly and he had not awakened her. She was lying on her back, one arm upflung over the pillow and covered with the murky blackness of her hair.

His knees creaked as he knelt on the floor beside the low cot and his hands poised over her, hesitating to wake her for fear she might cry out. There was a way to avoid that. He lowered his lips to hers to stifle any cry that she might make, and then let his hands touch her. She stirred and awoke and would have sat up, but the pressure of his lips and hands held her down.

"Don' be fearsome, Regine. It's Drumson. If'n you don' wan' me to stay, I go. But I hopes you do wan' me. I wan' you so much, Regine honey."

She turned her head to free her mouth.

"Drumson?"

"It's me, Regine."

"Oh, Drumson!" Her arms encircled his head and pulled him closer. He slid out of his trousers, easing himself up beside her without his lips leaving hers.

All that he had dreamed about for so long was actually happening, yet it seemed as strange and unreal as any dream. Was this soft, pliant, full-breasted woman under him the gentle, soft-spoken Regine of the downcast eyes? How different she was, as she writhed against him, overpowering him more completely than the Amazonian onslaughts of Big Pearl.

Never before had he felt the fire coursing through his veins with such fierce burning. He felt that he was going to faint from its very fierceness, only to be brought back from the brink of losing his senses to a newer intensity. Could this be the gentle Regine, this she-animal who shrank and clutched, moaned and cried, twined herself around him in one moment, only to withdraw in order to lead him on to greater abandon? This was not Regine, not one woman alone, but one woman multiplied into all the women of the world and each one of them a deadly tropical flower that opened wide its moist petals to ensnare him, and then closed around him, imprisoning him within their lush embrace, taking from him everything that he possessed and then giving it back to him in a round of ecstatic tortures that stretched on into an orgiastic eternity.

Even when the last gasping cry of complete and utter surrender had been wrung from his lips, she was unwilling to abandon him. Her mouth, fingers, hands, lips and cavernous depths united to produce another shrieking climax until, when every nerve fiber had been outraged and all his senses twisted into tight knots of unendurable rapture, his every sense again exploded in a cataclysmic deluge of molten fire that seared his eyes, lit up the walls and ceiling with scarlet flames, gilded her body and his with flickering tongues of unendurable heat and left him panting in a vermilion void of unreality.

Gradually the air came back into his strained lungs and he tried to orient himself in this strangely bright room, where the moaning woman, still writhing convulsively beside him, was tinged with a strange scarlet glow. Where was he? Had he passed in some strange journey of unearthly passion into an inferno where flames reached out to lick at his very body? With a gasp, he struggled to raise himself to his elbow but Regine pulled him back.

"My man," she panted in his ear. "If you only knew how I wanted you and how I still want you."

The strange light continued. It was not his imagination. The fire his flesh had fed on had become a strange reality, flickering and pulsating on the walls. The entire window was filled with a strange light which flickered and danced into the room. He raised her face to his, kissed her lightly and sprang out of bed. Over the treetops he could see a blazing inferno that sent streamers of flame high into the black sky.

"Fire!"

## chapter xv

DRUMSON RAN TO THE WINDOW. The night sky was bright with color and, high over the treetops, flames were rising in giant tongues of orange and scarlet, licking at the blackness of the sky and then cascading down in showers of golden sparks. Frozen in inarticulate terror, Drumson continued to stare out of the window, trying to gather his thoughts into some form of action.

Fire! The realization unfroze him and he ran to the door, frantic now. With his finger on the latch, he became conscious of his nakedness and snatched his pants from the floor, marveling for an instant how red-skinned his body was from the reflected light.

"Quick, Regine, dress!" He shocked her from her apathy, but she could only grab the hand that was shaking her and cover it with kisses. "Rouse all de servants on dis floor. Tell Merc or Jupe run out to de barn and git the men there. I'll go to Masta Hammond." He forgot to fasten the button on the waistband of his pants and now as he started down the stairs, the pants fell and tripped him. The second-floor landing broke his fall and as he stood up, dazed, to gather his trousers around him, he took another step and stumbled over the shoes he had left on the landing. He pushed open the door to his own room, which was also lit up by the fire, and noticed that Bruno had taken his suggestion and was now bedded with Brutus.

"Fire! Fire!" he cried. He shook them both, although it was needless for they were both awake, though quite oblivious to the strange light in the room.

Without waiting for them to get up, he rushed down the stairs and through the main house to Hammond's room. The door was bolted on the inside. His fists beat a frenzied tattoo on the panels.

"Masta Hammond, Masta Hammond," he screamed. "It's me, Drumson. Get up! Fire, Masta Hammond, fire!"

He could hear hasty footsteps in the room, footsteps that seemed too light for a man. He heard the bolt inside being slipped back. Then the door flew open under his pounding, with such force that it hit Hammond on the forehead, nearly stunning him.

"You goddam nigger son of a bitch. What you mean a-poundin' on the do' fer?" It was dark in Hammond's room because the shutters, despite the heat, were all tightly closed, but some of the brightness filtered in around the edges, enough so that Drumson could see a froth of white flounces scurrying up the stairs.

Miss Augusta! the thought flashed across his mind.

"Open de shutters, Masta Hammond. Somethin' a-burnin' over to de ol' house. Fire goin' up in de sky."

Hammond hurried to the windows. One look told him the story. In the light Drumson saw Hammond's nightshirt, a pool of white on the floor. Grabbing up his master's trousers he handed them to him, then dashed up the stairs to the room above where he found Augusta tying the belt of her dressing gown.

"Fire, Miz 'Gusta," he cried, and ran on through the house to awaken the guests. Each of the Rowe sisters sat bolt upright in bed, believing the end of the world had come when they saw a half naked Negro running through their room yelling "fire." He roused the Holcombs, the Gasaways and the Redfields and then returned to the lower floor. Hammond was in the kitchen and all the servants were down, except Clytie. Ajax, Caleb, the Holcomb coachman and the old man who drove for the Rowe sisters were in from the barn.

"Get all the kettles, buckets and big pans out and we'll take 'em over to the old house," Hammond ordered. "Don' jes' know what we kin do. That ol' house made of pine and she go up like tinder. Shore hope Ellen and the kids got out. Hope it don' spread to the cabins and the sheds. Here," he fumbled in his pocket and withdrew a key which he threw to Brute. "Run over and unlock the sheds and let the boys and girls out. Tell 'em we'll all be over in a minute."

He was interrupted by a knocking on the outside kitchen door. The pounding was enough to break the door down and Drumson ran to open it. It was Big Pearl. She paused on the step outside, not daring to enter, and she was panting so it was almost impossible for her to speak. Her eyes were rolling wildly and she leaned against the side of the door, trying to support herself.

"Don' go out, Masta Hammond. Don' go out. They's a-comin' here. They's a-goin' to kill you, Masta Hammond."

"Who's a-comin'? Who's a-goin' to kill me?" Hammond helped Drumson pull her inside.

"Clees, Masta Hammond." Big Pearl was screaming in her hysteria. "Clees and that Meg and Alph and them niggers what come las' night. Some o' our boys too. They got pitchforks and they on they way over here. Heard 'em I did. Lucy say fer me to run over here to tell you. Lucy said fer you not to leave de house."

Lewis Gasaway, Doc Redfield and Holcomb came into the kitchen.

"Wha's happenin', Ham?" Redfield spoke.

"Don' jes' know. Big Pearl here say the niggers are loose. Clees a-leadin' a uprise. Don' know how many of my boys are in on it, maybe all of 'em, maybe none but those Montgomery niggers are loose. They're bad 'uns. Old house a-burnin' but cain' do nothin' to save it." He turned back to Big Pearl.

"See anythin' of Miz Ellen and the kids?"

It set her off into another fit of screaming and now Lucretia Borgia added her high-pitched wails.

"Ain' seen 'em, ain' seen hide nor hair of 'em. They's burnt, Masta Hammond. Burnt to a crisp." A new series of hysterics had been touched off and now all the women in the kitchen were wailing.

Hammond saw Augusta coming through the doorway, followed by Lou-ella Gasaway.

"For God's sakes, get these screaming women out o' here and get 'em upstairs. Cain' do nothin' in this bedlam."

Augusta managed to slap Lucretia Borgia into sensibility and between the two of them they led Big Pearl away. The rest of the women followed and as Regine passed Drumson, she laid a surreptitious hand on his and squeezed hard.

In the momentary lull of quiet that followed they heard a distant rumble of voices.

"Wha's that?" Ajax held up a warning hand.

Drumson opened the back door a crack and listened. From down in the hollow that separated the two houses, he could hear a shouting that swelled in volume. It sounded like the voices of a hundred men approaching, and as it increased in volume he could distinguish individual words that rose above the tumult.

"Kill 'em! Kill the white bastards! Don' kill de wimmin. I wants me a white woman."

As he stood in the open door listening, he could discern the heads of the shouting men, appearing now over the rise, and then their running forms, silhouetted against the bright light. He slammed the door shut and bolted it.

"They's comin', Masta Hammond. They's comin'."

"You Brute, and you Ajax! Merc, Jupe! You boy"—he pointed to Bruno—"and you otherns. Pile furniture up agin all the windows." Hammond stepped to the door but Drumson tried to halt him.

"Don' go out, Masta Hammond, don' go out."

"Ain' a-goin', boy. Just goin' to take a peek."

The slaves had massed on the edge of the woods. Shouts were still to be heard but they had stopped their advance. Evidently they had halted for some sort of a council. They were too far away to be seen plainly and if it had not been for the light from the burning house, they would have been invisible. Hammond was relieved to see that there were no flickering torches among them. Evidently they had forgotten to light them from the flames of the old house or had not thought them necessary. He knew that none of them had tinderboxes and without torches there would be little danger of the house burning. It had been his greatest worry—that the house would be turned into a blazing inferno, driving them out into the open where they would be easily overcome by sheer force of numbers.

He had seen all he wanted to see. He knew that he and his guests were in great danger. Slave uprisings were rare indeed but there had been a few instances when they had burned the big house, killed all the whites, and scattered, seeking hiding places in the swamps or mountains. Hammond could not bring himself to believe that his own slaves were all taking part in the revolt. He knew himself to be admired and respected if not actually loved by most of them, but he did not discount the fact that the seeds of rebellion found fertile soil in any slave's mind. He turned to the group of white men who had remained in the kitchen.

"Any of you men got any side arms? All I got here is a brace of pistols. Other guns over to the ol' house. Probably those black bastards found 'em but don' think any of 'em kin shoot. Don' think they ever had a gun in they hands afore."

"Never thought to bring no gun sech a little ways," Gasaway excused himself.

"Nor I," Doc Redfield added.

"Brought a brace of pistols, but they're out in my coach," Holcomb said.

"If'n them varmints armed, and if'n any of Montgomery's men knows how to shoot, we ain' got much of a chance to hold this place 'ginst 'em with only four pistols. Lewis, looks like it all depends on you." Hammond singled out Lewis Gasaway.

"What you mean, Ham?"

"Think you kin sneak out to the barn and get a horse and then ride to Benson?"

"Think I kin."

"Then Ajax, you goes with him. Help him saddle. Then you look in Holcomb's coach and get his brace of pistols and bring 'em back. That'll give us four."

Bruno stepped forward from the dark shadows of the wall to stand in front of his master.

"Them pistols hidden in de coach, Masta Holcomb, suh Hidden in de little secret cupboard 'hind de seat. Ajax he never fin' 'em. Better let me go with 'im. I finds 'em fast and gets 'em back to the house afore Ajax finish saddlin' the horse."

"All right for Bruno to go?" Holcomb recognized Hammond as in command.

"Kin you trus' him?" Hammond said. "Won' take the guns and run wid 'em?"

"Trust him, I do. Bruno's a good boy. Can we trust you, Bruno?"

"You knows you kin, Masta Holcomb, suh. Ain' a-wantin to go with them niggers."

"I'd let him go, Maxwell, and besides, we'll need him You wouldn't think it to look at him but that boy's a crack shot. His other master taught him. Kin pick the eyes out of a squirrel, never knew him to miss."

Hammond nodded. "Put out the candle."

With the room in darkness, he slowly opened the door and looked out. He saw nothing nearer than the distant groups and even they were becoming more indistinct as the flames of the old house were dying down. "Now, Lewis, scrouch down and run for the barn. Ajax and Bruno will be behind you. Ride across the fields till you gets to the road. That way the barn will be behind you and the niggers. Wake every-one along the road and tell all the men folks to git here as soon as possible. Tell 'em to wait down at the gates so's they n come in a body. When you gits to Benson, ring the fire ll. Git as many as you kin. God knows how many we got ainst us. And hurry, man." He gave Gasaway a slight push he bent low to run to the barn, then pushed Ajax and uno out after him. He kept the door open a crack until saw all three gain the barn in safety and then a figure nning out from the barn. Bruno reached the back door fely with Holcomb's pistols. In a few moments a horse d rider came out and galloped down across the field, but Ajax started back to the house, another figure appeared t of the darkness running towards him.

Bruno, without even asking Hammond's permission, shed the door open wide and knelt on the threshold.

"Come on, Ajax," Hammond yelled. "Look out for the stard behin' you." He could see a flash of light glitter om the scythe blade in the man's hand.

Bruno fired. The pursuer dropped in his tracks. Hamond reached down, grabbed the boy by the shoulders and lled him back, waited for Ajax to get inside, then slammed e door and bolted it.

"Good boy. You got that one. Sorry I doubted you. You eps that gun and guards the back do.' Got more powder d shot?"

Bruno was reloading in the darkness and when he had fined, he pushed a silver powder horn and shot into Hamond's hand. Hammond summoned them all, except Bruno, to the pantry and there lit a candle. He handed Holcomb e other of the two pistols, gave one of his own to Redfield d retained the third.

"Know how to load, Drumson?"

"Don' know, Masta Hammond, suh."

Hammond showed him how to put the powder in, how to e the little ramrod, how to insert the ball, and cock it.

"If'n I fires, I hand it to you to reload. You keep 'hind me. olcomb, you take this side of the house. Doc, you goes to e other. That boy guards the back and I takes the front. ach one of you get some of my boys to watch with you. ome 'long, Drumson." Hammond walked out into the front ll, Drumson behind him. He heard the swish of skirts scending the staircase and turned to look at Augusta. She me up to Hammond and laid a hand on his arm. He could e Lucretia Borgia's wide face behind her.

"Go back upstairs," he whispered. "You're safer up there d 'sides," he added, remembering her punctiliousness, "you got a duty to your guests. You got to keep them fro hysterickin'."

"I've got another duty that's far more important—beir with you. The slaves are rising, aren't they? What chance d we have?"

"I don' know. We got four pistols and no tellin' what the got. Lewis got away on a horse and he's gone to rouse th neighbors. He'll tell 'em all to wait down at the gate, but things git hot, they'll know 'bout it and not wait for th others. Lewis should get to Benson in 'bout a half hour. Gi or take 'nother hour for the men to get dressed and bac here. If'n we kin hol' out for two hours, we pretty safe."

"But can we?"

"Might not. Them niggers wantin' blood tonight. The gone back to Africa. Pizen in their blood tonight. Turns 'e from bein' docile into savages and I don' know how mar of them there is."

"I'm not afraid of dying, Hammond. There is only or thing I fear."

"Fear they mistreat you? Don' blame you."

"No, not even that. I'm afraid that I might die before I te you I love you. I love you more than anything in the worl Now that I have told you, it doesn't matter what happens me."

Hammond opened his arms wide and she stood inside the strong security for a brief moment while he kissed her an then gently pushed her away.

Drumson kept his back turned to them, surprised at th new tenderness between the two, the emotion of their qui embrace. In another moment he heard Hammond walk the door and saw Augusta and Lucretia Borgia step back in the shadows.

Hammond himself was surprised. He was unable to classi his own feelings for this white woman; he had always thoug himself incapable of loving a woman of his own race. No he knew suddenly, for the first time in his life, what it w to love another. It was not the passion he had lavished on th young Ellen nor the taken-for-granted ecstasy he had accept from Regine. It was something far beyond either of thes and he felt within him a quiet joy he had never known befor

As he stood by the door with his hand on the big irc bolt, he could hear the noises outside growing louder an louder. There was a crash of glass in the fanlight above th door, and a rock landed on the floor of the hall. Vile wor from the stables and the slave pens were screamed, yelled and shouted by the milling slaves, and one black fellow, bolder than the rest, leaped up the steps of the portico and pounded on the front door, swinging the big brass knocker so that its sound reverberated throughout the house.

"We goin' to kill you, Maxwell. Then we goin' to pleasure ourselves wid yo' women."

Hammond pushed back the bolt and swung the front door open. He took quick aim at the black figure hardly more than a foot away. There was a flash from his pistol and a loud report. The fellow's head was knocked backwards as if it had been hit with a hammer, and he crumpled to the floor. Hammond stood in the doorway and handed his pistol to Drumson who was behind him, to reload it. With legs spread wide apart, he stood, hands firmly planted on his hips, and regarded the sea of faces in the semicircle surrounding the portico. The dying light of the fire gilded the long curved blades of the scythes, the tines of the pitchforks and the black faces, most of which were strange to Hammond.

"Who's a-goin' to kill who?" Hammond pointed to the long black legs and arms stretched out on the white floor. "What you goddam fool niggers think you doin'?" He looked at the row of faces below him, trying to recognize one of them.

"What you a-doin' here, Meg?" He pointed straight at him. "Who let you out?"

"Masta Hammond, suh." Meg was almost apologetic. "They tells me you going to nut me and Alph tomorrow."

"And what if I do? You're mine, ain' you? Kin do as I please wid you. Cuts yo' balls off if'n I want to. Chop yo' hands off if'n I want to. But don' plan on geldin' you tomorrow. Not a-goin' to geld you, goin' to hang you. Goin' to put a rope 'round yo' neck and string you up. And you too, Clees." He had located Clees standing a few men away from Meg. "Goin' to hang you, too, but goin' to strip the meat off'n yo' back 'fore I do. Goin' to flog you till you wants to be hung. But perhaps, if'n you lays down them pitchforks and scythes, I'll leave out the floggin'. Jes' hang you 'thout strippin' the meat off'n yo' back."

Hammond saw Clees raise his hand and caught the glint of light on the steel barrel of a pistol. So . . . Clees was armed.

Clees flourished the pistol. "We free, Masta Hammond. Ain' a-goin' back to be hung. We a-goin' north and you cain't stop us."

Hammond felt the solid weight of the pistol being slipped into his hand by Drumson behind him. It gave him reassurance. He stepped out onto the portico, remembering that these were not men, only animals;—remembering that they had only the intelligence which his mind gave them;—remembering that they had never thought for themselves but had been conditioned to obey white men always.

"You-all know you ain' got a chance of gettin' away with this. Soon's you leave this place, patrols after you. You won' git five mile."

"Who goin' to send de patrols?" Clees had not noticed the gun in Hammond's hand and he swaggered up on the steps of the portico.

"I'm a-goin' to send 'em, goddamit. Goin' to give 'em orders to shoot every one of you varmints on sight but not shoot to kill. I'm a-goin' to hang you myse'f."

"You ain' a-goin' to send them if'n you dead." Clees started to aim the pistol but it was clumsy in his hands. He fumbled, trying to get his oversized finger on the trigger.

Hammond fired and Clees stumbled and clapped his hand to his thigh, his face contorted with pain. Drumson ran out onto the porch, grabbed the empty pistol from Hammond's hand and started to reload it, while keeping his eye on Clees. He saw Clees slowly raise his arm and steady his stance against a pillar. The pistol pointed directly at Hammond but Hammond did not move. Drumson hurled himself at his master to push him aside just as the pistol in Clees' hand barked and spit fire.

He felt a thundering impact as though he had been kicked in the chest with a heavy boot, and he slumped to the floor, across Hammond's body.

"Masta Hammond, suh." He dimly realized that he had no right to be lying this way on his master but it was hard for him to speak for his mouth was filled with blood. He felt Hammond's body being pulled out from under him and heard the slam of the front door. He closed his eyes in a strange red light which seemed to come from within. A great volcano of pain burst in his chest and he tried to cry out for Hammond but he couldn't. With a last effort he opened his eyes to see black feet around, padding noiselessly on the floor. There was a flash of the cruel blade of a scythe and another shattering pain and then he remembered no more. Pitchforks stabbed at the body that mercifully no longer could feel them, and the body was lifted by cruel hands that sought to tear it to pieces. The maniacal blacks had found an outlet for their years of oppression and once again they were back along the sluggish Niger, in the mangrove swamps of Calabar and on the sunburned plains of Senegal. They were no longer the English-speaking slaves who had been taught to obey the white man. For this brief moment they had become warriors with only the inherited savagery of their ancestors to govern them. Drumson's body was dragged to the edge of the portico, his head lolling over the step until a scythe blade, as sharp and as effective as any African sword, severed his head and it was clutched by black fingers and impaled on the tines of a pitchfork to become a tribal symbol of victory. His unseeing eyes were open, staring wide at the milling crowd that rushed at the house, oblivious of the bullets that came from the broken windows as the defenders shot at them.

Then there were other shots, coming up the long lane that led to the big house from the main road, and the sound of hoofbeats and the avenging yells of the white men as they galloped up to defend not only the occupants of the house but their own way of life. Without dismounting, they rode into the melee, shooting, killing and trampling in a relentless and methodical destruction which quickly ended the brief triumph of the blacks. It was all over in a few minutes, and Lewis Gasaway sprang down from his horse and walked over the scattered corpses, up the slippery, bloodstained steps of the portico to the front door. The bolt slipped on the inside and he entered.

A candle had been lit in a tall brass candlestick on the floor beside Hammond Maxwell, who lay with his head in Augusta's lap, while Lucretia Borgia knelt beside him.

"They got Ham?" Gasaway knelt beside Ham's stretched-out body.

"Not by a damn sight, Lew." Hammond opened his eyes. "Got me in the shoulder, tha's all."

"They's all dead, Ham." Lewis jerked his head in the direction of the door. "Didn't have to go all the way to Benson. Crowd of men down at the Johnstone place. Lucky we got here but think that Montgomery got away safe. Jes' as we a-comin' down the road, saw his wagon kitin' off in the other direction."

He waited for an answer from Hammond but Hammond had fainted.

# chapter xvi

As THE FIRST gray fingers of dawn crept through the shutters into Hammond's room, enfeebling the light of the candles burning on the table beside his bed, Augusta gently disengaged her fingers from his grasp and laid his hand back on the sheet that covered him. She marveled at the strong fingers with their blunt, clean nails, at the growth of short hairs on the back of his hand and on his arm which gave his body such a golden sheen. Now he belonged to her. No longer need she fear Regine nor the shadow of the woman who dwelt in the other house. If, that is, she were still alive, which Augusta doubted, for the report brought back by Ajax was that the old house was now nothing but a pile of still-glowing ashes.

Hammond was sleeping. His face was in repose and not the contorted mask it had been while Doc Redfield's clumsy fingers, aided only by a kitchen paring knife, had probed for the bullet which had passed through Drumson and landed in his shoulder. Then he had lain tense with agony, drops of sweat beading his forehead, while Lewis Gasaway had held him down and while, with his uninjured hand, he had clasped Augusta's so frantically her fingers were almost crushed. She had not minded the pain for she felt she was giving him her own strength. Then it was over and his hand had gone limp in hers as Redfield held up the lead slug with bloody fingers. She thought Hammond had fainted but he had not. He had even smiled at her and then she and Lou-ella Gasaway had washed the wound, and packed it with lint which Lou-ella had scraped from a napkin, and bound it with clean linen.

Augusta, at Redfield's suggestion, had given him laudanum and now he was sleeping.

She stroked the hair back from his forehead, adjusted the pillow, and quickly bending over, brushed his forehead with her lips and kissed his sleeping mouth. She tiptoed over to the big rocking chair where Lou-ella was sleeping. Lou-ella awakened at her touch and Augusta pointed to the bed.

"Will you sit with him, Lou-ella, dear?" she whispered. "It is daylight now and there is something I must do before the others get up." She crossed the floor, lifted the latch quietly and went into the big room where Lucretia Borgia was sitting bolt upright in a chair beside the door.

"How's he?" Lucretia Borgia pointed to the door.

"Sleeping now."

"Thank de good lord. Oh, Miz 'Gusta, what we all a-goin' ter do? To think that this should come ter Falconhurst. Ter think that my Meg and my Alph would try to kill Masta Hammond. Oh, Miz 'Gusta, cain't never face Masta Hammond 'gain. What're we a-goin' ter do?"

"We'll go on, Lucretia Borgia. We'll go on as usual. But first there's something I must do. I'll need help. Will you go up to the room over the kitchen and fetch Brutus for me?"

"Whaffor you wants that Brutus? I'se here."

"I'll need a strong man." Augusta hesitated. "It's Drumson."

"I jes' as strong as that Brute boy." Lucretia Borgia heaved herself out of the chair. "And 'sides, Miz 'Gusta, I got myself some work to do, too. Them two boys a-lyin' out there, they's my flesh and blood. Disowned 'em, I had, but now they's dead, they's mine 'gain. I goes wid you."

"Yes, come with me, but we'll still need Brutus, so go and wake him for me."

Lucretia Borgia lumbered out of the room and Augusta could hear the shuffling of her carpet slippers across the polished floors as she passed through the hall, the parlor and out into the dining room. When the pantry door closed behind her, Augusta turned and went out into the hall. She mounted the stairs one at a time, dragging herself up by the balustrade. All the doors along the upstairs hall were mutely closed—the guests had returned to their rooms after the horrors of the night. Augusta walked the length of the balcony to a big chest which stood under the windows. She opened it, smelling the faint aroma of cedar from the inside, and took from it a quilt, pieced together of myriad little diamonds of gaily colored silk. It was soft to her touch and rippled under her fingers with an iridescence of bright colors. With it over her arm, she descended the stairs and stood in the hall waiting for Lucretia and Brutus.

When they arrived, Brutus was sobbing.

"He done gone, Miz 'Gusta. What we goin' to do 'thout him, Miz 'Gusta? Misses him, I do. He good boy, Drumson was. He my fren."

"There's little more we can do for him, Brutus, but we'll do what we can. I want you to go over to the carpenter shop and make a coffin for Drumson. Can you do it?"

"Don' needs to Miz 'Gusta. Al'ays one or two over there. One for white folks, made of cypress and one for niggers, made of pine."

"The cypress one then, Brutus." Augusta was decisive.

"Ain' no white mans dead."

"The cypress one." She felt almost too tired to repeat the words. "It's none too good for Drumson. Now go, and bring it back. If you can't bring it alone, get someone to help you."

Brutus left, running through the house to carry out Augusta's orders. She stood for a long time with her finger on the doorlatch, trying to get up courage to open the door. A horrible scene awaited her outside and she dreaded having to look at it. Yet, she must go.

Lucretia Borgia came up behind her and laid a heavy arm around her waist.

"Don' go, Miz 'Gusta. Ain' no call fer you to go out there. Spare yo'self. You kin send Brute or Ajax or some other boy and I'll go wid him. Thinks that pore Drumson mus' be awful gory. Ain' no fittin' sight fer mist'ess to see."

"But if it wasn't for Drumson, Master Hammond would be out there. We must remember that, Lucretia Borgia. As it is, he is sleeping safely in his own bed, and he is alive." Her finger came down hard on the latch and she pulled the door open.

Her first impulse was to close it again. She could not face the horror that lay there before her. Let some slave do it—she could not. She shut her eyes to blot out the weirdly postured black corpses that littered the front of the house. And yet, even as she felt her inability to do what she had intended, she resolutely took a step out onto the portico, than another, trying to disregard the carnage before her. The remaining steps, which carried her to the edge of the portico, were easier. Now she could blot out everything except what she was seeking. She reached the edge of the steps. The headless body lying on the floor of the portico with its poor shoulders on the ground was Drumson's. The graveled drive where the shoulders rested was clotted with a pool of darkened blood. The arms, chest and abdomen were slashed with deep wounds and now green with the crawling iridescence of flies. A shred of black trousers was still buttoned around the waist but the tattered remnant could not cover the bloody gash of emasculation. Some six feet away, the severed head, lying on its cheek in the gravel, stared back at her through open eyes that seemed still to be terrified by what they had seen and experienced.

She knelt down beside the body and waved her hand to brush the buzzing flies away, beckoning to Lucretia Borgia to come closer. Gently Augusta reached out a hand and placed it on a spot on the cold flesh that was not mutilated.

"Thank you, Drumson. I'm very grateful. I wish you could hear me say it." She lingered, trying to picture this mutilated body as the grinning slave who had been at her beck and call daily; as the grave and dignified servant who had so deftly waited on them at table last night; and as the man who had offered his body as a shield for Hammond. While she was kneeling there, Brutus and another slave, each carrying one end of a wooden coffin, came around the corner of the house. To get to her, they had to step over the dead bodies of the slaves who had been killed the night before —a mass of black arms, rough homespun-covered legs and woolly black pates. They set the coffin down on the ground before the lowest step.

Augusta stood up slowly. It seemed as though she could never walk the few steps to where the head stared at her but she determinedly placed one foot in front of the other and then, her eyes wide open but her hands recoiling from the touch, she reached down and picked it up. Her revulsion passed and she brushed the sand and gravel from the matted, bloodied hair. Holding the head in both hands, she carried it back to Drumson's body and laid it down, as close to where it had been severed as possible. Then she looked around for Lucretia Borgia only to see her tugging at the arms of a corpse, pulling it away from the body that lay beneath it.

"Git yo' big arms and laigs off'n my boys," she was sputtering as she hauled the big fellow aside. "What you worthless trash a-doin', layin' on my Meg and Alph." She gave another heave and the corpse slid away from the two bodies under it. With some difficulty she managed to bend their arms, trying to fold their hands across their chests. Augusta watched her numbly for a moment, realizing that no matter what they had done, Meg and Alph were still a part of this woman who was trying to cover her sorrow by her brusque scolding. Then she went inside the house to fetch the silk quilt that shimmered in the dim light of the hall. She gathered it up and brought it outside, flinging it wide over the coffin and then, as it settled, straightening it out inside the box.

"Brutus."

"Yes, ma'am, Miz 'Gusta."

"Go in the ladies' sitting room and bring me one of those green velvet pillows from the couch."

Wide-eyed, he looked at her but he was back in a moment with the pillow, which she fitted into the coffin.

"Now, Brutus, lift poor Drumson in."

"Cain't touch him, Miz 'Gusta. Cain't touch him 'thout'n he got no head. No, Miz 'Gusta, cain't do it." Brutus backed away but he had not figured on Lucretia Borgia. With her own dead straightened out on the grass, she had come over to where Augusta was standing and as Brutus backed away he collided with her. She gave him a push with one hand and a resounding slap with the other.

"You do as yo' mist'ess tell you. Git that Drumson inter the box. Put his haid in too. If'n you don', nigger, they's goin' to be makin' 'nother box fo' you right soon, 'cause, nigger, I'se goin' to clobber you good."

And Brutus obeyed. With the rolling-eyed slave who had accompanied him, they lifted Drumson's body and then his head and placed them in the coffin, but it remained for Augusta to straighten the head and to wrap the silk coverlet around him, tucking it in well.

"Take him to the burying ground," she said, "and dig a grave for him."

"White folks' buryin' ground?" Lucretia Borgia asked in surprise.

"Exactly," Augusta answered. "Who has a better right to be there?" She stepped back as Brutus and the other slave lifted the coffin to their shoulders. Where Drumson's body had lain on the steps, she noticed a flash of light and she reached down and picked up a curious silver filigreed box, attached to a well worn chain. She remembered having caught glimpses of such a chain under Drumson's collar when he was working around the house in the morning. It belonged to him and her first impulse was to put it in his coffin but she remembered Elvira, now heavy with child and the Mandingo woman who was even now upstairs. Someday there might be another Drumson. She would keep it for him.

Her task was over. When Brutus returned, she would send him back to the slave shed and have him bring over a detail of slaves and the farm wagon. Somewhere, she did not much care where as long as it was far enough away from the house, they could dig a common grave for the men who had been in Montgomery's caffle and the Falconhurst slaves who had perished along with them. If Lucretia Borgia wanted to bury her two sons separately she could—it was immaterial to Augusta. Whatever their crime against Hammond had been, their death had wiped it out.

With the silver box and chain in her hand, she entered the house. It was cool and dark inside and the windows were still barricaded with furniture. She must tell Drumson to set things to rights—no, there was no Drumson to tell. Brutus would have to take over now.

Hammond was resting from the effects of the laudanum and she dreaded the time of his awakening and the pain that would return with his consciousness. Just now she wanted to be alone. She climbed the stairs slowly, clutching the bannister with one hand, the silver chain dangling from the other. The big chest under the front windows from which she had taken the silk quilt was open, and she closed the cover and sat down on it.

In the quiet of the upper hall she thought of what had transpired the night before between Hammond Maxwell and herself. Their sudden intimacy had been as much of a surprise to her as it must have been to him. And yet not truly a surprise, for the love each expressed for the other seemed perfectly natural, as natural as her marriage to Hammond that was sure to ensue. Yes, she had grown to love that man, and as time went on she would love him even more; each day would weave the pattern of their lives more closely together.

She looked out of the window, grateful that the balcony hid the twisted bodies in the drive below, and her eyes came to rest on the long line of saplings that stretched from the house to the main road. So Augusta Devereaux who had once been plain Gussie Delavan was now to become Mrs. Hammond Maxwell of Falconhurst. She could not deny that the thought made her glad. And yet there was no possessiveness in what she felt. She had come to love this house, this haven of security, just as she had come to love its master; in her heart she could not separate one from the other.

Her hand caressed the smooth polished mahogany of the chest, and she thought of Drumson. How much she owed—how much she and Hammond both owed—to this great-hearted Negro who would soon be resting under the live oaks in the burying ground. Drumson had died for them as he had lived for them. That she must never forget, as long as she lived.

Her hand still clutched the silver chain and she studied the little box attached to it. What did it contain? Some conjure, some weird talisman? Her fingers found the catch and opened it, but inside the box she saw only a piece of stained discolored cloth. The cloth was so old that it crumbled as she unwrapped it, and inside there was only a handful of gray dust.

Although its history was unknown to her, she felt that this precious dust had come a long way—and still had a long way to go. Some day soon there would be a son to Drumson, and she would hang it around his neck. She would keep it in trust for him, she told herself as she fastened the chain around her own neck and let the little silver box fall into the bosom of her dress. At first it was cold against her skin, cold as the touch of death, but soon it grew warm and comforting and it seemed to her that the dead slave had come back to life.

Now there were footsteps upstairs and a door slammed while voices spoke and answered each other in the hall. Hearing them, she sat upright on the chest. She searched for a handkerchief but found none and dabbed at her eyes with the hem of her petticoat, running her fingers through her hair and buttoning a button of her dress before she stood up. Her one moment of weakness was over and she started counting, on her fingers, the number of places to set for breakfast. But first she would run downstairs to see if Hammond was resting. She hoped he was still sleeping and had not awakened to pain. Drumson too was sleeping and he would not awaken to pain either. Nothing would ever disturb him again. He was no longer a slave. His death had at last earned him his freedom.